Gothic Parodies: Northanger Abbey, Nightmare Abbey &
The Heroine: or, Adventures of Cherubina (Volumes I, II, III)

I0561062

Jane Austen
Thomas Love Peacock
Eaton Stannard Barrett

Edited by Yona Rodrigue Cohen

**Gothic Parodies: Northanger Abbey, Nightmare Abbey &
The Heroine: or, Adventures of Cherubina (Volumes I, II , III)**

Published by
ELL Reading, LLC
P.O. Box 1137
Mason, OH 45040, USA

Library of Congress Control Number: 2011927456

ISBN: 978-0-9844098-3-9

Printed in United States of America

Table of Contents

NORTHANGER ABBEY
by Jane Austen

ADVERTISEMENT BY THE AUTHORESS
TO
NORTHANGER ABBEY

THIS little work was finished in the year 1803, and intended for immediate publication. It was disposed of to a bookseller, it was even advertised, and why the business proceeded no farther, the author has never been able to learn. That any bookseller should think it worth while to purchase what he did not think it worth while to publish seems extraordinary. But with this, neither the author nor the public have any other concern than as some observation is necessary upon those parts of the work which thirteen years have made comparatively obsolete. The public are entreated to bear in mind that thirteen years have passed since it was finished, many more since it was begun, and that during that period, places, manners, books, and opinions have undergone considerable changes.

CHAPTER 1

No one who had ever seen Catherine Morland in her infancy would have supposed her born to be an heroine. Her situation in life, the character of her father and mother, her own person and disposition, were all equally against her. Her father was a clergyman, without being neglected, or poor, and a very respectable man, though his name was Richard--and he had never been handsome. He had a considerable independence besides two good livings--and he was not in the least addicted to locking up his daughters. Her mother was a woman of useful plain sense, with a good temper, and, what is more remarkable, with a good constitution. She had three sons before Catherine was born; and instead of dying in bringing the latter into the world, as any body might expect, she still lived on--lived to have six children more--to see them growing up around her, and to enjoy excellent health herself. A family of ten children will be always called a fine family, where there are heads and arms and legs enough for the number; but the Morlands had little other right to the word, for they were in general very plain, and Catherine, for many years of her life, as plain as any. She had a thin awkward figure, a sallow skin without colour, dark lank hair, and strong features;--so much for her person; --and not less unpropitious for heroism seemed her mind. She was fond of all boys' plays, and greatly preferred cricket not merely to dolls, but to the more heroic enjoyments of infancy, nursing a dormouse, feeding a canary-bird, or watering a rose-bush. Indeed she had no taste for a garden; and if she gathered flowers at all, it was chiefly for the pleasure of mischief -- at least so it was conjectured from her always preferring those which she was forbidden to take. -- Such were her propensities -- her abilities were quite as extraordinary. She never could learn or understand any thing before she was taught; and sometimes not even then, for she was often inattentive, and occasionally stupid. Her mother was three months in teaching her only to repeat the "Beggar's Petition"; and after all, her next sister, Sally, could say it better than she did. Not that Catherine was always stupid --by no means; she learnt the fable of "The Hare and Many Friends" as quickly as any girl in England. Her mother wished her to learn music; and Catherine was sure she should like it, for she was very fond of tinkling the keys of the old forlorn spinnet; so, at eight years old she began. She learnt a year, and could not bear it;--and Mrs. Morland, who did not insist on her daughters being accomplished in spite of incapacity or distaste, allowed her to leave off. The day which dismissed the music-master was one of the happiest of Catherine's life. Her taste for drawing was not superior; though whenever she could obtain the outside of a letter from her mother, or seize upon any other odd piece of paper, she did what she could in that way, by drawing houses and trees, hens and chickens, all very much like one another.--Writing and accounts she was taught by her father; French by her mother: her proficiency in either was not remarkable, and she shirked her lessons in both whenever she could. What a strange, unaccountable character!--for with all these symptoms of profligacy at ten years old, she had neither a bad heart nor a bad temper, was seldom stubborn, scarcely ever quarrelsome, and very kind to the little ones, with few interruptions of tyranny; she was moreover noisy and wild, hated confinement and cleanliness, and loved nothing so well in the world as rolling down the green slope at the back of the house.

Such was Catherine Morland at ten. At fifteen, appearances were mending; she began to curl her hair and long for balls; her complexion improved; her features were softened by plumpness and colour, her eyes gained more animation, and her figure more consequence. Her love of dirt gave way to an inclination for finery, and she grew clean as she grew smart; she had now the pleasure of sometimes hearing her father and mother remark on her personal improvement. "Catherine grows quite a good-looking girl--she is almost pretty to-day," were words which caught her ears now and then; and how welcome were the sounds! To look *almost* pretty is an acquisition of higher delight to a girl who has been looking plain the first fifteen years of her life than a beauty from her cradle can ever receive.

Mrs. Morland was a very good woman, and wished to see her children every thing they ought to be; but her time was so much occupied in lying-in and teaching the little ones, that her elder daughters were inevitably left to shift for themselves; and it was not very wonderful that Catherine, who had by nature nothing heroic about her, should prefer cricket, base ball, riding on horseback, and running about the country at the age of fourteen, to books--or at least books of information--for, provided that nothing like useful knowledge could be gained from them, provided they were all story and no reflection, she had never any objection to books at all. But from fifteen to seventeen she was in training for a heroine; she read all such works as heroines must read to supply their memories with those quotations which are so serviceable and so soothing in the vicissitudes of their eventful lives.

From Pope, she learnt to censure those who
       "bear about the mockery of woe."
From Gray, that
       "Many a flower is born to blush unseen,
       "And waste its fragrance on the desert air."
From Thompson, that--
       "It is a delightful task
       "To teach the young idea how to shoot."
And from Shakespeare she gained a great store of information-- amongst the rest, that--
       "Trifles light as air,
       "Are, to the jealous, confirmation strong,
       "As proofs of Holy Writ."
That
       "The poor beetle, which we tread upon,
       "In corporal sufferance feels a pang as great
       "As when a giant dies."
And that a young woman in love always looks--
       "like Patience on a monument
       "Smiling at Grief."

So far her improvement was sufficient -- and in many other points she came on exceedingly well; for though she could not write sonnets, she brought herself to read them; and though there seemed no chance of her throwing a whole party into raptures by a prelude on the pianoforte, of her own composition, she could listen to other people's performance with very little fatigue. Her greatest deficiency was in the pencil -- she had no notion of drawing -- not enough even to attempt a sketch of her lover's profile, that she might be detected in the design. There she fell miserably short of the true heroic height. At present she did not know her own poverty, for she had no lover to portray. She had reached the age of seventeen, without having seen one amiable youth who could call forth her sensibility, without having inspired one real passion, and without having excited even any admiration but what was very moderate and very transient. This was strange indeed! But strange things may be generally accounted for if their cause be fairly searched out. There was not one lord in the neighbourhood; no--not even a baronet. There was not one family among their acquaintance who had reared and supported a boy accidentally found at their door--not one young man whose origin was unknown. Her father had no ward, and the squire of the parish no children.

But when a young lady is to be a heroine, the perverseness of forty surrounding families cannot prevent her. Something must and will happen to throw a hero in her way.

Mr. Allen, who owned the chief of the property about Fullerton, the village in Wiltshire where the Morlands lived, was ordered to Bath for the benefit of a gouty constitution--and his lady, a good-humoured woman, fond of Miss Morland, and probably aware that if adventures will not befall a young lady in her own village, she must seek them abroad, invited her to go with them. Mr. and Mrs. Morland were all compliance, and Catherine all happiness.

CHAPTER 2

In addition to what has been already said of Catherine Morland's personal and mental endowments, when about to be launched into all the difficulties and dangers of a six weeks' residence in Bath, it may be stated, for the reader's more certain information, lest the following pages should otherwise fail of giving any idea of what her character is meant to be; that her heart was affectionate, her disposition cheerful and open, without conceit or affectation of any kind--her manners just removed from the awkwardness and shyness of a girl; her person pleasing, and, when in good looks, pretty--and her mind about as ignorant and uninformed as the female mind at seventeen usually is.

When the hour of departure drew near, the maternal anxiety of Mrs. Morland will be naturally supposed to be most severe. A thousand alarming presentiments of evil to her beloved Catherine from this terrific separation must oppress her heart with sadness, and drown her in tears for the last day or two of their being together; and advice of the most important and applicable nature must of course flow from her wise lips in their parting conference in her closet. Cautions against the violence of such noblemen and baronets as delight in forcing young ladies away to some remote farm-house, must, at such a moment, relieve the fulness of her heart. Who would not think so? But Mrs. Morland knew so little of lords and baronets, that she entertained no notion of their general mischievousness, and was wholly unsuspicious of danger to her daughter from their machinations. Her cautions were confined to the following points. "I beg, Catherine, you will always wrap yourself up very warm about the throat, when you come from the Rooms at night; and I wish you would try to keep some account of the money you spend;-- I will give you this little book on purpose."

Sally, or rather Sarah (for what young lady of common gentility will reach the age of sixteen without altering her name as far as she can?), must from situation be at this time the intimate friend and confidante of her sister. It is remarkable, however, that she neither insisted on Catherine's writing by every post, nor exacted her promise of transmitting the character of every new acquaintance, nor a detail of every interesting conversation that Bath might produce. Every thing indeed relative to this important journey was done, on the part of the Morlands, with a degree of moderation and composure, which seemed rather consistent with the common feelings of common life, than with the refined susceptibilities, the tender emotions which the first separation of a heroine from her family ought always to excite. Her father, instead of giving her an unlimited order on his banker, or even putting an hundred pounds bank-bill into her hands, gave her only ten guineas, and promised her more when she wanted it.

Under these unpromising auspices, the parting took place, and the journey began. It was performed with suitable quietness and uneventful safety. Neither robbers nor tempests befriended them, nor one lucky overturn to introduce them to the hero. Nothing more alarming occurred than a fear, on Mrs. Allen's side, of having once left her clogs behind her at an inn, and that fortunately proved to be groundless.

They arrived at Bath. Catherine was all eager delight;--her eyes were here, there, every where, as they approached its fine and striking environs, and afterwards drove through those streets which conducted them to the hotel. She was come to be happy, and she felt happy already.

They were soon settled in comfortable lodgings in Pulteney Street.

It is now expedient to give some description of Mrs. Allen, that the reader may be able to judge in what manner her actions will hereafter tend to promote the general distress of the work, and how she will, probably, contribute to reduce poor Catherine to all the desperate wretchedness of which a last volume is capable--whether by her imprudence, vulgarity, or jealousy--whether by intercepting her letters, ruining her character, or turning her out of doors.

Mrs. Allen was one of that numerous class of females, whose society can raise no other emotion than surprise at there being any men in the world who could like them well enough to marry them. She had neither beauty, genius, accomplishment, nor manner. The air of a gentlewoman, a great deal of quiet, inactive good temper, and a trifling turn of mind were all that could account for her being the choice of a sensible, intelligent man like Mr. Allen. In one respect she was admirably fitted to introduce a young lady into public, being as fond of going every where and seeing every thing herself as any young lady could be. Dress was her passion. She had a most harmless delight in being fine; and our heroine's entrée into life could not take place till after three or four days had been spent in learning what was mostly worn, and her chaperone was provided with a dress of the newest fashion. Catherine too made some purchases herself, and when all these matters were arranged, the important evening came which was to usher her into the Upper Rooms. Her hair was cut and dressed by the best hand, her clothes put on with care, and both Mrs. Allen and her maid declared she looked quite as she should do. With such encouragement, Catherine hoped at least to pass uncensored through the crowd. As for admiration, it was always very welcome when it came, but she did not depend on it.

Mrs. Allen was so long in dressing that they did not enter the ball-room till late. The season was full, the room crowded, and the two ladies squeezed in as well as they could. As for Mr. Allen, he repaired directly to the card-room, and left them to enjoy a mob by themselves. With more care for the safety of her new gown than for the comfort of her protegée, Mrs. Allen made her way through the throng of men by the door, as swiftly as the necessary caution would allow; Catherine, however, kept close at her side, and linked her arm too firmly within her friend's to be torn asunder by any common effort of a struggling assembly. But to her utter amazement she found that to proceed along the room was by no means the way to disengage themselves from the crowd; it seemed rather to increase as they went on, whereas she had imagined that when once fairly within the door, they should easily find seats and be able to watch the dances with perfect convenience. But this was far from being the case, and though by unwearied diligence they gained even the top of the room, their situation was just the same; they saw nothing of the dancers but the high feathers of some of the ladies. Still they moved on -- something better was yet in view; and by a continued exertion of strength and ingenuity they found themselves at last in the passage behind the highest bench. Here there was something less of crowd than below; and hence Miss Morland had a comprehensive view of all the company beneath her, and of all the dangers of her late passage through them. It was a splendid sight, and she began, for the first time that evening, to feel herself at a ball: she longed to dance, but she had not an acquaintance in the room. Mrs. Allen did all that she could do in such a case by saying very placidly, every now and then, "I wish you could dance, my dear--I wish you could get a partner." For some time her young friend felt obliged to her for these wishes; but they were repeated so often, and proved so totally ineffectual, that Catherine grew tired at last, and would thank her no more.

They were not long able, however, to enjoy the repose of the eminence they had so laboriously gained. Every body was shortly in motion for tea, and they must squeeze out like the rest. Catherine began to feel something of disappointment--she was tired of being continually pressed against by people, the generality of whose faces possessed nothing to interest, and with all of whom she was so wholly unacquainted that she could not relieve the irksomeness of imprisonment by the exchange of a syllable with any of her fellow captives; and when at last arrived in the tea-room, she felt yet more the awkwardness of having no party to join, no acquaintance to claim, no gentleman to assist them. They saw nothing of Mr. Allen; and after looking about them in vain for a more eligible situation, were obliged to sit down at the end of a table, at which a large party were already placed, without having any thing to do there, or any body to speak to, except each other.

Mrs. Allen congratulated herself, as soon as they were seated, on having preserved her gown from injury. "It would have been very shocking to have it torn," said she, "would not it?-- It is such a delicate muslin.-- For my part I have not seen any thing I like so well in the whole room, I assure you."

"How uncomfortable it is," whispered Catherine, "not to have a single acquaintance here!"

"Yes, my dear," replied Mrs. Allen, with perfect serenity, "it is very uncomfortable indeed."

"What shall we do?-- The gentlemen and ladies at this table look as if they wondered why we came here--we seem forcing ourselves into their party."

"Aye, so we do.-- That is very disagreeable. I wish we had a large acquaintance here."

"I wish we had *any*;--it would be somebody to go to."

"Very true, my dear; and if we knew any body we would join them directly. The Skinners were here last year--I wish they were here now."

"Had not we better go away as it is?--Here are no tea things for us, you see."

"No more there are, indeed.--How very provoking! But I think we had better sit still, for one gets so tumbled in such a crowd! How is my head, my dear?-- Somebody gave me a push that has hurt it, I am afraid."

"No, indeed, it looks very nice.--But, dear Mrs. Allen, are you sure there is nobody you know in all this multitude of people? I think you *must* know somebody."

"I don't upon my word--I wish I did. I wish I had a large acquaintance here with all my heart, and then I should get you a partner.--I should be so glad to have you dance. There goes a strange-looking woman! What an odd gown she has got on!--How old-fashioned it is! Look at the back."

After some time they received an offer of tea from one of their neighbours; it was thankfully accepted, and this introduced a light conversation with the gentleman who offered it, which was the only time that any body spoke to them during the evening, till they were discovered and joined by Mr. Allen when the dance was over.

"Well, Miss Morland," said he, directly, "I hope you have had an agreeable ball."

"Very agreeable indeed," she replied, vainly endeavouring to hide a great yawn.

"I wish she had been able to dance," said his wife; "I wish we could have got a partner for her.--I have been saying how glad I should be if the Skinners were here this winter instead of last; or if the Parrys had come, as they talked of once, she might have danced with George Parry. I am so sorry she has not had a partner!"

"We shall do better another evening I hope," was Mr. Allen's consolation.

The company began to disperse when the dancing was over-- enough to leave space for the remainder to walk about in some comfort; and now was the time for a heroine, who had not yet played a very distinguished part in the events of the evening, to be noticed and admired. Every five minutes, by removing some of the crowd, gave greater openings for her charms. She was now seen by many young men who had not been near her before. Not one, however, started with rapturous wonder on beholding her, no whisper of eager inquiry ran round the room, nor was she once called a divinity by any body. Yet Catherine was in very good looks, and had the company only seen her three years before, they would *now* have thought her exceedingly handsome.

She *was* looked at, however, and with some admiration; for, in her own hearing, two gentlemen pronounced her to be a pretty girl. Such words had their due effect; she immediately thought the evening pleasanter than she had found it before--her humble vanity was contented--she felt more obliged to the two young men for this simple praise than a true-quality heroine would have been for fifteen sonnets in celebration of her charms, and went to her chair in good humour with every body, and perfectly satisfied with her share of public attention.

CHAPTER 3

Every morning now brought its regular duties;--shops were to be visited; some new part of the town to be looked at; and the Pump-room to be attended, where they paraded up and down for an hour, looking at every body and speaking to no one. The wish of a numerous acquaintance in Bath was still uppermost with Mrs. Allen, and she repeated it after every fresh proof, which every morning brought, of her knowing nobody at all.

They made their appearance in the Lower Rooms; and here fortune was more favourable to our heroine. The master of the ceremonies introduced to her a very gentlemanlike young man as a partner;--his name was Tilney. He seemed to be about four or five and twenty, was rather tall, had a pleasing countenance, a very intelligent and lively eye, and, if not quite handsome, was very near it. His address was good, and Catherine felt herself in high luck. There was little leisure for speaking while they danced; but when they were seated at tea, she found him as agreeable as she had already given him credit for being. He talked with fluency and spirit--and there was an archness and pleasantry in his manner which interested, though it was hardly understood by her. After chatting some time on such matters as naturally arose from the objects around them, he suddenly addressed her with--"I have hitherto been very remiss, madam, in the proper attentions of a partner here; I have not yet asked you how long you have been in Bath; whether you were ever here before; whether you have been at the Upper Rooms, the theatre, and the concert; and how you like the place altogether. I have been very negligent--but are you now at leisure to satisfy me in these particulars? If you are I will begin directly."

"You need not give yourself that trouble, sir."

"No trouble, I assure you, madam." Then forming his features into a set smile, and affectedly softening his voice, he added, with a simpering air, "Have you been long in Bath, madam?"

"About a week, sir," replied Catherine, trying not to laugh.

"Really!" with affected astonishment.

"Why should you be surprised, sir?"

"Why, indeed!" said he, in his natural tone --"but some emotion must appear to be raised by your reply, and surprise is more easily assumed, and not less reasonable than any other.--Now let us go on. Were you never here before, madam?"

"Never, sir."

"Indeed! Have you yet honoured the Upper Rooms?"

"Yes, sir, I was there last Monday."

"Have you been to the theatre?"

"Yes, sir, I was at the play on Tuesday."

"To the concert?"

"Yes, sir, on Wednesday."

"And are you altogether pleased with Bath?"

"Yes--I like it very well."

"Now I must give one smirk, and then we may be rational again."

Catherine turned away her head, not knowing whether she might venture to laugh.

"I see what you think of me," said he gravely--"I shall make but a poor figure in your journal to-morrow."

"My journal!"

"Yes, I know exactly what you will say: Friday, went to the Lower Rooms; wore my sprigged muslin robe with blue trimmings--plain black shoes--appeared to much advantage; but was strangely harassed by a queer, half-witted man, who would make me dance with him, and distressed me by his nonsense."

"Indeed I shall say no such thing."

"Shall I tell you what you ought to say?"

"If you please."

"I danced with a very agreeable young man, introduced by Mr. King; had a great deal of conversation with him--seems a most extraordinary genius--hope I may know more of him. *That*, madam, is what I *wish* you to say."

"But, perhaps, I keep no journal."

"Perhaps you are not sitting in this room, and I am not sitting by you. These are points in which a doubt is equally possible. Not keep a journal! How are your absent cousins to understand the tenour of your life in Bath without one? How are the civilities and compliments of every day to be related as they ought to be, unless noted down every evening in a journal? How are your various dresses to be remembered, and the particular state of your complexion, and curl of your hair to be described in all their diversities, without having constant recourse to a journal?-- My dear madam, I am not so ignorant of young ladies' ways as you wish to believe me; it is this delightful habit of journalizing which largely contributes to form the easy style of writing for which ladies are so generally celebrated. Every body allows that the talent of writing agreeable letters is peculiarly female. Nature may have done something, but I am sure it must be essentially assisted by the practice of keeping a journal."

"I have sometimes thought," said Catherine, doubtingly, "whether ladies do write so much better letters than gentlemen! That is--I should not think the superiority was always on our side."

"And what are they?"

"A general deficiency of subject, a total inattention to stops, and a very frequent ignorance of grammar."

"Upon my word! I need not have been afraid of disclaiming the compliment. You do not think too highly of us in that way."

"I should no more lay it down as a general rule that women write better letters than men, than that they sing better duets, or draw better landscapes. In every power, of which taste is the foundation, excellence is pretty fairly divided between the sexes."

They were interrupted by Mrs. Allen:--"My dear Catherine," said she, "do take this pin out of my sleeve; I am afraid it has torn a hole already; I shall be quite sorry if it has, for this is a favourite gown, though it cost but nine shillings a yard."

"That is exactly what I should have guessed it, madam," said Mr. Tilney, looking at the muslin.

"Do you understand muslins, sir?"

"Particularly well; I always buy my own cravats, and am allowed to be an excellent judge; and my sister has often trusted me in the choice of a gown. I bought one for her the other day, and it was pronounced to be a prodigious bargain by every lady who saw it. I gave but five shillings a yard for it, and a true Indian muslin."

Mrs. Allen was quite struck by his genius. "Men commonly take so little notice of those things," said she; "I can never get Mr. Allen to know one of my gowns from another. You must be a great comfort to your sister, sir."

"I hope I am, madam."

"And pray, sir, what do you think of Miss Morland's gown?"

"It is very pretty, madam," said he, gravely examining it; "but I do not think it will wash well; I am afraid it will fray."

"How can you," said Catherine, laughing, "be so--" She had almost said "strange."

"I am quite of your opinion, sir," replied Mrs. Allen; "and so I told Miss Morland when she bought it."

"But then you know, madam, muslin always turns to some account or other; Miss Morland will get enough out of it for a handkerchief, or a cap, or a cloak.-- Muslin can never be said to be wasted. I have heard my sister say so forty times, when she has been extravagant in buying more than she wanted, or careless in cutting it to pieces."

"Bath is a charming place, sir; there are so many good shops here.-- We are sadly off in the country; not but what we have very good shops in Salisbury, but it is so far to go;--eight miles is a long way; Mr. Allen says it is nine, measured nine; but I am sure it cannot be more than eight; and it is such a fag--I come back tired to death. Now, here one can step out of doors and get a thing in five minutes."

Mr. Tilney was polite enough to seem interested in what she said; and she kept him on the subject of muslins till the dancing recommenced. Catherine feared, as she listened to their discourse, that he indulged himself a little too much with the foibles of others. -- "What are you thinking of so earnestly?" said he, as they walked back to the ball-room; -- "not of your partner, I hope, for, by that shake of the head, your meditations are not satisfactory."

Catherine coloured, and said, "I was not thinking of any thing."

"That is artful and deep, to be sure; but I had rather be told at once that you will not tell me."

"Well then, I will not."

"Thank you; for now we shall soon be acquainted, as I am authorized to tease you on this subject whenever we meet, and nothing in the world advances intimacy so much."

They danced again; and, when the assembly closed, parted, on the lady's side at least, with a strong inclination for continuing the acquaintance. Whether she thought of him so much, while she drank her warm wine and water, and prepared herself for bed, as to dream of him when there, cannot be ascertained; but I hope it was no more than in a slight slumber, or a morning doze at most; for if it be true, as a celebrated writer has maintained, that no young lady can be justified in falling in love before the gentleman's love is declared,* it must be very improper that a young lady should dream of a gentleman before the gentleman is first known to have dreamt of her. How proper Mr. Tilney might be as a dreamer or a lover had not yet perhaps entered Mr. Allen's head, but that he was not objectionable as a common acquaintance for his young charge he was on inquiry satisfied; for he had early in the evening taken pains to know who her partner was, and had been assured of Mr. Tilney's being a clergyman, and of a very respectable family in Gloucestershire.

*Vide a letter from Mr. Richardson, No. 97, Vol. II, Rambler.

CHAPTER 4

With more than usual eagerness did Catherine hasten to the Pump-room the next day, secure within herself of seeing Mr. Tilney there before the morning were over, and ready to meet him with a smile;--but no smile was demanded -- Mr. Tilney did not appear. Every creature in Bath, except himself, was to be seen in the room at different periods of the fashionable hours; crowds of people were every moment passing in and out, up the steps and down; people whom nobody cared about, and nobody wanted to see; and he only was absent. "What a delightful place Bath is," said Mrs. Allen as they sat down near the great clock, after parading the room till they were tired; "and how pleasant it would be if we had any acquaintance here."

This sentiment had been uttered so often in vain that Mrs. Allen had no particular reason to hope it would be followed with more advantage now; but we are told to "despair of nothing we would attain," as "unwearied diligence our point would gain;" and the unwearied diligence with which she had every day wished for the same thing was at length to have its just reward, for hardly had she been seated ten minutes before a lady of about her own age, who was sitting by her, and had been looking at her attentively for several minutes, addressed her with great complaisance in these words:--"I think, madam, I cannot be mistaken; it is a long time since I had the pleasure of seeing you, but is not your name Allen?" This question answered, as it readily was, the stranger pronounced hers to be Thorpe; and Mrs. Allen immediately recognized the features of a former schoolfellow and intimate, whom she had seen only once since their respective marriages, and that many years ago. Their joy on this meeting was very great, as well it might, since they had been contented to know nothing of each other for the last fifteen years. Compliments on good looks now passed; and, after observing how time had slipped away since they were last together, how little they had thought of meeting in Bath, and what a pleasure it was to see an old friend, they proceeded to make inquiries and give intelligence as to their families, sisters, and cousins, talking both together, far more ready to give than to receive information, and each hearing very little of what the other said. Mrs. Thorpe, however, had one great advantage as a talker, over Mrs. Allen, in a family of children; and when she expatiated on the talents of her sons, and the beauty of her daughters, when she related their different situations and views--that John was at Oxford, Edward at Merchant Taylors', and William at sea -- and all of them more beloved and respected in their different station than any other three beings ever were, Mrs. Allen had no similar information to give, no similar triumphs to press on the unwilling and unbelieving ear of her friend, and was forced to sit and appear to listen to all these maternal effusions, consoling herself, however, with the discovery, which her keen eye soon made, that the lace on Mrs. Thorpe's pelisse was not half so handsome as that on her own.

"Here come my dear girls," cried Mrs. Thorpe, pointing at three smart-looking females who, arm in arm, were then moving towards her. "My dear Mrs. Allen, I long to introduce them; they will be so delighted to see you: the tallest is Isabella, my eldest; is not she a fine young woman? The others are very much admired too, but I believe Isabella is the handsomest."

The Miss Thorpes were introduced; and Miss Morland, who had been for a short time forgotten, was introduced likewise. The name seemed to strike them all; and, after speaking to her with great civility, the eldest young lady observed aloud to the rest, "How excessively like her brother Miss Morland is!"

"The very picture of him indeed!" cried the mother--and "I should have known her any where for his sister!" was repeated by them all, two or three times over. For a moment Catherine was surprised; but Mrs. Thorpe and her daughters had scarcely begun the history of their acquaintance with Mr. James Morland, before she remembered that her eldest brother had lately formed an intimacy with a young man of his own college, of the name of Thorpe; and that he had spent the last week of the Christmas vacation with his family, near London.

The whole being explained, many obliging things were said by the Miss Thorpes of their wish of being better acquainted with her; of being considered as already friends, through the friendship of their brothers, etc., which Catherine heard with pleasure, and answered with all the pretty expressions she could command; and, as the first proof of amity, she was soon invited to accept an arm of the eldest Miss Thorpe, and take a turn with her about the room. Catherine was delighted with this extension of her Bath acquaintance, and almost forgot Mr. Tilney while she talked to Miss Thorpe. Friendship is certainly the finest balm for the pangs of disappointed love.

Their conversation turned upon those subjects, of which the free discussion has generally much to do in perfecting a sudden intimacy between two young ladies: such as dress, balls, flirtations, and quizzes. Miss Thorpe, however, being four years older than Miss Morland, and at least four years better informed, had a very decided advantage in discussing such points; she could compare the balls of Bath with those of Tunbridge, its fashions with the fashions of London; could rectify the opinions of her new friend in many articles of tasteful attire; could discover a flirtation between any gentleman and lady who only smiled on each other; and point out a quiz through the thickness of a crowd. These powers received due admiration from Catherine, to whom they were entirely new; and the respect which they naturally inspired might have been too great for familiarity, had not the easy gaiety of Miss Thorpe's manners, and her frequent expressions of delight on this acquaintance with her, softened down every feeling of awe, and left nothing but tender affection. Their increasing attachment was not to be satisfied with half a dozen turns in the Pump-room, but required, when they all quitted it together, that Miss Thorpe should accompany Miss Morland to the very door of Mr. Allen's house; and that they should there part with a most affectionate and lengthened shake of hands, after learning, to their mutual relief, that they should see each other across the theatre at night, and say their prayers in the same chapel the next morning. Catherine then ran directly upstairs, and watched Miss Thorpe's progress down the street from the drawing-room window; admired the graceful spirit of her walk, the fashionable air of her figure and dress, and felt grateful, as well she might, for the chance which had procured her such a friend.

Mrs. Thorpe was a widow, and not a very rich one; she was a good-humoured, well-meaning woman, and a very indulgent mother. Her eldest daughter had great personal beauty, and the younger ones, by pretending to be as handsome as their sister, imitating her air, and dressing in the same style, did very well.

This brief account of the family is intended to supersede the necessity of a long and minute detail from Mrs. Thorpe herself, of her past adventures and sufferings, which might otherwise be expected to occupy the three or four following chapters; in which the worthlessness of lords and attorneys might be set forth, and conversations, which had passed twenty years before, be minutely repeated.

CHAPTER 5

Catherine was not so much engaged at the theatre that evening, in returning the nods and smiles of Miss Thorpe, though they certainly claimed much of her leisure, as to forget to look with an inquiring eye for Mr. Tilney in every box which her eye could reach; but she looked in vain. Mr. Tilney was no fonder of the play than the Pump-room. She hoped to be more fortunate the next day; and when her wishes for fine weather were answered by seeing a beautiful morning, she hardly felt a doubt of it; for a fine Sunday in Bath empties every house of its inhabitants, and all the world appears on such an occasion to walk about and tell their acquaintance what a charming day it is.

As soon as divine service was over, the Thorpes and Allens eagerly joined each other; and after staying long enough in the Pump-room to discover that the crowd was insupportable, and that there was not a genteel face to be seen, which every body discovers every Sunday throughout the season, they hastened away to the Crescent, to breathe the fresh air of better company. Here Catherine and Isabella, arm in arm, again tasted the sweets of friendship in an unreserved conversation;--they talked much, and with much enjoyment; but again was Catherine disappointed in her hope of re-seeing her partner. He was no where to be met with; every search for him was equally unsuccessful, in morning lounges or evening assemblies; neither at the Upper nor Lower Rooms, at dressed or undressed balls, was he perceivable; nor among the walkers, the horsemen, or the curricle-drivers of the morning. His name was not in the Pump-room book, and curiosity could do no more. He must be gone from Bath. Yet he had not mentioned that his stay would be so short! This sort of mysteriousness, which is always so becoming in a hero, threw a fresh grace in Catherine's imagination around his person and manners, and increased her anxiety to know more of him. From the Thorpes she could learn nothing, for they had been only two days in Bath before they met with Mrs. Allen. It was a subject, however, in which she often indulged with her fair friend, from whom she received every possible encouragement to continue to think of him; and his impression on her fancy was not suffered therefore to weaken. Isabella was very sure that he must be a charming young man, and was equally sure that he must have been delighted with her dear Catherine, and would therefore shortly return. She liked him the better for being a clergyman, "for she must confess herself very partial to the profession;" and something like a sigh escaped her as she said it. Perhaps Catherine was wrong in not demanding the cause of that gentle emotion -- but she was not experienced enough in the finesse of love, or the duties of friendship, to know when delicate raillery was properly called for, or when a confidence should be forced.

Mrs. Allen was now quite happy--quite satisfied with Bath. She had found some acquaintance, had been so lucky too as to find in them the family of a most worthy old friend; and, as the completion of good fortune, had found these friends by no means so expensively dressed as herself. Her daily expressions were no longer, "I wish we had some acquaintance in Bath!" They were changed into, "How glad I am we have met with Mrs. Thorpe!" and she was as eager in promoting the intercourse of the two families, as her young charge and Isabella themselves could be; never satisfied with the day unless she spent the chief of it by the side of Mrs. Thorpe, in what they called conversation, but in which there was scarcely ever any exchange of opinion, and not often any resemblance of subject, for Mrs. Thorpe talked chiefly of her children, and Mrs. Allen of her gowns.

The progress of the friendship between Catherine and Isabella was quick as its beginning had been warm, and they passed so rapidly through every gradation of increasing tenderness that there was shortly no fresh proof of it to be given to their friends or themselves. They called each other by their Christian name, were always arm in arm when they walked, pinned up each other's train for the dance, and were not to be divided in the set; and if a rainy morning deprived them of other enjoyments, they were still resolute in meeting in defiance of wet and dirt, and shut themselves up, to read novels together. Yes, novels;--for I will not adopt that ungenerous and impolitic custom so common with novel writers, of degrading by their contemptuous censure the very performances, to the number of which they are themselves adding--joining with their greatest enemies in bestowing the harshest epithets on such works, and scarcely ever permitting them to be read by their own heroine, who, if she accidentally take up a novel, is sure to turn over its insipid pages with disgust. Alas! If the heroine of one novel be not patronized by the heroine of another, from whom can she expect protection and regard? I cannot approve of it. Let us leave it to the reviewers to abuse such effusions of fancy at their leisure, and over every new novel to talk in threadbare strains of the trash with which the press now groans. Let us not desert one another; we are an injured body. Although our productions have afforded more extensive and unaffected pleasure than those of any other literary corporation in the world, no species of composition has been so much decried. From pride, ignorance, or fashion, our foes are almost as many as our readers. And while the abilities of the nine-hundredth abridger of the History of England, or of the man who collects and publishes in a volume some dozen lines of Milton, Pope, and Prior, with a paper from the Spectator, and a chapter from Sterne, are eulogized by a thousand pens,--there seems almost a general wish of decrying the capacity and undervaluing the labour of the novelist, and of slighting the performances which have only genius, wit, and taste to recommend them. "I am no novel reader --I seldom look into novels--Do not imagine that I often read novels--It is really very well for a novel."--Such is the common cant.--"And what are you reading, Miss--?" "Oh! It is only a novel!" replies the young lady, while she lays down her book with affected indifference, or momentary shame.--"It is only Cecilia, or Camilla, or Belinda"; or, in short, only some work in which the greatest powers of the mind are displayed, in which the most thorough knowledge of human nature, the happiest delineation of its varieties, the liveliest effusions of wit and humour are conveyed to the world in the best chosen language. Now, had the same young lady been engaged with a volume of the Spectator, instead of such a work, how proudly would she have produced the book, and told its name; though the chances must be against her being occupied by any part of that voluminous publication, of which either the matter or manner would not disgust a young person of taste: the substance of its papers so often consisting in the statement of improbable circumstances, unnatural characters, and topics of conversation, which no longer concern any one living; and their language, too, frequently so coarse as to give no very favourable idea of the age that could endure it.

CHAPTER 6

The following conversation, which took place between the two friends in the Pump-room one morning, after an acquaintance of eight or nine days, is given as a specimen of their very warm attachment, and of the delicacy, discretion, originality of thought, and literary taste which marked the reasonableness of that attachment.

They met by appointment; and as Isabella had arrived nearly five minutes before her friend, her first address naturally was, -- "My dearest creature, what can have made you so late? I have been waiting for you at least this age!"

"Have you, indeed! -- I am very sorry for it; but really I thought I was in very good time. It is but just one. I hope you have not been here long?"

"Oh! These ten ages at least. I am sure I have been here this half hour. But now, let us go and sit down at the other end of the room, and enjoy ourselves. I have an hundred things to say to you. In the first place, I was so afraid it would rain this morning, just as I wanted to set off; it looked very showery, and that would have thrown me into agonies! Do you know, I saw the prettiest hat you can imagine, in a shop window in Milsom Street just now -- very like yours, only with coquelicot ribbons instead of green; I quite longed for it. But, my dearest Catherine, what have you been doing with yourself all this morning? -- Have you gone on with Udolpho?"

"Yes, I have been reading it ever since I woke; and I am got to the black veil."

"Are you, indeed? How delightful! Oh! I would not tell you what is behind the black veil for the world! Are not you wild to know?"

"Oh! yes, quite; what can it be? -- But do not tell me -- I would not be told upon any account. I know it must be a skeleton, I am sure it is Laurentina's skeleton. Oh! I am delighted with the book! I should like to spend my whole life in reading it. I assure you, if it had not been to meet you, I would not have come away from it for all the world."

"Dear creature! how much I am obliged to you; and when you have finished Udolpho, we will read the Italian together; and I have made out a list of ten or twelve more of the same kind for you."

"Have you, indeed! How glad I am! -- What are they all?"

"I will read you their names directly; here they are, in my

pocket-book. Castle of Wolfenbach, Clermont, Mysterious Warnings, Necromancer of the Black Forest, Midnight Bell, Orphan of the Rhine, and Horrid Mysteries. Those will last us some time."

"Yes, pretty well; but are they all horrid, are you sure they are all horrid?"

"Yes, quite sure; for a particular friend of mine, a Miss Andrews, a sweet girl, one of the sweetest creatures in the world, has read every one of them. I wish you knew Miss Andrews, you would be delighted with her. She is netting herself the sweetest cloak you can conceive. I think her as beautiful as an angel, and I am so vexed with the men for not admiring her! -- I scold them all amazingly about it."

"Scold them! Do you scold them for not admiring her?"

"Yes, that I do. There is nothing I would not do for those who are really my friends. I have no notion of loving people by halves; it is not my nature. My attachments are always excessively strong. I told Captain Hunt at one of our assemblies this winter that if he was to tease me all night, I would not dance with him, unless he would allow Miss Andrews to be as beautiful as an angel. The men think us incapable of real friendship, you know, and I am determined to shew them the difference. Now, if I were to hear any body speak slightingly of you, I should fire up in a moment: -- but that is not at all likely, for *you* are just the kind of girl to be a great favourite with the men."

"Oh, dear!" cried Catherine, colouring. "How can you say so?"

"I know you very well; you have so much animation, which is exactly what Miss Andrews wants, for I must confess there is something amazingly insipid about her. Oh! I must tell you, that just after we parted yesterday, I saw a young man looking at you so earnestly--I am sure he is in love with you." Catherine coloured, and disclaimed again. Isabella laughed. "It is very true, upon my honour, but I see how it is; you are indifferent to every body's admiration, except that of one gentleman, who shall be nameless. Nay, I cannot blame you -- speaking more seriously -- your feelings are easily understood. Where the heart is really attached, I know very well how little one can be pleased with the attention of any body else. Every thing is so insipid, so uninteresting, that does not relate to the beloved object! I can perfectly comprehend your feelings."

"But you should not persuade me that I think so very much about Mr. Tilney, for perhaps I may never see him again."

"Not see him again! My dearest creature, do not talk of it. I am sure you would be miserable if you thought so!"

"No, indeed, I should not. I do not pretend to say that I was not very much pleased with him; but while I have Udolpho to read, I feel as if nobody could make me miserable. Oh! the dreadful black veil! My dear Isabella, I am sure there must be Laurentina's skeleton behind it."

"It is so odd to me, that you should never have read Udolpho before; but I suppose Mrs. Morland objects to novels."

"No, she does not. She very often reads Sir Charles Grandison herself; but new books do not fall in our way."

"Sir Charles Grandison! That is an amazing horrid book, is it not? -- I remember Miss Andrews could not get through the first volume."

"It is not like Udolpho at all; but yet I think it is very entertaining."

"Do you indeed! -- you surprise me; I thought it had not been readable. But, my dearest Catherine, have you settled what to wear on your head to-night? I am determined at all events to be dressed exactly like you. The men take notice of *that* sometimes, you know."

"But it does not signify if they do," said Catherine, very innocently.

"Signify! Oh, heavens! I make it a rule never to mind what they say. They are very often amazingly impertinent if you do not treat them with spirit, and make them keep their distance."

"Are they? --Well, I never observed *that*. They always behave very well to me."

"Oh! they give themselves such airs. They are the most conceited creatures in the world, and think themselves of so much importance! -- By the bye, though I have thought of it a hundred times, I have always forgot to ask you what is your favourite complexion in a man. Do you like them best dark or fair?"

"I hardly know. I never much thought about it. Something between both, I think. Brown -- not fair, and--and not very dark."

"Very well, Catherine. That is exactly he. I have not forgot your description of Mr. Tilney -- 'a brown skin, with dark eyes, and rather dark hair.' -- Well, my taste is different. I prefer light eyes, and as to complexion -- do you know -- I like a sallow better than any other.

You must not betray me, if you should ever meet with one of your acquaintance answering that description."

"Betray you! -- What do you mean?"

"Nay, do not distress me. I believe I have said too much. Let us drop the subject."

Catherine, in some amazement, complied, and after remaining a few moments silent, was on the point of reverting to what interested her at that time rather more than any thing else in the world, Laurentina's skeleton, when her friend prevented her, by saying, -- "For heaven's sake! let us move away from this end of the room. Do you know, there are two odious young men who have been staring at me this half hour. They really put me quite out of countenance. Let us go and look at the arrivals. They will hardly follow us there."

Away they walked to the book; and while Isabella examined the names, it was Catherine's employment to watch the proceedings of these alarming young men.

"They are not coming this way, are they? I hope they are not so impertinent as to follow us. Pray let me know if they are coming. I am determined I will not look up."

In a few moments Catherine, with unaffected pleasure, assured her that she need not be longer uneasy, as the gentlemen had just left the Pump-room.

"And which way are they gone?" said Isabella, turning hastily round. "One was a very good-looking young man."

"They went towards the church-yard."

"Well, I am amazingly glad I have got rid of them! And now, what say you to going to Edgar's Buildings with me, and looking at my new hat? You said you should like to see it."

Catherine readily agreed. "Only," she added, "perhaps we may overtake the two young men."

"Oh! never mind that. If we make haste, we shall pass by them presently, and I am dying to shew you my hat."

"But if we only wait a few minutes, there will be no danger of our seeing them at all."

"I shall not pay them any such compliment, I assure you. I have no notion of treating men with such respect. *That* is the way to spoil them."

Catherine had nothing to oppose against such reasoning; and therefore, to shew the independence of Miss Thorpe, and her

29

resolution of humbling the sex, they set off immediately as fast as they could walk, in pursuit of the two young men.

CHAPTER 7

Half a minute conducted them through the Pump-yard to the archway, opposite Union-passage; but here they were stopped. Every body acquainted with Bath may remember the difficulties of crossing Cheap Street at this point; it is indeed a street of so impertinent a nature, so unfortunately connected with the great London and Oxford roads, and the principal inn of the city, that a day never passes in which parties of ladies, however important their business, whether in quest of pastry, millinery, or even (as in the present case) of young men, are not detained on one side or other by carriages, horsemen, or carts. This evil had been felt and lamented, at least three times a day, by Isabella since her residence in Bath; and she was now fated to feel and lament it once more, for at the very moment of coming opposite to Union- passage, and within view of the two gentlemen who were proceeding through the crowds, and threading the gutters of that interesting alley, they were prevented crossing by the approach of a gig, driven along on bad pavement by a most knowing-looking coachman with all the vehemence that could most fitly endanger the lives of himself, his companion, and his horse.

"Oh, these odious gigs!" said Isabella, looking up, "how I detest them." But this detestation, though so just, was of short duration, for she looked again and exclaimed, "Delightful! Mr. Morland and my brother!"

"Good heaven! 'tis James!" was uttered at the same moment by Catherine; and, on catching the young men's eyes, the horse was immediately checked with a violence which almost threw him on his haunches, and the servant having now scampered up, the gentlemen jumped out, and the equipage was delivered to his care.

Catherine, by whom this meeting was wholly unexpected, received her brother with the liveliest pleasure; and he, being of a very amiable disposition, and sincerely attached to her, gave every proof on his side of equal satisfaction, which he could have leisure to do, while the bright eyes of Miss Thorpe were incessantly challenging his notice; and to her his devoirs were speedily paid, with a mixture of joy and embarrassment which might have informed Catherine, had she been more expert in the development of other people's feelings, and less simply engrossed by her own, that her brother thought her friend quite as pretty as she could do herself.

John Thorpe, who in the mean time had been giving orders about the horses, soon joined them, and from him she directly received the amends which were her due; for while he slightly and carelessly touched the hand of Isabella, on her he bestowed a whole scrape and half a short bow. He was a stout young man of middling height, who, with a plain face and ungraceful form, seemed fearful of being too handsome unless he wore the dress of a groom, and too much like a gentleman unless he were easy where he ought to be civil, and impudent where he might be allowed to be easy. He took out his watch: "How long do you think we have been running it from Tetbury, Miss Morland?"

"I do not know the distance." Her brother told her that it was twenty-three miles.

"*Three* and twenty!" cried Thorpe. "Five and twenty if it is an inch." Morland remonstrated, pleaded the authority of road-books, innkeepers, and milestones; but his friend disregarded them all; he had a surer test of distance. "I know it must be five and twenty," said he, "by the time we have been doing it. It is now half after one; we drove out of the inn-yard at Tetbury as the town clock struck eleven; and I defy any man in England to make my horse go less than ten miles an hour in harness; that makes it exactly twenty-five."

"You have lost an hour," said Morland; "it was only ten o'clock when we came from Tetbury."

"Ten o'clock! it was eleven, upon my soul! I counted every stroke. This brother of yours would persuade me out of my senses, Miss Morland; do but look at my horse; did you ever see an animal so made for speed in your life?" (The servant had just mounted the carriage and was driving off.) "Such true blood! Three hours and a half indeed coming only three-and-twenty miles! Look at that creature, and suppose it possible if you can."

"He *does* look very hot, to be sure."

"Hot! he had not turned a hair till we came to Walcot Church; but look at his forehead; look at his loins; only see how he moves; that horse *cannot* go less than ten miles an hour: tie his legs and he

31

will get on. What do you think of my gig, Miss Morland? A neat one, is not it? Well hung; town-built; I have not had it a month. It was built for a Christ-church man, a friend of mine, a very good sort of fellow; he ran it a few weeks, till, I believe, it was convenient to have done with it. I happened just then to be looking out for some light thing of the kind, though I had pretty well determined on a curricle too; but I chanced to meet him on Magdalen Bridge, as he was driving into Oxford, last term: 'Ah! Thorpe,' says he, 'do you happen to want such a little thing as this? It is a capital one of the kind, but I am cursed tired of it.' 'Oh! d--,' said I; 'I am your man; what do you ask?' And how much do you think he did, Miss Morland?"

"I am sure I cannot guess at all."

"Curricle-hung, you see; seat, trunk, sword-case, splashing-board, lamps, silver moulding, all you see complete; the iron-work as good as new, or better. He asked fifty guineas; I closed with him directly, threw down the money, and the carriage was mine."

"And I am sure," said Catherine, "I know so little of such things that I cannot judge whether it was cheap or dear."

"Neither one nor t'other; I might have got it for less, I dare say; but I hate haggling, and poor Freeman wanted cash."

"That was very good-natured of you," said Catherine, quite pleased.

"Oh! d---- it, when one has the means of doing a kind thing by a friend, I hate to be pitiful."

An inquiry now took place into the intended movements of the young ladies; and, on finding whither they were going, it was decided that the gentlemen should accompany them to Edgar's Buildings, and pay their respects to Mrs. Thorpe. James and Isabella led the way; and so well satisfied was the latter with her lot, so contentedly was she endeavouring to ensure a pleasant walk to him who brought the double recommendation of being her brother's friend, and her friend's brother, so pure and uncoquettish were her feelings, that, though they overtook and passed the two offending young men in Milsom Street, she was so far from seeking to attract their notice, that she looked back at them only three times.

John Thorpe kept of course with Catherine, and, after a few minutes' silence, renewed the conversation about his gig. -- "You will find, however, Miss Morland, it would be reckoned a cheap thing by some people, for I might have sold it for ten guineas more the next day; Jackson, of Oriel, bid me sixty at once; Morland was with me at the time."

"Yes," said Morland, who overheard this; "but you forget that your horse was included."

"My horse! oh, d---- it! I would not sell my horse for a hundred. Are you fond of an open carriage, Miss Morland?"

"Yes, very; I have hardly ever had an opportunity of being in one; but I am particularly fond of it."

"I am glad of it; I will drive you out in mine every day."

"Thank you," said Catherine, in some distress, from a doubt of the propriety of accepting such an offer.

"I will drive you up Lansdown Hill to-morrow."

"Thank you; but will not your horse want rest?"

"Rest! he has only come three-and-twenty miles to-day; all nonsense; nothing ruins horses so much as rest; nothing knocks them up so soon. No, no; I shall exercise mine at the average of four hours every day while I am here."

"Shall you indeed!" said Catherine very seriously, "that will be forty miles a day."

"Forty! aye, fifty, for what I care. Well, I will drive you up Lansdown to-morrow; mind, I am engaged."

"How delightful that will be!" cried Isabella, turning round. "My dearest Catherine, I quite envy you; but I am afraid, brother, you will not have room for a third."

"A third indeed! no, no; I did not come to Bath to drive my sisters about; that would be a good joke, faith! Morland must take care of you."

This brought on a dialogue of civilities between the other two; but Catherine heard neither the particulars nor the result. Her companion's discourse now sunk from its hitherto animated pitch to nothing more than a short decisive sentence of praise or condemnation on the face of every woman they met; and Catherine, after listening and agreeing as long as she could, with all the civility and deference of the youthful female mind, fearful of hazarding an opinion of its own in opposition to that of a self-assured man, especially where the beauty of her own sex is concerned, ventured at length to vary the subject by a question which had been long uppermost in her thoughts; it was, "Have you ever read Udolpho, Mr. Thorpe?"

"Udolpho! Oh, Lord! not I; I never read novels; I have something else to do."

Catherine, humbled and ashamed, was going to apologize for her question, but he prevented her by saying, "Novels are all so full of nonsense and stuff; there has not been a tolerably decent one come out since Tom Jones, except The Monk; I read that t'other day; but as for all the others, they are the stupidest things in creation."

"I think you must like Udolpho, if you were to read it; it is so very interesting."

"Not I, faith! No, if I read any, it shall be Mrs. Radcliffe's; her novels are amusing enough; they are worth reading; some fun and nature in *them*."

"Udolpho was written by Mrs. Radcliffe," said Catherine, with some hesitation, from the fear of mortifying him.

"No sure; was it? Aye, I remember, so it was; I was thinking of that other stupid book, written by that woman they make such a fuss about, she who married the French emigrant."

"I suppose you mean Camilla?"

"Yes, that's the book; such unnatural stuff! -- An old man playing at see-saw! I took up the first volume once and looked it over, but I soon found it would not do; indeed I guessed what sort of stuff it must be before I saw it: as soon as I heard she had married an emigrant, I was sure I should never be able to get through it."

"I have never read it."

"You had no loss, I assure you; it is the horridest nonsense you can imagine; there is nothing in the world in it but an old man's playing at see-saw and learning Latin; upon my soul there is not."

This critique, the justness of which was unfortunately lost on poor Catherine, brought them to the door of Mrs. Thorpe's lodgings, and the feelings of the discerning and unprejudiced reader of Camilla gave way to the feelings of the dutiful and affectionate son, as they met Mrs. Thorpe, who had descried them from above, in the passage. "Ah, mother! how do you do?" said he, giving her a hearty shake of the hand. "Where did you get that quiz of a hat? It makes you look like an old witch. Here is Morland and I come to stay a few days with you, so you must look out for a couple of good beds somewhere near." And this address seemed to satisfy all the fondest wishes of the mother's heart, for she received him with the most delighted and exulting affection. On his two younger sisters he then bestowed an equal portion of his fraternal tenderness, for he asked

34

each of them how they did, and observed that they both looked very ugly.

These manners did not please Catherine; but he was James's friend and Isabella's brother; and her judgment was further bought off by Isabella's assuring her, when they withdrew to see the new hat, that John thought her the most charming girl in the world, and by John's engaging her before they parted to dance with him that evening. Had she been older or vainer, such attacks might have done little; but, where youth and diffidence are united, it requires uncommon steadiness of reason to resist the attraction of being called the most charming girl in the world, and of being so very early engaged as a partner; and the consequence was that, when the two Morlands, after sitting an hour with the Thorpes, set off to walk together to Mr. Allen's, and James, as the door was closed on them, said, "Well, Catherine, how do you like my friend Thorpe?" instead of answering, as she probably would have done, had there been no friendship and no flattery in the case, "I do not like him at all," she directly replied, "I like him very much; he seems very agreeable."

"He is as good-natured a fellow as ever lived; a little of a rattle; but that will recommend him to your sex, I believe: and how do you like the rest of the family?"

"Very, very much indeed: Isabella particularly."

"I am very glad to hear you say so; she is just the kind of young woman I could wish to see you attached to; she has so much good sense, and is so thoroughly unaffected and amiable; I always wanted you to know her; and she seems very fond of you. She said the highest things in your praise that could possibly be; and the praise of such a girl as Miss Thorpe even you, Catherine," taking her hand with affection, "may be proud of."

"Indeed I am," she replied; "I love her exceedingly, and am delighted to find that you like her too. You hardly mentioned any thing of her when you wrote to me after your visit there."

"Because I thought I should soon see you myself. I hope you will be a great deal together while you are in Bath. She is a most amiable girl; such a superior understanding! How fond all the family are of her; she is evidently the general favourite; and how much she must be admired in such a place as this -- is not she?"

"Yes, very much indeed, I fancy; Mr. Allen thinks her the prettiest girl in Bath."

"I dare say he does; and I do not know any man who is a better judge of beauty than Mr. Allen. I need not ask you whether you are happy here, my dear Catherine; with such a companion and friend as Isabella Thorpe, it would be impossible for you to be otherwise; and the Allens, I am sure, are very kind to you?"

"Yes, very kind; I never was so happy before; and now you are come it will be more delightful than ever; how good it is of you to come so far on purpose to see *me*."

James accepted this tribute of gratitude, and qualified his conscience for accepting it too, by saying with perfect sincerity, "Indeed, Catherine, I love you dearly."

Inquiries and communications concerning brothers and sisters, the situation of some, the growth of the rest, and other family matters now passed between them, and continued, with only one small digression on James's part, in praise of Miss Thorpe, till they reached Pulteney Street, where he was welcomed with great kindness by Mr. and Mrs. Allen, invited by the former to dine with them, and summoned by the latter to guess the price and weigh the merits of a new muff and tippet. A pre-engagement in Edgar's Buildings prevented his accepting the invitation of one friend, and obliged him to hurry away as soon as he had satisfied the demands of the other. The time of the two parties uniting in the Octagon Room being correctly adjusted, Catherine was then left to the luxury of a raised, restless, and frightened imagination over the pages of Udolpho, lost from all worldly concerns of dressing and dinner, incapable of soothing Mrs. Allen's fears on the delay of an expected dress-maker, and having only one minute in sixty to bestow even on the reflection of her own felicity, in being already engaged for the evening.

CHAPTER 8

In spite of Udolpho and the dress-maker, however, the party from Pulteney Street reached the Upper Rooms in very good time. The Thorpes and James Morland were there only two minutes before them; and Isabella having gone through the usual ceremonial of meeting her friend with the most smiling and affectionate haste, of admiring the set of her gown, and envying the curl of her hair, they followed their chaperones, arm in arm, into the ballroom, whispering to each other whenever a thought occurred, and supplying the place of many ideas by a squeeze of the hand or a smile of affection.

The dancing began within a few minutes after they were seated; and James, who had been engaged quite as long as his sister, was very importunate with Isabella to stand up; but John was gone into the card-room to speak to a friend, and nothing, she declared, should induce her to join the set before her dear Catherine could join it too: "I assure you," said she, "I would not stand up without your dear sister for all the world; for if I did we should certainly be separated the whole evening." Catherine accepted this kindness with gratitude, and they continued as they were for three minutes longer, when Isabella, who had been talking to James on the other side of her, turned again to his sister and whispered, "My dear creature, I am afraid I must leave you, your brother is so amazingly impatient to begin; I know you will not mind my going away, and I dare say John will be back in a moment, and then you may easily find me out." Catherine, though a little disappointed, had too much good-nature to make any opposition, and the others rising up, Isabella had only time to press her friend's hand and say, "Good bye, my dear love," before they hurried off. The younger Miss Thorpes being also dancing, Catherine was left to the mercy of Mrs. Thorpe and Mrs. Allen, between whom she now remained. She could not help being vexed at the non-appearance of Mr. Thorpe, for she not only longed to be dancing, but was likewise aware that, as the real dignity of her situation could not be known, she was sharing with the scores of other young ladies still sitting down all the discredit of wanting a partner. To be disgraced in the eye of the world, to wear the appearance of infamy while her heart is all purity, her actions all innocence, and the misconduct of another the true source of her debasement, is one of those circumstances which peculiarly belong to the heroine's life, and her fortitude under it what particularly dignifies her character. Catherine had fortitude too; she suffered, but no murmur passed her lips.

From this state of humiliation, she was roused, at the end of ten minutes, to a pleasanter feeling, by seeing, not Mr. Thorpe, but Mr. Tilney, within three yards of the place where they sat; he seemed to be moving that way, but he did not see her, and therefore the smile and the blush, which his sudden reappearance raised in Catherine, passed away without sullying her heroic importance. He looked as handsome and as lively as ever, and was talking with interest to a fashionable and pleasing-looking young woman, who leant on his arm, and whom Catherine immediately guessed to be his sister; thus unthinkingly throwing away a fair opportunity of considering him lost to her for ever, by being married already. But guided only by what was simple and probable, it had never entered her head that Mr. Tilney could be married; he had not behaved, he had not talked, like the married men to whom she had been used; he had never mentioned a wife, and he had acknowledged a sister. From these circumstances sprang the instant conclusion of his sister's now being by his side; and therefore, instead of turning of a deathlike paleness, and falling in a fit on Mrs. Allen's bosom, Catherine sat erect, in the perfect use of her senses, and with cheeks only a little redder than usual.

Mr. Tilney and his companion, who continued, though slowly, to approach, were immediately preceded by a lady, an acquaintance of Mrs. Thorpe; and this lady stopping to speak to her, they, as belonging to her, stopped likewise, and Catherine, catching Mr. Tilney's eye, instantly received from him the smiling tribute of recognition. She returned it with pleasure, and then advancing still nearer, he spoke both to her and Mrs. Allen, by whom he was very civilly acknowledged. "I am very happy to see you again, sir, indeed; I was afraid you had left Bath." He thanked her for her fears, and said that he had quitted it for a week, on the very morning after his having had the pleasure of seeing her.

"Well, sir, and I dare say you are not sorry to be back again, for it is just the place for young people -- and indeed for everybody else too. I tell Mr. Allen, when he talks of being sick of it, that I am sure he should not complain, for it is so very agreeable a place, that it is much better to be here than at home at this dull time of year. I tell him he is quite in luck to be sent here for his health."

"And I hope, madam, that Mr. Allen will be obliged to like the place, from finding it of service to him."

"Thank you, sir. I have no doubt that he will. -- A neighbour of ours, Dr. Skinner, was here for his health last winter, and came away quite stout."

"That circumstance must give great encouragement."

"Yes, sir -- and Dr. Skinner and his family were here three months; so I tell Mr. Allen he must not be in a hurry to get away."

Here they were interrupted by a request from Mrs. Thorpe to Mrs. Allen, that she would move a little to accommodate Mrs. Hughes and Miss Tilney with seats, as they had agreed to join their party. This was accordingly done, Mr. Tilney still continuing standing before them; and after a few minutes' consideration, he asked Catherine to dance with him. This compliment, delightful as it was, produced severe mortification to the lady; and in giving her denial, she expressed her sorrow on the occasion so very much as if she really felt it, that had Thorpe, who joined her just afterwards, been half a minute earlier, he might have thought her sufferings rather too acute. The very easy manner in which he then told her that he had kept her waiting did not by any means reconcile her more to her lot; nor did the particulars which he entered into while they were standing up, of the horses and dogs of the friend whom he had just left, and of a proposed exchange of terriers between them, interest her so much as to prevent her looking very often towards that part of the room where she had left Mr. Tilney. Of her dear Isabella, to whom she particularly longed to point out that gentleman, she could see nothing. They were in different sets. She was separated from all her party, and away from all her acquaintance; -- one mortification succeeded another, and from the whole she deduced this useful lesson, that to go previously engaged to a ball does not necessarily increase either the dignity or enjoyment of a young lady. From such a moralizing strain as this, she was suddenly roused by a touch on the shoulder, and turning round, perceived Mrs. Hughes directly behind her, attended by Miss Tilney and a gentleman. "I beg your pardon, Miss Morland," said she, "for this liberty, -- but I cannot any how get to Miss Thorpe, and Mrs. Thorpe said she was sure you would not have the least objection to letting in this young lady by you." Mrs. Hughes could not have applied to any creature in the room more happy to oblige her than Catherine. The young ladies were introduced to each other, Miss Tilney expressing a proper sense of such goodness, Miss Morland with the real delicacy of a generous mind making light of the obligation; and Mrs. Hughes, satisfied with having so respectably settled her young charge, returned to her party.

Miss Tilney had a good figure, a pretty face, and a very agreeable countenance; and her air, though it had not all the decided pretension, the resolute stylishness of Miss Thorpe's, had more real elegance. Her manners shewed good sense and good breeding; they

39

were neither shy nor affectedly open; and she seemed capable of being young, attractive, and at a ball, without wanting to fix the attention of every man near her, and without exaggerated feelings of extatic delight or inconceivable vexation on every little trifling occurrence. Catherine, interested at once by her appearance and her relationship to Mr. Tilney, was desirous of being acquainted with her, and readily talked therefore whenever she could think of any thing to say, and had courage and leisure for saying it. But the hindrance thrown in the way of a very speedy intimacy, by the frequent want of one or more of these requisites, prevented their doing more than going through the first rudiments of an acquaintance, by informing themselves how well the other liked Bath, how much she admired its buildings and surrounding country, whether she drew, or played, or sang, and whether she was fond of riding on horseback.

The two dances were scarcely concluded before Catherine found her arm gently seized by her faithful Isabella, who in great spirits exclaimed, -- "At last I have got you. My dearest creature, I have been looking for you this hour. What could induce you to come into this set, when you knew I was in the other? I have been quite wretched without you."

"My dear Isabella, how was it possible for me to get at you? I could not even see where you were."

"So I told your brother all the time -- but he would not believe me. Do go and see for her, Mr. Morland, said I -- but all in vain -- he would not stir an inch. Was not it so, Mr. Morland? But you men are all so immoderately lazy! I have been scolding him to such a degree, my dear Catherine, you would be quite amazed. -- You know I never stand upon ceremony with such people."

"Look at that young lady with the white beads round her head," whispered Catherine, detaching her friend from James. -- "It is Mr. Tilney's sister."

"Oh! heavens! You don't say so! Let me look at her this moment. What a delightful girl! I never saw any thing half so beautiful! But where is her all-conquering brother? Is he in the room? Point him out to me this instant, if he is. I die to see him. Mr. Morland, you are not to listen. We are not talking about you."

"But what is all this whispering about? What is going on?"

"There now, I knew how it would be. You men have such restless curiosity! Talk of the curiosity of women, indeed! -- 'tis

40

nothing. But be satisfied, for you are not to know any thing at all of the matter."

"And is that likely to satisfy me, do you think?"

"Well, I declare I never knew any thing like you. What can it signify to you, what we are talking of? Perhaps we are talking about you; therefore I would advise you not to listen, or you may happen to hear something not very agreeable."

In this common-place chatter, which lasted some time, the original subject seemed entirely forgotten; and though Catherine was very well pleased to have it dropped for a while, she could not avoid a little suspicion at the total suspension of all Isabella's impatient desire to see Mr. Tilney. When the orchestra struck up a fresh dance, James would have led his fair partner away, but she resisted. "I tell you, Mr. Morland," she cried, "I would not do such a thing for all the world. How can you be so teasing; only conceive, my dear Catherine, what your brother wants me to do. He wants me to dance with him again, though I tell him that it is a most improper thing, and entirely against the rules. It would make us the talk of the place, if we were not to change partners."

"Upon my honour," said James, "in these public assemblies, it is as often done as not."

"Nonsense, how can you say so? But when you men have a point to carry, you never stick at any thing. My sweet Catherine, do support me; persuade your brother how impossible it is. Tell him that it would quite shock you to see me do such a thing; now would not it?"

"No, not at all; but if you think it wrong, you had much better change."

"There," cried Isabella, "you hear what your sister says, and yet you will not mind her. Well, remember that it is not my fault, if we set all the old ladies in Bath in a bustle. Come along, my dearest Catherine, for heaven's sake, and stand by me." And off they went, to regain their former place. John Thorpe, in the meanwhile, had walked away; and Catherine, ever willing to give Mr. Tilney an opportunity of repeating the agreeable request which had already flattered her once, made her way to Mrs. Allen and Mrs. Thorpe as fast as she could, in the hope of finding him still with them -- a hope which, when it proved to be fruitless, she felt to have been highly unreasonable. "Well, my dear," said Mrs. Thorpe, impatient for praise of her son, "I hope you have had an agreeable partner."

"Very agreeable, madam."

"I am glad of it. John has charming spirits, has not he?"

"Did you meet Mr. Tilney, my dear?" said Mrs. Allen.

"No, where is he?"

"He was with us just now, and said he was so tired of lounging about, that he was resolved to go and dance; so I thought perhaps he would ask you, if he met with you."

"Where can he be?" said Catherine, looking round; but she had not looked round long before she saw him leading a young lady to the dance.

"Ah! he has got a partner; I wish he had asked *you*," said Mrs. Allen; and after a short silence, she added, "he is a very agreeable young man."

"Indeed he is, Mrs. Allen," said Mrs. Thorpe, smiling complacently; "I must say it, though I *am* his mother, that there is not a more agreeable young man in the world."

This inapplicable answer might have been too much for the comprehension of many; but it did not puzzle Mrs. Allen, for after only a moment's consideration, she said, in a whisper to Catherine, "I dare say she thought I was speaking of her son."

Catherine was disappointed and vexed. She seemed to have missed by so little the very object she had had in view; and this persuasion did not incline her to a very gracious reply, when John Thorpe came up to her soon afterwards and said, "Well, Miss Morland, I suppose you and I are to stand up and jig it together again."

"Oh, no; I am much obliged to you, our two dances are over; and, besides, I am tired, and do not mean to dance any more."

"Do not you? -- then let us walk about and quiz people. Come along with me, and I will shew you the four greatest quizzers in the room; my two younger sisters and their partners. I have been laughing at them this half hour."

Again Catherine excused herself; and at last he walked off to quiz his sisters by himself. The rest of the evening she found very dull; Mr. Tilney was drawn away from their party at tea, to attend that of his partner; Miss Tilney, though belonging to it, did not sit near her, and James and Isabella were so much engaged in conversing together that the latter had no leisure to bestow more on her friend than one smile, one squeeze, and one "dearest Catherine."

CHAPTER 9

The progress of Catherine's unhappiness from the events of the evening was as follows. It appeared first in a general dissatisfaction with every body about her, while she remained in the rooms, which speedily brought on considerable weariness and a violent desire to go home. This, on arriving in Pulteney Street, took the direction of extraordinary hunger, and when that was appeased, changed into an earnest longing to be in bed; such was the extreme point of her distress; for when there she immediately fell into a sound sleep which lasted nine hours, and from which she awoke perfectly revived, in excellent spirits, with fresh hopes and fresh schemes. The first wish of her heart was to improve her acquaintance with Miss Tilney, and almost her first resolution, to seek her for that purpose, in the Pump-room at noon. In the Pump-room, one so newly arrived in Bath must be met with, and that building she had already found so favourable for the discovery of female excellence, and the completion of female intimacy, so admirably adapted for secret discourses and unlimited confidence, that she was most reasonably encouraged to expect another friend from within its walls. Her plan for the morning thus settled, she sat quietly down to her book after breakfast, resolving to remain in the same place and the same employment till the clock struck one; and from habitude very little incommoded by the remarks and ejaculations of Mrs. Allen, whose vacancy of mind and incapacity for thinking were such, that as she never talked a great deal, so she could never be entirely silent; and, therefore, while she sat at her work, if she lost her needle or broke her thread, if she heard a carriage in the street, or saw a speck upon her gown, she must observe it aloud, whether there were any one at leisure to answer her or not. At about half past twelve, a remarkably loud rap drew her in haste to the window, and scarcely had she time to inform Catherine of there being two open carriages at the door, in the first only a servant, her brother driving Miss Thorpe in the second, before John Thorpe came running up stairs, calling out, "Well, Miss Morland, here I am. Have you been waiting long? We could not come before; the old devil of a coachmaker was such an eternity finding out a thing fit to be got into, and now it is ten thousand to one, but they break down before we are out of the street. How do you do, Mrs. Allen? A famous ball last night, was not it? Come, Miss Morland, be quick, for the others are in a confounded hurry to be off. They want to get their tumble over."

"What do you mean?" said Catherine. "Where are you all going to?"

"Going to? Why, you have not forgot our engagement! Did not we agree together to take a drive this morning? What a head you have! We are going up Claverton Down."

"Something was said about it, I remember," said Catherine, looking at Mrs. Allen for her opinion; "but really I did not expect you."

"Not expect me! That's a good one! And what a dust you would have made, if I had not come."

Catherine's silent appeal to her friend, meanwhile, was entirely thrown away, for Mrs. Allen, not being at all in the habit of conveying any expression herself by a look, was not aware of its being ever intended by any body else; and Catherine, whose desire of seeing Miss Tilney again could at that moment bear a short delay in favour of a drive, and who thought there could be no impropriety in her going with Mr. Thorpe, as Isabella was going at the same time with James, was therefore obliged to speak plainer. "Well, ma'am, what do you say to it? Can you spare me for an hour or two? Shall I go?"

"Do just as you please, my dear," replied Mrs. Allen, with the most placid indifference. Catherine took the advice, and ran off to get ready. In a very few minutes she reappeared, having scarcely allowed the two others time enough to get through a few short sentences in her praise, after Thorpe had procured Mrs. Allen's admiration of his gig; and then receiving her friend's parting good wishes, they both hurried down stairs. "My dearest creature," cried Isabella, to whom the duty of friendship immediately called her before she could get into the carriage, "you have been at least three hours getting ready. I was afraid you were ill. What a delightful ball we had last night. I have a thousand things to say to you; but make haste and get in, for I long to be off."

Catherine followed her orders and turned away, but not too soon to hear her friend exclaim aloud to James, "What a sweet girl she is! I quite dote on her."

"You will not be frightened, Miss Morland," said Thorpe, as he handed her in, "if my horse should dance about a little at first setting off. He will, most likely, give a plunge or two, and perhaps take the rest for a minute; but he will soon know his master. He is full of spirits, playful as can be, but there is no vice in him."

Catherine did not think the portrait a very inviting one, but it was too late to retreat, and she was too young to own herself frightened; so, resigning herself to her fate, and trusting to the animal's boasted knowledge of its owner, she sat peaceably down, and saw Thorpe sit down by her. Every thing being then arranged, the servant who stood at the horse's head was bid in an important voice "to let him go," and off they went in the quietest manner imaginable, without a plunge or a caper, or any thing like one. Catherine, delighted at so happy an escape, spoke her pleasure aloud with grateful surprise; and her companion immediately made the matter perfectly simple by assuring her that it was entirely owing to the peculiarly judicious manner in which he had then held the reins, and the singular discernment and dexterity with which he had directed his whip. Catherine, though she could not help wondering that with such perfect command of his horse, he should think it necessary to alarm her with a relation of its tricks, congratulated herself sincerely on being under the care of so excellent a coachman; and perceiving that the animal continued to go on in the same quiet manner, without shewing the smallest propensity towards any unpleasant vivacity, and (considering its inevitable pace was ten miles an hour) by no means alarmingly fast, gave herself up to all the enjoyment of air and exercise of the most invigorating kind, in a fine mild day of February, with the consciousness of safety. A silence of several minutes succeeded their first short dialogue; -- it was broken by Thorpe's saying very abruptly, "Old Allen is as rich as a Jew -- is not he?" Catherine did not understand him -- and he repeated his question, adding in explanation, "Old Allen, the man you are with."

"Oh! Mr. Allen, you mean. Yes, I believe, he is very rich."

"And no children at all?"

"No -- not any."

"A famous thing for his next heirs. He is *your* godfather, is not he?"

"My godfather! -- no."

"But you are always very much with them."

"Yes, very much."

"Aye, that is what I meant. He seems a good kind of old fellow enough, and has lived very well in his time, I dare say; he is not gouty for nothing. Does he drink his bottle a-day now?"

45

"His bottle a-day! -- no. Why should you think of such a thing? He is a very temperate man, and you could not fancy him in liquor last night?"

"Lord help you! -- You women are always thinking of men's being in liquor. Why, you do not suppose a man is overset by a bottle? I am sure of *this* -- that if every body was to drink their bottle a-day, there would not be half the disorders in the world there are now. It would be a famous good thing for us all."

"I cannot believe it."

"Oh! Lord, it would be the saving of thousands. There is not the hundredth part of the wine consumed in this kingdom that there ought to be. Our foggy climate wants help."

"And yet I have heard that there is a great deal of wine drunk in Oxford."

"Oxford! There is no drinking at Oxford now, I assure you. Nobody drinks there. You would hardly meet with a man who goes beyond his four pints at the utmost. Now, for instance, it was reckoned a remarkable thing at the last party in my rooms, that upon an average we cleared about five pints a head. It was looked upon as something out of the common way. *Mine* is famous good stuff, to be sure. You would not often meet with any thing like it in Oxford-- and that may account for it. But this will just give you a notion of the general rate of drinking there."

"Yes, it does give a notion," said Catherine warmly, "and that is, that you all drink a great deal more wine than I thought you did. However, I am sure James does not drink so much."

This declaration brought on a loud and overpowering reply, of which no part was very distinct, except the frequent exclamations, amounting almost to oaths, which adorned it, and Catherine was left, when it ended, with rather a strengthened belief of there being a great deal of wine drunk in Oxford, and the same happy conviction of her brother's comparative sobriety.

Thorpe's ideas then all reverted to the merits of his own equipage, and she was called on to admire the spirit and freedom with which his horse moved along, and the ease which his paces, as well as the excellence of the springs, gave the motion of the carriage. She followed him in all his admiration as well as she could. To go before or beyond him was impossible. His knowledge and her ignorance of the subject, his rapidity of expression, and her diffidence of herself put that out of her power; she could strike out nothing new in commendation, but she readily echoed whatever he chose to assert, and it was finally settled between them without any difficulty that his equipage was altogether the most complete of its kind in England, his carriage the neatest, his horse the best goer, and himself the best coachman.-- "You do not really think, Mr. Thorpe," said Catherine, venturing after some time to consider the matter as entirely decided, and to offer some little variation on the subject, "that James's gig will break down?"

"Break down! Oh! Lord! Did you ever see such a little tittuppy thing in your life? There is not a sound piece of iron about it. The wheels have been fairly worn out these ten years at least--and as for the body! Upon my soul, you might shake it to pieces yourself with a touch. It is the most devilish little rickety business I ever beheld! Thank God! We have got a better. I would not be bound to go two miles in it for fifty thousand pounds."

"Good heavens!" cried Catherine, quite frightened. "Then pray let us turn back; they will certainly meet with an accident if we go on. Do let us turn back, Mr. Thorpe; stop and speak to my brother, and tell him how very unsafe it is."

"Unsafe! Oh, lord! What is there in that? They will only get a roll if it does break down; and there is plenty of dirt; it will be excellent falling. Oh, curse it! The carriage is safe enough, if a man knows how to drive it; a thing of that sort in good hands will last above twenty years after it is fairly worn out. Lord bless you! I would undertake for five pounds to drive it to York and back again, without losing a nail."

Catherine listened with astonishment; she knew not how to reconcile two such very different accounts of the same thing; for she had not been brought up to understand the propensities of a rattle, nor to know to how many idle assertions and impudent falsehoods the excess of vanity will lead. Her own family were plain, matter-of-fact people, who seldom aimed at wit of any kind; her father, at the utmost, being contented with a pun, and her mother with a proverb; they were not in the habit therefore of telling lies to increase their importance, or of asserting at one moment what they would contradict the next. She reflected on the affair for some time in much perplexity, and was more than once on the point of requesting from Mr. Thorpe a clearer insight into his real opinion on the subject; but she checked herself, because it appeared to her that he did not excel in giving those clearer insights, in making those things

47

plain which he had before made ambiguous; and, joining to this, the consideration that he would not really suffer his sister and his friend to be exposed to a danger from which he might easily preserve them, she concluded at last that he must know the carriage to be in fact perfectly safe, and therefore would alarm herself no longer. By him the whole matter seemed entirely forgotten; and all the rest of his conversation, or rather talk, began and ended with himself and his own concerns. He told her of horses which he had bought for a trifle and sold for incredible sums; of racing matches, in which his judgment had infallibly foretold the winner; of shooting parties, in which he had killed more birds (though without having one good shot) than all his companions together; and described to her some famous day's sport, with the fox-hounds, in which his foresight and skill in directing the dogs had repaired the mistakes of the most experienced huntsman, and in which the boldness of his riding, though it had never endangered his own life for a moment, had been constantly leading others into difficulties, which he calmly concluded had broken the necks of many.

Little as Catherine was in the habit of judging for herself, and unfixed as were her general notions of what men ought to be, she could not entirely repress a doubt, while she bore with the effusions of his endless conceit, of his being altogether completely agreeable. It was a bold surmise, for he was Isabella's brother; and she had been assured by James that his manners would recommend him to all her sex; but in spite of this, the extreme weariness of his company, which crept over her before they had been out an hour, and which continued unceasingly to increase till they stopped in Pulteney Street again, induced her, in some small degree, to resist such high authority, and to distrust his powers of giving universal pleasure.

When they arrived at Mrs. Allen's door, the astonishment of Isabella was hardly to be expressed, on finding that it was too late in the day for them to attend her friend into the house: -- "Past three o'clock!" It was inconceivable, incredible, impossible! and she would neither believe her own watch, nor her brother's, nor the servant's; she would believe no assurance of it founded on reason or reality, till Morland produced his watch, and ascertained the fact; to have doubted a moment longer *then* would have been equally inconceivable, incredible, and impossible; and she could only protest, over and over again, that no two hours and a half had ever gone off so swiftly before, as Catherine was called on to confirm; Catherine could not tell a falsehood even to please Isabella; but the latter was spared the misery of her friend's dissenting voice, by not waiting for her answer. Her own feelings entirely engrossed her; her wretchedness was most acute on finding herself obliged to go directly home. It was ages since she had had a moment's conversation with her dearest Catherine; and, though she had such thousands of things to say to her, it appeared as if they were never to be together again; so, with smiles of most exquisite misery, and the laughing eye of utter despondency, she bade her friend adieu and went on.

Catherine found Mrs. Allen just returned from all the busy idleness of the morning, and was immediately greeted with, "Well, my dear, here you are," a truth which she had no greater inclination than power to dispute; "and I hope you have had a pleasant airing?"

"Yes, ma'am, I thank you; we could not have had a nicer day."

"So Mrs. Thorpe said; she was vastly pleased at your all going."

"You have seen Mrs. Thorpe, then?"

"Yes, I went to the Pump-room as soon as you were gone, and there I met her, and we had a great deal of talk together. She says there was hardly any veal to be got at market this morning, it is so uncommonly scarce."

"Did you see any body else of our acquaintance?"

"Yes; we agreed to take a turn in the Crescent, and there we met Mrs. Hughes, and Mr. and Miss Tilney walking with her."

"Did you indeed? And did they speak to you?"

"Yes, we walked along the Crescent together for half an hour. They seem very agreeable people. Miss Tilney was in a very pretty spotted muslin, and I fancy, by what I can learn, that she always dresses very handsomely. Mrs. Hughes talked to me a great deal about the family."

"And what did she tell you of them?"

"Oh! A vast deal indeed; she hardly talked of any thing else."

"Did she tell you what part of Gloucestershire they come from?"

"Yes, she did; but I cannot recollect now. But they are very good kind of people, and very rich. Mrs. Tilney was a Miss Drummond, and she and Mrs. Hughes were school-fellows; and Miss Drummond had a very large fortune; and, when she married, her father gave her twenty thousand pounds, and five hundred to buy

49

wedding-clothes. Mrs. Hughes saw all the clothes after they came from the warehouse."

"And are Mr. and Mrs. Tilney in Bath?"

"Yes, I fancy they are, but I am not quite certain. Upon recollection, however, I have a notion they are both dead; at least the mother is; yes, I am sure Mrs. Tilney is dead, because Mrs. Hughes told me there was a very beautiful set of pearls that Mr. Drummond gave his daughter on her wedding-day and that Miss Tilney has got now, for they were put by for her when her mother died."

"And is Mr. Tilney, my partner, the only son?"

"I cannot be quite positive about that, my dear; I have some idea he is; but, however, he is a very fine young man, Mrs. Hughes says, and likely to do very well."

Catherine inquired no further; she had heard enough to feel that Mrs. Allen had no real intelligence to give, and that she was most particularly unfortunate herself in having missed such a meeting with both brother and sister. Could she have foreseen such a circumstance, nothing should have persuaded her to go out with the others; and, as it was, she could only lament her ill luck, and think over what she had lost, till it was clear to her that the drive had by no means been very pleasant and that John Thorpe himself was quite disagreeable.

CHAPTER 10

The Allens, Thorpes, and Morlands, all met in the evening at the theatre; and, as Catherine and Isabella sat together, there was then an opportunity for the latter to utter some few of the many thousand things which had been collecting within her for communication in the immeasurable length of time which had divided them. -- "Oh, heavens! My beloved Catherine, have I got you at last?" was her address on Catherine's entering the box and sitting by her. "Now, Mr. Morland," for he was close to her on the other side, "I shall not speak another word to you all the rest of the evening; so I charge you not to expect it. My sweetest Catherine, how have you been this long age? but I need not ask you, for you look delightfully. You really have done your hair in a more heavenly style than ever; you

50

mischievous creature, do you want to attract every body? I assure you, my brother is quite in love with you already; and as for Mr. Tilney--but *that* is a settled thing--even *your* modesty cannot doubt his attachment now; his coming back to Bath makes it too plain. Oh! What would not I give to see him! I really am quite wild with impatience. My mother says he is the most delightful young man in the world; she saw him this morning, you know; you must introduce him to me. Is he in the house now? -- Look about for heaven's sake! I assure you, I can hardly exist till I see him."

"No," said Catherine, "he is not here; I cannot see him anywhere."

"Oh, horrid! Am I never to be acquainted with him? How do you like my gown? I think it does not look amiss; the sleeves were entirely my own thought. Do you know I get so immoderately sick of Bath; your brother and I were agreeing this morning that, though it is vastly well to be here for a few weeks, we would not live here for millions. We soon found out that our tastes were exactly alike in preferring the country to every other place; really, our opinions were so exactly the same, it was quite ridiculous! There was not a single point in which we differed; I would not have had you by for the world; you are such a sly thing, I am sure you would have made some droll remark or other about it."

"No, indeed I should not."

"Oh, yes you would indeed; I know you better than you know yourself. You would have told us that we seemed born for each other, or some nonsense of that kind, which would have distressed me beyond conception; my cheeks would have been as red as your roses; I would not have had you by for the world."

"Indeed you do me injustice; I would not have made so improper a remark upon any account; and besides, I am sure it would never have entered my head."

Isabella smiled incredulously and talked the rest of the evening to James.

Catherine's resolution of endeavouring to meet Miss Tilney again continued in full force the next morning; and till the usual moment of going to the Pump-room, she felt some alarm from the dread of a second prevention. But nothing of that kind occurred, no visitors appeared to delay them, and they all three set off in good time for the Pump-room, where the ordinary course of events and conversation took place; Mr. Allen, after drinking his glass of water, joined some gentlemen to talk over the politics of the day and compare the accounts of their newspapers; and the ladies walked about together, noticing every new face, and almost every new bonnet in the room. The female part of the Thorpe family, attended by James Morland, appeared among the crowd in less than a quarter of an hour, and Catherine immediately took her usual place by the side of her friend. James, who was now in constant attendance, maintained a similar position, and separating themselves from the rest of their party, they walked in that manner for some time, till Catherine began to doubt the happiness of a situation which, confining her entirely to her friend and brother, gave her very little share in the notice of either. They were always engaged in some sentimental discussion or lively dispute, but their sentiment was conveyed in such whispering voices, and their vivacity attended with so much laughter, that though Catherine's supporting opinion was not unfrequently called for by one or the other, she was never able to give any, from not having heard a word of the subject. At length however she was empowered to disengage herself from her friend, by the avowed necessity of speaking to Miss Tilney, whom she most joyfully saw just entering the room with Mrs. Hughes, and whom she instantly joined, with a firmer determination to be acquainted, than she might have had courage to command, had she not been urged by the disappointment of the day before. Miss Tilney met her with great civility, returned her advances with equal goodwill, and they continued talking together as long as both parties remained in the room; and though in all probability not an observation was made, nor an expression used by either which had not been made and used some thousands of times before, under that roof, in every Bath season, yet the merit of their being spoken with simplicity and truth, and without personal conceit, might be something uncommon.

"How well your brother dances!" was an artless exclamation of Catherine's towards the close of their conversation, which at once surprised and amused her companion.

"Henry!" she replied with a smile. "Yes, he does dance very well."

"He must have thought it very odd to hear me say I was engaged the other evening, when he saw me sitting down. But I really had been engaged the whole day to Mr. Thorpe." Miss Tilney could only bow. "You cannot think," added Catherine after a moment's silence, "how surprised I was to see him again. I felt so sure of his being quite gone away."

"When Henry had the pleasure of seeing you before, he was in Bath but for a couple of days. He came only to engage lodgings for us."

"*That* never occurred to me; and of course, not seeing him anywhere, I thought he must be gone. Was not the young lady he danced with on Monday a Miss Smith?"

"Yes, an acquaintance of Mrs. Hughes."

"I dare say she was very glad to dance. Do you think her pretty?"

"Not very."

"He never comes to the Pump-room, I suppose?"

"Yes, sometimes; but he has rid out this morning with my father."

Mrs. Hughes now joined them, and asked Miss Tilney if she was ready to go. "I hope I shall have the pleasure of seeing you again soon," said Catherine. "Shall you be at the cotillion ball to-morrow?"

"Perhaps we--yes, I think we certainly shall."

"I am glad of it, for we shall all be there." -- This civility was duly returned; and they parted -- on Miss Tilney's side with some knowledge of her new acquaintance's feelings, and on Catherine's, without the smallest consciousness of having explained them.

She went home very happy. The morning had answered all her hopes, and the evening of the following day was now the object of expectation, the future good. What gown and what head-dress she should wear on the occasion became her chief concern. She cannot be justified in it. Dress is at all times a frivolous distinction, and excessive solicitude about it often destroys its own aim. Catherine knew all this very well; her great aunt had read her a lecture on the subject only the Christmas before; and yet she lay awake ten minutes on Wednesday night debating between her spotted and her tamboured muslin, and nothing but the shortness of the time prevented her buying a new one for the evening. This would have been an error in judgment, great though not uncommon, from which one of the other sex rather than her own, a brother rather than a great aunt might have warned her, for man only can be aware of the insensibility of man towards a new gown. It would be mortifying to the feelings of many ladies, could they be made to understand how little the heart of man is affected by what is costly or new in their

53

attire; how little it is biased by the texture of their muslin, and how unsusceptible of peculiar tenderness towards the spotted, the sprigged, the mull, or the jackonet. Woman is fine for her own satisfaction alone. No man will admire her the more, no woman will like her the better for it. Neatness and fashion are enough for the former, and a something of shabbiness or impropriety will be most endearing to the latter. But not one of these grave reflections troubled the tranquillity of Catherine.

She entered the rooms on Thursday evening with feelings very different from what had attended her thither the Monday before. She had then been exulting in her engagement to Thorpe, and was now chiefly anxious to avoid his sight, lest he should engage her again; for though she could not, dared not expect that Mr. Tilney should ask her a third time to dance, her wishes, hopes, and plans all centred in nothing less. Every young lady may feel for my heroine in this critical moment, for every young lady has at some time or other known the same agitation. All have been, or at least all have believed themselves to be, in danger from the pursuit of some one whom they wished to avoid; and all have been anxious for the attentions of some one whom they wished to please. As soon as they were joined by the Thorpes, Catherine's agony began; she fidgeted about if John Thorpe came towards her, hid herself as much as possible from his view, and when he spoke to her pretended not to hear him. The cotillions were over, the country-dancing beginning, and she saw nothing of the Tilneys. "Do not be frightened, my dear Catherine," whispered Isabella, "but I am really going to dance with your brother again. I declare positively it is quite shocking. I tell him he ought to be ashamed of himself, but you and John must keep us in countenance. Make haste, my dear creature, and come to us. John is just walked off, but he will be back in a moment."

Catherine had neither time nor inclination to answer. The others walked away, John Thorpe was still in view, and she gave herself up for lost. That she might not appear, however, to observe or expect him, she kept her eyes intently fixed on her fan; and a self-condemnation for her folly, in supposing that among such a crowd they should even meet with the Tilneys in any reasonable time, had just passed through her mind, when she suddenly found herself addressed and again solicited to dance, by Mr. Tilney himself. With what sparkling eyes and ready motion she granted his request, and with how pleasing a flutter of heart she went with him to the set, may be easily imagined. To escape, and, as she believed, so narrowly escape John Thorpe, and to be asked, so immediately on his joining her, asked by Mr. Tilney, as if he had sought her on purpose! -- it did not appear to her that life could supply any greater felicity.

Scarcely had they worked themselves into the quiet possession of a place, however, when her attention was claimed by John Thorpe, who stood behind her. "Heyday, Miss Morland!" said he. "What is the meaning of this? I thought you and I were to dance together."

"I wonder you should think so, for you never asked me." "That is a good one, by Jove! -- I asked you as soon as I came into the room, and I was just going to ask you again, but when I turned round, you were gone! -- This is a cursed shabby trick! I only came for the sake of dancing with *you*, and I firmly believe you were engaged to me ever since Monday. Yes; I remember, I asked you while you were waiting in the lobby for your cloak. And here have I been telling all my acquaintance that I was going to dance with the prettiest girl in the room; and when they see you standing up with somebody else, they will quiz me famously."

"Oh, no; they will never think of *me*, after such a description as that."

"By heavens, if they do not, I will kick them out of the room for blockheads. What chap have you there?" Catherine satisfied his curiosity. "Tilney," he repeated. "Hum--I do not know him. A good figure of a man; well put together. Does he want a horse? Here is a friend of mine, Sam Fletcher, has got one to sell that would suit any body. A famous clever animal for the road--only forty guineas. I had fifty minds to buy it myself, for it is one of my maxims always to buy a good horse when I meet with one; but it would not answer my purpose, it would not do for the field. I would give any money for a real good hunter. I have three now, the best that ever were backed. I would not take eight hundred guineas for them. Fletcher and I mean to get a house in Leicestershire, against the next season. It is so d-- uncomfortable, living at an inn."

This was the last sentence by which he could weary Catherine's attention, for he was just then borne off by the resistless pressure of a long string of passing ladies. Her partner now drew near, and said, "That gentleman would have put me out of patience, had he stayed with you half a minute longer. He has no business to withdraw the

55

attention of my partner from me. We have entered into a contract of mutual agreeableness for the space of an evening, and all our agreeableness belongs solely to each other for that time. Nobody can fasten themselves on the notice of one, without injuring the rights of the other. I consider a country-dance as an emblem of marriage. Fidelity and complaisance are the principal duties of both; and those men who do not chuse to dance or marry themselves, have no business with the partners or wives of their neighbours."

"But they are such very different things!"

"--That you think they cannot be compared together."

"To be sure not. People that marry can never part, but must go and keep house together. People that dance, only stand opposite each other in a long room for half an hour."

"And such is your definition of matrimony and dancing. Taken in that light certainly, their resemblance is not striking; but I think I could place them in such a view. You will allow, that in both, man has the advantage of choice, woman only the power of refusal; that in both, it is an engagement between man and woman, formed for the advantage of each; and that when once entered into, they belong exclusively to each other till the moment of its dissolution; that it is their duty, each to endeavour to give the other no cause for wishing that he or she had bestowed themselves elsewhere, and their best interest to keep their own imaginations from wandering towards the perfections of their neighbours, or fancying that they should have been better off with any one else. You will allow all this?"

"Yes, to be sure, as you state it, all this sounds very well; but still they are so very different. -- I cannot look upon them at all in the same light, nor think the same duties belong to them."

"In one respect, there certainly is a difference. In marriage, the man is supposed to provide for the support of the woman, the woman to make the home agreeable to the man; he is to purvey, and she is to smile. But in dancing, their duties are exactly changed; the agreeableness, the compliance are expected from him, while she furnishes the fan and the lavender water. *That*, I suppose, was the difference of duties which struck you, as rendering the conditions incapable of comparison."

"No, indeed, I never thought of that."

"Then I am quite at a loss. One thing, however, I must observe. This disposition on your side is rather alarming. You totally disallow any similarity in the obligations; and may I not thence infer that your notions of the duties of the dancing state are not so strict as your partner might wish? Have I not reason to fear that if the gentleman who spoke to you just now were to return, or if any other gentleman were to address you, there would be nothing to restrain you from conversing with him as long as you chose?"

"Mr. Thorpe is such a very particular friend of my brother's, that if he talks to me, I must talk to him again; but there are hardly three young men in the room besides him that I have any acquaintance with."

"And is that to be my only security? Alas, alas!"

"Nay, I am sure you cannot have a better; for if I do not know any body, it is impossible for me to talk to them; and, besides, I do not *want* to talk to any body."

"Now you have given me a security worth having; and I shall proceed with courage. Do you find Bath as agreeable as when I had the honour of making the inquiry before?"

"Yes, quite -- more so, indeed."

"More so! Take care, or you will forget to be tired of it at the proper time. -- You ought to be tired at the end of six weeks."

"I do not think I should be tired, if I were to stay here six months."

"Bath, compared with London, has little variety, and so everybody finds out every year. 'For six weeks, I allow Bath is pleasant enough; but beyond *that*, it is the most tiresome place in the world.' You would be told so by people of all descriptions, who come regularly every winter, lengthen their six weeks into ten or twelve, and go away at last because they can afford to stay no longer."

"Well, other people must judge for themselves, and those who go to London may think nothing of Bath. But I, who live in a small retired village in the country, can never find greater sameness in such a place as this than in my own home; for here are a variety of amusements, a variety of things to be seen and done all day long, which I can know nothing of there."

"You are not fond of the country."

"Yes, I am. I have always lived there, and always been very happy. But certainly there is much more sameness in a country life than in a Bath life. One day in the country is exactly like another."

"But then you spend your time so much more rationally in the country."

"Do I?"

"Do you not?"

"I do not believe there is much difference."

"Here you are in pursuit only of amusement all day long."

"And so I am at home--only I do not find so much of it. I walk about here, and so I do there; -- but here I see a variety of people in every street, and there I can only go and call on Mrs. Allen."

Mr. Tilney was very much amused. "Only go and call on Mrs. Allen!" he repeated. "What a picture of intellectual poverty! However, when you sink into this abyss again, you will have more to say. You will be able to talk of Bath, and of all that you did here."

"Oh! Yes. I shall never be in want of something to talk of again to Mrs. Allen, or any body else. I really believe I shall always be talking of Bath, when I am at home again -- I *do* like it so very much. If I could but have Papa and Mamma, and the rest of them here, I suppose I should be too happy! James's coming (my eldest brother) is quite delightful -- and especially as it turns out that the very family we are just got so intimate with are his intimate friends already. Oh! Who can ever be tired of Bath?"

"Not those who bring such fresh feelings of every sort to it as you do. But papas and mammas, and brothers and intimate friends are a good deal gone by, to most of the frequenters of Bath -- and the honest relish of balls and plays, and everyday sights, is past with them."

Here their conversation closed, the demands of the dance becoming now too importunate for a divided attention.

Soon after their reaching the bottom of the set, Catherine perceived herself to be earnestly regarded by a gentleman who stood among the lookers-on, immediately behind her partner. He was a very handsome man, of a commanding aspect, past the bloom, but not past the vigour of life; and with his eye still directed towards her, she saw him presently address Mr. Tilney in a familiar whisper. Confused by his notice, and blushing from the fear of its being excited by something wrong in her appearance, she turned away her head. But while she did so, the gentleman retreated, and her partner, coming nearer, said, "I see that you guess what I have just been asked. That gentleman knows your name, and you have a right to know his. It is General Tilney, my father."

Catherine's answer was only "Oh!"--but it was an "Oh!" expressing every thing needful: attention to his words, and perfect reliance on their truth. With real interest and strong admiration did her eye now follow the General, as he moved through the crowd, and "How handsome a family they are!" was her secret remark.

In chatting with Miss Tilney before the evening concluded, a new source of felicity arose to her. She had never taken a country walk since her arrival in Bath. Miss Tilney, to whom all the commonly frequented environs were familiar, spoke of them in terms which made her all eagerness to know them too; and on her openly fearing that she might find nobody to go with her, it was proposed by the brother and sister that they should join in a walk, some morning or other. "I shall like it," she cried, "beyond any thing in the world; and do not let us put it off -- let us go to-morrow." This was readily agreed to, with only a proviso of Miss Tilney's, that it did not rain, which Catherine was sure it would not. At twelve o'clock, they were to call for her in Pulteney Street; and "Remember--twelve o'clock," was her parting speech to her new friend. Of her other, her older, her more established friend, Isabella, of whose fidelity and worth she had enjoyed a fortnight's experience, she scarcely saw any thing during the evening. Yet, though longing to make her acquainted with her happiness, she cheerfully submitted to the wish of Mr. Allen, which took them rather early away, and her spirits danced within her, as she danced in her chair all the way home.

CHAPTER 11

The morrow brought a very sober-looking morning, the sun making only a few efforts to appear, and Catherine augured from it every thing most favourable to her wishes. A bright morning so early in the year, she allowed would generally turn to rain, but a cloudy one foretold improvement as the day advanced. She applied to Mr. Allen for confirmation of her hopes, but Mr. Allen, not having his own skies and barometer about him, declined giving any absolute promise of sunshine. She applied to Mrs. Allen, and Mrs. Allen's opinion was more positive. "She had no doubt in the world of its being a very fine day, if the clouds would only go off, and the sun keep out."

At about eleven o'clock, however, a few specks of small rain upon the windows caught Catherine's watchful eye, and "Oh! dear, I do believe it will be wet," broke from her in a most desponding tone.

"I thought how it would be," said Mrs. Allen.

"No walk for me to-day," sighed Catherine; -- "but perhaps it may come to nothing, or it may hold up before twelve."

"Perhaps it may, but then, my dear, it will be so dirty."

"Oh! That will not signify; I never mind dirt."

"No," replied her friend very placidly, "I know you never mind dirt."

After a short pause, "It comes on faster and faster!" said Catherine, as she stood watching at a window.

"So it does indeed. If it keeps raining, the streets will be very wet."

There are four umbrellas up already. How I hate the sight of an umbrella!"

"They are disagreeable things to carry. I would much rather take a chair at any time."

"It was such a nice-looking morning! I felt so convinced it would be dry!"

"Any body would have thought so indeed. There will be very few people in the Pump-room, if it rains all the morning. I hope Mr. Allen will put on his greatcoat when he goes, but I dare say he will not, for he had rather do any thing in the world than walk out in a greatcoat; I wonder he should dislike it, it must be so comfortable."

The rain continued--fast, though not heavy. Catherine went every five minutes to the clock, threatening on each return that, if it still kept on raining another five minutes, she would give up the matter as hopeless. The clock struck twelve, and it still rained. -- "You will not be able to go, my dear."

"I do not quite despair yet. I shall not give it up till a quarter after twelve. This is just the time of day for it to clear up, and I do think it looks a little lighter. There, it is twenty minutes after twelve, and now I *shall* give it up entirely. Oh! That we had such weather here as they had at Udolpho, or at least in Tuscany and the South of France!--the night that poor St. Aubin died!--such beautiful weather!"

At half past twelve, when Catherine's anxious attention to the weather was over, and she could no longer claim any merit from its amendment, the sky began voluntarily to clear. A gleam of sunshine took her quite by surprise; she looked round; the clouds were parting, and she instantly returned to the window to watch over and encourage the happy appearance. Ten minutes more made it certain that a bright afternoon would succeed, and justified the opinion of Mrs. Allen, who had "always thought it would clear up." But whether Catherine might still expect her friends, whether there had not been too much rain for Miss Tilney to venture, must yet be a question.

It was too dirty for Mrs. Allen to accompany her husband to the Pump-room; he accordingly set off by himself, and Catherine had barely watched him down the street when her notice was claimed by the approach of the same two open carriages, containing the same three people that had surprised her so much a few mornings back.

"Isabella, my brother, and Mr. Thorpe, I declare! They are coming for me perhaps -- but I shall not go -- I cannot go indeed, for you know Miss Tilney may still call." Mrs. Allen agreed to it. John Thorpe was soon with them, and his voice was with them yet sooner, for on the stairs he was calling out to Miss Morland to be quick. "Make haste! Make haste!" as he threw open the door. -- "Put on your hat this moment -- there is no time to be lost -- we are going to Bristol. -- How d'ye do, Mrs. Allen?"

"To Bristol! Is not that a great way off? -- But, however, I cannot go with you to-day, because I am engaged; I expect some friends every moment." This was of course vehemently talked down as no reason at all; Mrs. Allen was called on to second him, and the two others walked in, to give their assistance. "My sweetest Catherine, is not this delightful? We shall have a most heavenly drive. You are to thank your brother and me for the scheme; it darted into our heads at breakfast-time, I verily believe at the same instant; and we should have been off two hours ago if it had not been for this detestable rain. But it does not signify, the nights are moonlight, and we shall do delightfully. Oh! I am in such ecstasies at the thoughts of a little country air and quiet! -- So much better than going to the Lower Rooms. We shall drive directly to Clifton and dine there; and, as soon as dinner is over, if there is time for it, go on to Kingsweston."

"I doubt our being able to do so much," said Morland.

"You croaking fellow!" cried Thorpe. "We shall be able to do ten times more. Kingsweston! Aye, and Blaize Castle too, and any thing else we can hear of; but here is your sister says she will not go."

"Blaize Castle!" cried Catherine. "What is that?"

"The finest place in England -- worth going fifty miles at any time to see."

"What, is it really a castle, an old castle?"

"The oldest in the kingdom."

"But is it like what one reads of?"

"Exactly -- the very same."

"But now really -- are there towers and long galleries?"

"By dozens."

"Then I should like to see it; but I cannot -- I cannot go."

"Not go! -- My beloved creature, what do you mean?"

"I cannot go, because" -- looking down as she spoke, fearful of Isabella's smile -- "I expect Miss Tilney and her brother to call on me to take a country walk. They promised to come at twelve, only it rained; but now, as it is so fine, I dare say they will be here soon."

"Not they indeed," cried Thorpe; "for, as we turned into Broad Street, I saw them -- does he not drive a phaeton with bright chestnuts?"

"I do not know indeed."

"Yes, I know he does; I saw him. You are talking of the man you danced with last night, are not you?"

"Yes."

"Well, I saw him at that moment turn up the Lansdown Road, -- driving a smart-looking girl."

"Did you indeed?"

"Did upon my soul; knew him again directly, and he seemed to have got some very pretty cattle too."

"It is very odd! But I suppose they thought it would be too dirty for a walk."

"And well they might, for I never saw so much dirt in my life. Walk! You could no more walk than you could fly! It has not been so dirty the whole winter; it is ankle-deep every where."

Isabella corroborated it: -- "My dearest Catherine, you cannot form an idea of the dirt; come, you must go; you cannot refuse going now."

"I should like to see the castle; but may we go all over it? May we go up every staircase, and into every suite of rooms?"

"Yes, yes, every hole and corner."

"But then, if they should only be gone out for an hour till it is dryer, and call by and by?"

"Make yourself easy, there is no danger of that, for I heard Tilney hallooing to a man who was just passing by on horseback, that they were going as far as Wick Rocks."

"Then I will. Shall I go, Mrs. Allen?"

"Just as you please, my dear."

"Mrs. Allen, you must persuade her to go," was the general cry. Mrs. Allen was not inattentive to it: -- "Well, my dear," said she, "suppose you go." -- And in two minutes they were off.

Catherine's feelings, as she got into the carriage, were in a very unsettled state; divided between regret for the loss of one great pleasure, and the hope of soon enjoying another, almost its equal in degree, however unlike in kind. She could not think the Tilneys had acted quite well by her, in so readily giving up their engagement, without sending her any message of excuse. It was now but an hour later than the time fixed on for the beginning of their walk; and, in spite of what she had heard of the prodigious accumulation of dirt in the course of that hour, she could not from her own observation help thinking that they might have gone with very little inconvenience. To feel herself slighted by them was very painful. On the other hand, the delight of exploring an edifice like Udolpho, as her fancy represented Blaize Castle to be, was such a counterpoise of good as might console her for almost any thing.

They passed briskly down Pulteney Street, and through Laura Place, without the exchange of many words. Thorpe talked to his horse, and she meditated, by turns, on broken promises and broken arches, phaetons and false hangings, Tilneys and trap-doors. As they entered Argyle Buildings, however, she was roused by this address from her companion, "Who is that girl who looked at you so hard as she went by?"

"Who? Where?"

"On the right-hand pavement -- she must be almost out of sight now." Catherine looked round and saw Miss Tilney leaning on her brother's arm, walking slowly down the street. She saw them both looking back at her. "Stop, stop, Mr. Thorpe," she impatiently cried, "it is Miss Tilney; it is indeed. -- How could you tell me they were gone? -- Stop, stop, I will get out this moment and go to them." But to what purpose did she speak? -- Thorpe only lashed his horse into a brisker trot; the Tilneys, who had soon ceased to look after her, were in a moment out of sight round the corner of Laura Place, and

63

in another moment she was herself whisked into the marketplace. Still, however, and during the length of another street, she entreated him to stop. "Pray, pray stop, Mr. Thorpe. -- I cannot go on. -- I will not go on. -- I must go back to Miss Tilney." But Mr. Thorpe only laughed, smacked his whip, encouraged his horse, made odd noises, and drove on; and Catherine, angry and vexed as she was, having no power of getting away, was obliged to give up the point and submit. Her reproaches, however, were not spared. "How could you deceive me so, Mr. Thorpe? How could you say that you saw them driving up the Lansdown Road? I would not have had it happen so for the world. They must think it so strange, so rude of me! To go by them, too, without saying a word! You do not know how vexed I am; I shall have no pleasure at Clifton, nor in any thing else. I had rather, ten thousand times rather, get out now, and walk back to them. How could you say you saw them driving out in a phaeton?" Thorpe defended himself very stoutly, declared he had never seen two men so much alike in his life, and would hardly give up the point of its having been Tilney himself.

Their drive, even when this subject was over, was not likely to be very agreeable. Catherine's complaisance was no longer what it had been in their former airing. She listened reluctantly, and her replies were short. Blaize Castle remained her only comfort; towards *that*, she still looked at intervals with pleasure; though rather than be disappointed of the promised walk, and especially rather than be thought ill of by the Tilneys, she would willingly have given up all the happiness which its walls could supply--the happiness of a progress through a long suite of lofty rooms, exhibiting the remains of magnificent furniture, though now for many years deserted--the happiness of being stopped in their way along narrow, winding vaults, by a low, grated door; or even of having their lamp, their only lamp, extinguished by a sudden gust of wind, and of being left in total darkness. In the meanwhile, they proceeded on their journey without any mischance, and were within view of the town of Keynsham, when a halloo from Morland, who was behind them, made his friend pull up, to know what was the matter. The others then came close enough for conversation, and Morland said, "We had better go back, Thorpe; it is too late to go on to-day; your sister thinks so as well as I. We have been exactly an hour coming from Pulteney Street, very little more than seven miles; and, I suppose, we have at least eight more to go. It will never do.

We set out a great deal too late. We had much better put it off till another day, and turn round."

"It is all one to me," replied Thorpe rather angrily; and instantly turning his horse, they were on their way back to Bath.

"If your brother had not got such a d-- beast to drive," said he soon afterwards, "we might have done it very well. My horse would have trotted to Clifton within the hour, if left to himself, and I have almost broke my arm with pulling him in to that cursed broken-winded jade's pace. Morland is a fool for not keeping a horse and gig of his own."

"No, he is not," said Catherine warmly, "for I am sure he could not afford it."

"And why cannot he afford it?"

"Because he has not money enough."

"And whose fault is that?"

"Nobody's, that I know of." Thorpe then said something in the loud, incoherent way to which he had often recourse, about its being a d-- thing to be miserly; and that if people who rolled in money could not afford things, he did not know who could, which Catherine did not even endeavour to understand. Disappointed of what was to have been the consolation for her first disappointment, she was less and less disposed either to be agreeable herself or to find her companion so; and they returned to Pulteney Street without her speaking twenty words.

As she entered the house, the footman told her that a gentleman and lady had called and inquired for her a few minutes after her setting off; that, when he told them she was gone out with Mr. Thorpe, the lady had asked whether any message had been left for her; and on his saying no, had felt for a card, but said she had none about her, and went away. Pondering over these heart-rending tidings, Catherine walked slowly up stairs. At the head of them she was met by Mr. Allen, who, on hearing the reason of their speedy return, said, "I am glad your brother had so much sense; I am glad you are come back. It was a strange, wild scheme."

They all spent the evening together at Thorpe's. Catherine was disturbed and out of spirits; but Isabella seemed to find a pool of commerce, in the fate of which she shared, by private partnership with Morland, a very good equivalent for the quiet and country air of an inn at Clifton. Her satisfaction, too, in not being at the Lower Rooms was spoken more than once. "How I pity the poor creatures that are going there! How glad I am that I am not amongst them! I wonder whether it will be a full ball or not! They have not begun dancing yet. I would not be there for all the world. It is so delightful to have an evening now and then to oneself. I dare say it will not be a very good ball. I know the Mitchells will not be there. I am sure I pity every body that is. But I dare say, Mr. Morland, you long to be at it, do not you? I am sure you do. Well, pray do not let any body here be a restraint on you. I dare say we could do very well without you; but you men think yourselves of such consequence."

Catherine could almost have accused Isabella of being wanting in tenderness towards herself and her sorrows, so very little did they appear to dwell on her mind, and so very inadequate was the comfort she offered. "Do not be so dull, my dearest creature," she whispered. "You will quite break my heart. It was amazingly shocking, to be sure; but the Tilneys were entirely to blame. Why were not they more punctual? It was dirty, indeed, but what did that signify? I am sure John and I should not have minded it. I never mind going through any thing, where a friend is concerned; that is my disposition, and John is just the same; he has amazing strong feelings. Good heavens! What a delightful hand you have got! Kings, I vow! I never was so happy in my life! I would fifty times rather you should have them than myself."

And now I may dismiss my heroine to the sleepless couch, which is the true heroine's portion; to a pillow strewed with thorns and wet with tears. And lucky may she think herself, if she get another good night's rest in the course of the next three months.

CHAPTER 12

"Mrs. Allen," said Catherine the next morning, "will there be any harm in my calling on Miss Tilney to-day? I shall not be easy till I have explained every thing."

"Go, by all means, my dear; only put on a white gown; Miss Tilney always wears white."

Catherine cheerfully complied, and being properly equipped, was more impatient than ever to be at the Pump-room, that she might inform herself of General Tilney's lodgings, for though she believed they were in Milsom Street, she was not certain of the house, and Mrs. Allen's wavering convictions only made it more doubtful. To Milsom Street she was directed, and having made herself perfect in the number, hastened away with eager steps and a beating heart to pay her visit, explain her conduct, and be forgiven; tripping lightly through the church-yard, and resolutely turning away her eyes, that she might not be obliged to see her beloved Isabella and her dear family, who, she had reason to believe, were in a shop hard by. She reached the house without any impediment, looked at the number, knocked at the door, and inquired for Miss Tilney. The man believed Miss Tilney to be at home, but was not quite certain. Would she be pleased to send up her name? She gave her card. In a few minutes the servant returned, and with a look which did not quite confirm his words, said he had been mistaken, for that Miss Tilney was walked out. Catherine, with a blush of mortification, left the house. She felt almost persuaded that Miss Tilney *was* at home, and too much offended to admit her; and as she retired down the street, could not withhold one glance at the drawing-room windows, in expectation of seeing her there, but no one appeared at them. At the bottom of the street, however, she looked back again, and then, not at a window, but issuing from the door, she saw Miss Tilney herself. She was followed by a gentleman, whom Catherine believed to be her father, and they turned up towards Edgar's Buildings. Catherine, in deep mortification, proceeded on her way. She could almost be angry herself at such angry incivility; but she checked the resentful sensation; she remembered her own ignorance. She knew not how such an offence as hers might be classed by the laws of worldly politeness, to what a degree of unforgivingness it might with propriety lead, nor to what rigours of rudeness in return it might justly make her amenable.

Dejected and humbled, she had even some thoughts of not going with the others to the theatre that night; but it must be confessed that they were not of long continuance, for she soon recollected, in the first place, that she was without any excuse for staying at home; and, in the second, that it was a play she wanted very much to see. To the theatre accordingly they all went; no Tilneys appeared to plague or please her; she feared that, amongst the many perfections of the family, a fondness for plays was not to be ranked; but perhaps it was because they were habituated to the finer performances of the London stage, which she knew, on Isabella's authority, rendered every thing else of the kind "quite horrid." She was not deceived in her own expectation of pleasure; the comedy so well suspended her care that no one, observing her during the first four acts, would have supposed she had any wretchedness about her. On the beginning of the fifth, however, the sudden view of Mr. Henry Tilney and his father, joining a party in the opposite box, recalled her to anxiety and distress. The stage could no longer excite genuine merriment— no longer keep her whole attention. Every other look upon an average was directed towards the opposite box; and, for the space of two entire scenes, did she thus watch Henry Tilney, without being once able to catch his eye. No longer could he be suspected of indifference for a play; his notice was never withdrawn from the stage during two whole scenes. At length, however, he did look towards her, and he bowed--but such a bow! No smile, no continued observance attended it; his eyes were immediately returned to their former direction. Catherine was restlessly miserable; she could almost have run round to the box in which he sat and forced him to hear her explanation. Feelings rather natural than heroic possessed her; instead of considering her own dignity injured by this ready condemnation -- instead of proudly resolving, in conscious innocence, to shew her resentment towards him who could harbour a doubt of it, to leave to him all the trouble of seeking an explanation, and to enlighten him on the past only by avoiding his sight, or flirting with somebody else -- she took to herself all the shame of misconduct, or at least of its appearance, and was only eager for an opportunity of explaining its cause.

The play concluded -- the curtain fell -- Henry Tilney was no longer to be seen where he had hitherto sat, but his father remained, and perhaps he might be now coming round to their box. She was right; in a few minutes he appeared, and, making his way through the then thinning rows, spoke with like calm politeness to Mrs. Allen and her friend. -- Not with such calmness was he answered by the latter: "Oh! Mr. Tilney, I have been quite wild to speak to you, and make my apologies. You must have thought me so rude; but indeed it was not my own fault, -- was it, Mrs. Allen? Did not they tell me that Mr. Tilney and his sister were gone out in a phaeton together? And then what could I do? But I had ten thousand times rather have been with you; now had not I, Mrs. Allen?"

"My dear, you tumble my gown," was Mrs. Allen's reply.

Her assurance, however, standing sole as it did, was not thrown away; it brought a more cordial, more natural smile into his countenance, and he replied in a tone which retained only a little affected reserve: -- "We were much obliged to you at any rate for wishing us a pleasant walk after our passing you in Argyle Street: you were so kind as to look back on purpose."

"But indeed I did not wish you a pleasant walk; I never thought of such a thing; but I begged Mr. Thorpe so earnestly to stop; I called out to him as soon as ever I saw you; now, Mrs. Allen, did not -- Oh! You were not there; but indeed I did; and, if Mr. Thorpe would only have stopped, I would have jumped out and run after you."

Is there a Henry in the world who could be insensible to such a declaration? Henry Tilney at least was not. With a yet sweeter smile, he said every thing that need be said of his sister's concern, regret, and dependence on Catherine's honour. -- "Oh! Do not say Miss Tilney was not angry," cried Catherine, "because I know she was; for she would not see me this morning when I called; I saw her walk out of the house the next minute after my leaving it; I was hurt, but I was not affronted. Perhaps you did not know I had been there."

"I was not within at the time; but I heard of it from Eleanor, and she has been wishing ever since to see you, to explain the reason of such incivility; but perhaps I can do it as well. It was nothing more than that my father -- they were just preparing to walk out, and he being hurried for time, and not caring to have it put off -- made a point of her being denied. That was all, I do assure you. She was very much vexed, and meant to make her apology as soon as possible."

Catherine's mind was greatly eased by this information, yet a something of solicitude remained, from which sprang the following question, thoroughly artless in itself, though rather distressing to the gentleman: -- "But, Mr. Tilney, why were *you* less generous than your sister? If she felt such confidence in my good intentions, and could suppose it to be only a mistake, why should *you* be so ready to take offence?"

"Me! -- I take offence!"

"Nay, I am sure by your look, when you came into the box, you were angry."

"I angry! I could have no right."

"Well, nobody would have thought you had no right who saw your face." He replied by asking her to make room for him, and talking of the play.

He remained with them some time, and was only too agreeable for Catherine to be contented when he went away. Before they parted, however, it was agreed that the projected walk should be taken as soon as possible; and, setting aside the misery of his quitting their box, she was, upon the whole, left one of the happiest creatures in the world.

While talking to each other, she had observed with some surprise that John Thorpe, who was never in the same part of the house for ten minutes together, was engaged in conversation with General Tilney; and she felt something more than surprise when she thought she could perceive herself the object of their attention and discourse. What could they have to say of her? She feared General Tilney did not like her appearance: she found it was implied in his preventing her admittance to his daughter, rather than postpone his own walk a few minutes. "How came Mr. Thorpe to know your father?" was her anxious inquiry, as she pointed them out to her companion. He knew nothing about it; but his father, like every military man, had a very large acquaintance.

When the entertainment was over, Thorpe came to assist them in getting out. Catherine was the immediate object of his gallantry; and, while they waited in the lobby for a chair, he prevented the inquiry which had travelled from her heart almost to the tip of her tongue, by asking, in a consequential manner, whether she had seen him talking with General Tilney: "He is a fine old fellow, upon my soul! Stout, active--looks as young as his son. I have a great regard for him, I assure you: a gentleman-like, good sort of fellow as ever lived."

"But how came you to know him?"

"Know him! -- There are few people much about town that I do not know. I have met him for ever at the Bedford; and I knew his face again to-day the moment he came into the billiard-room. One of the best players we have, by the by; and we had a little touch together, though I was almost afraid of him at first: the odds were five to four against me; and, if I had not made one of the cleanest strokes that perhaps ever was made in this world -- I took his ball exactly -- but I could not make you understand it without a table; -- however, I *did* beat him. A very fine fellow; as rich as a Jew. I should like to dine with him; I dare say he gives famous dinners. But what do you think we have been talking of? You. Yes, by heavens! And the General thinks you the finest girl in Bath."

"Oh! Nonsense! How can you say so?"

"And what do you think I said?"--lowering his voice--"Well done, General, said I; I am quite of your mind."

Here Catherine, who was much less gratified by his admiration than by General Tilney's, was not sorry to be called away by Mr. Allen. Thorpe, however, would see her to her chair, and, till she entered it, continued the same kind of delicate flattery, in spite of her entreating him to have done.

That General Tilney, instead of disliking, should admire her, was very delightful; and she joyfully thought that there was not one of the family whom she need now fear to meet. The evening had done more, much more, for her than could have been expected.

CHAPTER 13

Monday, Tuesday, Wednesday, Thursday, Friday, and Saturday have now passed in review before the reader; the events of each day, its hopes and fears, mortifications and pleasures have been separately stated, and the pangs of Sunday only now remain to be described, and close the week. The Clifton scheme had been deferred, not relinquished, and on the afternoon's crescent of this day, it was brought forward again. In a private consultation between Isabella and James, the former of whom had particularly set her heart upon going, and the latter no less anxiously placed his upon pleasing her, it was agreed that, provided the weather were fair, the party should take place on the following morning; and they were to set off very early, in order to be at home in good time. The affair thus determined, and Thorpe's approbation secured, Catherine only remained to be apprised of it. She had left them for a few minutes to speak to Miss Tilney. In that interval the plan was completed, and as soon as she came again, her agreement was demanded; but instead of the gay acquiescence expected by Isabella, Catherine looked grave, was very sorry, but could not go. The engagement which ought to have kept her from joining in the former attempt would make it impossible for her to accompany them now. She had that moment settled with Miss Tilney to take their proposed walk to-morrow; it was quite determined, and she would not, upon any account, retract. But that she *must* and *should* retract was instantly the eager cry of both the Thorpes; they must go to Clifton to-morrow, they would not go without her, it would be nothing to put off a mere walk for one day longer, and they would not hear of a refusal. Catherine was distressed, but not subdued. "Do not urge me, Isabella. I am engaged to Miss Tilney. I cannot go." This availed nothing. The same arguments assailed her again; she must go, she should go, and they would not hear of a refusal. "It would be so easy to tell Miss Tilney that you had just been reminded of a prior engagement, and must only beg to put off the walk till Tuesday."

"No, it would not be easy. I could not do it. There has been no prior engagement." But Isabella became only more and more urgent, calling on her in the most affectionate manner, addressing her by the most endearing names. She was sure her dearest, sweetest Catherine would not seriously refuse such a trifling request to a friend who loved her so dearly. She knew her beloved Catherine to have so feeling a heart, so sweet a temper, to be so easily persuaded by those she loved. But all in vain; Catherine felt herself to be in the right, and though pained by such tender, such flattering supplication, could not allow it to influence her. Isabella then tried another method. She reproached her with having more affection for Miss Tilney, though she had known her so little a while, than for her best and oldest friends, with being grown cold and indifferent, in short, towards herself. "I cannot help being jealous, Catherine, when I see myself slighted for strangers, I, who love you so excessively! When once my affections are placed, it is not in the power of any thing to change them. But I believe my feelings are stronger than any body's; I am sure they are too strong for my own peace; and to see myself supplanted in your friendship by strangers does cut me to the quick, I own. These Tilneys seem to swallow up every thing else."

Catherine thought this reproach equally strange and unkind. Was it the part of a friend thus to expose her feelings to the notice of others? Isabella appeared to her ungenerous and selfish, regardless of every thing but her own gratification. These painful ideas crossed her mind, though she said nothing. Isabella, in the meanwhile, had applied her handkerchief to her eyes; and Morland, miserable at such a sight, could not help saying, "Nay, Catherine. I think you cannot stand out any longer now. The sacrifice is not much; and to oblige such a friend -- I shall think you quite unkind, if you still refuse."

This was the first time of her brother's openly siding against her, and anxious to avoid his displeasure, she proposed a compromise. If they would only put off their scheme till Tuesday, which they might easily do, as it depended only on themselves, she could go with them, and every body might then be satisfied. But "No, no, no!" was the immediate answer; "that could not be, for Thorpe did not know that he might not go to town on Tuesday." Catherine was sorry, but could do no more; and a short silence ensued, which was broken by Isabella, who in a voice of cold resentment said, "Very well, then there is an end of the party. If Catherine does not go, I cannot. I cannot be the only woman. I would not, upon any account in the world, do so improper a thing."

"Catherine, you must go," said James.

"But why cannot Mr. Thorpe drive one of his other sisters? I dare say either of them would like to go."

"Thank ye," cried Thorpe, "but I did not come to Bath to drive my sisters about, and look like a fool. No, if you do not go, d---- me if I do. I only go for the sake of driving you."

"That is a compliment which gives me no pleasure." But her words were lost on Thorpe, who had turned abruptly away.

The three others still continued together, walking in a most uncomfortable manner to poor Catherine; sometimes not a word was said, sometimes she was again attacked with supplications or reproaches, and her arm was still linked within Isabella's, though their hearts were at war. At one moment she was softened, at another irritated; always distressed, but always steady.

"I did not think you had been so obstinate, Catherine," said James; "you were not used to be so hard to persuade; you once were the kindest, best-tempered of my sisters."

"I hope I am not less so now," she replied, very feelingly; "but indeed I cannot go. If I am wrong, I am doing what I believe to be right."

"I suspect," said Isabella, in a low voice, "there is no great struggle."

Catherine's heart swelled; she drew away her arm, and Isabella made no opposition. Thus passed a long ten minutes, till they were again joined by Thorpe, who, coming to them with a gayer look, said, "Well, I have settled the matter, and now we may all go to-morrow with a safe conscience. I have been to Miss Tilney, and made your excuses."

"You have not!" cried Catherine.

"I have, upon my soul. Left her this moment. Told her you had sent me to say that, having just recollected a prior engagement of going to Clifton with us to-morrow, you could not have the pleasure of walking with her till Tuesday. She said very well, Tuesday was just as convenient to her; so there is an end of all our difficulties. A pretty good thought of mine -- hey?"

Isabella's countenance was once more all smiles and good humour, and James too looked happy again.

"A most heavenly thought indeed! Now, my sweet Catherine, all our distresses are over; you are honourably acquitted, and we shall have a most delightful party."

"This will not do," said Catherine; "I cannot submit to this. I must run after Miss Tilney directly and set her right."

Isabella, however, caught hold of one hand, Thorpe of the other, and remonstrances poured in from all three. Even James was quite angry. When every thing was settled, when Miss Tilney herself said that Tuesday would suit her as well, it was quite ridiculous, quite absurd to make any further objection.

"I do not care. Mr. Thorpe had no business to invent any such message. If I had thought it right to put it off, I could have spoken to Miss Tilney myself. This is only doing it in a ruder way; and how do I know that Mr. Thorpe has -- he may be mistaken again perhaps; he led me into one act of rudeness by his mistake on Friday. Let me go, Mr. Thorpe; Isabella, do not hold me."

Thorpe told her it would be in vain to go after the Tilneys; they were turning the corner into Brock Street, when he had overtaken them, and were at home by this time.

"Then I will go after them," said Catherine; "wherever they are I will go after them. It does not signify talking. If I could not be persuaded into doing what I thought wrong, I never will be tricked into it." And with these words she broke away and hurried off. Thorpe would have darted after her, but Morland withheld him. "Let her go, let her go, if she will go."

"She is as obstinate as--"

Thorpe never finished the simile, for it could hardly have been a proper one.

74

Away walked Catherine in great agitation, as fast as the crowd would permit her, fearful of being pursued, yet determined to persevere. As she walked, she reflected on what had passed. It was painful to her to disappoint and displease them, particularly to displease her brother; but she could not repent her resistance. Setting her own inclination apart, to have failed a second time in her engagement to Miss Tilney, to have retracted a promise voluntarily made only five minutes before, and on a false pretence too, must have been wrong. She had not been withstanding them on selfish principles alone, she had not consulted merely her own gratification; *that* might have been ensured in some degree by the excursion itself, by seeing Blaize Castle; no, she had attended to what was due to others, and to her own character in their opinion. Her conviction of being right, however, was not enough to restore her composure; till she had spoken to Miss Tilney she could not be at ease; and quickening her pace when she got clear of the Crescent, she almost ran over the remaining ground till she gained the top of Milsom Street. So rapid had been her movements that in spite of the Tilneys' advantage in the outset, they were but just turning into their lodgings as she came within view of them; and the servant still remaining at the open door, she used only the ceremony of saying that she must speak with Miss Tilney that moment, and hurrying by him proceeded up stairs. Then, opening the first door before her, which happened to be the right, she immediately found herself in the drawing-room with General Tilney, his son and daughter. Her explanation, defective only in being -- from her irritation of nerves and shortness of breath -- no explanation at all, was instantly given. "I am come in a great hurry -- It was all a mistake--I never promised to go -- I told them from the first I could not go. -- I ran away in a great hurry to explain it.-- I did not care what you thought of me. -- I would not stay for the servant."

The business, however, though not perfectly elucidated by this speech, soon ceased to be a puzzle. Catherine found that John Thorpe *had* given the message; and Miss Tilney had no scruple in owning herself greatly surprised by it. But whether her brother had still exceeded her in resentment, Catherine, though she instinctively addressed herself as much to one as to the other in her vindication, had no means of knowing. Whatever might have been felt before her arrival, her eager declarations immediately made every look and sentence as friendly as she could desire.

The affair thus happily settled, she was introduced by Miss Tilney to her father, and received by him with such ready, such solicitous politeness as recalled Thorpe's information to her mind, and made her think with pleasure that he might be sometimes depended on. To such anxious attention was the General's civility carried, that not aware of her extraordinary swiftness in entering the house, he was quite angry with the servant whose neglect had reduced her to open the door of the apartment herself. "What did William mean by it? He should make a point of inquiring into the matter." And if Catherine had not most warmly asserted his innocence, it seemed likely that William would lose the favour of his master for ever, if not his place, by her rapidity.

After sitting with them a quarter of an hour, she rose to take leave, and was then most agreeably surprised by General Tilney's asking her if she would do his daughter the honour of dining and spending the rest of the day with her. Miss Tilney added her own wishes. Catherine was greatly obliged; but it was quite out of her power. Mr. and Mrs. Allen would expect her back every moment. The General declared he could say no more; the claims of Mr. and Mrs. Allen were not to be superseded; but on some other day he trusted, when longer notice could be given, they would not refuse to spare her to her friend. "Oh, no; Catherine was sure they would not have the least objection, and she should have great pleasure in coming." The General attended her himself to the street-door, saying every thing gallant as they went downstairs, admiring the elasticity of her walk, which corresponded exactly with the spirit of her dancing, and making her one of the most graceful bows she had ever beheld, when they parted.

Catherine, delighted by all that had passed, proceeded gaily to Pulteney Street, walking, as she concluded, with great elasticity, though she had never thought of it before. She reached home without seeing any thing more of the offended party; and now that she had been triumphant throughout, had carried her point, and was secure of her walk, she began (as the flutter of her spirits subsided) to doubt whether she had been perfectly right. A sacrifice was always noble; and if she had given way to their entreaties, she should have been spared the distressing idea of a friend displeased, a brother angry, and a scheme of great happiness to both destroyed, perhaps through her means. To ease her mind, and ascertain by the opinion of an unprejudiced person what her own conduct had really been, she took occasion to mention before Mr. Allen the half-settled scheme of her brother and the Thorpes for the following day. Mr. Allen caught at it directly. "Well," said he, "and do you think of going too?"

"No; I had just engaged myself to walk with Miss Tilney before they told me of it; and therefore you know I could not go with them, could I?"

"No, certainly not; and I am glad you do not think of it. These schemes are not at all the thing. Young men and women driving about the country in open carriages! Now and then it is very well; but going to inns and public places together! It is not right; and I wonder Mrs. Thorpe should allow it. I am glad you do not think of going; I am sure Mrs. Morland would not be pleased. Mrs. Allen, are not you of my way of thinking? Do not you think these kind of projects objectionable?"

"Yes, very much so indeed. Open carriages are nasty things. A clean gown is not five minutes' wear in them. You are splashed getting in and getting out; and the wind takes your hair and your bonnet in every direction. I hate an open carriage myself."

"I know you do; but that is not the question. Do not you think it has an odd appearance, if young ladies are frequently driven about in them by young men, to whom they are not even related?"

"Yes, my dear, a very odd appearance indeed. I cannot bear to see it."

"Dear madam," cried Catherine, "then why did not you tell me so before? I am sure if I had known it to be improper, I would not have gone with Mr. Thorpe at all; but I always hoped you would tell me, if you thought I was doing wrong."

"And so I should, my dear, you may depend on it; for as I told Mrs. Morland at parting, I would always do the best for you in my power. But one must not be over particular. Young people *will* be young people, as your good mother says herself. You know I wanted you, when we first came, not to buy that sprigged muslin, but you would. Young people do not like to be always thwarted."

"But this was something of real consequence; and I do not think you would have found me hard to persuade."

"As far as it has gone hitherto, there is no harm done," said Mr. Allen; "and I would only advise you, my dear, not to go out with Mr. Thorpe any more."

"That is just what I was going to say," added his wife.

Catherine, relieved for herself, felt uneasy for Isabella, and after a moment's thought, asked Mr. Allen whether it would not be both proper and kind in her to write to Miss Thorpe, and explain the indecorum of which she must be as insensible as herself; for she considered that Isabella might otherwise perhaps be going to Clifton the next day, in spite of what had passed. Mr. Allen, however, discouraged her from doing any such thing. "You had better leave her alone, my dear; she is old enough to know what she is about, and if not, has a mother to advise her. Mrs. Thorpe is too indulgent beyond a doubt; but, however, you had better not interfere. She and your brother choose to go, and you will be only getting ill will."

Catherine submitted, and though sorry to think that Isabella should be doing wrong, felt greatly relieved by Mr. Allen's approbation of her own conduct, and truly rejoiced to be preserved by his advice from the danger of falling into such an error herself. Her escape from being one of the party to Clifton was now an escape indeed; for what would the Tilneys have thought of her, if she had broken her promise to them in order to do what was wrong in itself, if she had been guilty of one breach of propriety, only to enable her to be guilty of another?

CHAPTER 14

The next morning was fair, and Catherine almost expected another attack from the assembled party. With Mr. Allen to support her, she felt no dread of the event: but she would gladly be spared a contest, where victory itself was painful, and was heartily rejoiced therefore at neither seeing nor hearing any thing of them. The Tilneys called for her at the appointed time; and no new difficulty arising, no sudden recollection, no unexpected summons, no impertinent intrusion to disconcert their measures, my heroine was most unnaturally able to fulfil her engagement, though it was made with the hero himself. They determined on walking round Beechen Cliff, that noble hill whose beautiful verdure and hanging coppice render it so striking an object from almost every opening in Bath.

"I never look at it," said Catherine, as they walked along the side of the river, "without thinking of the south of France."

"You have been abroad then?" said Henry, a little surprised.

"Oh! No, I only mean what I have read about. It always puts me in mind of the country that Emily and her father travelled through, in The Mysteries of Udolpho. But you never read novels, I dare say?"

"Why not?"

"Because they are not clever enough for you -- gentlemen read better books."

"The person, be it gentleman or lady, who has not pleasure in a good novel, must be intolerably stupid. I have read all Mrs. Radcliffe's works, and most of them with great pleasure. The Mysteries of Udolpho, when I had once begun it, I could not lay down again; I remember finishing it in two days -- my hair standing on end the whole time."

"Yes," added Miss Tilney, "and I remember that you undertook to read it aloud to me, and that when I was called away for only five minutes to answer a note, instead of waiting for me, you took the volume into the Hermitage Walk, and I was obliged to stay till you had finished it."

"Thank you, Eleanor -- a most honourable testimony. You see, Miss Morland, the injustice of your suspicions. Here was I, in my eagerness to get on, refusing to wait only five minutes for my sister, breaking the promise I had made of reading it aloud, and keeping her in suspense at a most interesting part, by running away with the volume, which, you are to observe, was her own, particularly her own. I am proud when I reflect on it, and I think it must establish me in your good opinion."

"I am very glad to hear it indeed, and now I shall never be ashamed of liking Udolpho myself. But I really thought before, young men despised novels amazingly."

"It is *amazingly*; it may well suggest *amazement* if they do -- for they read nearly as many as women. I myself have read hundreds and hundreds. Do not imagine that you can cope with me in a knowledge of Julias and Louisas. If we proceed to particulars, and engage in the never-ceasing inquiry of 'Have you read this?' and 'Have you read that?' I shall soon leave you as far behind me as -- what shall I say? -- I want an appropriate simile; -- as far as your friend Emily herself left poor Valancourt when she went with her aunt into Italy. Consider how many years I have had the start of you. I had entered on my studies at Oxford, while you were a good little girl working your sampler at home!"

"Not very good, I am afraid. But now really, do not you think Udolpho the nicest book in the world?"

"The nicest -- by which I suppose you mean the neatest. That must depend upon the binding."

"Henry," said Miss Tilney, "you are very impertinent. Miss Morland, he is treating you exactly as he does his sister. He is for ever finding fault with me, for some incorrectness of language, and now he is taking the same liberty with you. The word 'nicest,' as you used it, did not suit him; and you had better change it as soon as you can, or we shall be overpowered with Johnson and Blair all the rest of the way."

"I am sure," cried Catherine, "I did not mean to say any thing wrong; but it is a nice book, and why should not I call it so?"

"Very true," said Henry, "and this is a very nice day, and we are taking a very nice walk, and you are two very nice young ladies. Oh! It is a very nice word indeed! -- It does for every thing. Originally perhaps it was applied only to express neatness, propriety, delicacy, or refinement; -- people were nice in their dress, in their sentiments, or their choice. But now every commendation on every subject is comprised in that one word."

"While, in fact," cried his sister, "it ought only to be applied to you, without any commendation at all. You are more nice than wise. Come, Miss Morland, let us leave him to meditate over our faults in the utmost propriety of diction, while we praise Udolpho in whatever terms we like best. It is a most interesting work. You are fond of that kind of reading?"

"To say the truth, I do not much like any other."

"Indeed!"

"That is, I can read poetry and plays, and things of that sort, and do not dislike travels. But history, real solemn history, I cannot be interested in. Can you?"

"Yes, I am fond of history."

"I wish I were too. I read it a little as a duty, but it tells me nothing that does not either vex or weary me. The quarrels of popes and kings, with wars or pestilences, in every page; the men all so good for nothing, and hardly any women at all -- it is very tiresome: and yet I often think it odd that it should be so dull, for a great deal of it must be invention. The speeches that are put into the heroes' mouths, their thoughts and designs -- the chief of all this must be invention, and invention is what delights me in other books."

"Historians, you think," said Miss Tilney, "are not happy in their flights of fancy. They display imagination without raising interest. I am fond of history -- and am very well contented to take the false with the true. In the principal facts they have sources of intelligence in former histories and records, which may be as much depended on, I conclude, as any thing that does not actually pass under one's own observation; and as for the little embellishments you speak of, they are embellishments, and I like them as such. If a speech be well drawn up, I read it with pleasure, by whomsoever it may be made -- and probably with much greater, if the production of Mr. Hume or Mr. Robertson, than if the genuine words of Caractacus, Agricola, or Alfred the Great."

"You are fond of history! And so are Mr. Allen and my father; and I have two brothers who do not dislike it. So many instances within my small circle of friends is remarkable! At this rate, I shall not pity the writers of history any longer. If people like to read their books, it is all very well, but to be at so much trouble in filling great volumes, which, as I used to think, nobody would willingly ever look into, to be labouring only for the torment of little boys and girls, always struck me as a hard fate; and though I know it is all very right and necessary, I have often wondered at the person's courage that could sit down on purpose to do it."

"That little boys and girls should be tormented," said Henry, "is what no one at all acquainted with human nature in a civilized state can deny; but in behalf of our most distinguished historians, I must observe that they might well be offended at being supposed to have no higher aim, and that by their method and style, they are perfectly well qualified to torment readers of the most advanced reason and mature time of life. I use the verb 'to torment,' as I observed to be your own method, instead of 'to instruct,' supposing them to be now admitted as synonymous."

"You think me foolish to call instruction a torment, but if you had been as much used as myself to hear poor little children first learning their letters and then learning to spell, if you had ever seen how stupid they can be for a whole morning together, and how tired my poor mother is at the end of it, as I am in the habit of seeing almost every day of my life at home, you would allow that 'to *torment*' and 'to *instruct*' might sometimes be used as synonymous words."

"Very probably. But historians are not accountable for the difficulty of learning to read; and even you yourself, who do not altogether seem particularly friendly to very severe, very intense application, may perhaps be brought to acknowledge that it is very well worth while to be tormented for two or three years of one's life, for the sake of being able to read all the rest of it. Consider -- if reading had not been taught, Mrs. Radcliffe would have written in vain -- or perhaps might not have written at all."

Catherine assented -- and a very warm panegyric from her on that lady's merits closed the subject. -- The Tilneys were soon engaged in another on which she had nothing to say. They were viewing the country with the eyes of persons accustomed to drawing, and decided on its capability of being formed into pictures, with all the eagerness of real taste. Here Catherine was quite lost. She knew nothing of drawing -- nothing of taste: -- and she listened to them with an attention which brought her little profit, for they talked in phrases which conveyed scarcely any idea to her. The little which she could understand, however, appeared to contradict the very few notions she had entertained on the matter before. It seemed as if a good view were no longer to be taken from the top of an high hill, and that a clear blue sky was no longer a proof of a fine day. She was heartily ashamed of her ignorance. A misplaced shame. Where people wish to attach, they should always be ignorant. To come with a well-informed mind is to come with an inability of administering to the vanity of others, which a sensible person would always wish to avoid. A woman especially, if she have the misfortune of knowing any thing, should conceal it as well as she can.

The advantages of natural folly in a beautiful girl have been already set forth by the capital pen of a sister author; -- and to her treatment of the subject I will only add, in justice to men, that though to the larger and more trifling part of the sex, imbecility in females is a great enhancement of their personal charms, there is a portion of them too reasonable and too well informed themselves to desire any thing more in woman than ignorance. But Catherine did not know her own advantages -- did not know that a good-looking girl, with an affectionate heart and a very ignorant mind, cannot fail of attracting a clever young man, unless circumstances are particularly untoward. In the present instance, she confessed and lamented her want of knowledge, declared that she would give any thing in the world to be able to draw; and a lecture on the picturesque immediately followed, in which his instructions were so clear that she soon began to see beauty in every thing admired by him, and her attention was so earnest that he became perfectly satisfied of her having a great deal of natural taste. He talked of foregrounds, distances, and second distances -- side-screens and perspectives -- lights and shades; -- and Catherine was so hopeful a scholar that when they gained the top of Beechen Cliff, she voluntarily rejected the whole city of Bath as unworthy to make part of a landscape. Delighted with her progress, and fearful of wearying her with too much wisdom at once, Henry suffered the subject to decline, and by an easy transition from a piece of rocky fragment and the withered oak which he had placed near its summit, to oaks in general, to forests, the enclosure of them, waste lands, crown lands and government, he shortly found himself arrived at politics; and from politics, it was an easy step to silence. The general pause which succeeded his short disquisition on the state of the nation was put an end to by Catherine, who, in rather a solemn tone of voice, uttered these words, "I have heard that something very shocking indeed will soon come out in London."

Miss Tilney, to whom this was chiefly addressed, was startled, and hastily replied, "Indeed! And of what nature?"

"That I do not know, nor who is the author. I have only heard that it is to be more horrible than any thing we have met with yet."

"Good heaven! Where could you hear of such a thing?"

"A particular friend of mine had an account of it in a letter from London yesterday. It is to be uncommonly dreadful. I shall expect murder and every thing of the kind."

"You speak with astonishing composure! But I hope your friend's accounts have been exaggerated; -- and if such a design is known beforehand, proper measures will undoubtedly be taken by government to prevent its coming to effect."

"Government," said Henry, endeavouring not to smile, "neither desires nor dares to interfere in such matters. There must be murder; and government cares not how much."

The ladies stared. He laughed, and added, "Come, shall I make you understand each other, or leave you to puzzle out an explanation as you can? No -- I will be noble. I will prove myself a man, no less by the generosity of my soul than the clearness of my head. I have no patience with such of my sex as disdain to let themselves sometimes down to the comprehension of yours. Perhaps the abilities of women are neither sound nor acute -- neither vigorous nor keen. Perhaps they may want observation, discernment, judgment, fire, genius, and wit."

"Miss Morland, do not mind what he says; -- but have the goodness to satisfy me as to this dreadful riot."

"Riot! What riot?"

"My dear Eleanor, the riot is only in your own brain. The confusion there is scandalous. Miss Morland has been talking of nothing more dreadful than a new publication which is shortly to come out, in three duodecimo volumes, two hundred and seventy-six pages in each, with a frontispiece to the first of two tombstones and a lantern -- do you understand? -- And you, Miss Morland -- my stupid sister has mistaken all your clearest expressions. You talked of expected horrors in London -- and instead of instantly conceiving, as any rational creature would have done, that such words could relate only to a circulating library, she immediately pictured to herself a mob of three thousand men assembling in St. George's Fields, the Bank attacked, the Tower threatened, the streets of London flowing with blood, a detachment of the Twelfth Light Dragoons (the hopes of the nation) called up from Northampton to quell the insurgents, and the gallant Captain Frederick Tilney, in the moment of charging at the head of his troop, knocked off his horse by a brickbat from an upper window. Forgive her stupidity. The fears of the sister have added to the weakness of the woman; but she is by no means a simpleton in general."

Catherine looked grave. "And now, Henry," said Miss Tilney, "that you have made us understand each other, you may as well make Miss Morland understand yourself -- unless you mean to have her think you intolerably rude to your sister, and a great brute in your opinion of women in general. Miss Morland is not used to your odd ways."

"I shall be most happy to make her better acquainted with them."

"No doubt; -- but that is no explanation of the present."

"What am I to do?"

"You know what you ought to do. Clear your character handsomely before her. Tell her that you think very highly of the understanding of women."

"Miss Morland, I think very highly of the understanding of all the women in the world -- especially of those -- whoever they may be -- with whom I happen to be in company."

"That is not enough. Be more serious."

"Miss Morland, no one can think more highly of the understanding of women than I do. In my opinion, nature has given them so much that they never find it necessary to use more than half."

"We shall get nothing more serious from him now, Miss Morland. He is not in a sober mood. But I do assure you that he must be entirely misunderstood, if he can ever appear to say an unjust thing of any woman at all, or an unkind one of me."

It was no effort to Catherine to believe that Henry Tilney could never be wrong. His manner might sometimes surprise, but his meaning must always be just: -- and what she did not understand, she was almost as ready to admire, as what she did. The whole walk was delightful, and though it ended too soon, its conclusion was delightful too; -- her friends attended her into the house, and Miss Tilney, before they parted, addressing herself with respectful form, as much to Mrs. Allen as to Catherine, petitioned for the pleasure of her company to dinner on the day after the next. No difficulty was made on Mrs. Allen's side, and the only difficulty on Catherine's was in concealing the excess of her pleasure.

The morning had passed away so charmingly as to banish all her friendship and natural affection, for no thought of Isabella or James had crossed her during their walk. When the Tilneys were gone, she became amiable again, but she was amiable for some time to little effect; Mrs. Allen had no intelligence to give that could relieve her anxiety; she had heard nothing of any of them. Towards the end of the morning, however, Catherine, having occasion for some indispensable yard of ribbon which must be bought without a moment's delay, walked out into the town, and in Bond Street overtook the second Miss Thorpe as she was loitering towards Edgar's Buildings between two of the sweetest girls in the world, who had been her dear friends all the morning. From her, she soon learned that the party to Clifton had taken place. "They set off at eight this morning," said Miss Anne, "and I am sure I do not envy them their drive. I think you and I are very well off to be out of the scrape. -- It must be the dullest thing in the world, for there is not a soul at Clifton at this time of year. Belle went with your brother, and John drove Maria."

Catherine spoke the pleasure she really felt on hearing this part of the arrangement.

"Oh! yes," rejoined the other, "Maria is gone. She was quite wild to go. She thought it would be something very fine. I cannot say I admire her taste; and for my part, I was determined from the first not to go, if they pressed me ever so much."

Catherine, a little doubtful of this, could not help answering, "I wish you could have gone too. It is a pity you could not all go."

"Thank you; but it is quite a matter of indifference to me. Indeed, I would not have gone on any account. I was saying so to Emily and Sophia when you overtook us."

Catherine was still unconvinced; but glad that Anne should have the friendship of an Emily and a Sophia to console her, she bade her adieu without much uneasiness, and returned home, pleased that the party had not been prevented by her refusing to join it, and very heartily wishing that it might be too pleasant to allow either James or Isabella to resent her resistance any longer.

CHAPTER 15

Early the next day, a note from Isabella, speaking peace and tenderness in every line, and entreating the immediate presence of her friend on a matter of the utmost importance, hastened Catherine, in the happiest state of confidence and curiosity, to Edgar's Buildings. The two youngest Miss Thorpes were by themselves in the parlour; and, on Anne's quitting it to call her sister, Catherine took the opportunity of asking the other for some particulars of their yesterday's party. Maria desired no greater pleasure than to speak of it; and Catherine immediately learnt that it had been altogether the most delightful scheme in the world, that nobody could imagine how charming it had been, and that it had been more delightful than any body could conceive. Such was the information of the first five minutes; the second unfolded thus much in detail -- that they had driven directly to the York Hotel, ate some soup, and bespoke an early dinner, walked down to the Pump-room, tasted the water, and laid out some shillings in purses and spars; thence adjoined to eat ice at a pastry-cook's, and hurrying back to the hotel, swallowed their dinner in haste, to prevent being in the dark; and then had a delightful drive back, only the moon was not up, and it rained a little, and Mr. Morland's horse was so tired he could hardly get it along.

Catherine listened with heartfelt satisfaction. It appeared that Blaize Castle had never been thought of; and, as for all the rest, there was nothing to regret for half an instant. Maria's intelligence concluded with a tender effusion of pity for her sister Anne, whom she represented as insupportably cross, from being excluded the party.

"She will never forgive me, I am sure; but, you know, how could I help it? John would have me go, for he vowed he would not drive her, because she had such thick ankles. I dare say she will not be in good humour again this month; but I am determined I will not be cross; it is not a little matter that puts me out of temper."

Isabella now entered the room with so eager a step, and a look of such happy importance, as engaged all her friend's notice. Maria was without ceremony sent away, and Isabella, embracing Catherine, thus began: -- "Yes, my dear Catherine, it is so indeed; your penetration has not deceived you. -- Oh! That arch eye of yours! -- It sees through every thing."

Catherine replied only by a look of wondering ignorance.

"Nay, my beloved, sweetest friend," continued the other, "compose yourself. -- I am amazingly agitated, as you perceive. Let us sit down and talk in comfort. Well, and so you guessed it the moment you had my note? -- Sly creature! -- Oh! My dear Catherine, you alone, who know my heart, can judge of my present happiness. Your brother is the most charming of men. I only wish I were more worthy of him. -- But what will your excellent father and mother say? -- Oh! Heavens! When I think of them I am so agitated!"

Catherine's understanding began to awake: an idea of the truth suddenly darted into her mind; and, with the natural blush of so new an emotion, she cried out, "Good heaven! My dear Isabella, what do you mean? Can you -- can you really be in love with James?"

This bold surmise, however, she soon learnt comprehended but half the fact. The anxious affection, which she was accused of having continually watched in Isabella's every look and action, had, in the course of their yesterday's party, received the delightful confession of an equal love. Her heart and faith were alike engaged to James. -- Never had Catherine listened to any thing so full of interest, wonder, and joy. Her brother and her friend engaged! – New to such circumstances, the importance of it appeared unspeakably great, and she contemplated it as one of those grand events, of which the ordinary course of life can hardly afford a return. The strength of her feelings she could not express; the nature of them, however, contented her friend. The happiness of having such a sister was their first effusion, and the fair ladies mingled in embraces and tears of joy.

Delighting, however, as Catherine sincerely did in the prospect of the connexion, it must be acknowledged that Isabella far surpassed her in tender anticipations. -- "You will be so infinitely dearer to me, my Catherine, than either Anne or Maria: I feel that I shall be so much more attached to my dear Morland's family than to my own."

This was a pitch of friendship beyond Catherine.

"You are so like your dear brother," continued Isabella, "that I quite doated on you the first moment I saw you. But so it always is with me; the first moment settles every thing. The very first day that Morland came to us last Christmas -- the very first moment I beheld him -- my heart was irrecoverably gone. I remember I wore my yellow gown, with my hair done up in braids; and when I came into the drawing-room, and John introduced him, I thought I never saw any body so handsome before."

Here Catherine secretly acknowledged the power of love; for, though exceedingly fond of her brother, and partial to all his endowments, she had never in her life thought him handsome.

"I remember too, Miss Andrews drank tea with us that evening, and wore her puce-coloured sarsenet; and she looked so heavenly that I thought your brother must certainly fall in love with her; I could not sleep a wink all night for thinking of it. Oh! Catherine, the many sleepless nights I have had on your brother's account! -- I would not have you suffer half what I have done! I am grown wretchedly thin, I know; but I will not pain you by describing my anxiety; you have seen enough of it. I feel that I have betrayed myself perpetually -- so unguarded in speaking of my partiality for the church! -- But my secret I was always sure would be safe with you."

Catherine felt that nothing could have been safer; but ashamed of an ignorance little expected, she dared no longer contest the point, nor refuse to have been as full of arch penetration and affectionate sympathy as Isabella chose to consider her. Her brother, she found, was preparing to set off with all speed to Fullerton, to make known his situation and ask consent; and here was a source of some real agitation to the mind of Isabella. Catherine endeavoured to persuade her, as she was herself persuaded, that her father and mother would never oppose their son's wishes. -- "It is impossible," said she, "for parents to be more kind, or more desirous of their children's happiness; I have no doubt of their consenting immediately."

"Morland says exactly the same," replied Isabella; "and yet I dare not expect it; my fortune will be so small; they never can consent to it. Your brother, who might marry any body!"

Here Catherine again discerned the force of love.

"Indeed, Isabella, you are too humble. -- The difference of fortune can be nothing to signify."

"Oh! My sweet Catherine, in *your* generous heart I know it would signify nothing; but we must not expect such disinterestedness in many. As for myself, I am sure I only wish our situations were reversed. Had I the command of millions, were I mistress of the whole world, your brother would be my only choice."

This charming sentiment, recommended as much by sense as novelty, gave Catherine a most pleasing remembrance of all the heroines of her acquaintance; and she thought her friend never looked more lovely than in uttering the grand idea. -- "I am sure they will consent," was her frequent declaration; "I am sure they will be delighted with you."

"For my own part," said Isabella, "my wishes are so moderate that the smallest income in nature would be enough for me. Where people are really attached, poverty itself is wealth; grandeur I detest: I would not settle in London for the universe. A cottage in some retired village would be extasy. There are some charming little villas about Richmond."

"Richmond!" cried Catherine. -- "You must settle near Fullerton. You must be near us."

"I am sure I shall be miserable if we do not. If I can but be near *you*, I shall be satisfied. But this is idle talking! I will not allow myself to think of such things, till we have your father's answer. Morland says that by sending it to-night to Salisbury, we may have it to-morrow. -- To-morrow? -- I know I shall never have courage to open the letter. I know it will be the death of me."

89

A reverie succeeded this conviction -- and when Isabella spoke again, it was to resolve on the quality of her wedding-gown.

Their conference was put an end to by the anxious young lover himself, who came to breathe his parting sigh before he set off for Wiltshire. Catherine wished to congratulate him, but knew not what to say, and her eloquence was only in her eyes. From them, however, the eight parts of speech shone out most expressively, and James could combine them with ease. Impatient for the realization of all that he hoped at home, his adieus were not long; and they would have been yet shorter, had he not been frequently detained by the urgent entreaties of his fair one that he would go. Twice was he called almost from the door by her eagerness to have him gone. "Indeed, Morland, I must drive you away. Consider how far you have to ride. I cannot bear to see you linger so. For Heaven's sake, waste no more time. There, go, go -- I insist on it."

The two friends, with hearts now more united than ever, were inseparable for the day; and in schemes of sisterly happiness the hours flew along. Mrs. Thorpe and her son, who were acquainted with every thing, and who seemed only to want Mr. Morland's consent, to consider Isabella's engagement as the most fortunate circumstance imaginable for their family, were allowed to join their counsels, and add their quota of significant looks and mysterious expressions to fill up the measure of curiosity to be raised in the unprivileged younger sisters. To Catherine's simple feelings, this odd sort of reserve seemed neither kindly meant, nor consistently supported; and its unkindness she would hardly have forborne pointing out, had its inconsistency been less their friend; but Anne and Maria soon set her heart at ease by the sagacity of their "I know what"; and the evening was spent in a sort of war of wit, a display of family ingenuity; on one side in the mystery of an affected secret, on the other of undefined discovery, all equally acute.

Catherine was with her friend again the next day, endeavouring to support her spirits and while away the many tedious hours before the delivery of the letters; a needful exertion, for as the time of reasonable expectation drew near, Isabella became more and more desponding, and before the letter arrived, had worked herself into a state of real distress. But when it did come, where could distress be found? "I have had no difficulty in gaining the consent of my kind parents, and am promised that every thing in their power shall be done to forward my happiness," were the first three lines, and in one moment all was joyful security. The brightest glow was instantly spread over Isabella's features, all care and anxiety seemed removed, her spirits became almost too high for control, and she called herself without scruple the happiest of mortals.

Mrs. Thorpe, with tears of joy, embraced her daughter, her son, her visitor, and could have embraced half the inhabitants of Bath with satisfaction. Her heart was overflowing with tenderness. It was "dear John" and "dear Catherine" at every word; -- "dear Anne and dear Maria" must immediately be made sharers in their felicity; and two "dears" at once before the name of Isabella were not more than that beloved child had now well earned. John himself was no skulker in joy. He not only bestowed on Mr. Morland the high commendation of being one of the finest fellows in the world, but swore off many sentences in his praise.

The letter, whence sprang all this felicity, was short, containing little more than this assurance of success; and every particular was deferred till James could write again. But for particulars Isabella could well afford to wait. The needful was comprised in Mr. Morland's promise; his honour was pledged to make every thing easy; and by what means their income was to be formed, whether landed property were to be resigned, or funded money made over, was a matter in which her disinterested spirit took no concern. She knew enough to feel secure of an honourable and speedy establishment, and her imagination took a rapid flight over its attendant felicities. She saw herself at the end of a few weeks, the gaze and admiration of every new acquaintance at Fullerton, the envy of every valued old friend in Putney, with a carriage at her command, a new name on her tickets, and a brilliant exhibition of hoop rings on her finger.

When the contents of the letter were ascertained, John Thorpe, who had only waited its arrival to begin his journey to London, prepared to set off. "Well, Miss Morland," said he, on finding her alone in the parlour, "I am come to bid you good bye." Catherine wished him a good journey. Without appearing to hear her, he walked to the window, fidgeted about, hummed a tune, and seemed wholly self-occupied.

"Shall not you be late at Devizes?" said Catherine. He made no answer; but after a minute's silence burst out with, "A famous good thing this marrying scheme, upon my soul! A clever fancy of

Morland's and Belle's. What do you think of it, Miss Morland? I say it is no bad notion."

"I am sure I think it a very good one."

"Do you? -- That's honest, by heavens! I am glad you are no enemy to matrimony, however. Did you ever hear the old song, 'Going to One Wedding Brings on Another?' I say, you will come to Belle's wedding, I hope."

"Yes; I have promised your sister to be with her, if possible."

"And then you know"-- twisting himself about and forcing a foolish laugh -- "I say, then you know, we may try the truth of this same old song."

"May we? But I never sing. Well, I wish you a good journey. I dine with Miss Tilney to-day, and must now be going home."

"Nay, but there is no such confounded hurry. -- Who knows when we may be together again? -- Not but that I shall be down again by the end of a fortnight, and a devilish long fortnight it will appear to me."

"Then why do you stay away so long?" replied Catherine -- finding that he waited for an answer.

"That is kind of you, however -- kind and good-natured. I shall not forget it in a hurry. But you have more good nature and all that, than any body living, I believe. A monstrous deal of good-nature, and it is not only good-nature, but you have so much, so much of every thing; and then you have such -- upon my soul, I do not know any body like you."

"Oh! dear, there are a great many people like me, I dare say, only a great deal better. Good morning to you."

"But I say, Miss Morland, I shall come and pay my respects at Fullerton before it is long, if not disagreeable."

"Pray do. My father and mother will be very glad to see you."

"And I hope -- I hope, Miss Morland, you will not be sorry to see me."

"Oh! dear, not at all. There are very few people I am sorry to see. Company is always cheerful."

"That is just my way of thinking. Give me but a little cheerful company, let me only have the company of the people I love, let me only be where I like and with whom I like, and the devil take the rest, say I. -- And I am heartily glad to hear you say the same. But I have a notion, Miss Morland, you and I think pretty much alike upon most matters."

"Perhaps we may; but it is more than I ever thought of. And as to *most matters*, to say the truth, there are not many that I know my own mind about."

"By Jove, no more do I. It is not my way to bother my brains with what does not concern me. My notion of things is simple enough. Let me only have the girl I like, say I, with a comfortable house over my head, and what care I for all the rest? Fortune is nothing. I am sure of a good income of my own; and if she had not a penny, why, so much the better."

"Very true. I think like you there. If there is a good fortune on one side, there can be no occasion for any on the other. No matter which has it, so that there is enough. I hate the idea of one great fortune looking out for another. And to marry for money I think the wickedest thing in existence. -- Good day. -- We shall be very glad to see you at Fullerton, whenever it is convenient." And away she went. It was not in the power of all his gallantry to detain her longer. With such news to communicate, and such a visit to prepare for, her departure was not to be delayed by any thing in his nature to urge; and she hurried away, leaving him to the undivided consciousness of his own happy address, and her explicit encouragement.

The agitation which she had herself experienced on first learning her brother's engagement made her expect to raise no inconsiderable emotion in Mr. and Mrs. Allen, by the communication of the wonderful event. How great was her disappointment! The important affair, which many words of preparation ushered in, had been foreseen by them both ever since her brother's arrival; and all that they felt on the occasion was comprehended in a wish for the young people's happiness, with a remark, on the gentleman's side, in favour of Isabella's beauty, and on the lady's, of her great good luck. It was to Catherine the most surprising insensibility. The disclosure, however, of the great secret of James's going to Fullerton the day before, did raise some emotion in Mrs. Allen. She could not listen to that with perfect calmness, but repeatedly regretted the necessity of its concealment, wished she could have known his intention, wished she could have seen him before he went, as she should certainly have troubled him with her best regards to his father and mother, and her kind compliments to all the Skinners.

CHAPTER 16

Catherine's expectations of pleasure from her visit in Milsom Street were so very high that disappointment was inevitable; and accordingly, though she was most politely received by General Tilney, and kindly welcomed by his daughter, though Henry was at home, and no one else of the party, she found, on her return, without spending many hours in the examination of her feelings, that she had gone to her appointment preparing for happiness which it had not afforded. Instead of finding herself improved in acquaintance with Miss Tilney, from the intercourse of the day, she seemed hardly so intimate with her as before; instead of seeing Henry Tilney to greater advantage than ever, in the ease of a family party, he had never said so little, nor been so little agreeable; and, in spite of their father's great civilities to her -- in spite of his thanks, invitations, and compliments -- it had been a release to get away from him. It puzzled her to account for all this. It could not be General Tilney's fault. That he was perfectly agreeable and good-natured, and altogether a very charming man, did not admit of a doubt, for he was tall and handsome, and Henry's father. He could not be accountable for his children's want of spirits, or for her want of enjoyment in his company. The former she hoped at last might have been accidental, and the latter she could only attribute to her own stupidity. Isabella, on hearing the particulars of the visit, gave a different explanation: "It was all pride, pride, insufferable haughtiness and pride! She had long suspected the family to be very high, and this made it certain. Such insolence of behaviour as Miss Tilney's she had never heard of in her life! Not to do the honours of her house with common good-breeding! -- To behave to her guest with such superciliousness! -- Hardly even to speak to her!"

"But it was not so bad as that, Isabella; there was no superciliousness; she was very civil."

"Oh! Don't defend her! And then the brother, he, who had appeared so attached to you! Good heavens! Well, some people's feelings are incomprehensible. And so he hardly looked once at you the whole day?"

"I do not say so; but he did not seem in good spirits."

"How contemptible! Of all things in the world inconstancy is my aversion. Let me entreat you never to think of him again, my dear Catherine; indeed he is unworthy of you."

"Unworthy! I do not suppose he ever thinks of me."

"That is exactly what I say; he never thinks of you. -- Such fickleness! Oh! How different to your brother and to mine! I really believe John has the most constant heart."

"But as for General Tilney, I assure you it would be impossible for any body to behave to me with greater civility and attention; it seemed to be his only care to entertain and make me happy."

"Oh! I know no harm of him; I do not suspect him of pride. I believe he is a very gentleman-like man. John thinks very well of him, and John's judgment --"

"Well, I shall see how they behave to me this evening; we shall meet them at the rooms."

"And must I go?"

"Do not you intend it? I thought it was all settled."

"Nay, since you make such a point of it, I can refuse you nothing. But do not insist upon my being very agreeable, for my heart, you know, will be some forty miles off. And as for dancing, do not mention it, I beg; *that* is quite out of the question. Charles Hodges will plague me to death, I dare say; but I shall cut him very short. Ten to one but he guesses the reason, and that is exactly what I want to avoid, so I shall insist on his keeping his conjecture to himself."

Isabella's opinion of the Tilneys did not influence her friend; she was sure there had been no insolence in the manners either of brother or sister; and she did not credit there being any pride in their hearts. The evening rewarded her confidence; she was met by one with the same kindness, and by the other with the same attention, as heretofore: Miss Tilney took pains to be near her, and Henry asked her to dance.

Having heard the day before in Milsom Street that their elder brother, Captain Tilney, was expected almost every hour, she was at no loss for the name of a very fashionable-looking, handsome young man, whom she had never seen before, and who now evidently belonged to their party. She looked at him with great admiration, and even supposed it possible that some people might think him handsomer than his brother, though, in her eyes, his air was more assuming, and his countenance less prepossessing. His taste and manners were beyond a doubt decidedly inferior; for, within her hearing, he not only protested against every thought of dancing himself, but even laughed openly at Henry for finding it possible.

From the latter circumstance it may be presumed that, whatever might be our heroine's opinion of him, his admiration of her was not of a very dangerous kind; not likely to produce animosities between the brothers, nor persecutions to the lady. He cannot be the instigator of the three villains in horsemen's greatcoats, by whom she will hereafter be forced into a travelling-chaise and four, which will drive off with incredible speed. Catherine, meanwhile, undisturbed by presentiments of such an evil, or of any evil at all, except that of having but a short set to dance down, enjoyed her usual happiness with Henry Tilney, listening with sparkling eyes to every thing he said; and, in finding him irresistible, becoming so herself.

At the end of the first dance, Captain Tilney came towards them again, and, much to Catherine's dissatisfaction, pulled his brother away. They retired whispering together; and, though her delicate sensibility did not take immediate alarm, and lay it down as fact, that Captain Tilney must have heard some malevolent misrepresentation of her, which he now hastened to communicate to his brother, in the hope of separating them for ever, she could not have her partner conveyed from her sight without very uneasy sensations. Her suspense was of full five minutes' duration; and she was beginning to think it a very long quarter of an hour, when they both returned, and an explanation was given, by Henry's requesting to know if she thought her friend, Miss Thorpe, would have any objection to dancing, as his brother would be most happy to be introduced to her. Catherine, without hesitation, replied that she was very sure Miss Thorpe did not mean to dance at all. The cruel reply was passed on to the other, and he immediately walked away.

"Your brother will not mind it, I know," said she, "because I heard him say before that he hated dancing; but it was very good-natured in him to think of it. I suppose he saw Isabella sitting down, and fancied she might wish for a partner; but he is quite mistaken, for she would not dance upon any account in the world."

Henry smiled, and said, "How very little trouble it can give you to understand the motive of other people's actions."

"Why? What do you mean?"

"With you, it is not, How is such a one likely to be influenced? What is the inducement most likely to act upon such a person's feelings, age, situation, and probable habits of life considered? --

but, how should *I* be influenced, what would be *my* inducement in acting so and so?"

"I do not understand you."

"Then we are on very unequal terms, for I understand you perfectly well."

"Me? -- yes; I cannot speak well enough to be unintelligible."

"Bravo! -- an excellent satire on modern language."

"But pray tell me what you mean."

"Shall I indeed? -- Do you really desire it? -- But you are not aware of the consequences; it will involve you in a very cruel embarrassment, and certainly bring on a disagreement between us."

"No, no; it shall not do either; I am not afraid."

"Well, then, I only meant that your attributing my brother's wish of dancing with Miss Thorpe to good-nature alone convinced me of your being superior in good-nature yourself to all the rest of the world."

Catherine blushed and disclaimed, and the gentleman's predictions were verified. There was a something, however, in his words which repaid her for the pain of confusion; and that something occupied her mind so much that she drew back for some time, forgetting to speak or to listen, and almost forgetting where she was; till, roused by the voice of Isabella, she looked up and saw her with Captain Tilney preparing to give them hands across.

Isabella shrugged her shoulders and smiled, the only explanation of this extraordinary change which could at that time be given; but as it was not quite enough for Catherine's comprehension, she spoke her astonishment in very plain terms to her partner.

"I cannot think how it could happen! Isabella was so determined not to dance."

"And did Isabella never change her mind before?"

"Oh! but, because -- and your brother! -- After what you told him from me, how could he think of going to ask her?"

"I cannot take surprise to myself on that head. You bid me be surprised on your friend's account, and therefore I am; but as for my brother, his conduct in the business, I must own, has been no more than I believed him perfectly equal to. The fairness of your friend was an open attraction; her firmness, you know, could only be understood by yourself."

"You are laughing; but, I assure you, Isabella is very firm in general."

"It is as much as should be said of any one. To be always firm must be to be often obstinate. When properly to relax is the trial of judgment; and, without reference to my brother, I really think Miss Thorpe has by no means chosen ill in fixing on the present hour."

The friends were not able to get together for any confidential discourse till all the dancing was over; but then, as they walked about the room arm in arm, Isabella thus explained herself: -- "I do not wonder at your surprise and I am really fatigued to death. He is such a rattle! -- Amusing enough, if my mind had been disengaged; but I would have given the world to sit still."

"Then why did not you?"

"Oh! My dear! It would have looked so particular; and you know how I abhor doing that. I refused him as long as I possibly could, but he would take no denial. You have no idea how he pressed me. I begged him to excuse me, and get some other partner -- but no, not he; after aspiring to my hand, there was nobody else in the room he could bear to think of; and it was not that he wanted merely to dance, he wanted to be with *me*. Oh! Such nonsense! -- I told him he had taken a very unlikely way to prevail upon me; for, of all things in the world, I hated fine speeches and compliments; -- and so--and so then I found there would be no peace if I did not stand up. Besides, I thought Mrs. Hughes, who introduced him, might take it ill if I did not: and your dear brother, I am sure he would have been miserable if I had sat down the whole evening. I am so glad it is over! My spirits are quite jaded with listening to his nonsense: and then, -- being such a smart young fellow, I saw every eye was upon us."

"He is very handsome indeed."

"Handsome! -- Yes, I suppose he may. I dare say people would admire him in general; but he is not at all in my style of beauty. I hate a florid complexion and dark eyes in a man. However, he is very well. Amazingly conceited, I am sure. I took him down several times, you know, in my way."

When the young ladies next met, they had a far more interesting subject to discuss. James Morland's second letter was then received, and the kind intentions of his father fully explained. A living, of which Mr. Morland was himself patron and incumbent, of about four hundred pounds yearly value, was to be resigned to his son as soon as he should be old enough to take it; no trifling deduction from the family income, no niggardly assignment to one of ten children. An estate of at least equal value, moreover, was assured as his future inheritance.

James expressed himself on the occasion with becoming gratitude; and the necessity of waiting between two and three years before they could marry, being, however unwelcome, no more than he had expected, was borne by him without discontent. Catherine, whose expectations had been as unfixed as her ideas of her father's income, and whose judgment was now entirely led by her brother, felt equally well satisfied, and heartily congratulated Isabella on having every thing so pleasantly settled.

"It is very charming indeed," said Isabella, with a grave face.

"Mr. Morland has behaved vastly handsome indeed," said the gentle Mrs. Thorpe, looking anxiously at her daughter. "I only wish I could do as much. One could not expect more from him, you know. If he finds he *can* do more by and by, I dare say he will, for I am sure he must be an excellent good-hearted man. Four hundred is but a small income to begin on indeed, but your wishes, my dear Isabella, are so moderate, you do not consider how little you ever want, my dear."

"It is not on my own account I wish for more; but I cannot bear to be the means of injuring my dear Morland, making him sit down upon an income hardly enough to find one in the common necessaries of life. For myself, it is nothing; I never think of myself."

"I know you never do, my dear; and you will always find your reward in the affection it makes every body feel for you. There never was a young woman so beloved as you are by every body that knows you; and I dare say when Mr. Morland sees you, my dear child -- but do not let us distress our dear Catherine by talking of such things. Mr. Morland has behaved so very handsome, you know. I always heard he was a most excellent man; and you know, my dear, we are not to suppose but what, if you had had a suitable fortune, he would have come down with something more, for I am sure he must be a most liberal-minded man."

"Nobody can think better of Mr. Morland than I do, I am sure. But every body has their failing, you know, and every body has a right to do what they like with their own money." Catherine was hurt by these insinuations. "I am very sure," said she, "that my father has promised to do as much as he can afford."

Isabella recollected herself. "As to that, my sweet Catherine, there cannot be a doubt, and you know me well enough to be sure that a much smaller income would satisfy me. It is not the want of more money that makes me just at present a little out of spirits; I hate money; and if our union could take place now upon only fifty pounds a year, I should not have a wish unsatisfied. Ah! my Catherine, you have found me out. There's the sting. The long, long, endless two years and half that are to pass before your brother can hold the living."

"Yes, yes, my darling Isabella," said Mrs. Thorpe, "we perfectly see into your heart. You have no disguise. We perfectly understand the present vexation; and every body must love you the better for such a noble honest affection."

Catherine's uncomfortable feelings began to lessen. She endeavoured to believe that the delay of the marriage was the only source of Isabella's regret; and when she saw her at their next interview as cheerful and amiable as ever, endeavoured to forget that she had for a minute thought otherwise. James soon followed his letter, and was received with the most gratifying kindness.

CHAPTER 17

The Allens had now entered on the sixth week of their stay in Bath; and whether it should be the last was for some time a question, to which Catherine listened with a beating heart. To have her acquaintance with the Tilneys end so soon was an evil which nothing could counterbalance. Her whole happiness seemed at stake, while the affair was in suspense, and every thing secured when it was determined that the lodgings should be taken for another fortnight. What this additional fortnight was to produce to her beyond the pleasure of sometimes seeing Henry Tilney made but a small part of Catherine's speculation. Once or twice indeed, since James's engagement had taught her what *could* be done, she had got so far as to indulge in a secret "perhaps," but in general the felicity of being with him for the present bounded her views: the present was now comprised in another three weeks, and her happiness being certain for that period, the rest of her life was at such a distance as to excite but little interest. In the course of the morning which saw this business arranged, she visited Miss Tilney, and poured forth her joyful feelings. It was doomed to be a day of trial. No sooner had she expressed her delight in Mr. Allen's lengthened stay than Miss Tilney told her of her father's having just determined upon quitting Bath by the end of another week. Here was a blow! The past suspense of the morning had been ease and quiet to the present disappointment. Catherine's countenance fell, and in a voice of most sincere concern she echoed Miss Tilney's concluding words, "By the end of another week!"

"Yes, my father can seldom be prevailed on to give the waters what I think a fair trial. He has been disappointed of some friends' arrival whom he expected to meet here, and as he is now pretty well, is in a hurry to get home."

"I am very sorry for it," said Catherine dejectedly; "if I had known this before --"

"Perhaps," said Miss Tilney in an embarrassed manner, "you would be so good -- it would make me very happy if --"

The entrance of her father put a stop to the civility, which Catherine was beginning to hope might introduce a desire of their corresponding. After addressing her with his usual politeness, he turned to his daughter and said, "Well, Eleanor, may I congratulate you on being successful in your application to your fair friend?"

"I was just beginning to make the request, sir, as you came in."

"Well, proceed by all means. I know how much your heart is in it. My daughter, Miss Morland," he continued, without leaving his daughter time to speak, "has been forming a very bold wish. We leave Bath, as she has perhaps told you, on Saturday se'nnight. A letter from my steward tells me that my presence is wanted at home; and being disappointed in my hope of seeing the Marquis of Longtown and General Courteney here, some of my very old friends, there is nothing to detain me longer in Bath. And could we carry our selfish point with you, we should leave it without a single regret. Can you, in short, be prevailed on to quit this scene of public triumph and oblige your friend Eleanor with your company in Gloucestershire? I am almost ashamed to make the request, though its presumption would certainly appear greater to every creature in Bath than yourself. Modesty such as yours -- but not for the world would I pain it by open praise. If you can be induced to honour us with a visit, you will make us happy beyond expression. 'Tis true, we can offer you nothing like the gaieties of this lively place; we can tempt you neither by amusement nor splendour, for our mode of living, as you see, is plain and unpretending; yet no endeavours shall be wanting on our side to make Northanger Abbey not wholly disagreeable."

Northanger Abbey! -- These were thrilling words, and wound up Catherine's feelings to the highest point of extasy. Her grateful and gratified heart could hardly restrain its expressions within the language of tolerable calmness. To receive so flattering an invitation! To have her company so warmly solicited! Every thing honourable and soothing, every present enjoyment, and every future hope was contained in it; and her acceptance, with only the saving clause of Papa and Mamma's approbation, was eagerly given. -- "I will write home directly," said she, "and if they do not object, as I dare say they will not --"

General Tilney was not less sanguine, having already waited on her excellent friends in Pulteney Street, and obtained their sanction of his wishes. "Since they can consent to part with you," said he, "we may expect philosophy from all the world."

Miss Tilney was earnest, though gentle, in her secondary civilities, and the affair became in a few minutes as nearly settled as this necessary reference to Fullerton would allow.

The circumstances of the morning had led Catherine's feelings through the varieties of suspense, security, and disappointment; but they were now safely lodged in perfect bliss; and with spirits elated to rapture, with Henry at her heart, and Northanger Abbey on her lips, she hurried home to write her letter. Mr. and Mrs. Morland, relying on the discretion of the friends to whom they had already entrusted their daughter, felt no doubt of the propriety of an acquaintance which had been formed under their eye, and sent therefore by return of post their ready consent to her visit in Gloucestershire. This indulgence, though not more than Catherine had hoped for, completed her conviction of being favoured beyond every other human creature, in friends and fortune, circumstance and chance. Every thing seemed to co-operate for her advantage. By the kindness of her first friends, the Allens, she had been introduced into scenes where pleasures of every kind had met her. Her feelings, her preferences, had each known the happiness of a return. Wherever she felt attachment, she had been able to create it. The affection of Isabella was to be secured to her in a sister. The Tilneys, they, by whom, above all, she desired to be favourably thought of, outstripped even her wishes in the flattering measures by which their intimacy was to be continued. She was to be their chosen visitor, she was to be for weeks under the same roof with the person whose society she mostly prized -- and, in addition to all the rest, this roof was to be the roof of an abbey! Her passion for ancient edifices was next in degree to her passion for Henry Tilney-- and castles and abbeys made usually the charm of those reveries which his image did not fill. To see and explore either the ramparts and keep of the one, or the cloisters of the other, had been for many weeks a darling wish, though to be more than the visitor of an hour had seemed too nearly impossible for desire. And yet, this was to happen. With all the chances against her of house, hall, place, park, court, and cottage, Northanger turned up an abbey, and she was to be its inhabitant. Its long, damp passages, its narrow cells and ruined chapel, were to be within her daily reach, and she could not entirely subdue the hope of some traditional legends, some awful memorials of an injured and ill-fated nun.

It was wonderful that her friends should seem so little elated by the possession of such a home, that the consciousness of it should be so meekly borne. The power of early habit only could account for it. A distinction to which they had been born gave no pride. Their superiority of abode was no more to them than their superiority of person.

Many were the inquiries she was eager to make of Miss Tilney; but so active were her thoughts, that when these inquiries were answered, she was hardly more assured than before, of Northanger Abbey having been a richly endowed convent at the time of the Reformation, of its having fallen into the hands of an ancestor of the Tilneys on its dissolution, of a large portion of the ancient building still making a part of the present dwelling although the rest was decayed, or of its standing low in a valley, sheltered from the north and east by rising woods of oak.

CHAPTER 18

With a mind thus full of happiness, Catherine was hardly aware that two or three days had passed away, without her seeing Isabella for more than a few minutes together. She began first to be sensible of this, and to sigh for her conversation, as she walked along the

Pump-room one morning, by Mrs. Allen's side, without any thing to say or to hear; and scarcely had she felt a five minutes' longing of friendship, before the object of it appeared, and inviting her to a secret conference, led the way to a seat. "This is my favourite place," said she as they sat down on a bench between the doors, which commanded a tolerable view of every body entering at either; "it is so out of the way."

Catherine, observing that Isabella's eyes were continually bent towards one door or the other, as in eager expectation, and remembering how often she had been falsely accused of being arch, thought the present a fine opportunity for being really so; and therefore gaily said, "Do not be uneasy, Isabella, James will soon be here."

"Psha! My dear creature," she replied, "do not think me such a simpleton as to be always wanting to confine him to my elbow. It would be hideous to be always together; we should be the jest of the place. And so you are going to Northanger! -- I am amazingly glad of it. It is one of the finest old places in England, I understand. I shall depend upon a most particular description of it."

"You shall certainly have the best in my power to give. But who are you looking for? Are your sisters coming?"

"I am not looking for any body. One's eyes must be somewhere, and you know what a foolish trick I have of fixing mine, when my thoughts are an hundred miles off. I am amazingly absent; I believe I am the most absent creature in the world. Tilney says it is always the case with minds of a certain stamp."

"But I thought, Isabella, you had something in particular to tell me?"

"Oh! Yes, and so I have. But here is a proof of what I was saying. My poor head! I had quite forgot it. Well, the thing is this: I have just had a letter from John; -- you can guess the contents."

"No, indeed, I cannot."

"My sweet love, do not be so abominably affected. What can he write about, but yourself? You know he is over head and ears in love with you."

"With *me*, dear Isabella!"

"Nay, my sweetest Catherine, this is being quite absurd! Modesty, and all that, is very well in its way, but really a little common honesty is sometimes quite as becoming. I have no idea of being so overstrained! It is fishing for compliments. His attentions

104

were such as a child must have noticed. And it was but half an hour before he left Bath that you gave him the most positive encouragement. He says so in this letter, says that he as good as made you an offer, and that you received his advances in the kindest way; and now he wants me to urge his suit, and say all manner of pretty things to you. So it is in vain to affect ignorance."

Catherine, with all the earnestness of truth, expressed her astonishment at such a charge, protesting her innocence of every thought of Mr. Thorpe's being in love with her, and the consequent impossibility of her having ever intended to encourage him. "As to any attentions on his side, I do declare, upon my honour, I never was sensible of them for a moment -- except just his asking me to dance the first day of his coming. And as to making me an offer, or any thing like it, there must be some unaccountable mistake. I could not have misunderstood a thing of that kind, you know! And, as I ever wish to be believed, I solemnly protest that no syllable of such a nature ever passed between us. The last half hour before he went away! -- It must be all and completely a mistake -- for I did not see him once that whole morning."

"But *that* you certainly did, for you spent the whole morning in Edgar's Buildings -- it was the day your father's consent came -- and I am pretty sure that you and John were alone in the parlour some time before you left the house."

"Are you? -- Well, if you say it, it was so, I dare say -- but for the life of me, I cannot recollect it. -- I *do* remember now being with you, and seeing him as well as the rest -- but that we were ever alone for five minutes -- However, it is not worth arguing about, for whatever might pass on his side, you must be convinced, by my having no recollection of it, that I never thought, nor expected, nor wished for any thing of the kind from him. I am excessively concerned that he should have any regard for me -- but indeed it has been quite unintentional on my side; I never had the smallest idea of it. Pray undeceive him as soon as you can, and tell him I beg his pardon -- that is -- I do not know what I ought to say -- but make him understand what I mean, in the properest way. I would not speak disrespectfully of a brother of yours, Isabella, I am sure; but you know very well that if I could think of one man more than another -- *he* is not the person." Isabella was silent. "My dear friend, you must not be angry with me. I cannot suppose your brother cares so very much about me. And, you know, we shall still be sisters."

"Yes, yes" (with a blush), "there are more ways than one of our being sisters. But where am I wandering to? Well, my dear Catherine, the case seems to be that you are determined against poor John -- is not it so?"

"I certainly cannot return his affection, and as certainly never meant to encourage it."

"Since that is the case, I am sure I shall not tease you any further. John desired me to speak to you on the subject, and therefore I have. But I confess, as soon as I read his letter, I thought it a very foolish, imprudent business, and not likely to promote the good of either; for what were you to live upon, supposing you came together? You have both of you something, to be sure, but it is not a trifle that will support a family nowadays; and after all that romancers may say, there is no doing without money. I only wonder John could think of it; he could not have received my last."

"You *do* acquit me, then, of anything wrong? -- You are convinced that I never meant to deceive your brother, never suspected him of liking me till this moment?"

"Oh! As to that," answered Isabella laughingly, "I do not pretend to determine what your thoughts and designs in time past may have been. All that is best known to yourself. A little harmless flirtation or so will occur, and one is often drawn on to give more encouragement than one wishes to stand by. But you may be assured that I am the last person in the world to judge you severely. All those things should be allowed for in youth and high spirits. What one means one day, you know, one may not mean the next. Circumstances change, opinions alter."

"But my opinion of your brother never did alter; it was always the same. You are describing what never happened."

"My dearest Catherine," continued the other without at all listening to her, "I would not for all the world be the means of hurrying you into an engagement before you knew what you were about. I do not think any thing would justify me in wishing you to sacrifice all your happiness merely to oblige my brother, because he is my brother, and who perhaps after all, you know, might be just as happy without you, for people seldom know what they would be at, young men especially, they are so amazingly changeable and inconstant. What I say is, why should a brother's happiness be dearer to me than a friend's? You know I carry my notions of friendship pretty high. But, above all things, my dear Catherine, do

106

not be in a hurry. Take my word for it, that if you are in too great a hurry, you will certainly live to repent it. Tilney says there is nothing people are so often deceived in as the state of their own affections, and I believe he is very right. Ah! Here he comes; never mind, he will not see us, I am sure."

Catherine, looking up, perceived Captain Tilney; and Isabella, earnestly fixing her eye on him as she spoke, soon caught his notice. He approached immediately, and took the seat to which her movements invited him. His first address made Catherine start. Though spoken low, she could distinguish, "What! Always to be watched, in person or by proxy!"

"Psha, nonsense!" was Isabella's answer in the same half whisper. "Why do you put such things into my head? If I could believe it -- my spirit, you know, is pretty independent."

"I wish your heart were independent. That would be enough for me."

"My heart, indeed! What can you have to do with hearts? You men have none of you any hearts."

"If we have not hearts, we have eyes; and they give us torment enough."

"Do they? I am sorry for it; I am sorry they find any thing so disagreeable in me. I will look another way. I hope this pleases you" (turning her back on him); "I hope your eyes are not tormented now."

"Never more so; for the edge of a blooming cheek is still in view -- at once too much and too little."

Catherine heard all this, and quite out of countenance, could listen no longer. Amazed that Isabella could endure it, and jealous for her brother, she rose up, and saying she should join Mrs. Allen, proposed their walking. But for this Isabella shewed no inclination. She was so amazingly tired, and it was so odious to parade about the Pump-room; and if she moved from her seat she should miss her sisters; she was expecting her sisters every moment; so that her dearest Catherine must excuse her, and must sit quietly down again. But Catherine could be stubborn too; and Mrs. Allen just then coming up to propose their returning home, she joined her and walked out of the Pump-room, leaving Isabella still sitting with Captain Tilney. With much uneasiness did she thus leave them. It seemed to her that Captain Tilney was falling in love with Isabella, and Isabella unconsciously encouraging him; unconsciously it must be, for Isabella's attachment to James was as certain and well acknowledged as her engagement. To doubt her truth or good intentions was impossible; and yet, during the whole of their conversation her manner had been odd. She wished Isabella had talked more like her usual self, and not so much about money, and had not looked so well pleased at the sight of Captain Tilney. How strange that she should not perceive his admiration! Catherine longed to give her a hint of it, to put her on her guard, and prevent all the pain which her too lively behaviour might otherwise create both for him and her brother.

The compliment of John Thorpe's affection did not make amends for this thoughtlessness in his sister. She was almost as far from believing as from wishing it to be sincere; for she had not forgotten that he could mistake, and his assertion of the offer and of her encouragement convinced her that his mistakes could sometimes be very egregious. In vanity, therefore, she gained but little; her chief profit was in wonder. That he should think it worth his while to fancy himself in love with her was a matter of lively astonishment. Isabella talked of his attentions; *she* had never been sensible of any; but Isabella had said many things which she hoped had been spoken in haste, and would never be said again; and upon this she was glad to rest altogether for present ease and comfort.

CHAPTER 19

A few days passed away, and Catherine, though not allowing herself to suspect her friend, could not help watching her closely. The result of her observations was not agreeable. Isabella seemed an altered creature. When she saw her indeed surrounded only by their immediate friends in Edgar's Buildings or Pulteney Street, her change of manners was so trifling that, had it gone no farther, it might have passed unnoticed. A something of languid indifference, or of that boasted absence of mind which Catherine had never heard of before, would occasionally come across her; but had nothing worse appeared, that might only have spread a new grace and inspired a warmer interest. But when Catherine saw her in public, admitting Captain Tilney's attentions as readily as they were offered, and allowing him almost an equal share with James in her notice and smiles, the alteration became too positive to be passed over. What could be meant by such unsteady conduct, what her friend could be at, was beyond her comprehension. Isabella could not be aware of the pain she was inflicting; but it was a degree of wilful thoughtlessness which Catherine could not but resent. James was the sufferer. She saw him grave and uneasy; and however careless of his present comfort the woman might be who had given him her heart, to *her* it was always an object. For poor Captain Tilney too she was greatly concerned. Though his looks did not please her, his name was a passport to her good will, and she thought with sincere compassion of his approaching disappointment; for, in spite of what she had believed herself to overhear in the Pump-room, his behaviour was so incompatible with a knowledge of Isabella's engagement that she could not, upon reflection, imagine him aware of it. He might be jealous of her brother as a rival, but if more had seemed implied, the fault must have been in her misapprehension. She wished, by a gentle remonstrance, to remind Isabella of her situation, and make her aware of this double unkindness; but for remonstrance, either opportunity or comprehension was always against her. If able to suggest a hint, Isabella could never understand it. In this distress, the intended departure of the Tilney family became her chief consolation; their journey into Gloucestershire was to take place within a few days, and Captain Tilney's removal would at least restore peace to every heart but his own. But Captain Tilney had at present no intention of removing; he was not to be of the party to Northanger; he was to continue at Bath. When Catherine knew this, her resolution was directly made. She spoke to Henry Tilney on the subject, regretting his brother's evident partiality for Miss Thorpe, and entreating him to make known her prior engagement.

"My brother does know it," was Henry's answer.

"Does he? Then why does he stay here?"

He made no reply, and was beginning to talk of something else; but she eagerly continued, "Why do not you persuade him to go away? The longer he stays, the worse it will be for him at last. Pray advise him for his own sake, and for every body's sake, to leave Bath directly. Absence will in time make him comfortable again; but he can have no hope here, and it is only staying to be miserable."

Henry smiled and said, "I am sure my brother would not wish to do that."

"Then you will persuade him to go away?"

"Persuasion is not at command; but pardon me, if I cannot even endeavour to persuade him. I have myself told him that Miss Thorpe is engaged. He knows what he is about, and must be his own master."

"No, he does not know what he is about," cried Catherine; "he does not know the pain he is giving my brother. Not that James has ever told me so, but I am sure he is very uncomfortable."

"And are you sure it is my brother's doing?"

"Yes, very sure."

"Is it my brother's attentions to Miss Thorpe, or Miss Thorpe's admission of them, that gives the pain?"

"Is not it the same thing?"

"I think Mr. Morland would acknowledge a difference. No man is offended by another man's admiration of the woman he loves; it is the woman only who can make it a torment."

Catherine blushed for her friend, and said, "Isabella is wrong. But I am sure she cannot mean to torment, for she is very much attached to my brother. She has been in love with him ever since they first met, and while my father's consent was uncertain, she fretted herself almost into a fever. You know she must be attached to him."

"I understand: she is in love with James, and flirts with Frederick."

"Oh! no, not flirts. A woman in love with one man cannot flirt with another."

"It is probable that she will neither love so well, nor flirt so well, as she might do either singly. The gentlemen must each give up a little."

After a short pause, Catherine resumed with, "Then you do not believe Isabella so very much attached to my brother?"

"I can have no opinion on that subject."

"But what can your brother mean? If he knows her engagement, what can he mean by his behaviour?"

"You are a very close questioner."

"Am I? I only ask what I want to be told."

"But do you only ask what I can be expected to tell?"

"Yes, I think so; for you must know your brother's heart."

"My brother's heart, as you term it, on the present occasion, I assure you I can only guess at."

"Well?"

"Well! Nay, if it is to be guess-work, let us all guess for ourselves. To be guided by second-hand conjecture is pitiful. The premises are before you. My brother is a lively and perhaps sometimes a thoughtless young man; he has had about a week's acquaintance with your friend, and he has known her engagement almost as long as he has known her."

"Well," said Catherine, after some moments' consideration, "you may be able to guess at your brother's intentions from all this; but I am sure I cannot. But is not your father uncomfortable about it? Does not he want Captain Tilney to go away? Sure, if your father were to speak to him, he would go."

"My dear Miss Morland," said Henry, "in this amiable solicitude for your brother's comfort, may you not be a little mistaken? Are you not carried a little too far? Would he thank you, either on his own account or Miss Thorpe's, for supposing that her affection, or at least her good behaviour, is only to be secured by her seeing nothing of Captain Tilney? Is he safe only in solitude? Or is her heart constant to him only when unsolicited by any one else? He cannot think this -- and you may be sure that he would not have you think it. I will not say, 'Do not be uneasy,' because I know that you are so, at this moment; but be as little uneasy as you can. You have no doubt of the mutual attachment of your brother and your friend; depend upon it, therefore, that real jealousy never can exist between them; depend upon it that no disagreement between them can be of any duration. Their hearts are open to each other, as neither heart can be to you; they know exactly what is required and what can be borne; and you may be certain that one will never tease the other beyond what is known to be pleasant."

Perceiving her still to look doubtful and grave, he added, "Though Frederick does not leave Bath with us, he will probably remain but a very short time, perhaps only a few days behind us. His leave of absence will soon expire, and he must return to his regiment. And what will then be their acquaintance? The mess-room will drink Isabella Thorpe for a fortnight, and she will laugh with your brother over poor Tilney's passion for a month."

Catherine would contend no longer against comfort. She had resisted its approaches during the whole length of a speech, but it now carried her captive. Henry Tilney must know best. She blamed herself for the extent of her fears, and resolved never to think so seriously on the subject again.

Her resolution was supported by Isabella's behaviour in their parting interview. The Thorpes spent the last evening of Catherine's stay in Pulteney Street, and nothing passed between the lovers to excite her uneasiness, or make her quit them in apprehension. James was in excellent spirits, and Isabella most engagingly placid. Her tenderness for her friend seemed rather the first feeling of her heart; but that at such a moment was allowable; and once she gave her lover a flat contradiction, and once she drew back her hand; but Catherine remembered Henry's instructions, and placed it all to judicious affection. The embraces, tears, and promises of the parting fair ones may be fancied.

CHAPTER 20

Mr. and Mrs. Allen were sorry to lose their young friend, whose good humour and cheerfulness had made her a valuable companion, and in the promotion of whose enjoyment their own had been gently increased. Her happiness in going with Miss Tilney, however, prevented their wishing it otherwise; and, as they were to remain only one more week in Bath themselves, her quitting them now would not long be felt. Mr. Allen attended her to Milsom Street, where she was to breakfast, and saw her seated with the kindest welcome among her new friends; but so great was her agitation in finding herself as one of the family, and so fearful was she of not doing exactly what was right, and of not being able to preserve their good opinion, that, in the embarrassment of the first five minutes, she could almost have wished to return with him to Pulteney Street.

Miss Tilney's manners and Henry's smile soon did away some of her unpleasant feelings; but still she was far from being at ease; nor could the incessant attentions of the General himself entirely reassure her. Nay, perverse as it seemed, she doubted whether she might not have felt less, had she been less attended to. His anxiety for her comfort -- his continual solicitations that she would eat, and his often-expressed fears of her seeing nothing to her taste -- though never in her life before had she beheld half such variety on a breakfast-table -- made it impossible for her to forget for a moment that she was a visitor. She felt utterly unworthy of such respect, and knew not how to reply to it. Her tranquillity was not improved by the General's impatience for the appearance of his eldest son, nor by the displeasure he expressed at his laziness when Captain Tilney at last came down. She was quite pained by the severity of his father's reproof, which seemed disproportionate to the offence; and much was her concern increased when she found herself the principal cause of the lecture, and that his tardiness was chiefly resented from being disrespectful to her. This was placing her in a very uncomfortable situation, and she felt great compassion for Captain Tilney, without being able to hope for his good-will.

He listened to his father in silence, and attempted not any defence, which confirmed her in fearing that the inquietude of his mind, on Isabella's account, might, by keeping him long sleepless, have been the real cause of his rising late. It was the first time of her being decidedly in his company, and she had hoped to be now able to form her opinion of him; but she scarcely heard his voice while his father remained in the room; and even afterwards, so much were his spirits affected, she could distinguish nothing but these words, in a whisper to Eleanor, "How glad I shall be when you are all off."

The bustle of going was not pleasant. The clock struck ten while the trunks were carrying down, and the General had fixed to be out of Milsom Street by that hour. His greatcoat, instead of being brought for him to put on directly, was spread out in the curricle in which he was to accompany his son. The middle seat of the chaise was not drawn out, though there were three people to go in it, and his daughter's maid had so crowded it with parcels that Miss Morland would not have room to sit; and, so much was he influenced by this apprehension when he handed her in, that she had some difficulty in saving her own new writing-desk from being thrown out into the street. At last, however, the door was closed upon the three females, and they set off at the sober pace in which the handsome, highly-fed four horses of a gentleman usually perform a journey of thirty miles: such was the distance of Northanger from Bath, to be now divided into two equal stages. Catherine's spirits revived as they drove from the door; for with Miss Tilney she felt no restraint; and, with the interest of a road entirely new to her, of an abbey before, and a curricle behind, she caught the last view of Bath without any regret, and met with every

113

milestone before she expected it. The tediousness of a two hours' wait at Petty France, in which there was nothing to be done but to eat without being hungry, and loiter about without any thing to see, next followed -- and her admiration of the style in which they travelled, of the fashionable chaise-and-four -- postilions handsomely liveried, rising so regularly in their stirrups, and numerous out-riders properly mounted, sunk a little under this consequent inconvenience. Had their party been perfectly agreeable, the delay would have been nothing; but General Tilney, though so charming a man, seemed always a check upon his children's spirits, and scarcely any thing was said but by himself; the observation of which, with his discontent at whatever the inn afforded, and his angry impatience at the waiters, made Catherine grow every moment more in awe of him, and appeared to lengthen the two hours into four. At last, however, the order of release was given; and much was Catherine then surprised by the General's proposal of her taking his place in his son's curricle for the rest of the journey: "the day was fine, and he was anxious for her seeing as much of the country as possible."

The remembrance of Mr. Allen's opinion, respecting young men's open carriages, made her blush at the mention of such a plan, and her first thought was to decline it; but her second was of greater deference for General Tilney's judgment; he could not propose any thing improper for her; and, in the course of a few minutes, she found herself with Henry in the curricle, as happy a being as ever existed. A very short trial convinced her that a curricle was the prettiest equipage in the world; the chaise-and-four wheeled off with some grandeur, to be sure, but it was a heavy and troublesome business, and she could not easily forget its having stopped two hours at Petty France. Half the time would have been enough for the curricle, and so nimbly were the light horses disposed to move, that, had not the General chosen to have his own carriage lead the way, they could have passed it with ease in half a minute. But the merit of the curricle did not all belong to the horses; Henry drove so well -- so quietly -- without making any disturbance, without parading to her, or swearing at them: so different from the only gentleman-coachman whom it was in her power to compare him with! And then his hat sat so well, and the innumerable capes of his greatcoat looked so becomingly important! To be driven by him, next to being dancing with him, was certainly the greatest happiness in the world. In addition to every other delight, she had now that of listening to her own praise; of being thanked at least, on his sister's account, for her kindness in thus becoming her visitor; of hearing it ranked as real friendship, and described as creating real gratitude. His sister, he said, was uncomfortably circumstanced -- she had no female companion -- and, in the frequent absence of her father, was sometimes without any companion at all.

"But how can that be?" said Catherine. "Are not you with her?"

"Northanger is not more than half my home; I have an establishment at my own house in Woodston, which is nearly twenty miles from my father's, and some of my time is necessarily spent there."

"How sorry you must be for that!"

"I am always sorry to leave Eleanor."

"Yes; but besides your affection for her, you must be so fond of the abbey! After being used to such a home as the abbey, an ordinary parsonage-house must be very disagreeable."

He smiled, and said, "You have formed a very favourable idea of the abbey."

"To be sure I have. Is not it a fine old place, just like what one reads about?"

"And are you prepared to encounter all the horrors that a building such as 'what one reads about' may produce? Have you a stout heart? Nerves fit for sliding panels and tapestry?"

"Oh! Yes -- I do not think I should be easily frightened, because there would be so many people in the house -- and besides, it has never been uninhabited and left deserted for years, and then the family come back to it unawares, without giving any notice, as generally happens."

"No, certainly. We shall not have to explore our way into a hall dimly lighted by the expiring embers of a wood fire -- nor be obliged to spread our beds on the floor of a room without windows, doors, or furniture. But you must be aware that when a young lady is (by whatever means) introduced into a dwelling of this kind, she is always lodged apart from the rest of the family. While they snugly repair to their own end of the house, she is formally conducted by Dorothy, the ancient housekeeper, up a different staircase, and along many gloomy passages, into an apartment never used since some cousin or kin died in it about twenty years before.

Can you stand such a ceremony as this? Will not your mind misgive you when you find yourself in this gloomy chamber -- too lofty and extensive for you, with only the feeble rays of a single lamp to take in its size -- its walls hung with tapestry exhibiting figures as large as life, and the bed, of dark green stuff or purple velvet, presenting even a funereal appearance? Will not your heart sink within you?"

"Oh! But this will not happen to me, I am sure."

"How fearfully will you examine the furniture of your apartment! And what will you discern? Not tables, toilettes, wardrobes, or drawers, but on one side perhaps the remains of a broken lute, on the other a ponderous chest which no efforts can open, and over the fireplace the portrait of some handsome warrior, whose features will so incomprehensibly strike you, that you will not be able to withdraw your eyes from it. Dorothy, meanwhile, no less struck by your appearance, gazes on you in great agitation, and drops a few unintelligible hints. To raise your spirits, moreover, she gives you reason to suppose that the part of the abbey you inhabit is undoubtedly haunted, and informs you that you will not have a single domestic within call. With this parting cordial she curtseys off -- you listen to the sound of her receding footsteps as long as the last echo can reach you -- and when, with fainting spirits, you attempt to fasten your door, you discover, with increased alarm, that it has no lock."

"Oh! Mr. Tilney, how frightful! This is just like a book! But it cannot really happen to me. I am sure your housekeeper is not really Dorothy. Well, what then?"

"Nothing further to alarm perhaps may occur the first night. After surmounting your *unconquerable* horror of the bed, you will retire to rest, and get a few hours' unquiet slumber. But on the second, or at farthest the third night after your arrival, you will probably have a violent storm. Peals of thunder so loud as to seem to shake the edifice to its foundation will roll round the neighbouring mountains -- and during the frightful gusts of wind which accompany it, you will probably think you discern (for your lamp is not extinguished) one part of the hanging more violently agitated than the rest. Unable of course to repress your curiosity in so favourable a moment for indulging it, you will instantly arise, and throwing your dressing-gown around you, proceed to examine this mystery. After a very short search, you will discover a division in the tapestry so artfully constructed as to defy the minutest

116

inspection, and on opening it, a door will immediately appear -- which door, being only secured by massy bars and a padlock, you will, after a few efforts, succeed in opening -- and, with your lamp in your hand, will pass through it into a small vaulted room."

"No, indeed; I should be too much frightened to do any such thing."

"What! Not when Dorothy has given you to understand that there is a secret subterraneous communication between your apartment and the chapel of St. Anthony, scarcely two miles off -- Could you shrink from so simple an adventure? No, no, you will proceed into this small vaulted room, and through this into several others, without perceiving any thing very remarkable in either. In one perhaps there may be a dagger, in another a few drops of blood, and in a third the remains of some instrument of torture; but there being nothing in all this out of the common way, and your lamp being nearly exhausted, you will return towards your own apartment. In repassing through the small vaulted room, however, your eyes will be attracted towards a large, old-fashioned cabinet of ebony and gold, which, though narrowly examining the furniture before, you had passed unnoticed. Impelled by an irresistible presentiment, you will eagerly advance to it, unlock its folding doors, and search into every drawer -- but for some time without discovering any thing of importance -- perhaps nothing but a considerable hoard of diamonds. At last, however, by touching a secret spring, an inner compartment will open -- a roll of paper appears: you seize it -- it contains many sheets of manuscript -- you hasten with the precious treasure into your own chamber, but scarcely have you been able to decipher 'Oh! Thou -- whomsoever thou mayst be, into whose hands these memoirs of the wretched Matilda may fall' -- when your lamp suddenly expires in the socket, and leaves you in total darkness."

"Oh! No, no -- do not say so. Well, go on."

But Henry was too much amused by the interest he had raised to be able to carry it farther; he could no longer command solemnity either of subject or voice, and was obliged to entreat her to use her own fancy in the perusal of Matilda's woes. Catherine, recollecting herself, grew ashamed of her eagerness, and began earnestly to assure him that her attention had been fixed without the smallest apprehension of really meeting with what he related. "Miss Tilney, she was sure, would never put her into such a chamber as he had described! She was not at all afraid."

117

As they drew near the end of their journey, her impatience for a sight of the abbey -- for some time suspended by his conversation on subjects very different -- returned in full force, and every bend in the road was expected with solemn awe to afford a glimpse of its massy walls of grey stone, rising amidst a grove of ancient oaks, with the last beams of the sun playing in beautiful splendour on its high Gothic windows. But so low did the building stand, that she found herself passing through the great gates of the lodge into the very grounds of Northanger, without having discerned even an antique chimney.

She knew not that she had any right to be surprised, but there was a something in this mode of approach which she certainly had not expected. To pass between lodges of a modern appearance, to find herself with such ease in the very precincts of the abbey, and driven so rapidly along a smooth, level road of fine gravel, without obstacle, alarm, or solemnity of any kind, struck her as odd and inconsistent. She was not long at leisure, however, for such considerations. A sudden scud of rain, driving full in her face, made it impossible for her to observe any thing further, and fixed all her thoughts on the welfare of her new straw bonnet; and she was actually under the abbey walls, was springing, with Henry's assistance, from the carriage, was beneath the shelter of the old porch, and had even passed on to the hall, where her friend and the General were waiting to welcome her, without feeling one awful foreboding of future misery to herself, or one moment's suspicion of any past scenes of horror being acted within the solemn edifice. The breeze had not seemed to waft the sighs of the murdered to her; it had wafted nothing worse than a thick mizzling rain; and having given a good shake to her habit, she was ready to be shewn into the common drawing-room, and capable of considering where she was.

An abbey! Yes, it was delightful to be really in an abbey! But she doubted, as she looked round the room, whether any thing within her observation would have given her the consciousness. The furniture was in all the profusion and elegance of modern taste. The fireplace, where she had expected the ample width and ponderous carving of former times, was contracted to a Rumford, with slabs of plain though handsome marble, and ornaments over it of the prettiest English china. The windows, to which she looked with peculiar dependence, from having heard the General talk of his preserving them in their Gothic form with reverential care, were yet less what her fancy had portrayed. To be sure, the pointed arch was preserved -- the form of them was Gothic -- they might be even casements -- but every pane was so large, so clear, so light! To an imagination which had hoped for the smallest divisions, and the heaviest stone-work, for painted glass, dirt and cobwcbs, thc difference was very distressing.

The General, perceiving how her eye was employed, began to talk of the smallness of the room and simplicity of the furniture, where every thing, being for daily use, pretended only to comfort, etc.; flattering himself, however, that there were some apartments in the Abbey not unworthy her notice -- and was proceeding to mention the costly gilding of one in particular, when, taking out his watch, he stopped short to pronounce it with surprise within twenty minutes of five! This seemed the word of separation, and Catherine found herself hurried away by Miss Tilney in such a manner as convinced her that the strictest punctuality to the family hours would be expected at Northanger.

Returning through the large and lofty hall, they ascended a broad staircase of shining oak, which, after many flights and many landing-places, brought them upon a long, wide gallery. On one side it had a range of doors, and it was lighted on the other by windows which Catherine had only time to discover looked into a quadrangle, before Miss Tilney led the way into a chamber, and scarcely staying to hope she would find it comfortable, left her with an anxious entreaty that she would make as little alteration as possible in her dress.

CHAPTER 21

A moment's glance was enough to satisfy Catherine that her apartment was very unlike the one which Henry had endeavoured to alarm her by the description of. It was by no means unreasonably large, and contained neither tapestry nor velvet. The walls were papered, the floor was carpeted; the windows were neither less perfect nor more dim than those of the drawing-room below; the furniture, though not of the latest fashion, was handsome and comfortable, and the air of the room altogether far from uncheerful. Her heart instantaneously at ease on this point, she resolved to lose no time in particular examination of any thing, as she greatly dreaded disobliging the General by any delay. Her habit therefore was thrown off with all possible haste, and she was preparing to unpin the linen package, which the chaise-seat had conveyed for her immediate accommodation, when her eye suddenly fell on a large high chest, standing back in a deep recess on one side of the fireplace. The sight of it made her start; and, forgetting every thing else, she stood gazing on it in motionless wonder, while these thoughts crossed her:-

"This is strange indeed! I did not expect such a sight as this! An immense heavy chest! What can it hold? Why should it be placed here? Pushed back too, as if meant to be out of sight! I will look into it -- cost me what it may, I will look into it -- and directly too -- by daylight. If I stay till evening my candle may go out." She advanced and examined it closely: it was of cedar, curiously inlaid with some darker wood, and raised, about a foot from the ground, on a carved stand of the same. The lock was silver, though tarnished from age; at each end were the imperfect remains of handles also of silver, broken perhaps prematurely by some strange violence; and, on the centre of the lid, was a mysterious cipher, in the same metal. Catherine bent over it intently, but without being able to distinguish any thing with certainty. She could not, in whatever direction she took it, believe the last letter to be a T; and yet that it should be any thing else in that house was a circumstance to raise no common degree of astonishment. If not originally theirs, by what strange events could it have fallen into the Tilney family?

Her fearful curiosity was every moment growing greater; and seizing, with trembling hands, the hasp of the lock, she resolved at all hazards to satisfy herself at least as to its contents. With difficulty, for something seemed to resist her efforts, she raised the lid a few inches; but at that moment a sudden knocking at the door of the room made her, starting, quit her hold, and the lid closed with alarming violence. This ill-timed intruder was Miss Tilney's maid, sent by her mistress to be of use to Miss Morland; and though Catherine immediately dismissed her, it recalled her to the sense of what she ought to be doing, and forced her, in spite of her anxious desire to penetrate this mystery, to proceed in her dressing without further delay. Her progress was not quick, for her thoughts and her eyes were still bent on the object so well calculated to interest and alarm; and though she dared not waste a moment upon a second attempt, she could not remain many paces from the chest. At length, however, having slipped one arm into her gown, her toilette seemed so nearly finished that the impatience of her curiosity might safely be indulged. One moment surely might be spared; and, so desperate should be the exertion of her strength, that, unless secured by supernatural means, the lid in one moment should be thrown back. With this spirit she sprang forward, and her confidence did not deceive her. Her resolute effort threw back the lid, and gave to her astonished eyes the view of a white cotton counterpane, properly folded, reposing at one end of the chest in undisputed possession!

She was gazing on it with the first blush of surprise when Miss Tilney, anxious for her friend's being ready, entered the room, and to the rising shame of having harboured for some minutes an absurd expectation, was then added the shame of being caught in so idle a search. "That is a curious old chest, is not it?" said Miss Tilney, as Catherine hastily closed it and turned away to the glass. "It is impossible to say how many generations it has been here. How it came to be first put in this room I know not, but I have not had it moved, because I thought it might sometimes be of use in holding hats and bonnets. The worst of it is that its weight makes it difficult to open. In that corner, however, it is at least out of the way."

Catherine had no leisure for speech, being at once blushing, tying her gown, and forming wise resolutions with the most violent dispatch. Miss Tilney gently hinted her fear of being late; and in half a minute they ran down stairs together, in an alarm not wholly unfounded, for General Tilney was pacing the drawing-room, his watch in his hand, and having, on the very instant of their entering, pulled the bell with violence, ordered "Dinner to be on table directly!"

Catherine trembled at the emphasis with which he spoke, and sat pale and breathless, in a most humble mood, concerned for his children, and detesting old chests; and the General, recovering his politeness as he looked at her, spent the rest of his time in scolding his daughter for so foolishly hurrying her fair friend, who was absolutely out of breath from haste, when there was not the least occasion for hurry in the world: but Catherine could not at all get over the double distress of having involved her friend in a lecture and been a great simpleton herself, till they were happily seated at the dinner-table, when the General's complacent smiles, and a good appetite of her own, restored her to peace. The dining-parlour was a noble room, suitable in its dimensions to a much larger drawing-room than the one in common use, and fitted up in a style of luxury and expense which was almost lost on the unpractised eye of Catherine, who saw little more than its spaciousness and the number of their attendants. Of the former, she spoke aloud her admiration; and the General, with a very gracious countenance, acknowledged that it was by no means an ill-sized room, and further confessed that, though as careless on such subjects as most people, he did look upon a tolerably large eating-room as one of the necessaries of life; he supposed, however, "that she must have been used to much better-sized apartments at Mr. Allen's?"

"No, indeed," was Catherine's honest assurance; "Mr. Allen's dining-parlour was not more than half as large," and she had never seen so large a room as this in her life. The General's good humour increased. -- Why, as he *had* such rooms, he thought it would be simple not to make use of them; but, upon his honour, he believed there might be more comfort in rooms of only half their size. Mr. Allen's house, he was sure, must be exactly of the true size for rational happiness.

The evening passed without any further disturbance, and, in the occasional absence of General Tilney, with much positive cheerfulness. It was only in his presence that Catherine felt the smallest fatigue from her journey; and even then, even in moments of languor or restraint, a sense of general happiness preponderated, and she could think of her friends in Bath without one wish of being with them.

The night was stormy; the wind had been rising at intervals the whole afternoon; and by the time the party broke up, it blew and rained violently. Catherine, as she crossed the hall, listened to the tempest with sensations of awe; and, when she heard it rage round a corner of the ancient building and close with sudden fury a distant door, felt for the first time that she was really in an abbey. Yes, these were characteristic sounds; they brought to her recollection a countless variety of dreadful situations and horrid scenes, which such buildings had witnessed, and such storms ushered in; and most heartily did she rejoice in the happier circumstances attending her entrance within walls so solemn! *She* had nothing to dread from midnight assassins or drunken gallants. Henry had certainly been only in jest in what he had told her that morning. In a house so furnished, and so guarded, she could have nothing to explore or to suffer, and might go to her bedroom as securely as if it had been her own chamber at Fullerton. Thus wisely fortifying her mind, as she proceeded up stairs, she was enabled, especially on perceiving that Miss Tilney slept only two doors from her, to enter her room with a tolerably stout heart; and her spirits were immediately assisted by the cheerful blaze of a wood fire. "How much better is this," said she, as she walked to the fender -- "how much better to find a fire ready lit, than to have to wait shivering in the cold till all the family are in bed, as so many poor girls have been obliged to do, and then to have a faithful old servant frightening one by coming in with a faggot! How glad I am that Northanger is what it is! If it had been like some other places, I do not know that, in such a night as this, I could have answered for my courage: but now, to be sure, there is nothing to alarm one."

She looked round the room. The window curtains seemed in motion. It could be nothing but the violence of the wind penetrating through the divisions of the shutters; and she stepped boldly forward, carelessly humming a tune, to assure herself of its being so, peeped courageously behind each curtain, saw nothing on either low window seat to scare her, and on placing a hand against the shutter, felt the strongest conviction of the wind's force. A glance at the old chest, as she turned away from this examination, was not without its use; she scorned the causeless fears of an idle fancy, and began with a most happy indifference to prepare herself for bed. "She should take her time; she should not hurry herself; she did not care if she were the last person up in the house. But she would not make up her fire; *that* would seem cowardly, as if she wished for the protection of light after she were in bed." The fire therefore died away, and Catherine, having spent the best part of an hour in her arrangements, was beginning to think of stepping into bed, when, on giving a parting glance round the room, she was struck by the appearance of a high, old-fashioned black cabinet, which, though in a situation conspicuous enough, had never caught her notice before. Henry's words, his description of the ebony cabinet which was to escape her observation at first, immediately rushed across her; and though there could be nothing really in it, there was something whimsical, it was certainly a very remarkable coincidence! She took her candle and looked closely at the cabinet. It was not absolutely ebony and gold; but it was Japan, black and yellow Japan of the handsomest kind; and as she held her candle, the yellow had very much the effect of gold. The key was in the door, and she had a strange fancy to look into it; not, however, with the smallest expectation of finding any thing, but it was so very odd, after what Henry had said. In short, she could not sleep till she had examined it. So, placing the candle with great caution on a chair, she seized the key with a very tremulous hand and tried to turn it; but it resisted her utmost strength. Alarmed, but not discouraged, she tried it another way; a bolt flew, and she believed herself successful; but how strangely mysterious! The door was still immovable. She paused a moment in breathless wonder. The wind roared down the chimney, the rain beat in torrents against the windows, and every thing seemed to speak the awfulness of her situation. To retire to bed, however, unsatisfied on such a point, would be vain, since sleep must be impossible with the consciousness of a cabinet so mysteriously closed in her immediate vicinity. Again, therefore, she applied herself to the key, and after moving it in every possible way for some instants with the determined celerity of hope's last effort, the door suddenly yielded to her hand: her heart leaped with exultation at such a victory, and having thrown open each folding door, the second being secured only by bolts of less wonderful construction than the lock, though that her eye could not discern any thing unusual, a double range of small drawers appeared in view, with some larger drawers above and below them; and in the centre, a small door, closed also with a lock and key, secured in all probability a cavity of importance.

Catherine's heart beat quick, but her courage did not fail her. With a cheek flushed by hope, and an eye straining with curiosity, her fingers grasped the handle of a drawer and drew it forth. It was entirely empty. With less alarm and greater eagerness she seized a second, a third, a fourth; each was equally empty. Not one was left unsearched, and in not one was any thing found. Well read in the art of concealing a treasure, the possibility of false linings to the drawers did not escape her, and she felt round each with anxious acuteness in vain. The place in the middle alone remained now unexplored; and though she had "never from the first had the smallest idea of finding any thing in any part of the cabinet, and was not in the least disappointed at her ill success thus far, it would be foolish not to examine it thoroughly while she was about it." It was some time however before she could unfasten the door, the same difficulty occurring in the management of this inner lock as of the outer; but at length it did open; and not vain, as hitherto, was her search; her quick eyes directly fell on a roll of paper pushed back into the further part of the cavity, apparently for concealment, and her feelings at that moment were indescribable. Her heart fluttered, her knees trembled, and her cheeks grew pale. She seized, with an unsteady hand, the precious manuscript, for half a glance sufficed to ascertain written characters; and while she acknowledged with awful sensations this striking exemplification of what Henry had foretold, resolved instantly to peruse every line before she attempted to rest.

The dimness of the light her candle emitted made her turn to it with alarm; but there was no danger of its sudden extinction; it had yet some hours to burn; and that she might not have any greater difficulty in distinguishing the writing than what its ancient date might occasion, she hastily snuffed it. Alas! It was snuffed and extinguished in one. A lamp could not have expired with more awful effect. Catherine, for a few moments, was motionless with horror. It was done completely; not a remnant of light in the wick could give hope to the rekindling breath. Darkness impenetrable and immovable filled the room. A violent gust of wind, rising with sudden fury, added fresh horror to the moment. Catherine trembled from head to foot. In the pause which succeeded, a sound like receding footsteps and the closing of a distant door struck on her affrighted ear. Human nature could support no more. A cold sweat stood on her forehead, the manuscript fell from her hand, and groping her way to the bed, she jumped hastily in, and sought some suspension of agony by creeping far underneath the clothes. To close her eyes in sleep that night, she felt must be entirely out of the question. With a curiosity so justly awakened, and feelings in every way so agitated, repose must be absolutely impossible. The storm too abroad so dreadful! -- She had not been used to feel alarm from wind, but now every blast seemed fraught with awful intelligence. The manuscript so wonderfully found, so wonderfully accomplishing the morning's prediction, how was it to be accounted for? -- What could it contain? -- To whom could it relate? -- By what means could it have been so long concealed? -- And how singularly strange that it should fall to her lot to discover it! Till she had made herself mistress of its contents, however, she could have neither repose nor comfort; and with the sun's first rays she was determined to peruse it. But many were the tedious hours which must yet intervene. She shuddered, tossed about in her bed, and envied every quiet sleeper. The storm still raged, and various were the noises, more terrific even than the wind, which struck at intervals on her startled ear. The very curtains of her bed seemed at one moment in motion, and at another the lock of her door was agitated, as if by the attempt of somebody to enter. Hollow murmurs seemed to creep along the gallery, and more than once her blood was chilled by the sound of distant moans. Hour after hour passed away, and the wearied Catherine had heard three proclaimed by all the clocks in the house before the tempest subsided or she unknowingly fell fast asleep.

CHAPTER 22

The housemaid's folding back her window-shutters at eight o'clock the next day was the sound which first roused Catherine; and she opened her eyes, wondering that they could ever have been closed, on objects of cheerfulness; her fire was already burning, and a bright morning had succeeded the tempest of the night. Instantaneously, with the consciousness of existence, returned her recollection of the manuscript; and springing from the bed in the very moment of the maid's going away, she eagerly collected every scattered sheet which had burst from the roll on its falling to the ground, and flew back to enjoy the luxury of their perusal on her pillow. She now plainly saw that she must not expect a manuscript of equal length with the generality of what she had shuddered over in books, for the roll, seeming to consist entirely of small disjointed sheets, was altogether but of trifling size, and much less than she had supposed it to be at first.

Her greedy eye glanced rapidly over a page. She started at its import. Could it be possible, or did not her senses play her false? An inventory of linen, in coarse and modern characters, seemed all that was before her! If the evidence of sight might be trusted, she held a washing-bill in her hand. She seized another sheet, and saw the same articles with little variation; a third, a fourth, and a fifth presented nothing new. Shirts, stockings, cravats, and waistcoats faced her in each. Two others, penned by the same hand, marked an expenditure scarcely more interesting, in letters, hair-powder, shoe-string, and breeches-ball. And the larger sheet, which had enclosed the rest, seemed by its first cramp line, "To poultice chestnut mare"--a farrier's bill! Such was the collection of papers (left perhaps, as she could then suppose, by the negligence of a servant in the place whence she had taken them) which had filled her with expectation and alarm, and robbed her of half her night's rest! She felt humbled to the dust. Could not the adventure of the chest have taught her wisdom? A corner of it, catching her eye as she lay, seemed to rise up in judgment against her. Nothing could now be clearer than the absurdity of her recent fancies. To suppose that a manuscript of many generations back could have remained undiscovered in a room such as that, so modern, so habitable! -- Or that she should be the first to possess the skill of unlocking a cabinet, the key of which was open to all!

How could she have so imposed on herself? -- Heaven forbid that Henry Tilney should ever know her folly! And it was in a great measure his own doing, for had not the cabinet appeared so exactly to agree with his description of her adventures, she should never have felt the smallest curiosity about it. This was the only comfort that occurred. Impatient to get rid of those hateful evidences of her folly, those detestable papers then scattered over the bed, she rose directly, and folding them up as nearly as possible in the same shape as before, returned them to the same spot within the cabinet, with a very hearty wish that no untoward accident might ever bring them forward again, to disgrace her even with herself.

Why the locks should have been so difficult to open, however, was still something remarkable, for she could now manage them with perfect ease. In this there was surely something mysterious, and she indulged in the flattering suggestion for half a minute, till the possibility of the door's having been at first unlocked, and of being herself its fastener, darted into her head, and cost her another blush.

She got away as soon as she could from a room in which her conduct produced such unpleasant reflections, and found her way with all speed to the breakfast-parlour, as it had been pointed out to her by Miss Tilney the evening before. Henry was alone in it; and his immediate hope of her having been undisturbed by the tempest, with an arch reference to the character of the building they inhabited, was rather distressing. For the world would she not have her weakness suspected, and yet, unequal to an absolute falsehood, was constrained to acknowledge that the wind had kept her awake a little. "But we have a charming morning after it," she added, desiring to get rid of the subject; "and storms and sleeplessness are nothing when they are over. What beautiful hyacinths! I have just learnt to love a hyacinth."

"And how might you learn? By accident or argument?"

"Your sister taught me; I cannot tell how. Mrs. Allen used to take pains, year after year, to make me like them; but I never could, till I saw them the other day in Milsom Street; I am naturally indifferent about flowers."

"But now you love a hyacinth. So much the better. You have gained a new source of enjoyment, and it is well to have as many holds upon happiness as possible. Besides, a taste for flowers is always desirable in your sex, as a means of getting you out of doors, and tempting you to more frequent exercise than you would otherwise take. And though the love of a hyacinth may be rather domestic, who can tell, the sentiment once raised, but you may in time come to love a rose?"

"But I do not want any such pursuit to get me out of doors. The pleasure of walking and breathing fresh air is enough for me, and in fine weather I am out more than half my time. Mamma says I am never within."

"At any rate, however, I am pleased that you have learnt to love a hyacinth. The mere habit of learning to love is the thing; and a teachableness of disposition in a young lady is a great blessing. Has my sister a pleasant mode of instruction?"

Catherine was saved the embarrassment of attempting an answer by the entrance of the General, whose smiling compliments announced a happy state of mind, but whose gentle hint of sympathetic early rising did not advance her composure.

The elegance of the breakfast set forced itself on Catherine's notice when they were seated at table; and, lucidly, it had been the General's choice. He was enchanted by her approbation of his taste, confessed it to be neat and simple, thought it right to encourage the manufacture of his country; and for his part, to his uncritical palate, the tea was as well flavoured from the clay of Staffordshire, as from that of Dresden or Seve. But this was quite an old set, purchased two years ago. The manufacture was much improved since that time; he had seen some beautiful specimens when last in town, and had he not been perfectly without vanity of that kind, might have been tempted to order a new set. He trusted, however, that an opportunity might ere long occur of selecting one -- though not for himself. Catherine was probably the only one of the party who did not understand him.

Shortly after breakfast Henry left them for Woodston, where business required and would keep him two or three days. They all attended in the hall to see him mount his horse, and immediately on re-entering the breakfast-room, Catherine walked to a window in the hope of catching another glimpse of his figure. "This is a somewhat heavy call upon your brother's fortitude," observed the General to Eleanor. "Woodston will make but a sombre appearance to-day."

"Is it a pretty place?" asked Catherine.

"What say you, Eleanor? Speak your opinion, for ladies can best tell the taste of ladies in regard to places as well as men. I think it would be acknowledged by the most impartial eye to have many recommendations. The house stands among fine meadows facing the south-east, with an excellent kitchen-garden in the same aspect; the walls surrounding which I built and stocked myself about ten years ago, for the benefit of my son. It is a family living, Miss Morland; and the property in the place being chiefly my own, you may believe I take care that it shall not be a bad one. Did Henry's income depend solely on this living, he would not be ill-provided for. Perhaps it may seem odd, that with only two younger children, I should think any profession necessary for him; and certainly there are moments when we could all wish him disengaged from every tie of business. But though I may not exactly make converts of you young ladies, I am sure your father, Miss Morland, would agree with me in thinking it expedient to give every young man some employment. The money is nothing, it is not an object, but employment is the thing. Even Frederick, my eldest son, you see, who will perhaps inherit as considerable a landed property as any private man in the county, has his profession."

The imposing effect of this last argument was equal to his wishes. The silence of the lady proved it to be unanswerable.

Something had been said the evening before of her being shewn over the house, and he now offered himself as her conductor; and though Catherine had hoped to explore it accompanied only by his daughter, it was a proposal of too much happiness in itself, under any circumstances, not to be gladly accepted; for she had been already eighteen hours in the Abbey, and had seen only a few of its rooms. The netting-box, just leisurely drawn forth, was closed with joyful haste, and she was ready to attend him in a moment. "And when they had gone over the house, he promised himself moreover the pleasure of accompanying her into the shrubberies and garden." She curtsied her acquiescence. "But perhaps it might be more agreeable to her to make those her first object. The weather was at present favourable, and at this time of year the uncertainty was very great of its continuing so. -- Which would she prefer? He was equally at her service. -- Which did his daughter think would most accord with her fair friend's wishes? -- But he thought he could discern. -- Yes, he certainly read in Miss Morland's eyes a judicious desire of making use of the present smiling weather. -- But when did she judge amiss? -- The Abbey would be always safe and dry. -- He yielded implicitly, and would fetch his hat and attend them in a moment." He left the room, and Catherine, with a disappointed, anxious face, began to speak of her unwillingness that he should be taking them out of doors against his own inclination, under a mistaken idea of pleasing her; but she was stopped by Miss Tilney's saying, with a little confusion, "I believe it will be wisest to take the morning while it is so fine; and do not be uneasy on my father's account; he always walks out at this time of day."

Catherine did not exactly know how this was to be understood. Why was Miss Tilney embarrassed? Could there be any unwillingness on the General's side to shew her over the Abbey? The proposal was his own. And was not it odd that he should always take his walk so early? Neither her father nor Mr. Allen did so. It was certainly very provoking. She was all impatience to see the house, and had scarcely any curiosity about the grounds. If Henry had been with them indeed! -- But now she should not know what was picturesque when she saw it. Such were her thoughts, but she kept them to herself, and put on her bonnet in patient discontent.

She was struck, however, beyond her expectation, by the grandeur of the Abbey, as she saw it for the first time from the lawn. The whole building enclosed a large court; and two sides of the quadrangle, rich in Gothic ornaments, stood forward for admiration. The remainder was shut off by knolls of old trees, or luxuriant plantations, and the steep woody hills rising behind to give it shelter were beautiful even in the leafless month of March. Catherine had seen nothing to compare with it; and her feelings of delight were so strong, that without waiting for any better authority, she boldly burst forth in wonder and praise. The General listened with assenting gratitude; and it seemed as if his own estimation of Northanger had waited unfixed till that hour.

The kitchen-garden was to be next admired, and he led the way to it across a small portion of the park.

The number of acres contained in this garden was such as Catherine could not listen to without dismay, being more than double the extent of all Mr. Allen's, as well her father's, including church-yard and orchard. The walls seemed countless in number, endless in length; a village of hot-houses seemed to arise among them, and a whole parish to be at work within the enclosure. The General was flattered by her looks of surprise, which told him almost as plainly, as he soon forced her to tell him in words, that she had never seen any gardens at all equal to them before; and he then modestly owned that, "without any ambition of that sort himself -- without any solicitude about it -- he did believe them to be unrivalled in the kingdom. If he had a hobby-horse, it was *that*. He loved a garden. Though careless enough in most matters of eating, he loved good fruit -- or if he did not, his friends and children did. There were great vexations, however, attending such a garden as his. The utmost care could not always secure the most valuable fruits. The pinery had yielded only one hundred in the last year. Mr. Allen, he supposed, must feel these inconveniences as well as himself."

"No, not at all. Mr. Allen did not care about the garden, and never went into it."

With a triumphant smile of self-satisfaction, the General wished he could do the same, for he never entered his, without being vexed in some way or other, by its falling short of his plan.

"How were Mr. Allen's succession-houses worked?" describing the nature of his own as they entered them.

"Mr. Allen had only one small hot-house, which Mrs. Allen had the use of for her plants in winter, and there was a fire in it now and then."

"He is a happy man!" said the General, with a look of very happy contempt.

Having taken her into every division, and led her under every wall, till she was heartily weary of seeing and wondering, he suffered the girls at last to seize the advantage of an outer door, and then expressing his wish to examine the effect of some recent alterations about the tea-house, proposed it as no unpleasant extension of their walk, if Miss Morland were not tired. "But where are you going, Eleanor? -- Why do you chuse that cold, damp path to it? Miss Morland will get wet. Our best way is across the park."

"This is so favourite a walk of mine," said Miss Tilney, "that I always think it the best and nearest way. But perhaps it may be damp."

It was a narrow winding path through a thick grove of old Scotch firs; and Catherine, struck by its gloomy aspect, and eager to enter it, could not, even by the General's disapprobation, be kept from stepping forward. He perceived her inclination, and having again urged the plea of health in vain, was too polite to make further opposition. He excused himself, however, from attending them: -- "The rays of the sun were not too cheerful for him, and he would meet them by another course." He turned away; and Catherine was shocked to find how much her spirits were relieved by the separation. The shock, however, being less real than the relief, offered it no injury; and she began to talk with easy gaiety of the delightful melancholy which such a grove inspired.

"I am particularly fond of this spot," said her companion, with a sigh. "It was my mother's favourite walk."

Catherine had never heard Mrs. Tilney mentioned in the family before, and the interest excited by this tender remembrance shewed itself directly in her altered countenance, and in the attentive pause with which she waited for something more.

"I used to walk here so often with her!" added Eleanor; "though I never loved it then, as I have loved it since. At that time indeed I used to wonder at her choice. But her memory endears it now."

"And ought it not," reflected Catherine, "to endear it to her husband? Yet the General would not enter it." Miss Tilney continuing silent, she ventured to say, "Her death must have been a great affliction!"

"A great and increasing one," replied the other, in a low voice. "I was only thirteen when it happened; and though I felt my loss perhaps as strongly as one so young could feel it, I did not, I could not then know what a loss it was." She stopped for a moment, and then added, with great firmness, "I have no sister, you know -- and though Henry -- though my brothers are very affectionate, and Henry is a great deal here, which I am most thankful for, it is impossible for me not to be often solitary."

"To be sure you must miss him very much."

"A mother would have been always present. A mother would have been a constant friend; her influence would have been beyond all other."

"Was she a very charming woman? Was she handsome? Was there any picture of her in the Abbey? And why had she been so partial to that grove? Was it from dejection of spirits?" -- were questions now eagerly poured forth; the first three received a ready affirmative, the two others were passed by; and Catherine's interest in the deceased Mrs. Tilney augmented with every question, whether answered or not. Of her unhappiness in marriage, she felt persuaded. The General certainly had been an unkind husband. He did not love her walk: could he therefore have loved her? And besides, handsome as he was, there was a something in the turn of his features which spoke his not having behaved well to her.

"Her picture, I suppose," blushing at the consummate art of her own question, "hangs in your father's room?"

"No; it was intended for the drawing-room; but my father was dissatisfied with the painting, and for some time it had no place. Soon after her death I obtained it for my own, and hung it in my bed-chamber -- where I shall be happy to shew it you; -- it is very like." Here was another proof. A portrait -- very like -- of a departed wife, not valued by the husband! He must have been dreadfully cruel to her!

Catherine attempted no longer to hide from herself the nature of the feelings which, in spite of all his attentions, he had previously excited; and what had been terror and dislike before, was now absolute aversion. Yes, aversion! His cruelty to such a charming woman made him odious to her. She had often read of such characters, characters which Mr. Allen had been used to call unnatural and overdrawn; but here was proof positive of the contrary.

She had just settled this point when the end of the path brought them directly upon the General; and in spite of all her virtuous indignation, she found herself again obliged to walk with him, listen to him, and even to smile when he smiled. Being no longer able, however, to receive pleasure from the surrounding objects, she soon began to walk with lassitude; the General perceived it, and with a concern for her health, which seemed to reproach her for her opinion of him, was most urgent for returning with his daughter to the house. He would follow them in a quarter of an hour. Again they parted -- but Eleanor was called back in half a minute to receive a strict charge against taking her friend round the Abbey till his return. This second instance of his anxiety to delay what she so much wished for struck Catherine as very remarkable.

CHAPTER 23

An hour passed away before the General came in, spent, on the part of his young guest, in no very favourable consideration of his character. "This lengthened absence, these solitary rambles, did not speak a mind at ease, or a conscience void of reproach." At length he appeared; and, whatever might have been the gloom of his meditations, he could still smile with *them*. Miss Tilney, understanding in part her friend's curiosity to see the house, soon revived the subject; and her father being, contrary to Catherine's expectations, unprovided with any pretence for further delay, beyond that of stopping five minutes to order refreshments to be in the room by their return, was at last ready to escort them.

They set forward; and, with a grandeur of air, a dignified step, which caught the eye, but could not shake the doubts of the well-read Catherine, he led the way across the hall, through the common drawing-room and one useless antechamber, into a room magnificent both in size and furniture -- the real drawing-room, used only with company of consequence. It was very noble -- very grand -- very charming!-- was all that Catherine had to say, for her indiscriminating eye scarcely discerned the colour of the satin; and all minuteness of praise, all praise that had much meaning, was supplied by the General: the costliness or elegance of any room's fitting-up could be nothing to her; she cared for no furniture of a more modern date than the fifteenth century. When the General had satisfied his own curiosity, in a close examination of every well-known ornament, they proceeded into the library, an apartment, in its way, of equal magnificence, exhibiting a collection of books, on which an humble man might have looked with pride. Catherine heard, admired, and wondered with more genuine feeling than before -- gathered all that she could from this storehouse of knowledge, by running over the titles of half a shelf, and was ready to proceed. But suites of apartments did not spring up with her wishes. Large as was the building, she had already visited the greatest part; though, on being told that, with the addition of the kitchen, the six or seven rooms she had now seen surrounded three sides of the court, she could scarcely believe it, or overcome the suspicion of there being many chambers secreted. It was some relief, however, that they were to return to the rooms in common use, by passing through a few of less importance, looking into the court, which, with occasional passages, not wholly unintricate, connected the different sides; and she was further soothed in her progress by being told that she was treading what had once been a cloister, having traces of cells pointed out, and observing several doors that were neither opened nor explained to her -- by finding herself successively in a billiard-room, and in the General's private apartment, without comprehending their connexion, or being able to turn aright when she left them; and lastly, by passing through a dark little room, owning Henry's authority, and strewed with his litter of books, guns, and greatcoats.

From the dining-room, of which, though already seen, and always to be seen at five o'clock, the General could not forgo the pleasure of pacing out the length, for the more certain information of Miss Morland, as to what she neither doubted nor cared for, they proceeded by quick communication to the kitchen -- the ancient kitchen of the convent, rich in the massy walls and smoke of former days, and in the stoves and hot closets of the present. The General's improving hand had not loitered here: every modern invention to facilitate the labour of the cooks had been adopted within this, their spacious theatre; and, when the genius of others had failed, his own had often produced the perfection wanted. His endowments of this spot alone might at any time have placed him high among the benefactors of the convent.

With the walls of the kitchen ended all the antiquity of the Abbey; the fourth side of the quadrangle having, on account of its decaying state, been removed by the General's father, and the present erected in its place. All that was venerable ceased here. The new building was not only new, but declared itself to be so; intended only for offices, and enclosed behind by stable-yards, no uniformity of architecture had been thought necessary. Catherine could have raved at the hand which had swept away what must have been beyond the value of all the rest, for the purposes of mere domestic economy; and would willingly have been spared the mortification of a walk through scenes so fallen, had the General allowed it; but if he had a vanity, it was in the arrangement of his offices; and as he was convinced that, to a mind like Miss Morland's, a view of the accommodations and comforts, by which the labours of her inferiors were softened, must always be gratifying, he should make no apology for leading her on. They took a slight survey of all; and Catherine was impressed, beyond her expectation, by their multiplicity and their convenience. The purposes for which a few shapeless pantries and a comfortless scullery were deemed sufficient at Fullerton, were here carried on in appropriate divisions, commodious and roomy. The number of servants continually appearing did not strike her less than the number of their offices. Wherever they went, some pattened girl stopped to curtsy, or some footman in dishabille sneaked off. Yet this was an abbey! How inexpressibly different in these domestic arrangements from such as she had read about -- from abbeys and castles, in which, though certainly larger than Northanger, all the dirty work of the house was to be done by two pair of female hands at the utmost. How they could get through it all had often amazed Mrs. Allen; and, when Catherine saw what was necessary here, she began to be amazed herself.

They returned to the hall, that the chief staircase might be ascended, and the beauty of its wood, and ornaments of rich carving might be pointed out: having gained the top, they turned in an opposite direction from the gallery in which her room lay, and shortly entered one on the same plan, but superior in length and breadth. She was here shewn successively into three large bed-chambers, with their dressing-rooms, most completely and handsomely fitted up; every thing that money and taste could do, to give comfort and elegance to apartments, had been bestowed on these; and, being furnished within the last five years, they were perfect in all that would be generally pleasing, and wanting in all that could give pleasure to Catherine. As they were surveying the last, the General, after slightly naming a few of the distinguished characters by whom they had at times been honoured, turned with a smiling countenance to Catherine, and ventured to hope that henceforward some of their earliest tenants might be "our friends from Fullerton." She felt the unexpected compliment, and deeply regretted the impossibility of thinking well of a man so kindly disposed towards herself, and so full of civility to all her family.

The gallery was terminated by folding doors, which Miss Tilney, advancing, had thrown open, and passed through, and seemed on the point of doing the same by the first door to the left, in another long reach of gallery, when the General, coming forwards, called her hastily, and, as Catherine thought, rather angrily back, demanding whither she were going? -- And what was there more to be seen?-- Had not Miss Morland already seen all that could be worth her notice? -- And did she not suppose her friend might be glad of some refreshment after so much exercise? Miss Tilney drew back directly, and the heavy doors were closed upon the mortified Catherine, who, having seen, in a momentary glance beyond them, a narrower passage, more numerous openings, and symptoms of a winding staircase, believed herself at last within the reach of something worth her notice; and felt, as she unwillingly paced back the gallery, that she would rather be allowed to examine that end of the house than see all the finery of all the rest. The General's evident desire of preventing such an examination was an additional stimulant. Something was certainly to be concealed; her fancy, though it had trespassed lately once or twice, could not mislead her here; and what that something was, a short sentence of Miss Tilney's, as they followed the General at some distance down stairs, seemed to point out: "I was going to take you into what was my mother's room -- the room in which she died--" were all her words; but few as they were, they conveyed pages of intelligence to Catherine. It was no wonder that the General should shrink from the sight of such objects as that room must contain; a room in all probability never entered by him since the dreadful scene had passed, which released his suffering wife, and left him to the stings of conscience.

She ventured, when next alone with Eleanor, to express her wish of being permitted to see it, as well as all the rest of that side of the house; and Eleanor promised to attend her there, whenever they should have a convenient hour. Catherine understood her: -- the General must be watched from home, before that room could be entered. "It remains as it was, I suppose?" said she, in a tone of feeling.

"Yes, entirely."

"And how long ago may it be that your mother died?"

"She has been dead these nine years." And nine years, Catherine knew, was a trifle of time, compared with what generally elapsed after the death of an injured wife, before her room was put to rights.

"You were with her, I suppose, to the last?"

"No," said Miss Tilney, sighing; "I was unfortunately from home. Her illness was sudden and short; and, before I arrived it was all over."

Catherine's blood ran cold with the horrid suggestions which naturally sprang from these words. Could it be possible? Could Henry's father--? And yet how many were the examples to justify even the blackest suspicions! And, when she saw him in the evening, while she worked with her friend, slowly pacing the drawing-room for an hour together in silent thoughtfulness, with downcast eyes and contracted brow, she felt secure from all possibility of wronging him. It was the air and attitude of a Montoni! What could more plainly speak the gloomy workings of a mind not wholly dead to every sense of humanity, in its fearful review of past scenes of guilt? Unhappy man! And the anxiousness of her spirits directed her eyes towards his figure so repeatedly, as to catch Miss Tilney's notice. "My father," she whispered, "often walks about the room in this way; it is nothing unusual."

"So much the worse!" thought Catherine; such ill-timed exercise was of a piece with the strange unseasonableness of his morning walks, and boded nothing good.

After an evening, the little variety and seeming length of which made her peculiarly sensible of Henry's importance among them, she was heartily glad to be dismissed; though it was a look from the General not designed for her observation which sent his daughter to the bell. When the butler would have lit his master's candle, however, he was forbidden. The latter was not going to retire. "I have many pamphlets to finish," said he to Catherine, "before I can close my eyes, and perhaps may be poring over the affairs of the nation for hours after you are asleep. Can either of us be more meetly employed? My eyes will be blinding for the good of others, and yours preparing by rest for future mischief."

But neither the business alleged, nor the magnificent compliment, could win Catherine from thinking that some very different object must occasion so serious a delay of proper repose. To be kept up for hours, after the family were in bed, by stupid pamphlets was not very likely. There must be some deeper cause: something was to be done which could be done only while the household slept; and the probability that Mrs. Tilney yet lived, shut up for causes unknown, and receiving from the pitiless hands of her husband a nightly supply of coarse food, was the conclusion which necessarily followed. Shocking as was the idea, it was at least better than a death unfairly hastened, as, in the natural course of things, she must ere long be released. The suddenness of her reputed illness, the absence of her daughter, and probably of her other children, at the time -- all favoured the supposition of her imprisonment. Its origin -- jealousy perhaps, or wanton cruelty -- was yet to be unravelled.

In revolving these matters, while she undressed, it suddenly struck her as not unlikely that she might that morning have passed near the very spot of this unfortunate woman's confinement -- might have been within a few paces of the cell in which she languished out her days; for what part of the Abbey could be more fitted for the purpose than that which yet bore the traces of monastic division? In the high-arched passage, paved with stone, which already she had trodden with peculiar awe, she well remembered the doors of which the General had given no account. To what might not those doors lead? In support of the plausibility of this conjecture, it further occurred to her that the forbidden gallery, in which lay the apartments of the unfortunate Mrs. Tilney, must be, as certainly as her memory could guide her, exactly over this suspected range of cells, and the staircase by the side of those apartments of which she had caught a transient glimpse, communicating by some secret means with those cells, might well have favoured the barbarous proceedings of her husband. Down that staircase she had perhaps been conveyed in a state of well-prepared insensibility!

Catherine sometimes started at the boldness of her own surmises, and sometimes hoped or feared that she had gone too far; but they were supported by such appearances as made their dismissal impossible.

The side of the quadrangle, in which she supposed the guilty scene to be acting, being, according to her belief, just opposite her own, it struck her that, if judiciously watched, some rays of light from the General's lamp might glimmer through the lower windows, as he passed to the prison of his wife; and, twice before she stepped into bed, she stole gently from her room to the corresponding window in the gallery, to see if it appeared; but all abroad was dark, and it must yet be too early. The various ascending noises convinced her that the servants must still be up. Till midnight, she supposed it would be in vain to watch; but then, when the clock had struck twelve, and all was quiet, she would, if not quite appalled by darkness, steal out and look once more. The clock struck twelve -- and Catherine had been half an hour asleep.

CHAPTER 24

The next day afforded no opportunity for the proposed examination of the mysterious apartments. It was Sunday, and the whole time between morning and afternoon service was required by the General in exercise abroad or eating cold meat at home; and great as was Catherine's curiosity, her courage was not equal to a wish of exploring them after dinner, either by the fading light of the sky between six and seven o'clock, or by the yet more partial though stronger illumination of a treacherous lamp. The day was unmarked therefore by any thing to interest her imagination beyond the sight of a very elegant monument to the memory of Mrs. Tilney, which immediately fronted the family pew. By that her eye was instantly caught and long retained; and the perusal of the highly strained epitaph, in which every virtue was ascribed to her by the inconsolable husband, who must have been in some way or other her destroyer, affected her even to tears.

That the General, having erected such a monument, should be able to face it, was not perhaps very strange, and yet that he could sit so boldly collected within its view, maintain so elevated an air, look so fearlessly around, nay, that he should even enter the church, seemed wonderful to Catherine. Not, however, that many instances of beings equally hardened in guilt might not be produced. She could remember dozens who had persevered in every possible vice, going on from crime to crime, murdering whomsoever they chose, without any feeling of humanity or remorse; till a violent death or a religious retirement closed their black career. The erection of the monument itself could not in the smallest degree affect her doubts of Mrs. Tilney's actual decease. Were she even to descend into the family vault where her ashes were supposed to slumber, were she to behold the coffin in which they were said to be enclosed -- what could it avail in such a case? Catherine had read too much not to be perfectly aware of the ease with which a waxen figure might be introduced, and a supposititious funeral carried on.

The succeeding morning promised something better. The General's early walk, ill-timed as it was in every other view, was favourable here; and when she knew him to be out of the house, she directly proposed to Miss Tilney the accomplishment of her promise. Eleanor was ready to oblige her; and Catherine reminding her as they went of another promise, their first visit in consequence was to the portrait in her bed-chamber. It represented a very lovely woman, with a mild and pensive countenance, justifying, so far, the expectations of its new observer; but they were not in every respect answered, for Catherine had depended upon meeting with features, hair, complexion, that should be the very counterpart, the very image, if not of Henry's, of Eleanor's -- the only portraits of which she had been in the habit of thinking, bearing always an equal resemblance of mother and child. A face once taken was taken for generations. But here she was obliged to look and consider and study for a likeness. She contemplated it, however, in spite of this drawback, with much emotion, and, but for a yet stronger interest, would have left it unwillingly.

Her agitation as they entered the great gallery was too much for any endeavour at discourse; she could only look at her companion. Eleanor's countenance was dejected, yet sedate; and its composure spoke her inured to all the gloomy objects to which they were advancing. Again she passed through the folding doors, again her hand was upon the important lock, and Catherine, hardly able to breathe, was turning to close the former with fearful caution, when the figure, the dreaded figure of the General himself at the further end of the gallery, stood before her! The name of "Eleanor" at the same moment, in his loudest tone, resounded through the building, giving to his daughter the first intimation of his presence, and to Catherine terror upon terror. An attempt at concealment had been her first instinctive movement on perceiving him, yet she could scarcely hope to have escaped his eye; and when her friend, who with an apologizing look darted hastily by her, had joined and disappeared with him, she ran for safety to her own room, and, locking herself in, believed that she should never have courage to go down again. She remained there at least an hour, in the greatest agitation, deeply commiserating the state of her poor friend, and expecting a summons herself from the angry General to attend him in his own apartment. No summons, however, arrived; and at last, on seeing a carriage drive up to the Abbey, she was emboldened to descend and meet him under the protection of visitors. The breakfast-room was gay with company; and she was named to them by the General as the friend of his daughter, in a complimentary style, which so well concealed his resentful ire, as to make her feel secure at least of life for the present. And Eleanor, with a command of countenance which did honour to her concern for his character, taking an early occasion of saying to her, "My father only wanted me to answer a note," she began to hope that she had either been unseen by the General, or that from some consideration of policy she should be allowed to suppose herself so. Upon this trust she dared still to remain in his presence, after the company left them, and nothing occurred to disturb it.

In the course of this morning's reflections, she came to a resolution of making her next attempt on the forbidden door alone. It would be much better in every respect that Eleanor should know nothing of the matter. To involve her in the danger of a second detection, to court her into an apartment which must wring her heart, could not be the office of a friend. The General's utmost anger could not be to herself what it might be to a daughter; and, besides, she thought the examination itself would be more satisfactory if made without any companion. It would be impossible to explain to Eleanor the suspicions, from which the other had, in all likelihood, been hitherto happily exempt; nor could she therefore, in her presence, search for those proofs of the General's cruelty, which however they might yet have escaped discovery, she felt confident of somewhere drawing forth, in the shape of some fragmented journal, continued to the last gasp. Of the way to the apartment she was now perfectly mistress; and as she wished to get it over before Henry's return, who was expected on the morrow, there was no time to be lost. The day was bright, her courage high; at four o'clock, the sun was now two hours above the horizon, and it would be only her retiring to dress half an hour earlier than usual.

It was done; and Catherine found herself alone in the gallery before the clocks had ceased to strike. It was no time for thought; she hurried on, slipped with the least possible noise through the folding doors, and without stopping to look or breathe, rushed forward to the one in question. The lock yielded to her hand, and, luckily, with no sullen sound that could alarm a human being. On tiptoe she entered; the room was before her; but it was some minutes before she could advance another step. She beheld what fixed her to the spot and agitated every feature. She saw a large, well-proportioned apartment, an handsome dimity bed, arranged as unoccupied with an housemaid's care, a bright Bath stove, mahogany wardrobes and neatly painted chairs, on which the warm beams of a western sun gaily poured through two sash windows! Catherine had expected to have her feelings worked, and worked they were. Astonishment and doubt first seized them; and a shortly succeeding ray of common sense added some bitter emotions of shame. She could not be mistaken as to the room; but how grossly mistaken in everything else! -- in Miss Tilney's meaning, in her own calculation! This apartment, to which she had given a date so ancient, a position so awful, proved to be one end of what the General's father had built. There were two other doors in the chamber, leading probably into dressing-closets; but she had no inclination to open either. Would the veil in which Mrs. Tilney had last walked, or the volume in which she had last read, remain to tell what nothing else was allowed to whisper? No: whatever might have been the General's crimes, he had certainly too much wit to let them sue for detection. She was sick of exploring, and desired but to be safe in her own room, with her own heart only privy to its folly; and she was on the point of retreating as softly as she had entered, when the sound of footsteps, she could hardly tell where, made her pause and tremble. To be found there, even by a servant, would be unpleasant; but by the General (and he seemed always at hand when least wanted), much worse! She listened--the sound had ceased; and resolving not to lose a moment, she passed through and closed the door. At that instant a door underneath was hastily opened; someone seemed with swift steps to ascend the stairs, by the head of which she had yet to pass before she could gain the gallery. She had no power to move. With a feeling of terror not very definable, she fixed her eyes on the staircase, and in a few moments it gave Henry to her view. "Mr. Tilney!" she exclaimed in a voice of more than common astonishment. He looked astonished too. "Good God!" she continued, not attending to his address. "How came you here? How came you up that staircase?"

"How came I up that staircase!" he replied, greatly surprised. "Because it is my nearest way from the stable-yard to my own chamber; and why should I not come up it?"

Catherine recollected herself, blushed deeply, and could say no more. He seemed to be looking in her countenance for that explanation which her lips did not afford. She moved on towards the gallery. "And may I not, in my turn," said he, as he pushed back the folding doors, "ask how *you* came here? This passage is at least as extraordinary a road from the breakfast-parlour to your apartment, as that staircase can be from the stables to mine."

"I have been," said Catherine, looking down, "to see your mother's room."

"My mother's room! Is there any thing extraordinary to be seen there?"

"No, nothing at all. I thought you did not mean to come back till to-morrow."

"I did not expect to be able to return sooner, when I went away; but three hours ago I had the pleasure of finding nothing to detain me. You look pale. I am afraid I alarmed you by running so fast up those stairs. Perhaps you did not know -- you were not aware of their leading from the offices in common use?"

"No, I was not. -- You have had a very fine day for your ride."

"Very; and does Eleanor leave you to find your way into all the rooms in the house by yourself?"

"Oh! No; she shewed me over the greatest part on Saturday -- and we were coming here to these rooms -- but only" -- dropping her voice -- "your father was with us."

"And that prevented you," said Henry, earnestly regarding her. "Have you looked into all the rooms in that passage?"

"No, I only wanted to see -- Is not it very late? I must go and dress."

"It is only a quarter past four, (shewing his watch) and you are not now in Bath. No theatre, no rooms to prepare for. Half an hour at Northanger must be enough."

She could not contradict it, and therefore suffered herself to be detained, though her dread of further questions made her, for the first time in their acquaintance, wish to leave him. They walked slowly up the gallery. "Have you had any letter from Bath since I saw you?"

"No, and I am very much surprised. Isabella promised so faithfully to write directly."

"Promised so faithfully! A faithful promise! That puzzles me. I have heard of a faithful performance. But a faithful promise -- the fidelity of promising! It is a power little worth knowing, however, since it can deceive and pain you. My mother's room is very commodious, is it not? Large and cheerful-looking, and the dressing-closets so well disposed! It always strikes me as the most comfortable apartment in the house, and I rather wonder that Eleanor should not take it for her own. She sent you to look at it, I suppose?"

"No."

"It has been your own doing entirely?" Catherine said nothing. After a short silence, during which he had closely observed her, he added, "As there is nothing in the room in itself to raise curiosity, this must have proceeded from a sentiment of respect for my mother's character, as described by Eleanor, which does honour to her memory. The world, I believe, never saw a better woman. But it is not often that virtue can boast an interest such as this. The domestic, unpretending merits of a person never known do not often create that kind of fervent, venerating tenderness which would prompt a visit like yours. Eleanor, I suppose, has talked of her a great deal?"

"Yes, a great deal. That is -- no, not much, but what she did say was very interesting. Her dying so suddenly" (slowly, and with hesitation it was spoken), "and you -- none of you being at home -- and your father, I thought -- perhaps had not been very fond of her."

"And from these circumstances," he replied (his quick eye fixed on hers), "you infer perhaps the probability of some negligence -- some" -- (involuntarily she shook her head) -- or it may be -- of something still less pardonable." She raised her eyes towards him more fully than she had ever done before. "My mother's illness," he continued, "the seizure which ended in her death, was sudden. The malady itself, one from which she had often suffered, a bilious fever -- its cause therefore constitutional. On the third day, in short, as soon as she could be prevailed on, a physician attended her, a very respectable man, and one in whom she had always placed great confidence. Upon his opinion of her danger, two others were called in the next day, and remained in almost constant attendance for four-and-twenty hours. On the fifth day she died. During the progress of her disorder, Frederick and I (we were both at home) saw her repeatedly; and from our own observation can bear witness

145

to her having received every possible attention which could spring from the affection of those about her, or which her situation in life could command. Poor Eleanor was absent, and at such a distance as to return only to see her mother in her coffin."

"But your father," said Catherine, "was he afflicted?"

"For a time, greatly so. You have erred in supposing him not attached to her. He loved her, I am persuaded, as well as it was possible for him to -- we have not all, you know, the same tenderness of disposition -- and I will not pretend to say that while she lived, she might not often have had much to bear, but though his temper injured her, his judgment never did. His value of her was sincere; and, if not permanently, he was truly afflicted by her death."

"I am very glad of it," said Catherine; "it would have been very shocking!"

"If I understand you rightly, you had formed a surmise of such horror as I have hardly words to -- Dear Miss Morland, consider the dreadful nature of the suspicions you have entertained. What have you been judging from? Remember the country and the age in which we live. Remember that we are English, that we are Christians. Consult your own understanding, your own sense of the probable, your own observation of what is passing around you. Does our education prepare us for such atrocities? Do our laws connive at them? Could they be perpetrated without being known, in a country like this, where social and literary intercourse is on such a footing, where every man is surrounded by a neighbourhood of voluntary spies, and where roads and newspapers lay every thing open? Dearest Miss Morland, what ideas have you been admitting?"

They had reached the end of the gallery, and with tears of shame she ran off to her own room.

CHAPTER 25

The visions of romance were over. Catherine was completely awakened. Henry's address, short as it had been, had more thoroughly opened her eyes to the extravagance of her late fancies than all their several disappointments had done. Most grievously was she humbled. Most bitterly did she cry. It was not only with herself that she was sunk -- but with Henry. Her folly, which now seemed even criminal, was all exposed to him, and he must despise her for ever. The liberty which her imagination had dared to take with the character of his father -- could he ever forgive it? The absurdity of her curiosity and her fears -- could they ever be forgotten? She hated herself more than she could express. He had -- she thought he had, once or twice before this fatal morning, shewn something like affection for her. But now -- in short, she made herself as miserable as possible for about half an hour, went down when the clock struck five, with a broken heart, and could scarcely give an intelligible answer to Eleanor's inquiry if she was well. The formidable Henry soon followed her into the room, and the only difference in his behaviour to her was that he paid her rather more attention than usual. Catherine had never wanted comfort more, and he looked as if he was aware of it.

The evening wore away with no abatement of this soothing politeness; and her spirits were gradually raised to a modest tranquillity. She did not learn either to forget or defend the past; but she learned to hope that it would never transpire farther, and that it might not cost her Henry's entire regard. Her thoughts being still chiefly fixed on what she had with such causeless terror felt and done, nothing could shortly be clearer than that it had been all a voluntary, self-created delusion, each trifling circumstance receiving importance from an imagination resolved on alarm, and every thing forced to bend to one purpose by a mind which, before she entered the Abbey, had been craving to be frightened. She remembered with what feelings she had prepared for a knowledge of Northanger. She saw that the infatuation had been created, the mischief settled long before her quitting Bath, and it seemed as if the whole might be traced to the influence of that sort of reading which she had there indulged.

Charming as were all Mrs. Radcliffe's works, and charming even as were the works of all her imitators, it was not in them perhaps that human nature, at least in the Midland counties of England, was to be looked for. Of the Alps and Pyrenees, with their pine forests and their vices, they might give a faithful delineation; and Italy, Switzerland, and the south of France might be as fruitful in horrors as they were there represented. Catherine dared not doubt beyond her own country, and even of that, if hard pressed, would have yielded the northern and western extremities. But in the central part

147

of England there was surely some security for the existence even of a wife not beloved, in the laws of the land, and the manners of the age. Murder was not tolerated, servants were not slaves, and neither poison nor sleeping potions to be procured, like rhubarb, from every druggist. Among the Alps and Pyrenees, perhaps, there were no mixed characters. There, such as were not as spotless as an angel might have the dispositions of a fiend. But in England it was not so; among the English, she believed, in their hearts and habits, there was a general though unequal mixture of good and bad. Upon this conviction, she would not be surprised if even in Henry and Eleanor Tilney, some slight imperfection might hereafter appear; and upon this conviction she need not fear to acknowledge some actual specks in the character of their father, who, though cleared from the grossly injurious suspicions which she must ever blush to have entertained, she did believe, upon serious consideration, to be not perfectly amiable.

Her mind made up on these several points, and her resolution formed, of always judging and acting in future with the greatest good sense, she had nothing to do but to forgive herself and be happier than ever; and the lenient hand of time did much for her by insensible gradations in the course of another day. Henry's astonishing generosity and nobleness of conduct, in never alluding in the slightest way to what had passed, was of the greatest assistance to her; and sooner than she could have supposed it possible in the beginning of her distress, her spirits became absolutely comfortable, and capable, as heretofore, of continual improvement by any thing he said. There were still some subjects, indeed, under which she believed they must always tremble -- the mention of a chest or a cabinet, for instance -- and she did not love the sight of japan in any shape: but even *she* could allow that an occasional memento of past folly, however painful, might not be without use.

The anxieties of common life began soon to succeed to the alarms of romance. Her desire of hearing from Isabella grew every day greater. She was quite impatient to know how the Bath world went on, and how the Rooms were attended; and especially was she anxious to be assured of Isabella's having matched some fine netting-cotton, on which she had left her intent; and of her continuing on the best terms with James. Her only dependence for information of any kind was on Isabella. James had protested against writing to her till his return to Oxford; and Mrs. Allen had given her no hopes of a letter till she had got back to Fullerton. But Isabella had promised and promised again; and when she promised a thing, she was so scrupulous in performing it! This made it so particularly strange!

For nine successive mornings, Catherine wondered over the repetition of a disappointment, which each morning became more severe: but, on the tenth, when she entered the breakfast-room, her first object was a letter, held out by Henry's willing hand. She thanked him as heartily as if he had written it himself. " 'Tis only from James, however," as she looked at the direction. She opened it; it was from Oxford; and to this purpose:

"Dear Catherine,

"Though, God knows, with little inclination for writing, I think it my duty to tell you that every thing is at an end between Miss Thorpe and me. I left her and Bath yesterday, never to see either again. I shall not enter into particulars -- they would only pain you more. You will soon hear enough from another quarter to know where lies the blame; and I hope will acquit your brother of every thing but the folly of too easily thinking his affection returned. Thank God! I am undeceived in time! But it is a heavy blow! After my father's consent had been so kindly given -- but no more of this. She has made me miserable for ever! Let me soon hear from you, dear Catherine; you are my only friend; your love I do build upon. I wish your visit at Northanger may be over before Captain Tilney makes his engagement known, or you will be uncomfortably circumstanced. Poor Thorpe is in town: I dread the sight of him; his honest heart would feel so much. I have written to him and my father. Her duplicity hurts me more than all; till the very last, if I reasoned with her, she declared herself as much attached to me as ever, and laughed at my fears. I am ashamed to think how long I bore with it; but if ever man had reason to believe himself loved, I was that man. I cannot understand even now what she would be at, for there could be no need of my being played off to make her secure of Tilney. We parted at last by mutual consent -- happy for me had we never met! I can never expect to know such another woman! Dearest Catherine, beware how you give your heart.

"Believe me," &c.

Catherine had not read three lines before her sudden change of countenance, and short exclamations of sorrowing wonder, declared her to be receiving unpleasant news; and Henry, earnestly watching her through the whole letter, saw plainly that it ended no better than it began. He was prevented, however, from even looking his surprise by his father's entrance. They went to breakfast directly; but Catherine could hardly eat any thing. Tears filled her eyes, and even ran down her cheeks as she sat. The letter was one moment in her hand, then in her lap, and then in her pocket; and she looked as if she knew not what she did. The General, between his cocoa and his newspaper, had luckily no leisure for noticing her; but to the other two her distress was equally visible. As soon as she dared leave the table she hurried away to her own room; but the housemaids were busy in it, and she was obliged to come down again. She turned into the drawing-room for privacy, but Henry and Eleanor had likewise retreated thither, and were at that moment deep in consultation about her. She drew back, trying to beg their pardon, but was, with gentle violence, forced to return; and the others withdrew, after Eleanor had affectionately expressed a wish of being of use or comfort to her.

After half an hour's free indulgence of grief and reflection, Catherine felt equal to encountering her friends; but whether she should make her distress known to them was another consideration. Perhaps, if particularly questioned, she might just give an idea -- just distantly hint at it -- but not more. To expose a friend, such a friend as Isabella had been to her -- and then their own brother so closely concerned in it! She believed she must waive the subject altogether. Henry and Eleanor were by themselves in the breakfast-room; and each, as she entered it, looked at her anxiously. Catherine took her place at the table, and, after a short silence, Eleanor said, "No bad news from Fullerton, I hope? Mr. and Mrs. Morland -- your brothers and sisters -- I hope they are none of them ill?"

"No, I thank you" (sighing as she spoke); "they are all very well. My letter was from my brother at Oxford."

Nothing further was said for a few minutes; and then speaking through her tears, she added, "I do not think I shall ever wish for a letter again!"

"I am sorry," said Henry, closing the book he had just opened; "if I had suspected the letter of containing any thing unwelcome, I should have given it with very different feelings."

"It contained something worse than any body could suppose! Poor James is so unhappy! You will soon know why."

"To have so kind-hearted, so affectionate a sister," replied Henry warmly, "must be a comfort to him under any distress."

"I have one favour to beg," said Catherine, shortly afterwards, in an agitated manner, "that, if your brother should be coming here, you will give me notice of it, that I may go away."

"Our brother! Frederick!"

"Yes; I am sure I should be very sorry to leave you so soon, but something has happened that would make it very dreadful for me to be in the same house with Captain Tilney."

Eleanor's work was suspended while she gazed with increasing astonishment; but Henry began to suspect the truth, and something, in which Miss Thorpe's name was included, passed his lips.

"How quick you are!" cried Catherine: "you have guessed it, I declare! And yet, when we talked about it in Bath, you little thought of its ending so. Isabella -- no wonder *now* I have not heard from her -- Isabella has deserted my brother, and is to marry yours! Could you have believed there had been such inconstancy and fickleness, and every thing that is bad in the world?"

"I hope, so far as concerns my brother, you are misinformed. I hope he has not had any material share in bringing on Mr. Morland's disappointment. His marrying Miss Thorpe is not probable. I think you must be deceived so far. I am very sorry for Mr. Morland -- sorry that any one you love should be unhappy; but my surprise would be greater at Frederick's marrying her than at any other part of the story."

"It is very true, however; you shall read James's letter yourself. Stay -- There is one part --" recollecting with a blush the last line.

"Will you take the trouble of reading to us the passages which concern my brother?"

"No, read it yourself," cried Catherine, whose second thoughts were clearer. "I do not know what I was thinking of" (blushing again that she had blushed before); "James only means to give me good advice."

He gladly received the letter, and, having read it through, with close attention, returned it saying, "Well, if it is to be so, I can only say that I am sorry for it. Frederick will not be the first man who has chosen a wife with less sense than his family expected. I do not envy his situation, either as a lover or a son."

151

Miss Tilney, at Catherine's invitation, now read the letter likewise, and, having expressed also her concern and surprise, began to inquire into Miss Thorpe's connexions and fortune.

"Her mother is a very good sort of woman," was Catherine's answer.

"What was her father?"

"A lawyer, I believe. They live at Putney."

"Are they a wealthy family?"

"No, not very. I do not believe Isabella has any fortune at all: but that will not signify in your family. Your father is so very liberal! He told me the other day that he only valued money as it allowed him to promote the happiness of his children." The brother and sister looked at each other. "But," said Eleanor, after a short pause, "would it be to promote his happiness, to enable him to marry such a girl? She must be an unprincipled one, or she could not have used your brother so. And how strange an infatuation on Frederick's side! A girl who, before his eyes, is violating an engagement voluntarily entered into with another man! Is not it inconceivable, Henry? Frederick too, who always wore his heart so proudly! Who found no woman good enough to be loved!"

"That is the most unpromising circumstance, the strongest presumption against him. When I think of his past declarations, I give him up. Moreover, I have too good an opinion of Miss Thorpe's prudence to suppose that she would part with one gentleman before the other was secured. It is all over with Frederick indeed! He is a deceased man -- defunct in understanding. Prepare for your sister-in-law, Eleanor, and such a sister-in-law as you must delight in! Open, candid, artless, guileless, with affections strong but simple, forming no pretensions, and knowing no disguise."

"Such a sister-in-law, Henry, I should delight in," said Eleanor with a smile.

"But perhaps," observed Catherine, "though she has behaved so ill by our family, she may behave better by yours. Now she has really got the man she likes, she may be constant."

"Indeed I am afraid she will," replied Henry; "I am afraid she will be very constant, unless a baronet should come in her way; that is Frederick's only chance. I will get the Bath paper, and look over the arrivals."

"You think it is all for ambition, then? And, upon my word, there are some things that seem very like it. I cannot forget that, when she first knew what my father would do for them, she seemed quite disappointed that it was not more. I never was so deceived in any one's character in my life before."

"Among all the great variety that you have known and studied."

"My own disappointment and loss in her is very great; but, as for poor James, I suppose he will hardly ever recover it."

"Your brother is certainly very much to be pitied at present; but we must not, in our concern for his sufferings, undervalue yours. You feel, I suppose, that in losing Isabella, you lose half yourself: you feel a void in your heart which nothing else can occupy. Society is becoming irksome; and as for the amusements in which you were wont to share at Bath, the very idea of them without her is abhorrent. You would not, for instance, now go to a ball for the world. You feel that you have no longer any friend to whom you can speak with unreserve, on whose regard you can place dependence, or whose counsel, in any difficulty, you could rely on. You feel all this?"

"No," said Catherine, after a few moments' reflection, "I do not -- ought I? To say the truth, though I am hurt and grieved, that I cannot still love her, that I am never to hear from her, perhaps never to see her again, I do not feel so very, very much afflicted as one would have thought."

"You feel, as you always do, what is most to the credit of human nature. Such feelings ought to be investigated, that they may know themselves."

Catherine, by some chance or other, found her spirits so very much relieved by this conversation that she could not regret her being led on, though so unaccountably, to mention the circumstance which had produced it.

CHAPTER 26

From this time, the subject was frequently canvassed by the three young people; and Catherine found, with some surprise, that her two young friends were perfectly agreed in considering Isabella's want of consequence and fortune as likely to throw great difficulties in the way of her marrying their brother. Their persuasion that the General would, upon this ground alone, independent of the objection that might be raised against her character, oppose the connexion, turned her feelings moreover with some alarm towards herself. She was as insignificant, and perhaps as portionless as Isabella; and if the heir of the Tilney property had not grandeur and wealth enough in himself, at what point of interest were the demands of his younger brother to rest? The very painful reflections to which this thought led could only be dispersed by a dependence on the effect of that particular partiality, which, as she was given to understand by his words as well as his actions, she had from the first been so fortunate as to excite in the General; and by a recollection of some most generous and disinterested sentiments on the subject of money, which she had more than once heard him utter, and which tempted her to think his disposition in such matters misunderstood by his children.

They were so fully convinced, however, that their brother would not have the courage to apply in person for his father's consent, and so repeatedly assured her that he had never in his life been less likely to come to Northanger than at the present time, that she suffered her mind to be at ease as to the necessity of any sudden removal of her own. But as it was not to be supposed that Captain Tilney, whenever he made his application, would give his father any just idea of Isabella's conduct, it occurred to her as highly expedient that Henry should lay the whole business before him as it really was, enabling the General by that means to form a cool and impartial opinion, and prepare his objections on a fairer ground than inequality of situations. She proposed it to him accordingly; but he did not catch at the measure so eagerly as she had expected. "No," said he, "my father's hands need not be strengthened, and Frederick's confession of folly need not be forestalled. He must tell his own story."

"But he will tell only half of it."

"A quarter would be enough."

A day or two passed away and brought no tidings of Captain Tilney. His brother and sister knew not what to think. Sometimes it appeared to them as if his silence would be the natural result of the suspected engagement, and at others that it was wholly incompatible with it. The General, meanwhile, though offended every morning by Frederick's remissness in writing, was free from any real anxiety about him, and had no more pressing solicitude than that of making Miss Morland's time at Northanger pass pleasantly. He often expressed his uneasiness on this head, feared the sameness of every day's society and employments would disgust her with the place, wished the Lady Frasers had been in the country, talked every now and then of having a large party to dinner, and once or twice began even to calculate the number of young dancing people in the neighbourhood. But then it was such a dead time of year, no wild-fowl, no game, and the Lady Frasers were not in the country. And it all ended, at last, in his telling Henry one morning that when he next went to Woodston, they would take him by surprise there some day or other, and eat their mutton with him. Henry was greatly honoured and very happy, and Catherine was quite delighted with the scheme. "And when do you think, sir, I may look forward to this pleasure? I must be at Woodston on Monday to attend the parish meeting, and shall probably be obliged to stay two or three days."

"Well, well, we will take our chance some one of those days. There is no need to fix. You are not to put yourself at all out of your way. Whatever you may happen to have in the house will be enough. I think I can answer for the young ladies making allowance for a bachelor's table. Let me see; Monday will be a busy day with you, we will not come on Monday; and Tuesday will be a busy one with me. I expect my surveyor from Brockham with his report in the morning; and afterwards I cannot in decency fail attending the club. I really could not face my acquaintance if I stayed away now; for, as I am known to be in the country, it would be taken exceedingly amiss; and it is a rule with me, Miss Morland, never to give offence to any of my neighbours, if a small sacrifice of time and attention can prevent it. They are a set of very worthy men. They have half a buck from Northanger twice a year; and I dine with them whenever I can. Tuesday, therefore, we may say is out of the question. But on Wednesday, I think, Henry, you may expect us; and we shall be with you early, that we may have time to look about us. Two hours and three quarters will carry us to Woodston, I suppose; we shall be in the carriage by ten; so, about a quarter before one on Wednesday, you may look for us."

A ball itself could not have been more welcome to Catherine than this little excursion, so strong was her desire to be acquainted with Woodston; and her heart was still bounding with joy when Henry, about an hour afterwards, came booted and greatcoated into the room where she and Eleanor were sitting, and said, "I am come, young ladies, in a very moralizing strain, to observe that our pleasures in this world are always to be paid for, and that we often

155

purchase them at a great disadvantage, giving ready-monied actual happiness for a draft on the future, that may not be honoured. Witness myself, at this present hour. Because I am to hope for the satisfaction of seeing you at Woodston on Wednesday, which bad weather, or twenty other causes, may prevent, I must go away directly, two days before I intended it."

"Go away!" said Catherine, with a very long face. "And why?"

"Why! How can you ask the question? Because no time is to be lost in frightening my old housekeeper out of her wits, because I must go and prepare a dinner for you, to be sure."

"Oh! Not seriously!"

"Aye, and sadly too -- for I had much rather stay."

"But how can you think of such a thing, after what the General said? When he so particularly desired you not to give yourself any trouble, because *any thing* would do."

Henry only smiled. "I am sure it is quite unnecessary upon your sister's account and mine. You must know it to be so; and the General made such a point of your providing nothing extraordinary: besides, if he had not said half so much as he did, he has always such an excellent dinner at home, that sitting down to a middling one for one day could not signify."

"I wish I could reason like you, for his sake and my own. Good bye. As to-morrow is Sunday, Eleanor, I shall not return."

He went; and, it being at any time a much simpler operation to Catherine to doubt her own judgment than Henry's, she was very soon obliged to give him credit for being right, however disagreeable to her his going. But the inexplicability of the General's conduct dwelt much on her thoughts. That he was very particular in his eating, she had, by her own unassisted observation, already discovered; but why he should say one thing so positively, and mean another all the while, was most unaccountable! How were people, at that rate, to be understood? Who but Henry could have been aware of what his father was at?

From Saturday to Wednesday, however, they were now to be without Henry. This was the sad finale of every reflection: and Captain Tilney's letter would certainly come in his absence; and Wednesday she was very sure would be wet. The past, present, and future were all equally in gloom. Her brother so unhappy, and her loss in Isabella so great; and Eleanor's spirits always affected by Henry's absence! What was there to interest or amuse her? She was tired of the woods and the shrubberies -- always so smooth and so dry; and the Abbey in itself was no more to her now than any other house. The painful remembrance of the folly it had helped to nourish and perfect was the only emotion which could spring from a consideration of the building. What a revolution in her ideas! She, who had so longed to be in an abbey! Now, there was nothing so charming to her imagination as the unpretending comfort of a well-connected parsonage, something like Fullerton, but better: Fullerton had its faults, but Woodston probably had none. If Wednesday should ever come!

It did come, and exactly when it might be reasonably looked for. It came -- it was fine -- and Catherine trod on air. By ten o'clock, the chaise-and-four conveyed the two from the Abbey; and, after an agreeable drive of almost twenty miles, they entered Woodston, a large and populous village, in a situation not unpleasant. Catherine was ashamed to say how pretty she thought it, as the General seemed to think an apology necessary for the flatness of the country, and the size of the village; but in her heart she preferred it to any place she had ever been at, and looked with great admiration at every neat house above the rank of a cottage, and at all the little chandler's shops which they passed. At the further end of the village, and tolerably disengaged from the rest of it, stood the Parsonage, a new-built substantial stone house, with its semi-circular sweep and green gates; and, as they drove up to the door, Henry, with the friends of his solitude, a large Newfoundland puppy and two or three terriers, was ready to receive and make much of them.

Catherine's mind was too full, as she entered the house, for her either to observe or to say a great deal; and, till called on by the General for her opinion of it, she had very little idea of the room in which she was sitting. Upon looking round it then, she perceived in a moment that it was the most comfortable room in the world; but she was too guarded to say so, and the coldness of her praise disappointed him.

"We are not calling it a good house," said he. "We are not comparing it with Fullerton and Northanger -- we are considering it as a mere Parsonage, small and confined, we allow, but decent, perhaps, and habitable; and altogether not inferior to the generality; or, in other words, I believe there are few country parsonages in England half so good. It may admit of improvement, however. Far be it from me to say otherwise; and any thing in reason -- a bow thrown out, perhaps -- though, between ourselves, if there is one thing more than another my aversion, it is a patched-on bow."

Catherine did not hear enough of this speech to understand or be pained by it; and other subjects being studiously brought forward and supported by Henry, at the same time that a tray full of refreshments was introduced by his servant, the General was shortly restored to his complacency, and Catherine to all her usual ease of spirits.

The room in question was of a commodious, well-proportioned size, and handsomely fitted up as a dining-parlour; and on their quitting it to walk round the grounds, she was shewn, first into a smaller apartment, belonging peculiarly to the master of the house, and made unusually tidy on the occasion; and afterwards into what was to be the drawing-room, with the appearance of which, though unfurnished, Catherine was delighted enough even to satisfy the General. It was a prettily shaped room, the windows reaching to the ground, and the view from them pleasant, though only over green meadows; and she expressed her admiration at the moment with all the honest simplicity with which she felt it. "Oh! Why do not you fit up this room, Mr. Tilney? What a pity not to have it fitted up! It is the prettiest room I ever saw; it is the prettiest room in the world!"

"I trust," said the General, with a most satisfied smile, "that it will very speedily be furnished: it waits only for a lady's taste!"

"Well, if it was my house, I should never sit any where else. Oh! What a sweet little cottage there is among the trees -- apple trees, too! It is the prettiest cottage!"

"You like it -- you approve it as an object -- it is enough. Henry, remember that Robinson is spoken to about it. The cottage remains."

Such a compliment recalled all Catherine's consciousness, and silenced her directly; and, though pointedly applied to by the General for her choice of the prevailing colour of the paper and hangings, nothing like an opinion on the subject could be drawn from her. The influence of fresh objects and fresh air, however, was of great use in dissipating these embarrassing associations; and, having reached the ornamental part of the premises, consisting of a walk round two sides of a meadow, on which Henry's genius had begun to act about half a year ago, she was sufficiently recovered to think it prettier than any pleasure-ground she had ever been in before, though there was not a shrub in it higher than the green bench in the corner.

A saunter into other meadows, and through part of the village, with a visit to the stables to examine some improvements, and a charming game of play with a litter of puppies just able to roll about, brought them to four o'clock, when Catherine scarcely thought it could be three. At four they were to dine, and at six to set off on their return. Never had any day passed so quickly!

She could not but observe that the abundance of the dinner did not seem to create the smallest astonishment in the General; nay, that he was even looking at the side-table for cold meat which was not there. His son and daughter's observations were of a different kind. They had seldom seen him eat so heartily at any table but his own, and never before known him so little disconcerted by the melted butter's being oiled.

At six o'clock, the General having taken his coffee, the carriage again received them; and so gratifying had been the tenor of his conduct throughout the whole visit, so well assured was her mind on the subject of his expectations, that, could she have felt equally confident of the wishes of his son, Catherine would have quitted Woodston with little anxiety as to the How or the When she might return to it.

CHAPTER 27

The next morning brought the following very unexpected letter from Isabella:

Bath, April

My dearest Catherine,

I received your two kind letters with the greatest delight, and have a thousand apologies to make for not answering them sooner. I really am quite ashamed of my idleness; but in this horrid place one can find time for nothing. I have had my pen in my hand to begin a letter to you almost every day since you left Bath, but have always been prevented by some silly trifler or other. Pray write to me soon, and direct to my own home. Thank God, we leave this vile place to-

159

morrow. Since you went away, I have had no pleasure in it -- the dust is beyond any thing; and every body one cares for is gone. I believe if I could see you I should not mind the rest, for you are dearer to me than any body can conceive. I am quite uneasy about your dear brother, not having heard from him since he went to Oxford; and am fearful of some misunderstanding. Your kind offices will set all right: he is the only man I ever did or could love, and I trust you will convince him of it. The spring fashions are partly down; and the hats the most frightful you can imagine. I hope you spend your time pleasantly, but am afraid you never think of me. I will not say all that I could of the family you are with, because I would not be ungenerous, or set you against those you esteem; but it is very difficult to know whom to trust, and young men never know their minds two days together. I rejoice to say that the young man whom, of all others, I particularly abhor, has left Bath. You will know, from this description, I must mean Captain Tilney, who, as you may remember, was amazingly disposed to follow and tease me, before you went away. Afterwards he got worse, and became quite my shadow. Many girls might have been taken in, for never were such attentions; but I knew the fickle sex too well. He went away to his regiment two days ago, and I trust I shall never be plagued with him again. He is the greatest coxcomb I ever saw, and amazingly disagreeable. The last two days he was always by the side of Charlotte Davis: I pitied his taste, but took no notice of him. The last time we met was in Bath Street, and I turned directly into a shop that he might not speak to me; I would not even look at him. He went into the Pump-room afterwards; but I would not have followed him for all the world. Such a contrast between him and your brother! Pray send me some news of the latter -- I am quite unhappy about him; he seemed so uncomfortable when he went away, with a cold, or something that affected his spirits. I would write to him myself, but have mislaid his direction; and, as I hinted above, am afraid he took something in my conduct amiss. Pray explain every thing to his satisfaction; or, if he still harbours any doubt, a line from himself to me, or a call at Putney when next in town, might set all to rights. I have not been to the Rooms this age, nor to the Play, except going in last night with the Hodges, for a frolic, at half-price: they teased me into it; and I was determined they should not say I shut myself up because Tilney was gone. We happened to sit by the Mitchells, and they pretended to be quite surprised to see me out. I knew their spite: at one time they could not be civil to me, but now they are all friendship; but I am not such a fool as to be taken in by them. You know I have a pretty good spirit of my own. Anne Mitchell had tried to put on a turban like mine, as I wore it the week before at the concert, but made wretched work of it -- it happened to become my odd face, I believe, at least Tilney told me so at the time, and said every eye was upon me; but he is the last man whose word I would take. I wear nothing but purple now: I know I look hideous in it, but no matter -- it is your dear brother's favourite colour. Lose no time, my dearest, sweetest Catherine, in writing to him and to me,

Who ever am, &c.

Such a strain of shallow artifice could not impose even upon Catherine. Its inconsistencies, contradictions, and falsehood struck her from the very first. She was ashamed of Isabella, and ashamed of having ever loved her. Her professions of attachment were now as disgusting as her excuses were empty, and her demands impudent. "Write to James on her behalf! No, James should never hear Isabella's name mentioned by her again."

On Henry's arrival from Woodston, she made known to him and Eleanor their brother's safety, congratulating them with sincerity on it, and reading aloud the most material passages of her letter with strong indignation. When she had finished it -- "So much for Isabella," she cried, "and for all our intimacy! She must think me an idiot, or she could not have written so; but perhaps this has served to make her character better known to me than mine is to her. I see what she has been about. She is a vain coquette, and her tricks have not answered. I do not believe she had ever any regard either for James or for me, and I wish I had never known her."

"It will soon be as if you never had," said Henry.

"There is but one thing that I cannot understand. I see that she has had designs on Captain Tilney, which have not succeeded; but I do not understand what Captain Tilney has been about all this time. Why should he pay her such attentions as to make her quarrel with my brother, and then fly off himself?"

"I have very little to say for Frederick's motives, such as I believe them to have been. He has his vanities as well as Miss Thorpe, and the chief difference is, that, having a stronger head, they have not yet injured himself. If the effect of his behaviour does not justify him with you, we had better not seek after the cause."

"Then you do not suppose he ever really cared about her?"

"I am persuaded that he never did."

"And only made believe to do so for mischief's sake?"

Henry bowed his assent.

"Well, then, I must say that I do not like him at all. Though it has turned out so well for us, I do not like him at all. As it happens, there is no great harm done, because I do not think Isabella has any heart to lose. But, suppose he had made her very much in love with him?"

"But we must first suppose Isabella to have had a heart to lose -- consequently to have been a very different creature; and, in that case, she would have met with very different treatment."

"It is very right that you should stand by your brother."

"And if you would stand by yours, you would not be much distressed by the disappointment of Miss Thorpe. But your mind is warped by an innate principle of general integrity, and therefore not accessible to the cool reasonings of family partiality, or a desire of revenge."

Catherine was complimented out of further bitterness. Frederick could not be unpardonably guilty, while Henry made himself so agreeable. She resolved on not answering Isabella's letter, and tried to think no more of it.

CHAPTER 28

Soon after this, the General found himself obliged to go to London for a week; and he left Northanger earnestly regretting that any necessity should rob him even for an hour of Miss Morland's company, and anxiously recommending the study of her comfort and amusement to his children as their chief object in his absence. His departure gave Catherine the first experimental conviction that a loss may be sometimes a gain. The happiness with which their time now passed, every employment voluntary, every laugh indulged, every meal a scene of ease and good humour, walking where they liked and when they liked, their hours, pleasures, and fatigues at their own command, made her thoroughly sensible of the restraint which the General's presence had imposed, and most thankfully feel their present release from it. Such ease and such delights made her love the place and the people more and more every day; and had it not been for a dread of its soon becoming expedient to leave the one, and an apprehension of not being equally beloved by the other, she would at each moment of each day have been perfectly happy; but she was now in the fourth week of her visit; before the General came home, the fourth week would be turned, and perhaps it might seem an intrusion if she stayed much longer. This was a painful consideration whenever it occurred; and eager to get rid of such a weight on her mind, she very soon resolved to speak to Eleanor about it at once, propose going away, and be guided in her conduct by the manner in which her proposal might be taken.

Aware that if she gave herself much time, she might feel it difficult to bring forward so unpleasant a subject, she took the first opportunity of being suddenly alone with Eleanor, and of Eleanor's being in the middle of a speech about something very different, to start forth her obligation of going away very soon. Eleanor looked and declared herself much concerned. She had "hoped for the pleasure of her company for a much longer time -- had been misled (perhaps by her wishes) to suppose that a much longer visit had been promised -- and could not but think that if Mr. and Mrs. Morland were aware of the pleasure it was to her to have her there, they would be too generous to hasten her return." Catherine explained: "Oh! As to *that*, Papa and Mamma were in no hurry at all. As long as she was happy, they would always be satisfied."

"Then why, might she ask, in such a hurry herself to leave them?"

"Oh! Because she had been there so long."

"Nay, if you can use such a word, I can urge you no farther. If you think it long --"

"Oh! No, I do not indeed. For my own pleasure, I could stay with you as long again." And it was directly settled that, till she had, her leaving them was not even to be thought of. In having this cause of uneasiness so pleasantly removed, the force of the other was likewise weakened. The kindness, the earnestness of Eleanor's manner in pressing her to stay, and Henry's gratified look on being told that her stay was determined, were such sweet proofs of her importance with them, as left her only just so much solicitude as the human mind can never do comfortably without. She did -- almost always -- believe that Henry loved her, and quite always that his

163

father and sister loved and even wished her to belong to them; and believing so far, her doubts and anxieties were merely sportive irritations.

Henry was not able to obey his father's injunction of remaining wholly at Northanger in attendance on the ladies, during his absence in London, the engagements of his curate at Woodston obliging him to leave them on Saturday for a couple of nights. His loss was not now what it had been while the General was at home; it lessened their gaiety, but did not ruin their comfort; and the two girls agreeing in occupation, and improving in intimacy, found themselves so well sufficient for the time to themselves, that it was eleven o'clock, rather a late hour at the Abbey, before they quitted the supper-room on the day of Henry's departure. They had just reached the head of the stairs when it seemed, as far as the thickness of the walls would allow them to judge, that a carriage was driving up to the door, and the next moment confirmed the idea by the loud noise of the house-bell. After the first perturbation of surprise had passed away, in a "Good Heaven! What can be the matter?" it was quickly decided by Eleanor to be her eldest brother, whose arrival was often as sudden, if not quite so unseasonable, and accordingly she hurried down to welcome him.

Catherine walked on to her chamber, making up her mind as well as she could, to a further acquaintance with Captain Tilney, and comforting herself under the unpleasant impression his conduct had given her, and the persuasion of his being by far too fine a gentleman to approve of her, that at least they should not meet under such circumstances as would make their meeting materially painful. She trusted he would never speak of Miss Thorpe; and indeed, as he must by this time be ashamed of the part he had acted, there could be no danger of it; and as long as all mention of Bath scenes were avoided, she thought she could behave to him very civilly. In such considerations time passed away, and it was certainly in his favour that Eleanor should be so glad to see him, and have so much to say, for half an hour was almost gone since his arrival, and Eleanor did not come up.

At that moment Catherine thought she heard her step in the gallery, and listened for its continuance; but all was silent. Scarcely, however, had she convicted her fancy of error, when the noise of something moving close to her door made her start; it seemed as if some one was touching the very doorway -- and in another moment a slight motion of the lock proved that some hand must be on it. She trembled a little at the idea of any one's approaching so cautiously; but resolving not to be again overcome by trivial appearances of alarm, or misled by a raised imagination, she stepped quietly forward, and opened the door. Eleanor, and only Eleanor, stood there. Catherine's spirits, however, were tranquillized but for an instant, for Eleanor's cheeks were pale, and her manner greatly agitated. Though evidently intending to come in, it seemed an effort to enter the room, and a still greater to speak when there. Catherine, supposing some uneasiness on Captain Tilney's account, could only express her concern by silent attention, obliged her to be seated, rubbed her temples with lavender-water, and hung over her with affectionate solicitude. "My dear Catherine, you must not -- you must not indeed --" were Eleanor's first connected words. "I am quite well. This kindness distracts me -- I cannot bear it -- I come to you on such an errand!"

"Errand! To me!"

"How shall I tell you! Oh! How shall I tell you!"

A new idea now darted into Catherine's mind, and turning as pale as her friend, she exclaimed, " 'Tis a messenger from Woodston!"

"You are mistaken, indeed," returned Eleanor, looking at her most compassionately; "it is no one from Woodston. It is my father himself." Her voice faltered, and her eyes were turned to the ground as she mentioned his name. His unlooked-for return was enough in itself to make Catherine's heart sink, and for a few moments she hardly supposed there were any thing worse to be told. She said nothing; and Eleanor, endeavouring to collect herself and speak with firmness, but with eyes still cast down, soon went on. "You are too good, I am sure, to think the worse of me for the part I am obliged to perform. I am indeed a most unwilling messenger. After what has so lately passed, so lately been settled between us -- how joyfully, how thankfully on my side! -- as to your continuing here as I hoped for many, many weeks longer, how can I tell you that your kindness is not to be accepted -- and that the happiness your company has hitherto given us is to be repaid by -- but I must not trust myself with words. My dear Catherine, we are to part. My father has recollected an engagement that takes our whole family away on Monday. We are going to Lord Longtown's, near Hereford, for a fortnight. Explanation and apology are equally impossible. I cannot attempt either."

"My dear Eleanor," cried Catherine, suppressing her feelings as well as she could, "do not be so distressed. A second engagement must give way to a first. I am very, very sorry we are to part -- so soon, and so suddenly too; but I am not offended, indeed I am not. I can finish my visit here, you know, at any time; or I hope you will come to me. Can you, when you return from this lord's, come to Fullerton?"

"It will not be in my power, Catherine."

"Come when you can, then."

Eleanor made no answer; and Catherine's thoughts recurring to something more directly interesting, she added, thinking aloud, "Monday -- so soon as Monday; and you *all* go. Well, I am certain of -- I shall be able to take leave, however. I need not go till just before you do, you know. Do not be distressed, Eleanor, I can go on Monday very well. My father and mother's having no notice of it is of very little consequence. The General will send a servant with me, I dare say, half the way -- and then I shall soon be at Salisbury, and then I am only nine miles from home."

"Ah, Catherine! Were it settled so, it would be somewhat less intolerable, though in such common attentions you would have received but half what you ought. But -- how can I tell you? -- To-morrow morning is fixed for your leaving us, and not even the hour is left to your choice; the very carriage is ordered, and will be here at seven o'clock, and no servant will be offered you."

Catherine sat down, breathless and speechless. "I could hardly believe my senses, when I heard it; and no displeasure, no resentment that you can feel at this moment, however justly great, can be more than I myself -- but I must not talk of what I felt. Oh! That I could suggest any thing in extenuation! Good God! What will your father and mother say! After courting you from the protection of real friends to this -- almost double distance from your home, to have you driven out of the house, without the considerations even of decent civility! Dear, dear Catherine, in being the bearer of such a message, I seem guilty myself of all its insult; yet, I trust you will acquit me, for you must have been long enough in this house to see that I am but a nominal mistress of it, that my real power is nothing."

"Have I offended the General?" said Catherine in a faltering voice.

"Alas! For my feelings as a daughter, all that I know, all that I

166

answer for is that you can have given him no just cause of offence. He certainly is greatly, very greatly discomposed; I have seldom seen him more so. His temper is not happy, and something has now occurred to ruffle it in an uncommon degree; some disappointment, some vexation, which just at this moment seems important, but which I can hardly suppose you to have any concern in, for how is it possible?"

It was with pain that Catherine could speak at all; and it was only for Eleanor's sake that she attempted it. "I am sure," said she, "I am very sorry if I have offended him. It was the last thing I would willingly have done. But do not be unhappy, Eleanor. An engagement, you know, must be kept. I am only sorry it was not recollected sooner, that I might have written home. But it is of very little consequence."

"I hope, I earnestly hope, that to your real safety it will be of none; but to every thing else it is of the greatest consequence: to comfort, appearance, propriety, to your family, to the world. Were your friends, the Allens, still in Bath, you might go to them with comparative ease; a few hours would take you there; but a journey of seventy miles, to be taken post by you, at your age, alone, unattended!"

"Oh, the journey is nothing. Do not think about that. And if we are to part, a few hours sooner or later, you know, makes no difference. I can be ready by seven. Let me be called in time." Eleanor saw that she wished to be alone; and believing it better for each that they should avoid any further conversation, now left her with, "I shall see you in the morning."

Catherine's swelling heart needed relief. In Eleanor's presence friendship and pride had equally restrained her tears, but no sooner was she gone than they burst forth in torrents. Turned from the house, and in such a way! Without any reason that could justify, any apology that could atone for the abruptness, the rudeness, nay, the insolence of it. Henry at a distance -- not able even to bid him farewell. Every hope, every expectation from him suspended, at least, and who could say how long? Who could say when they might meet again? And all this by such a man as General Tilney, so polite, so well-bred, and heretofore so particularly fond of her! It was as incomprehensible as it was mortifying and grievous. From what it could arise, and where it would end, were considerations of equal perplexity and alarm. The manner in which it was done so grossly uncivil, hurrying her away without any reference to her own convenience, or allowing her even the appearance of choice as to the time or mode of her travelling; of two days, the earliest fixed on, and of that almost the earliest hour, as if resolved to have her gone before he was stirring in the morning, that he might not be obliged even to see her. What could all this mean but an intentional affront? By some means or other she must have had the misfortune to offend him. Eleanor had wished to spare her from so painful a notion, but Catherine could not believe it possible that any injury or any misfortune could provoke such ill-will against a person not connected, or, at least, not supposed to be connected with it.

Heavily passed the night. Sleep, or repose that deserved the name of sleep, was out of the question. That room, in which her disturbed imagination had tormented her on her first arrival, was again the scene of agitated spirits and unquiet slumbers. Yet how different now the source of her inquietude from what it had been then -- how mournfully superior in reality and substance! Her anxiety had foundation in fact, her fears in probability; and with a mind so occupied in the contemplation of actual and natural evil, the solitude of her situation, the darkness of her chamber, the antiquity of the building were felt and considered without the smallest emotion; and though the wind was high, and often produced strange and sudden noises throughout the house, she heard it all as she lay awake, hour after hour, without curiosity or terror.

Soon after six Eleanor entered her room, eager to show attention or give assistance where it was possible; but very little remained to be done. Catherine had not loitered; she was almost dressed, and her packing almost finished. The possibility of some conciliatory message from the General occurred to her as his daughter appeared. What so natural, as that anger should pass away and repentance succeed it? And she only wanted to know how far, after what had passed, an apology might properly be received by her. But the knowledge would have been useless here; it was not called for; neither clemency nor dignity was put to the trial -- Eleanor brought no message. Very little passed between them on meeting; each found her greatest safety in silence, and few and trivial were the sentences exchanged while they remained up stairs, Catherine in busy agitation completing her dress, and Eleanor with more good-will than experience intent upon filling the trunk. When every thing was done they left the room, Catherine lingering only half a minute behind her friend to throw a parting glance on every well-known, cherished object, and went down to the breakfast-parlour, where breakfast was prepared. She tried to eat, as well to save herself from the pain of being urged as to make her friend comfortable; but she had no appetite, and could not swallow many mouthfuls. The contrast between this and her last breakfast in that room gave her fresh misery, and strengthened her distaste for every thing before her. It was not four-and-twenty hours ago since they had met there to the same repast, but in circumstances how different! With what cheerful ease, what happy, though false, security, had she then looked around her, enjoying every thing present, and fearing little in future, beyond Henry's going to Woodston for a day! Happy, happy breakfast! For Henry had been there; Henry had sat by her and helped her. These reflections were long indulged undisturbed by any address from her companion, who sat as deep in thought as herself; and the appearance of the carriage was the first thing to startle and recall them to the present moment. Catherine's colour rose at the sight of it; and the indignity with which she was treated, striking at that instant on her mind with peculiar force, made her for a short time sensible only of resentment. Eleanor seemed now impelled into resolution and speech.

"You *must* write to me, Catherine," she cried; "you *must* let me hear from you as soon as possible. Till I know you to be safe at home, I shall not have an hour's comfort. For *one* letter, at all risks, all hazards, I must entreat. Let me have the satisfaction of knowing that you are safe at Fullerton, and have found your family well, and then, till I can ask for your correspondence as I ought to do, I will not expect more. Direct to me at Lord Longtown's, and, I must ask it, under cover to Alice."

"No, Eleanor, if you are not allowed to receive a letter from me, I am sure I had better not write. There can be no doubt of my getting home safe."

Eleanor only replied, "I cannot wonder at your feelings. I will not importune you. I will trust to your own kindness of heart when I am at a distance from you." But this, with the look of sorrow accompanying it, was enough to melt Catherine's pride in a moment, and she instantly said, "Oh, Eleanor, I *will* write to you indeed."

There was yet another point which Miss Tilney was anxious to settle, though somewhat embarrassed in speaking of. It had occurred to her that after so long an absence from home, Catherine might not be provided with money enough for the expenses of her journey, and, upon suggesting it to her with most affectionate offers of accommodation, it proved to be exactly the case. Catherine had never thought on the subject till that moment, but, upon examining her purse, was convinced that but for this kindness of her friend, she might have been turned from the house without even the means of getting home; and the distress in which she must have been thereby involved filling the minds of both, scarcely another word was said by either during the time of their remaining together. Short, however, was that time. The carriage was soon announced to be ready; and Catherine, instantly rising, a long and affectionate embrace supplied the place of language in bidding each other adieu; and, as they entered the hall, unable to leave the house without some mention of one whose name had not yet been spoken by either, she paused a moment, and with quivering lips just made it intelligible that she left "her kind remembrance for her absent friend." But with this approach to his name ended all possibility of restraining her feelings; and, hiding her face as well as she could with her handkerchief, she darted across the hall, jumped into the chaise, and in a moment was driven from the door.

CHAPTER 29

Catherine was too wretched to be fearful. The journey in itself had no terrors for her; and she began it without either dreading its length or feeling its solitariness. Leaning back in one corner of the carriage, in a violent burst of tears, she was conveyed some miles beyond the walls of the Abbey before she raised her head; and the highest point of ground within the park was almost closed from her view before she was capable of turning her eyes towards it. Unfortunately, the road she now travelled was the same which only ten days ago she had so happily passed along in going to and from Woodston; and, for fourteen miles, every bitter feeling was rendered more severe by the review of objects on which she had first looked under impressions so different. Every mile, as it brought her nearer Woodston, added to her sufferings, and when within the distance of five, she passed the turning which led to it, and thought of Henry, so near, yet so unconscious, her grief and agitation were excessive.

The day which she had spent at that place had been one of the happiest of her life. It was there, it was on that day that the General had made use of such expressions with regard to Henry and herself, had so spoken and so looked as to give her the most positive conviction of his actually wishing their marriage. Yes, only ten days ago had he elated her by his pointed regard -- had he even confused her by his too significant reference! And now -- what had she done, or what had she omitted to do, to merit such a change?

The only offence against him of which she could accuse herself had been such as was scarcely possible to reach his knowledge. Henry and her own heart only were privy to the shocking suspicions which she had so idly entertained; and equally safe did she believe her secret with each. Designedly, at least, Henry could not have betrayed her. If, indeed, by any strange mischance his father should have gained intelligence of what she had dared to think and look for, of her causeless fancies and injurious examinations, she could not wonder at any degree of his indignation. If aware of her having viewed him as a murderer, she could not wonder at his even turning her from his house. But a justification so full of torture to herself, she trusted would not be in his power.

Anxious as were all her conjectures on this point, it was not, however, the one on which she dwelt most. There was a thought yet nearer, a more prevailing, more impetuous concern. How Henry would think, and feel, and look, when he returned on the morrow to Northanger and heard of her being gone, was a question of force and interest to rise over every other, to be never ceasing, alternately irritating and soothing; it sometimes suggested the dread of his calm acquiescence, and at others was answered by the sweetest confidence in his regret and resentment. To the General, of course, he would not dare to speak; but to Eleanor -- what might he not say to Eleanor about her?

In this unceasing recurrence of doubts and inquiries, on any one article of which her mind was incapable of more than momentary repose, the hours passed away, and her journey advanced much faster than she looked for. The pressing anxieties of thought, which prevented her from noticing any thing before her, when once beyond the neighbourhood of Woodston, saved her at the same time from watching her progress; and though no object on the road could engage a moment's attention, she found no stage of it tedious. From this, she was preserved too by another cause, by feeling no eagerness for her journey's conclusion; for to return in such a manner to Fullerton was almost to destroy the pleasure of a meeting with those she loved best, even after an absence such as hers -- an eleven weeks' absence. What had she to say that would not humble herself and pain her family, that would not increase her own grief by the confession of it, extend an useless resentment, and perhaps involve the innocent with the guilty in undistinguishing ill-will? She could never do justice to Henry and Eleanor's merit; she felt it too strongly for expression; and should a dislike be taken against them, should they be thought of unfavourably, on their father's account, it would cut her to the heart.

With these feelings, she rather dreaded than sought for the first view of that well-known spire which would announce her within twenty miles of home. Salisbury she had known to be her point on leaving Northanger; but after the first stage she had been indebted to the post-masters for the names of the places which were then to conduct her to it; so great had been her ignorance of her route. She met with nothing, however, to distress or frighten her. Her youth, civil manners and liberal pay procured her all the attention that a traveller like herself could require; and stopping only to change horses, she travelled on for about eleven hours without accident or alarm, and between six and seven o'clock in the evening found herself entering Fullerton.

A heroine returning, at the close of her career, to her native village, in all the triumph of recovered reputation, and all the dignity of a countess, with a long train of noble relations in their several phaetons, and three waiting-maids in a travelling chaise-and-four, behind her, is an event on which the pen of the contriver may well delight to dwell; it gives credit to every conclusion, and the author must share in the glory she so liberally bestows. But my affair is widely different; I bring back my heroine to her home in solitude and disgrace; and no sweet elation of spirits can lead me into minuteness. A heroine in a hack post-chaise is such a blow upon sentiment, as no attempt at grandeur or pathos can withstand. Swiftly therefore shall her post-boy drive through the village, amid the gaze of Sunday groups, and speedy shall be her descent from it.

But, whatever might be the distress of Catherine's mind, as she thus advanced towards the parsonage, and whatever the humiliation of her biographer in relating it, she was preparing enjoyment of no every-day nature for those to whom she went; first, in the appearance of her carriage -- and secondly, in herself. The chaise of a traveller being a rare sight in Fullerton, the whole family were immediately at the window; and to have it stop at the sweep-gate was a pleasure to brighten every eye and occupy every fancy -- a pleasure quite unlooked for by all but the two youngest children, a boy and girl of six and four years old, who expected a brother or sister in every carriage. Happy the glance that first distinguished Catherine! Happy the voice that proclaimed the discovery! But whether such happiness were the lawful property of George or Harriet could never be exactly understood.

Her father, mother, Sarah, George, and Harriet, all assembled at the door to welcome her with affectionate eagerness, was a sight to awaken the best feelings of Catherine's heart; and in the embrace of each, as she stepped from the carriage, she found herself soothed beyond any thing that she had believed possible. So surrounded, so caressed, she was even happy! In the joyfulness of family love every thing for a short time was subdued, and the pleasure of seeing her, leaving them at first little leisure for calm curiosity, they were all seated round the tea-table, which Mrs. Morland had hurried for the comfort of the poor traveller, whose pale and jaded looks soon caught her notice, before any inquiry so direct as to demand a positive answer was addressed to her.

Reluctantly, and with much hesitation, did she then begin what might perhaps, at the end of half an hour, be termed by the courtesy of her hearers, an explanation; but scarcely, within that time, could they at all discover the cause, or collect the particulars of her sudden return. They were far from being an irritable race; far from any quickness in catching, or bitterness in resenting, affronts: but here, when the whole was unfolded, was an insult not to be overlooked, nor, for the first half hour, to be easily pardoned. Without suffering any romantic alarm, in the consideration of their daughter's long and lonely journey, Mr. and Mrs. Morland could not but feel that it might have been productive of much unpleasantness to her; that it was what they could never have voluntarily suffered; and that, in forcing her on such a measure, General Tilney had acted neither honourably nor feelingly -- neither as a gentleman nor as a parent. Why he had done it, what could have provoked him to such a breach of hospitality, and so suddenly turned all his partial regard for their daughter into actual ill-will, was a matter which they were at least as far from divining as Catherine herself; but it did not oppress them by any means so long; and, after a due course of useless conjecture, that "it was a strange business, and that he must be a very strange man," grew enough for all their indignation and wonder; though Sarah indeed still indulged in the sweets of incomprehensibility, exclaiming and conjecturing with youthful ardour. "My dear, you give yourself a great deal of needless trouble," said her mother at last; "depend upon it, it is something not at all worth understanding."

"I can allow for his wishing Catherine away, when he recollected this engagement," said Sarah, "but why not do it civilly?"

"I am sorry for the young people," returned Mrs. Morland; "they must have a sad time of it; but as for any thing else, it is no matter now; Catherine is safe at home, and our comfort does not depend upon General Tilney." Catherine sighed. "Well," continued her philosophic mother, "I am glad I did not know of your journey at the time; but now it is all over, perhaps there is no great harm done. It is always good for young people to be put upon exerting themselves; and you know, my dear Catherine, you always were a sad little scatter-brained creature; but now you must have been forced to have your wits about you, with so much changing of chaises and so forth; and I hope it will appear that you have not left any thing behind you in any of the pockets."

Catherine hoped so too, and tried to feel an interest in her own amendment, but her spirits were quite worn down; and, to be silent and alone becoming soon her only wish, she readily agreed to her mother's next counsel of going early to bed. Her parents, seeing nothing in her ill looks and agitation but the natural consequence of mortified feelings, and of the unusual exertion and fatigue of such a journey, parted from her without any doubt of their being soon slept away; and though, when they all met the next morning, her recovery was not equal to their hopes, they were still perfectly unsuspicious of there being any deeper evil. They never once thought of her heart, which, for the parents of a young lady of seventeen, just returned from her first excursion from home, was odd enough!

As soon as breakfast was over, she sat down to fulfil her promise to Miss Tilney, whose trust in the effect of time and distance on her friend's disposition was already justified, for already did Catherine

174

reproach herself with having parted from Eleanor coldly, with having never enough valued her merits or kindness, and never enough commiserated her for what she had been yesterday left to endure. The strength of these feelings, however, was far from assisting her pen; and never had it been harder for her to write than in addressing Eleanor Tilney. To compose a letter which might at once do justice to her sentiments and her situation, convey gratitude without servile regret, be guarded without coldness, and honest without resentment -- a letter which Eleanor might not be pained by the perusal of -- and, above all, which she might not blush herself, if Henry should chance to see, was an undertaking to frighten away all her powers of performance; and, after long thought and much perplexity, to be very brief was all that she could determine on with any confidence of safety. The money therefore which Eleanor had advanced was enclosed with little more than grateful thanks, and the thousand good wishes of a most affectionate heart.

"This has been a strange acquaintance," observed Mrs. Morland, as the letter was finished; "soon made and soon ended. I am sorry it happens so, for Mrs. Allen thought them very pretty kind of young people; and you were sadly out of luck too in your Isabella. Ah! Poor James! Well, we must live and learn; and the next new friends you make I hope will be better worth keeping."

Catherine coloured as she warmly answered, "No friend can be better worth keeping than Eleanor."

"If so, my dear, I dare say you will meet again some time or other; do not be uneasy. It is ten to one but you are thrown together again in the course of a few years; and then what a pleasure it will be!"

Mrs. Morland was not happy in her attempt at consolation. The hope of meeting again in the course of a few years could only put into Catherine's head what might happen within that time to make a meeting dreadful to her. She could never forget Henry Tilney, or think of him with less tenderness than she did at that moment; but he might forget her; and in that case, to meet --! Her eyes filled with tears as she pictured her acquaintance so renewed; and her mother, perceiving her comfortable suggestions to have had no good effect, proposed, as another expedient for restoring her spirits, that they should call on Mrs. Allen.

The two houses were only a quarter of a mile apart; and, as they walked, Mrs. Morland quickly dispatched all that she felt on the score of James's disappointment. "We are sorry for him," said she; "but otherwise there is no harm done in the match going off; for it could not be a desirable thing to have him engaged to a girl whom we had not the smallest acquaintance with, and who was so entirely without fortune; and now, after such behaviour, we cannot think at all well of her. Just at present it comes hard to poor James; but that will not last for ever; and I dare say he will be a discreeter man all his life, for the foolishness of his first choice."

This was just such a summary view of the affair as Catherine could listen to; another sentence might have endangered her complaisance, and made her reply less rational; for soon were all her thinking powers swallowed up in the reflection of her own change of feelings and spirits since last she had trodden that well-known road. It was not three months ago since, wild with joyful expectation, she had there run backwards and forwards some ten times a day, with an heart light, gay, and independent; looking forward to pleasures untasted and unalloyed, and free from the apprehension of evil as from the knowledge of it. Three months ago had seen her all this; and now, how altered a being did she return!

She was received by the Allens with all the kindness which her unlooked-for appearance, acting on a steady affection, would naturally call forth; and great was their surprise, and warm their displeasure, on hearing how she had been treated -- though Mrs. Morland's account of it was no inflated representation, no studied appeal to their passions. "Catherine took us quite by surprise yesterday evening," said she. "She travelled all the way post by herself, and knew nothing of coming till Saturday night; for General Tilney, from some odd fancy or other, all of a sudden grew tired of having her there, and almost turned her out of the house. Very unfriendly, certainly; and he must be a very odd man; but we are so glad to have her amongst us again! And it is a great comfort to find that she is not a poor helpless creature, but can shift very well for herself."

Mr. Allen expressed himself on the occasion with the reasonable resentment of a sensible friend; and Mrs. Allen thought his expressions quite good enough to be immediately made use of again by herself. His wonder, his conjectures, and his explanations became in succession hers, with the addition of this single remark -- "I really have not patience with the General" -- to fill up every accidental pause. And, "I really have not patience with the General," was uttered twice after Mr. Allen left the room, without any relaxation of anger, or any material digression of thought. A more considerable degree of wandering attended the third repetition; and, after completing the fourth, she immediately added, "Only think, my dear, of my having got that frightful great rent in my best Mechlin so charmingly mended, before I left Bath, that one can hardly see where it was. I must shew it you some day or other. Bath is a nice place, Catherine, after all. I assure you I did not above half like coming away. Mrs. Thorpe's being there was such a comfort to us, was not it? You know, you and I were quite forlorn at first."

"Yes, but *that* did not last long," said Catherine, her eyes brightening at the recollection of what had first given spirit to her existence there.

"Very true: we soon met with Mrs. Thorpe, and then we wanted for nothing. My dear, do not you think these silk gloves wear very well? I put them on new the first time of our going to the Lower Rooms, you know, and I have worn them a great deal since. Do you remember that evening?"

"Do I! Oh! Perfectly."

"It was very agreeable, was not it? Mr. Tilney drank tea with us, and I always thought him a great addition, he is so very agreeable. I have a notion you danced with him, but am not quite sure. I remember I had my favourite gown on."

Catherine could not answer; and, after a short trial of other subjects, Mrs. Allen again returned to -- "I really have not patience with the General! Such an agreeable, worthy man as he seemed to be! I do not suppose, Mrs. Morland, you ever saw a better-bred man in your life. His lodgings were taken the very day after he left them, Catherine. But no wonder; Milsom Street, you know."

As they walked home again, Mrs. Morland endeavoured to impress on her daughter's mind the happiness of having such steady well-wishers as Mr. and Mrs. Allen, and the very little consideration which the neglect or unkindness of slight acquaintance like the Tilneys ought to have with her, while she could preserve the good opinion and affection of her earliest friends. There was a great deal of good sense in all this; but there are some situations of the human mind in which good sense has very little power; and Catherine's feelings contradicted almost every position her mother advanced. It was upon the behaviour of these very slight acquaintance that all her present happiness depended; and while Mrs. Morland was successfully confirming her own opinions by the justness of her own representations, Catherine was silently reflecting that *now* Henry must have arrived at Northanger; *now* he must have heard of her departure; and *now*, perhaps, they were all setting off for Hereford.

CHAPTER 30

Catherine's disposition was not naturally sedentary, nor had her habits been ever very industrious; but whatever might hitherto have been her defects of that sort, her mother could not but perceive them now to be greatly increased. She could neither sit still nor employ herself for ten minutes together, walking round the garden and orchard again and again, as if nothing but motion was voluntary; and it seemed as if she could even walk about the house rather than remain fixed for any time in the parlour. Her loss of spirits was a yet greater alteration. In her rambling and her idleness she might only be a caricature of herself; but in her silence and sadness she was the very reverse of all that she had been before.

For two days Mrs. Morland allowed it to pass even without a hint; but when a third night's rest had neither restored her cheerfulness, improved her in useful activity, nor given her a greater inclination for needlework, she could no longer refrain from the gentle reproof of, "My dear Catherine, I am afraid you are growing quite a fine lady. I do not know when poor Richard's cravats would be done, if he had no friend but you. Your head runs too much upon Bath; but there is a time for every thing -- a time for balls and plays, and a time for work. You have had a long run of amusement, and now you must try to be useful."

Catherine took up her work directly, saying, in a dejected voice, that "her head did not run upon Bath -- much."

"Then you are fretting about General Tilney, and that is very simple of you; for ten to one whether you ever see him again. You should never fret about trifles." After a short silence -- "I hope, my Catherine, you are not getting out of humour with home because it is not so grand as Northanger. That would be turning your visit into an evil indeed. Wherever you are you should always be contented, but especially at home, because there you must spend the most of

178

your time. I did not quite like, at breakfast, to hear you talk so much about the French bread at Northanger."

"I am sure I do not care about the bread. It is all the same to me what I eat."

"There is a very clever essay in one of the books up stairs upon much such a subject, about young girls that have been spoilt for home by great acquaintance -- The Mirror, I think. I will look it out for you some day or other, because I am sure it will do you good."

Catherine said no more, and, with an endeavour to do right, applied to her work; but, after a few minutes, sunk again, without knowing it herself, into languor and listlessness, moving herself in her chair, from the irritation of weariness, much oftener than she moved her needle. Mrs. Morland watched the progress of this relapse; and seeing, in her daughter's absent and dissatisfied look, the full proof of that repining spirit to which she had now begun to attribute her want of cheerfulness, hastily left the room to fetch the book in question, anxious to lose no time in attacking so dreadful a malady. It was some time before she could find what she looked for; and other family matters occurring to detain her, a quarter of an hour had elapsed ere she returned down stairs with the volume from which so much was hoped. Her avocations above having shut out all noise but what she created herself, she knew not that a visitor had arrived within the last few minutes, till, on entering the room, the first object she beheld was a young man whom she had never seen before. With a look of much respect, he immediately rose, and being introduced to her by her conscious daughter as "Mr. Henry Tilney," with the embarrassment of real sensibility began to apologize for his appearance there, acknowledging that after what had passed he had little right to expect a welcome at Fullerton, and stating his impatience to be assured of Miss Morland's having reached her home in safety, as the cause of his intrusion. He did not address himself to an uncandid judge or a resentful heart. Far from comprehending him or his sister in their father's misconduct, Mrs. Morland had been always kindly disposed towards each, and instantly, pleased by his appearance, received him with the simple professions of unaffected benevolence; thanking him for such an attention to her daughter, assuring him that the friends of her children were always welcome there, and entreating him to say not another word of the past.

He was not ill-inclined to obey this request, for, though his heart was greatly relieved by such unlooked-for mildness, it was not just at that moment in his power to say any thing to the purpose. Returning in silence to his seat, therefore, he remained for some minutes most civilly answering all Mrs. Morland's common remarks about the weather and roads. Catherine meanwhile -- the anxious, agitated, happy, feverish Catherine -- said not a word; but her glowing cheek and brightened eye made her mother trust that this good-natured visit would at least set her heart at ease for a time, and gladly therefore did she lay aside the first volume of The Mirror for a future hour.

Desirous of Mr. Morland's assistance, as well in giving encouragement, as in finding conversation for her guest, whose embarrassment on his father's account she earnestly pitied, Mrs. Morland had very early dispatched one of the children to summon him; but Mr. Morland was from home -- and being thus without any support, at the end of a quarter of an hour she had nothing to say. After a couple of minutes' unbroken silence, Henry, turning to Catherine for the first time since her mother's entrance, asked her, with sudden alacrity, if Mr. and Mrs. Allen were now at Fullerton? And on developing, from amidst all her perplexity of words in reply, the meaning, which one short syllable would have given, immediately expressed his intention of paying his respects to them, and, with a rising colour, asked her if she would have the goodness to shew him the way. "You may see the house from this window, sir," was information on Sarah's side, which produced only a bow of acknowledgment from the gentleman, and a silencing nod from her mother; for Mrs. Morland, thinking it probable, as a secondary consideration in his wish of waiting on their worthy neighbours, that he might have some explanation to give of his father's behaviour, which it must be more pleasant for him to communicate only to Catherine, would not on any account prevent her accompanying him. They began their walk, and Mrs. Morland was not entirely mistaken in his object in wishing it. Some explanation on his father's account he had to give; but his first purpose was to explain himself, and before they reached Mr. Allen's grounds he had done it so well that Catherine did not think it could ever be repeated too often. She was assured of his affection; and that heart in return was solicited, which, perhaps, they pretty equally knew was already entirely his own; for, though Henry was now sincerely attached to her, though he felt and delighted in all the excellencies of her character and truly loved her society, I must confess that his affection originated in nothing better than gratitude, or, in other words, that a persuasion of her partiality for him had been the only cause of giving her a serious thought. It is a new circumstance in romance, I acknowledge, and dreadfully derogatory of an heroine's dignity; but if it be as new in common life, the credit of a wild imagination will at least be all my own.

A very short visit to Mrs. Allen, in which Henry talked at random, without sense or connexion, and Catherine, wrapt in the contemplation of her own unutterable happiness, scarcely opened her lips, dismissed them to the ecstasies of another tête-à-tête; and before it was suffered to close, she was enabled to judge how far he was sanctioned by parental authority in his present application. On his return from Woodston, two days before, he had been met near the Abbey by his impatient father, hastily informed in angry terms of Miss Morland's departure, and ordered to think of her no more.

Such was the permission upon which he had now offered her his hand. The affrighted Catherine, amidst all the terrors of expectation, as she listened to this account, could not but rejoice in the kind caution with which Henry had saved her from the necessity of a conscientious rejection, by engaging her faith before he mentioned the subject; and as he proceeded to give the particulars, and explain the motives of his father's conduct, her feelings soon hardened into even a triumphant delight. The General had had nothing to accuse her of, nothing to lay to her charge, but her being the involuntary, unconscious object of a deception which his pride could not pardon, and which a better pride would have been ashamed to own. She was guilty only of being less rich than he had supposed her to be. Under a mistaken persuasion of her possessions and claims, he had courted her acquaintance in Bath, solicited her company at Northanger, and designed her for his daughter-in-law. On discovering his error, to turn her from the house seemed the best, though to his feelings an inadequate proof of his resentment towards herself, and his contempt of her family.

John Thorpe had first misled him. The General, perceiving his son one night at the theatre to be paying considerable attention to Miss Morland, had accidentally inquired of Thorpe if he knew more of her than her name. Thorpe, most happy to be on speaking terms with a man of General Tilney's importance, had been joyfully and proudly communicative; and being at that time not only in daily expectation of Morland's engaging Isabella, but likewise pretty well resolved upon marrying Catherine himself, his vanity induced him to represent the family as yet more wealthy than his vanity and avarice had made him believe them. With whomsoever he was, or was likely to be connected, his own consequence always required that theirs should be great, and as his intimacy with any acquaintance grew, so regularly grew their fortune. The expectations of his friend Morland, therefore, from the first overrated, had ever since his introduction to Isabella been gradually increasing; and by merely adding twice as much for the grandeur of the moment, by doubling what he chose to think the amount of Mr. Morland's preferment, trebling his private fortune, bestowing a rich aunt, and sinking half the children, he was able to represent the whole family to the General in a most respectable light. For Catherine, however, the peculiar object of the General's curiosity, and his own speculations, he had yet something more in reserve, and the ten or fifteen thousand pounds which her father could give her would be a pretty addition to Mr. Allen's estate. Her intimacy there had made him seriously determine on her being handsomely legacied hereafter; and to speak of her therefore as the almost acknowledged future heiress of Fullerton naturally followed. Upon such intelligence the General had proceeded; for never had it occurred to him to doubt its authority. Thorpe's interest in the family, by his sister's approaching connexion with one of its members, and his own views on another (circumstances of which he boasted with almost equal openness), seemed sufficient vouchers for his truth; and to these were added the absolute facts of the Allens being wealthy and childless, of Miss Morland's being under their care, and -- as soon as his acquaintance allowed him to judge -- of their treating her with parental kindness. His resolution was soon formed. Already had he discerned a liking towards Miss Morland in the countenance of his son; and thankful for Mr. Thorpe's communication, he almost instantly determined to spare no pains in weakening his boasted interest and ruining his dearest hopes. Catherine herself could not be more ignorant at the time of all this, than his own children. Henry and Eleanor, perceiving nothing in her situation likely to engage their father's particular respect, had seen with astonishment the suddenness, continuance and extent of his attention; and though latterly, from some hints which had accompanied an almost positive command to his son of doing every thing in his power to attach her, Henry was convinced of his father's believing it to be an advantageous connexion, it was not till the late explanation at Northanger that they had the smallest idea of the false calculations which had hurried him on. That they were false, the General had learnt from the very person who had suggested them, from Thorpe himself, whom he had chanced to meet again in town, and who, under the influence of exactly opposite feelings, irritated by Catherine's refusal, and yet more by the failure of a very recent endeavour to accomplish a reconciliation between Morland and Isabella, convinced that they were separated for ever, and spurning a friendship which could be no longer serviceable, hastened to contradict all that he had said before to the advantage of the Morlands -- confessed himself to have been totally mistaken in his opinion of their circumstances and character, misled by the rhodomontade of his friend to believe his father a man of substance and credit, whereas the transactions of the two or three last weeks proved him to be neither; for after coming eagerly forward on the first overture of a marriage between the families, with the most liberal proposals, he had, on being brought to the point by the shrewdness of the relator, been constrained to acknowledge himself incapable of giving the young people even a decent support. They were, in fact, a necessitous family; numerous, too, almost beyond example; by no means respected in their own neighbourhood, as he had lately had particular opportunities of discovering; aiming at a style of life which their fortune could not warrant; seeking to better themselves by wealthy connexions; a forward, bragging, scheming race.

The terrified General pronounced the name of Allen with an inquiring look; and here too Thorpe had learnt his error. The Allens, he believed, had lived near them too long, and he knew the young man on whom the Fullerton estate must devolve. The General needed no more. Enraged with almost every body in the world but himself, he set out the next day for the Abbey, where his performances have been seen.

I leave it to my reader's sagacity to determine how much of all this it was possible for Henry to communicate at this time to Catherine, how much of it he could have learnt from his father, in what points his own conjectures might assist him, and what portion must yet remain to be told in a letter from James. I have united for their case what they must divide for mine. Catherine, at any rate, heard enough to feel that in suspecting General Tilney of either murdering or shutting up his wife, she had scarcely sinned against his character, or magnified his cruelty.

Henry, in having such things to relate of his father, was almost as pitiable as in their first avowal to himself. He blushed for the narrow-minded counsel which he was obliged to expose. The conversation between them at Northanger had been of the most unfriendly kind. Henry's indignation on hearing how Catherine had been treated, on comprehending his father's views, and being ordered to acquiesce in them, had been open and bold. The General, accustomed on every ordinary occasion to give the law in his family, prepared for no reluctance but of feeling, no opposing desire that should dare to clothe itself in words, could ill brook the opposition of his son, steady as the sanction of reason and the dictate of conscience could make it. But, in such a cause, his anger, though it must shock, could not intimidate Henry, who was sustained in his purpose by a conviction of its justice. He felt himself bound as much in honour as in affection to Miss Morland, and believing that heart to be his own which he had been directed to gain, no unworthy retraction of a tacit consent, no reversing decree of unjustifiable anger, could shake his fidelity, or influence the resolutions it prompted.

He steadily refused to accompany his father into Herefordshire, an engagement formed almost at the moment to promote the dismissal of Catherine, and as steadily declared his intention of offering her his hand. The General was furious in his anger, and they parted in dreadful disagreement. Henry, in an agitation of mind which many solitary hours were required to compose, had returned almost instantly to Woodston, and, on the afternoon of the following day, had begun his journey to Fullerton.

CHAPTER 31

Mr. and Mrs. Morland's surprise on being applied to by Mr. Tilney for their consent to his marrying their daughter was, for a few minutes, considerable, it having never entered their heads to suspect an attachment on either side; but as nothing, after all, could be more natural than Catherine's being beloved, they soon learnt to consider it with only he happy agitation of gratified pride, and, as far as they alone were concerned, had not a single objection to start. His pleasing manners and good sense were self-evident recommendations; and having never heard evil of him, it was not their way to suppose any evil could be told. Good-will supplying the place of experience, his character needed no attestation. "Catherine would make a sad, heedless young house-keeper to be sure," was her mother's foreboding remark; but quick was the consolation of there being nothing like practice.

There was but one obstacle, in short, to be mentioned; but till that one was removed, it must be impossible for them to sanction the engagement. Their tempers were mild, but their principles were steady, and while his parent so expressly forbade the connexion, they could not allow themselves to encourage it. That the General should come forward to solicit the alliance, or that he should even very heartily approve it, they were not refined enough to make any parading stipulation; but the decent appearance of consent must be yielded, and that once obtained -- and their own hearts made them trust that it could not be very long denied -- their willing approbation was instantly to follow. His consent was all that they wished for. They were no more inclined than entitled to demand his money. Of a very considerable fortune, his son was, by marriage settlements, eventually secure; his present income was an income of independence and comfort, and under every pecuniary view, it was a match beyond the claims of their daughter.

The young people could not be surprised at a decision like this. They felt and they deplored -- but they could not resent it; and they parted, endeavouring to hope that such a change in the General, as each believed almost impossible, might speedily take place, to unite them again in the fullness of privileged affection. Henry returned to what was now his only home, to watch over his young plantations, and extend his improvements for her sake, to whose share in them he looked anxiously forward; and Catherine remained at Fullerton to cry. Whether the torments of absence were softened by a clandestine correspondence, let us not inquire. Mr. and Mrs. Morland never did -- they had been too kind to exact any promise; and whenever Catherine received a letter, as, at that time, happened pretty often, they always looked another way.

The anxiety, which in this state of their attachment must be the portion of Henry and Catherine, and of all who loved either, as to its final event, can hardly extend, I fear, to the bosom of my readers, who will see in the tell-tale compression of the pages before them, that we are all hastening together to perfect felicity. The means by which their early marriage was effected can be the only doubt: what probable circumstance could work upon a temper like the General's? The circumstance which chiefly availed was the marriage of his daughter with a man of fortune and consequence, which took place in the course of the summer -- an accession of dignity that threw him into a fit of good-humour, from which he did not recover till after Eleanor had obtained his forgiveness of Henry, and his permission for him "to be a fool if he liked it!"

The marriage of Eleanor Tilney, her removal from all the evils of such a home as Northanger had been made by Henry's banishment, to the home of her choice and the man of her choice, is an event which I expect to give general satisfaction among all her acquaintance. My own joy on the occasion is very sincere. I know no one more entitled, by unpretending merit, or better prepared by habitual suffering, to receive and enjoy felicity. Her partiality for this gentleman was not of recent origin; and he had been long withheld only by inferiority of situation from addressing her. His unexpected accession to title and fortune had removed all his difficulties; and never had the General loved his daughter so well in all her hours of companionship, utility, and patient endurance as when he first hailed her, "Your Ladyship!" Her husband was really deserving of her; independent of his peerage, his wealth, and his attachment, being to a precision the most charming young man in the world. Any further definition of his merits must be unnecessary; the most charming young man in the world is instantly before the imagination of us all. Concerning the one in question, therefore, I have only to add -- aware that the rules of composition forbid the introduction of a character not connected with my fable -- that this was the very gentleman whose negligent servant left behind him that collection of washing-bills, resulting from a long visit at Northanger, by which my heroine was involved in one of her most alarming adventures.

The influence of the Viscount and Viscountess in their brother's behalf was assisted by that right understanding of Mr. Morland's circumstances which, as soon as the General would allow himself to be informed, they were qualified to give. It taught him that he had been scarcely more misled by Thorpe's first boast of the family wealth than by his subsequent malicious overthrow of it; that in no sense of the word were they necessitous or poor, and that Catherine would have three thousand pounds. This was so material an amendment of his late expectations that it greatly contributed to smooth the descent of his pride; and by no means without its effect was the private intelligence, which he was at some pains to procure, that the Fullerton estate, being entirely at the disposal of its present proprietor, was consequently open to every greedy speculation.

On the strength of this, the General, soon after Eleanor's marriage, permitted his son to return to Northanger, and thence made him the bearer of his consent, very courteously worded in a page full of empty professions to Mr. Morland. The event which it authorized soon followed: Henry and Catherine were married, the bells rang, and every body smiled; and, as this took place within a twelvemonth from the first day of their meeting, it will not appear, after all the dreadful delays occasioned by the General's cruelty, that they were essentially hurt by it. To begin perfect happiness at the respective ages of twenty-six and eighteen is to do pretty well; and professing myself moreover convinced that the General's unjust interference, so far from being really injurious to their felicity, was perhaps rather conducive to it, by improving their knowledge of each other, and adding strength to their attachment, I leave it to be settled, by whomsoever it may concern, whether the tendency of this work be altogether to recommend parental tyranny, or reward filial disobedience.

NIGHTMARE ABBEY

by Thomas Love Peacock

*   *   *   *   *

There's a dark lantern of the spirit,
Which none see by but those who bear it,
That makes them in the dark see visions
And hag themselves with apparitions,
Find racks for their own minds, and vaunt
Of their own misery and want.

BUTLER.

*   *   *   *   *

Matthew. Oh! it's your only fine humour, sir. Your true melancholy breeds your perfect fine wit, sir. I am melancholy myself, divers times, sir; and then do I no more but take pen and paper presently, and overflow you half a score or a dozen of sonnets at a sitting.
Stephen. Truly, sir, and I love such things out of measure.
Matthew. Why, I pray you, sir, make use of my study: it's at your service.
Stephen. I thank you, sir, I shall be bold, I warrant you. Have you a stool there, to be melancholy upon?

BEN JONSON, *Every Man in his Humour*, Act 3, Sc. 1

Ay esleu gazouiller et siffler oye, comme dit le commun proverbe, entre les cygnes, plutoust que d'estre entre tant de gentils poëtes et faconds orateurs mut du tout estimé.

RABELAIS, Prol. L. 5

189

CHAPTER 1

Nightmare Abbey, a venerable family-mansion, in a highly picturesque state of semi-dilapidation, pleasantly situated on a strip of dry land between the sea and the fens, at the verge of the county of Lincoln, had the honour to be the seat of Christopher Glowry, Esquire. This gentleman was naturally of an atrabilarious temperament, and much troubled with those phantoms of indigestion which are commonly called *blue devils*. He had been deceived in an early friendship: he had been crossed in love; and had offered his hand, from pique, to a lady, who accepted it from interest, and who, in so doing, violently tore asunder the bonds of a tried and youthful attachment. Her vanity was gratified by being the mistress of a very extensive, if not very lively, establishment; but all the springs of her sympathies were frozen. Riches she possessed, but that which enriches them, the participation of affection, was wanting. All that they could purchase for her became indifferent to her, because that which they could not purchase, and which was more valuable than themselves, she had, for their sake, thrown away. She discovered, when it was too late, that she had mistaken the means for the end -- that riches, rightly used, are instruments of happiness, but are not in themselves happiness. In this wilful blight of her affections, she found them valueless as means: they had been the end to which she had immolated all her affections, and were now the only end that remained to her. She did not confess this to herself as a principle of action, but it operated through the medium of unconscious self-deception, and terminated in inveterate avarice. She laid on external things the blame of her mind's internal disorder, and thus became by degrees an accomplished scold. She often went her daily rounds through a series of deserted apartments, every creature in the house vanishing at the creak of her shoe, much more at the sound of her voice, to which the nature of things affords no simile; for, as far as the voice of woman, when attuned by gentleness and love, transcends all other sounds in harmony, so far does it surpass all others in discord, when stretched into unnatural shrillness by anger and impatience.

Mr. Glowry used to say that his house was no better than a spacious kennel, for every one in it led the life of a dog. Disappointed both in love and in friendship, and looking upon human learning as vanity, he had come to a conclusion that there was but one good thing in the world, videlicet, a good dinner; and this his parsimonious lady seldom suffered him to enjoy: but, one morning, like Sir Leoline in Christabel, "he woke and found his lady dead," and remained a very consolate widower, with one small child.

This only son and heir Mr. Glowry had christened Scythrop, from the name of a maternal ancestor, who had hanged himself one rainy day in a fit of toedium vitae, and had been eulogised by a coroner's jury in the comprehensive phrase of felo de se; on which account, Mr. Glowry held his memory in high honour, and made a punchbowl of his skull.

When Scythrop grew up, he was sent, as usual, to a public school, where a little learning was painfully beaten into him, and from thence to the University, where it was carefully taken out of him; and he was sent home like a well-threshed ear of corn, with nothing in his head: having finished his education to the high satisfaction of the master and fellows of his college, who had, in testimony of their approbation, presented him with a silver fish-slice, on which his name figured at the head of a laudatory inscription in some semi-barbarous dialect of Anglo-Saxonised Latin.

His fellow-students, however, who drove tandem and random in great perfection, and were connoisseurs in good inns, had taught him to drink deep ere he departed. He had passed much of his time with these choice spirits, and had seen the rays of the midnight lamp tremble on many a lengthening file of empty bottles. He passed his vacations sometimes at Nightmare Abbey, sometimes in London, at the house of his uncle, Mr. Hilary, a very cheerful and elastic gentleman, who had married the sister of the melancholy Mr. Glowry. The company that frequented his house was the gayest of the gay. Scythrop danced with the ladies and drank with the gentlemen, and was pronounced by both a very accomplished charming fellow, and an honour to the University.

At the house of Mr. Hilary, Scythrop first saw the beautiful Miss Emily Girouette. He fell in love; which is nothing new. He was favourably received; which is nothing strange. Mr. Glowry and Mr. Girouette had a meeting on the occasion, and quarrelled about the terms of the bargain; which is neither new nor strange. The lovers were torn asunder, weeping and vowing everlasting constancy; and, in three weeks after this tragical event, the lady was led a smiling bride to the altar, by the Honourable Mr. Lackwit; which is neither strange nor new.

Scythrop received this intelligence at Nightmare Abbey, and was half distracted on the occasion. It was his first disappointment, and preyed deeply on his sensitive spirit. His father, to comfort him, read him a Commentary on Ecclesiastes, which he had himself composed, and which demonstrated incontrovertibly that all is vanity. He insisted particularly on the text, "One man among a thousand have I found, but a woman amongst all those have I not found."

"How could he expect it," said Scythrop, "when the whole thousand were locked up in his seraglio? His experience is no precedent for a free state of society like that in which we live."

"Locked up or at large," said Mr. Glowry, "the result is the same: their minds are always locked up, and vanity and interest keep the key. I speak feelingly, Scythrop."

"I am sorry for it, sir," said Scythrop. "But how is it that their minds are locked up? The fault is in their artificial education, which studiously models them into mere musical dolls, to be set out for sale in the great toy-shop of society."

"To be sure," said Mr. Glowry, "their education is not so well finished as yours has been; and your idea of a musical doll is good. I bought one myself, but it was confoundedly out of tune; but, whatever be the cause, Scythrop, the effect is certainly this, that one is pretty nearly as good as another, as far as any judgment can be formed of them before marriage. It is only after marriage that they shew their true qualities, as I know by bitter experience. Marriage is therefore a lottery, and the less choice and selection a man bestows on his ticket the better; for, if he has incurred considerable pains and expense to obtain a lucky number, and his lucky number proves a blank, he experiences not a simple, but a complicated disappointment; the loss of labour and money being superadded to the disappointment of drawing a blank, which, constituting simply and entirely the grievance of him who has chosen his ticket at random, is, from its simplicity, the more endurable." This very excellent reasoning was thrown away upon Scythrop, who retired to his tower as dismal and disconsolate as before.

The tower which Scythrop inhabited stood at the south-eastern angle of the Abbey; and, on the southern side, the foot of the tower opened on a terrace, which was called the garden, though nothing grew on it but ivy, and a few amphibious weeds. The south-western tower, which was ruinous and full of owls, might, with equal propriety, have been called the aviary. This terrace or garden, or terrace-garden, or garden-terrace (the reader may name it *ad libitum*), took in an oblique view of the open sea, and fronted a long tract of level sea-coast, and a fine monotony of fens and windmills.

The reader will judge, from what we have said, that this building was a sort of castellated abbey; and it will, probably, occur to him to inquire if it had been one of the strong-holds of the ancient church militant. Whether this was the case, or how far it had been indebted to the taste of Mr. Glowry's ancestors for any transmutations from its original state, are, unfortunately, circumstances not within the pale of our knowledge.

The north-western tower contained the apartments of Mr. Glowry. The moat at its base, and the fens beyond, comprised the whole of his prospect. This moat surrounded the Abbey, and was in immediate contact with the walls on every side but the south.

The north-eastern tower was appropriated to the domestics, whom Mr. Glowry always chose by one of two criterions, -- a long face, or a dismal name. His butler was Raven; his steward was Crow; his valet was Skellet. Mr. Glowry maintained that the valet was of French extraction, and that his name was Squelette. His grooms were Mattocks and Graves. On one occasion, being in want of a footman, he received a letter from a person signing himself Diggory Deathshead, and lost no time in securing this acquisition; but on Diggory's arrival, Mr. Glowry was horror-struck by the sight of a round ruddy face, and a pair of laughing eyes. Deathshead was always grinning, -- not a ghastly smile, but the grin of a comic mask; and disturbed the echoes of the hall with so much unhallowed laughter, that Mr. Glowry gave him his discharge. Diggory, however, had stayed long enough to make conquests of all the old gentleman's maids, and left him a flourishing colony of young Deathsheads to join chorus with the owls, that had before been the exclusive choristers of Nightmare Abbey.

The main body of the building was divided into rooms of state, spacious apartments for feasting, and numerous bed-rooms for visitors, who, however, were few and far between.

Family interests compelled Mr. Glowry to receive occasional visits from Mr. and Mrs. Hilary, who paid them from the same motive; and, as the lively gentleman on these occasions found few conductors for his exuberant gaiety, he became like a double-charged electric jar, which often exploded in some burst of outrageous merriment to the signal discomposure of Mr. Glowry's nerves.

Another occasional visitor, much more to Mr. Glowry's taste, was Mr. Flosky,* a very lachrymose and morbid gentleman, of some note in the literary world, but in his own estimation of much more merit than name. The part of his character which recommended him to Mr. Glowry was his very fine sense of the grim and the tearful. No one could relate a dismal story with so many minutiæ of supererogatory wretchedness. No one could call up a raw-head and bloody-bones with so many adjuncts and circumstances of ghastliness. Mystery was his mental element. He lived in the midst of that visionary world in which nothing is but what is not. He dreamed with his eyes open, and saw ghosts dancing round him at noontide. He had been in his youth an enthusiast for liberty, and had hailed the dawn of the French Revolution as the promise of a day that was to banish war and slavery, and every form of vice and misery, from the face of the earth. Because all this was not done, he deduced that nothing was done; and from this deduction, according to his system of logic, he drew a conclusion that worse than nothing was done; that the overthrow of the feudal fortresses of tyranny and superstition was the greatest calamity that had ever befallen mankind; and that their only hope now was to rake the rubbish together, and rebuild it without any of those loopholes by which the light had originally crept in. To qualify himself for a coadjutor in this laudable task, he plunged into the central opacity of Kantian metaphysics, and lay *perdu* several years in transcendental darkness, till the common daylight of common sense became intolerable to his eyes. He called the sun an *ignis fatuus*; and exhorted all who would listen to his friendly voice, which were about as many as called "God save King Richard," to shelter themselves from its delusive radiance in the obscure haunt of Old Philosophy. This word Old had great charms for him. The good old times were always on his lips; meaning the days when polemic theology was in its prime, and rival prelates beat the drum ecclesiastic with Herculean vigour, till the one wound up his series

---

* Mr. Flosky: A corruption of Filosky, quasi *Philoschios*, a lover, or sector, of shadows.

of syllogisms with the very orthodox conclusion of roasting the other.

But the dearest friend of Mr. Glowry, and his most welcome guest, was Mr. Toobad, the Manichaean Millenarian. The twelfth verse of the twelfth chapter of Revelations was always in his mouth: "Woe to the inhabiters of the earth and of the sea, for the devil is come among you, having great wrath, because he knoweth that he hath but a short time." He maintained that the supreme dominion of the world was, for wise purposes, given over for a while to the Evil Principle; and that this precise period of time, commonly called the enlightened age, was the point of his plenitude of power. He used to add that by and by he would be cast down, and a high and happy order of things succeed; but he never omitted the saving clause, "Not in our time"; which last words were always echoed in doleful response by the sympathetic Mr. Glowry.

Another and very frequent visitor was the Reverend Mr. Larynx, the vicar of Claydyke, a village about ten miles distant; -- a good-natured accommodating divine, who was always most obligingly ready to take a dinner and a bed at the house of any country gentleman in distress for a companion. Nothing came amiss to him, -- a game at billiards, at chess, at draughts, at backgammon, at piquet, or at all-fours in a tête-à-tête, -- or any game on the cards, round, square, or triangular, in a party of any number exceeding two. He would even dance among friends, rather than that a lady, even if she were on the wrong side of thirty, should sit still for want of a partner. For a ride, a walk, or a sail, in the morning, -- a song after dinner, a ghost story after supper, -- a bottle of port with the squire, or a cup of green tea with his lady, -- for all or any of these, or for any thing else that was agreeable to any one else, consistently with the dye of his coat, the Reverend Mr. Larynx was at all times equally ready. When at Nightmare Abbey, he would condole with Mr. Glowry, -- drink Madeira with Scythrop, -- crack jokes with Mr. Hilary, -- hand Mrs. Hilary to the piano, take charge of her fan and gloves, and turn over her music with surprising dexterity, -- quote Revelations with Mr. Toobad, -- and lament the good old times of feudal darkness with the transcendental Mr. Flosky.

CHAPTER 2

Shortly after the disastrous termination of Scythrop's passion for Miss Emily Girouette, Mr. Glowry found himself, much against his will, involved in a lawsuit, which compelled him to dance attendance on the High Court of Chancery. Scythrop was left alone at Nightmare Abbey. He was a burnt child, and dreaded the fire of female eyes. He wandered about the ample pile, or along the garden-terrace, with "his cogitative faculties immersed in cogibundity of cogitation." The terrace terminated at the south-western tower, which, as we have said, was ruinous and full of owls. Here would Scythrop take his evening seat, on a fallen fragment of mossy stone, with his back resting against the ruined wall, -- a thick canopy of ivy, with an owl in it, over his head, -- and the Sorrows of Werter in his hand. He had some taste for romance reading before he went to the university, where, we must confess, in justice to his college, he was cured of the love of reading in all its shapes; and the cure would have been radical, if disappointment in love, and total solitude, had not conspired to bring on a relapse. He began to devour romances and German tragedies, and, by the recommendation of Mr. Flosky, to pore over ponderous tomes of transcendental philosophy, which reconciled him to the labour of studying them by their mystical jargon and necromantic imagery. In the congenial solitude of Nightmare Abbey, the distempered ideas of metaphysical romance and romantic metaphysics had ample time and space to germinate into a fertile crop of chimæras, which rapidly shot up into vigorous and abundant vegetation.

He now became troubled with the *passion for reforming the world*.* He built many castles in the air, and peopled them with secret tribunals, and bands of illuminati, who were always the imaginary instruments of his projected regeneration of the human species. As he intended to institute a perfect republic, he invested himself with absolute sovereignty over these mystical dispensers of liberty. He slept with Horrid Mysteries under his pillow, and dreamed of venerable eleutherarchs and ghastly confederates holding midnight conventions in subterranean caves. He passed whole mornings in his study, immersed in gloomy reverie, stalking

---

* *passion for reforming the world*: See Forsyth's *Principles of Moral Science.*

about the room in his nightcap, which he pulled over his eyes like a cowl, and folding his striped calico dressing-gown about him like the mantle of a conspirator.

"Action," thus he soliloquised, "is the result of opinion, and to new-model opinion would be to new-model society. Knowledge is power; it is in the hands of a few, who employ it to mislead the many, for their own selfish purposes of aggrandisement and appropriation. What if it were in the hands of a few who should employ it to lead the many? What if it were universal, and the multitude were enlightened? No. The many must be always in leading-strings; but let them have wise and honest conductors. A few to think, and many to act; that is the only basis of perfect society. So thought the ancient philosophers: they had their esoterical and exoterical doctrines. So thinks the sublime Kant, who delivers his oracles in language which none but the initiated can comprehend. Such were the views of those secret associations of illuminati, which were the terror of superstition and tyranny, and which, carefully selecting wisdom and genius from the great wilderness of society, as the bee selects honey from the flowers of the thorn and the nettle, bound all human excellence in a chain, which, if it had not been prematurely broken, would have commanded opinion, and regenerated the world."

Scythrop proceeded to meditate on the practicability of reviving a confederation of regenerators. To get a clear view of his own ideas, and to feel the pulse of the wisdom and genius of the age, he wrote and published a treatise, in which his meanings were carefully wrapt up in the monk's hood of transcendental technology, but filled with hints of matter deep and dangerous, which he thought would set the whole nation in a ferment; and he awaited the result in awful expectation, as a miner who has fired a train awaits the explosion of a rock. However, he listened and heard nothing; for the explosion, if any ensued, was not sufficiently loud to shake a single leaf of the ivy on the towers of Nightmare Abbey; and some months afterwards he received a letter from his bookseller, informing him that only seven copies had been sold, and concluding with a polite request for the balance.

Scythrop did not despair. "Seven copies," he thought, "have been sold. Seven is a mystical number, and the omen is good. Let me find the seven purchasers of my seven copies, and they shall be the seven golden candle-sticks with which I will illuminate the world."

Scythrop had a certain portion of mechanical genius, which his romantic projects tended to develop. He constructed models of cells and recesses, sliding panels and secret passages, that would have baffled the skill of the Parisian police. He took the opportunity of his father's absence to smuggle a dumb carpenter into the Abbey, and between them they gave reality to one of these models in Scythrop's tower. Scythrop foresaw that a great leader of human regeneration would be involved in fearful dilemmas, and determined, for the benefit of mankind in general, to adopt all possible precautions for the preservation of himself.

The servants, even the women, had been tutored into silence. Profound stillness reigned throughout and around the Abbey, except when the occasional shutting of a door would peal in long reverberations through the galleries, or the heavy tread of the pensive butler would wake the hollow echoes of the hall. Scythrop stalked about like the grand inquisitor, and the servants flitted past him like familiars. In his evening meditations on the terrace, under the ivy of the ruined tower, the only sounds that came to his ear were the rustling of the wind in the ivy, the plaintive voices of the feathered choristers, the owls, the occasional striking of the Abbey clock, and the monotonous dash of the sea on its low and level shore. In the mean time, he drank Madeira, and laid deep schemes for a thorough repair of the crazy fabric of human nature.

CHAPTER 3

Mr. Glowry returned from London with the loss of his lawsuit. Justice was with him, but the law was against him. He found Scythrop in a mood most sympathetically tragic, and they vied with each other in enlivening their cups by lamenting the depravity of this degenerate age, and occasionally interspersing divers grim jokes about graves, worms, and epitaphs. Mr. Glowry's friends, whom we have mentioned in the first chapter, availed themselves of his return to pay him a simultaneous visit. At the same time arrived Scythrop's friend and fellow-collegian, the Honourable Mr. Listless. Mr. Glowry had discovered this fashionable young gentleman in London, "stretched on the rack of a too easy chair," and devoured with a gloomy and misanthropical *nil curo*, and had pressed him so earnestly to take the benefit of the pure country air, at Nightmare Abbey, that Mr. Listless, finding it would give him more trouble to refuse than to comply, summoned his French valet, Fatout, and told him he was going to Lincolnshire. On this simple hint, Fatout went to work, and the imperials were packed, and the post-chariot was at the door, without the Honourable Mr. Listless having said or thought another syllable on the subject.

Mr. and Mrs. Hilary brought with them an orphan niece, a daughter of Mr. Glowry's youngest sister, who had made a runaway love-match with an Irish officer. The lady's fortune disappeared in the first year: love, by a natural consequence, disappeared in the second: the Irishman himself, by a still more natural consequence, disappeared in the third. Mr. Glowry had allowed his sister an annuity, and she had lived in retirement with her only daughter, whom, at her death, which had recently happened, she commended to the care of Mrs. Hilary.

Miss Marionetta Celestina O'Carroll was a very blooming and accomplished young lady. Being a compound of the *Allegro Vivace* of the O'Carrolls, and of the *Andante Doloroso* of the Glowries, she exhibited in her own character all the diversities of an April sky. Her hair was light-brown; her eyes hazel, and sparkling with a mild but fluctuating light; her features regular; her lips full, and of equal size; and her person surpassingly graceful. She was a proficient in music. Her conversation was sprightly, but always on subjects light in their nature and limited in their interest: for moral sympathies, in any general sense, had no place in her mind. She had some coquetry, and more caprice, liking and disliking almost in the same moment; pursuing an object with earnestness while it seemed unattainable, and rejecting it when in her power as not worth the trouble of possession.

Whether she was touched with a *penchant* for her cousin Scythrop, or was merely curious to see what effect the tender passion would have on so *outré* a person, she had not been three days in the Abbey before she threw out all the lures of her beauty and accomplishments to make a prize of his heart. Scythrop proved an easy conquest. The image of Miss Emily Girouette was already sufficiently dimmed by the power of philosophy and the exercise of reason: for to these influences, or to any influence but the true one, are usually ascribed the mental cures performed by the great physician Time. Scythrop's romantic dreams had indeed given him

200

many *pure anticipated cognitions* of combinations of beauty and intelligence, which, he had some misgivings, were not exactly realised in his cousin Marionetta; but, in spite of these misgivings, he soon became distractedly in love; which, when the young lady clearly perceived, she altered her tactics, and assumed as much coldness and reserve as she had before shown ardent and ingenuous attachment. Scythrop was confounded at the sudden change; but, instead of falling at her feet and requesting an explanation, he retreated to his tower, muffled himself in his nightcap, seated himself in the president's chair of his imaginary secret tribunal, summoned Marionetta with all terrible formalities, frightened her out of her wits, disclosed himself, and clasped the beautiful penitent to his bosom.

While he was acting this reverie -- in the moment in which the awful president of the secret tribunal was throwing back his cowl and his mantle, and discovering himself to the lovely culprit as her adoring and magnanimous lover, the door of the study opened, and the real Marionetta appeared.

The motives which had led her to the tower were a little penitence, a little concern, a little affection, and a little fear as to what the sudden secession of Scythrop, occasioned by her sudden change of manner, might portend. She had tapped several times unheard, and of course unanswered; and at length, timidly and cautiously opening the door, she discovered him standing up before a black velvet chair, which was mounted on an old oak table, in the act of throwing open his striped calico dressing-gown, and flinging away his nightcap -- which is what the French call an imposing attitude.

Each stood a few moments fixed in their respective places -- the lady in astonishment, and the gentleman in confusion. Marionetta was the first to break silence. "For heaven's sake," said she, "my dear Scythrop, what is the matter?"

"For heaven's sake, indeed!" said Scythrop, springing from the table; "for your sake, Marionetta, and you are my heaven, -- distraction is the matter. I adore you, Marionetta, and your cruelty drives me mad." He threw himself at her knees, devoured her hand with kisses, and breathed a thousand vows in the most passionate language of romance.

Marionetta listened a long time in silence, till her lover had exhausted his eloquence and paused for a reply. She then said, with a very arch look, "I prithee deliver thyself like a man of this world." The levity of this quotation, and of the manner in which it was delivered, jarred so discordantly on the high-wrought enthusiasm of the romantic inamorato, that he sprang upon his feet, and beat his forehead with his clenched fist. The young lady was terrified; and, deeming it expedient to soothe him, took one of his hands in hers, placed the other hand on his shoulder, looked up in his face with a winning seriousness, and said, in the tenderest possible tone, "What would you have, Scythrop?"

Scythrop was in heaven again. "What would I have? What but you, Marionetta? You, for the companion of my studies, the partner of my thoughts, the auxiliary of my great designs for the emancipation of mankind."

"I am afraid I should be but a poor auxiliary, Scythrop. What would you have me do?"

"Do as Rosalia does with Carlos, divine Marionetta. Let us each open a vein in the other's arm, mix our blood in a bowl, and drink it as a sacrament of love. Then we shall see visions of transcendental illumination, and soar on the wings of ideas into the space of pure intelligence."

Marionetta could not reply; she had not so strong a stomach as Rosalia, and turned sick at the proposition. She disengaged herself suddenly from Scythrop, sprang through the door of the tower, and fled with precipitation along the corridors. Scythrop pursued her, crying, "Stop, stop, Marionetta -- my life, my love!" and was gaining rapidly on her flight, when, at an ill-omened corner, where two corridors ended in an angle, at the head of a staircase, he came into sudden and violent contact with Mr. Toobad, and they both plunged together to the foot of the stairs, like two billiard-balls into one pocket. This gave the young lady time to escape, and enclose herself in her chamber; while Mr. Toobad, rising slowly, and rubbing his knees and shoulders, said, "You see, my dear Scythrop, in this little incident, one of the innumerable proofs of the temporary supremacy of the devil; for what but a systematic design and concurrent contrivance of evil could have made the angles of time and place coincide in our unfortunate persons at the head of this accursed staircase?"

"Nothing else, certainly," said Scythrop: "you are perfectly in the right, Mr. Toobad. Evil, and mischief, and misery, and confusion, and vanity, and vexation of spirit, and death, and disease, and assassination, and war, and poverty, and pestilence, and famine, and avarice, and selfishness, and rancour, and jealousy, and spleen, and malevolence, and the disappointments of philanthropy, and the faithlessness of friendship, and the crosses of love -- all prove the accuracy of your views, and the truth of your system; and it is not impossible that the infernal interruption of this fall downstairs may throw a colour of evil on the whole of my future existence."

"My dear boy," said Mr. Toobad, "you have a fine eye for consequences."

So saying, he embraced Scythrop, who retired, with a disconsolate step, to dress for dinner; while Mr. Toobad stalked across the hall, repeating, "Woe to the inhabiters of the earth, and of the sea, for the devil is come among you, having great wrath."

CHAPTER 4

The flight of Marionetta, and the pursuit of Scythrop, had been witnessed by Mr. Glowry, who, in consequence, narrowly observed his son and his niece in the evening; and, concluding from their manner, that there was a better understanding between them than he wished to see, he determined on obtaining the next morning from Scythrop a full and satisfactory explanation. He, therefore, shortly after breakfast, entered Scythrop's tower, with a very grave face, and said, without ceremony or preface, "So, sir, you are in love with your cousin."

Scythrop, with as little hesitation, answered, "Yes, sir."

"That is candid, at least; and she is in love with you."

"I wish she were, sir."

"You know she is, sir."

"Indeed, sir, I do not."

"But you hope she is."

"I do, from my soul."

"Now that is very provoking, Scythrop, and very disappointing: I could not have supposed that you, Scythrop Glowry, of Nightmare Abbey, would have been infatuated with such a dancing, laughing, singing, thoughtless, careless, merry-hearted thing, as Marionetta -- in all respects the reverse of you and me. It is very disappointing, Scythrop. And do you know, sir, that Marionetta has no fortune?"

"It is the more reason, sir, that her husband should have one."

"The more reason for her; but not for you. My wife had no fortune, and I had no consolation in my calamity. And do you reflect, sir, what an enormous slice this lawsuit has cut out of our family estate? we who used to be the greatest landed proprietors in Lincolnshire."

"To be sure, sir, we had more acres of fen than any man on this coast: but what are fens to love? What are dykes and windmills to Marionetta?"

"And what, sir, is love to a windmill? Not grist, I am certain: besides, sir, I have made a choice for you. I have made a choice for you, Scythrop. Beauty, genius, accomplishments, and a great fortune into the bargain. Such a lovely, serious creature, in a fine state of high dissatisfaction with the world, and every thing in it. Such a delightful surprise I had prepared for you. Sir, I have pledged my honour to the contract -- the honour of the Glowries of Nightmare Abbey: and now, sir, what is to be done?"

"Indeed, sir, I cannot say. I claim, on this occasion, that liberty of action which is the co-natal prerogative of every rational being."

"Liberty of action, sir? there is no such thing as liberty of action. We are all slaves and puppets of a blind and unpathetic necessity."

"Very true, sir; but liberty of action, between individuals, consists in their being differently influenced, or modified, by the same universal necessity; so that the results are unconsentaneous, and their respective necessitated volitions clash and fly off in a tangent."

"Your logic is good, sir: but you are aware, too, that one individual may be a medium of adhibiting to another a mode or form of necessity, which may have more or less influence in the production of consentaneity; and, therefore, sir, if you do not comply with my wishes in this instance (you have had your own way in every thing else), I shall be under the necessity of disinheriting you, though I shall do it with tears in my eyes."

Having said these words, he vanished suddenly, in the dread of Scythrop's logic.

Mr. Glowry immediately sought Mrs. Hilary, and communicated to her his views of the case in point. Mrs. Hilary, as the phrase is, was as fond of Marionetta as if she had been her own child: but-- there is always a *but* on these occasions -- she could do nothing for her in the way of fortune, as she had two hopeful sons, who were finishing their education at Brazen-nose, and who would not like to encounter any diminution of their prospects, when they should be brought out of the house of mental bondage -- i.e. the university -- to the land flowing with milk and honey -- i.e. the west end of London.

Mrs. Hilary hinted to Marionetta, that propriety, and delicacy, and decorum, and dignity, &c. &c. &c.,* would require them to leave the Abbey immediately. Marionetta listened in silent submission, for she knew that her inheritance was passive obedience; but, when Scythrop, who had watched the opportunity of Mrs. Hilary's departure, entered, and, without speaking a word, threw himself at her feet in a paroxysm of grief, the young lady, in equal silence and sorrow, threw her arms round his neck and burst into tears. A very tender scene ensued, which the sympathetic susceptibilities of the soft-hearted reader can more accurately imagine than we can delineate. But when Marionetta hinted that she was to leave the Abbey immediately, Scythrop snatched from its repository his ancestor's skull, filled it with Madeira, and presenting himself before Mr. Glowry, threatened to drink off the contents if Mr. Glowry did not immediately promise that Marionetta should not be taken from the Abbey without her own consent. Mr. Glowry, who took the Madeira to be some deadly brewage, gave the required promise in dismal panic. Scythrop returned to Marionetta with a joyful heart, and drank the Madeira by the way.

Mr. Glowry, during his residence in London, had come to an agreement with his friend Mr. Toobad, that a match between Scythrop and Mr. Toobad's daughter would be a very desirable occurrence. She was finishing her education in a German convent, but Mr. Toobad described her as being fully impressed with the

---

* decorum, and dignity, &c. &c. &c: We are not masters of the whole vocabulary. See any novel by any literary lady.

truth of his Ahrimanic philosophy,* and being altogether as gloomy and antithalian a young lady as Mr. Glowry himself could desire for the future mistress of Nightmare Abbey. She had a great fortune in her own right, which was not, as we have seen, without its weight in inducing Mr. Glowry to set his heart upon her as his daughter-in-law that was to be; he was therefore very much disturbed by Scythrop's untoward attachment to Marionetta. He condoled on the occasion with Mr. Toobad; who said, that he had been too long accustomed to the intermeddling of the devil in all his affairs, to be astonished at this new trace of his cloven claw; but that he hoped to outwit him yet, for he was sure there could be no comparison between his daughter and Marionetta in the mind of any one who had a proper perception of the fact, that, the world being a great theatre of evil, seriousness and solemnity are the characteristics of wisdom, and laughter and merriment make a human being no better than a baboon. Mr. Glowry comforted himself with this view of the subject, and urged Mr. Toobad to expedite his daughter's return from Germany. Mr. Toobad said he was in daily expectation of her arrival in London, and would set off immediately to meet her, that he might lose no time in bringing her to Nightmare Abbey. "Then," he added, "we shall see whether Thalia or Melpomene -- whether the Allegra or the Penserosa -- will carry off the symbol of victory." – "There can be no doubt," said Mr. Glowry, "which way the scale will incline, or Scythrop is no true scion of the venerable stem of the Glowrys."

---

*his Ahrimanic philosophy: Ahrimanes, in the Persian mythology, is the evil power, the prince of the kingdom of darkness. He is the rival of Oromazes, the prince of the kingdom of light. These two powers have divided and equal dominion. Sometimes one of the two has a temporary supremacy. -- According to Mr. Toobad, the present period would be the reign of Ahrimanes. Lord Byron seems to be of the same opinion, by the use he has made of Ahrimanes in "Manfred"; where the great Alastor, or [Greek: Kachos Daimôn], of Persia, is hailed king of the world by the Nemesis of Greece, in concert with three of the Scandinavian Valkyrae, under the name of the Destinies; the astrological spirits of the alchemists of the middle ages; an elemental witch, transplanted from Denmark to the Alps; and a chorus of Dr Faustus's devils, who come in the last act for a soul. It is difficult to conceive where this heterogeneous mythological company could have originally met, except at a *table d'hôte*, like the six kings in "Candide".

CHAPTER 5

Marionetta felt secure of Scythrop's heart; and notwithstanding the difficulties that surrounded her, she could not debar herself from the pleasure of tormenting her lover, whom she kept in a perpetual fever. Sometimes she would meet him with the most unqualified affection; sometimes with the most chilling indifference; rousing him to anger by artificial coldness -- softening him to love by eloquent tenderness -- or inflaming him to jealousy by coquetting with the Honourable Mr. Listless, who seemed, under her magical influence, to burst into sudden life, like the bud of the evening primrose. Sometimes she would sit by the piano, and listen with becoming attention to Scythrop's pathetic remonstrances; but, in the most impassioned part of his oratory, she would convert all his ideas into a chaos, by striking up some Rondo Allegro, and saying, "Is it not pretty?" Scythrop would begin to storm; and she would answer him with,

> "Zitti, zitti, piano, piano,
> Non facciamo confusione,"

or some similar *facezia*, till he would start away from her, and enclose himself in his tower, in an agony of agitation, vowing to renounce her, and her whole sex, for ever; and returning to her presence at the summons of the billet, which she never failed to send with many expressions of penitence and promises of amendment. Scythrop's schemes for regenerating the world, and detecting his seven golden candlesticks, went on very slowly in this fever of his spirit.

Things proceeded in this train for several days; and Mr. Glowry began to be uneasy at receiving no intelligence from Mr. Toobad; when one evening the latter rushed into the library, where the family and the visitors were assembled, vociferating, "The devil is come among you, having great wrath!" He then drew Mr. Glowry aside into another apartment, and after remaining some time together, they re-entered the library with faces of great dismay, but did not condescend to explain to any one the cause of their discomfiture.

The next morning, early, Mr. Toobad departed. Mr. Glowry sighed and groaned all day, and said not a word to any one. Scythrop had quarrelled, as usual, with Marionetta, and was enclosed in his tower, in a fit of morbid sensibility. Marionetta was comforting herself at the piano, with singing the airs of *Nina pazza per amore*; and the Honourable Mr. Listless was listening to the harmony, as he lay supine on the sofa, with a book in his hand, into which he peeped at intervals. The Reverend Mr. Larynx approached the sofa, and proposed a game at billiards.

THE HONOURABLE MR. LISTLESS

Billiards! Really I should be very happy; but, in my present exhausted state, the exertion is too much for me. I do not know when I have been equal to such an effort. (*He rang the bell for his valet. Fatout entered.*) Fatout! when did I play at billiards last?

FATOUT

De fourteen December de last year, Monsieur. (*Fatout bowed and retired.*)

THE HONOURABLE MR. LISTLESS

So it was. Seven months ago. You see, Mr. Larynx; you see, sir. My nerves, Miss O'Carroll, my nerves are shattered. I have been advised to try Bath. Some of the faculty recommend Cheltenham. I think of trying both, as the seasons don't clash. The season, you know, Mr. Larynx -- the season, Miss O'Carroll -- the season is every thing.

MARIONETTA

And health is something. *N'est-ce pas*, Mr. Larynx?

THE REVEREND MR. LARYNX

Most assuredly, Miss O'Carroll. For, however reasoners may dispute about the *summum bonum*, none of them will deny that a very good dinner is a very good thing: and what is a good dinner without a good appetite? and whence is a good appetite but from good health? Now, Cheltenham, Mr. Listless, is famous for good appetites.

THE HONOURABLE MR. LISTLESS

The best piece of logic I ever heard, Mr. Larynx; the very best, I assure you. I have thought very seriously of Cheltenham: very seriously and profoundly. I thought of it -- let me see -- when did I think of it? (*He rang again, and Fatout reappeared.*) Fatout! When did I think of going to Cheltenham, and did not go?

FATOUT

De Juillet twenty-von, de last summer, Monsieur. (*Fatout retired.*)

THE HONOURABLE MR. LISTLESS

So it was. An invaluable fellow that, Mr. Larynx -- invaluable, Miss O'Carroll.

MARIONETTA

So I should judge, indeed. He seems to serve you as a walking memory, and to be a living chronicle, not of your actions only, but of your thoughts.

THE HONOURABLE MR. LISTLESS

An excellent definition of the fellow, Miss O'Carroll,--excellent, upon my honour. Ha! ha! he! Heigho! Laughter is pleasant, but the exertion is too much for me.

A parcel was brought in for Mr. Listless; it had been sent express. Fatout was summoned to unpack it; and it proved to contain a new novel, and a new poem, both of which had long been anxiously expected by the whole host of fashionable readers; and the last number of a popular Review, of which the editor and his coadjutors were in high favour at court, and enjoyed ample pensions* for their services to church and state. As Fatout left the room, Mr. Flosky entered, and curiously inspected the literary arrivals.

MR. FLOSKY

(*Turning over the leaves.*) "Devilman, a novel." Hm. Hatred -- revenge -- misanthropy -- and quotations from the Bible. Hm. This is the morbid anatomy of black bile. -- "Paul Jones, a poem." Hm. I see how it is. Paul Jones, an amiable enthusiast -- disappointed in his affections -- turns pirate from ennui and magnanimity -- cuts various masculine throats, wins various feminine hearts -- is hanged at the yard-arm! The catastrophe is very awkward, and very unpoetical. -- "The Downing Street Review." Hm. First article -- An Ode to the Red Book, by Roderick Sackbut, Esquire. Hm. His own poem reviewed by himself. Hm--m--m.

(*Mr. Flosky proceeded in silence to look over the other articles of the review; Marionetta inspected the novel, and Mr. Listless the poem.*)

THE REVEREND MR. LARYNX

For a young man of fashion and family, Mr. Listless, you seem to be of a very studious turn.

---

*pensions: "PENSION. Pay given to a slave of state for treason to his country." -- *Johnson's Dictionary.*

THE HONOURABLE MR. LISTLESS

Studious! You are pleased to be facetious, Mr. Larynx. I hope you do not suspect me of being studious. I have finished my education. But there are some fashionable books that one must read, because they are ingredients of the talk of the day; otherwise, I am no fonder of books than I dare say you yourself are, Mr. Larynx.

THE REVEREND MR. LARYNX

Why, sir, I cannot say that I am indeed particularly fond of books; yet neither can I say that I never do read. A tale or a poem, now and then, to a circle of ladies over their work, is no very heterodox employment of the vocal energy. And I must say, for myself, that few men have a more Job-like endurance of the eternally-recurring questions and answers that interweave themselves, on these occasions, with the crisis of an adventure, and heighten the distress of a tragedy.

THE HONOURABLE MR. LISTLESS

And very often make the distress when the author has omitted it.

MARIONETTA

I shall try your patience some rainy morning, Mr. Larynx; and Mr. Listless shall recommend us the very newest new book, that every body reads.

THE HONOURABLE MR. LISTLESS

You shall receive it, Miss O'Carroll, with all the gloss of novelty; fresh as a ripe green-gage in all the downiness of its bloom. A mail-coach copy from Edinburgh, forwarded express from London.

MR. FLOSKY

This rage for novelty is the bane of literature. Except my works and those of my particular friends, nothing is good that is not as old as Jeremy Taylor: and, *entre nous*, the best parts of my friends' books were either written or suggested by myself.

THE HONOURABLE MR. LISTLESS

Sir, I reverence you. But I must say, modern books are very consolatory and congenial to my feelings. There is, as it were, a delightful north-east wind, an intellectual blight breathing through them; a delicious misanthropy and discontent, that demonstrates the nullity of virtue and energy, and puts me in good humour with myself and my sofa.

MR. FLOSKY

Very true, sir. Modern literature is a north-east wind -- a blight of the human soul. I take credit to myself for having helped to make it so. The way to produce fine fruit is to blight the flower. You call this a paradox. Marry, so be it. Ponder thereon.

The conversation was interrupted by the re-appearance of Mr. Toobad, covered with mud. He just shewed himself at the door, muttered "The devil is come among you!" and vanished. The road which connected Nightmare Abbey with the civilised world was artificially raised above the level of the fens, and ran through them in a straight line as far as the eye could reach, with a ditch on each side, of which the water was rendered invisible by the aquatic vegetation that covered the surface. Into one of these ditches the sudden action of a shy horse, which took fright at a windmill, had precipitated the travelling chariot of Mr. Toobad, who had been reduced to the necessity of scrambling in dismal plight through the window. One of the wheels was found to be broken; and Mr. Toobad, leaving the postilion to get the chariot as well as he could to Claydyke for the purpose of cleaning and repairing, had walked back to Nightmare Abbey, followed by his servant with the imperial, and repeating all the way his favourite quotation from the Revelations.

CHAPTER 6

Mr. Toobad had found his daughter, Celinda, in London, and after the first joy of meeting was over, told her he had a husband ready for her. The young lady replied, very gravely, that she should take the liberty to choose for herself. Mr. Toobad said he saw the devil was determined to interfere with all his projects, but he was resolved on his own part, not to have on his conscience the crime of passive obedience and non-resistance to Lucifer, and therefore she should marry the person he had chosen for her. Miss Toobad replied, *très posément*, she assuredly would not. "Celinda, Celinda," said Mr. Toobad, "you most assuredly shall." -- "Have I not a fortune in my own right, sir?" said Celinda. "The more is the pity," said Mr. Toobad: "but I can find means, miss; I can find means. There are more ways than one of breaking in obstinate girls." They parted for the night with the expression of opposite resolutions, and in the morning the young lady's chamber was found empty, and what was become of her Mr. Toobad had no clue to

211

conjecture. He continued to investigate town and country in search of her; visiting and revisiting Nightmare Abbey at intervals, to consult with his friend, Mr. Glowry. Mr. Glowry agreed with Mr. Toobad that this was a very flagrant instance of filial disobedience and rebellion; and Mr. Toobad declared, that when he discovered the fugitive, she should find that "the devil was come unto her, having great wrath."

In the evening, the whole party met, as usual, in the library. Marionetta sat at the harp; the Honourable Mr. Listless sat by her and turned over her music, though the exertion was almost too much for him. The Reverend Mr. Larynx relieved him occasionally in this delightful labour. Scythrop, tormented by the demon Jealousy, sat in the corner, biting his lips and fingers. Marionetta looked at him every now and then with a smile of most provoking good humour, which he pretended not to see, and which only the more exasperated his troubled spirit. He took down a volume of Dante, and pretended to be deeply interested in the Purgatorio, though he knew not a word he was reading, as Marionetta was well aware; who, tripping across the room, peeped into his book, and said to him, "I see you are in the middle of Purgatory." -- "I am in the middle of hell," said Scythrop furiously. "Are you?" said she; "then come across the room, and I will sing you the finale of Don Giovanni."

"Let me alone," said Scythrop. Marionetta looked at him with a deprecating smile, and said, "You unjust, cross creature, you." -- "Let me alone," said Scythrop, but much less emphatically than at first, and by no means wishing to be taken at his word. Marionetta left him immediately, and returning to the harp, said, just loud enough for Scythrop to hear -- "Did you ever read Dante, Mr. Listless? Scythrop is reading Dante, and is just now in Purgatory." -- "And I" said the Honourable Mr. Listless, "am not reading Dante, and am just now in Paradise," bowing to Marionetta.

MARIONETTA

You are very gallant, Mr. Listless; and I dare say you are very fond of reading Dante.

THE HONOURABLE MR. LISTLESS

I don't know how it is, but Dante never came in my way till lately. I never had him in my collection, and if I had had him, I should not have read him. But I find he is growing fashionable, and I am afraid I must read him some wet morning.

MARIONETTA

No, read him some evening, by all means. Were you ever in love, Mr. Listless?

THE HONOURABLE MR. LISTLESS

I assure you, Miss O'Carroll, never -- till I came to Nightmare Abbey. I dare say it is very pleasant; but it seems to give so much trouble that I fear the exertion would be too much for me.

MARIONETTA

Shall I teach you a compendious method of courtship, that will give you no trouble whatever?

THE HONOURABLE MR. LISTLESS

You will confer on me an inexpressible obligation. I am all impatience to learn it.

MARIONETTA

Sit with your back to the lady and read Dante; only be sure to begin in the middle, and turn over three or four pages at once -- backwards as well as forwards, and she will immediately perceive that you are desperately in love with her -- desperately.

(*The Honourable Mr. Listless sitting between Scythrop and Marionetta, and fixing all his attention on the beautiful speaker, did not observe Scythrop, who was doing as she described.*)

THE HONOURABLE MR. LISTLESS

You are pleased to be facetious, Miss O'Carroll. The lady would infallibly conclude that I was the greatest brute in town.

MARIONETTA

Far from it. She would say, perhaps, some people have odd methods of shewing their affection.

THE HONOURABLE MR. LISTLESS

But I should think, with submission --

MR. FLOSKY (*joining them from another part of the room*)

Did I not hear Mr. Listless observe that Dante is becoming fashionable?

THE HONOURABLE MR. LISTLESS

I did hazard a remark to that effect, Mr. Flosky, though I speak on such subjects with a consciousness of my own nothingness, in the presence of so great a man as Mr. Flosky. I know not what is the colour of Dante's devils, but as he is certainly becoming fashionable I conclude they are blue; for the blue devils, as it seems to me, Mr. Flosky, constitute the fundamental feature of fashionable literature.

MR. FLOSKY

The blue are, indeed, the staple commodity; but as they will not always be commanded, the black, red, and grey may be admitted as substitutes. Tea, late dinners, and the French Revolution, have played the devil, Mr. Listless, and brought the devil into play.

MR. TOOBAD (*starting up*)

Having great wrath.

MR. FLOSKY

This is no play upon words, but the sober sadness of veritable fact.

THE HONOURABLE MR. LISTLESS

Tea, late dinners, and the French Revolution. I cannot exactly see the connexion of ideas.

MR. FLOSKY

I should be sorry if you could; I pity the man who can see the connexion of his own ideas. Still more do I pity him, the connexion of whose ideas any other person can see. Sir, the great evil is, that there is too much common-place light in our moral and political literature; and light is a great enemy to mystery, and mystery is a great friend to enthusiasm. Now the enthusiasm for abstract truth is an exceedingly fine thing, as long as the truth, which is the object of the enthusiasm, is so completely abstract as to be altogether out of the reach of the human faculties; and, in that sense, I have myself an enthusiasm for truth, but in no other, for the pleasure of metaphysical investigation lies in the means, not in the end; and if the end could be found, the pleasure of the means would cease. The mind, to be kept in health, must be kept in exercise. The proper exercise of the mind is elaborate reasoning. Analytical reasoning is a base and mechanical process, which takes to pieces and examines, bit by bit, the rude material of knowledge, and extracts therefrom a few hard and obstinate things called facts, every thing in the shape of which I cordially hate. But synthetical reasoning, setting up as its goal some unattainable abstraction, like an imaginary quantity in algebra, and commencing its course with taking for granted some two assertions which cannot be proved, from the union of these two assumed truths produces a third assumption, and so on in infinite series, to the unspeakable benefit of the human intellect. The beauty of this process is, that at every step it strikes out into two branches, in a compound ratio of ramification; so that you are perfectly sure of losing your way, and keeping your mind in perfect health by the perpetual exercise of an interminable quest; and for these reasons I have christened my eldest son Emanuel Kant Flosky.

THE REVEREND MR. LARYNX

Nothing can be more luminous.

THE HONOURABLE MR. LISTLESS

And what has all that to do with Dante, and the blue devils?

MR. HILARY

Not much, I should think, with Dante, but a great deal with the blue devils.

MR. FLOSKY

It is very certain, and much to be rejoiced at, that our literature is hag-ridden. Tea has shattered our nerves; late dinners make us slaves of indigestion; the French Revolution has made us shrink from the name of philosophy, and has destroyed, in the more refined part of the community (of which number I am one), all enthusiasm for political liberty. That part of the *reading public* which shuns the solid food of reason for the light diet of fiction, requires a perpetual adhibition of *sauce piquante* to the palate of its depraved imagination. It lived upon ghosts, goblins, and skeletons (I and my friend, Mr. Sackbut, served up a few of the best), till even the devil himself, though magnified to the size of Mount Athos, became too base, common, and popular, for its surfeited appetite. The ghosts have therefore been laid, and the devil has been cast into outer darkness, and now the delight of our spirits is to dwell on all the vices and blackest passions of our nature, tricked out in a masquerade dress of heroism and disappointed benevolence; the whole secret of which lies in forming combinations that contradict all our experience, and affixing the purple shred of some particular virtue to that precise character, in which we should be most certain not to find it in the living world; and making this single virtue not only redeem all the real and manifest vices of the character, but make them actually pass for necessary adjuncts, and indispensable accompaniments and characteristics of the said virtue.

MR. TOOBAD

That is, because the devil is come among us, and finds it for his interest to destroy all our perceptions of the distinctions of right and wrong.

MARIONETTA

I do not precisely enter into your meaning, Mr. Flosky, and should be glad if you would make it a little more plain to me.

215

MR. FLOSKY

One or two examples will do it, Miss O'Carroll. If I were to take all the mean and sordid qualities of a money-dealing Jew, and tack on to them, as with a nail, the quality of extreme benevolence, I should have a very decent hero for a modern novel, and should contribute my quota to the fashionable method of administering a mass of vice, under a thin and unnatural covering of virtue, like a spider wrapt in a bit of gold leaf, and administered as a wholesome pill. On the same principle, if a man knocks me down, and takes my purse and watch by main force, I turn him to account, and set him forth in a tragedy as a dashing young fellow, disinherited for his romantic generosity, and full of a most amiable hatred of the world in general, and his own country in particular, and of a most enlightened and chivalrous affection for himself: then, with the addition of a wild girl to fall in love with him, and a series of adventures in which they break all the Ten Commandments in succession (always, you will observe, for some sublime motive, which must be carefully analysed in its progress), I have as amiable a pair of tragic characters as ever issued from that new region of the belles lettres, which I have called the Morbid Anatomy of Black Bile, and which is greatly to be admired and rejoiced at, as affording a fine scope for the exhibition of mental power.

MR. HILARY

Which is about as well employed as the power of a hot-house would be in forcing up a nettle to the size of an elm. If we go on in this way, we shall have a new art of poetry, of which one of the first rules will be: To remember to forget that there are any such things as sunshine and music in the world.

THE HONOURABLE MR. LISTLESS

It seems to be the case with us at present, or we should not have interrupted Miss O'Carroll's music with this exceedingly dry conversation.

MR. FLOSKY

I should be most happy if Miss O'Carroll would remind us that there are yet both music and sunshine --

THE HONOURABLE MR. LISTLESS

In the voice and the smile of beauty. May I entreat the favour of -- (*turning over the pages of music.*)

All were silent, and Marionetta sung:

216

Why are thy looks so blank, grey friar?
Why are thy looks so blue?
Thou seem'st more pale and lank, grey friar,
Than thou wast used to do:--
Say, what has made thee rue?

Thy form was plump, and a light did shine
In thy round and ruby face,
Which showed an outward visible sign
Of an inward spiritual grace:--
Say, what has changed thy case?

Yet will I tell thee true, grey friar,
I very well can see,
That, if thy looks are blue, grey friar,
'Tis all for love of me,--
'Tis all for love of me.

But breathe not thy vows to me, grey friar,
Oh, breathe them not, I pray;
For ill beseems in a reverend friar,
The love of a mortal may;
And I needs must say thee nay.

But, could'st thou think my heart to move
With that pale and silent scowl?
Know, he who would win a maiden's love,
Whether clad in cap or cowl,
Must be more of a lark than an owl.

Scythrop immediately replaced Dante on the shelf, and joined the circle round the beautiful singer. Marionetta gave him a smile of approbation that fully restored his complacency, and they continued on the best possible terms during the remainder of the evening. The Honourable Mr. Listless turned over the leaves with double alacrity, saying, "You are severe upon invalids, Miss O'Carroll: to escape your satire, I must try to be sprightly, though the exertion is too much for me."

CHAPTER 7

A new visitor arrived at the Abbey, in the person of Mr. Asterias, the ichthyologist. This gentleman had passed his life in seeking the living wonders of the deep through the four quarters of the world: he had a cabinet of stuffed and dried fishes, of shells, sea-weeds, corals, and madrepores, that was the admiration and envy of the Royal Society. He had penetrated into the watery den of the Sepia Octopus, disturbed the conjugal happiness of that turtle-dove of the ocean, and come off victorious in a sanguinary conflict. He had been becalmed in the tropical seas, and had watched, in eager expectation, though unhappily always in vain, to see the colossal polypus rise from the water, and entwine its enormous arms round the masts and the rigging. He maintained the origin of all things from water, and insisted that the polypodes were the first of animated things, and that, from their round bodies and many-shooting arms, the Hindoos had taken their gods, the most ancient of deities. But the chief object of his ambition, the end and aim of his researches, was to discover a Triton and a Mermaid, the existence of which he most potently and implicitly believed, and was prepared to demonstrate, *a priori, a posteriori, a fortiori*, synthetically and analytically, syllogistically and inductively, by arguments deduced both from acknowledged facts and plausible hypotheses. A report that a mermaid had been seen "sleeking her soft alluring locks" on the sea-coast of Lincolnshire, had brought him in great haste from London, to pay a long-promised and often-postponed visit to his old acquaintance, Mr. Glowry.

Mr. Asterias was accompanied by his son, to whom he had given the name of Aquarius, -- flattering himself that he would, in the process of time, become a constellation among the stars of ichthyological science. What charitable female had lent him the mould in which this son was cast, no one pretended to know; and, as he never dropped the most distant allusion to Aquarius's mother, some of the wags of London maintained that he had received the favours of a mermaid, and that the scientific perquisitions which kept him always prowling about the sea-shore, were directed by the less philosophical motive of regaining his lost love.

Mr. Asterias perlustrated the sea-coast for several days, and reaped disappointment, but not despair. One night, shortly after his arrival, he was sitting in one of the windows of the library, looking towards the sea, when his attention was attracted by a figure which was moving near the edge of the surf, and which was dimly visible through the moonless summer-night. Its motions were irregular, like those of a person in a state of indecision. It had extremely long hair, which floated in the wind. Whatever else it might be, it certainly was not a fisherman. It might be a lady; but it was neither Mrs. Hilary nor Miss O'Carroll, for they were both in the library. It might be one of the female servants; but it had too much grace, and too striking an air of habitual liberty, to render it probable. Besides, what should one of the female servants be doing there at this hour, moving to and fro, as it seemed, without any visible purpose? It could scarcely be a stranger; for Claydyke, the nearest village, was ten miles distant; and what female would come ten miles across the fens, for no purpose but to hover over the surf under the walls of Nightmare Abbey? Might it not be a mermaid? It was possibly a mermaid. It was probably a mermaid. It was very probably a mermaid. Nay, what else could it be but a mermaid? It certainly was a mermaid. Mr. Asterias stole out of the library on tiptoe, with his finger on his lips, having beckoned Aquarius to follow him.

The rest of the party was in great surprise at Mr. Asterias's movement, and some of them approached the window to see if the locality would tend to elucidate the mystery. Presently they saw him and Aquarius cautiously stealing along on the other side of the moat, but they saw nothing more; and Mr. Asterias returning, told them, with accents of great disappointment, that he had had a glimpse of a mermaid, but she had eluded him in the darkness, and was gone, he presumed, to sup with some enamoured Triton, in a submarine grotto.

"But, seriously, Mr. Asterias," said the Honourable Mr. Listless, "do you positively believe there are such things as mermaids?"

MR. ASTERIAS

Most assuredly; and Tritons too.

THE HONOURABLE MR. LISTLESS

What! things that are half human and half fish?

MR. ASTERIAS

Precisely. They are the Oran-outangs of the sea. But I am persuaded that there are also complete sea men, differing in no respect from us, but that they are stupid, and covered with scales: for, though our organization seems to exclude us essentially from the class of amphibious animals, yet anatomists well know that the *foramen ovale* may remain open in an adult, and that respiration is, in that case, not necessary to life: and how can it be otherwise explained that the Indian divers, employed in the pearl fishery, pass whole hours under the water? and that the famous Swedish gardener of Troningholm lived a day and a half under the ice without being drowned? A Nereid, or mermaid, was taken in the year 1403 in a Dutch lake, and was in every respect like a French woman, except that she did not speak. Towards the end of the seventeenth century, an English ship, a hundred and fifty leagues from land, in the Greenland seas, discovered a flotilla of sixty or seventy little skiffs, in each of which was a Triton, or sea man: at the approach of the English vessel, the whole of them, seized with simultaneous fear, disappeared, skiffs and all, under the water, as if they had been a human variety of the Nautilus. The illustrious Don Feijoo has preserved an authentic and well-attested story of a young Spaniard, named Francis de la Vega, who, bathing with some of his friends in June 1674, suddenly dived under the sea and rose no more. His friends thought him drowned: they were plebeians and pious Catholics; but a philosopher might very legitimately have drawn the same conclusion.

THE REVEREND MR. LARYNX

Nothing could be more logical.

MR. ASTERIAS

Five years afterwards, some fishermen, near Cadiz, found in their nets a Triton, or sea man; they spoke to him in several languages --

THE REVEREND MR. LARYNX

They were very learned fishermen.

MR. HILARY

They had the gift of tongues by especial favour of their brother fisherman, Saint Peter.

THE HONOURABLE MR. LISTLESS

Is Saint Peter the tutelar saint of Cadiz?

(*None of the company could answer this question, and MR. ASTERIAS proceeded.*)

They spoke to him in several languages, but he was as mute as a fish. They handed him over to some holy friars, who exorcised him; but the devil was mute too. After some days, he pronounced the name Lierganes. A monk took him to that village. His mother and brothers recognised and embraced him; but he was as insensible to their caresses as any other fish would have been. He had some scales on his body, which dropped off by degrees; but his skin was as hard and rough as shagreen. He stayed at home nine years, without recovering his speech or his reason: he then disappeared again; and one of his old acquaintance, some years after, saw him pop his head out of the water near the coast of the Asturias. These facts were certified by his brothers, and by Don Gaspardo de la Riba Aguero, Knight of Saint James, who lived near Lierganes, and often had the pleasure of our Triton's company to dinner. -- Pliny mentions an embassy of the Olyssiponians to Tiberius, to give him intelligence of a Triton which had been heard playing on its shell in a certain cave; with several other authenticated facts on the subject of Tritons and Nereids.

THE HONOURABLE MR. LISTLESS

You astonish me. I have been much on the sea-shore, in the season, but I do not think I ever saw a mermaid. (*He rang, and summoned Fatout, who made his appearance half-seas-over.*) Fatout! did I ever see a mermaid?

FATOUT

Mermaid! mer-r-m-m-aid! Ah! merry maid! Oui, monsieur! Yes, sir, very many. I vish dere vas von or two here in de kitchen -- ma foi! Dey be all as melancholic as so many tombstone.

THE HONOURABLE MR. LISTLESS

I mean, Fatout, an odd kind of human fish.

FATOUT

De odd fish! Ah, oui! I understand de phrase: ve have seen nothing else since ve left town -- ma foi!

THE HONOURABLE MR. LISTLESS

You seem to have a cup too much, Sir.

FATOUT

Non, Monsieur: de cup too little. De fen be very unwholesome, and I drink-a-de ponch vid Raven de butler, to keep out de bad air.

THE HONOURABLE MR. LISTLESS

Fatout! I insist on your being sober.

FATOUT

Oui, Monsieur; I vil be as sober as de révérendissime père Jean. I should be ver glad of de merry maid; but de butler be de odd fish, and he swim in de bowl de ponch. Ah! ah! I do recollect de leetle-a song: -- "About fair maids, and about fair maids, and about my merry maids all." (*Fatout reeled out, singing.*)

221

THE HONOURABLE MR. LISTLESS

I am overwhelmed: I never saw the rascal in such a condition before. But will you allow me, Mr. Asterias, to inquire into the *cui bono* of all the pains and expense you have incurred to discover a mermaid? The *cui bono*, Sir, is the question I always take the liberty to ask, when I see any one taking much trouble for any object. I am myself a sort of Signor Pococurante, and should like to know if there be any thing better or pleasanter, than the state of existing and doing nothing?

MR. ASTERIAS

I have made many voyages, Mr. Listless, to remote and barren shores: I have travelled over desert and inhospitable lands: I have defied danger -- I have endured fatigue -- I have submitted to privation. In the midst of these I have experienced pleasures which I would not at any time have exchanged for that of existing and doing nothing. I have known many evils, but I have never known the worst of all, which, as it seems to me, are those which are comprehended in the inexhaustible varieties of *ennui*: spleen, chagrin, vapours, blue devils, time-killing, discontent, misanthropy, and all their interminable train of fretfulness, querulousness, suspicions, jealousies, and fears, which have alike infected society, and the literature of society; and which would make an Arctic ocean of the human mind, if the more humane pursuits of philosophy and science did not keep alive the better feelings and more valuable energies of our nature.

THE HONOURABLE MR. LISTLESS

You are pleased to be severe upon our fashionable belles lettres.

MR. ASTERIAS

Surely not without reason, when pirates, highwaymen, and other varieties of the extensive genus Marauder, are the only *beau idéal* of the active, as splenetic and railing misanthropy is of the speculative energy. A gloomy brow and a tragical voice seem to have been, of late, the characteristics of fashionable manners; and a morbid, withering, deadly, antisocial sirocco, loaded with moral and political despair, breathes through all the groves and valleys of the modern Parnassus; while science moves on in the calm dignity of its course, affording to youth delights equally pure and vivid -- to maturity, calm and grateful occupation -- to old age, the most pleasing recollections and inexhaustible materials of agreeable and salutary reflection; and, while its votary enjoys the disinterested pleasure of enlarging the intellect and increasing the comforts of society, he is himself independent of the caprices of human intercourse and the accidents of human fortune. Nature is his great and inexhaustible treasure. His days are always too short for his enjoyment: *ennui* is a stranger to his door. At peace with the world and with his own mind, he suffices to himself, makes all around him happy, and the close of his pleasing and beneficial existence is the evening of a beautiful day.*

THE HONOURABLE MR. LISTLESS

Really, I should like very well to lead such a life myself, but the exertion would be too much for me. Besides, I have been at college. I contrive to get through my day by sinking the morning in bed, and killing the evening in company, dressing and dining in the intermediate space, and stopping the chinks and crevices of the few vacant moments that remain with a little easy reading. And that amiable discontent and antisociality, which you reprobate in our present drawing-room-table literature, I find, I do assure you, a very fine mental tonic, which reconciles me to my favourite pursuit of doing nothing, by shewing me that nobody is worth doing any thing for.

MARIONETTA

But is there not in such compositions a kind of unconscious self-detection, which seems to carry their own antidote with them? For surely, no one who cordially and truly either hates or despises the world will publish a volume every three months to say so.

MR. FLOSKY

There is a secret in all this, which I will elucidate with a dusky remark. According to Berkeley, the *esse* of things is *percipi*. They exist as they are perceived. But, leaving for the present, as far as relates to the material world, the materialists, hyloists, and antihyloists, to settle this point among them, which is indeed

A subtle question, raised among
Those out o' their wits, and those i' the wrong:

for only we transcendentalists are in the right: we may very safely assert that the *esse* of happiness is *percipi*. It exists as it is

---

*...of a beautiful day: See Denys Montfort: *Histoire Naturelle des Mollusques; Vues Générales*, pp. 37, 38.

223

perceived. "It is the mind that maketh well or ill." The elements of pleasure and pain are every where. The degree of happiness that any circumstances or objects can confer on us depends on the mental disposition with which we approach them. If you consider what is meant by the common phrases, a happy disposition and a discontented temper, you will perceive that the truth for which I am contending is universally admitted.

(*Mr. Flosky suddenly stopped: he found himself unintentionally trespassing within the limits of common sense.*)

MR. HILARY

It is very true; a happy disposition finds materials of enjoyment every where. In the city, or the country -- in society, or in solitude -- in the theatre, or the forest -- in the hum of the multitude, or in the silence of the mountains, are alike materials of reflection and elements of pleasure. It is one mode of pleasure to listen to the music of "Don Giovanni," in a theatre glittering with light, and crowded with elegance and beauty: it is another to glide at sunset over the bosom of a lonely lake, where no sound disturbs the silence but the motion of the boat through the waters. A happy disposition derives pleasure from both, a discontented temper from neither, but is always busy in detecting deficiencies, and feeding dissatisfaction with comparisons. The one gathers all the flowers, the other all the nettles, in its path. The one has the faculty of enjoying every thing, the other of enjoying nothing. The one realises all the pleasure of the present good; the other converts it into pain, by pining after something better, which is only better because it is not present, and which, if it were present, would not be enjoyed. These morbid spirits are in life what professed critics are in literature: they see nothing but faults, because they are predetermined to shut their eyes to beauties. The critic does his utmost to blight genius in its infancy: that which rises in spite of him he will not see; and then he complains of the decline of literature. In like manner, these cankers of society complain of human nature and society, when they have wilfully debarred themselves from all the good they contain, and done their utmost to blight their own happiness and that of all around them. Misanthropy is sometimes the product of disappointed benevolence; but it is more frequently the offspring of overweening and mortified vanity, quarrelling with the world for not being better treated than it deserves.

SCYTHROP (*to Marionetta*)

These remarks are rather uncharitable. There is great good in human nature, but it is at present ill-conditioned. Ardent spirits cannot but be dissatisfied with things as they are; and, according to their views of the probabilities of amelioration, they will rush into the extremes of either hope or despair, -- of which the first is enthusiasm, and the second misanthropy: but their sources, in this case, are the same, as the Severn and the Wye run in different directions, and both rise in Plinlimmon.

MARIONETTA

"And there is salmon in both:" for the resemblance is about as close as that between Macedon and Monmouth.

CHAPTER 8

Marionetta observed, the next day, a remarkable perturbation in Scythrop, for which she could not imagine any probable cause. She was willing to believe, at first, that it had some transient and trifling source, and would pass off in a day or two; but, contrary to this expectation, it daily increased. She was well aware that Scythrop had a strong tendency to the love of mystery, for its own sake; that is to say, he would employ mystery to serve a purpose, but would first choose his purpose by its capability of mystery. He seemed now to have more mystery on his hands than the laws of the system allowed, and to wear his coat of darkness with an air of great discomfort. All her little playful arts lost by degrees much of their power either to irritate or to soothe, and the first perception of her diminished influence produced in her an immediate depression of spirits, and a consequent sadness of demeanour, that rendered her very interesting to Mr. Glowry; who, duly considering the improbability of accomplishing his wishes with respect to Miss Toobad (which improbability naturally increased in the diurnal ratio of that young lady's absence), began to reconcile himself by degrees to the idea of Marionetta being his daughter.

Marionetta made many ineffectual attempts to extract from Scythrop the secret of his mystery; and, in despair of drawing it from himself, began to form hopes that she might find a clue to it from Mr. Flosky, who was Scythrop's dearest friend, and was more frequently than any other person admitted to his solitary tower. Mr. Flosky, however, had ceased to be visible in a morning. He was engaged in the composition of a dismal ballad; and, Marionetta's uneasiness overcoming her scruples of decorum, she determined to seek him in the apartment which he had chosen for his study. She tapped at the door, and, at the sound "Come in," entered the apartment. It was noon, and the sun was shining in full splendour, much to the annoyance of Mr. Flosky, who had obviated the inconvenience by closing the shutters, and drawing the window curtains. He was sitting at his table by the light of a solitary candle, with a pen in one hand, and a muffineer in the other, with which he occasionally sprinkled salt on the wick, to make it burn blue. He sate with "his eye in a fine frenzy rolling," and turned his inspired gaze on Marionetta as if she had been the ghastly ladie of a magical vision; then placed his hand before his eyes, with an appearance of manifest pain -- shook his head -- withdrew his hand -- rubbed his eyes, like a waking man -- and said, in a tone of ruefulness most jeremitaylorically pathetic, "To what am I to attribute this very unexpected pleasure, my dear Miss O'Carroll?"

MARIONETTA

I must apologise for intruding on you, Mr. Flosky; but the interest which I -- you -- take in my cousin Scythrop --

MR. FLOSKY

Pardon me, Miss O'Carroll; I do not take any interest in any person or thing on the face of the earth; which sentiment, if you analyse it, you will find to be the quintessence of the most refined philanthropy.

MARIONETTA

I will take it for granted that it is so, Mr. Flosky; I am not conversant with metaphysical subtleties, but --

MR. FLOSKY

Subtleties! my dear Miss O'Carroll. I am sorry to find you participating in the vulgar error of the *reading public*, to whom an unusual collocation of words, involving a juxtaposition of antiperistatical ideas, immediately suggests the notion of hyperoxysophistical paradoxology.

MARIONETTA

Indeed, Mr. Flosky, it suggests no such notion to me. I have sought you for the purpose of obtaining information.

226

MR. FLOSKY (*shaking his head*)

No one ever sought me for such a purpose before.

MARIONETTA

I think, Mr. Flosky -- that is, I believe -- that is, I fancy -- that is, I imagine --

MR. FLOSKY

The [Greek: toytesti], the *id est*, the cioè, the *c'est à dire*, the *that is*, my dear Miss O'Carroll, is not applicable in this case -- if you will permit me to take the liberty of saying so. Think is not synonymous with believe -- for belief, in many most important particulars, results from the total absence, the absolute negation of thought, and is thereby the sane and orthodox condition of mind; and thought and belief are both essentially different from fancy, and fancy, again, is distinct from imagination. This distinction between fancy and imagination is one of the most abstruse and important points of metaphysics. I have written seven hundred pages of promise to elucidate it, which promise I shall keep as faithfully as the bank will its promise to pay.

MARIONETTA

I assure you, Mr. Flosky, I care no more about metaphysics than I do about the bank; and, if you will condescend to talk to a simple girl in intelligible terms --

MR. FLOSKY

Say not condescend! Know you not that you talk to the most humble of men, to one who has buckled on the armour of sanctity, and clothed himself with humility as with a garment?

MARIONETTA

My cousin Scythrop has of late had an air of mystery about him, which gives me great uneasiness.

MR. FLOSKY

That is strange. Nothing is so becoming to a man as an air of mystery. Mystery is the very key-stone of all that is beautiful in poetry, all that is sacred in faith, and all that is recondite in transcendental psychology. I am writing a ballad, which is all mystery: it is "such stuff as dreams are made of," and is, indeed, stuff made of a dream: for, last night I fell asleep, as usual, over my book, and had a vision of pure reason. I composed five hundred lines in my sleep; so that, having had a dream of a ballad, I am now officiating as my own Peter Quince, and making a ballad of my dream, and it shall be called Bottom's Dream, because it has no bottom.

MARIONETTA

I see, Mr. Flosky, you think my intrusion unseasonable, and are inclined to punish it, by talking nonsense to me. (*Mr. Flosky gave a start at the word nonsense, which almost overturned the table.*) I assure you, I would not have intruded if I had not been very much interested in the question I wish to ask you. -- (*Mr. Flosky listened in sullen dignity.*) -- My cousin Scythrop seems to have some secret preying on his mind. -- (*Mr. Flosky was silent.*) -- He seems very unhappy -- Mr. Flosky. -- Perhaps you are acquainted with the cause. -- (*Mr. Flosky was still silent.*) -- I only wish to know -- Mr. Flosky -- if it is anything -- that could be remedied by anything -- that any one -- of whom I know anything -- could do.

MR. FLOSKY (*after a pause*)

There are various ways of getting at secrets. The most approved methods, as recommended both theoretically and practically in philosophical novels, are eaves-dropping at key-holes, picking the locks of chests and desks, peeping into letters, steaming wafers, and insinuating hot wire under sealing wax; none of which methods I hold it lawful to practise.

MARIONETTA

Surely, Mr. Flosky, you cannot suspect me of wishing to adopt or encourage such base and contemptible arts.

MR. FLOSKY

Yet are they recommended, and with well-strung reasons, by writers of gravity and note, as simple and easy methods of studying character, and gratifying that laudable curiosity which aims at the knowledge of man.

MARIONETTA

I am as ignorant of this morality which you do not approve, as of the metaphysics which you do: I should be glad to know, by your means, what is the matter with my cousin: I do not like to see him unhappy, and I suppose there is some reason for it.

MR. FLOSKY

Now I should rather suppose there is no reason for it. It is the fashion to be unhappy. To have a reason for being so would be exceedingly common-place: to be so without any is the province of genius: the art of being miserable, for misery's sake, has been brought to great perfection in our days; and the ancient Odyssey, which held forth a shining example of the endurance of real misfortune, will give place to a modern one, setting out a more instructive picture of querulous impatience under imaginary evils.

MARIONETTA

Will you oblige me, Mr. Flosky, by giving me a plain answer to a plain question?

MR. FLOSKY

It is impossible, my dear Miss O'Carroll. I never gave a plain answer to a question in my life.

MARIONETTA

Do you, or do you not, know what is the matter with my cousin?

MR. FLOSKY

To say that I do not know, would be to say that I am ignorant of something: and God forbid, that a transcendental metaphysician, who has pure anticipated cognitions of every thing, and carries the whole science of geometry in his head without ever having looked into Euclid, should fall into so empirical an error as to declare himself ignorant of any thing: to say that I do know, would be to pretend to positive and circumstantial knowledge touching present matter of fact, which, when you consider the nature of evidence, and the various lights in which the same thing may be seen --

MARIONETTA

I see, Mr. Flosky, that either you have no information, or are determined not to impart it; and I beg your pardon for having given you this unnecessary trouble.

MR. FLOSKY

My dear Miss O'Carroll, it would have given me great pleasure to have said any thing that would have given you pleasure; but, if any person living could make report of having any information on any subject from Ferdinando Flosky, my transcendental reputation would be ruined for ever.

CHAPTER 9

Scythrop grew every day more reserved, mysterious, and *distrait*; and gradually lengthened the duration of his diurnal seclusions in his tower. Marionetta thought she perceived in all this very manifest symptoms of a warm love cooling.

It was seldom that she found herself alone with him in the morning, and, on these occasions, if she was silent, in the hope of his speaking first, not a syllable would he utter: if she spoke to him indirectly, he assented monosyllabically: if she questioned him, his answers were brief, constrained, and evasive. Still, though her spirits were depressed, her playfulness had not so totally forsaken her, but that it illuminated, at intervals, the gloom of Nightmare Abbey; and, if, on any occasion, she observed in Scythrop tokens of unextinguished or returning passion, her love of tormenting her lover immediately got the better both of her grief and her sympathy, though not of her curiosity, which Scythrop seemed determined not to satisfy. This playfulness, however, was in a great measure artificial, and usually vanished with the irritable Strephon, to whose annoyance it had been exerted. The Genius Loci, the *tutela* of Nightmare Abbey, the spirit of black melancholy, began to set his seal on her pallescent countenance. Scythrop perceived the change, found his tender sympathies awakened, and did his utmost to comfort the afflicted damsel, assuring her that his seeming inattention had only proceeded from his being involved in a profound meditation on a very hopeful scheme for the regeneration of human society. Marionetta called him ungrateful, cruel, cold-hearted, and accompanied her reproaches with many sobs and tears; poor Scythrop growing every moment more soft and submissive, -- till, at length, he threw himself at her feet, and declared, that no competition of beauty however dazzling, genius however transcendent, talents however cultivated, or philosophy however enlightened, should ever make him renounce his divine Marionetta.

"Competition!" thought Marionetta, and suddenly, with an air of the most freezing indifference, she said, "You are perfectly at liberty, sir, to do as you please: I beg you will follow your own plans, without any reference to me."

Scythrop was confounded. What was become of all her passion and her tears? Still kneeling, he kissed her hand with rueful timidity, and said, in most pathetic accents, "Do you not love me, Marionetta?"

"No," said Marionetta, with a look of cold composure: "No." Scythrop still looked up incredulously. "No, I tell you."

"Oh! very well, madam," said Scythrop, rising, "if that is the case, there are those in the world --"

"To be sure there are, sir; -- and do you suppose I do not see through your designs, you ungenerous monster?"

"My designs? Marionetta!"

"Yes, your designs, Scythrop. You have come here to cast me off, and artfully contrive that it should appear to be my doing, and not yours, thinking to quiet your tender conscience with this pitiful stratagem. But do not suppose that you are of so much consequence to me. Do not suppose it. You are of no consequence to me at all. None at all. Therefore, leave me. I renounce you. Leave me. Why do you not leave me?"

Scythrop endeavoured to remonstrate, but without success. She reiterated her injunctions to him to leave her, till, in the simplicity of his spirit, he was preparing to comply. When he had nearly reached the door, Marionetta said, "Farewell." Scythrop looked back. "Farewell, Scythrop," she repeated, "you will never see me again."

"Never see you again, Marionetta?"

"I shall go from hence to-morrow, perhaps to-day; and, before we meet again, one of us will be married, and we might as well be dead, you know, Scythrop."

The sudden change of her voice in the last few words, and the burst of tears that accompanied them, acted like electricity on the tender-hearted youth; and in another instant a complete reconciliation was accomplished without the intervention of words.

There are, indeed, some learned casuists, who maintain that love has no language, and that all the misunderstandings and dissensions of lovers arise from the fatal habit of employing words on a subject to which words are inapplicable; that love, beginning with looks, that is to say, with the physiognomical expression of congenial mental dispositions, tends, through a regular gradation of signs and symbols of affection, to that consummation which is most devoutly to be wished; and that it neither is necessary that there should be, nor probable that there would be, a single word spoken from first to last between two sympathetic spirits, were it not that the arbitrary institutions of society have raised, at every step of this very simple process, so many complicated impediments and barriers in the shape of settlements and ceremonies, parents and guardians, lawyers, jew-brokers, and parsons; whence many an adventurous knight (who, in order to obtain the conquest of the Hesperian fruit, is obliged to fight his way through all these monsters), is either repulsed at the onset or vanquished before the achievement of his enterprise: and such a quantity of unnatural talking is rendered inevitably necessary through all the stages of the progression, that the tender and volatile spirit of love often takes flight on the pinions of some of the [Greek: epea pteroenta], or *winged words* which are pressed into his service in despite of himself.

At this conjuncture, Mr. Glowry entered, and, sitting down near them, said, "I see how it is; and, as we are all sure to be miserable, do what we may, there is no need of taking pains to make one another more so; therefore, with God's blessing and mine, there"-- joining their hands as he spoke.

Scythrop was not exactly prepared for this decisive step: but he could only stammer out, "Really, sir, you are too good;" and Mr. Glowry departed to bring Mr. Hilary to ratify the act.

Now, whatever truth there may be in the theory of love and language, of which we have so recently spoken, certain it is, that during Mr. Glowry's absence, which lasted half an hour, not a single word was said by either Scythrop or Marionetta.

Mr. Glowry returned with Mr. Hilary, who was delighted at the prospect of so advantageous an establishment for his orphan niece, of whom he considered himself in some manner the guardian, and nothing remained, as Mr. Glowry observed, but to fix the day.

Marionetta blushed, and was silent. Scythrop was also silent for a time, and at length hesitatingly said, "My deal sir, your goodness overpowers me; but really you are so precipitate."

Now, this remark, if the young lady had made it, would, whether she thought it or not -- for sincerity is a thing of no account on these occasions, nor indeed on any other, according to Mr. Flosky -- this remark, if the young lady had made it, would have been perfectly *comme il faut*; but, being made by the young gentleman, it was *toute autre chose*, and was, indeed, in the eyes of his mistress, a most heinous and irremissible offence. Marionetta was angry, very angry, but she concealed her anger, and said, calmly and coldly, "Certainly, you are much too precipitate, Mr. Glowry. I assure you, sir, I have by no means made up my mind; and, indeed, as far as I know it, it inclines the other way: but it will be quite time enough to think of these matters seven years hence." Before surprise permitted reply, the young lady had locked herself up in her own apartment.

"Why, Scythrop," said Mr. Glowry, elongating his face exceedingly, "the devil is come among us, sure enough, as Mr. Toobad observes: I thought you and Marionetta were both of a mind."

"So we are, I believe, sir," said Scythrop, gloomily, and stalked away to his tower.

"Mr. Glowry," said Mr. Hilary, "I do not very well understand all this."

"Whims, brother Hilary," said Mr. Glowry; "some little foolish love quarrel, nothing more. Whims, freaks, April showers. They will be blown over by to-morrow."

"If not," said Mr. Hilary, 'these April showers have made us April fools."

"Ah!" said Mr. Glowry, "you are a happy man, and in all your afflictions you can console yourself with a joke, let it be ever so bad, provided you crack it yourself. I should be very happy to laugh with you, if it would give you any satisfaction; but, really, at present, my heart is so sad, that I find it impossible to levy a contribution on my muscles."

CHAPTER 10

On the evening on which Mr. Asterias had caught a glimpse of a female figure on the sea-shore, which he had translated into the visual sign of his interior cognition of a mermaid, Scythrop, retiring to his tower, found his study pre-occupied. A stranger, muffled in a cloak, was sitting at his table. Scythrop paused in surprise. The stranger rose at his entrance, and looked at him intently a few minutes, in silence. The eyes of the stranger alone were visible. All the rest of the figure was muffled and mantled in the folds of a black cloak, which was raised, by the right hand, to the level of the eyes. This scrutiny being completed, the stranger, dropping the cloak, said, "I see, by your physiognomy, that you may be trusted;" and revealed to the astonished Scythrop a female form and countenance

233

of dazzling grace and beauty, with long flowing hair of raven blackness, and large black eyes of almost oppressive brilliancy: which strikingly contrasted with a complexion of snowy whiteness. Her dress was extremely elegant, but had an appearance of foreign fashion, as if both the lady and her mantua-maker were of "a far countree."

> "I guess 'twas frightful there to see
> A lady so richly clad as she,
> Beautiful exceedingly."

For, if it be terrible to one young lady to find another under a tree at midnight, it must, *a fortiori*, be much more terrible to a young gentleman to find a young lady in his study at that hour. If the logical consecutiveness of this conclusion be not manifest to my readers, I am sorry for their dulness, and must refer them, for more ample elucidation, to a treatise which Mr. Flosky intends to write, on the Categories of Relation, which comprehend Substance and Accident, Cause and Effect, Action and Re-action.

Scythrop, therefore, either was or ought to have been frightened: at all events, he was astonished; and astonishment, though not in itself fear, is nevertheless a good stage towards it, and is, indeed, as it were, the half-way house between respect and terror, according to Mr. Burke's graduated scale of the sublime.*

---

*Mr. Burke's graduated scale of the sublime: There must be some mistake in this, for the whole honourable band of gentlemen-pensioners has resolved unanimously, that Mr. Burke was a very sublime person, particularly after he had prostituted his own soul, and betrayed his country and mankind, for *1200l.* a year: yet he does not appear to have been a very terrible personage, and certainly went off with a very small portion of human respect, though he contrived to excite, in a great degree, the astonishment of all honest men. Our immaculate laureate (who gives us to understand that, if he had not been purified by holy matrimony into a mystical type, he would have died a virgin,) is another sublime gentleman of the same genus: he very much astonished some persons when he sold his birthright for a pot of sack; but not even his *Sosia* has a grain of respect for him, though, doubtless, he thinks his name very terrible to the enemy, when he flourishes his criticopoeticopolitical tomahawk, and sets up his Indian yell for the blood of his old friends: but, at best, he is a mere political scarecrow, a man of straw, ridiculous to all who know of what materials he is made; and to none more so, than to those who have stuffed him, and set him up, as the Priapus of the garden of the golden apples of corruption.

"You are surprised," said the lady; "yet why should you be surprised? If you had met me in a drawing-room, and I had been introduced to you by an old woman, it would have been a matter of course: can the division of two or three walls, and the absence of an unimportant personage, make the same object essentially different in the perception of a philosopher?"

"Certainly not," said Scythrop; "but when any class of objects has habitually presented itself to our perceptions, in invariable conjunction with particular relations, then, on the sudden appearance of one object of the class, divested of those accompaniments, the essential difference of the relation is, by an involuntary process, transferred to the object itself, which thus offers itself to our perceptions with all the strangeness of novelty."

"You are a philosopher," said the lady, "and a lover of liberty. You are the author of a treatise, called 'Philosophical Gas; or, a Project for a General Illumination of the Human Mind.' "

"I am," said Scythrop, delighted at this first blossom of his renown.

"I am a stranger in this country," said the lady; "I have been but a few days in it, yet I find myself immediately under the necessity of seeking refuge from an atrocious persecution. I had no friend to whom I could apply, and, in the midst of my difficulties, accident threw your pamphlet in my way. I saw that I had, at least, one kindred mind in this nation, and determined to apply to you."

"And what would you have me do?" said Scythrop, more and more amazed, and not a little perplexed.

"I would have you," said the young lady, "assist me in finding some place of retreat, where I can remain concealed from the indefatigable search that is being made for me. I have been so nearly caught once or twice already, that I cannot confide any longer in my own ingenuity."

Doubtless, thought Scythrop, this is one of my golden candle-sticks. "I have constructed," said he, "in this tower, an entrance to a small suite of unknown apartments in the main building, which I defy any creature living to detect. If you would like to remain there a day or two, till I can find you a more suitable concealment, you may rely on the honour of a transcendental eleutherarch."

"I rely on myself," said the lady. "I act as I please, go where I please, and let the world say what it will. I am rich enough to set it

235

at defiance. It is the tyrant of the poor and the feeble, but the slave of those who are above the reach of its injury."

Scythrop ventured to inquire the name of his fair *protégée*. "What is a name?" said the lady: "any name will serve the purpose of distinction. Call me Stella. -- I see by your looks," she added, "that you think all this very strange. When you know me better, your surprise will cease. I submit not to be an accomplice in my sex's slavery. I am, like yourself, a lover of freedom, and I carry my theory into practice. *They alone are subject to blind authority who have no reliance on their own strength.*"

Stella took possession of the recondite apartments. Scythrop intended to find her another asylum, but from day to day he postponed his intention, and by degrees forgot it. The young lady reminded him of it from day to day, till she also forgot it. Scythrop was anxious to learn her history; but she would add nothing to what she had already communicated, that she was shunning an atrocious persecution. Scythrop thought of Lord C. and the Alien Act, and said, "As you will not tell your name, I suppose it is in the green-bag." Stella, not understanding what he meant, was silent; and Scythrop, translating silence into acquiescence, concluded that he was sheltering an *illuminée,* whom Lord S. suspected of an intention to take the Tower, and set fire to the Bank: exploits, at least, as likely to be accomplished by the hands and eyes of a young beauty, as by a drunken cobbler and doctor, armed with a pamphlet and an old stocking.

Stella, in her conversations with Scythrop, displayed a highly cultivated and energetic mind, full of impassioned schemes of liberty, and impatience of masculine usurpation. She had a lively sense of all the oppressions that are done under the sun; and the vivid pictures which her imagination presented to her of the numberless scenes of injustice and misery which are being acted at every moment in every part of the inhabited world, gave an habitual seriousness to her physiognomy, that made it seem as if a smile had never once hovered on her lips. She was intimately conversant with the German language and literature; and Scythrop listened with delight to her repetitions of her favourite passages from Schiller and Goethe, and to her encomiums on the sublime Spartacus Weishaupt, the immortal founder of the sect of the Illuminati. Scythrop found that his soul had a greater capacity of love than the image of Marionetta had filled. The form of Stella took possession of every

236

vacant corner of the cavity, and by degrees displaced that of Marionetta from many of the outworks of the citadel, though the latter still held possession of the *keep*. He judged, from his new friend calling herself Stella, that, if it were not her real name, she was an admirer of the principles of the German play from which she had taken it, and took an opportunity of leading the conversation to that subject: but, to his great surprise, the lady spoke very ardently of the singleness and exclusiveness of love, and declared that the reign of affection was one and indivisible; that it might be transferred, but could not be participated. "If I ever love," said she, "I shall do so without limit or restriction. I shall hold all difficulties light, all sacrifices cheap, all obstacles gossamer. But, for love so total, I shall claim a return as absolute. I will have no rival: whether more or less favoured will be of little moment. I will be neither first nor second -- I will be alone. The heart which I shall possess I will possess entirely, or entirely renounce."

Scythrop did not dare to mention the name of Marionetta: he trembled lest some unlucky accident should reveal it to Stella, though he scarcely knew what result to wish or anticipate, and lived in the double fever of a perpetual dilemma. He could not dissemble to himself that he was in love, at the same time, with two damsels of minds and habits as remote as the Antipodes. The scale of predilection always inclined to the fair one who happened to be present, but the absent was never effectually outweighed, though the degrees of exaltation and depression varied according to accidental variations in the outward and visible signs of the inward and spiritual graces of his respective charmers. Passing and re-passing several times a day from the company of the one to that of the other, he was like a shuttlecock between two battledores, changing its direction as rapidly as the oscillations of a pendulum, receiving many a hard knock on the cork of a sensitive heart, and flying from point to point on the feathers of a super-sublimated head. This was an awful state of things. He had now as much mystery about him as any romantic transcendentalist or transcendental romancer could desire. He had his esoterical and his exoterical love. He could not endure the thought of losing either of them, but he trembled when he imagined the possibility that some fatal discovery might deprive him of both. The old proverb concerning two strings to a bow gave him some gleams of comfort: but that concerning two stools occurred to him more frequently, and covered his forehead with a cold perspiration. With Stella, he could indulge freely in all his romantic and philosophical visions. He could build castles in the air, and she would pile towers and turrets on the imaginary edifices. With Marionetta, it was otherwise: she knew nothing of the world and society beyond the sphere of her own experience. Her life was all music and sunshine, and she wondered what any one could see to complain of in such a pleasant state of things. She loved Scythrop, she hardly knew why: indeed, she was not always sure that she loved him at all: she felt her fondness increase or diminish in an inverse ratio to his. When she had manoeuvred him into a fever of passionate love, she often felt, and always assumed indifference: if she found that her coldness was contagious, and that Scythrop either was, or pretended to be, as indifferent as herself, she would become doubly kind, and raise him again to that elevation from which she had previously thrown him down. Thus, when his love was flowing, hers was ebbing: when his was ebbing, hers was flowing. Now and then there were moments of level tide, when reciprocal affection seemed to promise imperturbable harmony: but Scythrop could scarcely resign his spirit to the pleasing illusion, before the pinnace of the lover's affections was caught in some eddy of the lady's caprice, and he was whirled away from the shore of his hopes, without rudder or compass, into an ocean of mists and storms. It resulted, from this system of conduct, that all that passed between Scythrop and Marionetta consisted in making and unmaking love. He had no opportunity to take measure of her understanding by conversations on general subjects, and on his favourite designs; and, being left, in this respect, to the exercise of indefinite conjecture, he took it for granted, as most lovers would do in similar circumstances, that she had great natural talents, which she wasted at present on trifles: but coquetry would end with marriage, and leave room for philosophy to exert its influence on her mind. Stella had no coquetry, no disguise: she was an enthusiast in subjects of general interest; and her conduct to Scythrop was always uniform, or rather shewed a regular progression of partiality, which seemed fast ripening into love.

CHAPTER 11

Scythrop, attending one day the summons to dinner, found in the drawing-room his friend Mr. Cypress, the poet, whom he had known at college, and who was a great favourite of Mr. Glowry. Mr. Cypress said, he was on the point of leaving England, but could not think of doing so without a farewell look at Nightmare Abbey and his respected friends, the moody Mr. Glowry and the mysterious Mr. Scythrop, the sublime Mr. Flosky and the pathetic Mr. Listless; to all of whom, and the morbid hospitality of the melancholy dwelling, in which they were then assembled, he assured them he should always look back with as much affection as his lacerated spirit could feel for any thing. The sympathetic condolence of their respective replies was cut short by Raven's announcement of "dinner on table."

The conversation that took place when the wine was in circulation, and the ladies were withdrawn, we shall report with our usual scrupulous fidelity.

MR. GLOWRY

You are leaving England, Mr. Cypress. There is a delightful melancholy in saying farewell to an old acquaintance, when the chances are twenty to one against ever meeting again. A smiling bumper to a sad parting, and let us all be unhappy together.

MR. CYPRESS (*filling a bumper*)

This is the only social habit that the disappointed spirit never unlearns.

THE REVEREND MR. LARYNX (*filling*)

It is the only piece of academical learning that the finished educatee retains.

MR. FLOSKY (*filling*)

It is the only objective fact which the sceptic can realise.

SCYTHROP (*filling*)

It is the only styptic for a bleeding heart.

THE HONOURABLE MR. LISTLESS (*filling*)

It is the only trouble that is very well worth taking.

MR. ASTERIAS (*filling*)

It is the only key of conversational truth.

MR. TOOBAD (*filling*)

It is the only antidote to the great wrath of the devil.

MR. HILARY (*filling*)

It is the only symbol of perfect life. The inscription "HIC NON BIBITUR" will suit nothing but a tomb-stone.

MR. GLOWRY

You will see many fine old ruins, Mr. Cypress, crumbling pillars, and mossy walls -- many a one-legged Venus and headless Minerva -- many a Neptune buried in sand -- many a Jupiter turned topsy-turvy -- many a perforated Bacchus doing duty as a water-pipe -- many reminiscences of the ancient world, which I hope was better worth living in than the modern; though, for myself, I care not a straw more for one than the other, and would not go twenty miles to see any thing that either could shew.

MR. CYPRESS

It is something to seek, Mr. Glowry. The mind is restless, and must persist in seeking, though to find is to be disappointed. Do you feel no aspirations towards the countries of Socrates and Cicero? no wish to wander among the venerable remains of the greatness that has passed for ever?

MR. GLOWRY

Not a grain.

SCYTHROP

It is, indeed, much the same as if a lover should dig up the buried form of his mistress, and gaze upon relics which are any thing but herself, to wander among a few mouldy ruins, that are only imperfect indexes to lost volumes of glory, and meet at every step the more melancholy ruins of human nature -- a degenerate race of stupid and shrivelled slaves, grovelling in the lowest depths of servility and superstition.

THE HONOURABLE MR. LISTLESS

It is the fashion to go abroad. I have thought of it myself, but am hardly equal to the exertion. To be sure, a little eccentricity and originality are allowable in some cases; and the most eccentric and original of all characters is an Englishman who stays at home.

SCYTHROP

I should have no pleasure in visiting countries that are past all hope of regeneration. There is great hope of our own; and it seems to me that an Englishman, who, either by his station in society, or by his genius, or (as in your instance, Mr. Cypress,) by both, has the power of essentially serving his country in its arduous struggle with its domestic enemies, yet forsakes his country, which is still so rich in hope, to dwell in others which are only fertile in the ruins of memory, does what none of those ancients, whose fragmentary memorials you venerate, would have done in similar circumstances.

MR. CYPRESS

Sir, I have quarrelled with my wife; and a man who has quarrelled with his wife is absolved from all duty to his country. I have written an ode to tell the people as much, and they may take it as they list.

SCYTHROP

Do you suppose, if Brutus had quarrelled with his wife, he would have given it as a reason to Cassius for having nothing to do with his enterprise? Or would Cassius have been satisfied with such an excuse?

MR. FLOSKY

Brutus was a senator; so is our dear friend: but the cases are different. Brutus had some hope of political good: Mr. Cypress has none. How should he, after what we have seen in France?

SCYTHROP

A Frenchman is born in harness, ready saddled, bitted, and bridled, for any tyrant to ride. He will fawn under his rider one moment, and throw him and kick him to death the next; but another adventurer springs on his back, and by dint of whip and spur on he goes as before. We may, without much vanity, hope better of ourselves.

MR. CYPRESS

I have no hope for myself or for others. Our life is a false nature: it is not in the harmony of things: it is an all-blasting upas, whose root is earth, and whose leaves are the skies which rain their poison-dews upon mankind. We wither from our youth: we gasp with unslaked thirst for unattainable good: lured from the first to the last by phantoms -- love, fame, ambition, avarice -- all idle, and all ill-- one meteor of many names, that vanishes in the smoke of death.*

MR. FLOSKY

A most delightful speech, Mr. Cypress. A most amiable and instructive philosophy. You have only to impress its truth on the minds of all living men, and life will then, indeed, be the desert and the solitude; and I must do you, myself, and our mutual friends, the justice to observe, that let society only give fair play at one and the

---

*... vanishes in the smoke of death: *Childe Harold*, canto 4. cxxiv. cxxvi.

same time, as I flatter myself it is inclined to do, to your system of morals, and my system of metaphysics, and Scythrop's system of politics, and Mr. Listless's system of manners, and Mr. Toobad's system of religion, and the result will be as fine a mental chaos as even the immortal Kant himself could ever have hoped to see; in the prospect of which I rejoice.

MR. HILARY

"Certainly, ancient, it is not a thing to rejoice at:" I am one of those who cannot see the good that is to result from all this mystifying and blue-devilling of society. The contrast it presents to the cheerful and solid wisdom of antiquity is too forcible not to strike any one who has the least knowledge of classical literature. To represent vice and misery as the necessary accompaniments of genius, is as mischievous as it is false, and the feeling is as unclassical as the language in which it is usually expressed.

MR. TOOBAD

It is our calamity. The devil has come among us, and has begun by taking possession of all the cleverest fellows. Yet, forsooth, this is the enlightened age. Marry, how? Did our ancestors go peeping about with dark lanterns, and do we walk at our ease in broad sunshine? Where is the manifestation of our light? By what symptoms do you recognise it? What are its signs, its tokens, its symptoms, its symbols, its categories, its conditions? What is it, and why? How, where, when is it to be seen, felt, and understood? What do we see by it which our ancestors saw not, and which at the same time is worth seeing? We see a hundred men hanged, where they saw one. We see five hundred transported, where they saw one. We see five thousand in the workhouse, where they saw one. We see scores of Bible Societies, where they saw none. We see paper, where they saw gold. We see men in stays, where they saw men in armour. We see painted faces, where they saw healthy ones. We see children perishing in manufactories, where they saw them flourishing in the fields. We see prisons, where they saw castles. We see masters, where they saw representatives. In short, they saw true men, where we see false knaves. They saw Milton, and we see Mr. Sackbut.

MR. FLOSKY

"The false knave, sir, is my honest friend; therefore, I beseech you, let him be countenanced. God forbid but a knave should have some countenance at his friend's request."

242

MR. TOOBAD

"Good men and true" was their common term, like the chalos chagathos of the Athenians. It is so long since men have been either good or true, that it is to be questioned which is most obsolete, the fact or the phraseology.

MR. CYPRESS

There is no worth nor beauty but in the mind's idea. Love sows the wind and reaps the whirlwind.* Confusion, thrice confounded, is the portion of him who rests even for an instant on that most brittle of reeds -- the affection of a human being. The sum of our social destiny is to inflict or to endure.*

MR. HILARY

Rather to bear and forbear, Mr. Cypress -- a maxim which you perhaps despise. Ideal beauty is not the mind's creation: it is real beauty, refined and purified in the mind's alembic, from the alloy which always more or less accompanies it in our mixed and imperfect nature. But still the gold exists in a very ample degree. To expect too much is a disease in the expectant, for which human nature is not responsible; and, in the common name of humanity, I protest against these false and mischievous ravings. To rail against humanity for not being abstract perfection, and against human love for not realizing all the splendid visions of the poets of chivalry, is to rail at the summer for not being all sunshine, and at the rose for not being always in bloom.

MR. CYPRESS

Human love! Love is not an inhabitant of the earth. We worship him as the Athenians did their unknown God: but broken hearts are the martyrs of his faith, and the eye shall never see the form which phantasy paints, and which passion pursues through paths of delusive beauty, among flowers whose odours are agonies, and trees whose gums are poison.*

MR. HILARY

You talk like a Rosicrucian, who will love nothing but a sylph, who does not believe in the existence of a sylph, and who yet quarrels with the whole universe for not containing a sylph.

MR. CYPRESS

The mind is diseased of its own beauty, and fevers into false

---

*... and reaps the whirlwind: *Childe Harold*, Canto 4. cxxiii.
*... or to endure: *Ibid*. Canto 3. lxxi.
*... whose gums are poison: *Ibid*. Canto 4. cxxi. cxxxvi.

creation. The forms which the sculptor's soul has seized exist only in himself.*

MR. FLOSKY

Permit me to discept. They are the mediums of common forms combined and arranged into a common standard. The ideal beauty of the Helen of Zeuxis was the combined medium of the real beauty of the virgins of Crotona.

MR. HILARY

But to make ideal beauty the shadow in the water, and, like the dog in the fable, to throw away the substance in catching at the shadow, is scarcely the characteristic of wisdom, whatever it may be of genius. To reconcile man as he is to the world as it is, to preserve and improve all that is good, and destroy or alleviate all that is evil, in physical and moral nature -- have been the hope and aim of the greatest teachers and ornaments of our species. I will say, too, that the highest wisdom and the highest genius have been invariably accompanied with cheerfulness. We have sufficient proofs on record that Shakespeare and Socrates were the most festive of companions. But now the little wisdom and genius we have seem to be entering into a conspiracy against cheerfulness.

MR. TOOBAD

How can we be cheerful with the devil among us?

THE HONOURABLE MR. LISTLESS

How can we be cheerful when our nerves are shattered?

MR. FLOSKY

How can we be cheerful when we are surrounded by a *reading public*, that is growing too wise for its betters?

SCYTHROP

How can we be cheerful when our great general designs are crossed every moment by our little particular passions?

MR. CYPRESS

How can we be cheerful in the midst of disappointment and despair?

MR. GLOWRY

Let us all be unhappy together.

MR. HILARY

Let us sing a catch.

MR. GLOWRY

No: a nice tragical ballad. The Norfolk Tragedy to the tune of the

---

*... exist only in himself: *Childe Harold*, Canto 4. cxxii.

Hundredth Psalm.
MR. HILARY
    I say a catch.
MR. GLOWRY
    I say no. A song from Mr. Cypress.
ALL
    A song from Mr. Cypress.
MR. CYPRESS *sung* --

    There is a fever of the spirit,
    The brand of Cain's unresting doom,
    Which in the lone dark souls that bear it
    Glows like the lamp in Tullia's tomb:
    Unlike that lamp, its subtle fire
    Burns, blasts, consumes its cell, the heart,
    Till, one by one, hope, joy, desire,
    Like dreams of shadowy smoke depart.

    When hope, love, life itself, are only
    Dust -- spectral memories -- dead and cold --
    The unfed fire burns bright and lonely,
    Like that undying lamp of old:
    And by that drear illumination,
    Till time its clay-built home has rent,
    Thought broods on feeling's desolation --
    The soul is its own monument.

MR. GLOWRY
    Admirable. Let us all be unhappy together.
MR. HILARY
    Now, I say again, a catch.
THE REVEREND MR. LARYNX
    I am for you.
MR. HILARY
    "Seamen three."
THE REVEREND MR. LARYNX
    Agreed. I'll be Harry Gill, with the voice of three. Begin.
MR. HILARY AND THE REVEREND MR. LARYNX

    Seamen three! What men be ye?
245

Gotham's three wise men we be.
Whither in your bowl so free?
To rake the moon from out the sea.
The bowl goes trim. The moon doth shine.
And our ballast is old wine;
And your ballast is old wine.

Who art thou, so fast adrift?
I am he they call Old Care.
Here on board we will thee lift.
No: I may not enter there.
Wherefore so? 'Tis Jove's decree,
In a bowl Care may not be;
In a bowl Care may not be.

Fear ye not the waves that roll?
No: in charmed bowl we swim.
What the charm that floats the bowl?
Water may not pass the brim.
The bowl goes trim. The moon doth shine.
And our ballast is old wine;
And your ballast is old wine.

This catch was so well executed by the spirit and science of Mr.
Hilary, and the deep tri-une voice of the reverend gentleman, that
the whole party, in spite of themselves, caught the contagion, and
joined in chorus at the conclusion, each raising a bumper to his lips:

The bowl goes trim: the moon doth shine:
And our ballast is old wine.

Mr. Cypress, having his ballast on board, stepped, the same evening,
into his bowl, or travelling chariot, and departed to rake seas and
rivers, lakes and canals, for the moon of ideal beauty.

CHAPTER 12

It was the custom of the Honourable Mr. Listless, on adjourning from the bottle to the ladies, to retire for a few moments to make a second toilette, that he might present himself in becoming taste. Fatout, attending as usual, appeared with a countenance of great dismay, and informed his master that he had just ascertained that the Abbey was haunted. Mrs. Hilary's *gentlewoman*, for whom Fatout had lately conceived a *tendresse*, had been, as she expressed it, "fritted out of her seventeen senses" the preceding night, as she was retiring to her bed-chamber, by a ghastly figure, which she had met stalking along one of the galleries, wrapped in a white shroud, with a bloody turban on its head. She had fainted away with fear; and, when she recovered, she found herself in the dark, and the figure was gone. "*Sacre--cochon--bleu!*" exclaimed Fatout, giving very deliberate emphasis to every portion of his terrible oath – "I vould not meet de *revenant*, de ghost -- *non* -- not for all de *bowl-de-ponch* in de vorld."

"Fatout," said the Honourable Mr. Listless, "did I ever see a ghost?"

"*Jamais*, monsieur, never."

"Then I hope I never shall, for, in the present shattered state of my nerves, I am afraid it would be too much for me. There -- loosen the lace of my stays a little, for really this plebeian practice of eating -- Not too loose -- consider my shape. That will do. And I desire that you bring me no more stories of ghosts; for, though I do not believe in such things, yet, when one is awake in the night, one is apt, if one thinks of them, to have fancies that give one a kind of a chill, particularly if one opens one's eyes suddenly on one's dressing-gown, hanging in the moonlight, between the bed and the window."

The Honourable Mr. Listless, though he had prohibited Fatout from bringing him any more stories of ghosts, could not help thinking of that which Fatout had already brought; and, as it was uppermost in his mind, when he descended to the tea and coffee cups, and the rest of the company in the library, he almost involuntarily asked Mr. Flosky, whom he looked up to as a most oraculous personage, whether any story of any ghost that had ever appeared to any one, was entitled to any degree of belief?

MR. FLOSKY

By far the greater number, to a very great degree.

THE HONOURABLE MR. LISTLESS

Really, that is very alarming!

MR. FLOSKY

Sunt geminoe somni portoe. There are two gates through which ghosts find their way to the upper air: fraud and self-delusion. In the latter case, a ghost is a *deceptio visûs*, an ocular spectrum, an idea with the force of a sensation. I have seen many ghosts myself. I dare say there are few in this company who have not seen a ghost.

THE HONOURABLE MR. LISTLESS

I am happy to say, I never have, for one.

THE REVEREND MR. LARYNX

We have such high authority for ghosts, that it is rank scepticism to disbelieve them. Job saw a ghost, which came for the express purpose of asking a question, and did not wait for an answer.

THE HONOURABLE MR. LISTLESS

Because Job was too frightened to give one.

THE REVEREND MR. LARYNX

Spectres appeared to the Egyptians during the darkness with which Moses covered Egypt. The witch of Endor raised the ghost of Samuel. Moses and Elias appeared on Mount Tabor. An evil spirit was sent into the army of Sennacherib, and exterminated it in a single night.

MR. TOOBAD

Saying, The devil is come among you, having great wrath.

MR. FLOSKY

Saint Macarius interrogated a skull, which was found in the desert, and made it relate, in presence of several witnesses, what was going forward in hell. Saint Martin of Tours, being jealous of a pretended martyr, who was the rival saint of his neighbourhood, called up his ghost, and made him confess that he was damned. Saint Germain, being on his travels, turned out of an inn a large party of ghosts, who had every night taken possession of the *table d'hôte*, and consumed a copious supper.

MR. HILARY

Jolly ghosts, and no doubt all friars. A similar party took possession of the cellar of M. Swebach, the painter, in Paris, drank his wine, and threw the empty bottles at his head.

THE REVEREND MR. LARYNX

An atrocious act.

MR. FLOSKY

Pausanias relates, that the neighing of horses and the tumult of combatants were heard every night on the field of Marathon: that those who went purposely to hear these sounds suffered severely for their curiosity; but those who heard them by accident passed with impunity.

THE REVEREND MR. LARYNX

I once saw a ghost myself, in my study, which is the last place where any one but a ghost would look for me. I had not been into it for three months, and was going to consult Tillotson, when, on opening the door, I saw a venerable figure in a flannel dressing-gown, sitting in my arm-chair, and reading my Jeremy Taylor. It vanished in a moment, and so did I; and what it was or what it wanted I have never been able to ascertain.

MR. FLOSKY

It was an idea with the force of a sensation. It is seldom that ghosts appeal to two senses at once; but, when I was in Devonshire, the following story was well attested to me. A young woman, whose lover was at sea, returning one evening over some solitary fields, saw her lover sitting on a stile over which she was to pass. Her first emotions were surprise and joy, but there was a paleness and seriousness in his face that made them give place to alarm. She advanced towards him, and he said to her, in a solemn voice, "The eye that hath seen me shall see me no more. Thine eye is upon me, but I am not." And with these words he vanished; and on that very day and hour, as it afterwards appeared, he had perished by shipwreck.

The whole party now drew round in a circle, and each related some ghostly anecdote, heedless of the flight of time, till, in a pause of the conversation, they heard the hollow tongue of midnight sounding twelve.

MR. HILARY

All these anecdotes admit of solution on psychological principles. It is more easy for a soldier, a philosopher, or even a saint, to be frightened at his own shadow, than for a dead man to come out of his grave. Medical writers cite a thousand singular examples of the force of imagination. Persons of feeble, nervous, melancholy temperament, exhausted by fever, by labour, or by spare diet, will readily conjure up, in the magic ring of their own phantasy, spectres, gorgons, chimaeras, and all the objects of their hatred and their love. We are most of us like Don Quixote, to whom a windmill was a giant, and Dulcinea a magnificent princess: all more or less the dupes of our own imagination, though we do not all go so far as to see ghosts, or to fancy ourselves pipkins and teapots.

MR. FLOSKY

I can safely say I have seen too many ghosts myself to believe in their external existence. I have seen all kinds of ghosts: black spirits and white, red spirits and grey. Some in the shapes of venerable old men, who have met me in my rambles at noon; some of beautiful young women, who have peeped through my curtains at midnight.

THE HONOURABLE MR. LISTLESS

And have proved, I doubt not, "palpable to feeling as to sight."

MR. FLOSKY

By no means, sir. You reflect upon my purity. Myself and my friends, particularly my friend Mr. Sackbut, are famous for our purity. No, sir, genuine untangible ghosts. I live in a world of ghosts. I see a ghost at this moment.

Mr. Flosky fixed his eyes on a door at the farther end of the library. The company looked in the same direction. The door silently opened, and a ghastly figure, shrouded in white drapery, with the semblance of a bloody turban on its head, entered and stalked slowly up the apartment. Mr. Flosky, familiar as he was with ghosts, was not prepared for this apparition, and made the best of his way out at the opposite door. Mrs. Hilary and Marionetta followed, screaming. The Honourable Mr. Listless, by two turns of his body, rolled first off the sofa and then under it. The Reverend Mr. Larynx leaped up and fled with so much precipitation, that he overturned the table on the foot of Mr. Glowry. Mr. Glowry roared with pain in the ear of Mr. Toobad. Mr. Toobad's alarm so bewildered his senses, that, missing the door, he threw up one of the windows, jumped out in his panic, and plunged over head and ears in the moat. Mr. Asterias and his son, who were on the watch for their mermaid, were attracted by the splashing, threw a net over him, and dragged him to land.

Scythrop and Mr. Hilary meanwhile had hastened to his assistance, and, on arriving at the edge of the moat, followed by several servants with ropes and torches, found Mr. Asterias and Aquarius busy in endeavouring to extricate Mr. Toobad from the net, who was entangled in the meshes, and floundering with rage. Scythrop was lost in amazement; but Mr. Hilary saw, at one view, all the circumstances of the adventure, and burst into an immoderate fit of laughter; on recovering from which, he said to Mr. Asterias, "You have caught an odd fish, indeed." Mr. Toobad was highly exasperated at this unseasonable pleasantry; but Mr. Hilary softened his anger, by producing a knife, and cutting the Gordian knot of his reticular envelopment. "You see," said Mr. Toobad, "you see, gentlemen, in my unfortunate person, proof upon proof of the present dominion of the devil in the affairs of this world; and I have no doubt but that the apparition of this night was Apollyon himself in disguise, sent for the express purpose of terrifying me into this complication of misadventures. The devil is come among you, having great wrath, because he knoweth that he hath but a short time."

CHAPTER 13

Mr. Glowry was much surprised, on occasionally visiting Scythrop's tower, to find the door always locked, and to be kept sometimes waiting many minutes for admission: during which he invariably heard a heavy rolling sound, like that of a ponderous mangle, or of a waggon on a weighing-bridge, or of theatrical thunder.

He took little notice of this for some time: at length his curiosity was excited, and, one day, instead of knocking at the door, as usual, the instant he reached it, he applied his ear to the key-hole, and like Bottom, in the Midsummer Night's Dream, "spied a voice," which he guessed to be of the feminine gender, and knew to be not Scythrop's, whose deeper tones he distinguished at intervals. Having attempted in vain to catch a syllable of the discourse, he knocked violently at the door, and roared for immediate admission. The voices ceased, the accustomed rolling sound was heard, the door opened, and Scythrop was discovered alone. Mr. Glowry looked round to every corner of the apartment, and then said, "Where is the lady?"

"The lady, sir?" said Scythrop.

"Yes, sir, the lady."

"Sir, I do not understand you."

"You don't, sir?"

"No, indeed, sir. There is no lady here."

"But, sir, this is not the only apartment in the tower, and I make no doubt there is a lady up-stairs."

"You are welcome to search, sir."

"Yes, and while I am searching, she will slip out from some lurking-place, and make her escape."

"You may lock this door, sir, and take the key with you."

"But there is the terrace-door: she has escaped by the terrace."

"The terrace, sir, has no other outlet, and the walls are too high for a lady to jump down."

"Well, sir, give me the key."

Mr. Glowry took the key, searched every nook of the tower, and returned.

"You are a fox, Scythrop; you are an exceedingly cunning fox, with that demure visage of yours. What was that lumbering sound I heard before you opened the door?"

"Sound, sir?"

"Yes, sir, sound."

"My dear sir, I am not aware of any sound, except my great table, which I moved on rising to let you in."

"The table! -- let me see that. No, sir; not a tenth part heavy enough, not a tenth part."

"But, sir, you do not consider the laws of acoustics: a whisper becomes a peal of thunder in the focus of reverberation. Allow me to explain this: sounds striking on concave surfaces are reflected from them, and, after reflection, converge to points which are the foci of these surfaces. It follows, therefore, that the ear may be so placed in one, as that it shall hear a sound better than when situated nearer to the point of the first impulse: again, in the case of two concave surfaces placed opposite to each other -- "

"Nonsense, sir. Don't tell me of foci. Pray, sir, will concave surfaces produce two voices when nobody speaks? I heard two voices, and one was feminine; feminine, sir: what say you to that?"

"Oh, sir, I perceive your mistake: I am writing a tragedy, and was acting over a scene to myself. To convince you, I will give you a specimen; but you must first understand the plot. It is a tragedy on the German model. The Great Mogul is in exile, and has taken lodgings at Kensington, with his only daughter, the Princess Rantrorina, who takes in needle-work, and keeps a day-school. *The Princess is discovered hemming a set of shirts for the parson of the parish: they are to be marked with a large R. Enter to her the Great Mogul. A pause, during which they look at each other expressively. The Princess changes colour several times. The Mogul takes snuff in great agitation. Several grains are heard to fall on the stage. His heart is seen to beat through his upper benjamin.*--THE MOGUL (*with a mournful look at his left shoe*). "My shoe-string is broken."-- THE PRINCESS (*after an interval of melancholy reflection*), "I know it." -- THE MOGUL. "My second shoe-string! The first broke when I lost my empire: the second has broken to-day. When will my poor heart break?" -- THE PRINCESS, "Shoe-strings, hearts, and empires! Mysterious sympathy!"

"Nonsense, sir," interrupted Mr. Glowry. "That is not at all like the voice I heard."

"But, sir," said Scythrop, "a key-hole may be so constructed as to act like an acoustic tube, and an acoustic tube, sir, will modify sound in a very remarkable manner. Consider the construction of the ear, and the nature and causes of sound. The external part of the ear is a cartilaginous funnel."

"It won't do, Scythrop. There is a girl concealed in this tower, and find her I will. There are such things as sliding panels and secret closets." -- He sounded round the room with his cane, but detected no hollowness. -- "I have heard, sir," he continued, "that during my absence, two years ago, you had a dumb carpenter closeted with you day after day. I did not dream that you were laying contrivances for carrying on secret intrigues. Young men will have their way: I had my way when I was a young man: but, sir, when your cousin Marionetta -- "

Scythrop now saw that the affair was growing serious. To have clapped his hand upon his father's mouth, to have entreated him to be silent, would, in the first place, not have made him so; and, in the second, would have shown a dread of being overheard by somebody. His only resource, therefore, was to try to drown Mr. Glowry's voice; and, having no other subject, he continued his description of the ear, raising his voice continually as Mr. Glowry raised his.

"When your cousin Marionetta," said Mr. Glowry, "whom you profess to love -- whom you profess to love, sir -- "

"The internal canal of the ear," said Scythrop, "is partly bony and partly cartilaginous. This internal canal is -- "

"Is actually in the house, sir; and, when you are so shortly to be-- as I expect --"

"Closed at the further end by the *membrana tympani* --"

"Joined together in holy matrimony --"

"Under which is carried a branch of the fifth pair of nerves --"

"I say, sir, when you are so shortly to be married to your cousin Marionetta --"

"The *cavitas tympani*--"

A loud noise was heard behind the book-case, which, to the astonishment of Mr. Glowry, opened in the middle, and the massy compartments, with all their weight of books, receding from each other in the manner of a theatrical scene, with a heavy rolling sound (which Mr. Glowry immediately recognised to be the same which had excited his curiosity,) disclosed an interior apartment, in the entrance of which stood the beautiful Stella, who, stepping forward, exclaimed, "Married! Is he going to be married? The profligate!"

"Really, madam," said Mr. Glowry, "I do not know what he is going to do, or what I am going to do, or what any one is going to do; for all this is incomprehensible."

"I can explain it all," said Scythrop, "in a most satisfactory manner, if you will but have the goodness to leave us alone."

"Pray, sir, to which act of the tragedy of the Great Mogul does this incident belong?"

"I entreat you, my dear sir, leave us alone."

Stella threw herself into a chair, and burst into a tempest of tears. Scythrop sat down by her, and took her hand. She snatched her hand away, and turned her back upon him. He rose, sat down on the other side, and took her other hand. She snatched it away, and turned from him again. Scythrop continued entreating Mr. Glowry to leave them alone; but the old gentleman was obstinate, and would not go.

"I suppose, after all," said Mr. Glowry maliciously, "it is only a phænomenon in acoustics, and this young lady is a reflection of sound from concave surfaces."

Some one tapped at the door: Mr. Glowry opened it, and Mr. Hilary entered. He had been seeking Mr. Glowry, and had traced him to Scythrop's tower. He stood a few moments in silent surprise, and then addressed himself to Mr. Glowry for an explanation.

"The explanation," said Mr. Glowry, "is very satisfactory. The Great Mogul has taken lodgings at Kensington, and the external part of the ear is a cartilaginous funnel."

"Mr. Glowry, that is no explanation."

"Mr. Hilary, it is all I know about the matter."

"Sir, this pleasantry is very unseasonable. I perceive that my niece is sported with in a most unjustifiable manner, and I shall see if she will be more successful in obtaining an intelligible answer." And he departed in search of Marionetta.

Scythrop was now in a hopeless predicament. Mr. Hilary made a hue and cry in the Abbey, and summoned his wife and Marionetta to Scythrop's apartment. The ladies, not knowing what was the matter, hastened in great consternation. Mr. Toobad saw them sweeping along the corridor, and judging from their manner that the devil had manifested his wrath in some new shape, followed from pure curiosity.

Scythrop, meanwhile, vainly endeavoured to get rid of Mr. Glowry and to pacify Stella. The latter attempted to escape from the tower, declaring she would leave the Abbey immediately, and he should never see her or hear of her more. Scythrop held her hand and detained her by force, till Mr. Hilary re-appeared with Mrs. Hilary and Marionetta. Marionetta, seeing Scythrop grasping the hand of a strange beauty, fainted away in the arms of her aunt. Scythrop flew to her assistance; and Stella, with redoubled anger, sprang towards the door, but was intercepted in her intended flight by being caught in the arms of Mr. Toobad, who exclaimed -- "Celinda!"

"Papa!" said the young lady disconsolately.

"The devil is come among you," said Mr. Toobad, "how came my daughter here?"

"Your daughter!" exclaimed Mr. Glowry.

"Your daughter!" exclaimed Scythrop, and Mr. and Mrs. Hilary.

"Yes," said Mr. Toobad, "my daughter Celinda."

Marionetta opened her eyes and fixed them on Celinda. Celinda, in return, fixed hers on Marionetta. They were at remote points of the apartment. Scythrop was equidistant from both of them, central and motionless, like Mahomet's coffin.

"Mr. Glowry," said Mr. Toobad, "can you tell by what means my daughter came here?"

"I know no more," said Mr. Glowry, "than the Great Mogul."

"Mr. Scythrop," said Mr. Toobad, "how came my daughter here?"

"I did not know, Sir, that the lady was your daughter."

"But how came she here?"

"By spontaneous locomotion," said Scythrop, sullenly.

"Celinda," said Mr. Toobad, "what does all this mean?"

"I really do not know, Sir."

"This is most unaccountable. When I told you in London that I had chosen a husband for you, you thought proper to run away from him; and now, to all appearance, you have run away to him."

"How, Sir! was that your choice?"

"Precisely; and, if he is yours too, we shall be both of a mind, for the first time in our lives."

"He is not my choice, Sir. This lady has a prior claim: I renounce him."

"And I renounce him," said Marionetta.

Scythrop knew not what to do. He could not attempt to conciliate the one without irreparably offending the other; and he was so fond of both, that the idea of depriving himself for ever of the society of either was intolerable to him: he, therefore, retreated into his stronghold, mystery; maintained an impenetrable silence; and contented himself with stealing occasionally a deprecating glance at each of the objects of his idolatry. Mr. Toobad and Mr. Hilary, in the mean time, were each insisting on an explanation from Mr. Glowry, who, they thought, had been playing a double game on this occasion. Mr. Glowry was vainly endeavouring to persuade them of his innocence in the whole transaction. Mrs. Hilary was endeavouring to mediate between her husband and brother. The Honourable Mr. Listless, the Reverend Mr. Larynx, Mr. Flosky, Mr. Asterias, and Aquarius, were attracted by the tumult to the scene of action, and were appealed to severally and conjointly by the respective disputants. Multitudinous questions and answers, *en masse*, composed a *charivari*, to which the genius of Rossini alone could have given a suitable accompaniment, and which was only terminated by Mrs. Hilary and Mr. Toobad retreating with the captive damsels. The whole party followed, with the exception of Scythrop, who threw himself into his arm-chair, crossed his left foot over his right knee, placed the hollow of his left hand on the interior ancle of his left leg, rested his right elbow on the elbow of the chair, placed the ball of his right thumb against his right temple, curved the forefinger along the upper part of his forehead, rested the point of the middle finger on the bridge of his nose, and the points of the two others on the lower part of the palm, fixed his eyes intently on the veins in the back of his left hand, and sat in this position like the immoveable Theseus, who, as is well known to many who have not been at college, and to some few who have, *sedet, oeternumque sedebit.** We hope the admirers of the *minutiæ* in poetry and romance will appreciate this accurate description of a pensive attitude.

CHAPTER 14

Scythrop was still in this position when Raven entered to announce that dinner was on table.

"I cannot come," said Scythrop.

Raven sighed. "Something is the matter," said Raven: "but man is born to trouble."

"Leave me," said Scythrop: "go, and croak elsewhere."

"Thus it is," said Raven. "Five-and-twenty years have I lived in Nightmare Abbey, and now all the reward of my affection is -- Go, and croak elsewhere. I have danced you on my knee, and fed you with marrow."

"Good Raven," said Scythrop, "I entreat you to leave me."

"Shall I bring your dinner here?" said Raven. "A boiled fowl and a glass of Madeira are prescribed by the faculty in cases of low spirits. But you had better join the party: it is very much reduced already."

"Reduced! how?"

"The Honourable Mr. Listless is gone. He declared that, what with family quarrels in the morning, and ghosts at night, he could get neither sleep nor peace; and that the agitation was too much for his nerves: though Mr. Glowry assured him that the ghost was only

---

*sedet, oeternumque sedebit: Sits, and will sit for ever.

poor Crow walking in his sleep, and that the shroud and bloody turban were a sheet and a red nightcap."

"Well, sir?"

"The Reverend Mr. Larynx has been called off on duty, to marry or bury (I don't know which) some unfortunate person or persons, at Claydyke: but man is born to trouble!"

"Is that all?"

"No. Mr. Toobad is gone too, and a strange lady with him."

"Gone!"

"Gone. And Mr. and Mrs. Hilary, and Miss O'Carroll: they are all gone. There is nobody left but Mr. Asterias and his son, and they are going to-night."

"Then I have lost them both."

"Won't you come to dinner?"

"No."

"Shall I bring your dinner here?'

"Yes."

"What will you have?"

"A pint of port and a pistol."*

"A pistol!"

"And a pint of port. I will make my exit like Werter. Go. Stay. Did Miss O'Carroll say any thing?"

"No."

"Did Miss Toobad say any thing?"

"The strange lady? No."

"Did either of them cry?"

"No."

"What did they do?'

"Nothing."

"What did Mr. Toobad say?"

"He said, fifty times over, the devil was come among us."

"And they are gone?"

"Yes; and the dinner is getting cold. There is a time for every thing under the sun. You may as well dine first, and be miserable afterwards."

"True, Raven. There is something in that. I will take your advice: therefore, bring me -- "

---

*a pint of port and a pistol: See *The Sorrows of Werter*, Letter 93.

"The port and the pistol?"

"No; the boiled fowl and Madeira."

Scythrop had dined, and was sipping his Madeira alone, immersed in melancholy musing, when Mr. Glowry entered, followed by Raven, who, having placed an additional glass and set a chair for Mr. Glowry, withdrew. Mr. Glowry sat down opposite Scythrop. After a pause, during which each filled and drank in silence, Mr. Glowry said, "So, sir, you have played your cards well. I proposed Miss Toobad to you: you refused her. Mr. Toobad proposed you to her: she refused you. You fell in love with Marionetta, and were going to poison yourself, because, from pure fatherly regard to your temporal interests, I withheld my consent. When, at length, I offered you my consent, you told me I was too precipitate. And, after all, I find you and Miss Toobad living together in the same tower, and behaving in every respect like two plighted lovers. Now, sir, if there be any rational solution of all this absurdity, I shall be very much obliged to you for a small glimmering of information."

"The solution, sir, is of little moment; but I will leave it in writing for your satisfaction. The crisis of my fate is come: the world is a stage, and my direction is *exit*."

"Do not talk so, sir; -- do not talk so, Scythrop. What would you have?"

"I would have my love."

"And pray, sir, who is your love?"

"Celinda -- Marionetta -- either -- both."

"Both! That may do very well in a German tragedy; and the Great Mogul might have found it very feasible in his lodgings at Kensington; but it will not do in Lincolnshire. Will you have Miss Toobad?"

"Yes."

"And renounce Marionetta?"

"No."

"But you must renounce one."

"I cannot."

"And you cannot have both. What is to be done?"

"I must shoot myself."

"Don't talk so, Scythrop. Be rational, my dear Scythrop. Consider, and make a cool, calm choice, and I will exert myself in your behalf."

"Why should I choose, sir? Both have renounced *me*: I have no hope of either."

"Tell me which you will have, and I will plead your cause irresistibly."

"Well, sir, -- I will have -- no, sir, I cannot renounce either. I cannot choose either. I am doomed to be the victim of eternal disappointments; and I have no resource but a pistol."

"Scythrop -- Scythrop; -- if one of them should come to you -- what then?"

"That, sir, might alter the case: but that cannot be."

"It can be, Scythrop; it will be: I promise you it will be. Have but a little patience -- but a week's patience; and it shall be."

"A week, sir, is an age: but, to oblige you, as a last act of filial duty, I will live another week. It is now Thursday evening, twenty-five minutes past seven. At this hour and minute, on Thursday next, love and fate shall smile on me, or I will drink my last pint of port in this world."

Mr. Glowry ordered his travelling chariot, and departed from the Abbey.

CHAPTER 15

The day after Mr. Glowry's departure was one of incessant rain, and Scythrop repented of the promise he had given. The next day was one of bright sunshine: he sat on the terrace, read a tragedy of Sophocles, and was not sorry, when Raven announced dinner, to find himself alive. On the third evening, the wind blew, and the rain beat, and the owl flapped against his windows; and he put a new flint in his pistol. On the fourth day, the sun shone again; and he locked the pistol up in a drawer, where he left it undisturbed, till the morning of the eventful Thursday, when he ascended the turret with a telescope, and spied anxiously along the road that crossed the fens from Claydyke: but nothing appeared on it. He watched in this manner from ten A.M. till Raven summoned him to dinner at five; when he stationed Crow at the telescope, and descended to his own funeral-feast. He left open the communications between the tower and turret, and called aloud at intervals to Crow, -- "Crow, Crow, is any thing coming?" Crow answered, "The wind blows, and the windmills turn, but I see nothing coming;" and, at every answer, Scythrop found the necessity of raising his spirits with a bumper. After dinner, he gave Raven his watch to set by the Abbey clock. Raven brought it. Scythrop placed it on the table, and Raven departed. Scythrop called again to Crow; and Crow, who had fallen asleep, answered mechanically, "I see nothing coming." Scythrop laid his pistol between his watch and his bottle. The hour-hand passed the VII. -- the minute-hand moved on; -- it was within three minutes of the appointed time. Scythrop called again to Crow: Crow answered as before. Scythrop rang the bell: Raven appeared.

"Raven," said Scythrop, "the clock is too fast."

"No, indeed," said Raven, who knew nothing of Scythrop's intentions; "if any thing, it is too slow."

"Villain!" said Scythrop, pointing the pistol at him; "it is too fast."

"Yes -- yes -- too fast, I meant," said Raven, in manifest fear.

"How much too fast?" said Scythrop.

"As much as you please," said Raven.

"How much, I say?" said Scythrop, pointing the pistol again.

"An hour, a full hour, sir," said the terrified butler.

"Put back my watch," said Scythrop.

Raven, with trembling hand, was putting back the watch, when the rattle of wheels was heard in the court; and Scythrop, springing down the stairs by three steps together, was at the door in sufficient time to have handed either of the young ladies from the carriage, if she had happened to be in it; but Mr. Glowry was alone.

"I rejoice to see you," said Mr. Glowry; "I was fearful of being too late, for I waited till the last moment in the hope of accomplishing my promise; but all my endeavours have been vain, as these letters will shew."

Scythrop impatiently broke the seals. The contents were these:

Almost a stranger in England, I fled from parental tyranny, and the dread of an arbitrary marriage, to the protection of a stranger and a philosopher, whom I expected to find something better than, or at least something different from, the rest of his worthless species. Could I, after what has occurred, have expected nothing more from you than the common-place impertinence of sending your father to treat with me, and with mine, for me? I should be a little moved in your favour, if I could believe you capable of carrying into effect the resolutions which your father says you have taken, in the event of my proving inflexible; though I doubt not you will execute them, as far as relates to the pint of wine, twice over, at least. I wish you much happiness with Miss O'Carroll. I shall always cherish a grateful recollection of Nightmare Abbey, for having been the means of introducing me to a true transcendentalist; and, though he is a little older than myself, which is all one in Germany, I shall very soon have the pleasure of subscribing myself

CELINDA FLOSKY.

I hope, my dear cousin, that you will not be angry with me, but that you will always think of me as a sincere friend, who will always feel interested in your welfare; I am sure you love Miss Toobad much better than me, and I wish you much happiness with her. Mr. Listless assures me that people do not kill themselves for love now-a-days, though it is still the fashion to talk about it. I shall, in a very short time, change my name and situation, and shall always be happy to see you in Berkeley Square, when, to the unalterable designation of your affectionate cousin, I shall subjoin the signature of

MARIONETTA LISTLESS.

Scythrop tore both the letters to atoms, and railed in good set terms against the fickleness of women.

"Calm yourself, my dear Scythrop," said Mr. Glowry; "there are yet maidens in England."

"Very true, sir," said Scythrop.

"And the next time," said Mr. Glowry, "have but one string to your bow."

"Very good advice, sir," said Scythrop.

"And, besides," said Mr. Glowry, "the fatal time is past, for it is now almost eight."

"Then that villain, Raven," said Scythrop, "deceived me when he said that the clock was too fast; but, as you observe very justly, the time has gone by, and I have just reflected that these repeated crosses in love qualify me to take a very advanced degree in misanthropy; and there is, therefore, good hope that I may make a figure in the world. But I shall ring for the rascal Raven, and admonish him."

Raven appeared. Scythrop looked at him very fiercely two or three minutes; and Raven, still remembering the pistol, stood quaking in mute apprehension, till Scythrop, pointing significantly towards the dining-room, said, "Bring some Madeira."

THE END

THE

HEROINE,

OR

ADVENTURES

OF

CHERUBINA,

BY

EATON STANNARD BARRETT, ESQ,

———

"L'Histoire d'une femme est toujours un Roman."

———

Second Edition,

WITH CONSIDERABLE ADDITIONS AND ALTERATIONS.

———

IN THREE VOLUMES,
VOL. I.

———

THE HEROINE TO THE READER.

ATTEND, gentle and intelligent reader; for I am not the fictitious personage whose memoirs you will peruse in "The Heroine;" but I am a corporeal being, and an inhabitant of another world.

Know, that the moment a mortal manuscript is written in a legible hand, and the word End or Finis annexed thereto, whatever characters happen to be sketched in it (whether imaginary, biographical, or historical), acquire the quality of creating and effusing a sentient soul or spirit, which instantly takes flight, and ascends through the regions of air, till it arrives at the MOON; where it is then embodied, and becomes a living creature: the precise counterpart, in mind and person, of its literary prototype.

Know farther, that all the towns, villages, rivers, hills, and vallies of the moon, owe their origin, in a similar manner, to the descriptions which writers give of those on earth; and that all the lunar trades and manufactures, fleets and coins, stays for men, and boots for ladies, receive form and substance here, from terrestrial books on war and commerce, pamphlets on bullion, and fashionable magazines.

267

Works consisting of abstract argument, ethics, metaphysics, polemics, &c. which, from their very nature, cannot become tangible essences, send their ideas, in whispers, up to the moon; where the tribe of talking birds receive, and repeat them for the Lunarians. So that it is not unusual to hear a mitred parrot screaming a political sermon, or a fashionable jay twittering a compiled bravura. These birds then are our philosophers; and so great is their value, that they sell for as much as your patriots.

The moment, however, that a book becomes obsolete on earth, the personages, countries, manners, and things recorded in it, lose, by the law of sympathy, their existence in the moon.

This, most grave reader, is but a short and imperfect sketch of the way we Moonites live and die. I shall now give you some account of what has happened to me since my coming hither.

It is something more than three lunar hours; or, in other words, about three terrestrial days ago, that, owing to the kindness of some human gentleman or other (to whom I take this occasion of returning my grateful thanks), I became a living inhabitant of the Moon. Like the Miltonic Eve, almost the first thing I did was to peep into the water and admire my face; -- a very pretty one, I assure you, dear reader. I then perceived advancing a lank and grimly figure in armour, who introduced himself as Don Quixote; and we soon found each other kindred souls.

We walked, hand in hand, through a beautiful tract of country, called Terra Fertilitatis; for your Selenographers, Langrenus, Florentius, Grimaldus, Ricciolus, and Hevelius, have given proper names to the various portions of our hemisphere.

As I proceeded, 1 met the Radcliffian, Rochian, and other heroines; but they tossed their heads, and told me pertly that I was a slur on the sisterhood; while some went so far as to say that I had a design upon their lives. They likewise shunned the Edgeworthian heroines, whom they thought too comic, moral, and natural.

I met the Lady of the Lake, and shook hands with her; but her hand felt rather hard from the frequent use of the oar; and I spoke to the Widow Dido, but she had her old trick of turning on her heel, without answering a civil question.

I found the Homeric Achilles broiling his own beefsteaks, as usual; the Homeric Princesses drawing water, and washing linen; the Virgilian Trojans eating their tables; and the Livian Hannibal melting mountains with the patent vinegar of an advertisement.

The little boy in the Æneid had introduced the amusement of whipping tops; and Musidora had turned bathing-woman at a halfpenny a dip.

A Caesar, an Alexander, and an Alfred, were talking politics, and quaffing the Horatian Falernian, at the Garter Inn of Shakespeare. A Catiline was holding forth on Reform, and a Hanno was advising the recall of a victorious army.

As I walked along, a mob of statesmen, just created by your newspapers, popped up their heads, nodded, and died. About twenty come to us in this manner, almost every day; and though some of them are of the same name, and drawn from the same original, they are often as unlike each other as so many clouds. The Buonapartes, thus sent, are, in general hideous fellows. However, your parliamentary Reports sometimes agreeably surprize us with most respectable characters of that name.

On my way, I could observe numbers of patients dying, according as the books that had created them were sinking into oblivion. The Foxian James was paraded about in a sedan chair, and considered just gone; and a set of politicians, entitled All the Talents, who had once made a terrible noise among us, lay sprawling in their last agonies. But the most extensive mortality ever known here was caused by the burning of the Alexandrian Library. This forms quite an æra in the Lunar Annals; and is called The great Conflagration.

I had attempted to pluck an apple from a tree which grew near the road; but instead of a substance, grasped a vacuum; and while Don Quixote was instructing me that this phænomenon arose from the Berkeleian system of immaterialism, and that this apple was only a globular idea, I heard a squeaking voice just beside me cry:

"I must remark, Madam, that the writer who sent you amongst us, had far too much to say, and too little to do."

I looked round, but saw nobody.

"Tis Junius," observed Don Quixote. "He was invisible on earth, and therefore must be so here. Do not mind his bitter sayings."

"An author" continued the satirist, "who has judgment enough to write wit, should have judgment enough to prevent him from writing it."

" Sir," said Don Quixote, "if, by his works of wit, he can attain popularity, he will ensure a future attention to his works of judgment. So here is at thee, caitiff!" and closing his visor, he ran atilt at pure space.

"Nay," cried Junius, "let us not quarrel, though we differ. Mind unopposed by mind, fashions false opinions, and degenerates from its original rectitude. The stagnant pool resolves into putridity. It is the conflict of the waters which keeps them pure."

"Except in dropsical cases, I presume," said Tristram Shandy, who just then came up, with his Uncle Toby. "How goes it, heroine? How goes it? -- By the man in the moon, the moment 1 heard of your arrival here, I gave three exulting flourishes of my hand, thus 1 2 3 then applying my middle finger to my thumb, and compressing both with the flexory muscles, I shot them asunder transversely; so that the finger coming plump upon the aponeurosis --

* * * *

In short, -- for I don't much like how I am getting on with the description -- I snapped my fingers.

"Now, Madam, I will bet the whole of Kristmanus's, Capuanus's, Schihardus's, Phocylides's and Hanzelius's estates, -- which are the best on our disk, -- to as much landed property as could be spooned into your shoe--that you will get miserably mauled by their reverences, the Reviewers. My life for it, they will say that your character is a mere daub drawn in distemper -- the hair too golden -- an eyelash too much -- then, that the book itself has too little of the rational and argumentative; -- that the fellow merely wrote it to make the world laugh, -- and, by the bye, to make the world laugh is the gravest occupation an author can chuse. It is no trifle, splitting the sides of people, who are not to live till a thousand years after. In fine, Madam, it will appear that the work has every fault which must convict it Aristotellically and Edinburgo -- reviewically, in the eyes of ninety-nine barbati; but which will leave it not the ninety-ninth part of a gry the worse in the eyes of fifteen millions of honest Britons; besides several very respectable ladies and gentleman yet unborn, and nations yet undiscovered, who will read translations of it in languages yet unspoken. Bless me, what hacking these Critics will have at you! Small sword and broad sword -- staff and stiletto -- flankonnade and cannonade -- hurry-scurry -- right wing and left wing --"

But Tristram paused short in consternation; for his animated description of a fight had roused the military spirits of Don Quixote and Captain Shandy, who were already at hard knocks; the one with his spear, and the other with his crutch. I therefore took this occasion of escaping.

And now day begins to decline; and your globe, which never sets to us, will soon shed her pale earthshine over the landscape. O how serene, are these regions! Here are no hurricanes, or clouds, or vapours. Here heroines cannot sigh; for here there is no air to sigh withal. Here in our great pits, poetically called vallies, we retire from all moonly cares; or range through the meads of Cysatus or Gruemberget, and luxuriate in the coolness of the Conical Penumbra.

I trust you will feel, dear reader, that you now owe more to my discoveries, than to those of Endymion, Copernicus, Tycho Brahe, Galileus, and Newton. I pray you, therefore, reward my services with a long and happy life; though much I fear I shall not obtain it. For, I am told, that two little shining specks, called England and Ireland (which we can just see with our glasses on your globe), are the places upon whose health and prosperity mine must depend. If they fall, I must fall with them; and I fancy they have already seen the best of their days. A parrot informs me, that they are at open war with a prodigious blotch just beside them; and that their most approved patriots daily indite pamphlets to shew how they cannot hold out ten years longer. The Sternian Starling assured me just now, that these patriots write the triumphs of their country in the most commiserating language; and portray her distresses with exultation. Of course, therefore, they conceive that her glories would undo her, and that nothing can save her but her calamities. So since she is the most flourishing nation in the world, I may fairly infer that she is on her last legs.

Before I conclude, I must inform you how I shall have this letter conveyed to your world. Laplace, and other philosophers, have already proved that a stone projected by a volcano, from the moon, and with the velocity of a mile and a half per second, would be thrown beyond the sphere of the moon's attraction, and enter into the confines of the earth's.

Now, hundreds have attested upon oath, that they have seen luminous meteors moving through the sky; and falling on the earth, in stony or semimetallic masses. Ergo (say the philosophers), they

271

came all the way from the moon; and the philosophers have a right to say so, for it is thought that they themselves are moonstruck by blows from these very stones.

One of these very stones, therefore, shall convey this letter to you. I have written it on asbestus, in liquid gold (as both these substances are the least consumable by fire); and I will fasten it to the top of a volcanic mountain, which is expected to explode in another hour,

Alas, alas, short-sighted Earthites! how little ye foresee the havock that will happen hereafter, from the pelting of these pitiless stones. For, about the time of the millennium, the doctrine of projectiles will be so prodigiously improved, that while there is universal peace upon earth, the planets will go to war with each other. Then shall we Lunarians, like true satellites, turn upon our benefactors and instead of merely trying our small shot (as at present), we will fire off whole mountains; while you, from your superior attraction, will find it difficult to hit us at all. The consequence must be, our losing so much weight, that we shall approach, by degrees, nearer and nearer to you; 'till at last, both globes will come slap together, flatten each other out, like the pancakes of Glasse's Cookery, and rush headlong into primeval chaos.

Such will be the consummation of all things.

Adieu.

THE HEROINE.

LETTER I.

AH! my good Governess, guardian of my youth, must I then behold you no more? No more at breakfast, find your melancholy features shrouded in an umbrageous cap, a novel in the one hand, a cup in the other, and tears springing from your eyes, at the tale too tender, or at the tea too hot? Must I no longer wander with you through painted meadows, and by purling rivulets? Motherless, am I to be bereft of my more than mother, at the sensative age of fifteen? What though papa caught the Butler kissing you in the pantry? What though he turned you by the venerable shoulder out of his house? I am well persuaded that the kiss was maternal, not amorous, and that the interesting Butler, Simon Snaggs, is your son.

Perhaps you married early in life, and without the knowledge of your parents. A gipsy stole the pretty pledge of your love; and, at length, you have recognized him by some improbable concurrence of events. Happy, happy mother!

Happy too, perhaps, in being cast upon the world, unprotected and defamed; while I am doomed to endure the security of a home, and the dullness of an unimpeached reputation. For me, there is no hope whatever of being reduced to despair. I am condemned to waste my health, bloom, and youth, in a series of uninterrupted prosperity.

It is not, my friend, that I wish for ultimate unhappiness, but that I am anxious to suffer present sorrow, in order to secure future felicity: an improvement, you will own, on the system of other girls, who, to enjoy the passing moment, run the risk of being wretched ever after. Have not all persons their favourite pursuits in life, and do not all brave fatigue, vexation, and calumny, for the purpose of accomplishing them? One woman aspires to be a beauty, another a title, a third a belle esprit; and to effect these objects, health is sacrificed, reputation tainted, and peace of mind destroyed. Now my ambition is to be a Heroine, and how can I hope for success in my vocation, unless I, too, suffer privations and inconveniences?

Besides, have I not far greater merit in getting a husband by sentiment, adventure, and melancholy, than by dressing, gadding, dancing, and singing? For heroines are just as much on the alert to get husbands, as other young ladies; and in truth, I would never voluntarily subject myself to misfortunes, were I not certain that matrimony would be the last of them. But even misery itself has its consolations and advantages. It makes one, at least, look interesting, and affords an opportunity for ornamental murmurs. Besides, it is the mark of a refined mind. Only fools, children, and savages, are happy.

With these sentiments, no wonder I should feel discontented at my present mode of life. Such an insipid routine, always, always, always the same. Rising with no better prospect than to make breakfast for papa. Then 'tis, "Good morrow, Cherry," or "is the paper come, Cherry?" or "more cream, Cherry," or "what shall we have for dinner, Cherry?" At dinner, nobody but a farmer or the parson; and nothing talked but politics and turnips. After tea I am made sing some fal lal la of a ditty, and am sent to bed with a "Good night, pretty miss," or "sweet dear." The Clowns!

Now instead of this, just conceive me a child of misery, in a castle, a convent, or a cottage; becoming acquainted with the hero by his saving my life -- I in beautiful confusion -- "Good Heaven, what an angel!" cries he -- then sudden love on both sides -- in two days my hand kissed. Embarrassments--my character suspected -- a quarrel -- a reconciliation -- "fresh embarrassments. -- O Biddy, what an irreparable loss to the public, that a victim of thrilling sensibility, like me, should be thus idling her precious time over the common occupations of life! -- prepared as I am, too, by a five years' course of novels (and you can bear witness that I have read little else), to embody and ensoul those enchanting reveries, which I am accustomed to indulge in bed and bower, and which really constitute almost the whole happiness of my life.

That I am not deficient in the qualities requisite for a heroine is indisputable. I know nothing of the world, or of human nature; I have lived in utter seclusion, and every one says I am handsome. My form is tall and aerial, my face Grecian, my tresses flaxen, my eyes blue and sleepy. Then, not only peaches, roses, and Aurora, but snow, lilies, and alabaster, may, with perfect propriety, be applied to a description of my skin. I confess I differ from other heroines in one point. They, you may remark, are always unconscious of their charms; whereas, I am, I fear, convinced of mine, beyond all hope of retraction.

There is but one serious flaw in my title to Heroine -- the mediocrity of my lineage. My father is descended from nothing better than a decent and respectable family. He began life with a thousand pounds, purchased a farm, and by his honest and disgusting industry, has realized fifty thousand. Were even my legitimacy suspected, it would be a comfort; since, in that case, I should assuredly start forth, at one time or other, the daughter of some plaintive nobleman, who lives retired, and occasionally slaps his forehead.

Another subject perplexes me. It is my name; and what a name -- Cherry! It reminds one so much of plumpness and ruddy health. Cherry -- better be called Pine-apple at once. There is a green and yellow melancholy in pine-apple, that is infinitely preferable. I wonder whether Cherry could possibly be an abbreviation of CHERUBINA. 'Tis only changing y into ubina, and the name becomes quite classic. Celestina, Angelina, Seraphina, are all of the same family. But Cherubina sounds so empyrean, so something or other beyond mortality; and besides I have just a face for it. Yes, Cherubina I am resolved to be called, now and for ever.

But you must naturally wish to learn what has happened here since your departure. I was in my boudoir, reading the Delicate Distress, when I heard a sudden bustle below, and "Out of the house, this moment," vociferated by my father. The next minute he was in my room with a face like fire.

"There!" cried he, "I knew what your famous romances would do for us at last."

"Fie!" said I, playfully spreading my fingers over his face. "Don't frown so, but tell me what these famous romances have done?"

"Only a kissing match between the Governess and the Butler," answered he. "I caught them at the sport in the pantry."

I was petrified. "Dear Sir," said I, "you must surely mistake."

"No such thing," cried he. "The kiss was too much of a smacker for that. -- Egad, it rang through the pantry like the smash of twenty plates. But she shall never darken my doors again, never. I have just packed the pair of wrinkled sweethearts off together; and what is better, I have ordered all the novels in the house to be burnt, by way of purification. They talk so much of flames, that I suppose they will like to feel them." He spoke, and ran raging out of the room.

275

Adieu, then, ye dear romances, adieu for ever. No more shall I sympathize with your heroines, while they faint and blush, and weep, through four half-bound octavos. Adieu, ye Edwins, Edgars, and Edmunds; ye Selinas, Evelinas, Malvinas: ye inas all adieu! The flames will consume all. The melody of Emily, the prattle of Annette, and the hoarseness of Ugo, will be confounded in one indiscriminate crackle. The Casa and Castello will blaze with equal fury; nor will the virtue of Pamela aught avail to save; nor Wolmar delighting to see his wife in a swoon; nor Werter shelling peas and reading Homer, nor Charlotte cutting bread and butter for the children.

Write to me, my friend, and advise me in this emergency. Alas! I am torn with grief at the destruction of my romances, and the discharge of my loved governess, who was not even permitted to take and receive a hysterical farewell. Adieu.

CHERUBINA.

LETTER II.

A thousand thanks, my dear Governess, for your inestimable letter; and though I must ever regret our separation as the greatest misfortune of my life, yet I cannot but consider it auspicious in this respect, that it has irritated you to inform me of your suspicions respecting my birth.

And so you really think I am not the daughter of my reputed father, but a child of mystery? Enchanting! And so the hypocrite calls me Cherry Bounce, and all sorts of nicknames behind my back, and often wishes me out of his house? The traitor! Yes, I will comply with his desire, and with your excellent advice, by quitting the iniquitous mansion for ever.

Your letter on the subject reached me just before breakfast. Heavens! how my noble blood throbbed in my veins! What a new prospect of things opened on my soul! I might be an heiress. I might be a title. I might be -- I would not wait to think; I would not wait to bind my hair. I flew down stairs, rushed into the parlour, and in a moment was at the feet of my persecutor. My hands were folded on my bosom, and my agitated eyes raised to his face.

276

"Heyday, Cherry," said he, laughing, "this is a new flourish. There, child, now fancy yourself stabbed, and come to breakfast."

"Hear me," cried I.

"Why, said he, "you keep your countenance as stiff and steady as the face on our rapper."

"A countenance," cried I, "is worth keeping, when the features are a proof of the descent, and vindicate the noble birth from the baseness of the adoption."

"Come, come," said he, "your cup is full all this time."

"And so is my heart," cried I, pressing it expressively.

"What the mischief can be the meaning of this mummery?" said he.

"Hear me, Wilkinson," cried the fair sufferer, rising with dignified tranquillity. "Candor is at once the most amiable and the most difficult of virtues; and there is more magnanimity in confessing an error, than in never committing one."

"Confound your written sentences," cried he, "can't you come to the point?"

"Then, Sir," said I, "to be plain and explicit, learn, that I have discovered a mystery in my birth, and that you -- you, Wilkinson, are not -- my real Father!"

I pronounced these words with a measured emphasis, and one of my ineffable looks. Wilkinson coloured like scarlet, and stared steadily in my face.

"Would you scandalize the mother that bore you?" cried he, fiercely.

"No, Wilkinson," answered I, "but you would by calling yourself the father of her daughter."

"And if *I* am not," said he, "what must *you* be?"

"An illustrious heiress," cried I, "snatched from her parents in her infancy; -- snatched by thee, vile agent of the diabolical conspiracy!"

He looked aghast.

"Tell me then," continued I, "miserable man, tell me where my dear, my distracted father lingers out the remnant of his wretched days? My mother too -- or say, am I indeed an orphan?"

Still he remained mute, and gazed on me with a searching intensity. I raised my voice:

"Expiate thine offences, restore an outcast to her birthright, make atonement, ox *tremble at retribution!*"

277

I thought the farmer would sink into the ground.

"Nay," continued I, lowering my voice, "think not I thirst for vengeance. I myself will intercede to stay the sword of Justice. Poor wretch! I want not thy blood."

The culprit was now at the climax of his agony; he writhed through every limb and feature, and by this time had torn the newspaper to tatters.

"What!" cried I, "can nothing move thee to confess thy crimes? Then listen. Ere Aurora with rosy fingers shall unbar the eastern gate--"

"My child, my child, my dear darling daughter!" exclaimed this accomplished crocodile, bursting into tears, and snatching me to his bosom, "what have they done to you? What phantom, what horrid disorder is distracting my treasure?"

"Unhand me, guileful adulator," cried I, "and try thy powers of tragedy elsewhere, for-- *I know thee!*" I spoke, and extricated myself from his embrace.

"Dreadful, dreadful!" muttered he. "Her sweet senses are lost. My love, my life, do not speak thus to your poor old father."

"Father!" exclaimed I, accomplishing with much accuracy that hysterical laugh, which (gratefully let me own) I owe to your instruction; "Father? Oh, no Sir, no thank you. 'Tis true you have blue eyes like myself, but have you my pouting lip and dimple? You have the flaxen hair, but can you execute the rosy smile? Besides, is it possible, that I, who was born a Heroine, and who must, therefore, have sprung from an idle and illustrious family, should be the daughter of a fat funny farmer? Oh, no Sir; no thank you."

The fat funny farmer covered his face with his hands, and rushed out of the room, nor left a doubt of his guilt behind.

You see I relate the several conversations, in a dramatic manner, and word for word, as well as I can recollect them, since heroines do the same. Indeed, I cannot too much admire the fortitude of these charming creatures, who, even while they are in momentary expectation of losing their honors, sit down with the utmost unconcern, and indite the sprightliest letters in the world. They have even presence of mind enough to copy the vulgar dialect, uncouth phraseology, and bad grammar, of villains, who, perhaps, are in the next room to them, and who would not matter annihilating them with a poignard, while they are mending a pen.

Adieu.

278

LETTER III.

Soon after my last letter, I was summoned to dinner. What heroine in distress but starves? so I sent a message that I was unwell, and then solaced myself with a volume of the Mysteries of Udolpho, which had escaped the conflagration. Afterwards I flung myself on my bed, in hopes to have dreams portentous of my future fate; for heroines are remarkably subject to a certain prophetic sort of night-mare. You remember the story which Ludovico read, of a spectre that beckons a Baron from his castle in the dead of night, and leading him into a forest, points to its own corpse, and bids him bury it. Well, owing, I suppose, to my having just read this episode, and to my having fasted so long, 1 had the following dreams.

Methought a delicious odour of viands attracted me to the kitchen, where I found an iron pot upon the fire simmering in unison with my sighs. As I looked at it with a longing eye, the lid began to rise, and I beheld a half-boiled turkey stalk majestically forth. It beckoned me with its claw. I followed. It led me into the yard, and pointed to its own head and feathers, which were lying in a corner.

What a vulgar, what a disgusting vision, when I ought to have dreamt of nothing but coffins and ladies in black!

At tea (which I could not resist taking, I was so hungry), Wilkinson affected the most tender solicitude for my health; and as I now watched his words, I could discover in almost all that he said, something to confirm my surmise of his not being my father.

After tea, a letter was handed to him, which he read, and then gave to me. It ran thus:

London.

In accepting your invitation to Sylvan Lodge, my respected friend, I confer a far greater favour on myself, than, as you kindly tell me, I shall on you. After an absence of seven years, spent in the seclusion of a college, and the fatigues of a military life, how delightful to revisit the scene of my childhood, and those who contribute to render its memory so dear! I left you while you were my guardian; I return to you with your assurances that I shall find you a friend. Let me but find you what I left you, and you shall take what title you please.

Yet, much as I flatter myself with your retaining all your former feelings towards me, I must expect a serious alteration in those of

279

my friend Cherry. Will she again make me her playmate? Again climb my shoulders, and gallop me round the lawn? Are we to renew all our little quarrels, then kiss and be friends? Shall we even recognize each others' features, through their change from childhood to maturity? There is, at least, one feature of our early days, that, I trust, has undergone no alteration -- our mutual affection and friendship.

My servant, whom I send forward, takes this letter. At ten to-night I shall see you myself.

Ever affectionately your's,

ROBERT STUART.

To Gregory Wilkinson, Esq.

"There," cries the farmer, "if I have deprived you of an old woman, I have got you a young man. Large estates, you know; -- handsome, fashionable; -- come, pluck up a heart, my girl; ay, egad, and steal one too."

I rose, gave him one of my ineffable looks, and retired to my chamber.

"So," said I, locking my door, and flinging myself on the bed, "this is something like misery. Here is another precious project against my peace. I am to be forced into marriage, am I? And with whom? A man whose legitimacy is unimpeached, and whose friends would certainly consent. His name Robert too: -- master Bobby, as the servants used to call him. A fellow that mewed like a cat, when he was whipt. O my Bob! what a pretty monosyllable for a girl like me to pronounce. Now, indeed, my wretchedness is complete; the cup is full, even to overflowing. An orphan, or at least an outcast; robbed of my birthright, immured in a farm-house -- threatened with a husband of decent birth, parentage and education -- my governess gone, my novels burnt, what is left to me but flight? Yes, I will roam through the wide world in search of my parents; I will ransack all the sliding pannels and tapestries in Italy; I will explore Il Castello Di Udolpho, and will then enter the convent of Ursulines, or Carmelites, or Santa della Pieta, or the Abbey of La Trappe. Here I meet with little better than smiling faces and honest hearts. No precious scoundrels are here, no horrors, or atrocities, worth tolerating. But abroad I shall encounter banditti, monks, daggers, racks -- O ye celebrated terrors, when shall I taste of you?"

I then rose, and stole into Wilkinson's study, in hopes of finding, before my flight, some record or relic that might aid me in unravelling the mystery of my birth. As heroines are privileged to ransack private drawers, and read whatever they find there, I opened his scrutoire, without ceremony. But what were my sensations, when I discovered in a corner of it, an antique scrap of tattered parchment, scrawled all over with this frightful fragment.

This Indenture
For and in consideration of
Doth grant, bargain, release
Possession, and to his heirs and assigns
Lands of Sylvan Lodge, in the
Trees, stones, quarries, &c,

Reasonable amends and satisfaction
This demise
Molestation of him the said Gregory Wilkinson
The natural life of
Cherry Wilkinson only daughter of
De Willoughby eldest son of Thomas
Lady Gwyn of Gwyn Castle.

O Biddy, does not your blood run cold at this excruciating manuscript? for already you must have decyphered its terrific import. The part lost may be gathered from the part left. In short, it is a written covenant between this Gregory Wilkinson, and the miscreant (whom my being an heiress had prevented from enjoying the title and estate that would devolve to him at my death), stipulating to give Wilkinson "Sylvan Lodge," together with, "trees, stones, quarries, &c." as "reasonable amends and satisfaction, "for being the instrument of my "Demise;" and declaring that there shall be "no molestation of him the said Gregory Wilkinson" for taking away " the natural life of Cherry Wilkinson" --"only daughter of--" somebody "De Willoughby, eldest son of Thomas" --Then follows, "Lady Gwyn of Gwyn Castle." So that it is evident I am a De Willoughby, and related to Lady Gwyn! What perfectly confirms me in the latter supposition is an old portrait which I found soon after, among Wilkinson's papers, representing a young and beautiful

281

female superbly dressed; and underneath, in large letters, the name of, "NELL GWYN."

Distraction! what shall I do? Whither turn? To sleep another night under the same roof with a wretch, who has bound himself to assassinate me, would be little short of madness. Besides Stuart arrives here to-night; so, if I remain any longer, I must endure his odious addresses. My plan of escape, therefore, is already arranged, and this very evening I mean to begin my pilgrimage.

The picture and parchment I will keep in my bosom during my journey; and I will also carry a small bandbox, containing my satin petticoat, satin shoes, a pair of silk stockings, my spangled muslin, and all my jewels. For as some benevolent duchess may possibly receive me into her family, and her son persecute me, I might just as well look decent, you know.

On mature deliberation, I have resolved to take but five guineas with me, since more would only make me too comfortable, and tempt me, in some critical moment, to extricate myself from distress.

I shall leave the following billet on my toilet.

To Gregory Wilkinson, Farmer.

Sir,

When this letter meets your eye, the writer will be far, far distant. She will be wandering the convex earth in pursuit of those parents, from whose dear embraces you have torn her. She will be flying from a Stuart, to whose detestable embraces you have destined her.

Your motive for this hopeful match I can guess. As you obtained one property by undertaking my death, you are probably promised another on effecting my marriage. Learn that the latter fate has more terrors for me than the former. But I shall escape both.

Alas! Sir, I once doated upon you as the best of fathers. Think then of my consternation at finding you the worst of persecutors. Yet I pity more than hate you; and the first moment of your repentance shall be the last of my animosity.

The much injured,
CHERUBINA DE WILLOUGHBY.

All is prepared, and in ten minutes I commence my interesting expedition. As London is the most approved refuge for distressed

Heroines, and the most likely place for obtaining information about my birth, I mean to bend my steps thither.

O peaceful shades, why must I leave you? In your retreats I should still find pleasure and repose.

Adieu.

LETTER IV.

The hail rattled and the wind whistled, as I tied on my bonnet for my journey. With the bandbox under my arm, I descended the stairs, and paused in the hall to listen. I heard a distant door shut, and steps advancing. I sprang forward, opened the door, and ran down the shrubbery.

I then hastened into the road, and pressed onward with a hurried step, while a violent tempest beat full against my face.

In this manner I walked four long and toilsome miles. At length, finding myself fatigued, I resolved to rest awhile, in the lone and uninhabited house, which lies, you may recollect, on the grey common, about a hundred paces from the road. Besides, I was in duty bound to explore it, as a ruined pile.

I approached. The wind moaned through the broken windows, and the rank grass rustled in the court. I entered. All was dark within; the boards creaked as I trod, the shutters flapped, and an ominous owl was hooting in the chimney. I groped my way along the hall, thence into a parlour -- up stairs and down -- not a horror to be found. No dead hand met my left hand; no huge eye-ball glared at me through a crevice. How disheartening!

The cold was now creeping through my veins; my teeth chattered, and my frame shook. I had seated myself on the stairs, and was weeping piteously, wishing myself at home, and in bed, and deploring the dire necessity which had compelled me to this frightful undertaking, when on a sudden I heard the sound of approaching steps. I sprang upon my feet with renovated spirits. Presently several persons entered the hall, and a vulgar accent cried: --

"Jem, run down to the cellar and strike a light."

"What can you want of me, now that you have robbed me?" said the voice of a gentleman.

"Why, young man," answered a ruffian, "we want you to write home for a hundred pounds, or some such trifle, which we will have the honour of spending. You must manufacture some confounded good lie about where you are, and why you send for the money; and one of us will carry the letter."

"I assure you," said the youth, "I shall forge no such falsehood."

"As you please, master," replied the ruffian, "but, the money or your life we must have, and that soon."

"Will you trust my solemn promise to send you a hundred pounds?" said the other. "My name is Stuart: I am on my way to Mr. Wilkinson, of Sylvan Lodge, so you may depend upon my sending you, by his assistance, the sum that you require, and I will promise not to betray you."

"No, curse me if I trust," cried the robber.

"Then curse me if I write," said Stuart.

"Look you, Squire," cried the robber: "we cannot stand parlying with you now; we have other matters on hands. But we will lock you safe in the cellar, with pen, ink, and paper, and a lantern; and if you have not a fine bouncing lie of a letter, ready written when we come back, you are a dead man -- that is all."

"I am almost a dead man already," said Stuart, "for the wound you gave me is bleeding torrents."

They now carried him down to the cellar, where they remained a few minutes, then returned, and locked the door outside.

"Leave the key in it," says one, "for we do not know which of us may come back first." They then went away.

Now was the fate of my bitter enemy, the wily, the wicked Stuart, in my power; I could either liberate him, or let him perish. It struck me, that to miss such a fruitful interview, would be stupid in the extreme; and I felt a sort of glow at the idea of saying to him, live! Besides he could not possibly recognize me, since I was but eight years old when we saw each other last. So I descended the steps, unlocked the door, and bursting into the cellar, stood in an unparalleled attitude before him. He was sitting on the ground, and fastening a handkerchief about his wounded leg, but at my entrance, he sprang upon his feet.

"Away, save thyself!" cried I. "She who restores thee to freedom flies herself from captivity. Look on these features -- Thou wouldest have wrung them with despair. Look on this form -- Thou wouldest have prest it in depravity. Hence, unhappy sinner, and learn, that innocence is ever victorious and ever merciful."

"I am all amazement!" exclaimed he. "Who are you? Whence come you? Why speak so angrily, yet act so kindly?"

I smiled disdain, and turned to depart.

"One moment more," cried he. "Here is some mistake, for I never even saw you before."

"Often, often," exclaimed I, and was again going.

"So you will leave me, my sweet preserver," said he, smiling. "Now you have all this time prevented me from binding my wound, and you owe me some compensation for loss of blood."

I paused.

"I would ask you to assist me," continued he, "but in binding one wound, I fear you would only inflict another."

Mere curiosity made me return two steps.

"I think, however, there would be healing in the touch of so fair a hand," and he took mine as he spoke.

Mere humanity made me kneel down, and begin to fasten the bandage; but I resolutely resolved on not uttering another word.

"What kindness!" cried he. "And pray to whom am I indebted for it?"

No reply.

"At least, may I learn whether I can, in any manner, repay it?"

No reply.

"You will stain your beautiful locks," said he. "My blood would flow to defend, but shall not flow to disfigure them. Pray let me collect these charming tresses."

"Oh! dear, thank you, Sir!" stammered I.

"And thank you, ten thousand times," said he, as I finished my disagreeable task; "and now never will I quit you till I see you safe to your friends."

"You!" exclaimed I. "Ah, traitor!"

He gazed at me with a look of pity. "Farewell, then," said he: "'tis a long way to the next habitation, and should my wound open afresh, and should I faint with loss of blood --"

"Dear me," cried I, springing forward, "let me assist you."

He smiled. "We will assist each other," answered he; "and now let us not lose a moment, as the robbers may return."

He took the lantern to search the cellar for his watch and money. However, we saw nothing there except a couple of portmanteaus, some rusty pistols, and a small barrel, half full of gunpowder. We then left the house; but had hardly proceeded twenty yards, when he began to totter.

"I can go no farther," said he, sinking down. "I have lost so much blood, that my strength is entirely exhausted."

"Pray, dear Sir," said I, "exert yourself, and lean on me."

"Impossible," answered he; "but fly and save your own life."

"I will run for assistance," said I, and flew towards the road, where I had just heard the sound of an approaching carriage. But on a sudden it stopped, voices began disputing, and soon after a pistol was fired. I paused in great terror, for I judged that these were the robbers again. What was I to do? When a heroine is reduced to extremities, she always does one of two things -- either faints on the spot, or exhibits energies almost superhuman.

Faint I could not, so nothing remained for me, but energies almost superhuman. I pondered a moment, and a grand thought struck me. Recollecting the gunpowder in the cellar, I flew for it back to the ruin, carried it up to the hall, threw most of it on the floor, and with the remainder, strewed a train, as I walked towards Stuart.

When I was within a few paces of him, I heard quick steps; and a hoarse voice vociferating, "Who goes yonder with the light?" for I had brought the lantern.

"Fly!" cried Stuart, "or you are lost."

I snatched the candle from the lantern, applied it to the train, and the next moment dropped down at the shock of the tremendous explosion that took place. A noise of falling timbers resounded through the ruin, and the robbers were heard scampering off in every direction.

"There!" whispered I, after a pause; "there is an original horror for you; and all of my own contrivance. The villains have fled, the neighbours will flock to the spot, and you will obtain assistance."

By this time we heard the people of the carriage running towards us.

"Stuart!" cried I, in an awful voice.

"My name, indeed!" said he. "This is completely inexplicable."

"Stuart," cried I, "hear my parting words. *Never again*" (quoting his own letter), "*will I make you my playmate! never again climb your shoulders, and gallop you round the lawn!* Ten o'clock is past.

Go not to Sylvan Lodge to-night. She departed two hours ago. Look to your steps."

I spoke this portentous warning, and fled across the common, Miss Wilkinson! Miss Wilkinson! sounded on the blast; but the wretch had discovered me too late. I ran about half a mile, and then looking behind me, beheld the ruin in a blaze. Renovated by the sight of this admirable horror, I walked another hour, without once stopping; till, to my surprise and dismay, I found myself utterly unable to proceed a step farther. This was the more provoking, because heroines often perform journies on foot that would founder fifty horses.

However, I crossed into a field, and contrived to make a nest of hay, where I remained till day began to dawn. Then, stiff and shivering, I proceeded on my journey; and in a short time, met a little girl with a pail of milk. She consented to let me change my wet dress at her cottage, and conducted me thither.

It was a family of frights. Flat noses and thick lips without mercy. No Annettes and Lubins, or Amorets and Phyllidas, or Florimels and Florellas; no rosy little fatlings, or Cherubim and Seraphim amongst them. However, I slipped on (for *slipping on* is the heroic mode of dressing) my spangled muslin, silk stockings, and satin shoes, and joined their uglinesses at breakfast, resolving to bear patiently with their features.

On the whole, I see much reason to be pleased with what has happened hitherto. How fortunate that I went to the house upon the common! I see plainly, that if adventure does not come to me, I must go to adventure. And, indeed, I am authorized in doing so by the example of my sister heroines; who, with a noble disinterestedness, are ever the chief artificers of their own misfortunes: for, in nine cases out of ten, were they to manage matters like mere common mortals, they would avoid all those charming mischiefs which adorn their memoirs.

As for this Stuart, I know not what to think of him. I will, however, do him the justice to say, that he has a reputable Roman nose; and although he neither kissed my hand, nor knelt to me, yet he had the decency to talk of "wounds," and my "charming tresses." Perhaps, if he had saved my life, instead of my having saved his; and his name had consisted of three syllables ending in i or o; and, in fine, if he were not an unprincipled profligate, the man might have made a tolerable Hero.

287

A public coach to London passes shortly, so I shall take a place in it.

Adieu.

LETTER V.

"I SHALL find in the coach," said I, approaching it, "some emaciated Adelaide, or sister Olivia. We will interchange congenial looks -- she will sigh, so will I -- and we shall commence a vigorous friendship on the spot."

Yes, I did sigh; but it was at the huge and hideous Adelaide that presented herself, as I got into the coach. In describing her, our wittiest novelists would say, that her nose lay modestly retired between her cheeks; that her eyes, which pointed inwards, seemed looking for it, and that her teeth were

"Like angels' visits; short, and far between."

She first eyed me with a supercilious sneer, and then addressed a diminutive old gentleman opposite, in whose face Time had ploughed furrows, and Luxury sown pimples.

"And so, Sir, as I was telling you, when my poor man died, I so bemoaned myself, that between swoons and hystorics, I got nervous all over, and was obliged to go through a regiment."

I stared in astonishment. "What!" thought I, "a woman of her magnitude and vulgarity, faint, and have nerves? Impossible!"

"Howsomdever," continued she, "my Bible and my Moll are great consolations to me. Moll is the dearest little thing in the world; as straight as a popular; then such dimples; and her eyes are the very squintessence of perfection. She has all her catechism by heart, and moreover, her mind is uncontaminated by romances and novels, and such abominations."

"Pray, Ma'am," said I, civilly, "may I presume to ask how romances and novels contaminate the mind?"

"Why, Mem," answered she tartly, and after another survey, "by teaching little misses to go gadding, Mem, and to be fond of the men, Mem, and of spangled muslin, Mem."

288

"Ma'am," said I, reddening, "I wear spangled muslin because I have no other dress: and you should be ashamed of yourself for saying that I am fond of the men."

"The cap fits you then," cried she.

"Were it a fool's cap," said I, "perhaps I might return the compliment."

I thought it expedient on my first outset in life to practise apt repartee, and emulate the infatuating sauciness, and elegant vituperation of Amanda, the Beggar Girl, and other heroines; who, when irritated, disdain to speak below an epigram.

"Pray, Sir," said she, addressing our fellow traveller, "what is your opinion of novels? An't they all love and nonsense, and the most unpossible lies possible?"

"They are fictions, certainly," said he.

"Surely, Sir," exclaimed I, "you do not mean to call them fictions?"

"Why, no," replied he, "not absolute fictions."

"But," cried the big lady, "you don't pretend to call them true."

"Why no," said he, "not absolutely true."

"Then," cried I, "you are on both sides of the question at once."

He trod on my foot.

"Ay, that you are," said the big lady.

He trod on her foot.

"I am too much of a courtier," said he, "to differ from the ladies," and he trod on both our feet.

"A courtier!" cried I: "I should rather have imagined you a musician."

"Pray why?" said he.

"Because," answered I, "you are playing the pedal harp on this lady's foot and mine."

"I wished to produce harmony," said he, bowing.

"If you wish it with me," said I, "you must confess that novels are more true than histories, because historians often contradict each other, but novelists never do."

"Yet do not novelists contradict themselves?" said he.

"Certainly," replied I, "and there lies the surest proof of their veracity. For as human actions are always contradicting themselves, so those books which faithfully relate them must do the same."

"Admirable!" exclaimed he. "And yet what proof have we that such personages as Shedoni, Vivaldi, Camilla, or Cecilia, ever existed?"

"And what proof have we," cried I, "that such personages as Alfred the Great, Henry the Fifth, Elfrida, or Mary Queen of Scots, ever existed? Why, Sir, at this rate you might just as well question the truth of Guy Faux's attempt to blow up the Parliament-House, or of my having blown up a house last night."

"You blow up a house!" exclaimed the big lady with amazement.

"Madam," said I, modestly, "I scorn ostentation, but on my word and honour, 'tis fact."

"Of course you did it accidentally," said the gentleman.

"You wrong me, Sir," replied I; "I did it by design."

"You will swing for it, however," cried the big lady.

"Swing for it!" said I; "a heroine swing? Excellent! I presume, Madam, you are unacquainted with the common law of romance."

"Just," said she, "as you seem to be with the common law of England."

"I despise the common law of England," cried I.

"Then I fancy," said she, "it would not be much amiss if you were hanged."

"And I fancy," retorted I, nodding at her big figure, "it would not be much amiss if you were quartered."

Meantime the gentleman coincided with every syllable that I said, praised my parts and knowledge, and discovered evident symptoms of a discriminating mind, and an amiable heart. That I am right in my good opinion of him is most certain; for he himself assured me it would be quite impossible to deceive me, I am so penetrating. In short, I have set him down as the benevolent guardian, who is destined to save me several times from destruction.

Indeed he has already done so once; for, when our journey was almost over, he told me, that my having set fire to the ruin might prove a most fatal affair; and whispered that the big lady would probably inform against me. On my pleading the prescriptive immunities of heroines, he solemnly swore, that he once knew a golden-haired, azure-eyed heroine, called Angelica Angela Angelina, who was hanged at the Old Bailey for stealing a broken lute out of a haunted chamber; and while my blood was running cold at the recital, he pressed me so cordially to take refuge in his house, that I threw myself on the protection of the best of men.

I now write from his mansion in Grosvenor Square, where we have just dined. His name is Betterton; he has no family, but possesses a splendid independence. Multitudes of liveried menials watch his nod; and he does me the honour to call me cousin. My chamber too is charming. The curtains hang quite in a new style, but I do not like the pattern of the drapery.

To-morrow I mean to go shopping; and I may, at the same time, pick up some adventures on my way; for business must be minded.

Adieu.

LETTER VI.

Soon after my last letter, I was summoned to supper. Betterton appeared much interested in my destiny, and I took good care to inspire him with a proper sense of my forlorn and unprotected state. I told him that I had not a friend in the wide world, related to him my lamentable tale, and as a proof of my veracity produced the parchment and the picture.

To my surprise, he said that he considered my high birth improbable; and then began advising me to descend from my romantic flights, as he called them, and to seek after happiness instead of misery.

"In this town," continued he, after a long preamble, "your charms would be despotic, if unchained by legal constraints. But for ever distant from you be that cold and languid tie which erroneous policy invented. For you be the mystic union, whose tie of bondage is passion, the wish the licence, and impulse the law."

"Pretty expressions enough," said I, "only I cannot comprehend them."

"Charming girl!" cried he, while he conjured up a fiend of a smile, and drew a brilliant from his finger, "accept this ring, and the signature of the hand that has worn it, securing to you five hundred a-year, while you remain under my protection."

"Ha, monster!" exclaimed I, "and is this thy vile design?"

So saying, I flung the ruffian from me, then rushed down stairs, opened the door, and quick as lightning darted along the streets.

At last, panting for breath, I paused underneath a portico. It was now midnight. Not a wheel, not a hoof fatigued the pavement, or disturbed the slumbering mud of the metropolis. But soon steps and voices broke the silence, and a youth, encircling a maiden's waist with his arm, and modulating the most mellifluent phraseology, passed by me. Another couple succeeded, and another, and another. The town seemed swarming with heroes and heroines. "Fortunate pairs!" ejaculated I, "at length ye enjoy the reward of your incomparable constancy and virtue. Here, after a long separation, meeting by chance, and in extreme distress, ye pour forth your unpolluted souls. O blissful termination of unexampled miseries!"

I now perceived, on the steps of a house, a fair and slender form. She was sitting with her elbow in her lap, and her head leaning on one side, within her hand.

"She seems a congenial outcast," said I; "so, should she but have a Madona face, and a name ending in a, we will live, we will die together."

I then approached, and discovered a countenance so pale, so pensive, so Roman, that I could almost have knelt and worshipped it.

"Fair unfortunate," said I, taking her hand and pressing it; "interesting unknown, say by what name am I to address so gentle a sister in misery."

"Eh? What?" cried she, with a voice somewhat coarser than I was prepared to expect.

"May I presume on my sudden predilection," said I, "and inquire your name?"

"Maria," replied she, rising from her seat: "and now I must be gone."

"And where are you going, Maria?" said I.

"To the Devil!" said she.

I started. "Alas! my love," whispered I, "sorrow hath bewildered thee. I am myself a miserable orphan; but happy, thrice happy, could I clasp a sympathetic bosom, in this frightful wilderness of houses and faces, where, alas! I know not a human being."

"Then you are a stranger here?" said she quickly.

"I am here but a few hours," answered I.

"Have you money?" she demanded.

"Only four guineas and a half," replied I, taking out my purse. "Perhaps you are in distress -- perhaps -- forgive this officiousness-- not for worlds would I wound your delicacy, but if you want assistance--"

292

"I have only this old sixpence upon earth," interrupted she, "and there 'tis for you, Miss."

So saying, she put sixpence into my purse, which I had opened while I was speaking."

"Generous angel!" cried I.

"Now we are in partnership, a'nt we?" said she.

"Yes, sweet innocent," answered I, "we are partners in grief."

"And as grief is dry," cried she, "we will go moisten it."

"And where shall we moisten it, Maria?" said I.

"In a public-house," cried she. "It will do us good."

"O my Maria!" said I, " never, never!"

"Why then give me back my sixpence," cried she, snatching at my purse; but I held it fast, and, springing from her, ran away.

"Stop thief, stop thief!" vociferated she.

In an instant, I heard a sort of rattling noise from several quarters, and a huge fellow, called a watchman, came striding out of a wooden box, and grasped me by the shoulder.

"She has robbed me of my purse," exclaimed the wily wanton. "'Tis a green one, and has four guineas and a half in it, besides a curious old sixpence."

The watchman took it from me, and examined it.

"'Tis my purse," cried I, "and I can swear to it."

"You lie!" said the little wretch; "you know well that you snatched it from my hand, when I was going to give you sixpence, out of charity."

Horror and astonishment struck me dumb; and when I told my tale, the watchman declared that both of us must remain in custody, till next morning; and then be carried before the magistrate. Accordingly, he escorted us to the watchhouse, a room filled with smoke and culprits; where we stayed all night, amidst a concert of swearing, snoring, laughing, and crying.

In the morning we were carried before a magistrate; and with step superb, and neck erect, I entered the room.

"Pert enough," said the magistrate; and turning from me, continued his examination of two men who stood near him.

It appeared that one of them (whose name was Jerry Sullivan) had assaulted the other, on the following occasion. A joint sum of money had lately been deposited in Sullivan's hands, by this other, and a third man, his partner; which sum Sullivan had consented to keep for them, and had bound himself to return, whenever both should go together to him, and demand it. Sometime afterwards, one of them went to him, and told him that the other, being ill, and therefore unable to come for the money, had empowered him (the partner) to get it. Sullivan, believing him, gave the money, and when he next met the other, mentioned the circumstance. The other denied having authorized the act, and demanded his own share of the deposit from Sullivan, who refused it. Words ensued, and Sullivan having knocked him down, was brought before the magistrate, to be committed for an assault.

"Have you any defence?" said the magistrate to him.

"None that I know of," answered Sullivan, "only my arm is subject to a kind of a sort of jerking spasm, ever since I was bewitched by Molly Cranahan the Fairy Woman; so I do suppose it was a jerking spasm that knocked the man down."

"And is this your defence?" said the magistrate.

"It is so," replied Sullivan, "and I hope your worship likes it, as well as I like your worship."

"So we," said the magistrate, "that I now mean to do you a signal service."

"Why then," cried Sullivan, "the heavens smile on you for a kind gentleman."

"And that service," continued the magistrate, "is to commit you immediately."

"Why then," cried Sullivan, "the Devil inconvenience you for a big blackguard."

"By your insolence, you should be an Irishman," said the magistrate.

"I was an Irishman forty years ago," replied the other; "and I don't suppose I am any thing else now. Though I have left my country, I scorn to change my birth-place."

"Commit him," said the magistrate.

Just then, a device struck me, which I thought might extricate the poor fellow; so, having received permission, I went across, and whispered it to him.

He half crushed me with a hug, and then addressed his accuser: "Now, Sir, if I can prove to you that I have not broken our agreement about the money, will you promise not to prosecute me for this assault ?"

"With all my heart," answered the man; "for if you have not broken our agreement, you must give me the money, which is all I want."

"And will your worship," said Sullivan, "approve of this compromise, and stand umpire between us?"

"I have not the least objection," answered the magistrate; "for I would rather be the means of your fulfilling an agreement, than of your suffering a punishment."

"Well then," said Jerry to his accuser; "was not our agreement that I should return the money to yourself and your partner, whenever both of you came together to me, and asked for it?"

"Certainly," said the man.

"And did both of you ever come together to me, and ask for it?"

"Never," said the man.

"Then I have not broken our agreement," cried Sullivan.

"But you cannot keep it," said the man; "because you have already given the money away."

"No matter," cried Sullivan, "provided I have it whenever both of you come together and demand it. But I believe that will be never at all at all, for the fellow who ran off with it won't much like to shew his face again. So now will your worshipful honor decide?"

The magistrate, after complimenting me upon my ingenious suggestion, confessed, he said, with much unwillingness, that Sullivan had made out his case clearly. The poor accuser was therefore obliged to abide by his covenant, and Sullivan was dismissed, snapping his fingers, and offering to treat the whole world with a tankard.

My cause came after, and the treacherous Maria was ordered to state her evidence.

But what think you, Biddy, of my keeping you in suspense till my next letter? The practice of keeping in suspense, so common among novelists, is always interesting, and often necessary. In the Romance of the Highlands, a lady terminates, not her letter, but her life, much in the same style, and with great effect; for when dying, she was about to disclose the circumstances of a horrid murder, which, had she done, not a single incident that afterwards happened, would then have happened. But fortunately, just as she was on the point of telling all, she chanced to expend her last breath in a beautiful description of the verdant hills, rising sun, all nature smiling, and a few streaks of purple in the east.

Adieu.

LETTER VII.

Maria being ordered to state her evidence, "That I will," said she.

"I was walking innocently home, from my aunt's, with my poor eyes fixed upon the ground, for fear of the fellors, when what should I see, but this girl, talking on some steps, with a pickpocket, I fancy, 'cause he looked pretty decent. So I ran past them, for I was so ashamed you can't think; and this girl runs after me, and says, says she, 'The fellor wouldn't give me a little shilling,' says she, 'so by Jingo, you must,' says she."

"By Jingo! I say by Jingo?" cried I. "St. Catherine guard me! Indeed, your Excellenza, my only oath is Santa Maria."

"She swore at me like a bilking trooper," continued the little imp, "so I pulled out my purse in a fright, and she snatched it from me, and ran away, and I after her, calling stop thief; and this is the whole truth 'pon my honor and word, and as I hope to be married."

The watchman declared that he had caught me running away, that he had found the purse upon my person, and that Maria had described it, and the money contained in it, accurately.

"And will your worship," said Maria, "ask the girl to describe the sixpence that is in it?"

The magistrate turned to me.

"Really," said I, "as I never even saw it, I cannot possibly pretend to describe it."

"Then I can," cried she. " 'Tis bent in two places, and stamped on one of its sides with a D and an H."

The sixpence was examined, and answered her description of it.

"The case is clear enough," said the magistrate, "so now, Miss, try whether you can advocate your own cause as well as Jerry Sullivan's."

Jerry, who still remained in the room, came behind me, and whispered, "Troth, Miss, I have no brains, but I have a bit of an oath, if that is of any use to you. I would sell my soul to Old Nick out of gratitude, at any time."

"Alas! your Excellenza," said I to the magistrate, " frail is the tenure of that character which has Innocence for its friend, and Infamy for its foe. Life is a chequered scene of light and shade--"

"Talking of life is not the way to save it," said the magistrate. "Less sentiment and more point, if you please."

I was silent, but looked anxiously towards the door.

"Are you meditating an escape?" asked he.

"No," said I, "but just wait a little, and you shall see what an interesting turn affairs will take."

"Come," cried he, "proceed at once, or say you will not."

"Ah, now," said I, "can't you stop one moment, and not spoil everything by your impatience. I am only watching for the tall, elegant young stranger, with an oval face, who is to enter just at this crisis, and snatch me from perdition."

"Did he promise to come?" said the magistrate.

"Not at all," answered I, "for I have never seen the man in my life. But whoever rescues me now, you know, is destined to marry me hereafter. That is the rule."

"You are an impudent minx," said the magistrate, "and shall pay dear for your jocularity. Have you parents?"

"I cannot tell."

"Friends?"

"None."

"Where do you live?"

"No where."

"At least 'tis plain where you will die. What is your name?"

"Cherubina."

"Cherubina what?"

"I know not."

"Not know? I protest this is the most hardened profligate I have ever met. Commit her instantly."

I now saw that something must be done; so summoning all my most atsuasive airs, I related the whole adventure, just as it had occurred.

Not a syllable obtained belief. The fatal sixpence carried all before it. I recollected the fate of Angelica Angela Angelina, and shuddered. What should 1 do? One desperate experiment remained.

"There were four guineas and half a guinea in the purse," said I to the girl.

"To be sure there were," replied she. "Bless us, how obliging you are to tell me my own news!"

"Now," said I, "answer me at once, and without hesitation, whether is it the half guinea or one of the guineas that is notched in three places, like the teeth of a saw?"

She paused a little, and looked confused.

"Nay," said I, "no thinking."

"I have a long story to tell about those same notches," said she at length. "I wanted a silk handkerchief yesterday, so I went into a shop to buy one, and an impudent ugly young fellor was behind the counter. Well, he began ogling me so, I was quite ashamed; and says he to me, there is the change of your two pound note, says he, a guinea and a half in gold, says he, and you are vastly handsome, says he. And there are three notches in one of the coins, says he; guess which, says he, but it will pass all the same, says he, and you are prodigious pretty, says he. So indeed, I was so ashamed, that though I looked at the money, and saw the three notches, I have quite forgotten which they were in -- guinea or half guinea; for my sight spread so, with shame at his compliments, that the half guinea looked as big as the guinea; and I frowned so, you can't think. And I am sure, I never remembered to look at the money since; and this is the whole truth, I pledge you my credit and honour, and *by the immaculate Wenus*, as the gentlemen say."

The accusing witness who insulted the magistrate's bench with the oath, leered as she gave it in; and the recording clerk, as he wrote it down, drew a line under the words, and pointed them out for ever.

"Then you saw the three notches?" said I.

"As plain as I see you now," replied she, "and a guilty poor object you look."

"And yet," said I, "if his Worship will try, he will find that there is not a single notch in any one of the coins!"

" 'Tis the case indeed," said the magistrate, after accurately examining them.

Then turning to me, "Your conduct, young woman, is unaccountable: but as your accuser has certainly belied herself, she has probably belied you. The money, by her own account, cannot be her's, but as it was found in your possession, it may be your's. I therefore feel fully justified in restoring it to you, and in acquitting you of the crime laid to your charge."

I received the purse, gave Maria back her sixpence, and hurried out of the room.

Jerry followed me.

"Why then," cried he, shaking me heartily by the hand, as we walked along, "only tell me how I can serve you, and 'tis I that will; though, to be sure, you must be the greatest little reprobate (bless your heart!) in the three kingdoms."

"Alas!" said I, "you mistake my character. I am no reprobate, but a heroine -- the proudest title that can adorn a woman."

"I never heard of the title before," said Jerry, "and I warrant 'tis no better than it should be."

"You shall judge for yourself," said I. "A heroine is a young lady, rather taller than usual, and often an orphan; at all events, with the finest eyes in the world. She blushes to the tips of her fingers, and when mere misses would laugh, she faints. Besides, she has tears, sighs, and half sighs, at command; can live a month on a mouthful, and is addicted to the pale consumption."

"Why then, much good may it do her," cried Jerry; "but in my mind, a tisicky girl is no great treasure; and as to the fashion of living a month on a mouthful, let me have a potatoe and chop for my dinner, and a herring at nights, and I would not give a farthing for all the starvation you could offer me. So when I finish my bit of herring, wife says to me, winking, ' a fish loves water,' says she, and immediately she fetches me a dram."

"These are the delights of vulgar life," said I. "But to be thin, innocent, and lyrical; to bind and unbind her hair; in a word, to be the most miserable creature that ever augmented a brook with tears, these, my friend, are the glories of a heroine."

"Famous glories, by dad!" cried Jerry; "but as I am a poor man, and not over particular, I can contrive to make shift with health and happiness, and to rub through life without binding my hair. - Bind it? by the powers, 'tis seldom I even comb it."

As I was all this time without my bonnet (for in my hurry from Betterton's I had left it behind me), I determined to purchase one. So I went into a shop, and asked for an interesting and melancholy turn of bonnet.

The woman looked at me with some surprise, but produced several; and I fixed upon one which resembled a bonnet that I had once seen in a picture of a wood nymph. So I put it on me, wished the woman good morning, and was walking away.

"You have forgotten to pay me, Miss," said she.

"True," replied I, "but I will call another time. Adieu."

"You shall pay me, however," cried she, ringing a bell, and a man entered instantly from an inner room.

"Here is a hussey," exclaimed she, "who refuses to pay me for a bonnet."

"My sweet friend," said I to her, "a distressed heroine, which I assure you, I am, runs in debt every where. Besides, as I like your face, I mean to implicate you in my plot, and make you one of the *dramatis personæ* in the history of my life. Probably you will turn out to be my mother's nurse's daughter. At all events, I give you my word I will pay you at the *denouement*, when the other characters come to be provided for; and meantime, to secure your acquaintance, I must insist on owing you money."

"By dad," said Jerry, "that is the first of all ways to lose an acquaintance."

"The bonnet or the money!" cried the man, stepping between me and the door.

Jerry jumped forward, and arrested his arm. "Hands off, bully," cried the shopman.

"No, in troth," said Jerry; "and the more you bid me, the more I won't let you go."

"Do you want to rob me?" cried the shopman.

"If her ladyship has set her heart on a robbery," said Jerry, "I am not the man to baulk her fancy. Sure, did'nt she save me from a gaol? And sure, would'nt I help her to a bonnet ? A bonnet? 'Pon my conscience, she shall have half a dozen. 'Tis I that would not mind being hanged for her!"

So saying, he snatched a parcel of bonnets from the counter, and was instantly knocked down by the shopman. He rose, and both began a furious conflict. In the midst of it, I was attempting to rush from the shop, when I found my spangled muslin barbarously grasped by the woman, who tore it to pieces in the struggle; and pulling off the bonnet, pushed me into the street, just as Jerry had stunned his adversary with a blow. Taking this opportunity of escape, he dragged me through several streets without uttering a word.

At length I was so much exhausted, that we stopped; and strange figures we looked. Jerry's face was smeared with blood, nothing was on my head: my long locks were hanging loose about me, and my poor spangled muslin was all in rags.

"Here," said Jerry to an old woman who sold apples at a corner, "take care of this young body, while I fetch her a coach." And off he ran.

The woman looked at me with a suspicious eye, so I resolved to gain her good opinion. It struck me that I might extract pathos from an apple, and taking one from her stall, "An apple, my charming old friend," said I, "is the symbol of discord. Eve lost Paradise by tasting it, Paris exasperated Juno by throwing it." -- A burst of laughter made me turn round, and I perceived a crowd already at my elbow.

"Who tore her gown?" said one.

"Ask her spangles," said another.

"Or her hair," cried a third.

" 'Tis long enough to hang her," cried a fourth.

"The king's hemp will do that job for her," added a fifth.

A pull at my muslin assailed me on the one side, and when I turned about, my hair was thrown over my face on the other.

I was just beginning to cry, when a butcher's boy advanced: "Will your ladyship," said he, "permit me to hand you into that there shop?"

I bowed assent, and he led me, nothing loath. Peals of laughter followed us.

"Now," said I as I stood at the door, "I will reward your gallantry with half a guinea."

As I drew forth my money, I saw his face reddening, his cheeks swelling, and his mouth pursing up.

"What sensibility!" said I, "but positively you must not refuse this trifle."

He took it, and then just think, the brute laughed in my face!

"I will give this guinea," cried I, quite enraged, " to the first who chastises that ungrateful!"

Hardly had I spoken, when he was laid prostrate. He fell against the stall, upset it, and instantly the street was strewn with apples, nuts, and cakes. He rose. The battle raged. Some sided with him, some against him. The furious stall-woman pelted both parties with her own apples; while the only discreet person there was a ragged

301

little girl, who stood laughing at a distance, and eating one of the cakes.

In the midst of the fray, Jerry returned with a coach. I sprang into it, and he after me.

"The guinea, the guinea!" cried twenty voices at once. At once twenty apples came rattling against the glasses.

"Pay me for my apples!" cried the woman.

"Pay me for my windows!" cried the coachman.

"Drive like a devil," cried Jerry, "and I will pay you like an emperor!"

"Much the same sort of persons, now-a-days," said the coachman, and away we flew. The guinea, the guinea! died along the sky. I thought I should drop with laughter.

I write from Jerry's house, where I have taken refuge for the present.

I am extremely distracted, I assure you.

Adieu.

LETTER VIII.

Jerry Sullivan is a petty woollen-draper in St. Giles's, and occupies the lower floor of a small house. At first his wife and daughter eyed me with some suspicion; but when he told them how I had saved him from ruin, they became very civil, and gave me a tolerable breakfast. Soon afterwards I threw myself on a bed, and slept several hours.

I woke with pains in all my limbs; but anxious to forward the adventures of my life, I rose, and called mother and daughter on a consultation about my dress. As my spangled muslin was in ruins, they furnished me with the best of their wardrobe. I bargained to give them two guineas; and I then began equipping myself.

While thus employed, I heard the voices of husband and wife in the next room, rising gradually to the matrimonial key. At last the wife exclaims,

"A Heroine? I will take my corpular oath, there is no such title in all England; she's a fragrant impostume and if she has the four guineas, she never came honestly by them; so the sooner she parts with them the better; and not a step shall she stir in our clothes till she launches forth three of them. So that's that, and mine's my own, and how do you like my manners, Ignoramus?"

"How dare you call me Ignoramus?" cried Jerry. "Blackguard if you like, but no ignoramus, I believe. I know what I could call you, though."

"Well?" cried she, "well? saving a drunkard and a scold, what else can you call me?"

"I won't speak another word to you," said Jerry. "I would not speak to you, if you were lying dead in the kennel."

"Then," cried she, "you're an ugly unnatural beast, so you are; and your Miss is no better than a bad one, so she is; and I warrant you understand one another well, so you do!"

This last insinuation was perfectly sufficient for me. What! remain in a house where suspicion attached to my character? What! act so diametrically, so outrageously contrary from the principle of aspersed heroines, who are sure on such occasions to pin up a bundle, and set off? I spurned the puny notion, and resolved to decamp instantly. So having hastened my toilette, I threw three guineas on the table, and then looked for a pen and ink, to write a sonnet. I could find nothing, however, but a bit of chalk, and with this substitute, I scratched the following lines upon the wall.

SONNET,

To J. Sullivan, on leaving his House,

As some deputed angel downward steers,
  His golden wings, with glittering nectar dew'd;
Mid firmamental wilds and radiant spheres,
  To starless tracts of black infinitude--

Here the chalk failed me, and just at the critical moment; for my simile had also failed me, nor could I have ever gotten beyond infinitude. I got to the hall-door, however, and without fear of being overheard: to such an altitude of tone had ribaldry arisen between husband and wife, who were now contesting a most delicate point -- which of them had beaten the other last.

"I know," cried Jerry, "that I gave you the last blow."

"Then take the first now," cried his wife, as I shut the door.

Anticipating that I should probably have occasion for Jerry's services again, I marked the number of his house, and then hastened along the street. It was swarming and humming like a hive of bees, and I felt as if I could never escape alive out of it. Here a carriage almost ran over me; there a sweep brushed against me. "Beauty!" cried a man like a monkey, and chucked my chin, while a fellow with a trunk shoved me aside.

The shops soon attracted my attention, and I stopped to look at some of them. You cannot conceive any thing more charming: Turkish turbans, Indian shawls, pearls, diamonds, fans, feathers, laces; all shewn for nothing at the windows. Alas! I had but one guinea remaining!

At length I reached an immense edifice, which appeared to me the castle of some Marquis or Baron. Ponderous columns supported it, and statues stood in the niches. The portal lay open. I glided into the hall: As I looked anxiously around, I beheld a cavalier descending a flight of steps. He paused, muttered some words, laid his hand upon his heart, shook his head, and advanced.

I felt instantly interested in his fate; and as he came nearer, perceived, that surely never lighted on this orb, which he hardly seemed to touch, a more delightful vision. His form was tall, his face oval, and his nose aquiline. Once more he paused, frowned, and waving his arm, exclaimed, with an elegant energy of enunciation;

"If again this apparition come, he may approve our eyes, and speak to it."

That moment a pang, poignant, but delicious, transfixed my besom. Too well I felt and confessed it the dart of love. In sooth, too well I knew that my heart was lost to me for ever. Silly maiden! But fate had decreed it.

I rushed forward, and sank at the feet of the stranger.

"Pity and protect a destitute orphan!" cried I. "Here, in this hospitable castle, I may hope for repose and protection. Oh, Signor, conduct me to your illustrious mother, the Baroness, and let me pour into her ear my simple and pathetic tale."

"O ho! simple and pathetic!" cried he. "Come, my dear, let me hear it."

I seated myself on the steps, and told my whole story. During the recital, the noble youth betrayed extreme sensibility. Sometimes he turned his head aside to conceal his emotion; and sometimes stifled a hysterical laugh of agony.

I ceased, he heaved a profound sigh, and begged to know whether I was quite certain that I had ten thousand pounds in my power; -- I replied, that as Wilkinson's daughter, I certainly had; but that the property must devolve to some one else, as soon as I should prove myself a nobleman's daughter."

He then made still more accurate inquiries about it; and having satisfied himself:

"Beshrew my heart!" exclaimed he; "but I will avenge your injuries; and ere long you shall be proclaimed and acknowledged the Lady Cherubina De Willoughby. Meantime, as prudence demands that you should lie concealed from the search of your enemies, hear the project which I propose. I lodge in Drury-lane, an obscure street; one apartment of the house is unoccupied, you can hire it, and remain there, a beautiful recluse, till fortune and my indefatigable efforts shall rescue from oppression the most enchanting of her sex."

He spoke, and seizing my hand, carried it to his lips.

"What!" cried I, "do you not live in this castle, and are you not its heir?"

"This is no castle," said he, "but Covent Garden Theatre."

"And you?" asked I with anxiety.

"Am an actor," answered he.

"And your name?"

"Is Abraham Grundy."

"Then, Mr. Abraham Grundy, allow me to have the satisfaction of wishing you a very good evening."

"Stay!" cried he, detaining me, "and you shall know all. My extraction is illustrious, and my real name Lord Altamont Mortimer Montmorenci. But, like you, I am enveloped in a cloud of mysteries. Hereafter I will acquaint you with the most secret particulars of my life; but at present you must trust to my truth. Truth is the tie which binds society together, and those who have honour themselves, are ever forward to confide in the -- in the -- the--"

"Amiable Montmorenci!" exclaimed I, giving him my hand, "I repose implicit credence in your disclosure, and I throw myself on your protection."

"Now," said he, "you must pass at these lodgings as my near relation, or they will not admit you."

At first, I hesitated at deviating from veracity; but soon consented, on recollecting, that though propriety makes heroines begin with praising truth, necessity makes them end with being the greatest story-tellers in the world.

305

During our walk to the lodgings, Montmorenci instructed me how I should play my part. On our arrival, he introduced me to the landlady, who was about fifty, and who looked as if the goddess of fasting had bespoken her for a handmaid.

With an amiable effrontery, and a fine easy flow of falsehood, he told her, as we had concerted, that I was his second cousin, and an orphan; and that I had come to Town for the purpose of procuring, by his interest, an appointment at the Theatre.

The landlady said she would move heaven and earth, and her own bed, for so good a gentleman; and then consented to give me her sleeping-room on the lower floor, at some trifle or other, -- I forget what. I have also the use of a parlour adjoining it. There is, however, nothing mysterious in these chambers, but a dark closet belonging to the parlour, whither I may fly for refuge, when pursued by my persecutors.

Thus, my friend, the plot of my history begins to take a more interesting shape, and a fairer order of misfortune opens upon me. Trust me, there is a taste in distress as well as in millinery. Far be from me the loss of eyes or limbs, the sufferings of the pillory, or the grossness of a jail-fever. I would be sacrificed to the lawless, not to the laws; dungeoned in the holy Inquisition, not clapped into Bridewell; and recorded in a Novel, not in the Newgate Calender.

Yes, my Biddy, sensations hitherto unknown now heave my bosom, vary the carnation of my cheeks, and irradiate my azure eyes. I sigh, gaze on vacancy, start from a reverie; now bite, now moisten my lip, and pace my chamber with unequal steps. Too sure I am deeply, distractedly in love, and Altamont Mortimer Montmorenci is the first of men.

Adieu.

LETTER IX.

The landlady, his Lordship, and another lodger, are accustomed to dine in common; and his lordship persuaded me to join the party. Accordingly, just as I had finished my last letter, dinner was announced; so I tripped up stairs, and glided into the room. You must know I have practised tripping, gliding, flitting, and tottering, with great success. Of these, tottering ranks first, as it is the approved movement of heroic distress.

"I wonder where our mad poet can be?" said the hostess; and as she spoke, an uncouth figure entered, muttering in emphathic accents: --

"The hounds around bound on the sounding ground."

He started at seeing me, and when introduced by his Lordship, as Mr. Higginson, a fellow-lodger, and a celebrated poet, he made an unfathomable bow, rubbed his hands, and reddened to the roots of his hair.

This personage is tall, gaunt, and muscular; with a cadaverous countenance, and smutty hair hanging in strait strings. He seems to be one of those men who spend their lives in learning how the Greeks and Romans lived; how they spoke, dressed, ate; what were their coins and houses, &c; but neglect acquainting themselves with the manners and customs of their own limes. Montmorenci tells me that his brain is affected by excessive study; but that his manners are harmless.

At dinner, his Lordship looked all, said all, did all, which conscious nobility, united with ardent attachment, could inspire in a form unrivalled, and a face unexcelled. I perceived too that the landlady regarded him with eyes of tender attention, and languishing allurement, but in vain.

As to Higginson, he did not utter a word during dinner, except asking for a bit of *lambkin*; but he preserved a perpetuity of gravity in his lace, and stared at me the whole time, with a stupid and reverential fixedness. When I spoke, he stopped in whatever attitude he happened to be; whether with a glass at his mouth, or a fork half lifted to it.

After dinner, I proposed that each of us should relate our histories; an useful custom established by heroines, who seldom fail of finding their account in it, and discovering either a grandmother or a murder. Thus too, the confession of a monk, the prattle of an old woman, or the half-eaten words of a parchment, are the certain forerunners of virtue vindicated, vice punished, rights restored, and matrimony made easy.

The landlady was asked to begin.

"I have nothing to tell of myself," said she, "but that my mother left me this house, and desired me to look out for a good husband, Mr. Grundy; and I am not as old as I look; for I have had my griefs, as well as other folks, and every tear adds a year, as they say; and 'pon my veracity, Mr. Grundy, I was but thirty-two last month. And my bitterest enemies never impeached my character, that is what they did'nt, nor could'nt ; they dare'nt to my face. I am a perfect snowdrop for purity. Who presumes to go and say that a lord left me an annuity or any such abomination? Who, I ask? The wretches! But I got a prize in the lottery. So this is all I can tell of myself; and, Mr. Grundy, your health, and a good wife to you, Sir."

After this eloquent morsel of biography, I requested that Higginson would recount his adventures; and he read a sketch, which was to have accompanied a volume of poems, only unfortunately the booksellers refused to publish either. I copy it for you.

MEMOIRS OF JAMES HIGGINSON
BY HIMSELF.

"Of the lives of poets, collected from posthumous record, and oral tradition, as little is known with certainty, much must be left to conjecture. He, therefore, who presents his own memoirs to the public, may surely merit the reasonable applause of all, whose minds are emancipated from the petulance of envy, the fastidiousness of hypercriticism, and the exacerbation of party.

"I was born in the year 1771, at 24, Swallow Street; and should the curious reader wish to examine the mansion, he has every thing to hope from the alert urbanity of its present landlord, and the civil obsequiousness of his notable lady. He who gives civility, gives what costs him little, while remuneration may be multiplied in an indefinite ratio.

"My parents were reputable tobacconists, and kept me behind the counter, to negociate the titillating dust, and the tranquillizing quid. Of genius, the first spark which I elicited, was my reading a ballad in the shop, while the woman who sold it to me was stealing a canister of snuff. This specimen of mental abstraction shewed that I would never make a good tradesman; but it also evinced that I would make an excellent scholar. A tutor was accordingly appointed for me; and during a triennial course of study, I had passed from the insipidity of the incipient *hic, hœc, hoc*, to the music of a Virgil, and to the thunder of a Demosthenes.

"Debarred by my secluded life from copying the polished converse of high society, I have at least endeavoured to avoid the vulgar phraseology of low; and to discuss the very weather with polysyllabical ratiocination.

"For illustrations of my juvenile character, recollection affords me but small materiality. That I have always disliked the ceremony of diurnal ablution, and a hasty succession of linen, is a truth, which he who has a sensitive texture of skin will readily credit; which he who will not credit, may, if he pleases, deny; and may, if he can, controvert. Life, among its quiet blessings, can boast of few things more comfortable than indifference towards dress.

"To honey with my bread, and to apple-sauce with my goose, I have ever felt a romantic attachment, resulting from the classical allusions which they inspire. That man is little to be envied, whose honey would not remind him of the Hyblean honey, and whose apple-sauce would not suggest to him the golden apple.

"But notwithstanding my cupidity for such dainties, I have that happy adaptation of taste, which can banquet, with delight, upon hesternal offals; can nibble ignominious radishes, or masticate superannuated mutton.

"My first series of teeth I cut at the customary time, and the second succeeded them with sufficient punctuality. This fact I had from my mamma.

"My first poetical attempt was an epitaph on the expiration of my tutor.

EPITAPH.

Here lies the body of John Tomkins, who
Departed this life, aged fifty-two;
After a long and painful illness, that
He bore with Christian fortitude, tho' fat.
He died lamented deeply by this poem,
And all who had the happiness to know him."

"The first Latin verse which I ever composed was this :

"Fert roseos rores oriens Aurora per oras.

"And my tutor assured me that it was the most roaring line in the world.

"These compositions my father did not long survive; and mamma, to the management of the business feeling quite unequal,

309

relinquished it altogether, and retired with the respectable accumulation of a thousand pounds.

"I still pursued my studies, and from time to time accommodated confectionaries and band-boxes with printed sheets, which the world might have read, had it pleased, and might have been pleased with, had it read.

"On a pretty little maid of mamma's, I made my next poetical effort, which 1 present to the reader.

TO DOROTHY PULVERTAFT.

If Black-sea, White-sea, Red-sea ran
One title of ink to Ispahan;
If all the geese in Lincoln fens,
Produc'd spontaneous, well-made pens;
If Holland old, or Holland new,
One wond'rous sheet of paper grew;
Could I, by stenographic power,
Write twenty libraries an hour;
And should I sing but half the grace
Of half a freckle on thy face;
Each syllable I wrote, should reach
From Inverness to Bognor's beach;
Each hairstroke be a river Rhine.
Each verse an equinoctial line.

"Of the girl, an immediate dismission ensued; but for what reason, let the researches of future biographers decide.

"At length, having resolved on writing a volume of Eclogues, I undertook an excursion into the country to learn pastoral manners. An amputated loaf, and a contracted Theocritus, constituted my companions.

"In vain I questioned the youths and maidens about their Damons and Delias; their Dryads, and Hamadryads; their Amabœan contentions and amorous incantations. When I talked of Pan, they asked me if it was a pan of milk; when I requested to see the pastoral pipe, they shewed me a pipe of tobacco; when I spoke of satyrs with horns, they bade me go to the husbands; and when I spoke of fawns with cloven heel, they bade me go to the Devil. I met wrinkled shepherdesses, and humpy milkmaids: I recumbed on a bank of cowslips and primroses, and my features were transpierced by wasps, and ants, and nettles. I fell asleep under sunshine, and awoke under a torrent of rain. Dripping and disconsolate, I returned to my mamma, quaffed some whey; and since that misadventurous perambulation have never ruralized again. To him who subjects himself to a recurrence of disaster, the praise of boldness may possibly be accorded, but the praise of prudence must certainly be denied.

"A satirical Bucolic, however, was the fruit of this expedition. It is entituled Antiquated Amours, and is designed to shew that passions which are adapted to one time of life appear ridiculous in another. The reader shall have it.

ANTIQUATED AMOURS.
AN ECLOGUE.

'Tis eve. The sun his ardent axle cools
In ocean. Dripping geese shake off the pools.
An elm men's shadows measure by the sun;
The shattered leaves are rustling as they run;
While two antiques, a bachelor and maid,
Sit amorous under an old oaken shade.
He (for blue vapours damp the scanty grass)
Strews fodder underneath the hoary lass;
Then thus, -- O matchless piece of season'd clay,
'Tis Autumn, all things shrivel and decay.
Yet as in withered Autumn, charms we see,
Say, faded maiden, may we not in thee?
What tho' thy cheek have furrows? ne'er deplore;
For wrinkles are the dimples of threescore:
Come then, age urges, hours have winged feet,
Ah! press the wedding ere the winding sheet.
 To clasp that waist enwrapt in silken fold,
Of woof purpureal flowered with radiant gold;
Then, after stately kisses, to repair
That architectural edifice of hair,
These, these are blessings. -- O my grey delight,
O venerable nymph, O painted blight,
Give me to taste of these. By Heaven above,
My members tremble less with years than love;
Tho', while my husky whispers creak uncouth,
My words flow unobstructed by a tooth.
Come then, age urges, hours have winged feet,
Ah! press the wedding ere the winding sheet.
 Come, thou wilt ne'er provoke crimconic law,

311

Nor lie, maternal, on the pale-eyed straw.
Come, and in formal frolic intertwine,
The braided silver of thy hair with mine.
Then sing some bibulous and leering glee,
And quaff the grape upon my pranksome knee.
The wine loquacious let no brook dilute;
'Tis drinking water makes the fishes mute.
Come then, age urges, hours have winged feet;
Ah! press the wedding, ere the winding sheet.
    Thin as the spectre of a famished eel,
He spoke, and coughing shook from head to heel.
    Sharpening the blunted glances of her eyes
The virgin a decrepid ogle plies.
Then stretches unused simpers, which shew plain
Her passion, and some teeth that still remain.
    Innocent pair! But now the rain begins,
So both knot kerchiefs underneath their chins.
And homeward haste. Such loves our Poet wrote,
In the patch'd poverty of half a coat;
Then diadem'd with quills his brow sublime,
Magnanimously mad in mighty rhime.

"Whether the public will admire my works, as much as my mamma does, far be from me to determine. If they cannot boast of wit and judgment, to the praise of truth and modesty they may at least lay claim. To be unassuming in an age of impudence, and veracious in an age of mendacity, is to combat with a sword of glass against a sword of steel; the transparency of the one may appear more beautiful than the opacity of the other; yet let it be recollected, that the transparency is accompanied with brittleness, and the opacity with consolidation."

This evidence of a perverted intellect being read, my turn came next, and I repeated the fictitious tale that Montmorenci had taught me. He confirmed it; and when asked to relate his own life, gave us, with great taste, such a natural narrative of a man living on his wits, that any one who knew not his noble origin must have believed it.

Soon afterwards he repaired to the Theatre, and as I was now alone with Higginson, I determined to discover his real character; for his countenance belies his memoirs, and bespeaks the villain. Should he prove one, he may conduce to the horror and romance of my story.

"Your life, Mr. Higginson," said I, "has not near so much of the terrible in it, as I had expected from your appearance; for, to do you justice, you have a most fatal face -- pale and grim to a degree."

"Madam," returned he, with evident agitation, "my mamma says of my face, that though not regularly handsome, 'tis extremely interesting."

"Why now," cried I, "instead of the Hesperian curls, and slender eyebrows of a lover, have you not the bushy overshadowing eyebrows, and lank, raven hair of an assassin? Nay, start not, but answer me candidly -- for upon my honour you may find your account in it; -- can yon handle a dagger?"

"Dear, dear, dear!" muttered he, and made a precipitate retreat from the room.

As sure as fate, the man is an assassin.

Adieu.

LETTER X.

This morning, soon after breakfast, I heard a gentle knocking at my door, and, to my great astonishment, a figure, cased in shining armour, entered. Oh, ye conscious blushes, it was my Montmorenci! A plume of white feathers nodded on his helmet, and neither spear nor shield were wanting.

"I come," he cried, bending upon one knee, and taking my hand; "I come in the ancient armour of my family, to perform my promise of recounting my melancholy memoirs."

"My lord," said I, "rise and be seated. Cherubina knows how to appreciate the honour that Montmorenci confers."

He bowed; and having laid aside his spear, shield, and helmet, he placed himself by me on the sofa, and began his interesting history.

"All was dark. The hurricane howled, the wet rain fell, and the thunder rolled in an awful and Ossianly manner.

"On a beetling rock, lashed by the Gulph of Salerno, stood Il Castello di Grimgothico.

"My lads, are your carbines charged, and your sabres sharpened?" cried Stiletto.

"If they an't, we might load our carbines with this hail, and sharpen our sabres against this northwind," cried Poignardi.

313

"The wind is east-south-east," cried Daggeroni.

"At that moment the bell of Grimgothico tolled one. The sound vibrated through the long corridors, the spiral staircases, the suites of tapestried apartments, and the ears of the personage who has the honour to address you. Much alarmed, I started from my couch; but conceive my horror when I beheld my chamber filled with banditti! They were sent by Napoleon (that awful oddity) to dispatch me, because of my glorious struggle against him in Italy.

"Snatching my faulchion, I flew to the armoury for my coat of mail. The bravos rushed after me; but I fought and dressed, and dressed and fought, till I had perfectly completed my unpleasing toilette.

"Alack! there lies more peril in thine eye,
Than twenty of their swords."

"To describe the contest that followed, were beyond the pen of an Anacreon. The bullets flew round me, thick as hail,

"And whistled as they went for want of thought."

"At length I murdered my way down to my little skiff, embarked in it, and arrived at this island. As I first touched foot on its chalky beach, 'Hail, happy land,' cried I, 'hail, thrice hail!'

" 'There is no hail here, Sir,' said a child running by; 'but come with me, and I will shew you a wedding.'

"And who are to be married?" asked I, lifting the little innocent in my arms.

"The Marquis de Furioso, and the Lady Sympathina, daughter to Baron Hildebrand,' answered little Billy. 'Love is a primary principle, inculcated on the human heart, and consubstantiated with our beings.' And so saying, he playfully belaboured me with an infinitude of small thumps.

"Happy childhood! -- Ah, if when vitiated by the vile world, man, miserable man, could recall -- recall – poo! But to continue:

"As I walked towards the chapel, my heart dilated at beholding the picturesque scenery around. On the left were plantations or tufted turnips, on the right the venerable grandeur of a dilapidated dog kennel, and every where the eye caught monstrous mountains, and minute daisies; while groups of children and chickens added hilarity to the landscape. Rural beauties elevate the soul to virtue, and virtue alone is true nobility.

"At length I reached the chapel, and found the ceremony about to begin. But 1 must describe Lady Sympathina. Perhaps her face was not perfect, but it was more -- it was interesting, it was oval. Her eyes were of the real, original, old blue, and her eyelashes of the best silk. The roses of York and Lancaster united in her cheek, and a nose of the Grecian order surmounted the whole. She was habited in white drapery. Ten signs of the Zodiac, worked with spangles, sparkled over it; but Virgo was omitted at her own desire, and the bridegroom stipulated to dispense with Capricorn. Sweet delicacy!

"And now the ceremony had commenced, and was passing off with great spirit, till, in an evil moment, the bride happened to glance at me. I stood leaning on my sword. Seducing sweetness dwelled in my smile. She shrieked, turned pale: 'Comment vous portez vous,' cried she, as she rushed into my astonished arms, with distracted tresses, and a look that would have shocked the Humane Society.

"This, this is he,' she cried, 'who hath nightly haunted my dreams. This, this is my destined husband. Marquis De Furioso, never will I wed thee!'

"Flattered by her preference, I deposited a kiss on her cheek, and a blush was the rosy result. I therefore repeated the application. The domestics tore her from me. 'To arms!' cried the Mareschal: little Billy began screaming prodigiously for an urchin of his age, and the Marquis De Furioso, bowing gracefully to the bride, stabbed himself to the heart.

"The bride was carried off in a swoon, and from continual weeping, fell ill of an inverted eyelash.

"Meantime I was hurried from the chapel, and conveyed to the spectral chamber, where I strained my left leg in the composition of an extatic ode.

"One night I had thrown myself on the bed, to draw upon the contemplation of future misfortune for a supply of that melancholy which my immediate exigencies demanded, when to my particular consternation, a winged eyeball began flying about my face.

"Say little foolish fluttering thing."

315

"Much disconcerted, I walked to the glass, and was sleeking my slender brow with my finger, when lo! an impertinent apparition peeped over my shoulder, and made faces at me. I felt offended, and determined on asserting my dignity.

"Is it not enough,' said I, with an elevated voice, 'to be harassed by beings of this life, but those of the life to come must interfere? *En verité*, I would advise a certain inhabitant of a certain world (not the best, I fancy), to think less of my affairs, and more of his own.'

"The ghost looked confused, and adopted invisibility.

"At that moment a sudden thought struck me.

"Let me escape!" said I.

   "Gods, what a thought was there!"

"I then contrived this ingenious mode of accomplishing my object. My chamber had a window. I opened it, and got out of it. During eighteen months afterwards, I wandered about the country, an itinerant beggar; for Napoleon had confiscated all my patrimony.

"One day, the cattle lay panting under the broad umbrage; the sun had burst into an immoderate fit of splendour, and the struggling brook chided the matted grass for obstructing it. I sat beside a hedge, and began eating wild strawberries; when lo! a form, flexile as the flame that ascends from a censer, and undulates with the sighs of a dying vestal, flitted inaudible by me, nor crushed the daisies as it trod. What a divinity! she was fresh as the Anadyomene of Apelles, and beautiful as the Gnidus of Praxitiles, or the Helen of Zeuxis. Her eyes, which were sky-blue--"

"Sir," said I, "you need not mind her eyes: I dare say they were blue enough. But pray now, who was this immortal doll of your's?"

"Who!" cried he. "Why who but -- shall I speak it? Who but -- the LADY CHERUBINA DE WILLOUGHBY!"

"I?"

"You!"

"Ah, Montmorenci!"

"Ah, Cherubina! I followed you with cautious steps," continued he, "till I traced you into your -- you had a garden, had you not?"

"Yes."

"Into your garden. I thought ten thousand flowers would have leapt from their beds to offer you a nosegay.

316

"You disappeared, I was quite *au desespoir*, and next morning resumed my station at a corner of the garden."

"At which corner?" asked I.

"Why really," said he, "I cannot explain; for the place was then novel to me, and the ground was covered with snow."

"With snow!" cried I. "Why I thought you were eating wild strawberries only the day before."

"I? Sure you mistake."

"I declare most solemnly you told me so."

"Oons, Madam, I said no such thing."

"Sir, I must remark that your manners --"

"Now, by St. Bryde of Bothwell, I did say so, sure enough, and I did eat wild strawberries too; but they were *preserved* wild strawberries. I had gotten a crock of them from a nun, who was opening oysters in a meadow for a hysterical butcher; and her knife having snapt asunder, I lent her my sword; so, out of gratitude, she made me a present of the preserves. By the bye they were mouldy.

"One morning, as I sat at the side of the road, asking alms, some provincial players passed by. I accosted them, and offered my services. In short, they took me with them; I performed, was applauded: and at length my fame reached London, where I am at present acting understrappers wonderfully well, considering my genealogy.

"You may now wish to learn what has become of the personages mentioned in this narrative. The Baron Hildebrand still paces his chamber, and his eyebrows have gotten a portentous trick of meeting together. The Lady Sympathina remains immured in the northern turret. Little Billy died with the Bible before him, so the Coroner's Inquest brought in a verdict of Lunacy. Stiletto is dead, Poignardi is no more, Daggeroni has departed this life, and the rest of the bandits are in another, and I trust a better world.

"I shall conclude my tale with a moral remark, founded on circumstantial evidence -- that to suffer is an attribute of mortality.

"But wherefore," cried he, "wherefore talk of the past? Oh! let me tell you of the present and of the future. Oh! let me tell you, how dearly, how deeply, how devotedly I love you!"

"Love me!" cried I, giving such a start as the nature of the case required. "My lord, this is so -- really now, so --"

I remained silent, and with the elegant embarrassment of modesty, cast my blue eyes to the ground. I never looked so lovely.

"But I go!" cried he, springing on his feet. "I fly from you for ever! No more shall Cherubina be persecuted with my hopeless love. Yet, Cherubina! Cherubina! I will teach the songsters of the grove to articulate; and the hills and the vallies to echo Cherubina! Cherubina!

"I will turn hermit on Mount Caucasus, and I call all the stars of respectability to witness the vow. Then, Lady Cherubina," and he stopped short before me; "then, when maddened and emaciated, I shall pillow my haggard head on a hard rock, and lulled by the hurricanes of Heaven, shall sink into the sleep of the grave." –

"Dear Montmorenci!" said I, quite overcome, "live for my sake-- as you value my -- friendship, -- live."

"Friendship!" echoed he. "Oh! Cherubina, oh! my soul's precious treasure, say not that chilling word. Say hatred, disgust, horror; any thing but friendship."

"What shall I say?" cried I, ineffably affected, "or what shall I do?"

"What you please," muttered he, looking wild and pressing his forehead. "My brain is on fire. Hark! chains are clanking -- save me, Cherubina, save me, save me! Ha! she frowns at me -- she darts at me -- she pierces my heart with an arrow of ice!"

He threw himself on the floor, groaned grievously, and tore his hair. I was horror-struck.

"I declare," said I, "I would say any thing upon earth to relieve you; -- only tell me what."

"Angel of light!" exclaimed he, springing upon his feet, and beaming on me a smile that might liquefy marble. "Have I then hope? Dare I pronounce the divine words -- she loves me?"

"I will not be angry," murmured I, while the chamber swam before me.

He took both my hands in his own, pressed them to his forehead and lips, and leaned his burning cheek upon them. Then encircling my waist with his arm, he drew me to his heart. It was Cherubina's hand that fell on his shoulder, it was Cherubina's tress that played on his cheek, it was Cherubina's sigh that breathed on his lip.

"Moment of a pure and exquisite emotion!" cried he. "Now to die would be to die most blest!"

Suddenly he caught me under the chin, and kissed me. I struggled from him, and sprang to the farther end of the room; while my neck and face burst into a glow of indignation.

"Really," said I, panting with passion, "this is so unprovoked, so presuming."

He cast himself at my feet, execrated his folly, and besought my pardon.

"I fancy, my lord," said I, "you will find, that as far as a kiss on the hand, Heroines have no particular objection. But a salute on the lips is considered inaccurate. My lord, on condition that you never repeat that liberty, here is my hand."

He snatched it with ardor, and strained it to his throbbing bosom.

"And now," cried he, "make my happiness complete, by making this hand mine for ever."

On a sudden an air of grandeur involved my form. My mind, for the first time, was called upon to reveal its full force. It felt the solemnity of the appeal, and triumphed in its conscious ability.

"What!" exclaimed I, "can'st thou suppose the poor orphan Cherubina so destitute of principle and of pride, as to intrude herself unknown, unowned, unfriended, mysterious in her birth, and degraded in her situation, on the illustrious and Italian house of Montmorenci ?

"Here then I most inviolably vow never to wed, till the mystery which hangs over my birth be developed."

As soon as I had made this fatal vow, his lordship fell into the most afflicting agonies and attitudes.

"Oh!" cried he, "to be by your side, to see you, touch you, talk to you, love you, adore you, and yet find you lost to me for ever. Oh, 'tis too much, much too much!"

"The milliner is here, Miss," said the maid, tapping at the door.

"Bid her call again," said I; but as 1 spoke, in she came, with a charming assortment of bonnets and dresses.

"We will talk over the matter another time," whispered I to his lordship.

His lordship declared that he would drop dead that instant.

The milliner declared that she had brought the newest patterns.

"On my honour," said I to his lordship, "you shall finish this scene to-morrow morning, if you wish it."

"You may go and be -- Heigho!" said he, suddenly checking himself. What he was about to say, I know not; something mysterious, I should think, by the knitting of his brows. However, he snatched his spear, shield, and helmet; made a low bow, laid his hand on his heart, and stalked out of the chamber. Interesting youth!

I then ran in debt for some millinery, drank hartshorn, and chafed my temples.

I think I was right about the kiss. I confess I am not one of those girls who try to attract men by permitting liberties; and who thus excite passion at the expence of respect. Indeed, had I not been fortified by the precedent of other heroines, I should actually have felt, and I fear did feel, even the classical embrace of clasping to the heart too great a freedom. But I am certain I shall never attain hardihood enough to ravish a salute from a man's mouth, as the divine Heloise did; who once ran at St. Preux, and astonished him with the most balmy and remarkable kiss upon record. Poor fellow! he was never the same after it.

I must say too, that Montmorenci did not shew much judgment in urging me to matrimony, before I had undergone adventures for four volumes. Because, though the heroic etiquette allowed me to fall in love at first sight, and confess it at second sight, yet it would not authorize me to marry myself off, without agony and interruption. Even the ground must be lacerated, before it will bring forth fruits; and often we cannot reach the lovely violet, till we have torn our hands with brambles.

I met his lordship again at dinner; which we had almost finished, before the poet made his appearance, and his bow. His bow was as usual, but his appearance was oddly altered. His hair stood in stiff ringlets on his forehead, and he had pruned his bushy eyebrows, till hardly one bristle remained; while a pair of white gloves, small enough for myself, were forced upon his hands. He glanced at us with a conscious eye, and hurried to his seat.

"Ovid's Metamorphoses, by Jupiter!" exclaimed Montmorenci. "Why, Higginson, how shameful for the mice to have nibbled your eyebrows, while Apollo Belvidere was curling your hair!"

"I will tell my mamma of you!" cried the poet, half rising from his chair.

Now this mamma is an old bed-ridden cripple in one of the garrets. However, I pacified him so successfully by praising his Hesperian curls, that he consented not to lodge the complaint. An assassin! Ah, no. The hideous innocent would plunge into the ocean to save a drowning fly.

After dinner I requested ten pounds from his Lordship for the purpose of paying the milliner. Never was regret so finely pictured in a face, as in his, while he swore he had not a penny upon earth.

Indeed, so graceful was his lamentation, so interesting his penury, that though the poet stole out of the room for ten pounds, which he slipped into my hand, I preferred the refusal to the donation.

Yes, this amiable young nobleman increases in my estimation every moment. Never can you catch him out of a classical position. He would exhaust, at one sitting, all the attitudes of all the statues; aud when he talks tenderness, he brings in his heart with great effect. Then, too, his oaths are well conceived, and elegantly exprest. Thunderbolts and the fixed stars are ever at his elbow, nor can any man sink himself to perdition with so picturesque a frown. And yet sometimes his imprecations—

But my paper is almost filled.

O I could write of him, talk of him, think of him, hour after hour, minute after minute; even now, while the shadows of night are blackening the blushes of the rose, till dawn shall stain with her ruddy fire, the snows of the naked Appennine; till the dusky streams shall be pierced with darts of light, and the sun shall quaff his dewy beverage from the cup of the tulip and the chalice of the lily.

Adieu.

LETTER XI.

"It is my lady, O it is my love!" exclaimed Lord Altamont Mortimer Montmorenci, as he flew like a winged Mercury, into my apartment this morning. A rap at the door checked his eloquence, and spoiled a most promising posture.

My door was then thrown open, and who should waddle into the room, but fat Wilkinson!

My first feeling (could you believe it?) was of gladness at seeing him; nor had I presence of mind enough, either to repulse his embrace, or utter a piercing shriek. Happily my recollection soon returned, and I flung him from me.

"Cherry," said he, "dear Cherry, what have I done to you, that you should use me thus? Was there ever a wish of your heart left ungratified by me? And now to desert me in my old age! Only come home with me, my child, only come home with me, and I will forgive you all."

"Wilkinson," said I, "this interview must be short, pointed, and decisive. As to calling yourself my father, that is a stale trick, and will not pass; and as to personating (what I perceive you aspire to) the grand villain in my Memoirs, your corpulency, pardon me, puts that out of the question for ever. Ah! no, Sir, you are not at all a real villain. You are only a sleek, good-humoured, chuckle-headed schemer. For instance, you never murdered me, though you stipulated to do so fourteen years ago. Remain then, what nature made you; return to your plough; mow, reap, fatten your pigs and the parson; but never again attempt to get yourself thrust into the pages of a romance."

Disappointment and consternation imprinted his thick features with more angles than I thought practicable. The fact is, he had never imagined that my notions of what villains ought to be were so refined; and that I have formed my taste in these matters upon the purest models.

As a last effort of despair, the silly man flung himself on his knees before me, and grasping both my hands, looked up in my face with such an imploring expression, while the silent tears rolled down his cheeks, that I confess I was a little moved; and at the moment fancied him sincere.

"Now, goodness bless thee," said he, at length; "goodness bless thee, for these sweet tears of thine, my daughter!"

"Tears!" cried I, quite shocked.

"Yes, darling," said he, "and now with this kiss of peace and love we will blot out all the past."

I shrieked, started from my seat, and rushed into the expanded arms of Montmorenci.

"And pray, Sir," cried Wilkinson, advancing fiercely, "who are you?"

"A lodger in this house, Sir," answered his lordship, "and your best friend, as I trust you will acknowledge hereafter. I became acquainted with this lady at the table of our hostess; and learned from her that she had left your house in disgust. Yesterday morning, on entering her apartment, to make my respects, I found an old gentleman there, one Doctor Merrick, whom I recognized as a wretch of infamous character.

Sir, I was present at a trial, where the American Ambassador prosecuted him for stealing an olden tweezer-case; and where a flaw in the indictment saved his life, as he proved the stolen article a golden tooth-pick case.

Being well acquainted with this young lady's high respectability, I presumed to warn her against such a dangerous companion; when I found, unfortunate girl! that she had already promised her hand to him in marriage."

Wilkinson groaned: I stared.

"Once apprised of his character," continued Montmorenci, "the lady was willing enough to drop the connection; but unhappily, the ruffian had previously procured a written promise of marriage from her, which he now refuses to surrender; and at the moment you came, I was consulting with your daughter on what should be done."

"Lead me to the villain," cried Wilkinson, "and I will shew you what should be done!"

"I have already appointed an interview with him," said his Lordship; "but as your feelings might probably prompt you to too much warmth, perhaps you had better not accompany me. However, should I fail in persuading him to resign the fatal paper, you shall then see him yourself."

"You are a fine fellow!" cried the farmer, shaking his hand, "and have made a friend of me for ever."

"I will hasten to him now," said his Lordship; and with a significant glance towards me, went away, leaving me quite astonished, both at his story, and his motive for fabricating it. However, my business was to support the deception.

Wilkinson then told me that he learned my residence in London from the discharged Butler, who had heard it from you. The wretch made the disclosure for forty guineas; and Wilkinson says that he wants to marry you, merely for your annuity. Ah! how unlike the disinterested Montmorenci; who would rather marry me, at this moment, as plain, plebeian Cherry Wilkinson, with my paltry ten thousand pounds, than wait till I am the acknowledged Lady Cherubina De Willoughby, with all my restored estates.

Biddy, Biddy! if you knew as much of the world as I do, a fortune-hunter would not impose upon you.

But to return. In the midst of our conversation, the maid brought me this note.

"Will my soul's idol forgive the tale I told Wilkinson, since it was devised in order to save her from his fangs? This Doctor Merrick, whom I mentioned to him, keeps a private madhouse. I have just seen him, and informed him that I am about to put a lunatic gentleman, my honoured uncle, under his care. I told him, that this dear uncle (who, you may well suppose, is Wilkinson) has lucid intervals; that his madness arose from grief at an unfortunate amour of his daughter's; that he fancies every man he sees is attached to her, and has her written promise of marriage; and that the first demand he makes of every stranger, is to give him the paper containing it.

"Now, my love, let not a lurking kindness, which I fear you still retain for Wilkinson, prevent you from joining in this plot against him. Indeed, to confine him is an act of humanity; because if the ruffian be suffered to walk at large, he will probably (since he now knows that his designs are discovered) contrive to have you assassinated. With this conviction on my mind, I must declare, that if you betray my scheme to him, 1 shall feel myself perfectly justified in prosecuting him for a conspiracy against your life, and having him hanged.

Ever, ever, ever,

Your MONTMORENCI.

P. S. Excuse tender language, as I am in haste.

This advice my prudence induced me to adopt, and my desire of saving Wilkinson from an ignominious end; for unfortunately, such is my weakness, that I cannot divest myself of all my former feelings towards him. Nay, even when he presented me, during our conversation, with a hundred pounds, to purchase baubles, as he said, and reward me for my promises of discarding the Doctor, I thanked him with as much gratitude as if I had not known that he gave the money merely to decoy me home again, and perhaps imprison me for ever.

Soon afterwards, our hero returned, and told us that his interview had proved unsuccessful; so it was determined that the whole party should repair to the Doctor's, and make another attempt. Accordingly, off we set in a hired coach, and on our arrival were shewn into a parlour. After some minutes of anxious suspense, the Doctor, a shrivelled little figure, entered with two servants.

Wilkinson being introduced, the Doctor commenced operations, by trying the state of his brain.

"Any news to-day, Mr. Wilkinson?" said he.

"Very bad news for me, Sir," replied Wilkinson, sullenly.

"I mean public news," said the Doctor.

"A private grievance ought to be considered of public moment," said Wilkinson.

"Well remarked, Sir," cried the Doctor, "a clear-headed observation as possible. I give you credit. Sir, if you continue to talk so rationally, you will not remain long in my house, I promise you."

"I am sorry," replied Wilkinson, "that talking rationally is the way to get turned out of your house, because I have come for the purpose of talking rationally. I believe, Doctor, I talk rationally when I say, that it is the duty of every man to rescue his fellow-creature from misery."

"Few sentiments," answered the Doctor, "could do more honour both to your head and to your heart."

"I believe too," resumed Wilkinson, "it is the duty of a parent to consult the happiness of his child. Is that talking rationally, eh?"

"Clearly so," said the Doctor. " 'Tis a corollary from your first proposition."

"Why then, I have you in a fine quandary!" cried Wilkinson. "For since my child feels unhappy at having given you the paper containing her promise of marriage, it is my duty, by your own admission, to get this paper out of your hands. Aha, I have you there, I think. Egad, I have you there. An't that talking rationally, eh?"

"So far from it," said the Doctor, "that if you ask for the paper again, I must be under the disagreeable necessity of punishing you most severely. To be candid, Sir, I must handcuff you."

"Od's bobs, and bobbin, and bonbobbin, and bonbobinet!" shouted Wilkinson, with a yell of laughter. "Handcuff me? Great, very great! Any thing more, my fine fellow?"

"And as often as you persist in asking for the paper," said the Doctor, "I must -- excuse me -- I must have you plied with exemplary horsewhippings."

"Why, you ruffian!" cried Wilkinson, as he marched up, shaking his head, and clapping his hands to his sides; "I will ask you for it ten thousand times over and over. Give me the paper, give me the paper, give me the paper, the paper, the paper, the paper, paper, paper, paper! Confound you, you shall have a quire of it at once!"

"This is indeed a bad case," said the Doctor.

"Case?" exclaimed Wilkinson. "Is it a golden tweezer-case, eh? Or a golden tooth-pick case, eh? or a case where you were near being hanged by the American Ambassador, eh ? There are cases for you, my old buck!"

"Madder, and madder, I protest," whispered the Doctor.

"O you withered wasp, O you uncommon weasel!" cried Wilkinson, "how could the girl ever bring herself to fancy you? A fellow, by all that is horrid, as ugly as if he were bespoke: an old fellow, too, and twice as disgusting, and not half so interesting, as a monkey in a consumption!"

"Perfectly distracted, 'pon my conscience!" muttered the Doctor. "Here, John, Tom, secure the wretch this moment."

Wilkinson instantly darted at the Doctor, and knocked him down. The servants collared Wilkinson, who called to Montmorenci for assistance; but in vain; and after a furious scuffle, the farmer was handcuffed.

"Dear uncle, calm these transports!" said his Lordship. "Your dutiful and affectionate nephew beseeches you to compose yourself."

"Uncle! -- nephew!" cried the farmer. "What do you mean, fellow? Who the devil is this villain?"

"Are you so far gone as not to know your own nephew?" said the Doctor, grinning with anger.

"Never set eyes on the poltroon till an hour ago!" cried Wilkinson.

"Merciful powers!" exclaimed Montmorenci. "And when I was a baby, he dandled me; and when I was a child, he gave me whippings and sugar-plums; and when I came to man's estate, he cherished me in his bosom, and was unto me as a father!"

"Curse me, but the wretch is crazed !" cried Wilkinson.

"No, dear uncle," said Montmorenci, "but you are shockingly crazed; and to be candid with you, this is a madhouse, and this gentleman is the mad-doctor, and with him you must now remain, till you recover from the most afflicting attack of insanity that ever visited a country gentleman."

"Insanity!" faltered the farmer, turning deadly pale.

"You are the maddest man that ever bellowed in Bedlam," said the Doctor.

"Mad! I mad!" cried Wilkinson. "I vow to my veracity, Doctor, that I was always reckoned the quietest, merriest, sweetest -- sure every one knows honest Greg Wilkinson, and his bottle of claret.

Don't they, Cherry? Dear child, answer for your father. Am I mad? Am I, Cherry?"

"As butter in May," said Montmorenci.

"You lie like a thief!" vociferated the farmer, struggling and kicking. "You lie, you sneering, hook-nosed reprobate!"

"Why, my dear uncle," said Montmorenci, "don't you recollect the night you began jumping like a grasshopper, and scolding the full-moon in my deer-park?"

"Your deer-park? I warrant you are not worth a cabbage-garden! But now I see through the whole plot. Ay, I am to be kept a prisoner here, while my daughter marries that old mummy before my face. It would kill me, Cherry; I tell you I should die on the spot. Oh, my unfortunate girl, are you too conspiring against me? Are you, Cherry? Dear Cherry, speak. Only say you are not!"

"Indeed, my friend," said I, "you shall be treated with mildness. Doctor, I beg you will not act harshly towards him. Notwithstanding all his faults, the man is good natured and well tempered, and to do him justice, has always used me kindly."

"Have I not?" cried he. "Sweet Cherry, beautiful Cherry, blessings on you for that!"

"Come away," whispered Montmorenci hastily.

"Farewell, Doctor," said I. "Adieu, poor Wilkinson."

"For pity's sake, stay five minutes!" cried Wilkinson, struggling with the servants.

"Come, my love!" whispered Montmorenci.

"Only one minute -- one short minute!" cried the other.

"Well," said I, stopping, "one minute then."

"Not one moment!" cried his Lordship, and was hurrying me away.

"My child, my child!" shrieked Wilkinson, with a tone of such indescribable agony, as made my blood curdle in my veins.

"Dear Sir," said I, returning; "you know well I am not your child."

"You are," cried he. "By all that is just and good, you are my own, own child."

"By all that is just and good," exclaimed Montmorenci to me, "you shall come away this instant, or remain here for ever." And he dragged me out of the room.

"Now then," said the poor prisoner bursting into tears, as the door was closing, "now do what you please with me, for my heart is quite broken!"

I too began crying; nor for many minutes could Montmorenci reason me out of my folly. Yet, after all, I am not so very, very blameable. Were a wretch going to the gallows, I could not help feeling for him. How much more then must I feel for a man, who, villain as he indisputably is, had acted as a parent towards me, during fifteen years of my life.

On our way home, I shewed the hundred pounds to Montmorenci, whose joy at this seasonable acquisition was truly friendly. I purchased a charming scarf, a shawl, a bonnet, two dresses, and a pair of pearl earrings. His Lordship borrowed a guinea from me, and with it bought a little casket, which he instantly presented to me in the handsomest manner.

Adieu.

LETTER XII.

On my first arrival at these lodgings, I sent the servant to Betterton's house, for the bandbox which I had left behind, the night I fled from him.

To my amazement, who should enter my room, this morning, but Betterton himself! I dropped my book. He bowed to the dust.

"Your business, Sir?" said I.

"To make a personal apology," answered he, "for the disrespectful treatment which the loveliest of her sex experienced at my house."

"An apology for one insult," said I, "must seem insincere, when the mode adopted for making it, is another insult!"

"The retort is exquisitely elegant," answered he, "but I trust, not true. For, granting that I offered a second insult by my intrusion, still I may lessen the first so much by my apology, that the sum of both may be less than the first, as it originally stood."

"Really," said I, "you have blended politeness and arithmetic so happily together; you have clothed multiplication and subtraction in such polished phraseology--"

"Good!" cried he, "that is real wit."

"You have added so much algebra to so much sentiment --" continued I.

"Better, still better!" interrupted he again.

"In a word, you have apologized so gracefully by the rule of three, that I know not which has assisted you the most -- Chesterfield or Cocker."

"Inimitable," exclaimed he. "Really your retorting powers are superior to those of any heroine on record."

In short, my friend, I was so delighted with my repartee, that I could not, for my life, continue vexed with the object of it; and before he went, I said the best things in the world, found him the most agreeable old man in the universe, shook hands with him at parting, and gave him permission to visit me again.

On calm consideration, I do not disapprove of my having allowed him this liberty. Were he merely a good kind of good for nothing gentleman, it would only be losing time to cultivate an acquaintance with him. But as the man is a reprobate, I may find account in enlisting him amongst the other characters; particularly, since I am at present miserably off for villains. Indeed, I augur auspiciously of his intriguing talent, from the fact (which he confessed), of his having discovered my place of abode, by tracing the maid, when she was returning from his house with the bandbox.

But I have to inform you of another rencontre.

Last night, the landlady, Higginson, and myself, went to see his lordship perform in the new Spectacle. The first piece was called a melo-drame; a composition of horror and drollery, where scenery, dresses, and decorations, answered for nature, genius, and moral. As to the plot, I could make nothing of it; only that the hero and heroine were in very great trouble about trifles, and quite unconcerned amidst real distress. For instance, when the heroine had arrived at the height of her misery, she sang a song in thunder and lightning. Then the hero, resolving to revenge her wrongs, falls upon one knee, turns up his eyes, and calls on God for assistance. This invocation to the Divinity, might, perhaps, prove the hero's piety, but I am afraid it shewed the poet's want of any. Certainly, however, it produced a powerful effect on my feelings. I heard the glory of God made subservient to a theatrical clap-trap, and my blood ran cold. So, I fancy, did the blood of six or seven sweet little children behind the scenes, for they were presently sent upon the stage, to warm themselves with a dance. After dancing, came murder, and the hero gracefully staggered forward with a bullet in his head. He falls; and many well-meaning persons suppose that the curtain will fall with him. No such thing: Hector had a funeral, and so must Kemble. Accordingly, the corpse appears, handsomely dished up on an escutcheoned coffin; while certain virgins of the sun (who, I am told, support that character better than their own), chaunt a holy requiem round it. When horror was exhausted, the poet tried disgust.

After this piece came another, full of bannered processions, gilded pillars, paper snows, and living horses, that were far better actors than the men who rode them. It concluded with a grand battle, where twenty soldiers on horseback, and twenty on foot, beat each other indiscriminately, and with the utmost good humour. Armour clashed, sabres struck fire, a castle was burnt to the ground, the horses fell as dead, the audience rose shouting, and clapping the horses, and a man just below me exclaimed in an ecstasy: -- "I made their saddles! I made their saddles!"

As to Montmorenci's performance, nothing could equal it; and though his character was the meanest in the piece, he contrived to make it the most prominent. He had an emphasis for every word, an attitude for every emphasis, and a look for every attitude. The people, indeed, hissed him repeatedly, because they knew not, as I did, that his acting a drunken waiter like a dethroned monarch, proceeded from native nobility, not want of talent.

After the performance, we were pressing through the crowd in the lobby, when I saw Stuart (Bob Stuart!) at a distance. Now was my time to lay a foundation for future incident. I therefore separated myself from my party, like Evelina at the Opera, and contrived to cross his path.

"Miss Wilkinson!" exclaimed he.

"Hush!" whispered I; "conduct me from the Theatre in silence."

He put my hand under his arm, and hurried me away. When we had gained the street; "Where is your father?" said he. "Have you not seen him since he came to Town?"

"I have not," answered I; an evasive, yet conscientious declaration, because Wilkinson is not my father.

"How strange!" cried he, "for he left the hotel yesterday to call on you. Oh, Miss Wilkinson, what tempted you to leave home? How are you situated at present? with whom? and what is your object?"

"Alas!" said I, "a horrible mystery hangs over me, which I dare not now develope. It is enough, that in flying from one misfortune, I have plunged into a thousand others, that peace has fled from my heart, and that I am RUINED."

"Ruined!" exclaimed he, with a look of horror.

"Past redemption," said I, hiding my face in my hands.

"The very first night I came to Town, a gentleman decoyed me into his house, and treated me extremely ill.

"Afterwards I left him, and walked the streets, till I was arrested for a robbery, and put into the watchhouse; and to conclude my short, but eventful tale, a gentleman, a mysterious and amiable youth, met me by mere accident, after my acquittal; and I am, at present, under his protection."

"The villain!" exclaimed Stuart,

"Villain?" said I. "Ah, his large and piercing eye is but the index of a soul fraught with every human virtue. And now, here are my lodgings, and if you will sup with me to-night, you shall see him."

Stuart gladly consented. We then entered the house; but none of my party had returned. I therefore conducted him into my room, and apprized the maid that he would stay for supper.

"Can nothing," said he, as we sat down, "induce you to relinquish the mode of life you have adopted?"

"Nothing whatever," answered I. "It is by far the most exalted that a girl, with the requisite qualifications, could select."

"What!" cried he, "to form an improper connection with a libertine?"

"There now!" exclaimed I. "There is a pretty insinuation. Ay, this is always the way with us poor heroines. And so, Sir, you presume to say that I have formed an improper connection?"

"Did you not tell me you were ruined?" said he.

"Well," answered I, "and so I am ruined. Am I not expelled from my paternal home? Am I not deprived of my property? Am I not under sentence of assassination? Is not old Wilkinson, who calls himself my father, working heaven and earth to make me marry you? Ay, you, you, -- so no pretended stare, if you please. Ruined? to be sure I am ruined."

"At least, I rejoice to perceive," said he, "that it is your understanding only which is perverted, and that your moral conduct and principles remain undepraved."

At this moment, the maid beckoned me from the room. I found Montmorenci outside, who begged of me to accompany him up stairs. I went.

"The landlady tells me," said he, in much agitation, "that you strayed from your party to-night, picked up a young man, and have brought him home to sup with you."

" 'Tis true, my Lord," answered I.

"And who is the fallow?" cried he.

"Stuart," said I. " Master Bobby. I find him rather agreeable. An improper education has perverted his understanding, but has not depraved his principles. He says the same of me. His face improves on acquaintance, and I am sure you will like him."

"Like your grandmother!" cried he, discarding attitude, elegance, every thing. "O the varment, the circumventing villain! Pack him out of the house, pack him out, I say, or by the infernal turnspit, I will lend him such a bother on the side of the head, as shall do his business in no time."

I was thunderstruck. "Sir," said I, "you have agitated the gentle air with the discordance of inelegant oaths and idioms, uttered in the most ungraceful manner. Sir, your vulgarity is unpardonable, and we now part for ever."

"For ever!" exclaimed he, reverting into attitude, and interlacing his knuckles in a clasp of agony. "Hear me, Cherubina. By the shades of my immortal ancestors, my vulgarity was assumed!"

"Assumed, Sir?" said I, "and pray, for what possible purpose?"

"Alas!" cried he, "I must not, dare not tell. It is a sad story, and enveloped in a mysterious veil. Oh, fatal vow! Oh, cruel Marchesa!" Shocking were his contortions as he spoke.

"No!" cried I. "No vow could ever have produced so dreadful an effect on your language."

"Well," said he, after a painful pause, "sooner than incur the odium of falsehood, I must disclose to you the horrid secret.

"The young Count Di Narcissini was my friend. Educated together, we became competitors in our studies and accomplishments; and in none of them could either of us be said to excel the other; till, on our introduction at the Court of Naples, it was remarked by the Queen, that I surpassed the Count in shaking hands. 'Narcissini,' said her Majesty, 'knows well enough when, where, and how, to present a single finger, or perhaps two; but, for the positive pressure, or the negligent hand half offered with a

332

drooping wrist; or the cordial, honest, dislocating shake, give me Montmorenci. I cannot deny that the former has great taste in this accomplishment; but then the latter has more genius -- more execution -- more, as it were, of the *magnifique* and *aimable*.'

"His mother the Marchesa overheard this charming critique, turned as pale as ashes, and left the levee.

"That night hardly had I fallen into one of those gentle slumbers

which ever attends the virtuous, when a sudden noise aroused me; and on opening my eyes, I beheld the detested Marchesa, with an Italian assassin, standing over me.

"Montmorenci!' cried she, ' thou art the bane of my repose. Thou hast surpassed my son in the graces. Now listen. Either pledge thyself, by an irrevocable vow, henceforth to vitiate thy conversation with uncouth phrases, and colloquial barbarisms, or prepare to die!'

"Terrible alternative! What could I do? The dagger gleamed before my face. I shuddered, and took the fatal vow of vulgarity.

"The Marchesa then put into my hand the Blackguard's Dictionary, which I studied night and day with much success; and I have now the misfortune to state, that I can be, so far as language goes, the greatest blackguard in England.

"I must add, however, that the Marchesa permitted me to resume my natural elegance, as soon as my marriage should put an end to competition between her son and me."

"Well," cried I, "of all the extraordinary, unmeaning, execrable vows ever invented -- Oh, I have not common patience with it! Let us change the subject. And now, my Lord, I must insist on entertaining Stuart to-night. Indeed, I will own, that my principal motive in doing so, is to see the difference between a mere gentleman, and an actual hero. That you will gain by the comparison, I make no doubt; since I know you will surpass him in majesty of manner, amiable sentiment, and antithetical repartee. You have but a few minutes to prepare for the contest, so pray make the most of them."

His Lordship expostulated again, and swore that Stuart would unheroinize me, and supplant him. However, I rallied this devoted lover out of his jealous fears; then returned to Stuart, and remained with him till supper was announced.

At the introduction, both youths eyed each other earnestly; and as soon as we were seated round the table, his Lordship broke the pause.

"Ah," cried he, "how many thousands of our fellowmen are now sick, naked, and hungry; while we have health, raiment, and a festive board. Ah, how can we repay these blessings but by virtue?"

Stuart stared. Already he began to perceive, that his Lordship's was no common mind.

"Ah," resumed his Lordship, "how sweetly the fineness of this weather attuneth each harmonized soul to unison with virtue!"

"It is indeed a most favourable season for the crops," said Stuart.

I tittered.

"That is precisely what you have said, Sir," cried his Lordship, and winked at me. "But I must trouble you for another observation; as, I fancy, that is not quite original. I dare say, now, one hundred thousand gentlemen have made it within a week."

"And I dare say," returned Stuart, "that no gentleman, under the circumstances, ever made your last remark before."

"I am a gentleman, however," cried his Lordship.

"Perhaps, Sir," said Stuart, smiling, "that is another original observation."

Montmorenci writhed his remarkable sneer, but was mute.

"Say something pointed," whispered I.

"That I will," returned he. "Pray Sir -- talking of original observations -- how many legs has a sheep?"

"It has four in a field," answered Stuart. "But (and he measured Montmorenci with a most meaning eye) we do not allow it more than two at a table."

"Had the scoundrel answered as he ought," whispered his Lordship to me, "I would have said the wittiest thing in the world!"

So closed the first dialogue; and now the conversation became general, and on the topics of the day. These, Stuart discussed with much ease and animation; while his Lordship remained silent and contemptuous. I fancy his illustrious tongue disdained to trifle.

Meantime Higginson sat Anglicising the Latinity of his face, and aping the postures of Montmorenci; whom the simple man, I verily believe, is already endeavouring to rival.

At length we talked of the Theatre, and afterwards of acting in general; till his Lordship concluded a long harangue by declaring, that he thought actors the most useful members of the community, because they ridicule human foibles with the best effect.

"Sir," said Higginson, as he rubbed the crumbs from the elbow of his new coat, and began an attitude which he was ashamed to finish, "I must, in all humility, dissent from your exprest proposition, and support the superior claims of the writer."

"Observe," whispered I to his Lordship, "how the ruling passion betrays itself."

"For," continued the poet, "inasmuch as the works of the writer live for ever, while the player but ' lives and struts his hour,' it is an indisputable sequitur, that the writer must be the more useful member."

"Pardon me, gentlemen," said I, "the most useful members are, not actors who merely mimic, or writers who merely describe, but heroes and heroines, who really perform."

"If you mean the heroes and heroines of romance," said Stuart, "they are useful certainly; but it is in teaching us what we should shun, not what we should imitate. The heroine quits a comfortable home, takes extreme pains to lose her character, and none to recover it; blushes by the chapter; and after weeping tears enough to float her work-basket, weds some captious, passionate, and idle hero."

"Better," cried I, "than remain a domesticated rosy little Miss, who romps with the squire, plays an old tune upon an old piano, and reads prayers for the good family -- servants and all. At last marrying some honest gentleman, who resides on his saddle; she degenerates into a dangler of keys and whipper of children; trots up and down stairs, educates the poultry, and superintends the architecture of pies."

"Now, for my part," said Stuart, "I would have a young lady neither a mere homely drudge, nor a heroic sky-rocket, let off into the clouds. I would instruct her heart and head, as well as her fingers and feet. She should be at once the ornament of the social group, and the delight of the domestic circle; abroad attractive, at home endearing; the enchantress to whom levity would apply for mirth, and wisdom for admonition; and her mirth should be graceful, and her admonition fascinating. When solitary, she should have the power of contemplation, and if her needle broke, she should be capable of finding resource in a book. Finally, she should present a proof, that wit is not inconsistent with good-nature, nor liveliness with good-sense; and that to make the Virtues be admired and imitated, they ought to be accompanied by the Graces."

"So much for the Heroine," said I. "Now what is a Hero?"

"The first and best of men," answered he. "His proper province is to keep the wheels of a Novel going, by misconstruing the motives of his mistress, aspersing her purity, and on every decent occasion, picking a quarrel with her. He must hunt her from castle to convent, and from convent to cottage. He must watch under her window, in all weathers, without ever taking cold, and he must save her life once at least. Then when he has rescued her from the impending peril, he must bend on one knee, sigh through the amorous gamut, and ask her to marry. If she knows her business, she will refuse him; upon which, he must act the most heart-rending antics, summon planets, grow pathetically fretful, writhe with grace, and groan in melody. To sum all, if such an animal as a Hero ever existed on earth, he would certainly be something between a monkey and an angel."

"If a Hero ever existed!" cried I. "If he ever existed! *If!* -- Well, well, what infatuation! And so, Sir, your's is one of those distorted minds, which deny that Heroes ever existed on earth."

"It has the misfortune," said he.

"Then," cried I, "you will probably be somewhat surprised, when you learn, -- since you provoke me to it -- that so far from there being no Hero on earth, there is one in this very room, at this very moment. Here, Sir, is a Hero; and let me add, as incontrovertible a Hero as ever breathed a sigh. Nay, notwithstanding the very unpleasant drollery of your countenance, I will condescend so far as to inform you, that he is the actual inheritor--"

"Hush!" whispered Montmorenci.

"Never fear," said I. "I will not commit myself. The actual inheritor of a Gothic castle, situated on a beetling rock, and lashed by a certain Italian gulph, which shall be nameless."

"Has he told you so?" asked Stuart.

"Certainly," answered I. "Oh, I have it from the best authority."

"Why then, noble unknown," cried Stuart, "since Grundy must be but an assumed name, may I beg your real name?"

"My name is Norval on the Grampian hills!" said his Lordship, with infinite humour.

"And pray, Sir," said Stuart, assuming a severe countenance, "what name does that man deserve, who personates one of those imaginary Heroes, in order to play upon the passions of an innocent girl, and to make her harmless illusions become the fatal instruments of her destruction?"

Here an unpleasant pause took place, and his Lordship appeared unaccountably agitated.

"What is the matter with you?" whispered I to him. "For shame, my Lord. Never suffer him to bear you down."

"I take it, Sir," cried his Lordship, turning towards Stuart, "I take it -- or rather I give it -- I give it, Sir, as my decided opinion, that -- you are no -- Hero!"

"And yet," said I, anxious to assist his Lordship at this crisis, "though Master Bobby is no Hero, I dare be sworn he is a mighty good sort of a man."

"Oh, a decent, proper-behaved young person, no doubt," cried his Lordship.

"An honest bon diable!" cried I.

"A respectable citizen!" cried he.

"A loyal subject!" cried I.

"A humane and pious Christian!" cried he.

This last hit was irresistible, and both of us burst into laughter, while Stuart sat silent, and even affected a smile.

"Now is your time," whispered I, to his Lordship. "Another sarcasm, and your victory is decisive."

"I fancy, Master Bobby," said his Lordship, facing round upon Stuart, and laughing so long, that I thought he would never finish the sentence; "I fancy, my tight fellow, you may now knock under!"

"I am not always inclined to knock under, as you elegantly term it," answered Stuart; "neither am I often provoked to knock down."

"Knock down whom?" demanded his Lordship, with the most highly-finished frown I had ever beheld.

"A puppy," said Stuart coolly.

"You lie!" vociferated our hero.

"Leave the room, Sir," cried Stuart, starting from his seat.

Montmorenci rose, retreated towards the door; -- stopped -- went on -- stopped again -- moved -- stopped –

"I tell you what," said he, "if you want satisfaction, I am the manner of man that will accommodate you. I am none of your slovenly, slobbering shots. Damme, I scorn to pistol a gentleman about the ankles. I can teach the young idea how to shoot, damme."

"Vanish!" cried Stuart, advancing.

His lordship vanished.

I ran, snatched a pen, and wrote on a scrap of paper.

"VINDICATE YOUR HONOUR, OR NEVER APPEAR IN MY PRESENCE AGAIN."

I then rang the bell, and bade the maid deliver the paper to him.

During half an hour, I remained in a state of the most distracting suspense, for he never returned! Meantime, Stuart was privately pressing me to leave my lodgings, and remain with one of his relations, till Wilkinson should be found. Indignant at the cowardly conduct of his Lordship, I had almost consented; when on a sudden, the door flew open, and with a slow step and majestic deportment, Lord Altamont Mortimer Montmorenci entered. There was a dead silence. He walked towards Stuart, and fell upon one knee before him:

"I come, Sir," said he, "to retract that abuse which I gave you just now. I submit to whatever punishment you please; nor shall I think my honour re-established, till my fault is repaired. Then grant me the pardon that I beg, on whatever conditions you think proper."

" 'Tis granted, my hero," said Stuart.

"Hero!" exclaimed I, with an indignation which I could not suppress. "He a hero?"

His Lordship instantly snatched a book from his pocket, and opening a passage, presented it to me. The book was *La Nouvelle Heloise*.

"You see there," said he, "how Lord B., after having given St. Preux the lie, as I did Mr. Stuart, begs forgiveness on his knees, and in the precise words which I have just used. Will Cherubina condemn the conduct that Heloise applauded?"

"Ever excellent, ever exalted mortal!" cried I. "O thou art indeed, all that is just, dignified, magnanimous."

I presented my hand to him; he bowed over it. And now mirth ruled the night. The landlady laughed; Montmorenci sang; Stuart uttered a thousand witticisms; and even the poet, whom his lordship had amply plied with the grape, determined to be heard; for, in the midst of our merriment, I saw him, with his mouth open, and his neck stretched forward, ready to arrest the next moment of silence. It came.

"This is the fun,
  Equalled by none;
So never have done!"

cried the uncouth creature, and then protruded such an exorbitant laugh, as made amends for the gravity of his whole life.

"You are a happy mortal," said Stuart.

"So I am happy," cried he, "and every thing seems to be happy, for every thing seems to be dancing!"

He spoke, and rolled from his chair. Montmorenci carried him to bed; Stuart took leave; and the landlady and I separated to our apartments.

Think of Stuart, that never once fixed his eyes on me, with a speaking gaze! Nay, not only is the fellow far from a pathetic turn himself, but he has also an odd talent of detaching even me from my miseries, and of reducing me to horrid hilarity. It would vex a saint to see how he makes me laugh, though I am predetermined not to give him a single smile. But Montmorenci, the sentimental Montmorenci, timely interposes the fine melancholy of his features; --he looks, he sighs, he speaks; and in a moment I am recalled to the tender emotions, and to soft complaints of my deplorable destiny.

Adieu.

END OF VOL. I.

THE

HEROINE,

OR

ADVENTURES

OF

CHERUBINA,

BY

EATON STANNARD BARRETT, ESQ,

————

"L'Histoire d'une femme est toujours un Roman."

————

Second Edition,

WITH CONSIDERABLE ADDITIONS AND ALTERATIONS.

————

IN THREE VOLUMES,
VOL. II.

————————

THE HEROINE.

LETTER XIII.

About an hour ago, I was amusing myself with the Children of the Abbey; and just as I had read the scene where Amanda conceals Belgrave in the closet, Betterton came into my chamber, and the landlady after him with a bundle.

"Has my fair friend ever seen a masquerade ?" said he, as he sat down.

"Never," answered I; "but there is nothing I would rather see."

"Then," said he, "as a masquerade is to take place at the Pantheon to-morrow night, I will do myself the honour of escorting you thither; and your hostess shall matronize you. So now to call a council of dress. What think you of personating Sterne's Maria?"

"No character could please me more," replied I.

"Then," said he, "do me the favour to accept this dress;" and opening the bundle, he presented me with a most elegant and suitable costume.

"And here," continued he, "is a dress for the Widow Wadman, which character your good landlady will enact; and here is Trim's antique and tarnished regimental coat, and Montero cap, for myself. And now, my dear Madam, promise to keep this expedition a profound secret from Stuart."

"And from Grundy too," added the landlady.

"Why from Grundy?" asked I.

"Because," said she, "he might disapprove of my going without himself."

"And what were that to you?" cried I.

"Why, Ma'am," answered she, "to be very candid with you, he and I are betrothed together in marriage."

"Betrothed!" exclaimed I.

But a tap at my door prevented me from expressing my decided doubts of her veracity; and it struck me, that should the person outside be his Lordship, I might make her look excessively silly on the occasion.

343

"Here, hide yourselves in this dark closet," whispered I to my visitors. "I have particular reasons." They looked at each other, and hesitated.

"In, in!" said I; "for I suspect that this visit is from a villain; and I wish you to witness what passes."

They went into the closet. I then opened the door of my chamber, and the poet appeared at it, with his eyes half out of their sockets, and his jaw ajar.

"What is the matter?" asked I.

He gaped still wider, but said nothing.

"Speak!" cried I. "What shock awaits me? For what horror are you preparing me?"

"Oh Miss!" exclaimed he; "oh Miss, Miss! Don't go to the masquerade, Miss. Oh, don't Miss. My mamma has just overheard the gentleman who visited you yesterday — Betterton, methinks, is his appellation, — planning with the landlady, to carry you from it by fraudulence or by force. But, Miss, I have a fine sword above stairs, three feet and a half long, and I will rub off the rust, and — "

Another tap came at my door. I was in a hiding mood. Already the scene promised wonders; and I resolved not to damp its rising spirit; so made the simple Higginson wedge himself underneath the sofa.

The next moment my door opened and to my great delight Montmorenci entered.

"Sweet is the dawn of morning," cried he; "sweet is the song of the lark; sweet is the odour of the floweret; but ah! far sweeter is the face of my love."

"And yet, Sir" said I, with a freezing smile, "as there are many mornings, many larks, and many flowerets, so there are many loves."

"To me there is but one," cried he.

"And that one?" said I.

"Need I mention?"

"Need you hesitate?"

"You, you alone!" exclaimed he. "And oh, wherefore should you doubt my constancy?"

"That interjectoral, Oh ! may be very pretty" said I, "but it cannot refute fact, or eradicate suspicion."

"Why then," cried he, "by the fat-cheeked little cherubim, that flap their innocent wings, and fly through oceans of air in a minute, without having a hair of their heads discomposed—"

"Now," said I, "you are all this time considering what to say. But I will relieve you. Our hostess is a charming woman, very charming, remarkably charming indeed. You love her. Sir; and I felicitate you on your choice. Yes, a letter of lodgings is an admirable match for an understrapping actor."

"Love our hostess?" cried he: "I love our hostess? What! that pale decent woman, worn to a thread-paper? 'Tis true she has roses in her cheek, and lilies in her skin; but they are white roses, and orange lilies. Our hostess! Beshrew my heart, I would let cobwebs grow on her lips, before I would kiss them."

A knock at the hall-door interrupted us.

"If this be the person I suspect," exclaimed I, "both of us are undone — separated forever!"

"Who? what ? which? where shall I hide?" cried his Lordship.

"Yon dark closet," said I, pointing. "Fly!"

His Lordship sprang into the closet, and closed the door.

"I can hear no tidings of your father," said Stuart, entering the moment after. "I have searched every hotel in Town, and I really fear that some accident — "

"Mercy upon me! who's here? " cried his Lordship from the closet. "Oons! let me go; whoever the devil you are, let me go!"

"Take that— and that— and that: you, you, you— Oh you, you, — you poor, pitiful, fortune-hunting play-actorer!" screamed the landlady, buffetting him about."

That unhappy young nobleman bolted from the closet, with his face running blood, and the landlady fast at his heels.

"Yes, you dog!" exclaimed she, " I have discovered your treacherousness at last. So you bring your Miss into my house as your cousin, and make love to her; and all the time are promising me marriage, and sending me letters and trinkets!"

"I cannot believe he was so base, Madam," said I.

"But he was so base," Madam, said she. "There, read the letter he sent me yesterday, just after I had asked him to pay me for six months' diet and lodging. "

I read :

"Accept the pair of bracelets which accompany this note, and rest assured I will discharge my bill before another month.

"Before another month, too, I trust the manager will enlarge my salary. Then, emancipated from poverty, I need no longer delay that happiness which I anticipate, in leading my lovely hostess to the hymeneal altar.

" Your own, own, own,
"ABRAHAM GRUNDY. "

It was as much as I could do to suppress my indignation at this letter; but the heroine prevailed, and I merely cast on his lordship, my famous compound expression of contempt, pity, and beautiful rebuke; which I tinged with just fascination enough to remind him, what a jewel he had thrown away. Meantime he stood wiping his face, and did not utter a word.

"And now," cried I, "now for the grand developement. James Higginson, come forth!"

In a moment the poet was seen, creeping, like a huge tortoise, from under the sofa.

"Mr. Higginson," said I, "did not your mother tell you, that this amiable lady," (and I courtesied low to the hostess, and she still lower to me), " that this best of women," (and again we exchanged rival courtesies), "is plotting with Mr. Betterton, to betray me into his hands at the masquerade?"

"Madam," answered the poet, "I do certify and asseverate, that so my mamma told me."

"Then your mamma told you a confounded falsehood!" cried Betterton, popping out of the closet.

Higginson walked up to him, and knocked him down with the greatest gravity imaginable. The hostess ran at Higginson, and fastened her fangs in his face. Montmorenci laid hold of the hostess, and off came her wig. Stuart dropped into a chair with laughter. I too forgot both grace and grief; and clapped my hands, and danced with delight, while they kicked and scratched each other without mercy.

At length Stuart interfered, and separated the combatants. The landlady retired to refit her dismantled head; and his Lordship and Higginson to wash their wounds. Betterton too was about taking his departure.

"Sir," said Stuart, "I must beg leave to detain you a few moments."

Betterton bowed, and returned.

346

"Your name is Betterton, I believe."

"It is, Sir,"

"After Mr. Higginson's accusation of you," said Stuart, "I feel myself entitled, as the friend of this lady's father, to insist upon your soliciting her forgiveness for the designs which you have harboured against her; and to demand an unequivocal renunciation of them."

"You are an honest fellow," said Betterton, "and I respect your spirit. Most sincerely, most humbly, Miss Wilkinson, do I beg your pardon; and I trust you will believe, that nothing but a misrepresentation of your real character and history tempted me to treat you with such undeserved insult. I now declare, that you need not fear any farther improprieties from me."

"But before I can feel perfectly satisfied," said Stuart, "I must stipulate for the discontinuance of your visits to Miss Wilkinson, as a proof that you have relinquished all improper projects against her."

"I had formed that resolution before you spoke," answered Betterton. "Now we are friends. Faults I may have; but my heart — (and he tapped at it with his forefinger) all is right here."

With these words he bowed and retired. Stuart then began exhorting me to leave my lodgings; but I felt so much irritated at his officious interference about Betterton, that I would not even answer him. Finding all his efforts fruitless, he went away quite offended; and I greatly fear will never return.

Well, I am the most unfortunate girl that ever breathed! Think now, after all my prospects, to find myself on a sudden, deserted by every individual, who had talent and baseness enough for conducting my plot! Stuart takes upon him to turn off Betterton. Betterton is so wretchedly sneaking as to be turned off by him: then Stuart himself makes his bow and exit: and lastly, Mr. Montmorenci comes out to be — But I will not believe it. No, his intrigue with the landlady must involve some mystery or other, which a distracting interview will elucidate.

I confess I feel predisposed to credit any reasonable excuse which he can assign, rather than find myself deceived, outrivalled, and deprived of a lover, not alone dear to my heart, but indispensible to my memoirs.

Then, that closet scene, which contained within itself the seeds of the true pathetic, what a bear-garden it became! In short, I feel disgusted with the world. I half wish I were at home again. Do you know, since I have seen Stuart, I cannot avoid sometimes picturing the familiar fire-side, the walks, frolics, occupations of our childhood; and well I remember how he used to humour my whims.

But whither am I wandering? Pardon these homely sentiments. They escaped my pen. I am not often guilty of vulgarity. Forgive them.

Adieu.

LETTER XIV.

All is as I thought. My Montmorenci has proved himself the most aspersed of men; and has convinced me that the letter to the landlady was a FORGERY, written by herself. The wretch! He thinks of prosecuting her, next term.

As I had refused, after the closet scene to hear his personal vindication, he wrote, I answered; and the following is an extract from our correspondence. Having first penned a most satisfactory disquisition on the various circumstances tending to prove the forgery, he thus concludes:

"I have begun twenty letters, and have torn them all. I write on my knees, and the paper is blistered with my tears; but I have dried it with my sighs.

"When the girl brought your last note, the idea that your eyes had just been dwelling on her face, on her cap, ribbon, apron, made her and them so interesting, so dear to me, that though her face was smutty, her cap tattered, her ribbon green (which I hate), and her apron greasy, I should certainly have taken her in my arms, had I not been the most bashful of men.

"Though that note pierced my very heart, the words were hosts of angels to me, and the small paper the interminable regions of bliss. Any thing from you!

"How my heart beats, and my blood boils in my veins, when by chance, our feet meet under the table. How often I call to mind the sweet reproof you once gave me at dinner, when I trod on your toe in a transport.

"If you love me, tell me so,' said you, smiling; 'but do not hurt my foot.'

"Another little incident is always recurring to me. As we parted from each other, the night before last, you said, in a voice soft as the Creolian lyre, 'Good night, my dear Montmorenci.' It was the first time you had ever called me *dear*. The sound sank into my heart. I have repeated it a hundred times since; and when I went to bed, I said, good night, my dear Montmorenci. I recollected myself and laughed."

BILLET FROM CHERUBINA.

He who could be capable of writing the letter, could be capable of calling it a forgery.

BILLET FROM MONTMORENCI.

Misery with you, were better than happiness without you.

BILLET FROM CHERUBINA.

Treachery and hatred were better than love and treachery.

BILLET FROM MONTMORENCI.

Love is heaven and heaven is love.

BILLET FROM CHERUBINA.

If heaven be love, I fear heaven is not eternal.

BILLET FROM MONTMORENCI.

If my mind be kept in suspense, my body shall be suspended too.

BILLET FROM CHERUBINA.

Foolish youth! If my life be dear to thee, attempt not thine own.

BILLET FROM MONTMORENCI.

It were easier to kill myself than to fly from Cherubina.

BILLET FROM CHERUBINA.

Live. I believe you innocent.

BILLET FROM MONTMORENCI.

Angelic girl! But how can I live without the means? My landlady threatens me with an arrest. Heloise lent money to St. Preux.

BILLET FROM CHERUBINA.

In enclosing to you half of all I have, I feel, alas! that I am but half as liberal of my purse as of my heart.

BILLET FROM MONTMORENCI.

I promise to pay Lady Cherubina de Willoughby, or order, on demand, the sum of thirty-five pounds sterling, value received.

MONTMORENCI.

Soon after I had received this last billet, his Lordship came in person, to perfect the reconciliation; and when he left me, the landlady called, made an abject apology for her conduct, and instead of desiring me to leave her house, advised me so violently to remain, that I much suspect her of some sinister motive.

About dusk, a letter was brought to me by the maid, who said, that a man in a cloak, put it into her hand, and then ran away.

Conceive my sensations on reading this note, written in antiquated characters.

To the
Lady Cherubina de Willoughby

These, greeting.

Most fayre Ladie,

An aunciente and loyall Wassall that erewhyles appertained unto y^{re} ryghte noble Auncestrie, in y^e qualitie of Seneschal, hath, by chaunce, discovred y^{re} place of hiding, and doth crave y^e boon that

350

will not fayle to goe alone and withouten a visor, unto y^e Masquerade at y$_e$ Pantheon; where, anon he will joyn you, and unravel divers mysterys touching your pedigree.

What a crisis is at hand! Yes, thou excellent old man, I will meet thee there.

Adieu.

LETTER XV.

Last night, soon after I had retired to rest, I heard a whispering and rustling outside my window, which looks into the yard; and while I was awaiting the result, sleep surprised me.

This morning, I woke earlier, as I thought, than usual; for not a ray penetrated my curtainless window. I therefore tried to take another slumber, but in vain. I lay turning and tumbling about, eight or nine hours longer. At last I became alarmed. What can be the matter? thought I. Is the sun quenched or eclipsed? or has the globe ceased rolling? or am I struck stone blind?

But amidst my conjectures, a sudden cry of fire! fire! rang through the house. I sprang out of bed, huddled on me whatever clothes came to hand, and then rushed into the outer room; where my eyes were almost blinded by the sudden glare of light that shot through them.

However, I had presence of mind enough to snatch up Corporal Trim's coat, which still remained there, and to slip it on me; for I had no gown underneath; and besides I recollected that Harriet Byron, at a moment of distress, went wild about the country, in masquerade.

As I ran into the hall, I saw the street-door wide open, Stuart and Montmorenci struggling with each other near it, the landlady dragging a trunk down stairs, and looking like the ghost of a mad housemaid; and the poet just behind her, with his crippled mother, bed and bed-clothes, upon his back; she crying, I shall soon be in Heaven, and he crying, Heaven forbid! I darted by them, thence out of the house, and (will you believe me?) had fled twenty paces, before I discovered, that, so far from being night, it was broad, bright, obvious, incontrovertible day!

I had no time to reflect on this mystery, as I heard steps pursuing me, and my name called. I fled the faster, for I dreaded I knew not what. The portentous darkness of my room, the false alarm of fire, all betokened some diabolical conspiracy against my life; so I rushed along the street, to the horror and astonishment of all who saw me. For conceive me drest in a long-skirted scarlet coat, stiff with brassy lace; a satin petticoat, and my flaxen hair flaunting like a streamer, behind me!

Stop her, stop her! was now shouted on all sides. Hundreds seemed in pursui Panting, and almost exhausted, I still continued my flight. They gained upon me. What should I do? I saw the door of a carriage just opened; and two ladies, dressed for dinner, stepping into it. I sprang after them, crying, save me, save me! They screamed. The footman endeavoured to drag me out; I held fast: the mob gathered round shouting; and at last, the horses, frightened by the tumult, set off in an unmanageable gallop.

All this time the ladies supported one unbroken scream, and shrinking back, held their hands between themselves and me.

"Pray be not alarmed," cried I, "for I am only a Heroine; and if you will have patience, you shall hear my story.

"My name is Cherubina, and I am descended from the noble house of De Willoughby. But alas! by the machinations of vile conspirators, all my fair prospects are overturned — "

At this moment the carriage itself was overturned, and my story along with it. Several persons immediately ran forward, and extracted us through the door. Again I began running, and again a mob was at my heels. I felt certain they would tear me in pieces. On I flew. Knock it down! cried several voices.

A footman was just entering a house; I rushed by him, and darted into a parlour, where a large party were at dinner.

"Save me!" exclaimed I, and sank on my knees before them. All arose: — some, in springing to seize me, fell; and others began dragging me away. Quite bewildered, I grasped at the table-cloth, and the next instant, the whole dinner was strewn about the floor. Those who had fallen down, rose in piteous plight; one reeking with soup, another crowned with vegetables, and the face of a third all over harico.

They held me fast, and questioned me; then called me mad, and turned me into the street. The mob, who were still waiting for me

352

there, cheered me as I came out; so seeing a shop at hand, I ran through it, up the stairs, and into the drawing-room.

There I found a mother in the cruel act of whipping her child. Ever a victim to sensibility, I snatched the rod from her hand; she shrieked and alarmed the house; and again I was turned out of doors. Again, my friend the mob, received me with a shout; again I took to flight; rushed through another shop, was turned out — though another, was turned out. In short, I paid flying visits to twenty different houses, and witnessed twenty different domestic scenes. In this, they were singing, in that scolding: — here, I caught an old man kissing the maid, there, I found a young man reading the Bible. Entering another, I heard ladies laughing and dancing. I hurried past them to the garrets, and saw their aged servant dying.

Shocked by the sight, I paused at his half-opened door. Not a soul was in the room, and vials and basins strewed the table.

"Is that my daughter?" said he feebly. "Will nobody go for my daughter? To desert me thus, after first breaking my heart! Well then, I will go for her myself."

He made a sudden effort to rise, but it was fatal. His head and arms dropped down motionless, and hung out of the bed. He gave a convulsive sob, and expired.

Horrorstruck, I rushed into an adjoining garret; my heart and my brain were almost bursting. I felt guilty of I knew not what; and the picture of Wilkinson, dying in the madhouse, and calling upon his daughter, shot across me for a moment.

The noise of people searching the rooms below, and ascending the stairs, interrupted my disagreeable reflections; and I thought but of escape. Running to the window of the garret, I found that it looked upon the roof of a neighbouring house. Any thing rather than encounter the mob again; so I lifted the sash, and with some difficulty, made good my landing below. I then closed it after me, and ran along the leads.

At last I was stopped by a house higher than the rest, with a small window, similar to the other out of which I had escaped. This window happily lay open; so, looking into the garret, and finding nobody there, up I scrambled, entered, and then fastened the sash. A bed, a chair, a table, and a spacious chest, constituted all the furniture. The chest had nothing in it, but some rotten silks and satins; and I determined to make it my place of refuge, on any emergency.

353

I sat a few moments, and composed my spirits; then curious to discover whether I had any chance of escaping through the house after nightfall, I determined on exploring it. Besides, I felt a secret presentiment that this house was, some way or other, connected with my fate — a most natural idea.

I first traversed the garrets, but observed nothing particular in them; so I stole, with cautious steps, down to the first landing-place, and found the door of a room open. Hearing no noise inside, I put in my head, and perceived a large table, lighted with candles, and covered with half-finished dresses of various descriptions; besides bonnets, feathers, caps, and ribbons; whence I concluded that the people were milliners.

Here I sat some time, admiring the dresses, and trying at a mirror, how the caps became me; till I was interrupted by steps on the stairs. I ran immediately behind a window-curtain; and two young milliners came into the room.

I found by their conversation, that one of them was making a dress for the masquerade, after the pattern of the Tuscan girl's, as described in the Mysteries of Udolpho.

Conceive my horror, when I recollected, that this was, indeed, the night of the masquerade, appointed by the Seneschal, for unravelling the mystery of my birth! How should I escape? Where had I a dress? What should I do? Distraction!

As I stood pondering a thousand schemes, one of the milliners left the room: but the other, who was finishing the Tuscan habit, still remained.

Aware that were I to attempt an escape, I might be caught, and confined, as a thief, the whole of this important night, I suddenly determined upon making a friend of the milliner, and obtaining her assistance to quit the house. No sooner planned than accomplished.
I drew aside the curtain, and stood before her.

She raised her head, made a miserable imitation of the heroic scream, and ran down stairs.

I ran after her, as far as the landing-place; and on looking over the bannisters, into the hall, I saw a maid issue from the kitchen, and ask what was the matter.

"Matter enough!" cried the terrified milliner. "There is a madwoman above stairs, dressed half like a man, half like a woman, and with hair down to the ground." And so saying, she ran into the parlour.

"What is all this?" cried a second maid, who now appeared.

"Oh! Molly," said the first maid, "Miss Jane is just frightened to death by a monster above stairs, half man, half woman, and covered all over with hair!"

The mistress herself then came from the shop.

"Oh! Madam," cried the second maid, "Miss Jane is just killed by a great, huge, horrid monster above stairs, half man, half beast, all over covered with curly hair, and every sort of abomination and bedevilment."

"Folly!" cried the mistress. "I warrant I will soon put an end to these pranks;" and she began ascending the stairs. Where could I hide? I luckily recollected the large chest; and up I flew to the garret. It was now quite dark; but I found the chest, sprang into it, and having closed the lid, flung some of the old satins over me.

The moment after, "Edward, Edward!" whispered the mistress, just outside the garret.

"Here I am," answered the voice of a young gentleman, in another garret. "How came you to delay so late?"

"And how came you to dress yourself up, and frighten the girl?" said she. "Here is the whole house in an uproar. For shame! had they discovered you, my character was gone for ever."

"Upon my soul," cried he, "I was never once out of the garret; nor did I see a single being, though I thought I heard a foot on the stairs."

"Oh, mercy!" exclaimed she, "then as sure as fate, there is a monster in the house. — A wild beast, I am certain; for 'tis all over the most horrible, abominable hair, and I heard it howling from the very shop! Here, here, hasten with me, till I hide you safe, and then call the watch."

To my great alarm, they came running into my garret; to my still greater dismay, they approached the chest; but how shall I describe my unutterable horror, when the gentleman jumped into it, and the mistress locked both of us up together!

All was the work of an instant.
Down she ran.

Almost crushed by his weight, I could not help making a sudden and desperate effort to get from under him.

"Heaven and earth!" exclaimed he, feeling about. "What is this? Who is this? Holloa, I say. Who are you?"

I lay still, and said nothing.

355

"Help, help," vociferated he. " 'Tis the beast— Here is the hair. Help, help!"

"Hush!" said I, "or both of us are betrayed. Upon my word, I am no beast, but a woman."

"What woman, then?"

"That is a mystery."

"What brings you here?"

"That is a mystery."

"Are you young?"

"Yes."

"Handsome?"

"That is another mystery."

"Why then curse me if I don't unravel it this moment!"

But now we heard several persons upon the stairs.

"Hush!" whispered I.

We lay quiet. They came into the room, and examined it; then tried the remaining garrets; and at last, to my great relief, returned down stairs.

"I suspect," said the gentleman, "that you are the very person who has raised all this uproar."

"I fear so, indeed," answered I; "though really, without any evil design upon my part; as I trust you will acknowledge, when you hear my history.

"My father was a nobleman — illustrious, powerful, and wealthy; — blest in a beloved wife, and in the playful endearments of my infantine innocence. But ah, who can say, to-day I am happy, and happy will I be to-morrow? For amidst this fatal calm, I was privately inveigled from his castle, by the wretch between whom and the title I stood; and my assassination was actually concerted; as a parchment now in my possession, will prove to a demonstration."

"Oh, what shall I do?" muttered the young man.

"Ha!" exclaimed I, "what is this I hear? Speak, Sir; Are you a party concerned?"

"In the devil's name, who are you?" cried he.

"Now don't you know?" said I.

"Not I, from my soul."

"But can't you guess?"

"Not for the life of me can I form the most remote notion!"

"Then I am sure," said I, "I have already told you enough to convince you, that I am a Heroine— one of those fair unfortunates,

356

whom we read of in romances. I am, upon my honour. To-night, at the masquerade, the mystery of my birth is to be unfolded; and to-morrow, I trust that the wretched Cherubina, released from thraldom, and restored to the tender arms of her family, will attest the justice of this sensible maxim, — Innocence, though vexed awhile by the storms of misfortune."

"Now may the merciful powers protect and rescue me!" ejaculated he, gathering himself up into a ball; "for 'tis a Bedlamite broken loose!"

And now, between terror and want of air, the poor fellow appeared on the very point of suffocation. He gasped, and groaned, kicked and struggled, and called help, help! with the most piercing utterance; when, in the acme of his agony, the chest, on a sudden, was unlocked, opened; and the mistress herself, holding a candle, appeared over us.

The gentleman darted, like an arrow, out of the chest. I rose from it more slowly.

"What is that? What thing is that?" cried the mistress, grasping his arm, and shrinking back.

"The wretch who has frightened you all," said he. "A dreadful mad-woman!"

"What upon this good earth can be done?" cried the mistress.

"I will tell you, Madam," answered I. "Your character is in my power. This gentleman cannot leave the house without my first alarming it; and if I am myself seized, you must appear to prosecute, and must swear that you locked him up in the chest. Now listen: Only furnish me with decent apparel, and suffer me to quit the house quietly, and on the word of a Heroine, I will not betray your intrigue. There is that dress of the Tuscan girl. I want it for the masquerade. Name your terms. We shall not differ."

"Gracious me!" exclaimed she, wringing her hands, "what in this wide world shall I do ?"

"Do?" cried I. "Why sell me the dress of course. Sure the whole scene, since I came into this house, was obviously contrived for the especial purpose of my procuring that individual dress; and just conceive the ridiculous effect, if, after all, I do not get it. Let me tell you, 'tis a serious thing for a heroine like me, to appear at a masquerade, in a corporal's coat. Here, now, whole nations will be reading this incident; and I just ask you, as a matter of feeling, could you bear their united execrations? Surely, when they shall have read

357

as far as up to this moment, they cannot but suppose, that I must obtain the dress; and if this be their idea, woe betide her who disappoints them! What can you answer to arguments so reasonable?"

"That the person who could use them," said she, "will never listen to reason. I see what is the matter with you, and that I have no alternative, but to humour you, or be ruined."

In a word, I got the Tuscan dress, slipped it on me, promised payment; and then, conducted down by the mistress (who thought she could never lose me too soon), I bade her good evening, and once more issued into the street.

I dared not venture back to my former lodgings, lest the conspirators there should keep me from the masquerade; so having called a coach, I drove to Jerry Sullivan's.

The poor Irishman jumped with joy when he saw me; but I found him in much distress. His creditors had threatened an execution on his little shop, unless he would immediately discharge his debts; and he was now quite unable to complete the necessary sum. Thirty pounds were still wanting. I had somewhat more than this, at my lodgings; and I determined that I would relieve him. I therefore dispatched him with a letter, requesting of my landlady to give the bearer my clothes, jewels, parchment, picture, and money; and bidding her deduct from my purse the amount of my bill. This commission he soon executed; and I presented him with the thirty pounds.

"Why then long life to your beautiful face!'" cried he, "for 'tis that is Heaven's own finger-post! O th'n, O th'n, I am the man who is grateful; so now, to be sure, all I wish upon this earth, is some mischief or other to happen you!"

"Thank you, Jerry," said I. "And pray is that the way you prove yourself grateful?"

"That same is the way, sure enough," cried Jerry. " For then, you know, I would relieve you, just as you did me; and then why, I think I would feel aisy."

I write from his house; but must soon conclude my letter, as the time for the masquerade is approaching.

I confess I am not perfectly satisfied with the mode that I adopted to obtain the dress from the milliner; since I took advantage of her indiscretion in one instance, to make her do wrong in another. However, the code of moral law that heroines acknowledge, is often opposite from those maxims which govern other conditions of life. And, indeed, if we view the various ranks and departments, we shall perceive, that what constitutes criminality in some of them, appears unobjectionable in others. Thus: a servant is disgraced, who robs his master of wine; but his master boasts how he defrauded the King of the revenue arising from that very wine. Thus too, what is called wantonness in a little minx with a flat face, is called only susceptibility in a heroine with an oval one. We weep at the letters of Heloise; but were they written by an alderman's fat wife, we should laugh at them. The heroine may permit an amorous arm round her waist, disobey her parents, and make assignations in groves, yet be described as the most prudent of human creatures; but the mere Miss must abide by the hackneyed rules of modesty, decorum, and filial obedience. In a word, as different classes have distinct privileges, it appears to me, from what I have read of the Law National, and the Law Romantic, that the Heroine's prerogative resembles the King's; and that she, like him, can do no wrong.

Adieu.

LETTER XVI.

O Biddy, I have ascertained my genealogy! I am — but I must not anticipate. Take the particulars.

Having secured a comfortable bed at Jerry's, and eaten something, I repaired in a coach, to the Pantheon; and that faithful Irishman escorted me thither.

But I must first describe my Tuscan dress. It was a short petticoat of pale green, and a boddice of white silk; the sleeves were loose, and tied up at the shoulders, with ribbons and bunches of flowers. My hair, which fell in ringlets on my neck, was also ornamented with flowers, and with a rural hat of wheaten straw.

Fearfully and anxiously, I entered the assembly. Such a multitude of grotesque groups as presented themselves! Clowns, harlequins, nuns, devils; all talking and none listening. The clowns were happy to be called fools, the harlequins were as awkward as clowns, the nuns were impudent, and the devils were well-conducted.

Too much agitated to support my character with spirit, I hastened into a recess, and there awaited the arrival of the ancient vassal.

In a few minutes, a mask approached. It was an old man. His infirm figure leaned upon a staff, a palsy shook his venerable locks, and his garments had all the quaintness of antiquity.

For some minutes he stood gazing on me with earnestness; and at length, heaving a heavy sigh, he thus broke into tremulous utterance.

"A-well-a-day! how the antique tears do run adown my wrinkled cheeks; for well I wis, thou beest herself—the Lady Cherubina De Willoughby, the long-lost daughter of mine honoured mistress."

"And you," cried I, starting from my seat, "you are the ancient and loyal vassal!"

"Now by my truly, 'tis even so," said he.

I could have hugged the obsolete old man to my heart.

"Welcome, welcome, much respected menial!" cried I, grasping his hand. "But tell me at once all about it; — all about my family; and I will be the making of your fortune: dear good old man, depend upon it I will.'"

"Now by my fay," said he, "I will say forth my say. I am ycleped Whylome Eftsoones, and I was accounted comely when a younker. Good my lady, I must tell unto thee a right pleasant and quaint saying of a certain nun touching my face."

"For pity's sake," cried I, "pass it over for the present."

"Certes, my lady," said he. "Well, I was first taken, as a bonny page, into the service of thy great great grandfader's fader's brother; and I was in at the death of these four generations; till at last, I became seneschal unto thine honoured fader, Lord De Willoughby. His lordship married the Lady Hysterica Belamour, and thou wast the sole issue of that ill-fated union.

"Soon after thy birth, thy noble father died of an apparition. Returning, impierced with mickle dolour, from his funeral, I was stopped on a common, by a tall figure, with a mirksome cloak, and a flapped hat. I shook grievously, ne in that ghastly dreriment wist how myself to bear.

"Anon, he threw aside his disguise, and I beheld — Lord Gwyn! Lord Gwyn who was ywedded unto the sister of Lord De Willoughby, the Lady Eleanor."

"Then Lady Eleanor Gwyn is my own aunt!" cried I.

"Thou sayest truly," replied he. "My good Eftsoones,' whispered Lord Gwyn to me, 'know you not that my wife, Lady Eleanor Gwyn, would enjoy all the extensive estates of her brother, Lord De Willoughby, if his child, the little Cherubina, were no more?'

"I trow, ween, and wote, 'tis as your lordship saith,' answered I.

"His lordship then put into mine hand a stiletto.

"Eftsoones,' said he, 'if this dagger be planted in the heart of a child, it will grow, and bear a golden flower!'

"He spake, and incontinently took to striding away from me, in such wise, that maulgre and albe, I gan make effort after him, nathlesse and algates did child Gwyn forthwith flee from mine eyne."

"Bless me!" cried, quite provoked, "I cannot understand half you say. What do you mean by *Child* Gwyn? Surely his Lordship was no suckling."

"In good old times," answered Eftsoones, "childe signified a noble youth; and it is coming into fashion again. For instance, there is Childe Harold."

"Then," said I, "there is 'second childishness;' and I fancy there will be 'mere oblivion.' But if possible, finish your tale in more modern language."

"I will endeavour," said he. "Tempted by this golden flower, I stole you from your mother, secreted you at the house of a peasant, and bribed him to rear you as his own daughter. I then told Lord Gwyn that I had dispatched you; and the golden flower he gave me was three and four- pence!

"When the dear lady, your mother, missed you, she became insane, executed the most elegant outrages on society; and having plucked the last hair from her own head, ran into the woods, and has never been found since."

"Dear sainted sufferer!" exclaimed I.

"Till a few days ago," continued Eftsoones, "I heard no more of the peasant or of you; when, to my surprise, the peasant sent for me. I went. He was dying. Such a scene! He confessed that he had sold you to one farmer Wilkinson, about thirteen years before; who purchased you on speculation."

"Yes," cried I, "on the speculation of a reward from Lord Gwyn for assassinating me. I have a parchment which ascertains the fact."

"What! beginning with 'THIS INDENTURE," cried Eftsoones.

"Yes," said I, "and then, 'for and in consideration of—"

"Doth grant, bargain, release —" cried he.

"Possession, and to his heirs and assigns —" cried I.

"Huzza, huzza, huzza!" cried he, taking a stiff frisk; "your title is as clear as the sun; and I hereby and thereby hail you Lady Cherubina de Willoughby, rightful heiress of all the territory that now appertaineth, or that may hereinafter appertain unto the House of De Willoughby."

"Wonderful! most wonderful!" cried I. "Oh, I am the happiest, happiest creature in the world!"

"Now listen," said he. "Lady Gwyn, (for his lordship is long dead) resides at this moment, on your estate. I have a carriage in waiting: we will set off together this very night —"

"This very moment!" cried I; but as I spoke, a Domino came forward, took off its mask, and I beheld Stuart! The moment he saluted me, Whylome Eftsoones slunk away.

Much as I was annoyed at his unseasonable interruption, I felt sincerely delighted to find, that he had not deserted me altogether.

After mutual salutations; "I came hither," said he, "upon the mere chance of meeting you; since you intended being here, when I saw you last, and since I knew that the villain Betterton had planned the infernal plot of inveigling you hence. I called on you several times to-day, but was always answered that you were out. Suspecting that you were not, but that you meant to refuse my future visits; and well aware of the dangers which environed you, I determined upon seeing you, at any hazard; so having knocked once more, I rushed into the house, and raised a cry of fire.

"This manoeuvre had the desired effect, for an universal panic took place; and in the midst of it, I saw you issue forth, and effect your escape, while I was struggling with Grundy, who wanted to prevent my entrance. I pursued you, but soon lost all traces of your route. I therefore returned to your lodgings; where Higginson informed me, that Betterton had made the landlady fasten a carpet outside your window, for the purpose of darkening the chamber, and thus leading you to believe it night. Undoubtedly their object was to detain you in bed ail day, that you might not see me before the masquerade.

"I then called at Betterton's house, but he was not within; and now, Miss Wilkinson, pardon me when I say, that I will never leave your side again, till I restore you to your father, or entrust you to some careful friend."

362

Here a long argument arose; and at length I pretended to yield the point; but privately resolved upon giving him the slip, as soon as old Eftsoones should reappear.

I therefore walked about with him, several hours; but no Eftsoones. And now the people had begun to disperse, and now the room was almost empty. Still no Eftsoones. At last, when scarcely one creature remained, and when all hope of seeing him was over, I acceded to the frequent solicitations of Stuart, and left the place.

On our way back, I told him that I would comply with his wish of accompanying me, provided he would suffer me to go where I chose. He asked me where I chose to go? I answered, Lady Gwyn's; as I had a most mysterious and important transaction to settle in that quarter.

"Then," said he, "I will escort you thither; for I am acquainted with her Ladyship, and rest assured, she shall receive you very graciously."

We have now just returned to Jerry Sullivan's. I will sleep a couple of hours; Stuart will remain in the parlour; and to-morrow morning we will commence our expedition. I think I know enough of her husband's infamy to astonish and terrify her into some advantageous concession.

Well, Biddy, what say you now? A young, rich, titled heiress already — think of that, Biddy.

As soon as I can decently turn Lady Gwyn out of doors, I mean to set up a most magnificent establishment. But I will treat the poor woman (who perhaps is innocent of her husband's crime) with extreme delicacy. She shall never want a bed or a plate. By the bye, I must purchase plate. My livery shall be white and crimson; but I am sadly puzzled between bays and greys. Biddy, depend upon my patronage. With what importance the parson and music-master will boast of having known me! Then our village will swarm so, *to hear tell as how* Miss Cherry has grown a great lady; and no doubt, old mother Muggins, at the bottom of the hill, will live a week on the gossip. I think I must drive through some day or other. But I mean to nod quite familiarly, for there is nothing I hate like pride.

Yet, though the chief objection against my marriage will soon be removed, by the confirmation of my noble birth, I am not so ignorant of what heroines must suffer, as to imagine that no other impediments will interfere.

363

Ah, no, my friend; be well assured, misfortune will not desert me quite so quickly. A present good is often but the precursor of an approaching evil; and when prosperity points its sunshine in our faces, adversity, like our shadows, is ever at our heels.

Adieu.

LETTER XVII.

Early this morning, I packed my clothes, jewels, parchment, and picture into a little box. Then Stuart and I, having breakfasted, and remunerated our entertainers, set off for Lady Gwyn's; while Jerry ran at the side of the chaise, half way down the street, blessing me all over, and hoping that we might meet again in his house; or if the worst came to the worst, in heaven.

We had now accomplished more than half our journey, and were waiting, at an inn, for a change of horses; when the door opened, and in walked old Betterton! He bowed, I started, Stuart reddened.

"From my soul," cried the hoary deluder, "I rejoice at overtaking you before 'tis too late. Yes, my dear lady, I come to protect you against the treachery of pretended friends."

"Sir," said Stuart, "I do not understand —"

"But, Sir," cried Betterton, "I do understand. I understand, Sir, that you are eloping with this lady. Nay, frown not, but listen.

"Last night I happened to be at the Pantheon, and saw you there, escorting her. Even during our former interview, I had suspected your vile intentions; but now finding you with her, at a masquerade, and without a matron, I felt fully convinced of them. I therefore traced you from the Pantheon; and perceived, to my horror, that you stopped at an infamous house in St. Giles's, where you remained during the night. This morning too, a chaise stood there, ready as if for a journey; whence concluding, as I well might, that an elopement was in agitation, I determined, if possible, to prevent so disastrous a catastrophe, by hiring a carriage and pursuing you.

"Sir, you undertook to lecture me, when last I saw you; and plausibly you performed your part. I must now return the obligation. Mr. Stuart, Mr. Stuart, is it not a shame for you, Mr. Stuart? Is this the way you treat the daughter of your friend, Mr. Stuart? Go, silly boy, return home; say your prayers, and bless that chance which hath sent me to the protection of this lady's honour."

"Let me tell you, Sir," returned Stuart, "that neither grey hairs nor facetious admonition shall protect villainy from chastisement; and I must add, that if you, Sir, would take less trouble in protecting this lady's honour, you would stand a better chance of preserving your own."

"Young gentleman," answered Betterton, "I will have you to know, that I would sacrifice my life in defence of my honour."

"If so," said Stuart, "though your life has but little of the saint, it would, at least, have something of the martyr."

Betterton scowled at him askance, and grinned prospective vengeance.

"Gentlemen," said I, "each has accused the other of evil designs. Let not arguments, but actions, determine the point. Mr. Stuart, I have already asked you to escort me, conceiving that you will prove a protector. Mr. Betterton, I now give you the same invitation for the same motive. I am going down to Lady Gwyn's; and if you have leisure, would feel happy at your company."

"Then, assuredly, I will do myself the honour to join your party," said he, with a triumphant glance at Stuart, who stood as if he were shot.

The fact is, I felt grateful to the valuable old villain, for his unwearied industry in promoting the memoirs of my life.

We then got into one of the chaises, and proceeded several miles, without any particular occurrence.

At length it was evening. A few fleecy clouds floated through the blue depths of ether. The breezes brought coolness on their wings, and an inviting valley, watered by a rivulet, lay to the left; here whitened with sheep, and there dotted with little encampments of hay.

Tempted by the prospect, after my long confinement in the metropolis, I proposed to my companions, our walking the remainder of the journey through the fields. Each, whatever was his motive, caught at the proposal with delight, and we then directed the chaise to wait for us in the village which adjoins Gwyn Castle.

I now hastened to luxuriate in Arcadian beatitude. My pastoral garb of Tuscany was appropriate: nothing remained but to rival an Ida, or a Glorvina, in simple touches of nature; and to trip along the lawns, like a Daphne or a Hamadryad.

On a sudden, I sprang across a hedge, and fled towards the valley, light as a wood-nymph flying from a satyr. I then took up a most picturesque position. It was beside the streamlet, under a weeping willow, and on a grassy bank. A little farther, stood a romantic cottage, with a small garden behind it, encompassed by green paling. The stream prattled prettily; save where a projecting stone shattered its crystal, and made its music hoarse. Here and there, too, it purled and murmured; but no where could it be said to tinkle or gurgle, to chide or brawl.

Flinging off my hat, I shook my locks over my shoulders, and began braiding them in the manner of a simple shepherdess.

Stuart reached me the first; and at that moment a lambkin began its pretty bleat.

"Now," said I, "make me a simple tripping little ditty on a lambkin."

"You shall have it," answered he, "and such as an attorney's clerk would read to a milliner's apprentice."

> Dear sensibility, O la!
> I heard a little lamb cry, ba;
> Says I, so you have lost mamma?
> > Ah!

> The little lamb, as I said so,
> Frisking about the field did go,
> And frisking, trod upon my toe.
> > Oh!

"Neat enough," said I, "only that it wants the word LOVE."

"True," cried Stuart; "for our modern poems abound in the word, though they seldom have much of the feeling."

"And pray, my good friend," asked I archly, as I bound up my golden ringlets —"WHAT IS LOVE?"

"Nay," said he, "they say that talking of love is making it."

Plucking a thistle which sprang from the bank, I blew away its down with my balmy breath, merely to hide my confusion.

Surely I am the most sensitive of all created beings!

Betterton had now reached us, out of breath after his race, and utterly unable to articulate.

"Betterton,'" cried I, "what is love?"

" 'Tis," said he, gasping, " 'tis — 'tis —"

"The gentleman," cried Stuart, "gives as good a description of it as most of our modern poets; who make its chief ingredients panting and broken murmurs."

"Love," said I, "is a mystical sympathy, which unfolds itself in the glance that seeks the soul, — the sentiment that the soul embodies — the tender gaiety — the more delicious sadness — the stifled sigh — the soft and malicious smile — the thrill, the hope, the fear — each in itself a little bliss. Such is love."

"And if such be love," said Stuart, "I fear I shall never bring myself to make it."

"And pray," said I, "how would you make love?"

"There are many modes," answered he, "and the way to succeed with one girl is often the way to fail with another. Girls may be divided into the conversable and inconversable. He who can talk the best, has therefore the best chance of the former; but would a man make a conquest of one of the beautiful Inutilities, who sits in sweet stupidity, plays off the small simpers, and founds her prospects on the shape of her face, he has little more to do than call her a goddess, and make himself a monkey. Or if that should fail, as he cannot apply to her understanding, he must have recourse to her feeling, and try what the touch can do for him. The touch has a thousand virtues. Only let him establish a lodgment on the first joint of her little finger, he may soon set out upon his travels, and make the grand tour of her waist. This is, indeed, having wit at his fingers' ends; and this will soon gain the hearts of those demure misses, who think that silence is modesty, that to be insipid is to be innocent, and that because they have not a word for a young man in public, they may have a kiss for him in private."

"Come," said I, "since love is the subject, I want some amorous verses to swell my memoirs; so, Betterton, I call on you."

Betterton bowed and began:

Say, Fanny, why has bounteous heaven,
    In every end benign and wise,
Perfection to your features given?
    Enchantment to your witching eyes?

Was it that mortal man might view
    These charms at distance, and adore?
Ah, no! the man who would not woo,
    Were less than mortal, or were more.

367

The mossy rose, by humming bee,
    And painted butterfly carest,
We leave not lingering on the tree,
    But snatch it to the happy breast.

There, unsurpassed in sweets, it dwells; —
    Unless the breast be Fanny's own:
There blooming, every bloom excels; —
    Except of Fanny's blush alone.

O Fanny, life is on the wing,
    And years, like rivers, glide away:
To-morrow may misfortune bring,
    Then, gentle girl, enjoy to-day.

And while the whimpering kiss I sip,
    Ah, start not from these ardent arms;
As if afraid, my pressing lip
    Might desolate your own of charms.

For see, we crush not, tho' we tread.
    The cup and primrose. Fanny smiled.
Come then and press the cup, she said.
    Come then and press the primrose wild.

"Now," cried Stuart, "I can give you a poem, with just as much love in it, and twice as much kissing."

"That," said I, "would be a treasure indeed."

He then began:

Dawn with streaks of purple light,
    Paints her grey and fragrant fingers,
While no more, Creolian night,
    In the unstarred azure, lingers.

Upward poplars, downward willows,
    Rustle round us; zephyrs sprinkle
Scents of daffodillies, lilies,
    Mignionette, and periwinkle.

Rosy, balmy, honied, humid,
    Biting, burning, murmuring kisses,
Sally, I will snatch from you, mid
    Looks demure that tempt to blisses.

If your cheek grow cold, my dear,
    I will kiss it, till it flushes;
Or if warm, my raptured tear,
    Shall extinguish all its blushes.

Yes, that dimple is a valley,
    Where sports many a little true love;
And that glance you dart, my Sally,
    Might melt diamonds into dew, love.

But while idle thus I chat,
    I the war of lips am missing.
This, this, this, and that, that, that,
    These make kissing, kissing, kissing.

The style reminded me of Montmorenci; and at the same moment I heard a rustling sound behind me. I started. " 'Tis Montmorenci!" cried I. Agitated in the extreme, I turned to see — It was only a cock-sparrow.

I deserve the disappointment," said I, "for I have never once thought of that amiable youth, since I last beheld him. Sweetest and noblest of men," I exclaimed, in an audible soliloquy, such as heroines often practise; "say, dost thou mourn my mysterious absence? Perhaps the draught of air that I now inhale, is the same which thou hast breathed, in a sigh for the far distant Cherubina!"

"That cannot well be;" interrupted Stuart, "because, unless the sigh of this unknown was packed in a case, and hermetically sealed, it could hardly have come so far, without being dispersed on the way."

"There, you are mistaken," answered I. "For in the Hermit of the Rock, the heroine, while sitting on the Sardinian coast, thought it highly probable, that the billow then at her feet, might be the identical billow, which had drowned her lover, about a year before, off the coast of Martinique."

"That was not more improbable than the theory which Valancourt invented," said Stuart.

"What theory?" asked I.

"Why," said he, "that the sun sets, in different longitudes, at the same moment. For when his Emily was going to Italy, while he remained in France, he bade her watch the setting sun every evening, that both he and she might gaze upon it at once. Now, since the sun would set, where she was in Italy, much earlier than

369

where he was in France, they could not, according to common astronomy, pursue the gazing system, with any chance of success."

"But, Sir," said Betterton, "heroes and heroines are not bound to understand astronomy."

"And yet," answered Stuart, "they are greater star-gazers than the ancient Egyptians. To form an attachment for the moon, and write a sonnet on it, is the first symptom of a heroine."

As he spoke, a butterfly came fluttering about me. To chase butterflies is a classical amusement, introduced by Caroline of Lichfield; so springing on my feet, I began the pastime. The nimble insect eluded my fingers, and got over the paling, into the garden. I followed it through the gate, and caught it; but alas! bruised its body, and broke one of its wings. The poor thing took refuge in a lily; where it lay struggling awhile, and then its little spirit fled to the stars.

What an opportunity for a sonnet! I determined to compose one. A beautiful bush of roses was blushing near the lily, and reminded me how pastoral I should look, could I recline on roses, during my poetical ecstasy. But might I venture to pick some? Surely a few could do no harm. I glanced round. --- Nobody was in sight --- I picked a few. But what mattered a few for what I wanted? I picked a few more. The more I picked, the more I longed to pick --- 'Tis human nature; and was not Eve herself tempted in a garden? So from roses I went to lilies, from lilies to carnations, thence to jessamine, honeysuckle, eglantine; till I had filled my hat, and almost emptied the beds. I then hurried out of the garden; sentenced Stuart and Betterton to fifty yards' banishment, and just under the willow constructed a couch of flowers, which I inlaid with daisies, and moss.

I then flung myself upon my paradisaical carpet; and my recumbent form, as it pressed the perfumes, was indeed, that of the Mahometan Houri. Exercise and agitation had heightened the glow of my cheeks, and the wind had blown my yellow hair about my face, like withered leaves round a ripened peach. I never looked so lovely.

In a short time I was able to repeat this sonnet aloud.

Where the blue stream reflected flowerets pale,
  A fluttering butterfly, with many a freak,
Dipped into dancing bells, and spread its sail,
  White as the snow, and edged with jetty streak.

I snatched it passing; but a pinion frail,
    Besprent with mealy gold, I chanced to break.
The mangled insect, ill deserving bane,
    Falls in the hollow of a lily new.
My tears drop after it, but drop in vain.
    The cup, tho' fresh with azure air and dew,
And flowery dust and grains of fragrant seed,
Can ne'er revive it from the fatal deed.
So guileless nymphs attract some traiterous eye,
So by the spoiler crushed, reject all joy and die.

The pomp of composition over, I began to think that I had treated the owner of the garden ill. I felt guilty of little less than theft; and was deliberating on what I ought to do, when an old peasant came running towards me from the garden.

"Miss!" cried he, "have you seen any body pass this way with a parcel of flowers; for some thief has just robbed me of all I had?"

I raised myself a little to reply, and he perceived the flowers underneath.

"Odd's life!" cried he, "so you are the thief, are you? How dare you, hussey, commit such a robbery?"

"I am no hussey, and 'tis no robbery," cried I. "Hussey, indeed! Sir, it was all your own fault in leaving that uncouth gate of your's sprawling open. Pretty master of a house you are! Hussey, indeed!"

The peasant was just about to seize me, when Stuart ran forward, and prevented him. They had then some private conversation, and I saw Stuart give him a guinea. The talismanic touch of gold struck instant peace. Indeed, I have found, that even my face, with all its dimples, blushes, and glances, could never do half so much for me, as the royal face on a bit of gold.

The peasant was now very civil, and invited us to rest in his cottage. Thither we repaired, and found his daughter, a beautiful young woman, just preparing the dinner. I felt instantly interested in her fate. I likewise felt fatigued and hungry; and as evening was now near a close, my visit to Gwyn Castle might appear rather unseasonable. Under these circumstances, therefore, I called the girl aside, begged of her to give me a dinner, and, if possible, a bed, at the cottage; and assured her that I would recompense her liberally.

She said she would accommodate me, if her father would permit her; and she then went to consult him. After a private conference between them, she told me that he would let me remain. So we soon

371

agreed upon the terms; and a village was at hand, where Stuart and Betterton might dine and sleep.

Before these departed, they made me promise not to quit the cottage, till both of them should return, next morning; but I took an opportunity of whispering in Stuart's ear.

"At ten o'clock to-night, trill a canzonet beneath my casement. I will then open it, and admit you to a stolen interview."

In short, Biddy, I perceive, that the man, with a little encouragement, will soon become the unsuccessful lover, the Sir Charles Bingley of my Memoirs.

Dinner is announced.

Adieu.

LETTER XVIII.

At dinner, a young farmer joined us; and I soon perceived that he and the peasant's daughter, Mary, were born for each other. They betrayed their mutual tenderness by a thousand little endearments, which passed, as they thought, unobserved.

After dinner, when Mary was about accompanying me to walk, the youth stole after us, drew her back, and I heard him kiss her. She returned with her ringlets a little ruffled, and her ripe lips ruddier than before.

"Well, Mary," said I, "what was he doing to you?"

"Doing, Ma'am? Nothing, I am sure, Ma'am."

"Nothing, Mary?"

"Why, Ma'am, he only wanted to be a little rude, and kiss me, I believe."

"And you would not allow him, Mary?"

"Why should I tell a falsehood about the matter, Ma'am? To be sure I did not hinder him; for he is my sweetheart, and we shall be married next week."

"And do you love him, Mary?"

"Better than my life, Ma'am. There never was such a lad; he has not a fault in the wide world, and all the girls are dying of envy that I have got him."

"Well, Mary," said I, "we will take a rural repast down to the brook, and tell our loves. The contrast will be beautiful; mine, the refined, sentimental, pathetic story; your's the pretty, simple, artless tale. Come, my friend; let us return, and prepare the rustic banquet. No metropolitan Souchong; no brown, George and Stir-about. Oh! no, but creams, berries, and fruits; goat's milk, figs, and honey — Arcadian, pastoral, primeval dainties!"

However, on returning to the cottage, we could get nothing better than some currants, gooseberries, and a maple bowl of cream. Mary, indeed, poor thing, cut a large slice of bread and butter for her private amusement; and with these we repaired to the streamlet. I then threw myself on my flowery sofa, and my companion sat beside me.

We helped ourselves. I took rivulet to my cream, and scooped the brook with my rosy palm. Innocent nymph!

"How soft, how serene this evening!" exclaimed I. "It is a landscape for a Claud. But how much more charming is an Italian or a French, than an English landscape. O! to saunter over hillocks, covered with lavender, thyme, juniper and tamarisc, while shrubs fringe the points of the rocks, or patches of meagre vegetation tint their recesses! Almonds, cypresses, palms, olives, and dates stretch along; nor are the larch and ilex, the masses of granite, and forests of fir wanting; while the Garonne wanders from the Pyrenees, and winds its blue waves towards the Bay of Biscay.

"Then, Mary, though your own cottage is tolerable, yet is it, as in Italy, covered with vine-leaves, fig-trees, jessamine, and clusters of grapes? Is it tufted with myrtle, or shaded with a grove of lemon, orange, and bergamot?"

"But, Ma'am," said Mary, " 'tis shaded with some fine old elms."

"True," cried I, "but are the flowers of the agnus castus there? Is the pomegranate of Shemlek there? Are the Asiatic andrachne, the rose coloured nerit, and the verdant alia marina there? Are they, Mary?"

"I believe not, Ma'am," answered she. "But then our fields are all over daisies, butterflowers, clover-blossoms, and daffodowndillies."

"Daffodowndillies!" cried I. "Ah, Mary, Mary, you may be a very good girl, but you do not shine in description. Now I leave it to your own taste, which sounds better, — Asiatic andrachne, or daffodowndillies? Oh, my friend, never while you live, say daffodowndillies."

"Never, if I can help it, Ma'am," said Mary. "And I hope you do not think the worse of me, for having said it now; since I could safely make oath that I never heard, till this instant, of its being a naughty word."

"I am satisfied," said I. "So now let us tell our loves; and you shall begin."

"Indeed, Ma'am," said she, "I have nothing to tell."

"Impossible," cried I. "What! no quarrelling, no rivalling, no slandering, no any thing?"

"No, Ma'am. He took a small farm near us; and he liked me from the first, and I liked him, and both families wished for the match, Ma'am; and when he asked me to marry him, I said I would, Ma'am, and so we shall be married next week; and that is the whole story, Ma'am."

"A melancholy story, indeed!" said I. "What pity that an interesting pair, like you, who, without flattery, seem born for one of Marmontel's tales, should be so cruelly sacrificed."

I then began to consider whether any thing could yet be done in their behalf, or whether the matter was past redemption. I reflected that it were but an act of charity, — hardly deserving praise — to snatch them awhile from mere matrimony, and introduce them to a few sensibilities. Surely, with very little ingenuity, I might get up an incident or two between them; — a week's or a fortnight's torture, perhaps; — and afterwards enjoy the luxury of re-uniting them.

With this laudable intention, I sat meditating awhile; and at length hit upon an admirable plan. It was no less than to make Mary (without her own knowledge) write a letter, dismissing her William for ever! This appears impossible; but attend.

"My story," said I, to the unsuspecting girl, "is long and lamentable, and I fear, I have not spirits for relating it. I shall merely tell you, that I have eloped with the younger of the gentlemen who were here this morning, and have married him. I took this step, because my parents insisted that I should marry another, whom I disliked, and who, by the bye, is a namesake of your William's. Now, Mary, I have a favour to beg. This man must be informed of my marriage; and as I promised my husband that I would never hold a correspondence with him, will you just take the trouble of writing, in my name, what I shall desire you?"

"That I will, and welcome," said the simple girl; "only, Ma'am, I fear I shall disgrace a lady like you, with my bad writing. I am, out

374

and out, the worst scribbler in our family; and William says to me, ah, Mary, says he, if your tongue talked as your pen writes, you might die an old maid for me. Ah, William, says I, I would bite off my tongue sooner than die an old maid. So, to be sure, Willy laughed very hearty."

We then returned home, and retired into my chamber, where I dictated, and Mary wrote as follows:

"Dear William,

"Prepare your mind for receiving a great and unexpected shock. To keep you no longer in suspense, I am MARRIED.

"Before I had become acquainted with you, I loved another man, whose name, however, I must conceal. About a year ago, circumstances obliged his going abroad, but before his departure, he procured my promise to marry him on his return. You then came, and rivalled him.

"As he never once wrote during his absence, I concluded that he was dead. Yesterday, however, a letter from him announced his return, and appointed a private interview. I went. He had a clergyman in waiting to join our hands. I prayed, entreated, wept — all in vain.

" I BECAME HIS WIFE.

"O, William, pity, but do not blame me. If you are a man of honour and of feeling, never shew this letter, or tell its contents, as my father must not know of my marriage for many months. Do not even speak to myself on the subject.

"Adieu, dear William: adieu for ever."

We then returned to the parlour, and found William there. While we were conversing, I took an opportunity of slipping the letter, unperceived, into his hand, and of bidding him read it elsewhere. He retired with it, and we continued talking. But in a few minutes he hurried back into the room, with an agitated countenance; stopped opposite Mary, and fixed his eyes earnestly upon her.

"William!" cried she, "William! For shame then, don't frighten one so."

"No, Mary," said he, "I scorn to frighten you, or injure you either. But no wonder my last look at you should be frightful. There, take your true-lover's knot — there, take your hair — there, take your letters. So now, Mary, good-by, good-by; and that you may live and die happy, is what I pray Providence, from the bottom of my broken heart!"

With these words, and a piteous glance of anguish, he rushed from the room.

Mary remained motionless a moment; then half rose, sat down, rose again; and grew pale and red by turns.

" 'Tis so — so laughable," said she at length, while her quivering lip refused the attempted smile. "All my presents returned too. Sure — my heavens! — Sure he cannot want to break off with me? Well, I have as good a spirit as he, I believe. The base man; the cruel, cruel man!" and she burst into a passion of tears.

I tried to sooth her, but the more I said, the more she wept. She was certain, she said, she was quite certain, that he wanted to leave her; and then she sobbed so plaintively, that I was on the very point of undeceiving her; when, fortunately, she heard her father returning, and ran into her own room. He asked about her; I told him that she was not well; — the old excuse of a fretting heroine; — so he hastened to her, and with difficulty gained admittance. They have remained together ever since.

How delicious will be the happy denouement of this pathetic episode, this dear novellette; and how sweetly will it read in my memoirs!

Adieu.

LETTER XIX.

The night was dark when I repaired to the casement, and I had intended beginning this letter with a description of it, in the style of the best romances. But after summoning to my mind all the black articles of value that I can recollect — ebony, sables, palls, pitch, and even coal, I find I have nothing better to say, than, simply,— The night was dark.

Having seated myself at the casement, I composed this

SONNET.

Now while within their wings each feather'd pair,
    Hide the hush'd head, thy visit, moon, renew,

376

Shake thy pale tresses down, irradiate air,
   And tip the spicy flowers that scent the dew.
The lonely nightingale shall pipe to thee,
And I will moralize her minstrelsy.

The gorgeous Sun ten thousand warblers sing,
   One only bird proclaims the placid moon;
Thus for the great, how many wake the string,
   Thus for the good, how few the lyre attune.

   Just as I had finished it, a low and tremulous voice, close to the casement, sang these words:

Haste, my love, and come away;
   What is folly, what is sorrow?
'Tis to turn from joys to-day,
   'Tis to wait for cares to-morrow.

   By yon river,
   Aspins shiver:
Thus I tremble at delay.
   Light discovers,
   Whispering lovers:
See the stars with sharpened ray,
   Gathering thicker,
   Glancing quicker;
Haste, my love, and come away.

   I sat enraptured, and heaved a sigh.
   "Enchanting sigh!" exclaimed the singer, as he sprang through the window; but I screamed aloud, for it was not the voice of Stuart.
   "Hush!" cried the mysterious unknown, and advanced towards me: I retreated, still shrieking; and now the door was thrown open, and the man of the house entered, with Mary behind him, holding a candle.
   In the middle of the room, stood a man, clad in a black cloak, with black feathers in his hat, and a black mask upon his face.
   The peasant ran forward, and knocked him to the ground.
   "Unmask him!" cried I.
   The peasant, kneeling on his body, tore off the mask, and I beheld — Betterton!
   "Alarm the neighbours, Mary!" cried the peasant.

377

"I must appear in an unfavourable light to you, my good man," said this terrifying character; "but the young lady will inform you that I came hither at her request."

"For shame!" cried I. "What a falsehood!"

"Falsehood!" said he. "I have your own letter, desiring me to come."

"The man is mad," cried I. "I never wrote such a letter in my life!"

"I can produce it, however," said he, pulling a paper from his pocket, and to my great amazement reading these lines.

"Cherubina begs that Betterton will repair to her window, at ten o'clock to-night, disguised like an Italian. The signal is his singing an air under the casement, which she will open, and he may then enter her chamber."

"Santa Maria!" cried I, "why, I never wrote a line of it! But this wretch (a ruffian of the first pretensions, I assure you), has a base design upon my person, and has followed me from London, for the purpose of effecting it; so I suppose, he wrote the letter himself, to himself, as an excuse, in case of discovery."

"Then he shall march to the magistrate," said the peasant, "and I will indict him for house-breaking."

A man half so frantic as Betterton I never beheld. He foamed, he grinned, he grinded the remnants of his teeth; and he swore that Stuart was at the bottom of the whole plot.

By this time, Mary having returned with some neighbours, we set forward in a body to the magistrate, and delivered our depositions before him.

The magistrate, therefore, notwithstanding all that Betterton could say, committed him to prison without hesitation.

As they were leading him away, he cast a furious look at the magistrate, and said: —

"Ay, Sir, I suppose you are one of those pensioned justices, who minister our vague and sanguinary laws, and do dark deeds for an usurping oligarchy, that now makes our most innocent actions misdemeanours, determines points of law without appeal, imprisons our persons without trial, and breaks open our houses with the standing army. But till we have a reform in Parliament, neither peace nor war, commerce nor agriculture, nothing will go right."

"Not even clocks nor watches?" said the magistrate.

"Not even clocks nor watches," cried Betterton, in a rage. "For how can our mechanics make any thing good, while a packed parliament deprives them of capital, and a mart?"

"So then," said the magistrate, "since a reform in parliament would improve our time-pieces, you reformers will probably be the means of discovering the longitude."

"No sneering, Sir," cried Betterton. "But do your duty, as you call it, and abide the consequence."

This gallant grey Lothario was then led to prison; and our party returned home.

Adieu.

LETTER XX.

I ROSE early this morning, and sought my favourite willow. Flinging myself on the margin of the bank, I began to warble a rustic madrigal, while I let down my length of tresses, and laved them in the little urn of the dimpling Naiad.

This, you know, was romantic enough, but the accident that befel me was not; for, leaning too much over, I lost my balance, and rolled headlong into the rivulet. As it was shallow, I did not fear being drowned, but as I was a heroine, I hoped to be rescued. Therefore, instead of rising, there I lay, shrieking and listening, and now and then lifting my head, in hopes to see Stuart come flying on the wings of the wind. Oh no! my gentleman thought proper to make himself scarce; so dripping, shivering, and indignant, I scramble out of the stream, and bent my steps towards the cottage.

On turning the corner of the hedge, who should I perceive, but the hopeful youth himself, quite at his ease, and blowing a penny trumpet for a chubby boy.

"What has happened to you?" said he, seeing me wring a rivulet from my dress.

"Only that I fell into the brook," answered I, "and was under the disagreeable necessity of saving my own life, when I expected you would kindly have condescended to take the trouble off my hands."

"Expected!" cried he. "Surely you had no reason for supposing that I was so near as to render you assistance."

"And therefore," retorted I, "I had every reason for supposing that you would render me assistance."

"You deal in riddles," said he.

"Not at all," answered I. "Surely the farther off a distrest heroine in danger believes a hero, the nearer he is sure to be. Only let her have good grounds for imagining him at her Antipodes, and nine times out of ten she finds him at her elbow. But I beg pardon; you are no hero."

"Well," said he, laughing, "though I did not save your life then, I will not endanger it now, by detaining you in your wet garments. Pray go and change them."

I took his advice, and borrowed some clothes from Mary, while mine were put to the fire. After breakfast, I once more equipped myself in my Tuscan costume, and a carriage being ready, I took an affectionate leave of that interesting rustic. Poor girl! Her attempts at cheerfulness all the morning were truly tragical; and, absorbed in another sorrow, she felt but little for my departure.

On our way, Stuart confessed that he was the person who forged the letter to Betterton; and that he did so for the purpose of accomplishing his temporary arrest, and thus of separating me from so dangerous a companion. He was himself at the window during the whole adventure, as he meant to have intercepted Betterton, had the peasant failed in securing him.

"You will excuse this interference in your concerns," added he; "but gratitude commands me to protect the daughter of my guardian; and friendship for her converts the duty into a pleasure."

"Ah!" said I, "however it happens, I fear you now dislike me."

"Believe me, my lovely visionary, you mistake," answered he. "With a few foibles (which are themselves as fascinating as foibles can be), you possess many virtues; and, let me add, attractions. As I sometimes annoy you with animadversion, I must now conciliate you with flattery."

"Flattery," said I, pleased by his praises, and willing to please him in return by serious conversation; "flattery deserves censure, only when the motive is mean or vicious."

"True," returned he; "and even though a compliment may not be sincere, our motive for paying it may be good. Flattery, so far from injuring, may benefit; since it is possible to create a virtue in others, by persuading them that they possess it."

"Besides," said I, "may we not imply compliments, without intending to impose them as serious truths; but merely meaning to make ourselves agreeable by an effort of the wit? And since such an effort evinces that we consider the person worthy of it, the compliment proves a kind intention at least, and thus tends to cement affection and friendship."

In this manner we touched on a thousand topics, and continued a delightful conversation during the remainder of the journey. Sometimes he seemed greatly gratified at my sprightly sallies, or sober remarks; but never could I throw him off his guard, by the dangerous softness of my manner.

Would you believe that this Mentor is a poet, and a poet of feeling. But whether he wrote these lines on a real or an imaginary being, I cannot, by any art, extract from him.

THE FAREWELL.

Go, gentle muse, 'tis near the gloomy day,
    Long dreaded; go, and bid farewell for me:
Farewell to her who once endured thy lay.
    Since soon she hastens hence. Ah, hard decree!

Tell her I feel that at the parting hour,
    Not waves alone will heave in tumult wild;
Not skies alone will rain a gushing shower.
    Not winds alone will breathe a murmur mild.

Say that her influence flies not with her form,
    That distant she will still engage my mind:
That suns are most remote when they most warm.
    That flying Parthians scatter darts behind.

Long will I gaze upon her vacant home,
    As the bird lingers near its pilfered nest;
There, will I cry, she turned the studious tome;
    There sported, there her envied pet caressed.

There, while she sat at each accomplished art,
    I saw her form, inclined with Sapphic grace;
Her radiant eyes, blest emblems of her heart,
    And all the living treasures of her face.

The Parian forehead parting clustered hair,

The cheek of peachy tinct, the meaning brow;
The witching archness, and the simple air,
    So magical, it charmed I knew not how.

Light was her footstep as the silent flakes
    Of falling snow; her smile was blithe as morn;
Her dimple, like the print the berry makes,
    In some smooth lake, when dropping from the thorn.

To snatch her passing accents as she spoke,
    To see her slender hand, (that future prize)
Fling back a ringlet, oft I dared provoke,
    The gentle vengeance of averted eyes.

Yet ah, what wonder, if when shrinking awe
    Withheld me from her sight, I broke my chain?
Or when I made a single glance my law,
    What wonder if that law were made in vain?

And say, can nought but converse love inspire?
    What tho' her lips for me have never moved?
The vale that speaks but with its feathered choir,
    When long beheld, eternally is loved.

Go then, my muse, 'tis near the gloomy day
    Of parting; go, and bid farewell for me;
Farewell to her who once endured thy lay,
    Whate'er engage her, whereso'er she be.

If slumbering, tell her in my dreams she sways,
    If speaking, tell her in my words she glows;
If thoughtful, tell her in my thoughts she strays,
    If tuneful, tell her in my song she flows.

Tell her that soon my dreams will wander wild;
    That soon my words will intermingle moans;
That soon my thoughts will languish unbeguiled;
    That soon my song will trill lamenting tones.

Yet dream, word, thought, and song shall often frame,
    Dear scenes ideal, where we meet at last;
Where, by my peril, snatched from wreck or flame,
    She smiles reward and talks of all the past:

Now to the rural lark she hastes away.

Ah, could the bard some winged warbler be,
Following her form, no longer would he say,
   Go, gentle muse, and bid farewell for me.

I write from the village, where the chaise, with my box, had awaited our arrival. Another hour and my fate is decided.

Adieu.

LETTER XXI.

At length with a throbbing heart, I now, for the first time, beheld Gwyn Castle, the mansion of my revered ancestors, and the present abode of Lady Gwyn. That unfortunate usurper of my rights was at home; so leaving Stuart (whom I would not suffer to accompany me) in the chaise, I alighted, and was ushered into the sitting-room.

I entered with gentleness, yet majesty; while my Tuscan habit, which was soiled and shrivelled by the brook, gave me an air of complicated distress.

I found her Ladyship at a table, classifying fossils.

On seeing me, she looked surprised; but smiled, and inquired my business.

"It is a business," said I, "of the most vital importance to your honour and repose; and I lament that imperious necessity compels me to undertake the invidious task of acquainting your Ladyship with it. Could any thing heighten the painful nature of my feelings, it would be my finding that I had wounded your's."

"Your preamble alarms me," said she. "Do pray be explicit."

"I begin," said I, "with declaring my conviction of your ignorance, that any person alive, except yourself, has a right to the property which your Ladyship at present possesses."

"Assuredly the notion never entered my head," said she; "and indeed, were such a claim made, I should consider it utterly untenable."

"I regret," said I, "that it is quite undeniable. There are documents extant, and witnesses living, to prove it beyond all refutation."

Her Ladyship, I thought, changed colour, as she said:

383

"This is strange; but I cannot believe it. Who could possibly have the face to set up such a silly claim?"

"I am so unfortunate as to have that face," answered I in a tone of the most touching humility.

"You!" she exclaimed with amazement. "You!"

"Pardon the pain I give you," said I, "but such is the fact; and much as this interview must outrage our mutual feelings, I do assure your Ladyship, that I have sought it, solely to prevent the more grating process of a lawsuit."

"You are welcome to twenty lawsuits, if you wish them," cried she; "but I fancy they will not deprive me of my property."

"At least," said I, "they may be the means of subjecting your deceased husband to the most horrid imputations."

"I defy the whole universe to sully his character," cried she.

"Ah," said I, "little your Ladyship knows what that unfortunate nobleman once attempted — indeed, I trust, more from momentary impulse, than from inherent depravity; for often, in a moment of temptation, man perpetrates atrocities, which his better heart afterwards disowns; and — "

"But he attempted, you say;" cried she. "What did he attempt?"

"Ah!" said I, "your Ladyship will not compel me to mention."

"I will!" cried she. "I demand an unequivocal explanation. What did he attempt?"

"Well, since I must speak plain," replied I, "he attempted — no I will not tell."

"You shall!" cried she with encreasing agitation, "By heaven, you shall tell this instant!"

"Why then," said I, "he attempted —assassination!"

"Merciful powers!" said she, sinking back, and reddening violently. "What does the horrid woman mean?"

"At this moment," cried I, "a person is ready to make oath, that your unhappy husband bribed a servant to murder me, while an infant, in cold blood."

" 'Tis a falsehood!" shrieked she. "I would stake my life upon its being a vile, malicious, diabolical falsehood."

"Would it were!" said I, "but oh! Lady Gwyn, the circumstances, the circumstances — these cannot be contradicted. The morning was dreary; — the bones of my noble father had just been deposited in the grave; — when a tall muffled figure, armed with a dagger, stood before the seneschal. *It was the late Lord Gwyn!*"

"Who are you?" cried she, starting up quite pale and horror-struck. "In the name of all that is dreadful, who can you be?"

"Your own niece!" said I, meekly kneeling to receive her blessing — The Lady Cherubina De Willoughby, daughter to your Ladyship's deceased brother, Lord De Willoughby, and to his much injured wife, the Lady Hysterica Belamour!"

"Never heard of such persons in all my days!" cried she, ringing the bell furiously.

"Pray now," said I, "be calm. Though you lose your property, do not forget your birth. Dignify degradation by humility. On my honour, I mean to treat you with kindness, nay with friendship. I shall make it a point. After all, what is rank? what are riches? How heartless their charms compared with those of honour and of virtue! O, Lady Gwyn, O, my respected aunt; I conjure you by our common ties of blood, by your brother, who was my father, spurn the perilous toy, fortune, and retire in time, and without exposing your lost lord, into the peaceful bosom of obscurity!"

"Conduct this wretch out of the house," said her Ladyship as the servant entered. "She wants to extort money I believe."

"A moment more," cried I. "Where is old Eftsoones? Where is that worthy character?"

"I know no such person," said she. "Begone, impostor!"

"Impostor!" cried I. "That is a good one. But I have a certain parchment, I fancy —"

"And a great deal of insolence, I fancy," said she.

"Something like it, at least," cried I, "for I have your Ladyship's portrait."

"My portrait!" said she with a sneer.

"As sure as your name is Nell Gwyn," cried I; "for Nell Gwyn is written under it."

"You little impertinent reprobate! " exclaimed she. "Begone this moment, or I will have you drummed through the village."

"Never mind," said I: "if I am not even with you yet, I wonder at it." And I walked out of my own house.

"Well," said Stuart, as I got to the carriage, "have you finished your business? Is the mighty mystery elucidated, unravelled, developed?"

"Ah, don't teize me!" said I, and burst out crying.

"What can all this mean?" exclaimed he, as he jumped from the chaise, and vanished into the house.

I remained in the chaise till he came back.

"Good news!" cried he. "Her Ladyship wishes to see you, and apologize for her rudeness; and I fancy," added he with a significant nod, "all will go well in a certain affair."

"Then she has told you every thing?" said I. "Yes, yes, I flatter myself she now finds civility the best of her game."

I alighted, and her Ladyship ran forward to receive me. She pressed my hand, *my-deared* me twice in a breath, told me that Stuart had related my little history — that it was delicious — elegant --- exotic; and concluded with declaring, that positively I must remain at her house a few days, to talk over the great object of my visit.

Much as I mistrusted this sudden change in her conduct, I accepted her invitation, on the principle, that heroines usually go on a visit to their bitterest enemies. Besides, old Eftsoones would most probably seek me there.

Stuart appeared quite delighted at my determination, and after another private interview with her Ladyship, departed for London, to make further inquiries about Wilkinson.

Her Ladyship and I had then a long conversation, and she candidly confessed the probable justice of my claims. Poor creature! It will pain me to send her adrift upon the world; and, indeed, she was born for a better fate, her amusements are so elegant. She loves literature and perroquets, scrapes mezzotintos, and spends half her income in buying any thing that is hardly to be had. Then her cabinet contains vases of onyx and sardonyx, cameos and intaglios; subjects in marine teeth, by Fiamingo and Benvenuto Cellini; and antique gems in iadestonce, mochoa, coral, amber, and agate.

She has already presented me with several dresses, and she calls me the Lady Cherubina, — a sound which makes my little heart leap within me. Nay, she actually assured me, that her curiosity to know a real heroine was her chief inducement for having me on a visit; and that she considers an hour with me worth all her curiosities put together. What a delicate compliment! So could I do less, than assure her, in return, that when I dispossess her of the property, she shall never want a lodging or a meal?

Adieu.

LETTER XXII

Think of my never recollecting, till I retired for the night, that I might be murdered! How so probable a circumstance had escaped my penetration, is inconceivable; but I never once thought of it. Lady Gwyn might (for aught I could tell to the contrary) be just as capable of assassination as the Marchesa di Vivaldi; her motives were just as urgent; and besides, I now remembered, that wherever I walked, during the day, a footman was watching me. I therefore searched my chamber, for concealed doors, or sliding pannels, where assassins might enter, but I could find none. I then resolved on exploring the galleries, corridors, and suites of apartments, in hopes to discover some place of retreat, or some ragged record of my birth.

Accordingly, at the celebrated hour of midnight, I took the taper, and unbolting my door, stole softly along the lobby.

I stopped before one of our family pictures. It represented a lady, pale, pensive, and interesting; with flaxen hair and azure eyes, like my own. Was not that enough?

"Gentle image of my departed mother!" ejaculated I, kneeling before it, "may thy sainted original repose in peace!"

I then rose and glided onward. No sigh met my listening ear, no moan amidst the pauses of the gust.

With a trembling hand I opened a door, and found myself in a circular chamber, which was furnished with musical instruments. Intending to run my fingers over the keys of a piano, I walked towards it, till a low rustling made me pause. But what was my confusion, when I heard the mysterious machine on a sudden begin to sound; not loudly, but (more terrible still!) with a hurried murmur; as if all its chords were agitated at once, by the hand of some invisible spirit.

I did not faint, I did not shriek; but I stood transfixed to the spot. The music ceased. I recovered courage, and advanced. The music began again; and again I paused.

What! should I shrink from lifting the simple lid of a mere piano? What! should I resign the palm of hardihood to Emily, who drew aside the black veil, and discovered the terrific wax-doll underneath it?

Emulation, enthusiasm, curiosity prompted me, and I rushed undaunted to the piano. Louder and more rapid grew the notes —

my desperate hand raised the cover, and beneath it, I beheld a sight to me the most hideous and fearful upon earth, — a mouse!

I shrieked, and dropped the candle, which was instantly extinguished. The mouse ran by my feet; I flew towards the door, but missed it, and fell against a table; nor till after I had made a most alarming clamour, could I get out of the room. As I groped my way through the corridor, I heard voices and steps above stairs; and presently lights appeared. The whole house was in confusion.

"They are coming to murder me at last!" cried I, as I regained my chamber, and began heaping chairs and tables against the door. Presently several persons arrived at it, and called my name. I said not a word. They called louder, but still I was silent; till at length they burst open the door, and Lady Gwyn, with some of her domestics, entered. They found me kneeling in an attitude of supplication.

"Spare, oh, spare me!" cried I.

"My dear," said her Ladyship, "no harm shall happen you."

"Alas, then," exclaimed I, "what portends this nocturnal visit? this assault on my chamber? all these dreadful faces? Was it not enough, unhappy woman, that thy husband attempted my life; but must thou, too, thirst for my blood?"

Lady Gwyn whispered a servant, who left the room; the rest raised, and put me to bed; while I read her Ladyship such a lecture on murder, as absolutely astonished her.

The servant soon after returned with a cup.

"Here, my love, is a composing draught for you," said her Ladyship. "Drink it, and you will be quite well to-morrow."

I took it with gladness, for I felt my brain strangely bewildered by my recent terror.

They then left a candle in my room, and departed.

My mind still remains uneasy; but I have barricaded the door. I believe, however, I must now throw myself on the bed; for the draught has made me sleepy.

Adieu.

LETTER XXIII.

O BIDDY GRIMES, I am poisoned! That fatal draught last night — why did I drink it? — dreadful is my agony. When this reaches you, all will be over. --- But I would not die without letting you know.

Farewell for ever, my poor Biddy!

1 bequeath you all my ornaments.

LETTER XXIV.

Yes, my friend, you may well stare at receiving another letter from me; and at hearing that I have not been poisoned in the least!

I must unfold the mystery. When I woke this morning, after my nocturnal adventure, I found my limbs so stiff, and such pains in all my bones, that I was almost unable to move. Judge of my horror and despair; for instantly it flashed across my mind, that Lady Gwyn had poisoned me! My whole frame underwent a sudden revulsion; I grew sick, and rang the bell with violence; nor ceased an instant, till half the servants, and Lady Gwyn herself, had burst into my chamber.

"If you have a remnant of mercy left," cried I, "send for a doctor!"

"What is the matter, my dear," said her Ladyship.

"Only that you have poisoned me, my dear," cried I. "Dear, indeed! Oh, what will become of me! What will become of me!"

"Do, tell me," said she, "how are you unwell?"

"I am sick to death," cried I. "I have shooting pains in all my limbs, and half an hour sees me a corpse. Oh, indeed, you have done the business completely. Lady Eleanor Gwyn, I do here, on my death-bed, and with all my senses about me, solemnly, and, before your domestics, accuse you of having administered a deadly potion to me last night."

"Go for the physician," said her Ladyship to a servant.

"Yes," cried I. "Well may you feel alarmed. Your life will pay the forfeit of mine."

"You, however, need not feel alarmed," said her Ladyship, "for really, what I gave you last night, was to make you sleep."

389

"Yes," cried I, "the sleep of the grave! O Lady Gwyn, what have I done, to deserve death at your hands? And in such a manner too! Had you shewn so much respect for custom and common decency, as to have offered me the potion in a bowl or a goblet, I might perhaps have suspected the treacherous intent. But you have added insult to injury; --- you have tricked me out of my life with a paltry tea-cup; — you have poisoned a girl of my pretensions, as vulgarly as you would a rat. Oh, what shall I do? What upon earth shall I do?"

Her Ladyship again began assuring me that I had taken a mere soporific; but I would not hear her, and at length, I sent every one out of the chamber, that I might prepare for my approaching end.

How to prepare was the question; I had never thought of death seriously, heroines so seldom die. Should I follow the precedent of the dying Heloise, who called her friends about her, got her chamber sprinkled with flowers and perfumes, and then yielded her gentle spirit, in a state of elegant inebriation with home-made wine, which she passed for Spanish? Alas! I had no friends, no flowers, no perfumes; and as for wine, I could not abide the thoughts of it in a morning.

But amidst these reflections, a more grave, and less agreeable subject intruded itself --- a future state. I strove to banish it, but it would not be repulsed. Yet surely, said I, as a heroine, I am a pattern of virtue; and what more is necessary? Yet at church (seldom as I frequented it), I had heard a very different doctrine. There I had heard, that the foundation of virtue is religion; and that if we are unacquainted with the precepts which prepare us for another world, we cannot be well instructed in those which fit us for this. Religion! alas, I knew nothing of it, except from novels; and there, though the devotion of heroines is sentimental and graceful to a degree, it never influences their acts, or appears connected with their moral duties. It is so speculative and generalized, that it would answer the Greek or the Persian church, as well as the Christian; and none but the picturesque and enthusiastic part is presented; such as kissing a cross, chanting a vesper with elevated eyes, or composing a well-worded prayer.

The more I thought, the more horrible appeared my situation. I felt a confused idea, that I had led a worthless, if not a criminal life; that I had left myself without a friend in this world, and had not endeavoured to make one in the next. I became more and more agitated. I turned my thoughts back to the plan of expiring with a grace, but in vain; I then wrote the note to you; nothing could calm or divert my mind. The pains grew keener; I felt sick at heart, my palate was parched, and every breath that I drew, I believed my last. My soul recoiled from the thought, and my brain became a chaos. Hideous visions of futurity rushed into my mind; I lay shivering, groaning, and abandoned to the most deplorable despair.

In this state the physician found me. O what a relief, when he declared, that my disorder was nothing but a violent rheumatism, contracted, it appears, by my fall into the water the morning before! Never was such a change from distraction to transport.

He prescribed for me; but remarked, that I might remain ill a month, or recover in a week.

"Positively," said her Ladyship, "you must get well in three days; because then comes my ball, and I have set my heart on your doing wonders at it."

I thanked her Ladyship, and begged pardon for my giddiness, in having accused her of murder; while she laughed at my mistake, and made quite light of it. Noble relative! But I dare say magnanimity is the family virtue.

I now felt just as miserable about losing the ball, as I had before felt about leaving the world. To lose it from any cause was provoking; but to lose it by a rheumatism, was dreadful. Now, instead of being swathed in flannels, and making wry faces at labelled vials, had I some pale, genteel, sofa-reclining illness, I would bless my kind stars, and quaff heroic hartshorn, with delight. Yet disguise thyself as thou wilt, hartshorn, still thou art a bitter draught; and though heroines in all novels have been made to drink of thee, thou art no less bitter on that account.

Indeed, I have to lament, that I am utterly unacquainted with those refined ailments, which assail all other celebrated girls. The consequence is my wanting that beauty, which, touched with the delicacy of illness, gains from sentiment what it loses in bloom; so that really this horse's constitution of mine is a terrible disadvantage to me. I know, if I could invent my own indispositions, I would strike out something infinitely beyond even the hectics and head-aches of my fair rivals. I believe there is no such complaint as a sigh fever; but one might fall ill of a scald from a lover's tear, or a classic scratch from the thorn of a rose.

Adieu.

LETTER XXV.

This morning I woke almost well, and towards evening was able to appear below. Lady Gwyn had invited several of her friends; so that I passed a delightful afternoon; the charm, admiration, and astonishment of all.

When I retired to rest, I found this note on my toilette.

To the Lady Cherubina.

YOUR MOTHER LIVES! and is confined in a subterranean vault of the villa. At midnight two men will tap at your door, and conduct you to her. Be silent, courageous, and circumspect.

What a flood of new feelings gushed upon my soul, as I laid down the billet, and lifted my filial eyes to heaven! Mother --- endearing name! I pictured that unfortunate lady, stretched on a mattrass of straw, her eyes sunken in their sockets, yet retaining a portion of their youthful fire; her frame emaciated, her voice feeble, her hand damp and chill. Fondly did I depict our meeting --- our embrace; she gently pushing me from her, and baring my forehead to gaze on the lineaments of my countenance. All, all is convincing; and she calls me the softened image of my noble father!

Two tedious hours I waited in extreme anxiety. At length the clock struck twelve; my heart beat responsive, and immediately the promised signal was made. I unbolted the door, and beheld two men masked and cloaked. They blindfolded me, and each taking an arm, led me along. Not a word passed. We traversed apartments, ascended, descended stairs; now went this way, now that; obliquely, circularly, angularly; till I began to imagine we were all the time in one spot.

At length my conductors stopped.

"Unlock the postern gate," whispered one, "while I light a torch."

"We are betrayed!" said the other, "for this is the wrong key."

"Then thou beest the traitor," cried the first.

"Thou liest, dost lie, and art lying!'" cried the second.

"Take that!" exclaimed the first. A groan followed, and the wretch tumbled to the ground.

"You have killed him!" cried I, sickening with horror.

392

"I have only hamstrung him, my lady," said the fellow. "He will be lame while ever he lives; but by St. Cripplegate, that won't be long; for our captain has given him four ducats to murder himself in a month."

He then burst open the gate; a sudden current of wind met us, and we hurried forward with incredible speed, while moans and smothered shrieks were heard at either side.

"Gracious goodness, where are we?" cried I.

"In the cavern of death!" said my conductor; "but never fear, Signora mia illustrissima, for the bravo Abellino is your povero devotissimo."

On a sudden innumerable footsteps sounded behind us. We ran swifter.

"Fire!" cried a ferocious accent, almost at my ear; and there came a discharge of arms.

I stopped, unable to move, breathe, or speak.

"I am wounded all over, right and left, fore and aft, long ways and cross ways, Death and the Devil!" cried the bravo.

"Am I bleeding?" said I, feeling myself with my hands.

"No, blessed St. Fidget be praised!" answered he; "and now all is safe, for the banditti have turned into the wrong passage."

He then stopped, and unlocked a door.

"Enter," said he, "and behold your mother!"

He led me forward, tore the bandage from my eyes, and retiring, locked the door after him.

Agitated already by the terrors of my dangerous expedition, I felt additional horror in finding myself within a dismal cell, lighted with a lantern; where, at a small table, sat a woman suffering under a corpulency unparalleled in the memoirs of human monsters. Her dress was a patchwork of blankets and satins, and her grey tresses were like horse's tails. Hundreds of frogs leaped about the floor; a piece of mouldy bread, and a mug of water, lay on the table; some straw, strewn with dead snakes and sculls, occupied one corner, and the distant end of the cell was concealed behind a black curtain.

I stood at the door, doubtful, and afraid to advance; while the prodigious prisoner sat examining me all over.

At last I summoned courage to say, "I fear, Madam, I am an intruder here. I have certainly been shewn into the wrong room."

"It is, it is my own, my only daughter, my Cherubina!" cried she, with a tremendous voice. "Come to my maternal arms, thou living picture of the departed Theodore!"

"Why, Ma'am," said I, "I would with great pleasure, but I am afraid — Oh, Madam, indeed, indeed, I am quite sure you cannot be my mother!"

"Why not, thou unnatural girl?" cried she.

"Because, Madam," answered I, "my mother was of a thin habit; as her portrait proves."

"And so was I once," said she. "This deplorable plumpness is owing to want of exercise. But I thank the Gods I am as pale as ever!"

"Heavens! no," cried I. "Your face, pardon me, is a rich scarlet."

"And is this our tender meeting?" cried she. "To disown me, to throw my fat in my teeth, to violate the lilies of my skin, with a dash of scarlet. Hey diddle diddle, the cat and the fiddle! Tell me, girl, will you embrace me, or will you not?"

"Indeed, Madam," answered I, "I will presently."

"Presently!"

"Yes, depend upon it I will. Only let me get over the first shock."

"Shock!"

Dreading her violence, and feeling myself bound to do the duties of a daughter, I kneeled at her feet, and said:

"Ever respected, ever venerable author of my being, I beg thy maternal blessing!"

My mother raised me from the ground, and hugged me to her heart, with such cruel vigour, that, almost crushed, I cried out stoutly, and struggled for release.

"And now," said she, relaxing her grasp, "let me tell you of my sufferings. Ten long years, I have eaten nothing but bread. Oh, ye favourite pullets, oh, ye inimitable tit-bits, shall I never, never taste you more? It was but last night, that maddened by hunger, methought I beheld the Genius of dinner in my dreams. His mantle was laced with silver eels, and his locks were dropping with soups. He had a crown of golden fishes upon his head, and pheasants' wings at his shoulders. A flight of little tartlets fluttered about him, and the sky rained down comfits. As I gazed on him, he vanished in a sigh, that was impregnated with the fumes of brandy. Hey diddle diddle, the cat and the fiddle."

I stood shuddering, and hating her more and more every moment.

"Pretty companion of my confinement!" cried she, apostrophizing an enormous toad which she pulled out of her bosom; "dear, spotted fondling, thou, next to my Cherubina, art worthy of my love. Embrace each other, my friends." And she put the hideous pet into my hand. I screamed and dropped it.

"Oh!" cried I, in a passion of despair, "what madness possessed me to undertake this execrable enterprize!" and I began beating with my hand against the door.

"Do you want to leave your poor mother?" said she, in a whimpering tone.

"Oh! I am so frightened!" cried I.

"You will spend the night here, however," said she; "and your whole life too; for the ruffian who brought you hither was employed by Lady Gwyn to entrap you."

When I heard this terrible sentence, my blood ran cold, and I began crying bitterly.

"Come, my love!" said my mother, "and let me clasp thee to my heart once more!"

"For goodness sake!" cried I, "spare me!"

"What!" exclaimed she, "do you spurn my proffered embrace again?"

"Dear, no, Madam," answered I. "But — but indeed now, you squeeze one so!"

My mother made a huge stride towards me; then stood groaning and rolling her eyes.

"Help!" cried I, half frantic; "help! help!"

I was stopped by a suppressed titter of infernal laughter, as if from many demons; and on looking towards the black curtain, whence the sound came, I saw it agitated; while about twenty terrific faces appeared peeping through slits in it, and making grins of a most diabolical nature. I hid my face with my hands.

" 'Tis the banditti!" cried my mother.

As she spoke, the door opened, a bandage was flung over my eyes, and I was borne away half senseless, in some one's arms; till at length, I found myself alone in my own chamber.

Such was the detestable adventure of to-night. Oh, Biddy, that I should live to meet this mother of mine! How different from the mothers that other heroines rummage out in northern turrets and ruined chapels! I am out of all patience. Liberate her I must, of course, and make a suitable provision for her too, when I get my property; but positively, never will I sleep under the same roof with — (ye powers of filial love forgive me!) such a living mountain of human horror.

Adieu.

LETTER XXVI.

The morning of the ball, I woke free from all remains of my late indisposition, except that captivating paleness, which adds interest without diminishing beauty.

I rose with the sun, and taking a Chinese vase in my hand, tripped into the parterre, to collect the dew that glistened on the blossoms. I filled the piece of painted earth with the nectar of the sky, and returned.

During the day, I took nothing but honey, milk, and dried conserves; a repast the most likely to promote that ethereal character which I purposed adopting at night.

Towards evening, I laved my limbs in a bath; and just as the sun had waved his last crimson banner over the horizon, I began my toilette.

So variable is fashion, that I determined not to follow its laws; since these might be completely exploded in a month; and must become quite antiquated long before my life is written. For instance, do we not already abhor Evelina's and Harriet Byron's powdered, pomatumed, and frizzled hair? It was, therefore, my plan to dress by classical models, and to copy the immortal toilette of Greece.

Having first disrobed myself from head to foot, I took an entire piece of the finest cambric, and twice entwined it around my shoulders and bosom, and twice enveloped my limbs in its folds; till, while it delineated the outline of my shape, it veiled the tincture of my skin. I then flung over it a drapery of embroidered gauze, whose unimplicated simplicity gave to my perfect figure the spirit of an antique statue. An apparent tissue of woven air, it fell like a vapour round me. A zone and a clasp prettily imprisoned my waist; and my graceful arms, undegraded by gloves, were bare to the shoulder. Half my hair felt the bondage of a bodkin, and half floated over my neck in native ringlets. As I could not well wear my leg naked, I hid it under a texture of knitted silk; and lastly, I laced the picturesque sandal on my little foot; which resembled that of a youthful Thetis, or of a fugitive Atalanta.

I then bathed my face with the dew of the morning, refreshed my tresses with the balmy waters of the distilled rose, and sprinkled my drapery with liquid lavender; so that I really moved in an ambient atmosphere of odours.

Behold me now, dressed to a charm, to a criticism. Here was no sloping, or goring, or seaming, or frilling, or flouncing. Manufactured mechanism of millinery! No tedious papillotes, or un-poetical pins were here. A clasp, a zone, and a bodkin, accomplished all.

As I surveyed my form in the mirror, I was enraptured at its Sylphic delicacy. You would imagine that a sigh could dissipate the drapery; and its aerial effect was as if a fairy were to lift the filmy gossamer on her spear, and lightly fling it over a rose-bud.

I now sat down and read Ossian, to store my mind with ideas for conversation. I likewise turned over other books; since, having never mixed among fashionable circles, I could not talk that nothingness, which is every thing in high life. Nor, indeed, if I could, would I; because, as a heroine, it was my part to mould my sentences for immortality.

About appearing in a world, of whose laws and customs I was ignorant, I resolved to adopt such manners as should not be dependent upon place, time, or fashion. In short, to copy primeval, generalized, unsophisticated nature, and Grecian statues.

As I had formed myself on these models, long before I knew the world, my graces were all original, and fit for the pencil; so that if I had not the temporary mannerisms of a marchioness, I had, at least, the immortal movements of a seraph. Words are local, and become obsolete, but the language of gesture is universal and eternal.

As for smiles, I felt myself a perfect adept in all that were ever ascribed to heroines; — the fatal smile, the smile such as precedes the dissolution of sainted goodness, the fragment of a broken smile, and the sly smile that creates the little dimple on the left side of the little mouth.

At length the most interesting moment of my life arrived; the moment when I was to burst, like a new planet, on the fashionable hemisphere. All the company had assembled. I descended the stairs, and pausing at the door, tried to tranquillize my fluttered spirits. I then assumed an air-lifted figure, barely touching the ground, and glided into the room.

The company were walking in groups, or sitting.

"That is she; — there she is; — look, look!" was whispered on all sides. Every eye turned towards me, while I felt at once elevated and opprest.

Lady Gwyn advanced, took my hand, and led me to a sofa. A semicircle of astonished admirers, head over head, ranged itself in my front, and a cordial smile of approbation illuminated every countenance. There I sat, in all the diffidence of a simple and inexperienced recluse; while, with an expression of sweet wildness, and retiring consciousness, was observable a certain susceptibility too exquisite to admit of lasting peace.

At last a spruce and puny fop stepped from amidst the group, and seated himself beside me.

"This was a charming day, Ma'am," said he, as he admired the accurate turn of his ankle.

"Yes," answered I, "so blithe was the morn, when I strayed into the garden, that methought the twins of Latona had met to propitiate their rites. Blushes, like their own roses, coloured the vapours; and rays, pure as their thoughts, gilded the foliage."

The company murmured applause.

" 'Tis a pity that this evening was wet," said he; "for were it fine, what a beautiful description of it would you not have given us."

"Ah, my good friend," cried I, wreathing my favourite smile; and laying the rosy tip of my finger on his arm; "such, such is man. His morning rises in sunshine, and his evening sets in rain."

While the company were again expressing their approbation, I overheard one of them whisper to the fop: —

"Come, play the girl off, and let her have your best nonsense."

The fop winked at him, and again turned towards me; while I sat shocked and astonished, but collecting all my powers.

"See," said he, "how you have fascinated every eye. Actually you are the queen of the bees, with all your swarm about you."

"And with my drone too," said I, bowing slightly.

"Happy in being a drone," said he, "so he but sips of your honey."

"Rather say," cried I, "that he deserves my sting."

398

"Ah," said he, laying his hand on his heart; "your eyes have already fixed a sting here."

"Then your tongue," returned I, "is more innocent than my eyes; for though it has the venom of a sting, it wants the point."

The company laughed, and he coloured.

"Do I tease you?" said he, trying to rally. "How cruel! Actually I am so abashed, as you may perceive, that my modesty flies into my face."

"Then," said I, "your modesty must be very hard run for a refuge."

Here the room echoed with acclamations.

"I am not at a loss about an answer," said he, looking round him, and forcing a smile. "I am not indeed."

"Then pray let me have it," said I, "for folly never becomes truly ludicrous till it tries to be severe."

"Brava! Brava!" cried an hundred voices at once: away the little drone flew from my hive, and I tossed back my ringlets with an infantine shake of the head.

The best of it is, that every word he said will one day appear in print. Men who converse with a heroine should talk for the press, or they will make but a silly figure in her memoirs.

"I admire your spirit, my dear," said Lady Gwyn, sitting down beside me. "That puppy deserves every severity. Think of his sitting in his dressing-gown, a full hour after he has shaved, that the blood may subside from his face. He protests his surprise how men can find pleasure in running after a nasty fox; cuts out half his own coat at his tailor's; has a smile, and a 'pretty!' for every thing; sits silent till one of his four topics is introduced, and then lisping a descant on the last opera, the last boxing-match, the last race, or the last sonnet, he drains his last idea, and has nothing left for the remainder of the night, but a 'bless me,' and a bow. Such insects should come abroad only at butterfly-season; and even then, in a four-wheeled band-box, while monkeys strew the way with mignionette. No, I can never forgive his having gone to Lady Bontein's masquerade, though he had a card from me, and though he knew that she gave it on the same evening for the purpose of thinning my party."

"And pray," said I, "who is Lady Bontein?"

"That tall personage yonder," answered her Ladyship; "with a gentlemanly face, and one shoulder of the Gothic order. She has now been forty years endeavouring to look handsome, and she still trusts, that by diligent perseverance she will succeed. See how she freshens her smiles, and labours to look at ease; though she has all the awkwardness of a milkmaid, without the simplicity. She pored over Latin, till she made her mind as dead as the language itself. Then she writes well-bred sonnets about a tear, or a primrose, or a daisy; but nothing larger than a lark; and talks botany with the men, as she thinks science an excuse for indecency. Nay, she affects the bible too; but they say she once threw it at her footman's head, without any affectation at all. However, my party of to-night will distract her dearly; for I shall introduce a little *Scena*, classical, appropriate, and almost unique, which she can never outdo. The plan of it is a triumphal procession, and the object of it is to grace your entrance into life, by conferring a peculiar mark of distinction on you."

"On me!" cried I. "What mark? I deserve no mark, I am sure."

"Indeed you do," said she. "All the world acknowledges you the first heroine in it; and therefore, I mean to celebrate your merits, by crowning you, just as Corinne was crowned in the capitol."

"Dear Lady Gwyn," cried I, panting with delight; "sure you are not — Ah, are you serious?"

"Most serious, my love," answered she, "and the ceremony will soon commence. You may perceive that the young men and girls have left the room. It is to prepare for the procession; and now excuse me, as I must assist them."

During half an hour, I remained in an agony of anxious expectation.

At last, I heard a confused murmur about the door, and a gentleman ran forward, to clear a passage. A lane was soon formed of the guests; and fancy my feelings, when I beheld the promised procession entering.

First appeared several little children, who came tripping towards me; some with baskets of flowers, and others with vases of odorous waters, or censers of fragrant fire. After them advanced a tall youth of noble port, and conspicuous in a scarlet robe, that trailed behind him with graceful dignity. On his head was a plat of palm, his left hand held a long wand, and his right the destined crown of laurel and myrtle. Behind him came maidens, two by two, and hand in hand. They had each a drapery of white muslin flung negligently round them, and knotted just under the shoulder: while their luxuriant hair shaded their bosoms. The youths came next, habited in flowing vestments of white linen.

The leader approached, and making profound obeisance, took my hand. I rose, bowed, and we proceeded with a measured step out of the room; while the children ran before us, tossing their little censers, scattering pansies, and sprinkling liquid sweets. The nymphs and youths followed in couples, and the company closed the procession. We crossed the hall, ascended the staircase, and passed along the corridor, till we reached the ball-room. The folding doors then flew open, as if with wings; and a scene presented itself, which almost baffles description.

It was an oval apartment, walled all round with a luxuriant texture of interwoven foliage. Branches of the broad chesnut and berried arbutus were relieved by flowering lauristinas, and acacias; while here and there, within the branches, clusters of lamps intermixed their coloured rays, and poured a river of light upon the leaves. The floor was chalked into circular compartments, and each depicted some scene of romance. There I saw Mortimer and his Amanda, Delville and his Cecilia, Valancourt and his Emily. The ceiling was of moss, illuminated with circles of lamps; and from the centre of each circle, a basket was seen peeping, and half inverted, as if about to shower its chaplets and ripe fruitage upon our heads.

At the upper end, I beheld a large arbour, elevated on a sloping bank of turf. Its outside was intertwined with jessamine, honeysuckle, and eglantine; tufted with clumps of sunflowers, lilies, and hollyhocks, and hung with clusters of grapes, and trails of intricate ivy; while all its interior was so studded with innumerable lamp, that it formed one amazing arch of variegated fire. The seat was framed of transparent spars and crystals; and the footstool was a heap of roses. Just from under this footstool, and through the turf, came gushing a little rill, that first tumbled its waters down some jutting stones, then separated to the right and left, and ran along a channel, embroidered with flowery banks; till it was lost, at either side, amidst overshadowing branches.

The moment I set foot in the room, a stream of invisible music, as if from above, and softened by distance, came swelling on my enraptured ear. Thrice we circled this enchanted chamber, and trod to the solemn measure. I was amazed, entranced; I felt elevated to the empyrean. I moved with the grandeur of a goddess, and the grace of a vision.

At length my conductor led me across the rivulet, into the arbour. I sat down, and he stood beside me. The children lay in groups upon the grass, the youths and virgins ranged themselves along the opposite bank of the streamlet, and the company stood behind them.

The master of this august ceremony now waved his wand: the music ceased, all was silent, and he thus began.

"My countrymen and countrywomen.

"Behold our Cherubina; behold the most celebrated woman of our island. Need I recount her accomplishments? Her impassioned sensibility, her exquisite art in depicting the delicate and affecting relations between the beauties of nature, and the deep emotions of the soul? Need I dwell on those elegant adventures, those sorrows, and those horrors, which she has experienced; I might almost say, sought ? Oh! no. The globe already resounds with them, and their fame will descend to the most remote posterity.

"Who can question her eloquence? the pensiveness of her epithets, and the querulous sweetness of her style? Are not her ancestors illustrious? Are not her manners fascinating? Alas! to this question, some of our hearts beat audible response. Her's is the head of a Sappho, deficient alone in the voluptuous languor, which should characterize the countenance of that enamoured Lesbian.

"To CROWN her, therefore, as the patroness of arts, the paragon of charms, and the first of heroines, is to gratify our feelings, more than her own: by enabling us to confer immortal honours on loveliness and on virtue."

He ceased amidst peals of applause. I rose; — and in an instant, it was the stillness of death. Then with a timorous, yet ardent air, I thus addressed the assembly.

"My countrymen, my countrywomen!

"How I happen to deserve the beautiful eulogium just pronounced, I am sure I cannot conceive. Till this flattering moment, I never knew that the globe resounds with my praises, that my style is sweet, and my head a Sappho's. But unconsciousness of merit was ever the characteristic of a heroine,

"The gratitude which my words cannot express, my deeds shall prove. Depend upon it, I will persevere in the heroic career I have begun; I am fond of it almost to a folly; and I now pledge myself, that neither rank nor riches (which, from my vocation, I am peculiar liable to), shall ever make me shun refined Adversity. For, from her,

I have acquired whatever little sympathies and sensibilities I may possess; and surely, since adversity thus encreases virtue, it must be a virtue to seek adversity.

"England, my friends, is now the depository of all the virtue that survives. She is the ark that floats upon the waters of the deluge. But what preserves her virtuous? Her women. And whence arises their purity? From education.

"To you, then, my fair auditory, I would enjoin a diligent cultivation of learning. But oh! beware what books you peruse; for, trust me, some are as injurious as others are salutary. I cannot point out to you the mischievous class, because I have never read them; but indubitably, the most useful are novels and romances. Such as I am, these, these alone have made me. These, by depicting the heroines who were sublimated almost above terrestriality, teach the less gifted portion of womankind to reach what is uncommon, in striving at what is unattainable; to despise the follies and idlenesses of the mere worker of samplers, and to entertain a taste for that sensibility, whose tear is the melting of a pearl, whose blush is the sunshine of the cheek, and whose sigh is more costly than the breeze, which comes odoured with oriental frankincense."

I spoke, and a thousand thunders of acclamation shook the arbour.

The priest of the ceremony now raises the crown on high, then lowers it by slow degrees, and holds it suspended over my head. Letting down my tresses, and folding my hands across my bosom, I throw myself upon my knees, and incline forward to receive it.

I AM CROWNED.

At the same moment, shouts, and drums, and trumpets, burst upon my bewildered ear, in a storm of harmony. The youths and maidens make obeisance; I rise, press my hand to my heart, and bow deeply. Tears start into my eyes. I feel far above mortality.

A harp was now brought to the bower; and they requested that I would sing and play an improvisatore, like Corinne. What should I do? for I knew nothing of the harp, but a few chords! In this difficulty, I recollected a heroine, who lived in an old castle, with only old steward, his old wife, and an old lute; and who, notwithstanding, as soon as she stepped into society, played and sang, like, angels, by intuition.

I therefore felt reassured, and sat to the harp. I struck a few low Lydian notes, and cast a timid glance around me. For the first minute, my voice was not louder than a sigh; and my accompaniment was a harmonic chord, swept at intervals. The words came from the moment.

"Where is my blue-eyed chief? said the white-bosomed daughter of Erin, as the wave kissed her foot; and wherefore went he to the fight of heroes? She saw a dim figure rise before her, like a mist from the valley. Pale grew her cheek, as the blighted leaf in autumn. Your lover, it shrilly shrieked, sleeps among the dead, like a broken thistle amidst dandelions; but his spirit, like the thistly down, has ascended into the skies. The maiden heard; she ran, she flew, she sprang from a rock. The waves closed over her. Peace to the daughter of Erin!"

As I sang, "she ran, she flew," my winged fingers fluttered along the strings, light as a swallow along a little lake, when he touches it with the utmost feather of his pinion. But while I sang, "peace to the daughter of Erin!" my voice, as it died over the faint vibration of the chords, had all the heart-breaking softness of an Eolian lyre; so woeful was it, so wistful, so wildered. "Viva! viva!" resounded through the room. At the last cadence, I dropped one arm at my side, and hanging the other on the harp, leaned my languishing head upon it.

A sudden disturbance aroused me from my trance. I raised my head, and beheld — what? — Can you imagine what? No, my friend, not to the day of judgment. I saw, in short, my great mother come striding towards me, with outspread arms, and calling, "My daughter, my daughter!" in a voice that might waken the dead.

My heart died within me: down I darted from the arbour, and ran for shelter behind Lady Gwyn.

"Give me back my daughter!" vociferated the dreadful woman, advancing close to her ladyship.

"Oh! do no such thing!" whispered I, pulling her Ladyship by the sleeve. "Take half --- all my property; but don't be the death of me!"

"What are you muttering there, Miss?" cried my mother, espying me.

"Indeed, Ma'am," stammered I, "I am --- I am taking your part."

"Is it by grinning at me over that wretch's shoulder?" cried she.

"Grinning at you, Ma'am?" said I. "I never grinned at any lady since I was born, much less at my respected—"

"Respected what?"

"Mother, respected mother."

"Who presumed to liberate this woman?" cried Lady Gwyn.

"The Condottieri," said my mother, "headed by the great Damno Sulphureo Volcanoni."

"Then return to your prison, this moment," cried Lady Gwyn.

My mother fell on her knees, and began blubbering; while the guests got round and interceded for her. I too thought it my duty to say something (my mother all the time sobbing horribly); till, at length, Lady Gwyn consented — for my sake she said, — that the wretch should remain in the room one hour.

My mother then begged a morsel of meat, as she declared she had not eaten any these ten years. Immediately, a small table, furnished with a cold turkey and a decanter of wine, was laid in the bower. The moment she perceived it, she ran, sat down, and began devouring with such avidity, that I was thunderstruck. One wing soon went; the second shared the fate of its companion, and now she set about an inordinate slice of the breast.

"What a charming appetite your dear mother has got!" said several of the company to me. I confessed it, but assured them that hunger did not run in our family. Her appetite at last satiated, she next assailed the wine. Glass after glass disappeared with inconceivable rapidity, and every glass went to my heart. "She will be quite intoxicated!" thought I; while my fears for the hereditary honour of our house overcoming my personal terrors, I had the resolution to steal across, and whisper:

"Mother, if you have any regard for your daughter, and respect for your ancestors, drink no more."

"No more than this decanter lovee!" cried she, lifting it to her lips.

At that moment the violins quavered their invitation.

"Hey diddle, diddle, the cat and the fiddle!" said she, frightfully frisking down from the bower, "who is for a dance?"

"I am," answered my friend, the little fop, advancing and taking her hand.

"Then," said she, "we will waltz, if you please."

Santa Maria! — Waltz !

A circle was cleared, and they began whirling each other round at a fearful rate, — or rather she him; for he was like a plaything in her hands; and had he let go his grasp, up he would certainly have pitched among the branches, and have stuck there, like King Charles in the oak.

405

At last, while I was standing, a statue of shame, and wondering how any human being could act so ridiculous a part, this miserable woman, overcome with wine and waltzing, fell flat upon the floor; and was carried from the room between four grinning footmen.

I could contain no longer: the character of my family demanded a prompt explanation, and with tearful eyes, I desired to be heard. Silence was obtained.

"I beseech and implore of this assembly," said I, "to credit me, while I protest, that I had neither act, nor part, in the conduct of that unfortunate person, who has thus disgraced herself. Nay, I never even saw her, till I came to this house; and that I may never see her again, I pray heaven. I hate her, I dread her; and I now declare most unequivocally, that I do not believe the woman my mother at all. She bears no resemblance to the portrait above stairs; and as she is stark mad, her imagining herself to be my mother, might very well happen; for they say that mad persons are apt to fancy themselves great people. No, my malignant star ordained us to meet, that she might place me in awkward situations by her vulgarity; just as Mrs. Garnet, the supposed mother of the Beggar Girl, used to place her. I am certain this is the case; nothing can alter my opinion; and therefore, I thus publicly renounce her, disown her, and wash my hands of her, now, now, and for ever, and for ever!"

The company coincided in my sentiments, and applauded my determination.

Dancing was then proposed: the men sauntered about the room for partners; the mothers walked their daughters up and down, to shew their paces; and their daughters turned away their heads when they saw their favourites approaching to ask them. Ugliness and diamonds occupied the top of the set; the beauties stood in the centre, and the motley couples at the bottom; — patriarchs with misses of fifteen; and striplings, who were glad to be thought men, with antiques, who were sorry to be called maids. Other unfortunates, drest to a pin, yet noticed by nobody, sat protruding the supercilious lip at a distance.

And now the merry maze commenced. But what mutilated steps, what grotesque graces! One girl sprang and sprawled, the terror of every ankle; and with a clear idea of infinite space, shewed that she had no notion of time. Another, not deigning to dance, only moved; while her poor partner was seen helping her in, like a tired jade to the distance-post. This exchanged elegance for a flic flac; that swam down the set; a third cut her way through it; and a fourth, who, by her longevity could not be dancing for a husband, appeared, by her earnestness, to be dancing for her life.

All this delighted me highly, because it would shew my graces to the greater advantage. My partner was the gentleman who had crowned me; and now, when my turn came, a general whisper among the spectators, and their sudden hurry towards me, proved that much was expected from my performance. I would not disappoint them for worlds; besides, it was incumbent on me to stamp a marked dissimilarity between my supposed mother, and myself, in every thing; and to call forth admiration, as much as she had excited contempt.

And now, with my right foot behind, and the point of it but just touching the ground, I leaned forward on my left, and stood as if in act to ascend from this vale of tears into regions of eternal beatitude.

The next moment the music gave the signal, and I began. Despising the figure of the common dance, I meandered through all the intricacies of the dance of Ariadne; imitating in my circular and oblique motions the harmonious movements of the spheres; and resembling in my light and playful form, the Horae of Bathycles. Sometimes with a rapid flight, and glowing smile, I darted, like a herald Iris, through the mazes of the set; sometimes assuming the dignity of a young Diana, I floated in a swimming languishment; and sometimes, like a pastoral nymph of Languedoc, capriciously did I bend my head on one side, and dance up insidious. What a Hebe!

I happened not to see my partner from the time I began till I had ended; but when I flew, like a lapwing, to my seat, he followed, and requested that I would accept the assurances of his high admiration. I prettily reproved his flattery, with arch anger, and a pouting playfulness.

Soon afterwards, waltzing was introduced.

"You have already imitated Ida's dancing," said he. "Will you now imitate Charlotte's, and allow me, like Werter, to hold in my arms the most lovely of women; to fly with her, like the wind, and lose sight of every other object?"

I consented; he led me forth, and clasping my waist, began the circuitous exercise of waltzing. Round and round we flew, and swifter and swifter; till my head grew quite giddy. Lamps, trees, dresses, faces, all appeared to be shattered and huddled together, and sent whisking round the room in a vortex.

But, oh, my friend, how shall I find language to describe the fatal termination of an evening so propitious at the commencement? I blush as I write, till the reflected crimson dyes my paper. For in the midst of my rotatory motion, while heaven seemed earth, and earth seemed heaven; the zone, upon which all my attire depended, and by which it was all confined, on a sudden burst asunder, and in the next whirl, more than half my dress dropped at my feet! Another revolution, and I had acted Diana to fifty Acteons; but I shrieked, and extricating myself from my partner, sank upon the floor, amidst the wreck of my drapery. The ladies ran, ranged themselves round me, and cast a mantle over my half revealed charms. I felt too miserable, and indeed too giddy to rise; so they lifted me between them, and bore me, in slow procession, from the room. It was the funeral of Modesty; but the pall was supported by tittering Malice.

I hurried into bed, and cried myself asleep.

I cannot think, much less write of this disaster, with common fortitude. I wonder whether Musidora could be considered a palliative parallel? If not, and that my biographer records it, I am undone.

Adieu.

LETTER XXVII

Yesterday Lady Gwyn took me, at my particular request, to visit Monkton Castle, an old ruin, within a few miles of us. It forms part of that property which she now holds; and consequently must devolve to me, as soon as I substantiate my title and my birth.

The gateway was blockaded with stones, so that I could not enter the building; but outside, it looked admirably blank and desolate. I mean, at some future period, to furnish it like Udolpho, and other castles of romance, and to reside there during the howling months.

After dinner her Ladyship left me alone on the sofa, and went to superintend the unpacking of some beautiful china. Evening had flung her grey mantle over the flowerets; a delicious indolence thrilled through my limbs, and I felt all that languor and vacuity, which the want of incident must ever create in the feeling mind.

"Were even some youth on a visit here," thought I, "who would conceive an unhappy passion for me; — had her Ladyship but one persecuting son, what scenes might happen! Suppose at this moment, the door were to open, and he to enter, with a quick step, and booted and spurred. He starts on seeing me. Never had I looked so lovely. "Heavens!" murmurs he, " 'tis a divinity!" then recollecting himself, he advances with a respectful bow. "Pardon this intrusion," says he; "but I — really I —." I rise, and colouring violently, mutter, without looking at him: "I wonder where her Ladyship can be?" But as I am about to pass him, he snatches my hand, and leading me back, says: — "Suffer me to detain you a moment. This occasion, long desired, and at last obtained, must not be relinquished. Prevented by the jealous care of a fond mother, from beholding those charms, I have sought and found a thousand opportunities, on the stairs---in the garden---through the shrubbery. Fatal opportunities, which robbed me of my peace for ever! Yes, charming Cherubina, you have undone me. That airy form; those mild, yet animated eyes; those lips, more delicious than the banquet of the gods---" "Really, Signor," says I, in all the pleasing simplicity of maiden embarrassment, "this language is as improper for me to hear as for you to express." "It is improper," cries he, "for it is inadequate." "Yes," says I, "inadequate to the respect I deserve as the guest of your mother." "Ah!" exclaims he, "why should the guest imitate the harshness of the hostess?" "That she may not," says I, "countenance the follies of the son. Signor, I desire you will unhand me." "Never!" cries he; "till you say you pity me. O, my Cherubina; O, my soul's idol!" — and he drops upon his knee, and grasps my hand; when behold, the door opens, and Lady Gwyn appears at it! Astonishment and dismay make statues of the whole party. "Godfrey, Godfrey," says her Ladyship, "is this the conduct that I requested of you? This, to seek clandestine interviews, where I had prohibited even an open acquaintance? And for thee, fair unfortunate," turning towards me, with that mild look, which cuts more than a thousand sarcasms; "for thee, lovely frail one, thou must seek some other asylum." Her sweet eyes swim in tears. I fling myself at her feet. "I am innocent," I cry, "innocent as the little fawn that frisks itself to repose by the bubbling fountain." She smiles incredulous. "Come," says she, taking my hand, "let me lead you to your apartment." "Stay, in mercy stay!" cries Godfrey, rushing between us and the door. She waves him aside. I reach my room. Nothing can console me. I am all despair. The maid taps, with a slip of paper from Godfrey. "Oh, Cherubina," it says, "how my heart is torn for you! As you value your fame, perhaps your life, meet me to-night, at twelve, in the shrubbery." After a long struggle, I resolve to meet him. 'Tis twelve, the winds are abroad, the shower descends. I fling on something, and steal into the shrubbery. I find him there before me. He thanks me ten thousand, thousand times for my kindness, my condescension; and by degrees, leads me towards the avenue, where I see a chaise. I shrink back; he prays, implores; and at length, snatching me in his arms, is about to force me into the vehicle, when on a sudden--- "Hold, villain!" cries a voice. It is the voice of Stuart! I shriek, and drop to the ground. The clashing of swords resounds over my contested body, and I faint. On recovering, I find myself in a small, but decent chamber, with an old woman and a beautiful girl watching beside me. "St. Catherine be praised," exclaims the young peasant, "she comes to herself." "Tell me," I cry, "is he murdered?" "The gentleman is dead, sure enough, miss," says the woman. I laugh frantic, and point my finger. "Ha! look yonder," I cry; "see his mangled corpse, mildly smiling, even in death. See, they fight; he falls.--- Barbarous Godfrey! valiant, generous, unfortunate Stuart! And hark, hear you that? 'Tis the bell tolling, tolling, tolling!" During six weeks I languish under this dreadful brain-fever. Slowly I recover. A low melancholy preys upon me, and I am in the last stage of a consumption. But though I lose my bloom, illness touches my features with something more than human. One evening, I had gotten my chair on the green before the door, and was watching the sun as he set in a blaze of gold. "And oh!" exclaimed I, "soon must I set like thee, fair luminary;" --- when I am interrupted by a stifled sigh, just behind me. I turn. Heaven and earth! who should be leaning over me, with looks of unutterable love, but---Stuart! In an instant, I see him, I shriek, I run, I leap into his arms.—

"Unfortunate leap; for it wakened me from a delicious reverie, and I found myself in the arms,---not of Stuart,---but of the old butler! Down we came together, and smashed to atoms a vase of superb china, which he was just bringing into the room.

"What will my lady say?" cried he, rising and collecting the fragments.

"She will smile ineffably," answered I, "and make a moral reflection upon the instability of sublunary things."

He shook his head, and went on with his work of affliction; while I hastened to the glass, where I found my face flushed from my reverie, my hair dishevelled, and my long eyelashes wetted with tears. I perceived too that my dress had suffered a terrible rent by my fall.

Hardly was I recomposed, when her Ladyship returned, and called for tea.

"How did you tear your robe, my love?" said she.

"By a fall that I got just now;" replied I. "Sure never was such an unfortunate fall!"

"Nay, child," said she, rallying me, "though a martyr to the tender sensibilities, you must not become a victim to torn muslin."

"I am extremely distressed, however," said I.

"But why so?" cried she. "It was an accident, and all of us are awkward at times. Life has too many serious miseries to admit of vexation about trifles."

"There now!" cried I, with delight. "I declare I told the butler, when I broke the china vase, that you would make a moral reflection."

"Broke the--Oh! mercy, did you break my beautiful china vase?"

"I did, indeed," answered I, in a tone of the most assuasive sweetness.

" You did?" exclaimed she, with a voice that stunned me. "How dared you go near it? How dared you even look at it? You, who are not fit company for crockery, much less china; — a crazed creature, that I brought into my house to divert my guests. You a title? You a beauty?" "Pray, Lady Gwyn," said I, "be calm under this calamity. Trust me, life has too many serious miseries to admit of vexation about trifles."

Her Ladyship rose, with her cheeks inflamed, and her eyes glittering.

I ran terrified out of the room; then up stairs, and into the nearest bed-chamber. It was her Ladyship's; and this circumstance struck me as most providential; since, in her present mood, she would probably compel me to quit the house; so that I had now the only opportunity possible, of ransacking her caskets and cabinets, for memorials of my birth.

I therefore began the search; but was interrupted by hearing a small voice cry, "get out!"

Much amazed, I looked round, and perceived her Ladyship's favourite parrot.

"Get out!" said the parrot again.

"Yes," I will let thee out, cost what it will," cried I.

So with much sensibility, and indeed, very little spleen, I took the bird from its cage, and liberated it through the window.

At last, after having examined several drawers, I found a casket; opened it, and beheld within, a miniature set round with inestimable diamonds, and bearing a perfect resemblance to the portrait in the gallery, — face, attitude, attire, every thing!

"Relic of my much injured house!" exclaimed I. "Image of my sainted mother, never will I part with thee!"

"What are you doing in my room?" cried Lady Gwyn, as she burst into it. "How is this? All my dresses about the floor! my drawers, my casket open! — And, as I live, here is the miniature gone! Why, you graceless little thing, are you robbing me?"

"Madam," answered I, "that miniature belongs to my family; I have recovered it at last; and let me see who will take it from me."

"You are more knave than fool," said her Ladyship: "give it back this instant, or, on my honour, I will expose you before the servants."

"You dare not," cried I; "for you are ruined, should this swindling affair of the picture transpire. I do not mean to say I would hang your Ladyship;---far from it;---but then you know, I might blast your character beyond all recovery. O Lady Gwyn, where is your hereditary honour? where is your feeling? where is your dignity?"

"Where is my parrot?" shrieked her Ladyship.

"Inhaling life, and fragrance, and freedom amidst the clouds!" exclaimed I. "For I have sent it flying through the window."

Her Ladyship ran towards me, but I passed her, and made the best of my way down stairs; while she followed, calling, stop thief! Too well I knew and rued the dire expression; nor stopped an instant, but hurried out of the house — through the lawn — down the avenue— into a field; — the servants in hot pursuit. Not a moment was to be lost: a drowning man, you know, will grasp at straws, so the poor Cherubina crept for refuge under some hay.

But whether they found me there, or how long I remained there, or what has become of me since, or what is likely to become of me hereafter, you shall learn in my next.

Adieu.

LETTER XXVIII.

I REMAINED my disagreeable situation till night closed around, and the pursuit appeared over. I then rose, and walked through the fields, without any settled intention. Terror was now succeeded by bitter indignation at the conduct of Lady Gwyn, who had dared to drive me from my hereditary house, and vilify me as a common thief. Insupportable insult! Unparalleled degradation! Was there no revenge? no remedy?

Like a rapid ray from heaven, a thought at once simple and magnificent, shot through my brain, and made every nerve trepidate with transport. When I name Monkton Castle, need I tell you the rest? Need I tell you, I determined to seize on that antique abode of my ancestors, to fortify it against assaults, to procure domestics and suitable furniture for it, and to reside there, the present rival, and the future successor of the vile Lady Gwyn? Let her dispossess me if she dare, or if she can; particularly since possession is—I do not know how many—but I am told, a great many, points of the law in one's favour.

As for fitting up the castle, that will be quite a mere easy matter; because the tradespeople of London give unlimited credit to a personage of rank like me; and therefore I need only bid some agent there, bespeak furniture in my name.

And now, a light heart making a light foot, I took my airy way towards Monkton Castle, for the purpose of procuring an asylum in some cottage near it, till I could accomplish my plan.

It was starlight, and I had walked almost three miles, when a little girl overtook me, and began asking alms. Amidst her supplications, we came to the hut where she lived; and I followed her into it, with the hope of getting a bed there.

In this smoked and cobwebbed hovel, I found a wrinkled Beldame, and two smutty urchins, holding hands over a few faded

413

embers. I begged permission to rest myself for a short time: the woman, after eyeing me keenly, consented, and I sat down. I then entered into conversation, represented myself as a wandering stranger in distress, and inquired whether I could procure a lodging about the neighbourhood. The woman assured me that I could not; and on perceiving me much disconcerted at the disappointment, coarsely, but cordially, offered me accommodation in her hut. I had no possible alternative; so the fire was replenished, some brown bread and sour milk (the last of their store), produced; and while we sat round this unsavoury supper, I requested of the poor woman to relate her little history.

She told me, with many tears and episodes, that her daughter and son-in-law, who had hitherto supported her, died of a fever, about a month ago, and left these children behind, without any means of subsistence, except what they procured from the charitable.

Indeed, their appearances corroborated this account; for Famine had set her meagre finger on their faces. I wished to pity them, but their whining, their dirtiness, and their vulgarity, disgusted more than interested me. I nauseated the brats, and abhorred the haggard hostess. How it happens, I know not, but the misery that looks alluring on paper, is almost always repulsive in real life. I turn with distaste from a ragged beggar, or a distrest tradesman; while the recorded sorrows of a Belfield or a Rusbbrook, draw tears of pity from me as I read.

At length we began to think of rest. The children gave me their pallet: I threw myself upon it without undressing, and they nestled among some musty straw.

In the morning we presented a most dismal group. Not a morsel was for breakfast, and no means of obtaining any. The grey cripple, who had expected some assistance from me, sat grunting in a corner; the children whimpered and shivered; and I began considering what mode of immediate subsistence I ought to adopt. At last I hit upon a most pleasing and simple plan. As some days must elapse between my writing to Jerry Sullivan and his coming down, (for I shall have him here if possible), I mean to remain at the cottage, till his arrival; and to go forth every day in the character of a beggar-girl. Like another Rosa, I will earn my bread by asking alms. Even the shrivelled palm of age will expand at my supplication, and youths, offering compliments with eleemosynary silver, will call me the lovely vagabond, or the mendicant angel.

Thus my few days of beggary will prove quite delightful; and oh, how sweet, when these are over, to reward and patronize, as Lady of the Castle, those hospitable cottagers, who have pitied and sheltered me as the beggar-girl.

But my first step was a letter to Jerry Sullivan; and fortunately, I found the stump of a pen, some thick ink, and coarse paper, in the cottage, I send you a copy, that you may form some notion of my present projects.

"Honest Jerry,

"Since I saw you last, I have established all my claims, and am now the Lady Cherubina de Willoughby, illustrious mistress of Gwyn Castle, Monkton Castle, and other estates. If you feel grateful for those services, however trivial, which you once received from me, you will, doubtless, be happy at an opportunity of obliging me in return; and, as I mean to make Monkton Castle (which is now uninhabited), my future residence, and to furnish it in the style of those times when it was built, you will bespeak, at the best shops, such articles as I shall enumerate.

"1st. Antique tapestry for one entire wing.

"2nd. Painted glass, enriched with armorial bearings.

"3rd. Pennons and flags, stained with the best old blood; Feudal, if possible.

"4th. Black feathers, and black cloaks for liveries.

"5th. An old lute, or lyre, or harp.

"6th. Black hangings, black curtains, and a black velvet pall.

"7th. A Warder's trumpet.

"8th. A bell for the portal.

"Besides these, I shall want antique pictures, chairs, tables, beds; and, in a word, every possible pin's worth and cast-off of old castles.

"You must also purchase a handsome barouche, and four horses; and by merely mentioning my name (the Lady Cherubina de Willoughby of Monkton Castle), and by shewing this letter, no shopkeeper or mechanic will refuse you credit for any thing. Tell them that I will pass bills, as soon as the several articles arrive.

"I have now to make a proposal, which, I hope and trust, Jerry, will meet your approbation. Your present business does not appear prosperous: all the offices in my castle are still unoccupied, and as I entertain the highest opinion of your discretion and honesty, the

415

situation of Warden (a most ostensible one), is at your service. The salary shall be two hundred per annum. Consider of it.

"You might travel down in the barouche, and bring some of the smaller articles with you. Do not delay beyond three days.

" CHERUBINA DE WILLOUGHBY.
" *Monkton Castle*."

I now began to think that I should also summon, upon this important occasion, the assistance of other friends: and accordingly, wrote a few lines to Higginson.

"Dear Sir,

"Intending to take immediate possession of Monkton Castle, which has become mine by right of lineal descent; and wishing, in imitation of ancient times, for a wild and enthusiastic Minstrel, as part of my household, I acquaint you, that if you think such an office eligible, I shall be happy to bestow it upon you, and to recompense your poetical services with an annual stipend of two hundred pounds.

"Should this proposal prove acceptable, have the goodness to call on my trusty servant, Jerry Sullivan, St. Giles's, and to accompany him down in my barouche.

" CHERUBINA DE WILLOUGHBY.
" *Monkton Castle*."

I then scribbled a billet to Montmorenci; — ah, ask not why, but pity me. Yet mark how my burning pen can write ice.

"My Lord,

"Perfectly well assured that we shall not meet again; but conceiving that you still feel some portion of interest in my welfare, I take the liberty to acquaint you, that my birth and pretensions are already acknowledged by Lady Gwyn, and that I am assembling my friends in Monkton Castle, where I shall reside for the future.

"With sentiments of respect and esteem,
" I have the honour to be,
"My Lord,
"Your Lordship's most obedient,

"And most humble servant,
" CHERUBINA DE WILLOUGHBY.
"*Monkton Castle*."

Now this is precisely the formal sort of letter which a heroine sometimes indites to her lover: he cannot, for the soul of him, tell why; so down he comes, all distracted in a postchaise, and makes such a dishevelled entrance, as melts her heart at the first onset, and the scene ends with his arm about her waist.

Adieu.

LETTER XXIX.

As soon as I had written my letters, I put on a tattered gown, cap, and cloak, belonging to the deceased daughter of my hostess; and then, with the dear portrait in my bosom, I sallied forth, and took the road towards the neighbouring village.

It was Sunday. The nymphs looked trim, and the youths festive; the grandsires sat before their doors, the sun was shining; all things rejoiced but the miserable Cherubina.

I reached the village, and deposited my letters in the post. Then, as the people were just coming out of church, I ran and placed myself beside the sacred gate,—an auspicious station for the commencement of my begging career.

"How are you? How are you? How are you?" was gabbled on all sides.

"One penny,—one penny,—Oh, one penny!" softly faltered I.

It was the cooing of a dove amidst the chattering of magpies.

"What a painted doll sat in the next pew!" said a lady.

"One penny,"

"She thought herself too pretty to pray," said another.

"One penny, for the love of... "

"Perhaps motion does not become her lips," said another.

"One penny for the love of charity!"

But they had escaped into their carriages.

"If innocence in distress can touch your hearts," said I, following two old gentlemen down the road, "pity the destitute orphan, the hungry vagrant, the most injured of her sex. Gentlemen, good gentlemen, kind gentlemen."

"Go to hell," said they.

"There is something for you," cried a horrid voice from behind, while a halfpenny jingled at my foot. I turned to thank my benefactor, and found him a drunken man in the stocks.

Disgusted with my first attempt, I hurried out of the village; and then loitered along, addressing all I met; but all appeared too gay for pity. Hour after hour I wasted in fruitless efforts; till at length day began to close, and fatigue and hunger to weaken my limbs.

In this piteous condition, I determined upon returning home; for night had already blackened the hemisphere, the mountainous clouds hung low and the winds piped the portentous moan of a coming hurricane. By the little light that still remained, I saw a long avenue on my left, which, I thought, might lead to some hospitable house; and I began groping my way through it, as well as the gloom of the trees would permit.

After much labour, and many falls, I arrived at an opening; but by this time, the storm had burst upon my head, with tremendous violence; and I could scarcely keep my feet.

However, I fancied that I perceived a building in front; so bent my steps towards it; and as I drew nearer, found my way sometimes obstructed by heaps of stones, or broken pillars; whence I concluded that I was approaching some prodigious old castle, where I should be certain to find shelter, horror, owls, and one of my near relations. I therefore hastened onward, and soon my extended hands touched the structure. My heart struck a throb of joy, and I began to feel along the wall for some ruined portal or archway.

Hardly had I advanced ten paces, when my groping hands plunged into sudden vacancy. I stopped a moment, then entered through the opening, and to my great comfort, found myself under immediate shelter.

This then, I guessed, was the hall of the castle; and accordingly, I prepared my mind for the most terrible things.

I had not proceeded three yards farther, when I paused in much dismay; as I thought, I heard something stir just behind me. Again all was still, and again I ventured forward. I now fancied that I heard a gentle breathing; and at the same instant, I struck my foot against

418

something, which, with a quick movement, tripped up my heels. Down I came, shrieking and begging for mercy; while a frightful bustle arose all round me, — such passing and repassing, rustling and rushing, that I gave myself over as lost.

"Oh, gentlemen-banditti!" cried I, "spare my life, I beseech of you!"

They did not answer a syllable, but retired to some corner, where they held a horrid silence.

In a few minutes, I heard steps outside; and then two persons entered the building.

"This shelters us well enough," said one of them.

"Curse on the storm," cried the other, "it will hinder any more from coming out to-night. However we have killed four already, and, please goodness, not one will be alive on the estate this day month."

Oh, Biddy, how my soul sickened at the shocking reflection, that four of an estated family were already murdered in cold blood; and that the remainder would share the same fate before a month.

Unable to contain myself, I muttered: — "Mercy upon me!"

"Did you hear that?" whispered one of the men.

"I did," said the other. "Off with us this moment!" and off they ran.

I too determined to quit this nest of horrors, for my very life appeared in danger; so, rising, I began to grope my way towards the door, when I fell over something that lay upon the ground, and as I put out my hand, I touched, (oh, horrible !) a dead, cold, damp human face! Instantly the thought struck me that this was one of the four whom the ruffians had murdered, and I flung myself from it, with a shiver of horror; but in doing so, laid my hand upon another face; while a faint gleam of lightning, which flashed at the moment, shewed me two bodies, ghastly, haggard, naked, and half covered with straw.

I started up, screaming, and made a desperate effort to reach the door; but just as I was darting out of it, I found my shoulder griped with a ferocious grasp.

"I have caught one of them," cried the person. "Fetch the lantern."

"I am innocent of the murder!" cried I. "I swear to you that I am!"

" Who? what murder?" cried he. "Hollo, help! here is murder!"

"Not by me !" cried I. "Not by me! No, no, my hands are unstained with their blood."

And now a lantern being brought, I perceived several servants in liveries, who first examined my features, and then dragged me back into the building. The building! And what was the building, think you? Why nothing more than the shell of an unfinished house, — a mere modern morsel of a tasty temple! And what were the banditti who had knocked me down, think you? Why nothing more than a few harmless sheep, that now lay huddled together in a corner! And what were the two corpses, think you? Why nothing more than two Heathen statues for the temple! — And the ruffians who talked of their having killed, and having to kill, were only poachers, who had killed four hares, and whom the servants were waylaying when they seized me. Here then was the whole mystery developed, and a great deal of good fright gone for nothing.

However, the servants, swearing that I was either concerned with the poachers, or with the murder that I talked of, dragged me down a shrubbery, till we reached a large mansion. We then entered a lighted hall; one of them went to call his master; and after a few minutes, an elderly gentleman, with a troop of young men and women at his heels, came out of a parlour.

"Young woman, what murder is this you were talking of?" said the gentleman to me.

"I will tell you with pleasure," answered I. "You must know that I am a wandering beggar, without home, parents, or friends; and when the storm began, I ran, for shelter, into the young ladies' Temple of Taste, as your servants nicknamed it. So, thinking it a castle, and some sheep which threw me down, banditti, and a couple of statues, corpses; of course I naturally imagined, when two men entered, and began to talk of having killed something, that they meant these very corpses. And so that is the plain and simple narrative of the whole affair."

To my surprize, a general burst of laughter ran round the hall.

"Sheep banditti, and statues corpses! Dear me,— Bless me!" tittered the misses.

"Young woman," said the gentleman, "your incoherent account inclines me to believe you concerned in some atrocious transaction, which I must make my business to discover."

"I am sure," said a young lady, "she carries the gallows in her face."

"Then 'tis so pretty a gallows," said a young gentleman, "that I wish I were hanging upon it."

"Fie, brother," said the young lady, "how can you talk so to a murderess?"

"And how can you talk so," cried I, "before you know that I am a murderess? Is it just, is it generous, is it feminine? Men impelled by love, may deprive our sex of virtue; but we ourselves, actuated by the rancorous passions, rob each other of character."

"Oh! indeed," said the young lady, " 'tis now plain to see what you are. That sentence of morality has settled you completely."

"Then I presume you do not admire morality," said I.

"Not from the lips of a mean creature like you," said she.

"Yet, know, young woman," cried I, "that the current which runs through these veins, is registered in hereditary heraldry."

The company gave a most disgusting laugh.

"It is," cried I, "I tell you it is. I tell you I am of the blood noble."

"Oh blood!" squeaked a young gentleman.

What wonder that I forgot my prudence amidst these indignities? Yes, the proud spirit of my progenitors swelled my heart, all my house stirred within me, and the blood of the De Willoughbys rose into my face, as I drew the picture from my bosom, pointed a quivering finger at it, and exclaimed:

"Behold the portrait of my titled mother!"

"See, see!" cried the girls crowding round. " 'Tis covered all over with diamonds!"

"There!" said I. "There is proof irrefragable for you!"

"Proof enough to hang you?" cried the old gentleman, snatching it out of my hand. "So now, my lady, you must go, this moment, before the magistrate." I began weeping, kneeling, and entreating; till I found that his son, the young man who had paid my face the compliment, was to take charge of my person; so then, speculating upon a speedy deliverance, I submitted without another murmur; and escorted by him and a footman, left the house.

After we had proceeded about half a mile, the young man stopped, and whispered something to the servant, who instantly disappeared.

"Now," said the young man, "whether you are a pilferer of pictures, I know not; but this I know, that you are a pilferer of hearts; and I am determined to keep you in custody, till you restore mine, which you have stolen. To be plain, I intend extricating you

421

from your present emergency, and concealing you in a cottage, till to-morrow, when I will call, and have some further conversation with you."

I replied that I trusted he would not find me deficient in gratitude.

"Thank you;" said he. "And now here is the cottage."

He then tapped at a door: an elderly woman opened it, and on entering, I perceived a girl, with a bold, but handsome face, hastily adjusting her cap.

"Here is a wretched creature," said he, "whom I found starving on the road. Pray give her some refreshment, and a bed for the night."

The women looked at me, and then at each other.

"She shall have no bed in my house," said the elder, "for I warrant this is the hussey who has lately been setting you against Susan, and telling you lies about Tommy Hicks's visiting her."

"Ay, and Bob Saunders," cried the daughter.

"Sweet innocent!" cried the mother.

"And Ebenezer Solomons," cried the daughter.

"Tender lamb!" cried the mother.

"And Patrick O'Brien," cried the daughter.

"Think of that!" cried the mother.

"Yes, think of that!" cried the daughter. "Patrick O'Brien! the broad-shouldered, abominable man! Oh! I will cut my throat — I will — so I will!"

The whole truth now flashed upon me. Here then, if I minded my hits, was another exquisite episode. Yes, I would separate Susan from her seducer, and secure her everlasting gratitude. The reclaimed wanton might yet do wonders for me.

"Alas!" said I, "behold the fatal effects of licentious love. This girl, whom your money, perhaps, allured from the paths of virtue —"

"Oh! no," cried Susan, "it was his honour's handsome face, and his fine words, so bleeding and so sore; and he called me an angel above the heavens!"

"Yes," resumed I, "it is the tenderness of youth, the smile of joy, the blush of innocence, which allure the libertine; and yet these are what he would destroy. It is the heart of sensibility which he would engage, and yet in that heart he would plant every rankling pang, every bitter misery. Detestable passion! which accomplishes the

422

worst of purposes, by touching the best and sweetest affections. She whose mind ascribes to others the motives that actuate itself; she who confides, because she would not herself deceive, she who has a tear for real grief, and who melts at the simulated miseries of her lover, falls a sacrifice to his arts; while the cold vestal who walks through the world, armed with austerity, repulses his approaches with indignation, and calls her prudence virtue."

The young man gazed upon me with surprize, and the mother came closer; but Susan was peeping at her face in the glass.

"Look on that beautiful girl before you," cried I. "Heaven itself is not brighter than her brow; the tints of the morning cannot rival her blushes."

Susan held down her head, but cast a quick glance at the 'squire.

"Such is she now;" continued I, "but too soon we may behold her, pale, shivering, unsteady of step, and hoarse with nocturnal curses, one of those unhappy thousands, who strew our streets with the premature ruins of dilapidated beauty!"

"Yes, look at her!" cried the mother, who, flushing even through her wrinkles, and quivering in every limb, rushed towards her daughter, and snatching off her cap, bared her forehead. "Look at her! she was once my lovely pride, the blessing of my heart; and see what he has now made her; while I, miserable as I am, must assist her guilt, that I may save her from disgrace and ruin!"

"Oh! then," cried I, turning to the 'squire, "while still some portion of her fame remains, fly from her, fly for ever!"

"Upon my soul, I mean to do so," replied he, " so pray make your mind easy."

"And I am convinced, Susan," said I, "that you feel grateful for the pains which I have taken, to withdraw the 'squire from a connection so fatal."

"I am quite sure I do," cried Susan, "and I will pray for your health and happiness while I live. But, since I must lose him, I hope you will persuade him to leave me some money first; not that I ever valued him for his money; but you know, I could not see my mother go without her tea o'nights."

"Amiable creature!" cried I. "Yes I will intercede for you."

"My giving you money," said the 'squire, "will depend upon my finding, when I return to-morrow, that you have treated this girl kindly to-night."

" I will treat her like a sister," said Susan.

The 'squire now declared that he must depart; then taking me aside, "I shall see you early in the morning; whispered he, "and remove you elsewhere. You have talked virtue to a miracle. Continue the system, and these people will fancy you a saint."

I then overheard him enjoin the mother, as she valued his future favour, not to let me quit the Cottage; and with this injunction, he went away.

But as I had not the most remote intention of awaiting his return, I set my wits at work, and soon hit upon a plan to accomplish my escape. I told the woman that my mother, who lived about a mile from the cottage, was almost starving; and that if I could procure a little silver, and a loaf of bread, I would run to her hut with the relief, and come back immediately.

The kind eagerness, the sweet solicitude, which mother and daughter manifested, in loading me with victuals and money, were most gratifying. Suffice it, that they gave me two shillings, some bread, tea, and sugar; and Susan herself offered to carry them; but this favour I declined; and now, with a secret sigh at the probability that I might never see them again, I left their house, and hastened towards the cottage of the poor woman. Having reached it, I made the hungry inhabitants happy once more; while I solaced myself with some tea, and the pleasing reflection, that I had brought comfort to the distrest, and had reclaimed a deluded girl from ruin and infamy.

Adieu.

END OF VOL. II.

THE

HEROINE,

OR

ADVENTURES

OF

CHERUBINA,

BY

EATON STANNARD BARRETT, ESQ,

––––––

"L'Histoire d'une femme est toujours un Roman."

––––––

Second Edition,

WITH CONSIDERABLE ADDITIONS AND ALTERATIONS.

––––––

IN THREE VOLUMES,
VOL. III.

THE HEROINE.

LETTER XXX.

After my last letter, I spent two tedious days in employments which I now blush to relate — no less than doing all the dirty work of the house; sweeping the room, kindling the fire, cooking the victuals, and endeavouring, by dint of comb and soap, to make cherubs of the children. What bewitched me, I cannot conceive. The humanity of other Heroines is ever clean, elegant, and fit for the reader. They give silver and tears in abundance, but never descend to the bodily charity of working, like wire-drawers for withered old women and brats with rosy noses. And yet, as those who sheltered me, were poor and helpless themselves, surely their hospitality to me deserved some recompense. So you must not condemn me totally; for I can swear, that I would rather have relieved them with my purse, and soothed them with my sympathy, than have fried their herrings and washed their faces.

However, during this interval, I mixed the poetess with the house-maid, and composed a tale, which I copy for you.

CAROLINE.

Beneath a thatch, where gadding woodbin flower'd,
About the lattice and the porch embower'd,
An humble widow liv'd, whose grey decline,
Clung on one hope, her lovely Caroline.
Her lovely Caroline, in virtue blest,
Was pure as early snow by feet unprest.
Her tresses unadorn'd a braid controll'd,
Her pastoral russet knew no stain of gold.
In either cheek an eddying dimple play'd,
And blushes flitted with a rosy shade.
Her airy step appear'd to tread the sky,
And joy and frolic sparkled in her eye.
Yet would she weep at sorrows not her own,
And love foredoom'd her heart his panting throne.
For her the rustics strove a homely grace,

427

Clipped their redundant locks, and smooth'd their pace;
Lurk'd near her customed path, in trimmest guise,
And talk'd the untaught praises of her eyes.

But fatal hour, when she, by swains unmov'd,
Beheld the master of the vale, and lov'd.
Long had he tempted her reserve in vain,
Till one luxuriant eve that sunn'd the plain;
On the bent herbage, where a gushing brook,
Blue harebells and the tufted violet shook;
Where hung umbrageous branches overhead,
And the rain'd roses lay in fragments red,
He found the slumbering maid. Prophane he press'd
Her lip, till then by lover uncarest.
She starts alarmed, and as the dawning day,
Thro' the white moonbeam shoots its ruddy ray,
Or as on Alpine cliffs, a wounded doe
Sheds all its purple life upon the snow;
So her cheek blushes, while her humble eyes
Fear from a knot of primroses to rise;
And mute she sits, affecting to repair
The discomposed meanders of her hair.

Need I his arts unfold? Enough to tell,
The virgin listen'd, and believ'd, and fell.

Now by the traitor far from home decoy'd,
She plunges into pleasures unenjoy'd,
Nor dares reflect, till tidings reach her door,
That her heartbroken mother lives no more.
Pale with despair, " At least, at least," she cries,
"Sad let me linger where the victim lies.
Short shelter need the village now bestow,
Ere by her sacred grave they lay me low."

Then without nurture, and in weary plight,
She hastes her journey homeward, morn and night;
Till, as her steps a hill familiar gain,
Bursts on her filling eyes her native plain.
She pants, expands her arms, "Ah, peaceful scene!"
Exclaiming: "Ah, dear valley, lovely green,
Still ye remain the same; your hawthorn still,
All your white cottages, the rustic mill;
Its osiered brook, that prattles through the meads;
The plat where oft I danced to piping reeds.
All, all remain unalter'd. 'Tis but thine
To suffer change, weak, wicked Caroline!"

The setting sun now purples hill and lake,
And lengthen'd shadows shadows overtake.

A parting carol larks and throstles sing,
The swains aside their heated sickles fling.
Now dairies all arrang'd, the nymphs renew
The straggling tress, and tighten aprons blue;
Then, scattered by their trooping lovers, run,
In a blithe tumult to the pipe begun.
And now, while dance and laughter shake the vale,
Sudden the penitent, dishevelled, pale,
Stands in the midst. All pausing gather round,
And gaze amaz'd. The tabors cease to sound.
    "Yes, ye may well," the faltering suppliant cries,
"Well may ye frown with those repulsive eyes.
Yet pity one not vicious but deceiv'd,
Who vows of marriage, ere she fell, believ'd.
Without a parent, friend, or cheerful home,
Save, save me, leave me not forlorn to roam.
Not now the gifts ye once so fondly gave,
Not now the verse or rural wreath I crave;
Not now to lead your festive sports along,
Queen of the dance, and despot of the song;
One shed is all, oh, just one wretched shed,
To lay my weary limbs and aching head.
Then will I bless your bounty, then inure
My frame to toil, and earn a pittance poor.
Then, while ye mix in mirth, will I, forlorn,
Beside my murder'd parent sit and mourn."
    She paus'd, expecting answer. None replied.
"And have ye children, have ye hearts?" she cried.
"Save me now, mothers, as from future harms,
Ye hope to save the babies in your arms!
See, to you, maids, I bend on abject knee;
Youths, even to you, who bent before to me.
O, my companions, by our happy plays,
By dear remembrance of departed days;
By pity's self, your cruel parents move;
By sacred friendship; Oh! by those ye love!
Oft when ye trespassed, I for pardon pray'd;
Oft on myself your little mischiefs laid.
Did I not always sooth the wounded mind?
Was I not call'd the generous and the kind?
Still silent? What! no word, no look to cheer?
No gentle gesture? What, not even a tear?
Go then, sublime in heartless virtue live;
Let none plead for me, none my crime forgive.
Go — yet the culprit, by her God forgiven,

May plead for you before the throne of heaven!
Ye simple pleasures of my rural hours,
Ye skies all sunshine, and ye paths all flowers:
Home, where no more a soothing friend I see,
Dear happy home, a last farewell to thee!"

    Claspt are her hands, her features strewn with hair,
And her eyes sparkle with a keen despair.
But turning to depart, a burst of tears,
And efforts, as of one withheld, she hears.
"Speak!" she conjures, "ere yet to phrenzy driven,
Tell me who weeps? What angel sent from Heav'n?"
"I, I your friend !" exclaims, with panting charms,
A rosy girl, and darts into her arms.
"What! will you leave me? Me, your other heart.
Your favourite Ellen? No, we must not part;
No, never! come, and in our cottage live;
Come, for the cruel village shall forgive.
O, my own darling, come, and unreprov'd,
Here on this heart rest ever, ever lov'd;
Here on this constant heart!" While yet she spoke,
Her furious sire the link'd embraces broke.
Borne in his arms, she wept, entreated, rav'd;
Then fainted, as a mute farewell she wav'd.

    But now the wretch, with low and wildered cries,
Round and around revolving vacant eyes:
Slow from the green departs, and pauses now,
And gnaws her tresses, and contracts her brow.
Shock'd by the change, the matrons, stern no more,
Pursue her steps, and her return implore:
Soon a poor maniac, innocent of ill,
She wanders unconfined, and drinks the rill.
And plucks the simple cress. A hovel near
Her native vale defends her from the year.
With tender feet to flint and thistle bare,
And faded willows weeping in her hair,
She climbs some rock at morn, and all alone,
Chaunts hasty snatches of harmonious moan.
When moons empearl the leafy locks of bowers,
With liquid grain, and light the glistening flowers,
She gathers honeysuckle down the dells,
And tangled eglantine, and slumbering bells;
And with moist finger, painted by the leaves,
A coronet of roses interweaves;
Then steals unheard, and gliding thro' the yews,
The fragrant offering on her mother strews.

At morn with tender pause, the nymphs admire,
How recent chaplets still the grave attire;
And matrons nightly tell, how fairies seen,
Dance roundelays aslant its cowslipped green.
Ev'n when the dreary vale is white with snows,
That verdant spot the little Robin knows;
And sure to find the flakes at dawn remov'd,
Alights and chirps upon its turf belov'd.

    Such her employ; till now, one wintry day,
Some shepherds hurrying by the guarded clay,
Find the pale ruin, life for ever flown,
With her cheek pillow'd on its dripping stone.
The turf unfinish'd wreaths of ivy strew,
And her lank locks are dim with misty dew.
Poor Ellen hymns her requiem. Willows pine
Around her grave. Fallen, fallen Caroline!

This morning, having relinquished my rags, and resumed my muslins, I repaired to Monkton Castle, where, seated on a withered stump, I began an accurate investigation of the edifice, for the purpose of ascertaining whether it could stand a siege, should Lady Gwyn attempt to dispossess me.

It is situated about a quarter of a mile from the road, upon a flat morass, where a few shattered oaks are all that remain of a former forest. The castle itself (which, however, appears too small for corridors and suites of apartments) is an exact square, having a turret at each corner; and a large gateway, on the southern side. While I surveyed its roofless walls, overtopt with briony, grass, and nettles, and admired the Gothic points of the windows, where mantling ivy had supplied the place of glass, long suffering and murder came to my thoughts.

As I sat planning, from romances, the revival of the feudal customs and manners in my castle, and of the feudal system among my tenantry (all so favourable to heroines), I perceived a barouche, just turning from the road into the common. My heart beat high: the carriage approached, stopped; and who should alight, but Higginson and Jerry Sullivan!

After Higginson, with reverence, and Jerry, with familiarity, had congratulated me on my restoration to my estates, the latter began looking hard at the castle.

"The people told us this was Monkton Castle," said he; "but where is the Monkton Castle that your Ladyship is to live in?"

"There it is, my friend," answered I.

"What? there!"

"Yes, there."

"What? there, there!"

"Yes, there, there."

"Oh, murder, murder, murder!"

"Murder enough, I dare swear," said I; "and ghosts too."

The postillion now came forward, with his hat in his hand.

"How far might we be from your house, my lady?" said he. "For I have brought the horses a deadly long journey already."

"That castle is my house," answered I.

"Begging your Ladyship's pardon," said he; "what I mean is this: how far are we from where your Ladyship lives?"

"I live in that castle," answered I.

Jerry began making signs, over the fellow's shoulder, for me to hold my tongue.

"What are you grimacing about there, Mr. Sullivan?" cried I.

"Oh, 'tis only a way I have got," answered Jerry. "But your Ladyship, you know, is merely come down to this castle on a sort of au excursion, you know, to see if it wants repairing you know: you don't mean to live in it, you know." And at every 'you know,' he put his finger upon his nose, and winked.

"But I know I do mean to live in it," said I, "and so, Sir, I beg you will cease your grinning."

"And sure 'tis for your good I'm grinning," cried he. "And sure if 'twas even through a horse-collar, I'd grin for that."

The postillion now stood staring up at the venerable edifice, with an expression of the most insolent ridicule.

"What are you looking at, blockhead?" said Jerry.

"By all that is comical," cried the fellow, reddening with smothered laughter, "I am looking at the sky through the windows!"

"Why then," said Jerry, " 'tis I that will spoil your looking for ever, if you don't take the horses from the carriage, and set off with yourself in a twinkling."

"By St. Peter, not till I am paid for their journey down;" cried the postillion. "So will your Ladyship have the goodness to pay me?"

"Assuredly," said I. "Jerry, pay him."

"Deuce a rap have I," answered Jerry. "I laid out my last farthing in things for your Ladyship."

" Higginson," said I, "pay him."

"It irks me to represent," answered Higginson, "that in equipments for this expedition; — a nice little desk, a nice little comb, a nice little pocket-glass, a nice little —"

"In short, you have no money," cried I.

"Not a farthing," answered he.

"Neither have I," said I; "so, postillion, you must call another time."

"Here is a pretty to do!" cried the postillion. "Damme, this is a shy sort of a business. Not even the price of a feed of oats! Snuff my eyelights, I must have the money. I must, blow me."

"I tell you what, Mr. Blow me;" cried Jerry, "if you don't unloose your horses this moment, and pack off, by the powers, the three of us will give you such a thrashing between us, as does'nt often fall to an honest man's share."

The postillion took the horses from the carriage, in silence; then, having mounted one of them, and ridden a few paces off, he stopped.

"You set of vagabonds and swindlers," cried he, "without a roof over your heads, or a penny in your pockets, to go diddle me out of my day's labour! Wait till master takes you in hand: and if I don't tell the coachmaker what a fresh one he was, to give you his barouche on tick, may I be particularly horsewhipt ! Ladyship! a rummish sort of a tit for a Ladyship! And there is my Lord, I suppose. And t'other is the Marquis. Three pickpockets from Fleet-street, I'd bet a whip to a wisp. Ladyship! Oh, her ladyship!" and away he cantered, ladyshipping it, till he was out of hearing.

"That young person wants a moral lecture," said Higginson.

"He wants his money," said Jerry; "and no blame to him. But there is nothing like bullying a man, when one is bilking him. And now, 'pon your conscience, does your Ladyship intend to live in this old castle?"

"Upon my honour I do," replied I.

"And is there no decent house on the estate, that one of your tenants could lend you?" said he.

"Why," replied I, "though Lady Gwyn has actually acknowledged my right to the estate, still, as she has not yet put me in formal possession of it, the tenantry, most probably, will not yet treat me as their mistress. All I can now do, therefore, is to seize this uninhabited castle which lies on the estate. But rest assured, that a heroine of good taste, and anxious to rise in her profession, would

433

infinitely prefer the desolation of a Castle to the comforts of a Villa."

"Well, of all the wise freaks--" muttered Jerry, standing astride, sticking his knuckles in his ribs, and nodding his head leisurely, as he looked up at the castle.

"Mr. Sullivan," interrupted I, "if you have the slightest objection to remaining here, you may depart this moment."

"And do you think I would leave you?" cried he. " Oh th'n, oh th'n, 'tis I that would'nt ! And if it was a gallows itself, instead of a castle, I would assist you all the same. 'Pon my virtue, if your Ladyship even commanded me to jump over that said Castle, I'd -- no, I don't say I'd do it; but by the powers, I'd take a run at it!"

I shook his honest hand with warmth, and then asked him if he had performed my commissions.

"Your Ladyship shall hear," said he.

"As soon as ever I got your letter, I went with it in my hand, and shewed it at fifty different shops;---clothiers, and glaziers, and upholsterers, and feather-makers, and trumpet-makers; but neither old tapestry, nor old painted glass, nor old flags stained with old blood, nor old lutes, nor old any thing could I get; and moreover, as sure as ever I shewed them your letter, so sure they laughed at it."

"Laughed at it!" cried I.

"All but one," said Jerry,

"And he?" cried I.

"Was going to knock me down. Howsomever, since Moll and I are giving up shop, on the strength of the two hundred-a-year: and since you commanded me to get old goods, rather than new, by Dad, I have brought you out of our own shop, as much cloth as would furnish two rooms at the very farthest. Half is black cloth, and half red; and though both are motheaten, and musty, and rotten enough, I suppose your Ladyship will like them the better for that same. Well, I then went and bought a parcel of old funeral feathers, and an old velvet pall, from an undertaker; and a broken old harp with five strings, that will do any thing but play, from the blind Welsh girl who thrums through the streets; and a big cracked old bell, from the sexton of our parish; and a tin horn from the guard of a mail-coach; and a lot of old pictures of wiggy quizzes, from a sign-painter. And all these, together with my bed and trunk, and a box of Mr. Higginson's, I have got snug here in the barouche,"

"But the barouche?" said I; "how did you procure that?"

"Faith, then, by not shewing your letter," answered Jerry; "and by knowing the coachmaker myself. And I told him it was for Lady De Willoughby, as beautiful as an angel---but he did not mind that; and as rich as a Jew;---but he minded that; and so he gave me, not only the barouche, but a thousand thanks into the bargain."

"Well, my friend," said I, "if you and Higginson will pull down those stones that barricade the gateway, we will enter the building, and see what can be done with our present materials."

They commenced operations, and having soon cleared away the rubbish, conducted me into my castle.

A thrill of pride and joy ran through my frame, as I entered and took possession. But I found its interior in a far more ruinous state than I had imagined. Nothing remained except the four turrets, and the four walls which united them. These roofless walls were stained with the venerable verdure of damp, and the intervening area was overrun with nettles and thistles. Each turret had a small doorway. I looked in; but three turrets, despoiled even of their stairs, were inaccessible to human feet, and attainable only by an owl or an angel. However, on reconnoitering the fourth, or eastern turret, I found it in much better condition than the rest. There the stairs, which were winding, and of stone, still remained. I therefore ascended the first flight, and got into a room of about eight feet square, (the size of the turret itself), which would answer admirably for my accommodation. I then mounted the next flight, and found myself at the top of the Tower. Around it ran a broken parapet; and fragments of the battlements lay beneath my feet. This Tower, therefore, I determined to furnish and inhabit; and to leave the remaining three in a state of classical dilapidation, as receptacles for strange noises, horrid sights, and nocturnal Condottieri.

I now descended, and made the Minstrel and Warden (for I have already invested them in these offices) draw the barouche within the gateway, and convey the luggage up to the chamber, which I had chosen as my residence.

This done, the pieces of black cloth were opened and inspected. Nothing could answer the purpose better; so, without farther loss of time, we set about hanging the chamber with them. This we contrived to accomplish by means of wooden pegs, which the Warden cut with his knife; and drove, with a stone, through the drapery into the crevices of the walls. We then stationed the mutilated harp at a corner, and fastened the portraits against the

435

hangings. They are in fine old gilded frames; and I am not very fanciful, I believe; but certainly, three of them have the De Willoughby eyebrow to a hair. When the hangings, harp, and pictures were all arranged, I gazed upon their sombrous and antique effect with extreme transport. I then named this apartment, the BLACK CHAMBER, and gave orders that it should always be so denominated.

Our next object was to contrive a bed for me. Jerry, therefore, procured some branches of trees; and after much labour, and no small ingenuity, constructed a bedstead, as crazy as any that ever creaked under a heroine. He then hung it round with curtains of black cloth; and his own bed being placed upon it, he spread the velvet pall, as a coverlet. Never was a more funereal piece of furniture; and I saw clearly, that it rivalled the terrifying bed in the Mysteries of Udolpho.

The room underneath, which I designed for my household, we draperied with the pieces of red cloth. This room, therefore, I called the RED CHAMBER; and as the other turrets were all over verdant moss, ivy, nettles, grass, and groundsel, I called them the GREEN CHAMBERS.

The Minstrel all this time appeared to be stupified and awestruck; but worked like a horse, puffing and panting, and doing every thing that he was desired, without uttering a word.

The bell, the horn, and the boxes, being now deposited in the Red Chamber, dinner became our next consideration. I have, therefore, just dispatched the Warden (like Peter, in the Romance of the Forest) to procure provisions. Yet not a farthing has he to purchase any; since even the money which Susan gave me was exhausted at the cottage.

But the light that enters my ivied window begins to grow grey; and an appropriate gloom thickens through the chamber. Sitting on a temporary stool, which the Warden made for me, I write with the pen of the Minstrel. My knees are my desk.

Adieu.

LETTER XXXI.

Just at the close of evening, Jerry came running towards the castle, with a milk-pail upon his head.

"See," cried he, putting it down, "how nicely I have choused a little milk-maid! There was she, tripping along, as tight as her garter. 'Fly for your life,' cries I, striding up to her: 'there is the big bull at my heels, that has just killed two children, two sucking pigs, two--Here! let me hold your pail,' and I whips it off her head. So, what does she do, but she runs off without it, one way; and what does I do, but I runs off with it, another way! And besides this, I have got my hat filled with young potatoes, that I scraped from a field; and my pockets stuffed with ears of wheat, that I plucked from another; and if we can't eat a hearty dinner of these dainties, why may our next be fried fleas and toasted leather!"

Though I was angry at the means used by Jerry to get the provisions, yet (as dinner, just then, had more charms for me than moral sentiment), instead of instructing him in the lofty doctrines of the social compact, I merely shewed him how to pound the wheat between two flat stones. Meantime, I sent the Minstrel to the cottage, for a light and some fuel; and on his return, made him kindle a fire of wood, in the centre of the Black Chamber. As the floor was stone, it ran no risk of being burned.

This accomplished, I mixed some milk with the bruised wheat, kneaded a cake, and laid it upon the red embers; while Jerry himself took charge of roasting the potatoes.

As soon as our romantic repast was ready, I drew my stool to the fire: my household drew stones, and we made a tolerable meal; they on the potatoes, and I on the cake, which hunger had really rendered palatable.

The Warden then lifted the pail to my lips, and I took a draught of the rural nectar; while the Minstrel remarked, that Nestor himself had not a larger goblet.

As the cottage of my late hostess was not more than a quarter of a mile distant, I paid her a solitary visit, and carried the fragments of our dinner to her.

On my return, we resumed our seats, and hung over the expiring embers, which cast a gloomy glare upon the bed and the drapery; while now and then, a flash from the ashes shot a reddened light on the paleness of the Minstrel, and brightened the broad features of the

437

Warden. The wind had risen: there was a good deal of excellent howling round the turret: we sat silent, and looking for likenesses in the fire.

"Come, Warden," cried I, "repair these embers with a fresh splinter, and recount the memoirs of your life."

The Warden threw down a log, up blazed the fire, and then he began his history.

"Once upon a time when pigs were swine—"

"I will trouble you for a more respectable beginning," said I; "some striking, genteel little picture, to bespeak attention,— such as, "It was on a gloomy night in the month of November."

"November!" cried Jerry; "that would be a proper lie, because, as it happens, I was born in January; and by the same token, I was one of the youngest children that ever was born, for I saw light five months after my mother's marriage. Well, being born, up I grew, and the first word I said was mammy; and my hair was quite yellow at first, though 'tis so brown now; and I promised to be handsome, but the symptoms soon left me; and I remember, I was as proud as Lucifer, the first day I wore trowsers; and —"

"Why now, Jerry, what sort of homely trash is this?" said I. "Fie; a Warden like you! I really hoped to have heard something of the wonderful from you."

"Oh, if 'tis the wonderful you want," cried Jerry, "I won't disappoint you. Well, then, the fact is, I am of the O'Sullivans, who were once kings of Munster; and that is the very reason I have not Mister to my name, seeing as how I am of the blood royal. So, being of the blood royal, I was iddicated in great tenderness and ingenuity; and when I came of age, I went and seized upon O'Sullivan Castle, and fortified it, and got a crown and sceptre, and reigned in great peace many years. But as the devil would have it—"

"Jerry," said I, "I must insist on hearing no more of these monstrous untruths."

"Untruths!" cried he. "O murder! to think I would tell a falsehood!"

"Sir," said I, " 'tis a falsehood on the very face of it."

"Then, 'pon my conscience," cried he, " 'tis as like your own story as two peas. Sure did'nt you yourself seize upon a castle? And as to the crown and sceptre, sure half the gentlemen in Europe have them now-a-days. And I did not contradict you, (whatever I might think, and I have my thoughts too, I can tell you,) when you talked so glib of your great estates; though, to be sure, your Ladyship is as poor as a rat. Howsomever, since you will have it all a falsehood, 'tis all a falsehood, sure enough; but now you shall hear the real, real story; though, for that matter, any fool can tell truth, and no thanks to him.

"Well, then, my father was nothing more than a common labourer, and just poor enough to be honest, though not quite poor enough to be a rogue. Poverty is no great disgrace, provided one comes honestly by it; for one may grow poor as well as rich by knavery. So, being poor, father used to make me earn odd pennies, when I was a boy; and at last I got so clever, that he resolved on sending me to sell chickens at the next town. But as I could only speak Irish then, by reason we lived up the mountains, he sat down and taught me a little English, in case any gentlefolks should ask me about my chickens. 'Now, Jerry, says he, (in Irish,) if any gentleman addresses you, of course it will be to know the price of your chickens; so you must answer, *three shillings, Sir*. Then to be sure he will be for lowering the price; so you must say stoutly, *No less, Sir*; and if he shakes his head, or looks angry, 'tis a sign he won't buy unless you bate a little; so you are to say, *I believe I must take two, Sir.* '

"Well, I got my lesson pat, and off I set, with my hair cut as strait as a rule, and my face scowered bright, and thinking it the greatest day of my life; and sure enough, I had not walked a hundred yards from our cabin, when I met a gentleman.

"How far is it to the next village?' says he.

"Three shillings, Sir,' says I.

"You are a saucy fellow,' says he.

"No less, Sir,' says I.

"I will give you a box in the face,' says he.

"I believe I must take two, Sir,' says I.

"But, instead of two, egad, I got twice two, and as many kicks as would match 'em; and home I ran howling. — Well, that was very well; so when I told father that I was beaten for nothing:

"I warrant you were not,' says he; 'and if I had treated my poor father as you treat me,' says he, 'he would have broken every bone in my skin,' says he. 'But he was a better father than I am,' says he.

"How dare you say that your father was better than my father?' says I; and upon this, father takes me by the ear, and lugs me right out of the cabin. Well, that was very well. So, just as we got outside, the self-same gentleman was passing by; and he stopped, and began complaining of me to father; and then the whole mistake came out, and both of them laughed splittingly.

"But what do you think? 'Pon my conscience, the gentleman took me strait home with him, and set me cleaning the knives and boots. And then he sent me to school, where I learned English; and then he made me tend at table; till after some time, I became a regular servant in the family.

"Well, here I lived several years; and grew a great fellow for whiskey and whist; until one night, when mistress had company, bringing in the tray of cake and wine, down I came, and smash went all the glasses.

"By this and that,' says mistress; (only mistress did'nt swear) 'you are drunk,' says she.

"Never tasted a drop all day,' says I; and sure, it was true for me, 'cause I did not begin till evening.

"Who taught you to tell falsehoods?' says she.

"Troth, you did,' says I; ' 'cause you taught me to tell visitors you were not at home, when all the time you were peeping down the bannisters. Fine fashions, indeed! Nobody is ever at home now-a-days, but a snail,' says I. And I would have said more too, only master kicked me out of the house.

"Well, that was very well; and now my misfortunes were all before me, like a wheelbarrow.

"This happened in the year of the Rebellion; so, being out of service, I lived at alehouses; and there it was that I met gentlemen with rusty superfine on their backs, and with the longest, genteelest words in the world. They soon persuaded me that old Ireland was going to ruin; I forget how now, but I know I had the whole story pat at that time; and the end of it was, that I became an United Irishman.

"Howsomever, though I would have died for my country, it would be carrying the joke too far to starve for her; and I had now spent all my wages. So, at last, back I goes to my old master, and falls on my knees, and asks his pardon for my bad conduct, and prays of him to hire me once more. Well, he did; and it was only two nights after, that we heard a great noise outside; and master comes running into the kitchen.

"Jerry,' says he, 'here are the rebels attacking the house; and as I know you are a faithful fellow, take this sword and pistol, and stand by me.'

"By you? No, but I will stand before you,' says I. So we mustered our men, five in all, and posted ourselves upon the head of the stairs; when in burst the rebels, and their captain bade us surrender our arms. 'Why then, is that Barney Delany?' says I.

"Why then, is that Jerry Sullivan?' says he. 'You are one of us,' says he, 'so now, turn round and shoot your master,' says he.

"I will cut off both my hands first,' says I.

"Take that then,' says he; and he fires a shot, and I another; and at it we kept, pop, pop, pop; till we beat them all off.

"Well, in a few months afterwards, this same Barney being made prisoner, I was bound over as witness against him. So, some of the gentlemen with the long words came to me, and told me as how I had acted wrong in fighting for my master, instead of my country; and as how I must make amends by giving evidence in favour of Barney.

"Well, they puzzled me so, that from then, till now, I never could satisfy myself, whether I was right or wrong in standing by my master. But somehow, I think I was right; for though patriotism (one of the long words) is a fine thing, still, after all, there is nothing like gratitude. Why, now, if the devil himself did me a kind office, I believe I would make shift to do him another; and not act like the clergy, who spend their whole lives snubbing at him, and calling him all manner of names; though they well know, that, only for him, there would not be a clergyman or a fat living in the kingdom.

"Howsomever, I was over persuaded to do the genteel thing by Barney Delany; so, when the day for trial came, I drank myself pretty unintelligible; and I swore point blank, before judge and jury, that I did not know Barney good or bad, and that all I knew of him was good: and I bothered the lawyers, and they turned me from the table, and threatened to indite me for perjury. But how the people praised me, and called it iligant swearing, and mighty pretty evidence! And I was the great man of the day; and they took me to the fair that was hard by, where we tippled a little more, and then forth we sallied, ripe for fun.

"Well, as we were running, like mad, through the fair, what should I spy, but a man's bald head sticking out of a hole in one of the tents — to cool, I suppose,— so I just lifted my cudgel, and just

441

laid it down; when, behold you, out comes a whole set of fellows from the tent, and baldpate asks, which of us had broken his head?

"It was my own self,' says I, 'but confound me if I could help it, that skull of your's looked so inviting.'

"Accordingly, both parties began a battle; and then others, who had nothing better to do, came and joined; they did not know why or wherefore; but no matter for that. Any one may fight, when there is an occasion; but the beauty of it, is to fight when there is no occasion at all.

"Howsomever, in the midst of it, up came the military to spoil sport, as usual; and they dispersed us, and made some of us prisoners, — I among the rest, — and we were put into Bridewell. Well, that was very well. So at night, we contrived to break it open, beat the keepers, and make our escape. I then skulked about the country several days; till coming across some lads, who were going beyond seas, to reap the English harvest, I took the frolic, and went with them.

"But to be sure, to be sure, such a hurricane as we had at sea, and such tumbling and tossing; and then we were driven to the world's end, or the Land's End, or some end; but I know I thought I was come to my own end. In short, such adventures never were known."

"What adventures, my friend?" cried I.

"Why," said he, "we had an adventure every moment, for every moment we were near going to the bottom."

"Nonsense!" said I. "Ah, Jerry, these famous adventures of your's are ending in nothing."

"Wait awhile," said Jerry. "Then there was such pulling of ropes, and reefing and rigging; and starboarding and larboarding; and so many seas and channels; the Irish Channel, and the British Channel, and the Bristol Channel, and the Baltic Sea, and the Atlantic Sea, and---Oh! bad luck to me, but we sailed over almost every sea in the known world.

"Did you sail over the Red Sea?" said I.

"To be sure I did."

"And the Black Sea?"

"Not a doubt of it."

"And the White Sea, and the Pacific Ocean?"

"Every mother's soul of them."

"And what kind of seas are they?"

"Why," said he, "the Red Sea is as red as blood, and the Black Sea is as black as ink, and the White Sea is the colour of new milk, or nearer butter-milk, I think; and the Pacifi-ifi---What's that word?"

"Pacific," said I.

"And what is the meaning of Pacific?" said he.

"It means peaceful or calm," answered I.

"Gad, I thought so," cried he, "for the devil a wave that same ocean had on it at all at all. 'Pon my conscience, it was as smooth as the palm of my hand."

"Take care, Jerry," said I, laughing; "I am afraid—"

"Why then," cried he, "that I may never—"

"Hush!" said I. "No swearing."

"By dad," cried he, "at this rate you had better tell me my own story yourself; for you seem bent upon having it all just as you like. I know, 'tis a hard case, that a poor man can't—"

"Pray, my friend," interrupted I, "do not bravo the matter any more; but suppose yourself safely landed in England; and what happened you then?"

"Why, then," said he, "I made a little money by reaping, and afterwards, I trudged to London."

"And how did you subsist in London at first?" asked I.

"By spitting through my teeth," said Jerry.

"Take care," cried I. "This I susspect is another—"

"If you mean lie," said Jerry, "you are out at last. 'Tis as true, as true can be; and I will explain all about it. You must know, that 'tis now the fashion for gentlemen to be their own coachmen; and not only to drive like coachmen, but to talk, walk, dress, drink, swear, and even spit like coachmen. Well, two days after my arrival, as I was standing in the street, and looking about, I happened to spit through my teeth, to the envy and admiration of a gentleman that was just driving his own carriage by. For he stopped, and called me across, and offered me half a crown if I would teach him to do the same. Well, I went home with him, and in a short time, taught him to spit so well, that my fame spread through the town, and all the fashionable fellows flocked about me for instruction; till I had a good mind to set up a Spitting Academy.

"I had now spit myself into such affluence, that I refused a coachman's seat, with forty pounds a-year (for, as I said, even a curate had more than that); and perhaps, instead of a seat on the box, I might at last have risen to a seat in Parliament (for many a man has got there by dirtier tricks than mine), only unfortunatety, my profession being of a nature to dry up my mouth, made me frequent porter-houses; where, as more bad luck would have it, I met other gentlemen, just such as I had met before, and with just the same set of long words.

"In a little time, all of us came to a determination that our country was ruined, and that something must be done. So we formed ourselves into a club, for the purpose of writing ballads about the war, and the taxes, and a thousand lashes that a soldier got. And we used to set ten or twelve ballad-singers round a table, in our club-room, each with her pint of beer; and one of our club would teach them the tuəe with a little kit, while I was in a cock-loft overhead, composing the words. And they reckoned me the finest poet of them all; and told me that my writings would descend to my poster--- some long word or other; and often the thoughts came so quick on me, that I was obliged to chalk them down upon the back of the bellows. But whenever I wanted an inflammation of ideas, I got some gin, and Weekly Register; and then between both, up I worked myself to such a pitch of poetry, that my blood would sometimes run cold in the morning, at the thoughts of what I had planned in the night.

"Well, one evening, the ballad-singers were round the table, sipping and singing to the little kit, and I had just popt down my head through the trap-door of the cock-loft, to ask the chairman the rhime for *a Reform.*

"Confound you,' says he, ' didn't I tell you twenty times 'tis *a storm*; ' when in bursts the door, and a parcel of peace-officers seize himself and the whole set, for holding seditious meetings. Think of that! when faith and honour, our only object was to procure a speedy peace, by letting our enemies know that we could not carry on the war.

"Howsomever, I got out of the scrape by being concealed in the cock-loft; and well I remember, it was on the very same night I first saw my wife."

"Ah," said I, "give me the particulars of that event; the first meeting of lovers is always so interesting!"

"Why," said he, "going home sorrowful enough, after the ruin of our club, I resolved to drown care in drink; and accordingly turned into a porter-house; where I found three fruit-women from Covent Garden, bound on the same errand."

"What dram shall we have?' says they.

"Brandy,' says one.

"Gin,' says another.

"Anniseed-water,' says another. And so they fell to and drank.

'I am happy that I ever came to this City of Lunnun; for my fortune's made,' says Brandy.

"If my father lived, I would be brought up to good iddication,' says Gin.

" If my mother lived, I would be brought up at a boarding-school,' says Anniseed-water.

"Why, curse you,' says Gin, ' what was your mother but an old apple-woman?'

"And curse you,' says Anniseed-water, ' what was your father but a gallows-bird of a bum-bailiff?'

"And then they fell a fighting and scratching; and Anniseed-water (the present Mrs. Jerry Sullivan) was getting well cuffed, when I came to her assistance. So that was our first meeting."

"Defend me from all such first meetings!" cried I. "And I suppose your courtship was just a match for it."

"Ah, it was my masterpiece!" cried he. "Molly, you must know, felt so much obliged by my conduct, that she invited me home to tea, and I went. At that time she was a widow; a fine doorful of a woman, as blooming a wench as you would wish to see over a washing tub. And her daughter, and a great deal of good company were there;—the tailor's wife, and the barber's wife, and the pawnbroker's wife: and none so grand as they. And they told as many lies over a dish of tea, as a parcel of porters would over a barrel of beer. And a young valet swore, one might as well be out of the world as out of the fashion; and then whispered Molly that she looked killing genteel. But I only pinched her elbow, and I thought she liked that better."

"That was very vulgar, however," observed I. "The first process is to kiss the hand."

"Ogh!" cried Jerry. "Is it to be mumbling the knuckles, just as a pup niggles at a bone. Dad, I am the manner of man, that takes, at once, and flusters a woman, and reckons her ribs for her. No creeping up, and up, and up; and then down, and down, and down, for me—Why now, as I hope to be saved, I gave that same widow a thundering kiss, on three days acquaintance."

" Poor thing!" exclaimed I. "Well, and what did she say?"

"Say? why she said, 'Be quiet now,--- though I know you can't!' So, of course, I kissed her still more; while she changed colour in a minute, as often as a blackberry does in a month. ' Ha' done, then,' says she, ' or I will call out,--- only there is nobody at home;'--- when--- in pops the valet, and catches us lip to lip.

"Now he was a conceited sort of a chap, that used to set himself off with great airs, shew his white hands---which, I verily believe, he washed every day of his life;---curse and swear just like a gentleman, keep a toothbrush, and make both his heels meet when he bowed.

"Well, I had nothing upon earth to oppose against all this, but a bit of a quarrel;--- that was *my* strong point;---so, sure enough, I gave him such a beating for catching us kissing, that the widow thought me main stout, and married me in a week.

"With her money I set up shop; and I did not much mind her being ten years older than myself, since she was ten times richer. I only copied my own father there; for he once happened to be divided between a couple of girls, the prettiest of them portioned with one cow, and the ugliest with two; so he consulted his landlord which he should marry, and his landlord bade him marry the girl with the two cows; for, says he, there is not a cow difference between any two women."

"Nay," said the Minstrel, "even the ancients thought less of a woman than of a cow; inasmuch as often-times, the first prize allotted in their games, was a cow, and the second a woman."

But now sleep began to pour its opiate over my eyes. The Minstrel and the Warden took their nocturnal station in the Red Chamber. Each was to keep alternate watch at the gate of the castle, and to toll the passing hour upon the bell.

The wind still moaned around the turret; and the fire, ghastly in decay, tinged with a fainter crimson the projecting folds of the black hangings. Dismal looked the bed as I drew near; and while I lifted the velvet pall to creep beneath, I shivered, and almost expected to behold the apparition of a human face starting from under it. When I lay down, I closed my fearful eyes, lest I should see something hideous; nor was it till the third bell had tolled, that I fell asleep.

Adieu.

LETTER XXXII.

I ROSE early this morning, and summoned Jerry to the Black Chamber; for my head was teeming with the most important projects.

"My friend," said I, "though Lady Gwyn has already acknowledged me as the rightful owner, not alone of this castle, but of the house which she herself inhabits, yet I cannot apply to my tenantry for rent, or even raise the price of a breakfast, till she surrenders the deeds and parchments, and puts me into legal possession. Now, since I fear I shall find her rather obstinate in this affair, I have determined on proposing a compromise, and on waving all title to the house and estate of Gwyn Castle, provided she will establish my title to the house and estate of Monkton Castle.

I shall therefore pay her Ladyship a visit immediately; but, as I was once before driven out of her house in disgrace, I shall return thither now, with such a numerous train of domestics, as will enable me to set both insult and injury at defiance.

"You must therefore, my good Warden, go and hire, without farther delay, a set of servants for me. Inform them, that I will give each, according to the feudal system, a portion of ground; that I will allow them to live in the castle, and finally that I will constitute them my feudal vassals. A tempting offer like this, must draw half the servants in the neighbourhood about you; so pray cull the flower of them. Go, my friend."

"Why then, now, speaking in all sober reason," said Jerry, "who but madmen would come, as servants, to a house without a roof? Arrah, would you have them build swallows' nests for themselves, under the windows, and live upon suction like the snipes?"

"Mr. Sullivan," said I, "cast no sarcasms, but do as you are desired."

"Well, from this moment, I say nothing," cried Jerry. "So now, your Ladyship, how many of these same feudal Vessels, as you call 'em;--- these Vessels that are to have no drink—"

"Jerry!"

"Well, well, how many must I hire? --- tell me, quick--- and there is my hand upon my mouth till I am gone."

"About fifteen or twenty," said I. "But remember, I will have no dapper footmen, with smirking faces. I must have a clan like those

447

that adorned the middle ages; fellows with Norman noses, and all sorts of frowns---men of iron, fit to live in comets."

"Ay, or they could not live in an old--- " But Jerry clapped his hand upon his mouth just in time, and then ran down stairs.

During his absence, I paid a visit to the poor cottagers; and after having sat with them awhile, and promised them assistance before evening, I returned towards the castle.

On approaching it, I perceived, to my great surprise, Jerry also advancing, at the head of about twenty men, armed with bludgeons.

"Here are the boys!" cried Jerry. "Here are the true sort. Few Norman noses, I believe, but all honest hearts; and though they never lived in comets, egad, they lived in Ireland. Look at 'em. Hold up your heads, you dogs. Please your Ladyship, they came over only to save the hay, and reap the harvest; but when they found their own countryman, and a pretty girl in distress, they soon volunteered their services; and now here they are, ready for that same Lady Gwyn, or any lady in the land."

My heart dilated with exultation at beholding this mighty retinue of feudal vassals; and I welcomed them cordially. As it was expedient to inspire Lady Gwyn with respect and awe, I resolved on making the best possible display of my power, taste, and feudal magnificence. Having no horses for my barouche, I fixed to make some of my domestics draw it, as at a triumph; and to make the rest follow it in procession. However, ragged and uncelebrated dresses, such as they wore, would never do; but I think you will give me credit for my plan to supply them with a more creditable costume. Much of the black and of the red cloth still remained; so we had only to divide it into large pieces, which the vassals might wear as cloaks; and then by sticking black feathers in their hats, they would rival even the Udolphian soldiery.

I had myself made up some flowing black drapery for Higginson, whom I meant to take in the barouche. But as minstrels never wear hats, and are always bald; and as Higginson still cherished his locks, with a spruceness most unmeet for minstrelsy, I persuaded him, after repeated assurances how much handsomer he would look, to let Jerry shave the crown of his head.

Accordingly, the Warden performed the tonsoral operation in the Black Chamber, while I remained in the Red, to adjust the feathers and cloaks on my domestics. These poor fellows, who, I suppose, had never read even a primmer, much less a romance, stood gaping at each other with silent wonder; though some of them attempted unmeaning, and, I must say, troublesome jests on what was going forward.

When accoutered, a more formidable and picturesque group than they presented, you never beheld; and while I was still admiring them, down from the turret issued the Minstrel. But such a spectacle! Half his huge head was shorn of its hair: his black garments, knotted just under his bare neck, gave a new ghastliness to his face; while his eyes, which he rivetted upon me, were starting out of their sockets with anxiety and agitation. He looked preternatural. To contain was impossible; I began laughing, and the Irishmen uttered a shout.

The poor man turned as pale as ashes; his face began to work and quiver, and he burst into a piteous fit of crying. Then suddenly, lifting a prodigious stone, he whirled it at Jerry's head; who ducked for his life, and saved it.

"Why then, curse on you, what did I do to you?" cried Jerry.

"You shaved my head, so as to spoil my looks," cried the Minstrel. "And you are endeavouring to outrival me with my mistress, and she likes you better than me. Well, well, it cannot be holpen. Oh, dear, dear!"

I tried to sooth him; but he turned from me with a froward shoulder, mounted the turret again, and continued sobbing there, as long as I remained. Having posted two sentinels upon the top of the tower, I now got into my barouche. Six vassals, in red cloaks, were deputed to draw it; and the rest, in black, brought up the rear. Jerry, whose hat I had distinguished with three feathers; and on whose black cloak I had fastened a scarlet cape, headed the whole. Never was a more august procession; and I will venture to assert, that this country, at least, never saw any thing like it.

As we paraded along the road, the people ran from their houses to gaze upon us. Some said we were strolling actors, others swore we were going to a funeral: all were astonished; and a rabble of boys and girls capered at our heels, and gathered as we went.

It was not till towards evening, that we reached Lady Gwyn's avenue. We paused there a moment, while I made my attendants wipe the barouche, shake the dust from their cloaks, adjust their feathers, and hold up their heads. Then, with a beating heart, I found myself at the door.

The Warden pealed an authoritative rap. The door opened. The servant stared.

"Inform the Lady Gwyn," said I, "that her niece, the Lady Cherubina de Willoughby, desires the honour of a conference with her."

The fellow grinned, and disappeared. In a few minutes, out came her Ladyship, accompanied by several guests; some of whose faces I remembered having seen there before.

They greeted me with great kindness and respect.

Carelessly bowing to Lady Gwyn, as I sat half reclined, I thus addressed her.

"Lady Gwyn, I now come with a proposal, which it is as generous in me to offer, as it will be politic in you to accept. And first learn, that I am at this moment holding actual possession of Monkton Castle, the seat of my renowned ancestors. To that castle, and to this house, your Ladyship has already acknowledged my right; and to both I can hereafter establish my claim by a judiciary process.

"However, as I prefer a more amicable mode of adjustment, and am willing to spare the effusion of money; I now before the company present, declare, that I will make over this house and demesne to your Ladyship, and to your heirs for ever, provided you, upon your part, will surrender to me, without delay or reservation, the title-deeds of Monkton Castle, and of all the Monkton estate. What says your Ladyship? Yes or no?"

"Lady Cherubina," returned her Ladyship, "I cannot think of entering into terms with you, till you restore the portrait, which you purloined from this house. But, meantime, as a proof of my desire to settle matters amicably, I request the honour of your company at dinner."

"Your Ladyship must excuse me," said I, with a noble air. "During our present dispute respecting this house, I should deem my entering it as a guest, derogatory to my honour and my dignity."

"Why then, death and 'ounds!" cried Jerry, "will you refuse so good an offer, after starving all the morning!"

"Starving!" exclaimed Lady Gwyn.

"We have not put a morsel inside our mouths this blessed day," said Jerry; "and even yesterday we dined upon potatoes and milk, and a sort of a contrivance of a cake, that your Ladyship would'nt throw to your cat."

450

I thought I should drop at this exposure of our poverty, and I commanded him to be silent.

"Time enough for silence when one has spoken," cried he. "But sure, would'nt it vex a saint to hear you talking about honour and dignity, when all the time, that poor stomach of your's is as empty as a sack!"

"Sensibly remarked," said Lady Gwyn. "And pray, honest fellow, who are you?"

"Mr. Warden," answered I quickly, lest he should speak again. "And these are my feudal Vassals; and I have left my Minstrel, and the rest of my faithful people, on the battlements of the eastern tower, just over the Black Chamber, to guard my castle."

"And for all this fine talk," cried Jerry, "we have not so much as a rap farthing amongst the whole set of us! So pray, your Ladyship, do make her stay dinner—Do. Or may be," (said he, getting closer and whispering), "may be you would just lend her half-a-crown or so;—do now, and, 'pon my soul, I will pay you myself before this day week."

"Silence, traitor!" cried I, rising, and dignifying my manner. "I do not want a dinner: I would not accept of a dinner; but above all, of a dinner in this house, till I am mistress of it!"

"And now is it true," cried Jerry to Lady Gwyn, "that the poor soul is really mistress of this house?"

"Oh! certainly, certainly," said her Ladyship.

"Oh! certainly, certainly," said the guests.

"Well, bad luck to me, if ever I believed it, till this moment," cried Jerry. "And why then won't your Ladyship give it up to her?"

"Because," answered she, "the quiet surrender of an estate is a thing unknown in romances."

" 'Tis the only rational excuse that you can assign," cried I.

"Dinner is on the table, my lady," said the Butler coming to the door.

"Do you hear that?" cried Jerry. "And so you won't dine in this house till you are mistress of it?"

"Never, as I hope to see heaven!" answered I.

"And so," cried he to Lady Gwyn, "you won't make her mistress of it?"

"Never, as I hope to see heaven!" answered she.

"Why then," cried Jerry, "since one refuses to dine in it till she is

451

mistress of it; and since t'other owns, that she ought to be mistress of it, and yet won't make her mistress of it; by the powers, 'tis I will make her mistress of it in half a shake!"

So saying, he shouted some words of an uncouth jargon (Irish, I suppose) to my Vassals, several of whom instantly darted into the house; while others began brandishing their sticks in the faces of the guests. Jerry himself ran, lifted me from the barouche, and bore me into the hall; the rest beat back the gentlemen who were attempting to rush between us and the door, and then entered after us.

Jerry set me down, shut the door, and told me that I was now in quiet possession for ever and ever.

Meantime I stood motionless and amazed, while some of my domestics scudded, with merry uproar, through kitchen, parlour, drawing-room, garret; and drove footman, maid, valet, cook, scullion, lap-dog, all out of the house!

"Jerry," said I, "there is no knowing how this will end. But come into that parlour, for some of my people are making a sad riot there."

In we went; it was the dining-room, and to my great astonishment, I found about a dozen of my domestics already round the table, eating and drinking just as if nothing had happened. In vain the Warden and I desired them to desist; they did not even hear us. They laughed and capered; tore entire joints with their hands, and swilled the richest wines from the decanters. The rest soon flocked in; and then such a scene of confusion arose, as struck me with utter dismay. And now, having glutted themselves, they ran to the windows, and exhibited the mangled meat and diminished wine before the straining eyes of Lady Gwyn. There she stood, amidst her friends, gesticulating like a Bedlamite; and as soon as I appeared, she beckoned me wildly to open the window.

I called the Warden, and made him raise the sash.

"Let us in, let us in!" she shrieked. "My house will be ruined by those miscreants! Have you no pity? Oh, let us in, let us in!"

"Lady Gwyn," said I calmly, "these outrages are on my house, not on your's. But rest assured, whatever injury your personal property sustains, is contrary to my wishes, and shall, by me, be most amply compensated."

"Gracious Heavens!" exclaimed she. "My precious cabinet, and my furniture will all be demolished! Won't you save my house? dear Madam, won't you?"

"*Your* house?" cried Jerry. "Why just now you said it was my own lady's house. So, if you told a lie, take the consequence. But we have got possession, and let me see who will dare drive us out."

"Here are they that will soon drive you out!" cried a servant.

"Here they are, here they are!" echoed every one.

All eyes were directed down the avenue, and to my horror, I perceived a large party of soldiers, in full march towards the house.

"We shall have a bloody battle of it," said Jerry. "But never fear, my lady; we will fight to the last gasp. Hollo, lads, here is a battle for you!"

At that magic word, all the Irishmen clubbed their sticks, and ran forward.

"We must surrender," said I. "Never could I bear the dreadful contest."

"By the mother that bore me," cried Jerry, "I will defend the house in spite of you!"

"Then I will walk out of it," said I.

"Well, surrender away!" cried Jerry, "and may all the—Oh! murder, murder, to give up your own good and true house without a bit of a battle!"

By this time the soldiers had arrived, and the magistrate who was at their head, advancing under the window, commanded me to have the door opened instantly.

"Provided you pledge yourself that none of my brave fellows shall be punished," answered I.

"Both they and you shall be punished with the utmost rigour of the law," said the magistrate.

"Then, if so," cried I, "and since I cannot keep possession of my house, I am resolved that no one else shall. Know, Sir, I have, at this instant, six of my domestics, each with a lighted brand, stationed in different apartments; so the moment you order your men to advance, that moment I give the signal, and the house bursts into a blaze."

"If you dare," cried the magistrate.

"Dare!" cried Lady Gwyn. "The creature would dare any thing. Dare! why she burned a house once before; so pray make some conditions with her, or she will burn this now. Surely you must remember her being here last week, and how she—" And her Ladyship whispered something in his ear.

"Is this the girl?" said he, "Nay, that alters the affair."

453

"Well, Madam, (addressing me) "will you promise never to come here again, provided I now permit you and your gang to pass without detention or punishment?"

"I will," answered I. "But I too must make some conditions. "In the first place, will your Ladyship give me back the box, with my clothes, jewels, and other valuables, which I left behind here?"

" Undoubtedly," answered she.

"In the next place," said I, "will you promise not to prevent me from inhabiting Monkton Castle, until such time as the law shall determine, which of us has a right to the contested estates?"

"Undoubtedly," answered she.

"And finally," said I, "I must have the distinct and unequivocal declaration of every individual present, that neither myself nor my people shall suffer any molestation in consequence of what we have done."

All present pledged their honours.

"Very well," said I, "we will now open the door."

Accordingly, we descended. The Warden opened it, and out I issued, with a majestic demeanour; while my awful band marched after their triumphant mistress.

Lady Gwyn and her guests hastened into the house, without even wishing me good evening; and the soldiers ranged themselves before the door.

In a few minutes, a servant came with my box. Having received it, I got into my barouche; and then, drawn by my Vassals, proceeded homeward.

"Well, Jerry," cried I, in a cheering tone. "Well, Jerry, my lad!"

"Well, Ma'am," said Jerry.

"Well," cried I, "that was famous, I think."

"What was famous, Ma'am?" said Jerry.

"Why that, all that."

"Death and 'ounds, all what?"

"Stupid man!" cried I. "I say, then, have we not obtained the most decisive advantages? Don't you think it was a glorious affair?"

"I think," said Jerry, "it was the bluest business that ever a set of chicken-hearted poltroons botched amongst them!"

"You may walk on, Sir," said I.

Jerry tossed his hat at one side, and strutted forward.

"Come back, dear Jerry," cried I. "Here is my hand. You are a faithful fellow, and would have died for me."

"Ah, bless you!" cried he. "You make war like a cat; but you shake hands like an angel!"

And now we began consulting, in good earnest, upon what was to be done; for we had not a morsel of food or a farthing of money. I proposed assembling and haranguing the tenantry: Jerry suggested a petition to the charitable and humane. At last, after a long silence, he suddenly touched his forehead with his finger:

"I have a thought!" said he. "I heard your Ladyship mention something about jewels in your box. Egad, I will go, this moment, to the town where I found these Irish lads, pawn the jewels, and bring back a cargo of eatables in their stead."

I adopted the expedient. The casket was produced, off he set; and I proceeded homeward with my vassals.

Arrived, I dismissed them for the night; but bade them call next day, to receive five shillings a man. I then paid another visit at the cottage, and assured its inhabitants of speedy relief.

On my return, the Minstrel came sneaking towards me, with his head down, to beg my pardon for his passionate conduct in the morning. This I easily accorded; and he then informed me, that during my absence, he had composed a poem upon me, which he promises to recite to-morrow.

Soon afterwards, the Warden, crowned with success, came joyously jogging towards the castle, in a hired cart.

And now, having alighted, he put a heap of money into my hand.

"There," said he, "there are twenty pounds, clear of all expences and now come see what I have brought you besides. Look there, my lady: six bottles of brandy, — six of wine, — two joints of mutton, — a surloin of beef,— a barrel of potatoes, —six pounds of tea, — six of sugar, — six loaves of bread; — a score of eggs---salt, pepper, mustard. Then look you here: a kettle---six knives and forks---six plates---six glasses---six cups and saucers---six spoons---a gridiron, a saucepan, and a teapot. Well, an't Jerry Sullivan the fellow after all?"

"I could have just done the same myself said the Minstrel; "and I would have bought some books besides."

"And what would be the use of books?" cried the Warden. "The world is all the worse for books. Had Adam and Eve books?"

"No," said the Minstrel, in extreme wrath; "nor six bottles of brandy, nor a surloin of beef either."

"And by the same token they lost Paradise," cried the Warden. "I tell you what, my man: if Eve had known the comforts of a hot beefsteak, bad luck to me, but the devil could never have tempted her with an apple!"

The several articles being now deposited in the archives of the castle, and the cart being discharged, we kindled a fire, and cooked a most delicious repast. I then sent some victuals to the poor cottagers; and afterwards dismissed the Minstrel and Warden to their nightly post.

It is probable that I may reside some time at the castle. As to the villa, I wish Lady Gwyn joy of it. I would not live in it, if she paid me: for I think it a perfect fright. Conceive the difference between the two. The villa, mere modern lath and plaster; with its pretty little draperies, and its pretty little pillars, and its pretty little bronzes. Nice, new, neat, and charming, are the only adjectives applicable to it; whereas antique, sublime, terrible, picturesque, and Gothic, are the Epic epithets appropriate to my Castello. What signify laced footmen, Chinese vases, Grecian tripods, and Turkish sofas, in comparison with feudal Vassals, ruined towers, black hangings, dampness, and ivy? And to a person of real taste, a single stone of this old edifice, is worth a whole waggon of such stones as the onyx, and sardonyx, and those other barbarous baubles belonging to Lady Gwyn. But nothing diverts me more than the idea, that her poor Ladyship is twice as old as the house she lives in! I have got a famous simile on the occasion. What think you of a decayed nut in an unripe shell? The woman is sixty if she is a day.

Adieu.

LETTER XXXIII

The moist shadows of Night had fled, Dawn shook the dew from his rosy ringlets; and the Sun, that well-known gilder of Eastern Turrets, arose with his usual punctuality. I too rose, and having now recovered my wardrobe, enjoyed the luxury of changing my dress; for, as I had worn the same garb several successive days, I was become a shocking slattern. How other heroines manage, I cannot conceive. Many of them, I remember, were thrown among mountains, or confined in cells, and chambers, and caverns, full of slime, mud, vermin, dust, and cobwebs; where they remained whole months, without either linen or soap, water or towel, brush or comb: and yet at last, when rescued from captivity, forth they walked, glittering like the morning star; as fragrant as a lily, and as fresh as an oyster.

We breakfasted upon the top of the Tower; and after our repast, the Minstrel begged permission to repeat his poem. With an emphatic enunciation, he thus began:

MONKTON CASTLE.

A METRICAL ROMAUNT.

I.

Awake, my harp, sweet plaintiff, wake once more,
    While Evening, draped in shadowy amice dim,
Steals westward to the Mississippian shore,
    And edges Ocean with a fiery rim.
Dampt by her dews, tho' dull thy music grow,
    (As crabbed critics check my natural strain)
The morning shall return, the Sun shall glow,
    The damping dews shall fly, the harp shall sound again.

II.

It was a Castle of turrets grey,
    In nettles and grass bedight;
Withouten a curtained window for day,
    Withouten a roof for night.
Yet once it had chambers, meet, I am sure.
    For Wassail and Bell-accoyle;
Where a Belamay, and a Belamoure,
    In sly Bellgards mote moyl."

"By Dad," said the Warden, "those same chambers had bells enough to bother the Rookery of Thomastown, and that is the largest in Ireland!"

The bard resumed:

457

III.

Nathlesse, to stablish her rights, I ween,
Liv'd in this Castle young Cherubine;
Her cheeks, where dimples made beauteous breach,
Daintily dawned, and the down on each,
Was soft as fur of unfinger'd peach.
Her glances shot out a dewy flame.
And the sky is blue, and her eyes were the same.

IV.

The Minstrel to the Castle hied,
His mother's hope, his mother's pride.
Gramercy, how that mother cried!
' Here, my delight and darling, take
This bread, and chicken; and this cake,
That I have made the baker bake.
So now one kiss.---Ah, Jemmy, ah! '
Were the last words of his mamma.

V.

He was a gentle man of thought,
And grave, but not ungracious aught.
His face with thinking lines was wrought.
Yet, tho' he pledged expensive books,
To spend the money on his looks:
Felt Cherubina such disdain,
That the poor Minstrel, with his strain,
 From the hour which is natal,
 To the hour which is fatal,
Might sing his humble love in vain."

"Eh! what? what's all that?" cried Jerry. "Why sure—body o'me, sure you an't—Oh, confound me, but 'tis making love to the mistress you are!"

The minstrel reddened, and then more pointedly repeated:

VI.

"Yet her favoured Warden, could he but sing,
He not unlistened, would touch the string.
Tho' he was a man with unchisseled face;

From eye to eye too petty a space;
A jester withouten one Attic joke,
And the greatest liar that ever spoke!"

"Bad luck to you, what do you mean?" cried Jerry, running towards him. "I will box you for a shilling!"

" I will box you for your life;" exclaimed the Minstrel, starting up, "though that is not worth half the money."

"'Hold, my friends!" cried I. "Higginson, I declare, your conduct is that of a child."

"Because you treat me like one;" whimpered he, "while you treat him like a man."

"At least," said I, "you should treat him like a gentleman."

"Arrah," cried Jerry, "rouse yourself from your snivelling jealousies, and give us a shake of the fist."

" Well, well," said the Minstrel, "here is my hand, My. Sullivan. The propitiation of a conciliatory observation, is better than excitation to personal encounter."

"Or in plain English," said Jerry, "a word to the heart is better than a blow at the head. An't that it? But here, now, you and her Ladyship call me a liar: and for what? Why, merely because I happened to say I saw that unlucky Pacific Ocean, and those curst particoloured seas, when I did'nt. And now what harm was a lie like that? Harm? Hang me, but here are some lies worthier and better than some truths. An't it better to tell a lie of, 'I'm glad to see you;' than a truth of 'I don't care a button about you?' And give me the man that swears my mother will live, when he knows she won't, rather than the grim dog, that says, 'Sir, the woman will be a corpse to-morrow morning.' Why now, without lies, how could the world wag at all at all? Sure, an't Bonaparte, who conquered half the world, the greatest Bouncer in it? And sure, if I had'nt told lies for my mistress, about her not being at home, I could never have kept my place a day; and sure, the moment I told her a bit of a truth, I got kicked out of the house. Oh, yes, indeed! we call a man a terrible rascal, if he tells truths that make against us: but if he tells lies that make for us, 'tis, 'give me your hand, my good friend, and my dear friend;' ay, faith, 'and my honest friend.' And moreover, a poor man is ruined for telling the same lies that are thought nothing in the mouth of a gentleman. And sure, did'nt her Ladyship herself, tell the biggest lie in Christendom, when she swore to the magistrate, that she had six firebrands ready for setting the house on fire? Faith and conscience, I could not believe my ears! And sure, did'nt yourself, Mr. Higginson, say something in your poem, just now, about her Ladyship's having a cheek that dawned? A cheek dawn? 'Pon my salvation, Mr. Higginson, I wonder at you!"

"Why," said the Minstrel, in some confusion, "we poets are permitted a peculiar latitude of language; which enables us to tell Homeric falsehoods, without fear of prosecution from the society for discountenancing vice. Thus, when we speak of,

'The lightning of her smile,'

we do not expect one to believe that fire comes out of her mouth, when she laughs with it."

"Not unless her teeth were flints," said the Warden. " But if you said that fire came out of her eves, one would believe you sooner; for this I know, that many and many a time Molly has struck fire out of mine."

"A heroine's eye," said I, "gives a greater scope to the poet than any thing in the world. It is all fire and water. If it is not beaming, or sparkling, it is sure to be drowned or swimming — "

"In the Pacific Ocean, I hope," cried the Warden.

"No, but in tears," said the Minstrel. "And of these there is an infinite variety. There is the big tear, and the bitter tear, and the salt tear, and the scalding tear."

"And, ah!" cried I, "how delightful, when two lovers lay cheek to cheek, and mingle these tears; or when the tender youth kisses them from the cheek of his mistress."

"Troth, then," said Jerry, "that must be no small compliment, since they are so brackish and so scalding. Water itself is maukish at any time, but salt water is the devil. Well, if I took such a dose of tears, I would be after seasoning it with a dram, or my name is not Jerry."

"And, indeed, I wish Jerry were not your name," said I. " 'Tis so vulgar for a Warden. I have often thought of altering it to *Jeronymo*; which I fancy, is the Italian for *Jerry*. Nothing can equal Italian names ending in O."

"Except Irish names beginning with O," cried Jerry.

"Nay," said I, "what can be finer than Montalto, Stefano, Morano, Rinaldo, Ubaldo, Utaldo?"

"I will tell you what is finer," said Jerry. " O'Brien, O'Leary, O'Flaherty, O'Flannigan, O'Guggerty, O'Shaughnassy — "

460

"Oh, ecstasy!" exclaimed a voice just beneath the turret. I looked down, and beheld — Montmorenci himself, clad in complete steel, and raising his extended arms towards me, with a grace that mocked mortal pencil.

I waved my hand and smiled.

"What? whom do I behold?" cried he. "Ah, 'tis but a dream! Yet I spoke to her, I am sure I spoke to her; and she beckoned me. Merciful powers! Wherefore this terror? Is it not Cherubina, and would Cherubina harm her Montmorenci?"

"Jerry, Jerry," said I; "run down to the Black Chamber, and clean it out quick. Sweep the ashes into a corner, put the bottle in your pocket, slip the leg of mutton under the bed. Run, run, run! - My lord, the Lady Cherubina hastens to receive your Lordship at her ever-open portal."

I then descended, and met him beneath the gateway. His greeting was frantic, but decorous; mine tender, but reserved. Several very elegant things were said on both sides. Of course, he snatched my hand, and carried it to his lips.

At last, when I supposed that Jerry had regulated the room above, I conducted his Lordship up stairs; while I anxiously anticipated his delight at beholding so legendary, fatal, and inconvenient a chamber.

His astonishment, indeed, was excessive. He stared round and round, admired the hangings, the pictures, the bed, the nettles; every thing.

"I see," said he, approaching the ashes, "that you are even classical enough to burn a fire of wood. But ha! — (and he started), what do mine eyes behold beneath these embers? A BONE, by all that is horrible! Perhaps part of the skeleton of some hysterical Innocent, or some pathetic Count, who was murdered centuries ago, in the haunted apartment of this mysterious castle. Interesting relic! Speak, Lady Cherubina. Is it as I suspect?"

"Why," said I, "I believe—that is to say—for aught I can tell— "

"Bless your Ladyship!" cried Jerry, "sure 'tis nothing at all at all, but the blade-bone of mutton, which was broiled for your supper last night!"

"Impossible, Sir," said his Lordship.

"A heroine never eats any thing less delicate than the leg of a lark, or the wing of a chicken."

461

"Pray, Mr. Blunderer," whispered I to Jerry, "did I not bid you clean out the room?"

"You did'nt say a word about the blade-bone," answered Jerry.

"But did I not bid you clean out the room?" repeated I.

"Don't I tell you — " cried Jerry.

"Can't you speak low?" said I.

"Don't I tell you that not one syllable about the blade-bone ever came outside your lips?"

"Grant me patience!" said I. "Answer me yes or no. Did I, or did I not, order you to clean out the room?"

"Now curse me," said he, "if you an't all this time confounding the blade-bone of mutton, with the leg of mutton, that you bade me put under the bed. And accordingly— "

"Gracious goodness!" said I, "can't you speak within your breath?"

"And accordingly," whispered he, "I put it under the velvet pall, 'cause I thought it might be seen under the bed."

"Well, that, at least, shewed some sort of discretion," said I.

"Though, with all my pains," said Jerry, "there is the man in the tin clothes, has just stripped down that same pall, and discovered the mutton, and the saucepan, and the bag of salt, and the pewter spoons, and the brandy bottle, and the —"

"Oh, Jerry, Jerry!" said I, "after that, I give you up!"

I then called his Lordship, and drew off his attention, by commencing an account of what had happened me, since our parting. He listened with great eagerness; and, after my recital, begged of the Warden to accompany him down stairs, that they might consult together, upon my present situation.

They descended; I remained alone. Montmorenci had left his helmet, shield, and spear behind. I pressed each of them to my heart, heaved several sighs, and paced the chamber. Still I felt that I was not half tender enough; something was still wanting, and I had just asked myself, could that something be Love? when I heard a sudden disturbance below; his Lordship exclaiming, "Oh, what shall I do?" and Jerry crying, "grin and bear it!"

Down I hastened; and beheld Jerry belabouring that nobleman; whose mouth was already gushing blood.

"Wretch," cried I, "forbear."

462

"Not till I beat a rainbow into his face!" cried Jerry. "The ruffian! to go and offer me half your fortune, if I would assist him in running away with you."

" 'Tis false, Sirrah!" cried his Lordship.

"False as the Prince of Lies, my Montmorenci!" said I. "So now, Sullivan, take your choice---ask pardon, or quit my service, this very moment."

"But can his asking pardon, restore the teeth he has knocked down my throat?" exclaimed his Lordship, with a finger in his mouth.

"Teeth!" cried I, shuddering.

"Two teeth," lisped he.

"Two teeth!" exclaimed I, faintly.

"Two front upper teeth," lisped he again.

"Then all is over!" muttered I. "Matters have taken a dreadful turn."

"What do you mean?" cried he.

"My lord," said I, "are you quite, quite certain that you have lost those teeth?"

"See yourself," cried he, lifting his lip. "They are gone, gone for ever!"

"They are gone indeed," said I. "And now---you may be gone too!"

"I be gone?" cried he. "What the mischief —"

"My lord," said I, solemnly; "you must already be well aware, that a full, complete, and perfect set of teeth, are absolutely indispensible to a Hero."

"Well?" cried he, starting.

"Well then," said I, "since you have now lost two of your teeth, it follows---pardon me—that you are no longer a Hero."

"You stretch my heart-strings!" shouted he. "Speak! what hideous whim is this?"

"No whim, my lord," answered I; "but principle; principle founded upon the Law Heroic; founded upon that Law, which rejects as Heroes, the maimed, the blind, the deformed, and the crippled. Oh, my good lord, trust me, trust me, teeth are just as necessary in the formation of a Hero, as of a comb."

"By Heaven," cried he; "I can get other teeth at a Dentist's;---a composition of paste, which would amaze you! I can, by Heaven!"

"Then that you may, my lord," said I, "and be happy with them; for never will you be happy with me."

"I am wilder than madness itself!" exclaimed he; "I am more desperate than despair! I will fly to the ends of the earth, and throw my ideas into a sonnet. On a fine summer's evening, when you walk towards the mountains, sometimes think of me."

"Never as a lover, my lord;" said I; "and, oh, how it shocks me to think, that I should ever have received you as one!"

He commenced a tremendous imprecation; but was interrupted by the sudden arrival of a gentleman on horse-back, with two servants after him. The gentleman stopped, alighted, approached.

"Mr. Betterton!" exclaimed I; "can it be possible?"

"Nothing is impossible," said he, with his confirmed smile, "when the charming Cherubina prompts our efforts. You remember you left me in a dilemma, which your facetious friend, Stuart, had contrived;---it was an admirable manœuvre, 'pon my soul;---and I made my friends so merry with an account of it. Well, I remained in durance vile, till the Sessions; when none appearing to prosecute, the judge discharged me; so the earliest use I made of my liberty, was visiting Lady Gwyn; who told me that I should see you here:--- here, therefore, I am; and find you just as much of the angel as ever."

I thanked him; and then whispered the Warden to run towards the village, and call my Vassals; as the Castle lost much of its pomp without them,

Betterton and Montmorenci soon recognized each other; for you may remember they had met at the closet-scene; and already were they casting reciprocal looks of suspicion and jealousy, when, on a sudden, three men turned short round the western tower, and stood before me.

"There is the woman! " cried one of them, pointing me out.

I looked at the speaker, and perceived that he was the identical postillion who had brought down the barouche.

"Your name is Cherry Wilkinson," said another of them, advancing.

"Sir," said I, haughtily, "my name is Lady Cherubina de Willoughby."

"That is your *travelling* name," rejoined he: "and now, Miss, look at this warrant. I arrest you, in the King's name, for having swindled the coachmaker out of yonder barouche."

He seized me. I screamed.

"A rescue!" cried his Lordship, and collared him.

"A rescue!" cried Betterton, and collared another.

"A rescue!" cried the servants, and fell upon the third.

In short, the constables and the postillion soon got a dreadful drubbing; and at last, were happy to make their escape across the common.

"This rescue, however, may prove a serious affair," said Betterton. "Mr. Grundy, will you step aside, and advise with me?"

They retired, and talked together some time. At length they returned, and Betterton thus addressed me: —

"Lady Cherubina, our zeal for you has induced us to assault officers, in the discharge of their duty. If, therefore, we remain at this castle much longer, we shall certainly be arrested and hanged."

"Then, pray, fly this moment!" exclaimed I.

"Yes, if your Ladyship will fly with us," said Betterton.

"No, Sir," answered I. "I shall remain here; for I am innocent of the assault."

"But they will seize you for swindling," said. Betterton.

"Then I will go with them," answered I, "establish my innocence, and return triumphant; whereas, if I act upon the skulking system, I cannot reside here at all."

Montmorenci now joined his entreaties, but I remained immoveable. Again they retired to consult, and again came forward.

"Lady Cherubina," said Betterton, "you must excuse me when I say, that both this gentleman and myself conceive ourselves fully warranted, by principles of regard for your welfare, in compelling, if we cannot persuade you, to leave this castle."

"In compelling me?" cried I. "Santa Maria! But I disdain to hold farther parley with you. Farewell for ever."

"Stop her!" cried Betterton.

"Higginson!" cried I. "Help, Higginson!"

His Lordship ran forward, and caught me round the waist; just as the Minstrel, with his pen across his mouth, came issuing from the castle.

"Save me, save me!" exclaimed I.

The Minstrel, brandishing his collected knuckles, struck Montmorenci to the ground. Betterton and his servants instantly assailed the Minstrel; but he felled a man at every blow, and every blow was like the kick of a horse. Still what could he do against four? If one dropped, three stood. And now they had hemmed him round; and now his breath grew shorter, and his blow slower, and all appeared lost, when, transport to my sight! I beheld Jerry, with several Vassals, come running towards us. They reach us: the tide of battle turns; his Lordship and the servants are well beaten with bludgeons, and Jerry himself does the honours to Betterton, in a kicking.

Nobody could bear it more gently than he did; but after it was over, he mounted his horse, and vociferated: —

"Now, by all that is sacred, I will go this moment, raise the neighbourhood, and drive you from your nest, you vipers,---you common nuisances! Lady Gwyn's castle shall no longer be made the receptacle of maniacs and marauding Irishmen!"

So saying, off he gallopped on one horse, and his Lordship on another; while the servants retreated as well as they could.

We now held a grand Council of War; for affairs began to wear a most alarming aspect. If Betterton should really put his threat of raising the neighbourhood, into execution, a most formidable force might soon be collected against us. After much deliberation, therefore, it was decided, that some of the Vassals should instantly be dispatched to hasten the remainder; and to collect others of their countrymen, who were in adjoining villages.

At this crisis, I recollected Susan.

"Now is the time," thought I, "for the gratitude of this amiable girl to manifest itself. I have rescued her from a criminal attachment; she will rescue me from an inexorable foe; and so will end the Episode."

I therefore wrote a note, reminding her of past services, informing her of my present situation, and begging that she would immediately raise a counterposse in my favour. This I sent by a vassal.

During the awful interval which ensued, I ordered the Warden and the Minstrel up to the Black Chamber.

"Warden," said I, "both my person and my property hang upon the issue of this approaching contest. Will you stand by me? Will you, Warden?"

"Will you, Warden!" repeated he. "Why then, if ever your Ladyship deserved that I should'nt, 'tis for that very 'Will you, Warden!"

"And, will you, Minstrel?" said I.

"Till I drop," answered the Minstrel; "provided you promise not to tell my mamma."

"I will not, upon my word," said I.

"And honour?"

"And honour."

"Because," said he, "a few weeks ago, I got a black eye from a porter, who was insulting a turnspit; and when I returned home, mamma sent me to bed without my dinner."

"Now," said I, "I constitute you, Sullivan, Commander of the forces; and you, Higginson, Commander of the Castle. Go, therefore, Higginson; bring me up six picked men, as body-guards; and also the tin horn. Go, Sullivan, dispatch scouts, plant sentinels and outposts, repair the breaches, and blockade the windows with stones."

They retired. I paused to reflect upon the sublime part which I was about performing. I was about laying the foundation of a feudal colony. I was about restoring that chivalric age, when neighbouring Barons were deadly foes, and their sons and daughters clandestine lovers; that age, when Heroines headed armies; and when the Lady Buccleugh and Beatrice, Duchess of Cleves, flourished.

"And these," cried I, in an ecstasy of enthusiasm, "these shall now be the immortal models of the Lady Cherubina de Willoughby."

As I spoke, up came Higginson and the guards. I equipped them in black cloaks and feathers, and made them mount guard on the battlements above.

Not having a white and azure standard, as Beatrice had, I tore off the skirts of two rubes—a white and a blue; stitched them together, fastened them to the pole of the barouche, and then made Higginson plant this banner upon the top of the tower.

And now an outscout, quite breathless, arrived with the important intelligence, that a large party of Lady Gwyn's tenantry were already gathering, at Betterton's instigation, about half a mile distant.

Instantly afterwards, the messenger, whom I had sent to Susan, returned with the information, that she would certainly assemble her friends, and assist me.

Another vassal then came back, bringing a fresh accession of Irishmen; and every successive moment, more and more arrived; till, at last, we mustered to the amount of fifty.

467

All being ready, I determined upon ascending the battlements, and haranguing my men. But as I knew nothing whatever of popular orations, except what I had sometimes heard my reputed father read, my only alternative was to imitate these, and also the speech of Beatrice, in the Knights of the Swan.

However, that I might appear with a suitable degree of grandeur, and at once awe my foes and charm my friends, I first flung my embroidered gauze over my robe; next, (like ancient Heroines, who wore armour in the day of battle), I placed upon my head the helmet of Montmorenci; and lastly, I snatched his shield and his spear.

Thus equipped, I mounted, with a beating heart, to the top of the tower.

There I found every preparation complete. The white and azure standard was streaming gloriously. The guards lined the parapet; and underneath the turret, I beheld the whole of my troops, marshalled in a long line, and grasping their oaken arms.

The spectacle was grand and imposing. Lightly I leaned on my spear; and while my feathered casque pressed my ringlets, and my tissued drapery floated to the breeze, and glistened to the sun; I stood upon the battlements, mildly sublime, sweetly stern, amiable in arms, and adorned with all the terrible graces of Beauty Belligerent.

A profound silence prevailed. I waved my spear, and thus began:

"My brave associates, partners of my toil, my feelings and my fame. Two days have I now been sovereign of this castle; and I hope I may flatter myself, that I have added to its prosperity. Young, and without experience, I merely claim the merit of blameless sentiments and intentions.

"Threatened with a barbarous incursion from my deadliest enemies, I have deemed it indispensible to collect, for my defence, a faithful band of Vassals. They have flocked at my call, and I thank them.

"I promise them all such laws and institutions, as shall secure their happiness. I will acknowledge the Majesty of the People;— (Applause). I will institute a full, fair, and free Representation;— (Applause). And I will establish a Radical Reform; or, in other words, a revival of the Feudal System. (Shouts of applause).

"I promise that there shall be no dilapidated hopes and resources; no army of mercenaries, no army of spies, no inquisition of private property, no degraded aristocracy, no oppressed people, no confiding parliament, no irresponsible minister. (Acclamation). In short, I promise every thing. (Thunders of acclamation).

"Such is the constitution, such are the privileges, which I propose. Now, my brave fellows, will you consent, on these conditions, to rally round my standard; to live in my service, and to die in my defence?"

"Ay, ay, ay!" shouted they.

"Thank you, my generous followers; and the crisis is just approaching, when I shall prove your loyalty. Already my mortal foe prepares to storm my castle, and drive me from my hereditary domain. Already he has excited my tenantry to Rebellion. Should he conquer us, I must return to my tears, and you to your sickles. But should we repel him, the cause of Liberty will triumph. What heart but throbs, what voice but shouts, at the name of Liberty? (Huzza!) Is there a man amongst you, who would not lay down his life for Liberty? (Huzza!) And if, on this important occasion, I might take the liberty---(Huzza!) to dictate, I would demand of you to sacrifice every earthly consideration in her cause. I do demand it of you, my friends. I call upon your feelings, your principles, and your interest, to risk family, property, and life, in a cause so just, so wise, and so glorious. Let foot, eye, heart, hand; be firm, be stern, be valiant, be invincible!"

I ceased, the soldiery tore the blue air with acclamations, and the crows overhead flew swifter at the sound.

I now found that a popular speech was not difficult; and I judged, from my performance, that the same qualities which have made me so good a Heroine, would, if I were a man, have made me just as illustrious a Patriot.

"Silence, lads," cried Jerry, breaking into full brogue, "and I will make a bit of a speech; but as to the long words her Ladyship used, I got a surfeit of 'em once, so I'll pass 'em over now; tho' I do suppose her honourable Ladyship meant all for the best. Mind, lads, devil a hair are we to care, you know, whether her Ladyship is right or wrong about this business of the castle; only if she's wrong, 'tis more our duty to take her part. For people can find friends enough, when they're in the right, but the true friend is he that sticks by one, right or wrong. I say then, we don't know whether her Ladyship has justice on her side or not; but this we know, that she is a woman, and in distress; and that we are Irishmen, and have shillelaghs! (shouts) So, do you hear, boys? scratch out entirely that you are in

469

England; and just fancy yourselves at Donnybrook Fair, going to have a famous set to of sticks! (Huzzas) Eh, my boys? Don't you remember the good old fun at Donnybrook Fair? And how we used to break each other's heads there, without meaning any harm at all at all? And for certain, 'tis the finest thing in the world, when a body gives a body a neat, clean, bothering blow over the scull, and down

he drops like a sack; and then rises, and shakes himself, like a wet spaniel, and begins again as merrily as ever! (great huzzaing) So, now boys, if any of you tumble, mind you get up quick, and don't sneak with your noses on the ground, like shying Paddy Goggin. Fight it out, my hearties; egad fight it out, till you are as weak as a horse! (much laughter) Ay, lads, — for all your laughing — as weak as a horse. Sure an Irishman, when he's tired will be only as weak as a horse; for when he's not tired, by the powers, he's as strong as a lion! (shouts of applause) And if your right arms get disabled, fight with your left; just as I did, the day I was sawing off the branches of a tree, and by some mistake or other, sawed off the branch I was astride upon, and down I fell ten feet, and broke my arm. And a fellow begins a laughing. Oho, says I, if I don't soon make you laugh at the wrong side of your mouth, says I; and I whips up a branch, and we sets to, my left against his right; and never was such a threshing as he got — I mean as I know he would have got, only, somehow, he happened, first of all, to beat my head as soft as pap; — and that was cursed hard, you know, boys. So now, success, my hearties! Spit upon your hands, club your sticks, then hi for Donnybrook Fair; and never heed me if we hav'nt a nice comfortable fight of it. Fighting may be an Englishman's business; but, by the Lord Harry, 'tis an Irishman's amusement!"

Rude as was this rhetoric, it touched the domestic spring of their hearts; and my patriotic promises did not produce half such a roar of delight as succeeded it.

Silence was but just restored, when I beheld, from my turret, our enemies advancing, in vast numbers, across the common. I confess my heart sank at the sight; but I soon called to mind the courage of the Feudal Heroines; and besides, I recollected that I was in no personal danger myself. Then, the greatness of the cause animating me with ardour I exclaimed:

"Lo! yonder come our enemies. To arms, to arms! blow, blow the horn!"

The Trumpeter blew the horn.

The Warden then stationed his men just in front of the gateway, which was the only vulnerable entrance into the castle; and my guards, poising huge stones, leaned forward over the battlements. All were prepared.

And now the foe, having approached within forty paces, halted to reconnoitre. The traitor Montmorenci, divested of his armour, commanded in person. Betterton was seen on horseback, at a distance; and the hostile troops themselves, who were about seventy, stood brandishing stakes, bludgeons, and poles. As all my men, the guards included, were only fifty, I looked round, with anxious expectation for Susan and her succours; but no sign of them appeared.

Montmorenci now began to form his troops into a compact phalanx, with the poles and stakes in front; evidently for the purpose of piercing our line, and forcing the gateway. Jerry, therefore, called in both the wings, and strengthened the centre. At this instant a thought struck me.

"Soldiers," cried I, "the moment you hear the horn sound, whether you are conquering or not conquering, hurry back to the gateway and make a stand there. You will not forget?"

"No, no, no!"

"You will recollect?"

"Ay, ay, ay!"

"Three cheers!" cried the Warden.

They gave three cheers.

"And now, my brave defenders," cried I, "success attend your arms!"

As I spoke, the foe began advancing at a rapid rate: my troops awaited them with firmness. And now, when they had approached within fifteen paces of the castle, I gave the word to my guards, who hurled two vollies of stones in quick succession. Part of the foremost rank were staggered; some behind fell, and amidst the confusion, in rushed my troops, with a tremendous shout. Thick pressed the throng of waving heads, and loud grew the clamour of voices, and the clatter of staffs; while the wielded weapons appeared and disappeared, like fragments of a wreck on the tossing surges. For some moments, both armies fought in one unbroken mass; those struggling to gain the gateway, these to prevent them. But soon, as two streams, rushing from opposite mountains, and meeting in the valley, broaden into a lake, and run off in little rivulets; so the contending ranks, after the first encounter, began to widen by degrees, and scatter over the plain. And now they were seen intermingled with each other, and fighting man to man. Warriors dropped and rose, and dropped again. Here a small wing of my brave troops, hemmed round on all sides, were defending themselves with incredible fury. There, a larger division were maintaining a desperate contest: while up and down, a few straggling Vassals, engaged in single combat, were driving their antagonists before them. Just at this juncture, Montmorenci, with a chosen band, that he kept round his person, had attacked the Warden, and a few who fought beside him. These placed their backs against an old oak, and performed prodigies of valour; but at last, overpowered by numbers, were beginning to retire, covered with glory, when I sent forth four of my guards, as a corps de reserve. These rushed upon the chosen band, broke through it, and joined the Warden. Again the contest became equal, and the Warden made a sudden spring forward to attack Montmorenci. But this prudent general, who was always behind his men, eluded him; and at the same moment, received a reinforcement. I then saw him point out the Warden; and instantly a desperate charge was made, to take my Chief prisoner. And now I see him struck down, and his enemies over him, belabouring him furiously. I shriek, I call to spare him; I conjure Higginson and another vassal to run and rescue him. Higginson has no arms; but down he rushes, and soon issues from the portal, bareheaded, his cloak flying, and his hand brandishing the leg of mutton;---but to me he seems an angel of mercy. He reaches the spot, presses through the throng, stands astride over the Warden, and fells numbers. All now depends upon his prowess. I gasp, spread my hands, hang upon his blows; wince as the sticks strike him, and move as he moves, with agonized mimickry.

At length the Warden jumps up! But in the same instant, I perceive Montmorenci beckoning his men towards the turret; and I recollect that I have only one solitary defender remaining there. This is the crisis of the battle. If the foe now reach the turret, I am made a prisoner. A moment more, and all is lost.

"Blow the horn!" cried I.

The Trumpeter blew the horn.

At this signal, I see my dispersed troops come pouring from all quarters, towards the Castle. They reach the gateway, halt, and form a front before it. The foe, who had followed, in a confused and

472

scattered manner, seeing them, on a sudden, so formidable, stop short.

"Guards, come into the castle!" cried I.

The guards obeyed.

"Now, soldiers," cried I to the rest, "rush upon the foe, before they can collect again; keep in a body with your captain, and the day is our own. Spring on them like lions! Away, away!"

The whole army shouted, and burst forward in a mass. Jerry led the van. Montmorenci, with his sacred squadron, fled before them. They pursued, overtook the fugitives, and after a short skirmish, made the whole detachment prisoners; while the remainder, in scattered parties, stood at a distance, and dared not advance. Never was a more decisive victory. Jerry marched back, holding Montmorenci fast; the troops followed, escorting eight other prisoners, and Higginson, with his leg of mutton, worn to the bone, brought up the rear. They halted at the gateway, and gave three cheers.

Palpitating with transport, I commanded Jerry to tie the prisoners' hands behind their backs; to place sentinels over them, and to confine them in the Green Chamber of the Northern Tower.

As for Montmorenci, his rank demanded more respect; so I ordered his Lordship, unfettered, into the Black Chamber. There, amidst my guards, I stood to receive him; and surely, if ever grandeur and urbanity were blended in one countenance, they met in mine, at that immortal moment.

"My lord," said I, "Victory, who long flapped her doubtful pinions over the field, has at length descended upon my legions; and has crowned the scale of Justice with the laurel of Glory. But though she has also put the person of the hostile Chieftain in my power, think not I intend to exercise that power harshly. Within these walls, your Lordship shall experience hospitable treatment; but beyond them you cannot be permitted, till my rights are re-established, and my rebellious Vassals restored to their allegiance."

"Fal lal la, lal lal la," hummed his Lordship, as he began stepping a minuet.

"Pinion him hand and foot!" cried I, quite disgusted and enraged.

"That I will!" said Jerry, "his feet in particular; for though he talks big, he runs fast. Egad, he's all voice and legs like a grasshopper."

473

Leaving Jerry to perform this office, I descended, and found my men within the walls, wiping their faces, and bandaging their wounds; but they forgot all in their cordial greetings. I sent one of them to watch at the gateway, and one at the top of the tower; made others kindle a fire in the area of the castle, produced my provisions, and bade the whole army cook a dinner for themselves. So they put down the potatoes, cut the surloin into slices, portioned the bread, and laughed and joked, and were the happiest of human beings.

Meantime I got another fire lighted in the Black Chamber, bade the Warden untie Montmorenci's hands, and deputed four of my handsomest Vassals, elegantly cloaked and feathered, and with bread, meat, plates, two bottles of wine, &c. to tend his Lordship at dinner. I confess I felt a pleasure in thus displaying my munificence and hospitality, even before a foe.

And now dinner was almost ready; the beef was broiling, the potatoes roasting, and my people busied round the fire, when the sentinel from the turret came running down to tell me, that a number of men, with a girl at their head, were approaching the castle.

" 'Tis Susan!" exclaimed I, and hurried to the gateway. It was indeed, Susan herself, and a train of youths, advancing rapidly. However, as Betterton and the routed remains of his army were still between her and the castle, I trembled lest they should intercept her.

I therefore summoned forth my forces, and stood prepared to support her. Presently she approached the foe, stopped, and conversed some time with them. But just judge of my consternation, when I beheld, both herself and her minions, enrolling themselves among the hostile ranks; and when I heard the whole allied army utter a shout of exultation! I was horror-struck. Her ingratitude, her perfidy were incredible, execrable !

But I had no time for moral reflection. My own glory, and the interests of my people, demanded all my thoughts. What was I to do? We had taken but nine prisoners, and even these would require a strong guard; while Susan had brought the foe a reinforcement of forty men; so that to contend against such superior numbers in the field, were madness.

I therefore called the Warden, and held a Council of War. The result was, to draw all my troops, and all my prisoners, into the eastern turret; and there stand a regular siege. For, as we still retained a large stock of provisions, we might hold out several days;

474

while our enemies, having other occupations of more importance, would probably retire, and leave us in quiet possession.

This plan was put into immediate execution. First, the prisoners, well handcuffed, were conveyed up to the Black Chamber, and then we set about fortifying the castle.

All the loopholes had already been well stopped with stones; and now the only vulnerable points, were the gateway leading into the castle, and the doorway leading up to the turret.

We therefore set twenty vassals at work, who, in a short time, pulled down enormous fragments from one of the towers, and barricaded the gateway with an impenetrable pile five feet thick. The wall just above the gateway, being much dilapidated, was not more than ten feet from the ground; so this pile was made high enough and broad enough for four men to stand upon it, and command the pass underneath; while the wall itself would serve them as a breastwork.

The doorway was not stopped at all, because it might be found necessary as a chain of communication with those stationed at the gateway, and as an opening for their retreat; and also, because the winding, abrupt, and narrow stairs, would enable a few men to defend that pass against whole hosts.

When these important preparations were completed, I mounted the tower, for the purpose of observing the motions of the enemy. They still stood at some distance, watching our works; but I was astonished to find their numbers sensibly lessened. However, I was not long astonished; as I soon perceived some of their absent party returning, and bearing six long ladders, and two short; and after them, another party, escorting three large carts of hay.

What the hay meant, I could not imagine; but I quickly discovered, that the ladders were for the purpose of scaling the castle. This was quite an unforeseen manœuvre; and, I confess, staggered me. I therefore called the Warden, and asked him what I should do? Should I harangue my men? He said, a glass of brandy each, would answer better. So they got the brandy. I then stationed four of them upon the breastwork over the gateway, with orders to retreat into the turret, should the besiegers gain the wall. Next, I placed ten men, under Higginson, within the doorway, to guard the stairs; two to watch the prisoners in the Black Chamber; and the remainder, under Jerry, to man the battlements above.

I, too, took post upon the battlements, and standing there, gloried in my strength; for now the fortress appeared impregnable.

By this time, the besieging army had formed, and all things announced an immediate attack. I therefore ordered the horn to sound, and I stationed myself, still armed, just underneath the standard.

At length the enemy began his march. The scaling ladders and the carts of hay came first; Betterton, on horseback, was seen directing their route, and Susan walked in the midst of the troops, using the most masculine and vehement gesticulations.

They halted within about thirty yards of us. Then one storming party, with the short ladders, filed off opposite the gateway; while another, with the long ladders, and their heads protected by bundles of hay, stood ready to scale the turret. Our troops intrepidly awaited the onset; but I trembled.

And now Betterton gave the word, Away! That moment the carts were driven rapidly just under the turret; and all the hay upset and spread about, in despite of the stony storm, which my men hurled from above. Then the scaling ladders were applied; some held them fast, others mounted. But no sooner had these reached the summit of the ladders, than my troops flung them down headlong. They fell unharmed upon the hay; instantly those behind them pushed up, — down they went. Another set succeeded, and shared a similar fate; and another, and another, and another.

I was standing, a delighted spectator of the operations on this wing, when I heard the battle raging fiercely at the gateway. I ran towards that side, and saw numbers of the foe just leaping from the wall, down into the castle; and my discomfited outposts making good their retreat into the turret. The foe followed them with horrid huzzas; and I could hear the din of war at the very doorway. The stairs themselves were contested! And now the conflict on the battlements became more desperate. I heard Betterton ordering a general attack, and Susan bidding the men bring me to her, dead or alive. Almost instantly after, I beheld three of the assailants, struggling, scrambling up the parapet, and at last, jumping down into the tower. I beheld too, the Warden himself, flying before them, and rushing down the stairs. I scream more like a seagull than a Heroine; I call after him, I give all over as lost. And now the heads of other assailants, appear above the parapet; and I am in the act of flying after the Warden, when I meet him rushing up again, with a

476

reinforcement of five men, all holding lighted sticks. They run, they fling the brands from the battlements, they seize the three who had made a lodgement; and the battle rages with greater fury than ever.

And now the noise at the doorway grew louder, and now I heard Higginson cry from the Black Chamber, "The prisoners are breaking loose!" when twenty voices underneath the turret, shouted together, "The hay is on fire; come down, come down!"

In an instant those on the ladders disappear; and a tremendous blaze rises to the top of the turret. "Draw up the ladders!" cries the Warden, and the ladders are drawn up. "Put them down at this side," cries he again, and they are put down. Then all my troops, he heading them, descended into the area, and attacked the rear of those who were assailing the stairs. Those, quite surrounded and cut off, made but a feeble resistance, and soon surrendered; while their companions outside, deprived of ladders, stood at a cool distance from the conflagration of hay; idly gaping; and uselessly listening to the fate of the party within.

An universal and reverberating shout from my troops below, announced the completion of this important, decisive, and unrivalled victory.

I then descended to congratulate my friends. I found them securing the prisoners, with their own neckcloths and handkerchiefs; but on seeing me, these brave fellows pealed another exulting acclamation. I thanked them in silent gestures and tears of joy; and Jerry exclaimed :

"Well, mistress, wasn't burning the hay a fine device? Edad, I thought I'd just tip 'em a Moscow! Why then, your thundering lie about the six fire-brands, was what put it into my head; so you see the use of lies, after all!"

The prisoners taken in this battle, (which I call the Battle of Monkton), were thirty-five; besides arms, ladders, and bundles of hay. So having ordered my troops to renew their interrupted preparations for dinner, I mounted the battlements again. Thence, I perceived, that Betterton and the wretched remnant of his army, had not yet retreated from the field.

As soon, however, as Betterton espied me leaning over the battlements, he waved a white handkerchief, and advanced alone, under the walls. I summoned the Warden and the Minstrel.

"Lady Cherubina de Willoughby," said he. "I demand of you to surrender at discretion. Refuse, and I pledge myself, that I will drive

477

the Leopard into the sea, and plant my standard upon the towers of Monkton."

"Sir, I refuse, and I defy you," replied I.

"Well then," said he, "since the prosecution of the war is inevitable, I shall stand acquitted of all its consequences, if I now go through the mere formula of proposing a GENERAL PACIFICATION."

"Pacifi—oh, by dad!" cried Jerry, "a word beginning that way will never do. Try another."

"Nay, my honest fellow— "

"Never honest-fellow me," cried Jerry. "It won't take, old boy. Whenever a man calls me an honest fellow, I always suspect he wants to make me a rogue. And a rogue, I dare say, I am; and will be again, if it pleases heaven; but may Beelzebub and all his imps and impesses, take and fry me before my own face, if ever I play the rogue to her Ladyship here, who saved me and my wife and daughter from ruin!"

"Instead of giving her bad advice, then," said Betterton, "you would be much better at home, helping your wife and daughter to boil the potatoes."

"Why then, bad manners to you, and that is worse than bad luck!" cried Jerry, "if you're for boiling, go boil your own tongue hard, like a calve's, and then it won't wag so glib and sly;—ay, and go boil that nose of your's white, like veal. But you will neither beat us out, nor starve us out; for we have sticks and stones, and meat and wine; and will eat together, and drink together, and— "

"And sleep together," interrupted Betterton; "because, as we shall now turn the siege into a blockade, her Ladyship, out of her infinite patriotism, will think nothing whatever of sleeping in the same room with sixty or seventy men."

The fatal words fell upon me, like a thunderbolt! It was indeed, too true, that some of my troops and prisoners must remain all night, in the Black Chamber, since the Red would not hold half the number. How then, could I bring myself to sleep among so many men? Certain it is, that Ellena Di Rosalba travelled one whole night, and one whole day, in a carriage with two Ruffians, who never left her a single moment alone; and it was not till after Luxima and the missionary had journeyed together during several entire days, that (to quote the very words), "for the first time since the beginning of their pilgrimage, she was hidden from his view."

How these heroines managed about sleep, I knew not; but this I knew, that I could not abide the idea of sleeping in the presence of men.

And yet to surrender my sweet, my beloved, my venerable castle, the hereditary seat of my proud progenitors; at the moment of an immortal victory, ere yet the laurel was warmed upon the throbbings of my forehead;---and for what? For the most pitiful and unclassical reason, that ever disgraced a human creature. Why, I should be pointed at, scouted at. "Look, look, there is the heroine, who surrendered her castle, because—" and then a whisper and a titter, and a " 'Tis fact 'pon my honour," Oh, my friend, my friend, the thought was madness!

I considered, and reconsidered, but consideration and reconsideration only strengthened me more and more in the conviction, that there was no remedy.

"Jerry," said I, "dear Jerry, we must surrender."

"Surrender!" exclaimed Jerry, "Why then, death alive, for what?"

"Because," answered I, "my modesty would prevent me from sleeping before so many men."

"Your modesty!" cried he; "poo, do as I do. Have too much modesty to shew your modesty. Sleep? By my soul, you shall sleep;---and snore too, if you have a mind. Sleep? Sure, can't you pin the curtains round, so that we shan't see you? Sleep? Sure, how did the ladies manage, on board the packet I came over in? Sleep---sleep---sleep?

— — — — —

"O murder! I believe we must surrender, sure enough. O murder, murder, 'tis all over with us! For now that I think of it,---you know we shan't have room to lie down, you know."

"This is a sad affair," said I. "Can you devise no remedy, Higginson?"

"None," said he, blushing through his very eyeballs.

"We must surrender," said Jerry, shaking his head.

"We must," said Higginson, shaking his.

"We must," said I, shaking mine.

"Well," cried Betterton, "is the council over?"

"Yes, Sir," said I, "and I consent to conclude a peace."

"I thought so," said he. "Now then, for the terms."

After much altercation, these articles, (which Betterton wrote with his pencil,) were agreed upon, and ratified:

Art. 1.

All the prisoners in the castle, shall forthwith be released.

Art. 2.

The troops of the contending powers shall consign their arms into the hands of their respective leaders.

Art. 3.

On a given signal, the commandant of the besieged army, shall evacuate the castle, at the head of his men, and take a northerly direction; while the commandant of the besieging army shall lead his forces in a southerly direction.

Art. 4.

The Lady Cherubina De Willoughby shall depart from the castle, as soon as both armies are out of sight; and shall not hold communication, direct or indirect, with the Warden, for twenty-four hours.

Art. 6.

The Minstrel, Higginson, shall remain with the Lady Cherubina, as her escort.

(Signed)   BETTERTON.

The several articles were immediately executed in due form. First, the prisoners left the castle; but Montmorenci bad made himself so drunk with the wine, that he went actually staggering away; and thus completed my disgust. Next, the soldiers on both sides, laid down their arms: and lastly, the two armies filed off, at opposite directions, and quitted the field.

Before Jerry departed, however, I promised to call upon him in London, after the expiration of the twenty-four hours.

When Jerry had marched almost out of sight, he halted his men, faced them towards the castle, and made them give three last and parting cheers. I waved my handkerchief, and cried like a child.

I then took a tender leave of my dear, dear castle; and with a heavy heart, and tardy step, departed from it; till better days should enable me to visit it again. I proceeded towards the cottage of the poor woman; whence I now write; and I have just dispatched Higginson, for a chaise, as I shall return to London immediately.

My heart is almost broken.

Adieu.

LETTER XXXIV.

MS.

O YE, WHOEVER YE ARE, WHOM CHANCE OR MISFORTUNE MAY HEREAFTER CONDUCT TO THIS SPOT, TO YOU I SPEAK, TO YOU REVEAL THE STORY OF MY WRONGS, AND ASK YOU TO REVENGE THEM. VAIN HOPE! YET IT IMPARTS SOME COMFORT TO BELIEVE, THAT WHAT I NOW WRITE, MAY ONE DAY MEET THE EYE OF A FELLOW-CREATURE; THAT THE WORDS WHICH TELL MY SUFFERINGS, MAY ONE DAY DRAW PITY FROM THE FEELING HEART.

KNOW THEN, THAT ON THE NIGHT OF THE FATAL DAY, WHICH SAW ME DRIVEN FROM MY CASTLE, FOUR MEN, IN BLACK VISORS, ENTERED THE COTTAGE, WHERE I HAD TAKEN SHELTER, AND FORCED ME AND MY MINSTREL INTO A CARRIAGE. WE TRAVELLED MILES IN SILENCE. AT LENGTH THEY STOPPED, CAST A CLOAK OVER MY FACE, AND CARRIED ME ALONG WINDING PASSAGES, AND UP AND DOWN FLIGHTS OF STEPS. THEY THEN TOOK OFF THE CLOAK, AND I FOUND MYSELF IN AN ANTIQUE AND GOTHIC APARTMENT. MY CONDUCTORS LAID DOWN A LAMP, AND DISAPPEARED. I HEARD THE DOOR BARRED UPON ME. O SOUND OF DESPAIR! O MOMENT OF UNUTTERABLE ANGUISH! SHUT OUT FROM DAY, FROM FRIENDS, FROM LIFE---IN THE PRIME OF MY YEARS, IN THE HEIGHT OF MY TRANSGRESSIONS,--- I SINK UNDER THE—

*   *   *   *   *   *

ALMOST AN HOUR HAS NOW PASSED IN SOLITUDE AND SILENCE. WHY AM I BROUGHT HITHER? WHY CONFINED THUS RIGOROUSLY? O DIRE EXTREMITY! O STATE OF LIVING DEATH! IS THIS A VISION? ARE THESE THINGS REAL? ALAS, I AM BEWILDERED.

*   *   *   *   *   *

Such, Biddy, was the manuscript that I scribbled last night, after the mysterious event which it relates. You shall now hear what has occurred since.

According to common usage, I first took the lamp, and began examining the chamber. On one wall, hung Historical arras, worked in colourless and rotten worsted, and depicting scenes from the Provencal Romances;---the deeds of Charlemagne and his twelve peers; the Crusaders, Troubadours, and Saracens; and the Necromantic feats of the Magician Jurl. The remaining walls were wainscotted with black larchwood: and over the painted and escutcheoned windows, hung iron visors, tattered pennons, and broken shields. An antique bed of decayed damask, stood in a corner; and a few moth-eaten chairs, tissued and fringed with threads of tarnished gold, were round the room. At the farther end, a picture of a warrior on horseback, darting his spear into a prostrate soldier, was enclosed in a frame of uncommon magnitude, that reached down to the ground. An old harp, which occupied one corner, proved imprisonment; and some clots of blood upon the floor proved murder.

I gazed with delight at this admirable apartment. It was a perfect treasure: nothing could exceed it: all was in the best style of horror; and now, for the first time, I felt the full and unqualified consciousness of being as real a heroine as ever existed.

I then indulged myself with imagining the frightful scenes which I should undergo here. Such attempts to murder me, such ghosts, such mysteries! figures flitting in the dusty perspective, quick steps along the corridor; groans, and an assassin, with a visage of the most ruffianly sculpture.

But amidst this pleasing reverie, methought I heard a step approaching. It stopped at the door, the bolts were undrawn; and an antiquated waiting-woman, in fardingale, ruffles, flounces, and flowered silk, bustled into the room.

"My lady," said she, "my lord will do himself the honour of waiting on you immediately."

"And pray, good woman," said I, "who is your lord?"

"Good woman!" cried she bridling: "no more good woman than yourself: — Dame Ursulina, if you please."

"Well then, Dame Ursulina, who is your lord?"

"The Baron Hildebrand," answered she.

"What!" exclaimed I, "who has a daughter called Sympathina?"

"The same."

"Which daughter loves Lord Montmorenci?"

"The same."

"Oh, Heavens! but what have I to do with all this?"

The Dame laid her finger across her lips, and nodded volumes of mystery.

"At least," said I, "tell me how comes all that recent blood upon the floor?"

"Recent!" cried she. "Lauk! 'tis there these fifty years. Sure your ladyship has often read of blood upon floors, and daggers, that looked as fresh as a daisy, at the end of centuries. But, alas-o-day! modern blood won't keep like the good old blood. See that harp yonder: I warrant 'tis in tune, at this moment; albeit no human finger has touched it these ten years: and your Ladyship must remember reading of other cobwebbed harps, which required no tuning-hammer, after lying whole ages untweedled. But, indeed, they do say, that the ghost keeps this harp in order, by playing on it o'nights."

"The ghost!" exclaimed I.

"Ay, by my fackins," said she; "sure this is the Haunted Chamber of the Northern Tower; and such sights and noises—Santa Catharina of Sienna, and St. Bridget, and San Pietro, and Santa Benedicta, and St. Radagunda, defend me!"

Then, aspirating an ejaculation, she hastily hobbled out of the room; and locked the door.

However, the visit from Baron Hildebrand, occupied my mind more than the ghost. At last, I heard a heavy tread along the corridor: the door was unbarred, and a huge, but majestic figure, strode into the chamber. The black plume, towering on his cap; the armorial coat, Persian sash, and Spanish cloak, all set off with the most muscular frown imaginable, made him look truly tremendous.

As he hurled himself into a chair, he cast a Schedoniac scowl at me; while I felt, that one glance from the corner of a villain's eye, is worth twenty straight-forward looks from an honest man. My heart throbbed audible, my bosom heaved like billows: I threw into my features a Conventual smile; and stood before him in all the meek pomp of despair—something between Niobe, Patience, and a broken lily.

483

"Lady!" cried he, with a voice which vibrated through my brain; "I am the Baron Hildebrand, that celebrated ruffian. My plans are terrible and unsearchable. Hear me.

"My daughter, the Lady Sympathina, has long been enamoured of the Lord Montmorenci. But never, never shall a daughter of mine marry the man she loves. In vain I tried entreaties and imprecations: nothing would induce her to relinquish him; even though he himself confessed, that you alone reigned tormentress of his heart.

At length, my spies informed me of your having seized upon Monkton Castle; and of its being besieged by Montmorenci himself. The opportunity was auspicious. I therefore planted armed men about the castle, with orders to make you and him prisoners. These orders are executed, and his Lordship is a captive in the Western Tower.

"Now, Madam, you must already have penetrated my motive for this step. It is to secure your immediate marriage with Montmorenci; and thus to terminate my daughter's hopes and my own inquietude. In two days, therefore, you give him your hand, or suffer imprisonment for life."

"My lord," said I, "I am a poor, weak, timid girl; but yet not unmindful of my noble lineage. I cannot consent to disgrace it. My lord, I will not wed Montmorenci."

"You will not?" cried he, in a voice of the hoarsest fury.

"I will not," said I, in a tone of the sweetest obstinacy.

He started from his seat, and began to pace the chamber with Colossal strides. Conceive the scene;—the tall figure of Hildebrand passing along; his folded arms; the hideous desolation of the room, and my shrinking figure. It was fine, very fine. It resembled a Pandemonium, where a fiend was tormenting an angel of light. Yet insult and oppression had but added to my charms; as the rose throws forth fresh fragrance by being mutilated.

On a sudden the Baron stopped short before me.

"Why do you refuse to marry him?" said he.

"Because, my lord," answered I, "I do not feel for him the passion of love."

"Love!" cried he, grimly sneering. "There is no such passion as love. But mark me, Madam: soon shall you learn, that there is such a passion as Revenge!" And with these ominous words, he rushed out of the chamber.

484

Nothing in nature could be better than my conduct on this occasion. I was delighted with it, and with the castle, and with every thing. I therefore knelt, and chaunted a vesper hymn, so soft and so solemn; while my eyes, like a Magdalen's, were cast to the planets.

Adieu.

LETTER XXXV.

"GRACIOUSNESSOSITY!" cried Dame Ursulina, as she brought breakfast this morning, "here is the whole castle in such a fluster; hammering and clamouring, and paddling at all manner of possets, to make much of the fine company, that are coming down to the Baron."

"Heavens!" exclaimed I, "when will my troubles cease? Doubtless this fine company are a most dissolute set. An amorous Verezzi, an insinuating Cavigni, an abandoned Orsino; besides some lovely Voluptuary, some fascinating Desperado, who plays the harp, and poisons by the hour."

"La, not at all," said the dame.

"We shall have none but old Sir Charles Grandison, and his lady, Miss Harriet Byron, that was;— old Mr. Mortimer Delville, and his lady, Miss Cecilia, that was;— and old Lord Mortimer, and his lady, Miss Amanda, that was."

"Santa Maria!" cried I. "Why these are all heroes and heroines!"

" 'Pon my conversation, and as I am a true maiden, so they are," said she. "And we shall have such tickling and pinching; and fircumdandying, and cherrybrandying, and the genteel poison of bad wine; and the Warder blowing his horn, and the Baron in his scowered armour, and I in a coif plaited high with ribbons all about it, and in the most rustling silk I have. And Philip, the butler, meets me in the dark: 'Oddsboddikins,' says he, 'mayhap I should know the voice of that silk?' 'Oddspittikins,' says I, 'peradventure thou should'st;' and then he catches me round the neck, and —"

"There, there!" cried I, "you distract me."

"Marry come up!" muttered she. "Some people think some people—Marry come up, quotha!" And this frumpish old woman sailed out of the chamber in a great fume.

485

I sat down to breakfast, astonished at what I had just heard. Harriet Byron, Cecilia, Amanda, and their respective consorts, all alive and well! Oh, could I get but one glimpse of them, speak ten words with them, I should die content. I was interrupted by the return of Dame Ursulina.

"The Baron," said she, "has just left the castle, to consult physicians about his periodical madness, and government about a peace with France. So my young mistress, the Lady Sympathina, has sent me to tell you, that she will visit you, during his absence."

I felt infinite delight, and I prepared for an interview of congenial souls; nor was I long kept in suspense. Hardly had the Dame disappeared, when the door opened again, and a tall, thin, lovely girl, flew into the room. Her yellow ringlets hung round her pale face, like a mist round the moon. She ran forward, took both my hands, and stood gazing on my features.

"Ah," said she, "what wonder Montmorenci should be captivated by these charms! No, I will not, cannot take him from you. He is your's, my friend. Marry him, and leave me to the solitude of a cloister."

"Never!" cried I. "Ah, madam, ah, Sympathina, your magnanimity amazes, transports me. Yes, my friend; your's he shall, he must be; for you love him, and I hate him."

"Hate him!" cried she; "and wherefore? Ah, what a form is his, and ah, what a face! Locks, brown as cinnamon; eyes half dew, half lightning; lips like a casket of jewels, loveliest when open— ."

"And teeth like the Sybil's books," said I; "for two of them are wanting."

"Ah," cried she, "why should his want of teeth prevent you from marrying him? Do all his charms lie in his teeth, as all Sampson's strength centered in his hair?"

"Upon my honor," said I, "I would not marry him, if he had five hundred teeth. But you, my friend, you shall marry him, in spite of his teeth."

"Then," cried she; "my father will torture you to death?"

"And so will you," said I, "if you do not marry Montmorenci."

"And if I do," said she, "I will torture him."

"Then happen what may," said I, "some of us must be tortured."

"My torture were sweet," said she, "for it would be in the cause of justice."

"Mine were sweeter," said I; "for it would be in the cause of generosity."

"Is it generosity," said she, "to spurn the man who loves you?"

"Is it justice," said I, "to make me marry the man whom I do not love?"

"Ah, my friend," said she, "you may vanquish me in repartee, but never shall you conquer me in magnanimity."

"Then, let us swear an eternal friendship," said I.

"I swear!" cried she.

"I swear!" cried I.

We rushed into each other's arms!

"And now," said she, when the first transports had subsided, "how do you like being a Heroine?"

"Above all things in the world," said I.

"And how do you prosper at the profession?" asked she.

"It is not for me to say," answered I. "Only this, that ardor and assiduity are not wanting on my part."

"Of course, then," said she, "you shine in the requisite qualities. Do you blush well?"

"As well as can be expected," said I.

"Because," said she, "blushing is my *chef d'œuvre*. I blush one tint and three-fourths, with joy; two (including forehead and bosom), with modesty; and four, with love, to the points of my fingers. My father once blushed me against the Dawn, for a tattered banner to a rusty poniard."

"And who won?" said I.

"It was play or pay," replied she; "so the morning happening to be misty, we had no sport; but I fainted, which was just as good, if not better. Are you much addicted to fainting?"

"A little," said I.

" 'Pon honor?"

"Well, ma'am, to be honest with you, I am afraid I have never fainted yet; but at a proper opportunity, I flatter myself— "

"Nay, love," said she, "do not be distressed about the matter. If you weep well, 'tis a good substitute. Do you weep well?"

"Extremely well, indeed," said I.

"Come then," cried she, "we will weep on each other's necks." And she flung her arms about me. We remained some moments, in motionless endearment.

"Are you weeping? " said she, at length.

"No, ma'am," answered I.

"Ah, why don't you?" said she.

"I can't, ma'am," said I; "I can't."

"Ah, do," said she.

"Upon my word, I can't," said I: "sure I am trying all I can. But, bless me, how desperately you are crying. Your tears are running down my bosom, boiling hot. Excuse me, ma'am, but you will give me my death of cold."

"Ah, my fondling," said she, "tears are my sole consolation. Ofttimes I sit and weep, I know not why; and then I weep to find myself weeping. Then, when I can weep, I weep at having nothing to weep at; and then, when I have something to weep at, I weep that I cannot weep at it. This very morning, I bumpered a tulip with my tears, while reading a dainty ditty, which 1 must now repeat to you.

———————

"The moon had just risen, as a lover stole from his mistress. A sylph pursued her parting sigh, through the deserts of air; and bathed in its warmth, and enhaled its odours. As he flew over the ocean, he saw a sea-nymph sitting on the shore; and singing the fate of a shipwreck, that appeared at a distance, with broken masts, and floating rudder. Her instrument was her own long and blue tresses, which she had strung across rocks of coral. The sparkling spray struck them, and made sweet music. He saw, he loved, he hovered over her. But invisible, how could he attract her eyes? Incorporeal, how could he touch her? Even his voice could not be heard by her, amidst the dashing of the waves, and the melody of her ringlets. The sylphs, pitying his miserable state, exiled him to an arboret of blossoms.— There he droops his unused pinions, dips his ethereal pen in dewy moonshine, and writes his love on the bell of a lily."

———————

This charming tale led us to talk of moonshine. We moralized upon the uncertainty of it, and of life; discussed sighs, and agreed that they were charming things; enumerated the various kinds of tresses—flaxen, golden, chesnut, amber, sunny, jetty, carroty; and I suggested two new epithets—sorrel hair, and narcissine hair. Such a flow of soul as came from our rosy lips!

At last she rose to depart.

"Now, my love," said she, "I am in momentary expectation of Sir Charles Grandison, Mortimer Delville, and Lord Mortimer, with their amiable wives. Will you permit them, during the absence of the Baron, to visit you, this evening, and give you some good advice respecting your present predicament?"

I grasped at the proposal eagerly; and she flitted out of the chamber with a promissory smile.

What an angel is this Sympathina! Her face has the contour of a Madona, and the sensibility of a Magdalen. Her voice languishes like the last accents of a dying maid. Her sigh is melodious, her oh is sublime, and her ah is beautiful.

Adieu.

LETTER XXXVI.

And now the promised hour was approaching, when I should see the recorded personages of Romance. I therefore heroinized and Heloised myself as much as possible; and elegantly leaning on the harp, awaited their arrival.

Meantime, I figured them, adorned with all the venerable loveliness of a virtuous old age, even in greyness engaging, even in wrinkles interesting. Hand in hand they walk down the gentle slope of life, and often pause to look back upon the scenes which they have quitted; the happy vale of their childhood, the turretted castle, the cloistered monastery. I anticipated how this interview with them would improve me in my profession. No longer drawing from books alone, I might now copy from the very originals. The hand of a master would guide mine, and I should quaff primeval waters from the source itself.

As I thus sat rapt, I heard steps in the passage: the bolts were undrawn; and Sympathina, at the head of the company, entered, and announced their names.

"Bless me!" said I, involuntarily; for such a set of objects never were seen.

Sir Charles Grandison came forward the first. He was an emaciated old oddity, and wore flannels and a flowing wig.

Lady Grandison leaned on his arm, bursting with fat and laughter; and so unlike what I had conceived of Harriet Byron, that I turned from her quite disgusted.

Mortimer Delville came next; and my disappointment at finding him a plain, sturdy, hard-featured fellow, was soon absorbed in my still greater regret at seeing his Cecilia, — once the blue-eyed, sun-tressed Cecilia, — now flaunting in all the reverend graces of a painted grandmother.

After them, advanced Lord Mortimer and his Amanda; but he had fallen into flesh; and she, with a face like scorched parchment, appeared both broken-hearted and broken-winded; such a perpetual sighing and wheezing did she keep.

I was too much shocked and astonished to speak; but Sir Charles, bowing over my hand—his old custom you know—thus broke silence.

"Your Ladyship may recollect, that I have always been celebrated for giving advice. Let me then advise you to relieve yourself from your present embarrassment, by marrying Lord Montmorenci. It seems you do not love him. For that very reason marry him. Trust me, love before marriage is the surest preventative of love after it. Heroes and heroines exemplify the proposition. Why do their biographers always conclude the book just at their wedding? Simply because all beyond it, is unhappiness and hatred."

"Surely, Sir Charles," said I, "you mistake. Their biographers (who have such admirable information, as even to tell the thoughts of people, when not a soul is near them), always end the book, with comparing the connubial lives of their heroes and heroines, skies unclouded, streams unruffled, summer the year through; or some other gentle simile!"

"All irony," replied Sir Charles, "for I know most of these heroes and heroines myself; and I know, that nothing can equal their misery."

"Do you know Lord Orville and his Evelina?" said I; "and are they not happy?"

"Have you really never heard of their notorious miffs?" cried he. "Why, but yesterday, she flogged him with a boiled leg of mutton, because he had sent home no turnips."

"Astonishment!" exclaimed I. "And she, when a girl, so meek."

"Ay," said he. "One has never seen a white foal, or a cross girl; but often white horses, and cross wives."

"Pray," said I, addressing Amanda, "are not your brother Oscar and his Adela happy?"

"Alas, no," cried she. "Oscar became infatuated with the charms of Evelina's old governess, Madam Duval; so poor Adela left him; and she, who was once the soul of mirth, has now grown a confirmed methodist; curls a sacred sneer at gaiety, loves canting and decanting, piety and *eau de vie*. In short, the devil is very busy about her; though she sometimes drives him away with a thump of the Bible."

"Well, Rosa, the gentle beggar-girl,—what of her?" said I.

"Eloped with one Corporal Trim," answered Sir Charles.

"How shocking!" cried I. "But Pamela, the virtuous Pamela?" —

"Made somewhat a better choice," said Sir Charles; "for she ran off with Rasselas, Prince of Abyssinia, when he returned to the happy valley."

"Dreadful account indeed!" said I.

"So dreadful," said Sir Charles, bowing over my hand, "that I trust they will determine you to marry Montmorenci. 'Tis true, he has lost two teeth, and you do not love him. But was not Walstein a cripple? And did not Caroline of Lichfield fall in love with him after their marriage, though she had hated him before it?"

"I am inexorable," said I.

"Recollect," cried Cecilia, "what perils environ you here. The Baron is the first murderer of the age."

"I cannot help that," said I.

"Look at yonder blood," cried Mortimer Delville.

"It cannot appal me," said I.

"Think of the spectre that haunt this apartment," cried Lady Grandison.

"No matter if I even see it," said I.

"And above all," cried Sympathina, "bear in mind, that you may wake some morning, with a face like a pumpkin."

"Heavens!" exclaimed I, "what do you mean? My face like a pumpkin?"

"Yes," said she. "The dampness of this chamber once swelled up the face of the fair, but unfortunate Novellette, till the skin burst asunder, and was obliged to be stitched."

"Oh! ladies and gentlemen," exclaimed I, dropping upon my knees, "you see what shocking horrors surround me here. Oh! let me beseech of you to pity and to rescue me!"

"Fly!" cried Dame Ursulina, running in breathless. "The Baron has just returned, and is searching for you, through chapel, armoury, gallery; and west tower, and east tower, and south tower; and cedar chamber, and oaken chamber, and black chamber; and grey, brown, yellow, green, pale-pink, sky-blue; and every shade, tinge, and tint of chamber in the whole castle! Benedicite, Santa Maria! Come, come, come."

The guests vanished, the door was barred, and I remained alone.

I sat ruminating in sad earnest, on the necessity, now so evident, of my consenting to this hateful match; when (and I protest I had not thought it nine o'clock), a terrible bell, which I never heard before, tolled, with an appalling reverberation, that rang through my frame, the frightful hour of ONE!

At the same moment, I heard a noise; and looking towards the opposite end of the chamber, beheld the great picture on a sudden disappear; and, standing in its stead, a tall figure, cased with steel, and whose spectral visage was a perfect counterpart of the Baron's. Its left thumb rested upon its hip, and its right hand was held to the heavens.

I sat gasping. It uttered these sepulchral intonations.

"I am the spirit of the murdered Count Romancer. Montmorenci deserves thee. To-morrow morning consent to wed him, or to-morrow night I come again."

The superhuman appearance spoke; and (oh, soothing sound!) uttered a human sneeze!

"Damnation!" it muttered. "Al is blown!" And immediately the picture flew back to its place.

Well, I had never heard of a ghost's sneezing before; so you may judge, I soon got rid of my terror; and felt pretty certain, that this was no bloodless and marrowless apparition; but the Baron himself, who had adopted the ghosting system, so common in romances, for the purpose of frightening me into his schemes.

However, I had now discovered a concealed door; and with it, a chance of escape. This chance I determined to try; because, though the castle, the Baron, the Dame, and the several terrors, are all classical, and fit for immortality; yet conceive how Ridicule would handle me in the Annals of Laughter (to say nothing of the personal disfigurement), should I wake some morning with a face like a pumpkin! I have therefore formed a plan for escaping through the concealed door, whenever the ghost shall appear again.

While I was pondered upon this plan, in came Dame Ursulina, taking snuff, and sneezing at a furious rate.

"By the mass," said she, "it rejoiceth the reverend cockles of my heart to see your Ladyship safe; for, as I passed your door just now, methought I heard the ghost."

"You might well have heard it," said I, pretending infinite faintness, "for I have seen it; and it entered through yonder picture."

"Benedicite!" cried she: "but was it a true spectre?"

"A real, downright apparition," said I, "uncontaminated with the smallest mixture of mortality."

"And did'nt your Ladyship hear me sneeze at the door?" said she.

"I was too much alarmed to hear any thing," answered I. "But pray lend me that box; as a pinch or two of snuff may revive me." I had particular reasons for this request.

"A heroine take snuff!" cried she, laying the box upon the table. "Lack-a-daisy, how the times have degenerated! But now, my lady, don't be trying to move or cut that great picture; for though the ghost gets into the chamber through it, no mortal can get out through it. Never yet was a heroine could give old Ursulina the slip; and I will tell you a story to prove my profound knowledge of bolts and bars. When I was a girl, a young man lodged in the house; and one night he stole the stick that used to fasten the hasp and staple of my door. Well, my mother bade me put a carrot (as there was nothing else) in its place. So I put in a carrot—for I was a dutiful daughter; but I put in a boiled carrot—for I was a love-sick maiden. Eh, don't I understand the doctrine of bolts and bars?"

"You understand a great deal too much," said I, as the withered wanton went chuckling out of the chamber.

LETTER XXXVII.

About noon, the Baron Hildebrand paid me a visit; to hear, as he said, my final determination respecting my marriage with Montmorenci. I had prepared my lesson, and I told him, that though my mind was not entirely reconciled to such an event, it was much swayed by an extraordinary circumstance, which had occurred the night before. He desired me to relate it; and I, with apparent agitation, recounted the particulars of the apparition. I likewise declared, that should it come again, I would endeavour to preserve my presence of mind, and ask it whether my marriage with his Lordship would prove fortunate or otherwise; and that, should its answer be favourable, I would not hesitate another moment, to give him my hand.

The Baron, suppressing a smile, protested himself highly delighted with my determination of accosting the spectre. He remarked, that ghosts, so far from doing us harm, always warn us against harm; that if we were civil to them, they would be civil to us; but that no wonder they should speak so harshly as they usually do, we shew such evident aversion and horror at their appearance. He concluded by declaring, that this spectre was the best-hearted creature of the kind ever known; and by earnestly advising me to address it. He then took leave; and I spent the remainder of the day in reflecting upon the desperate enterprise which I had planned; and in recalling all the exemplary escapes of other heroines.

At last, the momentous hour drew nigh. The lamp and box of snuff lay on the table. I sat anxious, and kept a watchful eye upon the picture.

The bell tolled one: again the picture vanished, and again the spectre stood before me. I sent forth a shriek, and hid my face in my hands.

"*I come for the last time,*" it said. "*Wilt thou wed Montmorenci? Speak, lady, and fear not.*"

"Oh," cried I, "if you would only promise not to do me a mischief!"

"A spirit cannot harm a mortal," said the spectre.

"Well then," faltered I— "Perhaps—pardon me—perhaps, you would first have the goodness to walk in."

The spectre advanced a few paces, and paused.

"This is so kind, so condescending," said I, "that really—do take a chair."

The spectre shook its head mournfully.

"Pray do," said I, "you will oblige me."

The spectre seated itself in a chair; but atoned for the mortal act, by an immortal majesty of manner.

"As you are of another world," said I, "you know 'tis but fair to do the honours of this. "What sort of night is it abroad?"

"Quite charming and tempestuous," it answered. "Just the weather we ghosts like."

494

"Yes," said I, "you, ghosts, have odd tastes! Nothing will satisfy you, but a storm, and one o'clock at night."

"Indeed we keep such late hours," said the spectre, "that 'tis no wonder we look pale and thin."

"Why really," said I, "I do not recollect ever having read of a fat or a fresh-coloured ghost."

"Nor of a ghost wanting a limb or an eye," said the spectre.

"Nor of an ugly ghost," said I, bowing.

The spectre took the compliment, and bowed in return.

"And therefore," said the spectre, "as spirits are always accurate likenesses of the bodies, which they once inhabited, none but thin, pale, handsome and unmaimed persons can ever become ghosts."

"And by the same rule," said I, "none but blue-eyed and golden-haired persons can go to heaven; for our painters always represent angels so. I have never heard of a hazel-eyed angel, or a black-haired cherub."

"I know," said the spectre, "if angels are, as painters depict them, always sitting naked upon cold clouds, I would rather live the life of a ghost, to the end of the chapter."

"And pray," cried I, "where, and how do ghosts live?"

"Within this very globe," said the spectre. "For this globe is not, as most mortals imagine, a solid body; but a round crust, about ten miles thick; and the concave inside, is furnished just like the convex outside, with wood, water, vale and mountain. In the centre, stands a nice little golden Sun, about the size of a pippin, and lights our internal world; where, whatever enjoyments we had loved as men, we retain as ghosts. We banquet on visionary turtle, or play at aërial marbles, or drive a phantasmagoric four in hand. The young renew their amours, and the more aged sit yawning for the day of judgment.—But I scent the rosy air of dawn. Speak, lady; wilt thou wed Montmorenci?"

"If I do," said I, "shall I be happy with him?"

"Blissful as Eden," replied the spectre.

"Then I will wed him," said I. "But you are in a great hurry. I am sure, I am so obliged by this visit. I beg you will call again. I wish I had something to offer you. Perhaps you would do me the favour to take a pinch of snuff?" And as I spoke, I advanced by degrees.

"Avaunt!" it cried, motioning me from it with its hand.

But quick as thought, I flung the whole contents of the box full into its eyes!

"Blood and thunder!" exclaimed the astonished apparition.

I snatched the lamp, sprang through the frame of the picture, shut the concealed door, bolted it; while all the time, I heard the phantom within, dancing in agony, at its eyes; and sending mine to as many devils, as could well be called together on so short a notice.

Thus far my venturous enterprise had prospered. I now found myself in a narrow passage, with another door at the farther end of it; and I prepared to traverse winding stairs, subterranean passages, and suites of tapestried apartments. I therefore advanced, and opened the door; but instantly started back; for I had beheld a lighted hall of modern architecture, with gilded balustrades, ceiling painted in Fresco; Etruscan lamps, and stucco-work! Yes, it was a Villa, or a Casino, or a Pallazo; or any thing you please, but a Castello. Amazement! Horror! What should I do? whither turn? delay would be fatal. Again I peeped. The hall was empty; so, putting down my lamp, I stole across, towards an open door, and looked through the chink. I had just time to perceive a Persian saloon, and in the centre, a table laid for supper; when I heard several steps entering the hall. It was too late to retreat, so I sprang into the room; and recollecting, that a curtain had befriended me once before, I ran behind one, which I saw there.

Instantly afterwards, the persons entered. They were spruce footmen, bringing in supper. Not a scowl, not a mustachio amongst them.

As soon as the covers were laid, a crowd of company came laughing into the room; but, friend of my bosom, fancy, just fancy my revulsion of soul, my dismay, my disgust, my bitter indignation — oh! how shall I describe half what I felt, when I recognised these wretches, as the identical gang, who had visited me the day before, in the character of heroes and heroines! I knew them instantly, though they looked twice as young; and merrily amongst them, came Betterton and Montmorenci! My heart died at the sight, I foresaw horrid things.

After they had seated themselves, Betterton, (who headed the table, and therefore, was host), desired one of the servants to bring in 'the crazed Poet.' And now two footmen appeared, carrying a large meal-bag, filled with Higginson; which they placed by the table, on a vacant seat. The bag was fastened at the top, but a slit was cut in its side.

The wretches then began to banter him, and bade him put forth his head; but he would neither move nor speak. At last, I heard them mention my name.

"I wonder if he can be ghosting her, all this time?" said Betterton.

"I ought to have played the ghost, I am so much taller than he," said the fellow, who had personated Grandison.

"Not unless you could act it better than you did Sir Charles," said the fictitious Sympathina. "But did I not perform my part well, when I poured a vial of hot water down her neck, as tears; and frightened her out of her senses, by threatening her with a face like a pumpkin!"

A laugh. I thought I had never seen so ugly, so disgusting a girl.

"Blast me," cried Montmorenci, "but I touched off the best piece of acting you ever saw, when I first met her at the theatre, and persuaded her, that Abraham Grundy was Lord Altamont Mortimer Montmorenci!"

Another laugh. I actually groaned with anguish.

"Except," said Betterton, "when I enacted old Whylome Eftsoones, at the masquerade; and made her believe that Miss Cherry Wilkinson was Lady Cherubina de Willoughby!"

I now turned quite sick; but I had no time for thought, the thunderclaps came so thick upon me.

"She had cherished some mad crotchet of the kind before," said Grundy (I have done with calling him Montmorenci); for she fancied that an old tattered copy of a lease of lives, belonging to her poor Father, was an irrefragable proof of her being Lady de Willoughby!"

"Upon which wild notion," said Betterton, "she claps this poor father into a madhouse; where he should have clapt her long ago."

"He should, by Goles!" cried Grundy. "Those romances have turned her brain inside out. I protest, her imitation of the language and manners, which Authors give Heroines, would make a tiger titter. But the maddest prank of all, was her seizing on the Castle, furnishing it so shabby genteel, and wanting to pass a bladebone of mutton upon me, as the bone of an assassinated ancestor."

By this time, I was at the highest pitch of indignation.

"Nay, Grundy," cried Betterton, "was it not a madder whim, when she discarded you the moment you had lost two teeth? Ah, my

497

hero, that shews she could never have loved you so much as you boast."

"Not love me!" exclaimed Grundy. "Why the poor creature could not even bridle her passion in my presence. Such hugging and kissing as she went on with;—such slobbering and pawing;—such patting my cheek, and pulling my whiskers; that, as I hope for woman, I sometimes thought she would bite off my very face!"

" 'Tis false!" cried I, bursting into tears, and running from behind the curtain. "On my sacred credit, ladies and gentlemen, 'tis every word of it, a vile, malicious, execrable falsehood! Oh! what shall I do? what shall I do?" and I wrung my hands with agony.

The guests had risen from their seats, in amaze; and I now made a spring towards the door, but was intercepted by Betterton, who held me fast.

"In the name of wonder," cried he, "how came you here?"

"No matter," cried I, struggling. "I know all! I know all! You base, you cruel people, to use me so!"

"Keep yourself cool, my little lady," said he.

"I won't, I can't!" cried I. "To use me so. You vile set; you horrid, horrid, horrid set!"

"Go for another sack," said Betterton to the servant. "Now, Madam, you shall keep company with the bagged Poet."

"Mercy, mercy!" cried I. "What, will no one help me?"

"I will if I can!" exclaimed Higginson, thrusting his head out of the bag, like a snail; and down he slided from his seat, and began rolling, and tumbling, and struggling on the floor, till he got upon his feet; and then he came jumping towards me, now falling, now rising, while his face and bald forehead were all over meal, his eyes blaring, and his mouth wide open. The company, wherever he moved, kept in a circle round him, and clapped their hands, and shouted.

While Betterton still stood, holding me fast, he was suddenly flung from me, and my hand seized. I turned, and beheld—Stuart. "Oh! bless you, bless you!" cried I, catching his arm, "for you have come to save me from destruction!"

He pressed my hand, and pointing towards Betterton and Grundy, who stood thunderstruck, cried, "There are your men!"

A large posse of constables immediately rushed forward, and secured them.

" Heyday! what is all this for?" cried Betterton.

"For your rescuing that lady from an arrest," answered a man; and I recognized in the speaker, one of the constables who had arrested me about the barouche.

"This is government all over," cried Betterton. "This is the minister. This is the law"

"And let me tell you. Sir," said Stuart, "that nothing but my respect for the law, deters me, at this moment, from chastising you as you deserve."

"What do you mean, sirrah?" cried Betterton.

"That you are a ruffian," said Stuart; "and the same cowardice which made you offer insult to a woman, will make you bear it from a man. Now, Sir, I leave you to your fate." And we were quitting the room.

"What is that?" said Stuart, stopping short before the poet; who, with one arm, and his face out of the bag, lay upon his back, gasping and unable to stir.

"Cut it, cut it!" cried the sufferer, in choking accents.

"Higginson, I protest!" exclaimed Stuart, as he snatched a knife, and laid open the bag. Up rose the poet, resurrectionary from his hempen coffin, and was clenching his fist; but Stuart caught his arm, and hurried him and me out of the house.

We then got into Stuart's own chariot, and drove off.

This excellent fellow now began asking me, anxiously, the particulars of all that had occurred at Betterton's: and his rage, as I related them, was extreme.

Presently, he proceeded to tell me how he discovered my being there. After his departure from Lady Gwyn's, he spent some days in inquiries about my father. At last, when he found every effort unavailing, he returned. But how shocked was he to learn from her Ladyship, that I had robbed her, absconded, and afterwards made an assault on her house, at the head of an Irish mob. He next visited Monkton Castle, but found it evacuated. However, judging by the description which her Ladyship gave, that Sullivan was one of my party, back he posted to London, and sought out Jerry. Jerry, who had only just returned from the castle, told him all; and acquainted him with my promise of calling at the shop, the moment of my arrival in town.

Accordingly, Stuart waited there some time; but as I did not appear, he began to suspect that Betterton bad entrapped me. He therefore saw the coachmaker, paid him for the barouche, informed him that I was not a swindler, and brought Jerry to depose, that Betterton and Grundy were the persons who had assaulted the constables. By his desire, the coachmaker applied at the office of police, whence a party was dispatched to apprehend Betterton and Grundy. Stuart accompanied them, and thus gained admission into the house.

Higginson now told a lamentable tale of the pranks, which Betterton had played upon him; and amongst the rest, he mentioned, that a servant had seduced him into the bag, under the pretext of smuggling him out of the house, in the character of meal.

He could gather, from things said, while the company were tormenting him, that Grundy had agreed, first to marry me; and then, for a stipulated sum, to give Betterton every opportunity of prosecuting his infamous designs upon me. By this device, Betterton would escape the penalties of the law.

He likewise informed me, that the several chambers in this Villa, were furnished according to the fashions of different countries,—Grecian, Persian, Chinese, Italian; and that mine was the Gothic Chamber.

By this time, having stopped at an inn, where we meant to sleep, I desired a room, and bade Stuart a hasty good night.

Shocked, astonished, and ashamed at all that had passed, I threw myself on the bed, and unburdened my bursting heart in a bitter fit of crying. What! thought I, not the Lady Cherubina De Willoughby after all?—Whylome Eftsoones, Betterton; Montmorenci an impostor; and the parchment a lease of lives?—could these things be? Alas, no doubt of the fatal facts remained; for the wretches rejoiced over them, as indisputable truths, even when they knew not that I was overhearing them! O, to be ruined in my favourite speculation, in the sole business of my life; all to begin over again,—the wide world to be searched anew for my real name, my real family—or was Wilkinson, indeed, my father? If so, what a fall! and how horridly had I treated him! Then to be ridiculed, despised, insulted by dissolute creatures, calling themselves Lords and Barons, heroes and heroines; and I no heroine! Am I a heroine? I caught myself constantly muttering; and then I walked about wildly, then sat on the bed, then cast my body across it. Once I dropped into a doze, and dreamed of monsters following me swifter than the wind; while my lingering limbs could hut creep, and my voice, calling help, could not rise above a whisper. Then I woke, repeating;

am I a heroine? I believe I was delirious; for spite of all my efforts, I ran on rapidly, am I a heroine? am I? am I? am I? till my panting brain reeled, and my hands were clenched with perturbation.

Thus passed the night, and towards morning, I fell into a slumber.

Adieu.

LETTER XXXVIII.

This morning, my head felt rather better, and I appeared before Stuart, with the sprightliest air imaginable; not that my mind was tranquil; but that pride prevented me from betraying my distraction, at the unheroical result of my career.

After breakfast, Stuart and I took our departure in a chaise. Unable to counterfeit gaiety long, I soon relapsed into languor; nor could my companion, by any effort, divert me from the contemplation of my late disgrace.

As we drew near Lady Gwyn's, he represented the propriety of my letting her Ladyship know where she might recover the portrait. I consented: and he proceeded to the house, while I remained at the gate. Presently, however, I saw him return, accompanied by Lady Gwyn herself.

But now came a new mortification. For now, at the instance of Stuart, her Ladyship began acknowledging all the pranks, which she had practised upon me. She confessed, that the crowning ceremony was merely to amuse her friends, with my pretty caprices, as she called them; and that my great mother was her own nephew! But here I stopped her short, bade Stuart get into the chaise, and left the hateful woman, without even wishing her good morning.

After this unpleasant explanation, we proceeded some miles, silent and uncomfortable.

At last, I found myself in sight of the village, where William, whom I had separated from his Mary, resided; and as this was a favourable opportunity for reconciling the lovers, I now made Stuart acquainted with their quarrel. He shook his head at the recital; and desired the driver to stop at William's house. This was done, and in

501

a few moments, William made his appearance. He remembered me immediately.

"Well, William," said I, "how goes on your little quarrel with Mary? Are you reconciled?"

"No, Ma'am," answered he, with a doleful look, "and, I fear, never will."

"Yes, William," cried I, with an assuring nod, "I have the happiness to tell you that you will."

"Ah, Ma'am," said he, "I suppose you do not know what a sad misfortune has fallen upon her, since you were here. The poor creature has quite lost her senses."

"For shame!' cried I. "What are you saying? Lost her senses! Well, I am sure it was not my fault, however."

"Your's?" said he: "oh, no, Ma'am. But, indeed, she has never been in her reason, since the day you left her."

"Let us be gone," whispered I to Stuart, as I sank back in the carriage.

"Surely not," said he. " 'Tis at least your duty to repair, as far as possible, the mischief you have done."

"I should die before I could disclose it," cried I.

"Then I will disclose it for you," said he, leaping out of the chaise.

He went, with William, into the house; and I remained in such a state of mind, that I was often on the point of quitting the chaise, and escaping, I knew not whither; any where from the woeful scene awaiting me. At last, Stuart returned without William; and gave the driver directions to the cottage of poor Mary.

On our way, he said every thing kind and consolatory. He declared that William felt more rejoiced, than dejected at the intelligence; because, as the poor girl was quite harmless, and had only temporary fits of wandering, she might eventually recover from her derangement, when the circumstance of the fatal letter were explained to her, and a reconciliation effected.

Having now arrived near the cottage, we alighted, and walked towards it. With a faltering step, I crossed the threshold, and found the father in the parlour.

"Dear Miss," said he, "welcome here once more. I suppose you have come to see poor Mary. Oh! 'tis a piteous sight. There she does nothing but walk about, and sigh, and talk so wild; and nobody can tell the cause, but that William; and he will not, for he says she forbade him."

"Come with me," said Stuart, "and I will tell you the cause."

He led the miserable old man out of the room, and I remained at the window weeping.

But in a few minutes, I heard a step; and turning round, saw the father, with a face haggard and ghastly, come running towards me. Then grasping my shoulder, and lifting his tremulous and withered hand to heaven: "Now," cried he, "may the lightning of a just and good Providence—"

"Oh! pray," cried I, snatching down his hand— "oh, pray do not curse me! Do not curse a poor, silly, mad creature. It was a horrid affair; most horrid; but indeed, indeed, I meant no harm!"

"Be calm, my good man," said Stuart, "and let us go to the garden, where your daughter is walking. This young lady will accompany us, and do her utmost, in this critical moment."

"Oh, I will do any thing," cried I: "come along."

We now passed into the garden; and I shuddered, when I beheld the beautiful wreck, at a distance. She had just stopt short in a stepping posture: her cloak had half fallen from her shoulder; and as her head hung down, her forefinger was lightly laid on her lip.

Panting to tell her all, I flew towards her, and caught her hand.

"Do you remember me, Mary?" said I softly.

She looked at me, some moments, with a vacant smile; and at last, coloured faintly.

"Ah! yes, I remember you," said she. "You were with us that very evening. But I don't care about him now;---I don't indeed; and if I could only see him once more, I would tell him so. And then I would frown and turn from him; and then he would follow, so sad and so pale: don't you think he would? And I am keeping his presents to give him back, as he did mine; and see how I have my hair parted on my forehead, just as he used to like it; ready the moment I see him, to rumple it all about; and then he will cry so: don't you think he will? And then I will run, run, run from him like the wind, and never see him again; never, never again."

"Dear Mary," said I, "you shall see him again, and love him too; for the poor fellow still loves you better than his life. I met him myself, this moment; and he was talking of you."

"He was?" exclaimed she, gasping and reddening. "Oh! and what did he say? But hush, not a word before my father and that man;"

503

and she put one hand upon my mouth, and, with the other round my waist, hurried me towards a little arbour, where we sat down.

"And now," whispered she, stealing her arms about my neck, and looking earnestly into my eyes, while her whole frame trembled, "and now what did he say?"

"Mary, you must collect your ideas, and listen attentively; for I have much to disclose. Do you recollect a letter, which you wrote, by my direction, when I was here last?"

"Letter---" muttered she. "Letter.---Yes, I believe I do. Oh! yes, I now remember it well; for it was a sad letter to a poor young man, who loved you, telling him that you had married another; and his name was William too; and I thought, at the time, I would never write my own Willy such a letter."

"And yet, Mary," said I, "your own William, by some mishap, got that very letter, that very evening; and seeing it in your hand-writing, and addressed to William, he thought it was from you to him; and so he gave you back your presents, and---"

"What is all that?" cried Mary, starting up. "Merciful powers! say all that over again!"

I made her sit down, and I shewed her the letter; for Stuart had procured it from William. As she read, her colour changed, her lip quivered, her hand shook; and at the conclusion, she dropped it, with a dreadful groan, and remained quite motionless.

"Mary!" cried I, "dear Mary, do not look so. Speak, Mary," and I stirred her shoulder; but she still sat motionless, with a settled smile.

"I shall, I will see her!" cried the voice of William, at a distance; and the next instant, he was seated, breathless, by her side.

"Mary, my Mary!" cried he, with the most touching utterance.

At the well-known voice, so long unheard, she started, and suddenly turned towards him; but as suddenly turned from him, and rose deadly pale. Then snatching some letters and baubles from her bosom, she threw them into his lap. Then she began gently disarranging her hair, and all the time looking down at him, with an oblique eye of pretty dignity.

"Come," said she, taking my hand, and leading me slowly out of the arbour. When we were halfway through the garden; "Look behind," said she, "and tell me is he following me."

"No, indeed," answered I. "So be not alarmed."

"Well," said she, "well, no matter. Time was, though, when he would have followed me. I wonder will he follow me? Is he following me?"

"Surely not," answered I, "after all your cruelty to him, though I have explained about the letter."

"Ay, true, the letter. Well, but he should not have believed it my letter; and so I must punish him. And besides—"

"Besides what, Mary?"

"Besides, you see he won't follow me."

"He cannot," answered I. "The poor fellow is lying upon the ground; and sobbing ready to break his heart."

Mary stopped.

"Shall I call him?" said I.

"Why now, dear lady," said she, laying her hand on my shoulder, and whispering in my ear, "how can I prevent you?"

"William!" cried I. "Mary calls you."

At the sound of his rapid steps she turned, stretched forth her hands towards him, uttered a long and piercing cry;—and they were locked in each other's arms, and united for ever!

But the poor girl, quite overpowered by the sudden change, fell back insensible; while William, kissing her, and weeping over her, bore her into the house, and laid her on a bed.

It was so long before she shewed any symptoms of animation, that we began to feel serious alarm. However, by degrees, she grew better, and became more composed; though her mind was still wandering. At last, her hand grasped in her lover's, she fell asleep; and then, as our presence could prove no farther useful, we took leave of the venerable peasant; who, generous with recent hope, freely gave me his forgiveness and his blessing.

In my first transports of anguish after this scene, I told Stuart, what I had all day determined, but dreaded to disclose—the situation of my poor father. At the horrid account, the good young man turned pale, but said not a word. I saw that I was undone, and I burst into tears.

"Be comforted, my dear girl," said he, laying his hand on mine. "You have long been acting under the delusion of a dreadful dream; but this confession, and these tears, are I trust, only the first step towards a total renunciation of error. So now let us hasten to your father, and release him. Past follies shall be forgotten, past pleasures renewed; you shall return home, and Cherry Wilkinson shall again be the daughter of an honest squire."

"Mr. Stuart," said I, "as to my past follies, I know of none but two;—the separation of these lovers, and the confinement of my father. And as to that father, he may not be what you suppose him. I fancy, Sir, there are instances innumerable, of men who begin life with plain names, and end it with the most Italian in the world."

"Well?" cried Stuart, anxiously.

"Well," said I, "that honest squire, as you call him, may yet turn up a Marquis."

Stuart groaned, and put out his head to look at the prospect.

We have reached London, and Stuart is now procuring from Grundy, who lies in prison, such a statement, as must make the Doctor release my poor father, without hesitation.

How shall I support this approaching interview with him? I shall sink, I shall die under it. Indeed I wish to die; and I feel an irresistible presentiment, that my prayer will shortly be granted. All day long, a horrid gloom troubles me; besides a wildness of ideas, and an unusual irritability. My head is as if billows were tossing through it; by turns I have a glow and a creeping chillness in my skin; and I am unwilling even to move. Oh, could I only lock myself into a room, with heaps of romances, and shut out all the world for ever! But no, my friend; the grave will soon be my chamber, the worms my books; and if ever I write again, I must write from the bed of death. I know it, I feel it. I shall embrace my broken-hearted parent, acknowledge my follies and die.

Adieu.

LETTER XXXIX.

AGITATED beyond measure, I found myself in the madhouse: I hardly knew how. Stuart supported me to the room, where my father was confined; and gently urged me forward, as I paused, breathless, at the door. I saw, by the dusky light, a miserable object, shivering, and sitting upon a bed. A few rags and a blanket were cast about it: the face was haggard, and the chin overgrown with a grisly beard. Yet, amidst all this disfigurement, I could not mistake my father. I ran, prostrated myself at his feet, and clasping his knees, exclaimed, "Father, dear father!"

He started, and gazed upon me for a moment; then pushed me from him, and buried his face in the bed. I cast my body across his, and endeavoured, with both my hands, to turn his face round, that I might kiss it; but he resisted every effort.

"Father!" cried I, fondling his neck, "will you break my heart? Will you drive me to distraction, father? Speak, father! Oh, one word, one little word, to save me from death!"

Still he lay mute and immoveable.

"You are cold, father," said I. "You shiver. Shall I put something about you? shall I, father? Ah! I can be so careful and so tender, when I love one; and I love you dearly — Heaven knows I do, my father."

I laid my shawl on his shoulders, stole my hand into one of his, and lay caressing his forehead, and murmuring words of fondness in his ear. But he drew away his hand, by degrees, and covered his forehead with it. And now half frantic, I began to sob convulsively, beat the pillow, and moan, and utter the most deplorable complaints.

At last, I thought I saw him a little convulsed, as if with smothered tears.

"Ah," cried I, "you are relenting, you are weeping. Bless you for that! Oh, my own, my beloved father, look up, look up, and see with what joy your daughter can embrace you!"

"My child, my child!" cried he, suddenly turning round, and flinging himself upon my bosom. "A heart of stone could not withstand this! — There, darling, there, I forgive you all!"

Fast and fondly did we cling about each other; and sweet were the sighs that we breathed, and the tears that we shed.

But I suffered too much: the disorder which had long been engendering in my frame, now burst forth, with sudden vehemence; and I was conveyed, raving, into a carriage. On our arrival at the hotel, they sent for a physician, who pronounced me in a violent fever of a nervous nature. During a fortnight, I was not expected to recover; and I myself felt so convinced of my speedy dissolution, that I requested the presence of a clergyman.

He came; and his conversations, by composing my mind, contributed, in a great degree, to my recovery. At my request, he paid me daily visits. Our subject was religion—not those theological controversies, which make Christian feel an abhorrence to Christian;

but those plain and simple truths, which convince without confounding; and which shun both the bigotry, that would worship error, because it is hereditary; and the fanaticism, that would lay rash hands on the temple, because some of its smaller pillars appear unsound.

After detaining me some days, upon this important topic, he gradually led me to give him an account of my late adventures; and as I related, he made comments.

Affected by his previous precepts, and by my own awful prospect, I now became as desirous of conviction, as I had heretofore been averse from it. To be predisposed is to be half converted; and soon this exemplary pastor taught me how impious, and how immoral, was the tendency of my past life. He shewed me, that to the inordinate gratification of a particular caprice, I had sacrificed my duty towards my natural protectors, myself, and my God; that my ruling passion, though harmless in its nature, was injurious in its effects; that it gave me a distaste for sober occupations, perverted my judgment, and even threatened my reason. Religion itself, he said, if indulged with excessive enthusiasm, at last degenerates into zealotry; and leaves the poor devotee too rapturous to be rational, and too virulent to be religious.

In a word, I have risen from my bed, an altered being; and I now look back upon my past delusions, with horror and disgust. Though the new principles of conduct, which I have espoused, are not yet well rooted, or well regulated in my mind; and though the prejudices of a whole life, are not (and indeed, could not be), entirely eradicated within a few days; still, as I am resolved to rid myself of them, I trust that the final result of my rejecting what is erroneous, will be my adopting what is correct.

Adieu.

LETTER XL.

I HAVE now so far recovered my bodily health, that I am no longer confined to my room; while the good Stuart, by his lively advice and witty reasoning, more complimentary than reproachful, and more insinuated than expressed, is perfecting my mental reformation.

He had lately put Don Quixote into my hands; and on my returning it to him, with a confession of the benefit which I derived from it, the conversation naturally ran upon romances in general. He thus delivered his sentiments.

"I do not protest against the perusal of fictitious biography altogether; for many works of this kind, may be read without injury, and some with advantage. Novels such as the Vicar of Wakefield, The Fashionable Tales, and Cœlebs, which draw man as he is, imperfect, instead of man as he cannot be, superhuman; are both instructive and entertaining. Romances, such as The Mysteries of Udolpho, The Italian, and The Bravo of Venice, which address the imagination alone, are often captivating, and seldom detrimental. But unfortunately, so seductive is the latter class of composition, that people are apt to become too fond of it, and to neglect more useful books. This, however, is not the only evil. Romances, indulged in extreme, act upon the mind, like inebriating stimulants; first elevate, and at last enervate it. They make it admire ideal scenes of transport and distraction; and feel disgusted with the vulgarities of living misery. Besides, they incapacitate it from encountering the turmoils of active life; and teach it erroneous notions of the world, by relating adventures too improbable to happen, and depicting characters too perfect to exist.

"In a country where morals are on the decline, sentimental novels always become dissolute. For it is their province to represent the prevalent opinions; nay, to run forward and meet the coming vice, and sketch it with an anticipating and gigantic pencil. Thus, long before France arrived at her extreme of vicious refinement, her novels had adopted that last master-stroke of immorality, which wins by the chastest aphorisms, while it corrupts, by the most alluring pictures of villainy. Take Rousseau, for instance. What St. Preux is to Heloise, the book is to the reader. The lover fascinates his mistress with his honourable sentiments, till she cannot resist his criminal advances. The book infatuates the reader, till, in his admiration of its morality, he loses all horror of its licentiousness. It may be said, that an author ought to pourtray seductive vice, for the purpose of unmasking its arts, and thus warning the young and inexperienced. But let it be recollected, that though familiarity with voluptuous descriptions, may improve our prudence, it must undermine our delicacy; and that while it teaches the reason to resist, it entices the passions to yield. Rousseau, however, painted the scenes of a brothel, merely that he might talk the cant of a monastery; and thus has undone many an imitating miss or wife, who began by enduring the attempts of the libertine, that she might speak sentiment, and act virtue; and ended by falling a victim to them, because her heart had become entangled, her head bewildered, and her principles depraved.

"But I am happy to say, that in this country, there has arisen an improved order of Sentimental novels; which, gratifying the reason, more than the imagination, and interesting, not so much by the story as by the morality, are at once a test and a source of National virtue. Foremost among this superior class, I would number Rasselas and The Misanthropist.

"Still, however, most of our native Novels possess a certain strain of impracticable, if not pernicious sentiment; and I will add, that your principles, which have hitherto been formed upon such books alone, appear, at times, a little perverted by their influence. It should now, therefore, be your object to counteract these bad effects, with some more enlightened line of reading; and, as your present views of life are drawn merely from Romances; and as even your manners and your language are vitiated by them, I would likewise recommend your mixing much in the world, and learning the customs of actual, not ideal society."

With this opinion my father coincided: the system has already commenced, and I now pass my time both usefully and agreeably. Morality, history, languages, and music, occupy my mornings; and my evenings are enlivened by balls, operas, and familiar parties.

Stuart, my counsellor and my companion, sits beside me, directs my studies, re-assures my timidity, and corrects my mistakes. Indeed he has to correct them often; for I still retain some taints of my former follies and affectations. My postures are sometimes too picturesque, my phrases too flowery, and my sentiments too exotic.

This day, Betterton and Grundy stood their trials, for having assaulted the constables; but as the prosecutors did not appear, the culprits were discharged. It is supposed that Betterton, the great declaimer against bribery and corruption, tampered with the postillion and the police, and thus escaped the fate which had awaited him.

Adieu.

LETTER XLI.

In ridding ourselves of a particular fault, we sometimes run too far into its opposite virtue. I had poured forth my tender feelings to you, with such sentimental absurdity, when I fancied myself enamoured of one man, that afterwards, when I found myself actually attached to another, I determined on concealing my fondness from you, with the most scrupulous discretion of pen.

Know, then, that even at a time, when I thought it my bounden duty to love Grundy, I felt an unconscious partiality for Stuart. But after my reformation, this partiality became too decisive to be misinterpreted or concealed. And indeed he was so constantly with me, and so kind a comforter and friend; and then so fascinating are his manners, and so good his disposition; for I am certain there is no such young man—you see in his eyes, what he is; you see that his heart is all benevolence; and yet he has a fire in them, a fire that would delight you: and I could tell you a thousand anecdotes of him that would astonish you.—But what have I done with my sentence? Go back, good pen, and restore it to grammar; or rather leave it, as it is—a cripple for life, and hasten to the happy catastrophe.

Stuart had latterly become more assiduous, than usual; his manners had betrayed more tenderness, and his language more regard. I saw these attentions with secret transport, but with many a little tremor, lest my fancy was only building a castle for my wishes.

This morning, however, put the matter beyond a doubt. I was alone, when he paid his accustomed visit. At first he made some faint attempts to converse; but I could perceive an uneasiness and perturbation in his manner, that surprised me.

"Pray," said I, at length, "what makes you so dull and absent to-day?"

"You," replied he, with a smile.

"And what have I done?" said I.

"So much," said he, "that I must now ask you, what you will do."

He then changed to a nearer chair, and looked at me with agitation. I guessed what was coming; I had expected it some time; but when the moment arrived, I felt my heart fail; so I suddenly moved towards the door, saying, I was sure I heard my father call. Stuart sprang after me, and led me back by the hand.

"When I tell you," said he, "that on the possession of this hand depends my happiness, may I flatter myself, that my happiness would not be your misery?"

"As I am no longer a heroine," said I, smiling, "I do not intend getting up a scene. You happen to have my hand now; and I am afraid---very much afraid, that—"

"That what?" cried he, holding it faster.

"That it is not worth withdrawing," said I.

But in this effort to shun a romantic dialogue, I feared I had run into the contrary extreme, and betrayed an undue boldness; so I got sentimental in good earnest, and burst out crying. However, Stuart soon dissipated my uneasiness by his eloquent expressions of gratitude and delight, and by his lively pictures of our future happiness. I told him, that I wondered how he, who knew my failings so well, would venture to stake his happiness upon me.

"Had I not seen your fallings," answered he, "I should never have discovered your perfections. Those embarrassments of your life, which I witnessed, have enabled me to judge your real disposition more justly, than had I known you, only in the common routine of intercourse; because they have shewn me, that if you had weakness enough to court danger, you had firmness enough to withstand temptation; and that while the faulty part of your character was factitious and superinduced, all the gentle and generous feelings came from your heart."

Our conversation was interrupted by the sudden entrance of my father; and on hearing the favourable issue of our interview, the good old man hugged both of us in his arms.

To detain you no longer, a week hence is fixed for our wedding.

I have just received a line from Mary, which mentions her restoration to health, and her union with William. I shall offer no observation on your late marriage with the Butler; but I must remark, that your having instigated me against my father, at the outset of my follies, was an act, which even your repentant letter cannot atone. However, he has pardoned me, and from my heart, I forgive you. I am too happy for anger.

Adieu.

LETTER XLII.

I HAVE just time to tell you, before I leave town, that my fate was sealed this morning, and that I am a wife.

After the ceremony, poor Higginson, who had kept peeping for my return, at the corner of the street, came forward, dreadfully pale, and presented me with an Epithalalium. He then attempted to recite a premeditated compliment, but stammered; and after pulling at his lip some moments, gave a sudden stamp, and ran away.

Honest Jerry Sullivan (whom Stuart has enabled to set up a handsome shop), was at the house before me. He shook my hand, and danced round me in a fury of outrageous joy.

"Well," cried he, "often and often I thought your freaks would get you hanged; but may I be hanged, if ever I thought they would get you married!"

"There!" cried I to Stuart, "after all your pains to prevent me from imitating romances, see how you have made me terminate my adventures, like every romance—in a marriage. Pray with what moral will you now conclude the story?"

"Why," said Stuart, "if the story cannot suggest its own moral to the reader, I might just as well conclude with saying—instead of some flourishing sentence about Patience and Resignation, Innocence and Calamity—that Tommy Horner was a bad boy, and would not get plumcake; and that King Pepin was a good boy, and rode in a golden coach."

Adieu.

THE END